STONE TABLETS

STONE TABLETS

Wojciech Żukrowski

TRANSLATED BY

STEPHANIE KRAFT

PAUL DRY BOOKS

Philadelphia 2016

First Paul Dry Books Edition, 2016

Paul Dry Books, Inc.
Philadelphia, Pennsylvania
www.pauldrybooks.com

Printed in the United States of America

Library of Congress Cataloging-in-Publication Data

Names: Żukrowski, Wojciech, author. | Kraft, Stephanie, translator.
Title: Stone tablets / Wojciech Żukrowski ; translated by Stephanie Kraft.
Other titles: Kamienne tablice. English
Description: First Paul Dry Books edition. | Philadelphia : Paul Dry Books, 2016.
Identifiers: LCCN 2016001450 (print) | LCCN 2016006201 (ebook) |
ISBN 9781589881075 (alk. paper) | ISBN 9781589883109 (ebook)
Classification: LCC PG7158.Z78 K313 2016 (print) | LCC PG7158.Z78 (ebook) |
DDC 891.8/537—dc23
LC record available at http://lccn.loc.gov/2016001450

Chapter I

Over clumps of blinding white—the villas in this quarter of New Delhi—the sky was growing opaque. Yellow dust rose on the empty horizon, blurring the jagged lines of the treetops. The air was becoming heavy. The heat did not abate, only the source of it changed; fire beat from the blistered reddish earth and burning stones. The flat roofs on which whole families camped at nightfall were still deserted, though the sun had buried itself deep in the palm groves.

Istvan Terey looked reluctantly through the tightly closed window. Behind the glass, through the wire screen on which spider webs and rainbow-tinted dust glinted, he saw a wide lawn, bleached by a long drought. Its grass was trampled down, crushed under the feet of loitering passersby. In a glass clouded with dust he saw his own face, darkened by the tropical sun, its oval lines cut by the sharp white of his collar.

He had stuck at his post in India for two years—two springs, rather, for they were the most oppressive: the hot seasons, when work became a torment. A somnolence almost like fainting enveloped the entire Hungarian embassy. People napped over their documents, they wiped sticky palms on linen trousers; their gaping shirts laid chests gleaming with sweat bare to the stream of cool air driven by the fan.

He looked gloomily at the cracked earth, which was taking on a red and violet sheen. Huge flies crashed blindly, with a frenzied buzzing, against the taut screen behind the windowpane, trying to force their way into the house. The toneless knocking, as if someone were throwing dried peas, the angry voices of the insects, the wheezing air from the cooling machine, and the hiss of the blades in the great ceiling fan: this was the music of the Indian twilight. Air full of dead light was suspended over the gardens; fringes of sickly green trailed back into the sky like smoke. Measureless empty space hung calmly, nodding with the evening breeze.

Among the banana trees with their broad leaves like tattered flags stood a watchman in shorts, lavishly watering what greenery remained with a red rubber hose. Sparkling droplets played around the stream. Thirsty starlings dived into the spray, spreading their wings with delight, and waded in the wet grass.

Terey rubbed his forehead. He would have liked to awaken in himself a joy like that of those birds; it was no use. He knew that refreshment well, for he had come from the bathtub only a little while ago. The water had been waiting until he returned from the office. The cook had drawn it at dawn, for during the day the tin collector on the roof grew so hot that the water poured in boiling from the tap. "A few weeks more and one will be able to breathe," he sighed, staring dully at the vacant sky, where dust was beginning to pulsate with scent like tobacco.

Monsoons: one only had to hold out until the sudden downpour, and the world was transformed. Everyone waited until the little map appeared in the first pages of the New Delhi newspapers with a chart showing which way the winds bearing the life-restoring moisture were blowing, in which direction the longed-for rains were advancing.

He felt the pleasant coolness of a fresh shirt on his back, and thought with distaste of the white jacket he would soon put on. He dropped into an armchair, stretched his legs, and relaxed. The ceiling fan limped in lazy gyrations, but sent a puff of air that grazed his close-cropped hair. The electric current wavered and the fans mounted in the windows rumbled fitfully. Their sighings blew the aromas of oil, caoutchouc, and dust into his face. The smell of drying stone rose from floor tiles that had been scoured with a wet rag not long before. The dinner jacket hanging from the back of a chair smelled of camphor and insecticide.

Muffled shrieks came from the kitchen as the cook quarreled with his family, who were waiting for the remains of the midday dinner. The drone of motors, the piercing trills of cicadas hidden in the climbing plants on the veranda, made it impossible to doze even for a little while. He heard his own uneven pulse. He felt a desire to smoke a cigarette, but he did not want to reach for one.

The insanity of a sudden wedding in this heat! His face contorted with resentment.

He knew the young couple well, Grace Vijayaveda and Rajah Ramesh Khaterpalia, an officer of the president's guard. He was even a friend of theirs; he saw them when he attended picnics, rode in hunts. Sometimes they pressed him to stay until the crowd of guests had left, for a chat, as they put it, "just among ourselves." The leisurely conversations in a dusk barely lit by floor lamps—the long moments of agreeable silence with a glass in the hand and a cigarette, measured by the soft clinking of the golden hoops that shifted with the motion of the girl's floating wrist—assured him that he was one of their intimate, trusted circle, though he worked at a communist embassy. The notification of Grace's wedding had caused him pain; but since the groom himself had called to verify that the messenger had delivered the invitation with its gold engraving, he had to put in an appearance.

It seemed to Istvan that there was something unspoken, yet understood, between the young Hindu woman and himself. Only two weeks ago she had told him how her old *ayah* had gone on pilgrimage with her begging bowl to obtain a blessing from the gods for her young lady. She spoke in a mild monotone, as if she wanted to create with trivial confidences a camouflage for the wandering of her slender palm around the nape of his neck, the intimate stroking of the temple. He listened to the slow music of her words; he drank in the shy—one might almost think, involuntary—touches, the half-conscious caresses. Her hand said more than her full lips; it lured, it promised.

He found Grace pleasing. Her mother had been an Englishwoman; perhaps that was why she was less diffident than Indian women, why she did not wait with lowered eyelids and inclined head until a man condescended to notice her, to honor her with a nod. She herself would initiate the encounter.

Her slight, compact body, wrapped in a green sari that veiled her figure while drawing the eye to it, piqued his imagination. Her large, dark eyes seemed fiercely inquiring. Her black hair, gathered into a loose knot, was plaited with a garland of jasmine buds which shed a sweet breath in their dying. Apart from the gold bracelets that jingled on her wrist, she wore no jewelry. Her neck and ears needed no adornment. She knew that she was beautiful. Her narrow, diligently groomed hands were never soiled by work. She was a dowered young lady of the highest caste, an only child.

Upon meeting Istvan, she had asked none of the obligatory questions: Did he like India, how long would he stay, who was he, really, in Europe? Who was he? Or—what did he own? Land, factories, houses, stocks? As an employee of the embassy, dependent on the opinions of his superiors, the capricious valuations of other officials, he could be of no importance. He was only a young poet, a good-looking man who had come here for a brief time; a bird of passage, kindly welcomed by a group of people jaded with beauty.

He seized on the startled, knowing glances as they flashed from under the darkly tinted eyelids, signaling that it was worth her while to have him among her docile admirers. He preferred to keep his distance. Distance allowed for timely withdrawals, for escape from humiliation, from words and gestures affirming certain inviolable limits.

"Be careful, Istvan," warned Secretary Ferenc. "Be careful to keep them from talking about you too much, for that's the end. A report will go out, they will recall you, they will make mincemeat of your reputation, and for years you will be warming a chair in a ministry instead of sailing the wide world."

"We go places together, you and I, after all—the same parties, you see me—"

"Just so; I see how the high life is getting a hold on you."

"I do it for you, not for myself. Winning people over is one of our duties. Even when I leave, it will make it easier for my successor. I am feathering the nest for him."

"I only remind you not to fly from it too soon."

Istvan smiled derisively. "I do what everyone does. I am no different from the rest of you."

"You play the bachelor. We have our wives here. They are what they are, but at least we can look at the Indian beauties without losing our composure."

Now and again the people at the embassy would begin a probing conversation about the skin of Indian women, which was rough to the touch, about their hair, which was glistening and hard as horsehair, about odd or arcane lovemaking customs. He sensed that his colleagues wanted to sound him out about whether he had become familiar with such things, what experience he had acquired. Then against his better judgment he was silent; he changed the subject; he referred them to the Kamasutra in an English translation, illustrated with photographs of stone sculptures from the Black Pagoda.

"Be careful, Istvan. Look to yourself. Don't slip up," Ferenc warned him jokingly.

"I feel absolutely safe, for everyone is spying on me," he rejoined.

GRACE VIJAYAVEDA HAD FINISHED her studies in England.

"She wanted me to send her, though it was money thrown away since she did not marry an Englishman. She will not be a judge or advocate here, so why the training in law?" her father complained. "I can pay for her whims, within reasonable limits, of course."

Istvan was disturbed by the incongruity between the balding, obese owner of a weaving mill in Lucknow and his petite, athletic daughter. Gray hair like an aureole encircled the man's yellowish face, which was full of good-humored cunning. Only his large eyes with their warmth, their color like chocolate melting in the sun, resembled hers. The old manufacturer crossed his ankles, spreading heavy thighs that could be seen under his none too clean dhoti. He preferred the airy traditional dress to woolen trousers. He was one of the pillars of the Congress Party; once Gandhi himself, when the police were looking for him, had stayed overnight in his house.

He knew how to make the most of his past, in which he had been a little reckless and which now served him well. He did business, he squeezed out income, couching everything in noble phrases: for India one must earn one's bread by the sweat of one's brow, broaden the industrial base. A drive to lead awoke in him; he knew how to build capital, he had nerved himself to wrest it from others. As long as weaving mills belonged to the English, he fought them hard, using every means at his disposal. When he built portfolios of stock, when he took the property of foreigners, it did not bother him at all that he was behaving in the same way as the colonialists.

"I am a Hindu. I am a son of this country, not an interloper," he explained to Istvan. "That is the fundamental difference. Perhaps your turn will come soon. Take the power—yes, you, communists—and the factories will stand. You will come prepared." It was clear, however, that he spoke without conviction—that even as he was evoking sympathy and admiration for the risk he was taking, the thought of radical change did not figure seriously in his calculations. He had beaten that thought back for decades.

Istvan liked to banter with him. He spoke vividly of the way land had been distributed in Hungary, and factory owners dispossessed. The old man listened greedily, with a fear that afterward sweetened his sense of his own absolute power over thousands of tame, undernourished workers. As he savored that twofold joy, he sipped yet another double whiskey with ice.

His daughter wore her sari gracefully, but swathed in that silken drapery she seemed in disguise. Istvan preferred her in the habit of her riding club: cherry-red frock coat, canary vest, and long black skirt. She sat sidesaddle and galloped with a flowing motion, softly and with just a touch of bravura.

From his childhood he had been familiar with horses. He had ridden with the herdsmen on the steppes of Hungary. Toward the end of the summer the wild horses grew unruly; the stallions bit each other, reared, and struck out with their hooves. Their manes were full of prickles and sticky balls of burdock. Even their coats gave off a pungent steam. "First, learn how to fall off the horse . . . and you must get up at once, dust yourself off and mount him again. He must understand that he will not get rid of you, no matter how he bucks and kicks. That lesson will stand you in good stead all your life, for life is a spitfire mare that likes to run away with her rider," said the old *csikos* with a face like a copper kettle, twirling up the ends of his grizzled mustache.

Horses raised in India were of mixed breed, not overfed, accommodating. They heard one's voice and felt the pressure of the calf, they ran after the white ball of their own accord, as if they understood the rules of polo. They positioned themselves to make it easy to strike with the mallet when the dust rose from the hard-trampled, cracked clay. Trainers in red turbans, mustachioed Sikhs with beards rolled up and gleaming as if they had been soaked in black lacquer a moment before, goaded them on with shouts. The horses broke into a short gallop, then moved sideways above the white ball as it lay on the grass. They understood that the aim was to block the opponent's way so that he could not hit with the mallet. The taut legs, firmly planted hooves, and muzzles contorted as if in jeering smiles irritated Istvan. He made his horse trot in a tight circle; he wanted to go for the ball. Again the riders moved as in a cavalcade, swaying like waves on the horses' backs, in a joyful hubbub, with raised mallets that glinted white in the westering sun.

Later, as their muscles tingled with pleasant sensations of weariness, they dismounted and returned the horses to the stable boys, who ran up noiselessly; the good old school. In the hall of the club, the stench of horse sweat mingled with the fragrance of perfume. He relished the first swallow of cold whiskey as it bit his throat.

Grace breathed deeply; he saw her breasts disturbingly near, the hair on her temple moistened with drops of sweat, her lips parted.

The servants took back the mallets and brought towels, dampened in hot water and steaming, to wipe the red dust from faces and necks. The air in the dimly lit hall smelled of cigar smoke, was alive with the quiet tinkle of glasses, the soft rattle of crushed ice in a silver shaker, the throaty gurgling of tilted bottles.

Grace liked to turn up uninvited for the Sunday morning jackal hunt. As the traditional sport of the Queen's Lancers, the hunt was rather an occasion for displaying skill, for readying oneself to thrust at full gallop, for practice at pinning down a swiftly escaping quarry, than for shedding blood and displaying a trophy dangling lifeless. The jackals with their triangular, spiteful faces and long, fluffy tails dodged about among clumps of cane. Their little paws worked rapidly; they seemed to fly over the trampled turf. A horse, carried away with the lust of the sport and feeling the insistence of the spur, bore down on the prey; then came the moment to test the lances. The jackal's cries urged the furious hunters on. The light pole with its metal fittings was fixed under the arm, to jab with its point, to lift the animal from the earth.

The horse gave chase, almost trampling the fleeing jackal. A blow—a thrust—the victim jumped away, and the rider, his lance buried in the ground, rose like a pole vaulter, his spurs etched against the sky as he was lifted from his saddle, then fell heavily on his back, like a clown.

The jackal burrowed into the nearest clump of brambles; they had to frighten him out with shouts. The Hindu servants came running up, throwing rocks. Suddenly under the legs of the shuddering, foaming horses a slender form slid like red lightning and whisked itself away, eluding the chase.

Ditches on the course made falls likely, and the master of the hunt had checked before the group moved out to see if the riders were wearing cork helmets as prescribed by the rules of the club. Istvan had barely escaped breaking his neck tumbling among the burnt-out stalks. Though he had ridden in more than a dozen hunts, not once had he seen a jackal speared to death; they slipped away, they hid deep in thickets, they dived into dens. So another one had to be flushed out, and the amusement went on until foam red with dust ran over the horses' bellies, until their raw-throated riders ceased shouting and the call of the trumpet announced the end of the hunt. Exasperated voices, faltering for lack of breath, told of perfect thrusts, extolled the fleetness and spirit of the horses, and made a laughingstock of Major Stowne, whose lance was lodged irretrievably in the rocky ground.

Grace rode doggedly with the experienced hunters. She knew that she rode well, but she did not force herself on anyone; she simply was. She was aware that her presence excited men, that each of them wanted to show his prowess—to win her praise, to feel a friendly jostle on the arm with a glove darkened by horse sweat, to see her eyes kindle with admiration.

The Sunday morning sun was unbearably hot. Shirts stiffened with sweat. Voices were full of barely concealed rage. They really wanted to spear that skittish carcass, to pin it to the ground and raise it quivering on a lance—to cut short this senseless chase, which they had already had their fill of, though no one dared call a halt. A few of the riders fell back a little from the group in the lead, giving their mounts their heads, and the horses slowed to a walk, as if in quiet desertion. But Grace, with fiery cheeks, galloped on a black horse side by side with Istvan. The jackal, straining all its powers, hurtled in front of them, its narrow tongue hanging from its mouth, saliva trickling down. They heard the tormented animal's snorting moans.

"Strike!" Grace cried in a high voice full of cruelty.

Istvan jabbed with his lance. He must have grazed the animal, for it bolted sideways with a screeching bark. The nervous Hindu horse swerved and Grace went flying over its neck. She was dragged a few meters by her hands, which were tangled in the reins; the imprint of her splayed legs could be seen on the grass.

He leaped from his horse and lifted her from the waist, like a sheaf of grain. Her chin strap had come apart and her helmet had fallen into the brush. Her skirt was rolled up high; he saw her dark, shapely thighs.

"Are you hurt, Grace?" He shook her lightly in his arms until her forehead fell against his cheek. He smelled the fragrance of her hair, felt the warmth of her body, felt her lips, viscid from fatigue, sticking to his neck. She opened her eyes with such a piercing look that he shivered. He pressed his palms to her back and held her close. There was no incidental touching, only a chaste kiss.

"You were frightened, Istvan," she said in a low voice. "Would it have pained you if I had been killed?"

He wanted to kiss her on the lips instead of answering, but the riders had come up in a group and were dismounting. Grace's fall had provided a reason to end the torturous chase in the blazing noon sun. She stood leaning on him, brushing off her skirt. It seemed to him that she wanted to prolong their moment of closeness.

Her fiance rode up on a dappled gray Arabian. Seeing that Grace had risen to her feet, he did not even get off his horse.

"I had him when the trumpet call began," he cried excitedly. "Look, I caught him on the nape. His hair is on the point." He shoved the tip of the lance uncomfortably near their faces. Was there some meaning in the gesture, Istvan wondered fleetingly.

Servants came, leading back Grace's horse. "Can madam mount him?" Terey asked.

"Call me Grace. He has no objection, isn't that so, my rajah?"

"Yes, only I must give the word. Mr. Terey is a gentleman. Mr. Terey, help her into the saddle." He drove his lance into the red earth and gouged out a hole.

Istvan lifted the girl and placed her in the saddle. He slipped her foot into the stirrup and adjusted the reins, as if it were difficult for him to move away from her. Then, seeing that the rajah had turned his horse away and, without waiting, was taking a short cut through the meadows, Grace pushed away her skirt and showed him a bruise on her knee. "It hurts," she complained like a child, and he kissed the bluish spot quickly. Without a word she rode off at a trot after the disappearing rajah.

Istvan turned around. Behind him an old sergeant major with a thick mustache was sitting on a horse like a statue, the point of his lance jutting up above his red turban. "He saw?" Istvan wondered uneasily. "Did he make anything of it?"

When he had caught up with the couple and was riding at a walk so close to Grace that their stirrups jogged each other with a dull clatter, no one alluded to the accident; they talked of the merits of Arabian half-bloods, of pasturage, of the grooming of manes.

He dismounted hastily, but Grace was off her horse before he could help her. The sergeant major shouted to his batmen; in woolen stockings and shorts, they looked like overaged scouts. Istvan glanced at the sergeant major's whiskered face. Flashing eyes looked knowingly, indulgently, from under shaggy brows. "Good hunt, sir?" he asked insinuatingly, and put out his hand for a tip.

In the dark interior of the club, sparks of color fell from stained glass emblazoned with heraldic emblems and wandered on the air. The hunters crowded to the bar, though the solitude offered by the spacious hall was alluring. Deep leather chairs invited each one to take his ease, but the members stubbornly clustered in groups. Barefoot servants ran about noiselessly, handing around drinks and cigars. Someone turned on the fans, and the starched muslin projecting like birds' crests from the waiters' turbans moved with a life of its own; the newspapers tossed onto tables or fastened in wicker racks rustled as if the invisible hands of club members long dead were turning their pages, once again carelessly browsing through the society columns. Istvan deposited his lance in an umbrella stand.

"Come here," the rajah called. "We must complete the ritual. Sit by Grace."

The girl was swallowed up by the leather-encased frame of the chair. She was pensive and distant. He could see only that both her palms clasped the knee he had kissed. "It hurts her," the rajah said.

He looked with repugnance at the white dinner jacket that hung from the back of the chair. The blades of the fan overhead chased their own shadows around the ceiling. A lizard, as if molded from bread crumbs, wandered in slow motion around the wall.

After all, I did not fall in love. He shook his head; this sudden wedding galled him. When all is said and done, nothing has changed; they both will still be my friends, he thought. But he felt indefinably injured, as if he were saying goodbye to the girl, as if he had lost her.

Goodbyes. The winter of 1955. The dejected face of Bela Fekete at the station in Budapest.

"How lucky you are! I have always dreamed of seeing India. I will do it by proxy, through your eyes. Only write me about everything! I'm glad they are sending you. But it hurts to part with you."

"I'll be back before you know it. In three years you will be coming to welcome me home."

"Can one be sure of anything?" Bela said, looking sad. "Three years in these times of ours . . ."

Steam hissed and hardened into needles of frost on the pipe joints. The clank of iron, the huffing of the locomotive, deepened the feeling of cold and sent a shiver through them. But Bela could not be sad for long.

"When you have had enough of that India, let me know, and I'll fling such dirt at you in the Ministry of Foreign Affairs that you'll be recalled right away."

Istvan stood in the open door; the copper handle seemed to thaw in his hand. The train was moving and Bela, enveloped in steam, took a hurried step beside it, waving his wide-brimmed hat. The window was crusted by a thickening layer of ice and refused to open. Then the train burst out into the sunlight and the glassy fields pulsed with reflected glare until he had to blink.

He had left his friend at a time when the air seemed heavy with a feeling of impending change, a joyful restiveness. Tension, impatience were everywhere. In the coffeehouses, people shrouded in the party newspaper whispered of disruptions that would occur in the government before long. Soon the letters he was receiving—full of sardonic humor, skeptical remarks and hopeful interjections—amounted to a prognostication that something would surely happen. Only the newspapers remained the same, with their gray columns of print spouting tedium. In vain he searched them for signs that something was coming.

Then he began to envy Bela because he was still in Budapest, because he could feel this strong, unifying current. He smiled as he recalled his caustic words, "A man ought to be something more than a dung factory, living to acquire raw material for its production. Blood in the veins is like a flag furled. We must remember that."

As soon as I return from the wedding, I will write to Bela, he decided, and tell him about Grace. I will lay out the whole story in order, and then I will be easier in my mind.

He had prepared the wedding present with time to spare: an oblong package wrapped in white tissue paper, done up with golden ribbon, like a dancer's calf. He could not afford jewelry, he could not impress them with a lavish gift, so he had chosen an enameled pitcher that Grace had admired at an exhibit of Hungarian art. She had cradled it in her hands, and the chubby face with the walrus mustache, the work of a peasant artist, had looked back at her with round, somewhat astonished eyes. "I would have sworn it was from India," she had said. "You can see at once that the potter enjoyed himself, molding these shapes."

Into the center of the pitcher, under the lid, he tucked a bottle of plum brandy. He had remembered that the groom liked to observe the English custom of drinking a little glass of plum brandy before a meal.

He heard the biting of gravel under the tires of a braking car and the long, triumphant yelp of the horn. Outside the window he could see the stocky figure of the watchman, who was scratching at the screen, flattening his nose against it, shielding his face from both sides with his hands and straining to see Terey in the dim room.

"Krishan has driven up, sir."

"Good. I heard."

He had already been taught that he should accept such services with a casual impatience, since they were obligatory—demonstrations of appropriate deference, proof of loyalty. Thanks in the form of a word or smile would be a sign of weakness, a breakdown of authority. In this country one said thank you with money.

He put on the jacket and adjusted the ends of his narrow bow tie. When he reached for the package, the housekeeper, who must have been eavesdropping at the door or looking through the keyhole, glided in. He seized the present in his black, slender hands. The long, twiggy fingers on the white wrapping paper looked like the claws of a reptile. His blue-striped shirt was split on the arms; the tears bristled with fringes of starched thread.

Terey knew that the housekeeper was making a show of his poverty again; his shirt, falling outside his pants and frayed to pieces, was an eyesore. Still, in accord with Indian custom, he pretended not to see it, not to lower himself by noticing misery, suffering, disease. Apart from the agreed-on payment, he had given the man three shirts. But the "sweeper" obstinately went on wearing his tattered clothes. When Terey had pointed out that he was an embarrassment to the house in those rags, he had said serenely, "Sahib will tell me when he is having guests, and I will be dressed in a new shirt. Those you gave me I save; I set them aside after the holiday. Sahib will go away, and I do not know if I will get anything from the new master. The Hindus give nothing to servants. They have relatives who have uses for everything."

They passed through the hall; the sweeper, making certain that he could hold the package safely with one hand, carefully opened the first door. Through the second, the screen door, burst a wave of scorching air. They went out onto the veranda, which was overgrown by a golden rain tree. The shading foliage, thick and shaggy as sheepskin, rustled when it was stirred by a puff of wind. Lizards clambered up the thin, braided branches and jumped into the leaves as if they were water. A cane chair made a scraping sound and a short, slender man rose from it. Against his dark complexion his open collar glared bright white; his eyes were reddened and glittering as if he had been weeping a moment earlier.

"Mr. Ram Kanval! Why are you sitting here?"

"The watchman saw me with you once and assumed that I was a friend of yours. He offered to let me in, but gave me to understand that you would be going out right away, so I preferred to wait here."

"How can I help you?"

"I am very sorry for not calling to give you notice of my visit. I have brought you my picture; this will only take a moment." He bent over, drew a canvas wrapped in a sheet of paper from behind his chair, and tugged violently at the string. "You are fond of painting, sir. You will see its merits at once. Please be seated for a minute." He pulled up a wicker chair.

His importunity was so warm, so full of hope, that Terey yielded. He sat on the edge of the chair, making it clear by his very posture that he had no time to spare. The painter walked out onto the steps into the yellow western light and turned the canvas around, lamenting nervously that the varnish was still shiny.

"It's fine now," Terey soothed him.

From the shaded veranda, among the motionless festoons of leaves reddened with dust and the spiraling coils of dried blossoms, he looked at the painting. Against a red background, figures with slender legs, draped in coarse grayish-blue linen, carried great baskets the color of wasps' nests on their heads. He could hardly distinguish the human forms, whose shapes were distorted by their burdens; the picture was bold and ingeniously composed. The narrow, almost girlish hand of the painter, cut by a bright sleeve of raw silk, held it from the top. Beyond it trembled a sky the color of bile. The red turban of the sentry bent toward the sweeper's head, which was wound with a handkerchief, like an old lady's. They were looking with interest at the back of the painting, the taut dun-colored canvas with a pair of oil spots.

There was a long, uncomfortable silence. Terey savored the moment. It will be worth writing Bela about, he thought. He will understand. Finally the painter gave in and asked, "Do you like it, sir?"

"Yes. But I will not buy it," he answered firmly.

"I would like one hundred—" Ram Kanval hesitated so as not to put him off with too high a price, "one hundred and thirty rupees. I would give it to you for a hundred . . ."

"No—though I truly like it."

"Keep it," the other said softly. "I do not want to return home with it. Hang it here."

"Dear Mr. Ram Kanval, you are a master of your art. But I am not permitted to accept such expensive gifts."

"Everyone will think that you have bought it. You are in contact with so many Europeans; you will whisper a word on my behalf. You know, after all, that this is a good painting. But people must be told about it, simply persuaded. They know a few names and they look at price. You can double it. Only do not broach the matter in the presence of Hindus; they will think I contrived to cheat you."

"No," Terey said with exaggerated determination, for the composition pleased him more and more.

"When I walked out of the house, all my family gathered at the barsati. My uncles laughed at me. My wife was in tears. They think I am a lunatic, and an expensive one, for they must not only provide me with food and decent clothing, but put out money for frames, canvas, and paints. I will leave this picture with you. Hang it; perhaps you will grow accustomed to it and want to keep it. Do not take away my hope. You do not even know how I have learned to lie. At home I will tell them the whole story of the good fortune I met with. If only they will stop counting how much they give, stop reproaching me for being a freeloader."

It pained Istvan that he had forced such a confession from the man. He was troubled as he looked at the cream-colored jacket sleeve and dark palm that brandished the picture. Garlands of cascading branches veiled the Hindu's face.

"I have something to propose," he began cautiously. "Just now I am going to Rajah Ramesh Khaterpalia's wedding. Pack the painting nicely and come with me. We will try to persuade the groom to buy it as a present."

"He will not buy it. He does not appreciate it, it has no value for him," Ram Kanval reflected despondently. "But I will go with you to see what possibilities there are. I live this way—by illusions."

"I will help you. We must make a good sale with this painting," Terey said in an artificially sprightly tone. "The cream of society is gathered there, wealthy people. Your very presence in the group will raise your reputation in the city. You will begin to be a person of importance. Let's go! It's high time."

"One must not be late to a funeral. The dead cannot take their time in such heat. But we can go to a wedding any time. Is this a wedding after the English rite, or in Indian tradition? With registration in the office, with Brahmins, with blind men to tell fortunes from pebbles strewn about?"

"I don't know," Terey answered candidly.

"In our country the ceremonies go on for three days and three nights."

"And the young couple are present all that time? The poor groom!"

"They go off to a bed, they are enclosed by a curtain of red muslin, but they are not permitted to come together physically. Their families can call for them to come out at any moment. They must become familiar with each other's bodies, know each other, desire each other. There is no question of such rape as is carried out among you, in Europe. I have been told . . ." The painter talked passionately, as if he wanted to forget the defeat he had suffered a moment earlier.

They got into the car. Krishan slammed the doors and asked if they were ready to leave. Between them, like a partition over which only their heads showed, stood the unfortunate painting, wrapped in partly torn paper.

"You have been misinformed. In barbarian Europe, what you begin to permit after the wedding happens long before it. The wedding itself is becoming, more and more, a legal affirmation of an already existing state. Earlier, half a century ago, much importance was attached to virginity; the value of the goods was higher when they carried the seal," he jeered. "Not today. Now it is seen as a troublesome relic that nature itself creates."

"With us, virginity is important. A woman is supposed to pass straight from the hands of her mother to the hands of her husband. The bride's family vouches for her. A girl should not be in contact with men outside her family, or remain tête-à-tête—"

"According to you, then, is Miss Vijayaveda a woman of doubtful reputation?"

"Oh! She can allow herself anything; her father is rich. Anyway, she is not bound by our strict customs. She is more English than Hindu. She is, if not above these prohibitions, beyond their control."

They drove down the streets of the villa districts on an asphalt roadway. Bicyclists swarmed over it randomly, like handfuls of white moths with wings erect. They pedaled sluggishly in groups, their arms about each other's shoulders, chatting loudly and bursting into laughter. On the grass that served as sidewalks, whole families were sprawled.

Twilight fell quickly; the sky turned green. The odors of open sewers and garlicky sweat and the cloying sweet fragrances of hair oils gusted in through the car windows. Istvan became aware that the driver's crest of hair smelled like roses, while the painter's was scented with jasmine. They had the grace of pampered women, he thought, and involuntarily touched the hand that rested on the edge of the canvas. It was cool and moist. Ram Kanval turned his black, clouded eyes toward him and smiled comprehendingly, as if at an accomplice.

"We must make a good sale with this painting!" he said in a spasm of zeal.

Krishan drove his machine with daredevil insouciance. Conversation died down at moments because Terey had to be watchful as the car squeezed into a crowd or, at one bound, passed other vehicles. "He's sure to collide with someone," he thought a little angrily. "This isn't driving, it's acrobatics." The painter seemed not to take account of the danger; he was content to be sitting on soft cushions, pulling up his knees and chattering about the dishes that would be served at the wedding. At last they skirted so close to a bulky Dodge that the glare of the cars' headlights crossed and they heard the scream of brakes.

"Easy, there, Krishan!" Terey could not restrain his irritation. "He could have hit you!"

The driver turned his jubilant face around, flashing his small, catlike teeth. He was obviously amused by Terey's caution, which he took for a sign of fear. "He had to slow down, sahib. He could tell I wouldn't put on the brakes. He knows me. He knows I won't give way."

"But sometime someone you don't know will come along, and he will wreck your car."

"I have been driving for eight years and I have never had an accident," he gloated. "My father ordered my horoscope as soon as I was born. The stars favored me. The astrologer told my mother—and she remembers every word, that is why I know—that only one thing can bring doom on me: sweets. So I avoid them. I take cane syrup with water at most."

"Look in front of you! Watch out!" Terey shouted as the wide white breeches of cyclists gleamed in the lights. As if they had been swept off the road, they swerved violently into the darkness.

"He went onto the curb," Krishan laughed. "They are as silly as rabbits in the headlights. Oh, they fell in a heap!"

He flew on, leaving behind the jingling of bicycle bells and the cyclists' angry shouts.

The lights of a car moving in front of them flashed red. On both sides of the avenue, limousines stood in the deep darkness; headlights licked them, revealing their colors. Their parking lights were like the eyes of skulking animals, extinguished or winking. A policeman was directing traffic; his sunburned knees, shorts, and white gloves were visible in the headlights. His eyes flashed in the glare like a bull's. With an authoritative gesture he forced Krishan to turn off his headlights, then motioned him into the stream of automobiles that was turning into the driveway.

The front of the palace shone incandescent white. A myriad of colored light bulbs were attached to the shrubbery and hung in the branches of the trees, like varicolored bouquets blooming in the dark. They created an atmosphere of mystery, of fairy tale, a little reminiscent of the sets in a second-class theater. Servants in red uniforms with lavish loops of gold braid, like operetta costumes, leaped to open the car doors.

"Don't wait for me, Krishan."

"I will be at the end of the avenue, on the left," he answered as if he had not heard the order. It had no place in his thinking; it would have been an affront to his dignity if the counselor had returned home on foot, or if one of his friends had taken the opportunity to drive him. Anyway, he wanted to have a part in the festivities, to stare at the women's jewels. He thought as well that some treat would be prepared for the drivers.

The painter alighted first, a little intimidated, for over him, like chiefs reconnoitering the field of an oncoming battle, stood both hosts: old Vijayaveda, Grace's father, and Rajah Khaterpalia in a formal red dolman belted with a white sash. It seemed to him that their gazes, and those of the staff who formed a double line, were concentrated on the shabby paper wrappings exposed in all their trashiness by the low beam of a headlight hidden in the shiny leaves of a holly bush. Swiftly he removed the packaging; he thought of throwing the crumpled paper onto the seat, but the car, responding to the insistence of limousines vibrating impatiently, was sliding into motion. Worriedly he folded the paper in quarters, then once more, shoved the roll into the pocket of his pants, and bent to retrieve the strings. He wadded them hastily, partly concealed behind Istvan, who was entering the receiving line nursing the package done up with ribbon as if it had been a baby in a bunting.

"How nice that you have remembered us, sir," the old manufacturer greeted Terey. The white, youthful teeth in his dark, bloated face were jarring, like false teeth too well made.

"Congratulations," Istvan said quietly. "I have brought a present for the bridal couple."

But the rajah quickly interrupted, "Give it to Grace. She will be pleased. She is busy with guests just now. We will talk when I have finished here."

With boredom in his eyes the rajah extended a sleek hand to the next guest, from whom he took a gift and passed it carelessly to a servant standing behind him. The servant took off the wrappings with curiosity, under the supervision of a distant member of the family.

"My friend, the distinguished painter Ram Kanval."

"Very pleased." Vijayaveda did not even bother to turn his head. A servant snatched the painting from Ram Kanval and turned aside, looking askance at it. He shook his head in astonishment and handed it to the gray-haired old man.

"Beautiful," he muttered without conviction and set it on a chair, but the flow of gifts soon displaced it. The picture stood against a wall, its tomato-red background blazing while the shadows of the legs of passing guests swarmed over it.

"It seems that we have not brought it at a good time," the painter said dolefully, stuffing the coils of string into his pocket.

"Nothing is lost yet," Terey said consolingly. All at once he felt that the struggle to sell the painting was futile; the artist, dragging worry, poverty, and sadness in his wake, grated on his nerves with his air of helplessness. He who gathers old string and picks up buttons, went the old saw, will never be rich, for he does not know how to take a loss. "Come on, we must look for the bride. I want to get rid of this." He held up the wrapped pitcher.

"If you want something to drink, I will hold it," the painter offered, his eyes following a tray high above their heads. A bottle of whiskey the color of old gold, a silver basket with ice cubes, a siphon and glasses all clinked softly like music turned low, but behind the servant the crowd blocked the way.

They went out to the park. On the lawn the guests stood in a dense, sluggishly moving mass. The figures of women and the white jackets of men were articulated by a geyser of changing lights, blue, green, violet, orange—a foaming fountain, opening like ostrich feathers. Every few minutes a servant blundered as he changed the glass in the lantern; then in the white, denuding glare the peacock colors of saris flashed, and the diminutive sparkles of rings and bracelets, diadems and necklaces. Heavy bodies reeked overwhelmingly of perfume and Eastern spices. Above the din of conversation soared the nasal voice of a singer, accompanied by a trio of flute, three-stringed guitar, and drum. The noisy chatter did not disturb the vocalist, who sat crosslegged in white bouffant pants with his hands between his knees, crooning plaintively with closed eyes while the fleshy pulse of the drum supported the hovering melody.

Dr. Kapur in a white turban, adroitly elbowing his way through the crowd, folded his hands on his chest in the Hindu greeting. He caught Terey by the sleeve. "Are you looking for the bride?" he asked in a confidential tone. "Indeed, she is before us!"

Her movements circumscribed by a red cord, she bustled among the tables on which the gifts were displayed. Gold chains and expensive brooches glittered from opened cases—family jewels and presents from the rajah, who had been more generous because they remained his property. Behind one table two tall, bearded guards kept watch, hands crossed on their chests.

Grace floated about in a white lace gown, looking as if she were immersed in foam. Her deep decolletage left her bosom almost exposed. It was easy to imagine that her straps would slip down and she would be nude to the waist, beautiful, unashamed, defiant. When Terey approached her, apologizing for the modest keepsake he had brought, she had just been showing a chain with a medallion set with pearls that brought cries of delight from the friends who gathered around her.

"What did you get? Go on, look!" they begged in birdlike voices, pressing against the red cord. He was gratified by the childish hurry with which she undid the ribbons and took out the bewhiskered peasant with arms akimbo. He gazed with stolid satisfaction at the jewelry that was spread around the table.

"You remembered that I liked it? What deity is this? What good fortune does it ensure for me?"

"A wagoner. I got him from a friend, so he would bring me back safely to my country. So he would remind me of our steppes."

"Oh, good!" Filled with delight about something known only to herself, she set the pitcher in the center of the table above the jewelry. Suddenly that yellowish-black figure seemed to overshadow the entire glittering display.

"Istvan," she said a little defensively, "I must stick it out for a while in this zoo, and I want something to drink so badly. I sent Margit for a drink, but I don't know what has become of her. The servant is all the way out at the edge of the crowd. Be nice and bring me a double whiskey."

Then he saw that she was in low spirits. Her eyelids were dark with sleeplessness.

"This is not easy for me," she said in an intimate whisper, laying her hand on his. She spoke almost as though her flock of female friends counted for nothing—as if they were alone, alighting from horses in the wild pastures. He wanted to comfort her, to say a few good, simple words, but he was filled with bitter feelings. I am a stranger here, he thought, I will go away; that is why she can be frank with me. I am of no importance; she might vent these complaints if she were smoothing down a horse's neck on impulse.

"Well—here you are!" she cried joyfully.

A slender red-haired girl in a greenish gown, straight as a tunic and fastened on one shoulder with a large turquoise clip, was coming toward them, holding two tall glasses. Without hesitating Grace took them both from her and handed one to Istvan.

Looking at the bride's moist, full lips as she drank avidly, he tilted his glass. The throat-burning taste of the whiskey and bubbles of gas were pleasantly invigorating. In his thoughts he wished her happiness, but not the kind that was supposed to begin this evening with the wedding ceremony—a happiness that somehow included him, innocently, as cats, wandering in a stream of sunlight, want to doze together on a windowsill on a summer afternoon. He felt an easygoing tenderness for her, and for himself.

The friendly roar of conversation went on; the crowd of guests suddenly became nothing more than an inconsequential background for a meeting greatly desired.

"Grace," he said softly, "think of me sometimes."

"No." She shuddered. "Not for anything." She saw that he was stung, and stroked his palm. "Surely you don't want me to suffer. This wedding is like an iron gate; let them once shut it . . ."

She was speaking hurriedly, as if locked into her own thoughts. She squeezed the tips of his fingers, driving her nails into them. "But tomorrow you will be here, too, and the day after. If only I could order you: go away, or die! I can't. This is not an easy day for me, Istvan, though I'm smiling at everyone. I'd be glad to get dead drunk, but this is not London; it isn't done."

The red-haired girl was standing nearby, partially shielding them from inquisitive looks. She turned her face away, sensing that something particular was going on between the two of them. With a calm motion she took away the empty glasses, as if acknowledging that she had been cast in a menial role. Terey found this disturbing.

"I'm sorry. It was thoughtless of me to drink the whiskey. You surely brought it for yourself."

"A mere trifle. Grace is a despot. It's a good thing you and I are guests—lucky for us. The poor rajah!"

"Well, that is one thing you can't say about him. I will not allow anyone to jeer at my almost-husband. You are talking as if you were old acquaintances: Counselor Terey, Hungarian and, be careful, red," she warned, falling into a jocular tone. "Miss Ward, Australian. Look out, for she likes to devote herself to a cause. That is why she came to India. We have misery and suffering enough, so she is in her element. She wants to help people, to make their lives better; it makes her feel better at once. Perhaps she will even be a saint. Call her by her first name, Margit. Well, seize the opportunity, Istvan, kiss her. Both her hands are full. I'd rather you did it now than behind my back."

"You are getting married, and you are jealous?" laughed Miss Ward. "You've made your choice; give me a chance. Well, don't be shy—since she has given me her recommendation, kiss me, please," and she offered a cheek of tender rose with a humorous dimple. Istvan's lips touched her taut skin. She used no perfume; the freshness of her body was enough.

"It seems, madam doctor, that he is your first private patient in India. You have taken his fancy," Grace laughed. "You want me to introduce you, Istvan, to the prettiest girls in New Delhi, and that is quite a field to choose from!" She made a sweeping gesture with her hand as colored lights played over it, and suddenly her white dress was bathed in violet, then in scarlet. "Lakshmi, Jila! Come here!" she called to two young women draped in iridescent silks.

They came, holding their heads high—beautiful heads with helmets of dead-black hair. Their huge eyes looked about with sparks of humor. They were conscious of their beauty and of the eminence that wealth confers.

"Next to them I feel like a dry stick, ugly and ungraceful," Margit said. "Are they really that gorgeous?"

"Oh, yes—especially in those wrappings," he said sarcastically. But she was not listening. She had noticed a servant with a tray of empty crystal and taken the opportunity to slip into the crowd, apparently to dispose of the whiskey glasses.

He knew several of the girls from families whose names were prominent in India: Savitri Dalmia, whose family owned a virtual monopoly in South Asian coconut meat and coconut oil; Nelly Sharma of Electric Corporation, slender and with a wonderfully long neck; Dorothy Shankar Bhabha, whose father owned a coal mine operated as it would have been in England two centuries earlier—a gigantic molehill enveloped in sulphurous smoke that made the hair of the workers go red and the grass and trees dry up. The combined land holdings of these women's parents amounted to a latifundium hardly smaller than a quarter of Hungary, and their influence reached still further.

The girls' eyes, as Terey gazed into them, were mild as cows' eyes; their blue-painted eyelids drew out all their depth. Each of them wore her hair piled high and fastened with ruby and emerald clips. Ropes of pearls gleamed on both of Dorothy's wrists as she played with them, laughing at Istvan's jocular words of admiration and flashing her even teeth. They made cheerful small talk; the girls' good looks drew men like a magnet. A photographer stalked the jovial group, his camera flashing repeatedly as he took souvenir pictures. They had to flail with their arms to drive him away, as if he had been a prowler.

Dr. Kapur, in a turban immaculately done up with small tucks, seized Dorothy Shankar's hand, which was girlish and soft as a leaf.

Looking her in the eye with unpleasant insistence, he began to tell her fortune. "Squares and rectangles—the lines closing," he whispered. "Tables set by fate."

"Not much of a trick to say that, since everyone knows who her papa is," Grace objected. "Tell hers!" She pushed redheaded Margit's hand at him.

"Leave me alone. I don't believe in this," the girl protested. The surgeon had seized her palm in a tight grip. It was tilted into the light; the shifting glare from the fountain with its erupting sparks played over it.

"Not long ago madam flew here, and not long from now she will fly away. I hear a chorus of blessing—"

"Tell the future of her heart!"

"Yes," cried the girls, "we want to hear about love. Perhaps we will find her a husband here."

The doctor put the young woman's palm to his forehead, puffed out his hairy cheeks, closed his eyes in concentration. To Istvan the intimacy seemed improper. A cheap actor! The doctor's lips, swollen and gleaming as if they had been rubbed with grease, hung partly open as he smacked them. He mumbled something and then said, "Bad, very bad, dear friend. One cannot buy love."

The girls burst out laughing.

"Enough!" Margit snatched her hand away and hid it behind her back as if she were afraid to hear more. Her eyes were frightened, her lips tight.

Istvan moved quietly away from the bevy of girls. He felt a sudden sense of satiation; their beauty was too extravagant. Their walk was like music; their hips were wrapped tightly in silks; their bare waists had a warm bronze tint. Their long, slender hands moved gracefully, sprinkling sparkles from their jewels. One had to admire them, but they did not arouse desire.

He went on for a few steps and, to escape the crowd, turned onto a side path. Here the lights flashed less often. Several peacocks sat on the leafless branches, their drooping tails streaming with the shifting glare. The agitated birds emitted tortured cries, as if someone were pushing a rusty wicket gate. He walked onto a little bridge; at that season of the year, the artificial stream barely oozed along its swampy-smelling bed. In a dull, lusterless pool of water amid the fleecy overgrowth, reflected lights moved unsteadily. The water was full of life and motion; the insects that slid over its surface elongated the quivering gleams.

The hubbub of conversation, the wailing of the singer that could be heard momentarily above it, the slapping of the drum, and the birdlike trills of the flute brought on melancholy. Suddenly it seemed to Terey that he was on Gellert Hill, looking from the terrace toward the bridges over the Danube, which were outlined with lights. His eyes wandered over the streets of Buda and Pest—the darting automobiles, the neon signs—and a dry wind drifted around the hillside, carrying the chalky smell of warm grass and wormwood. Behind him he heard the distant tinkle of music in a hotel; in the sultry night the high bank around him rang with the chirping of a thousand crickets. Along a bridge below, a girl walked with a springing step, her sunburned hands flickering against her simple dress. She had black hair that fell loosely to her shoulders. She could be seen quite clearly from above as she walked into the white circles of lamplight. He felt a great tenderness for her; he would have longed to take her arm, to draw her away to a cafe that stayed open past midnight. But a feeling of inertia such as one has sometimes in a dream restrained him.

He did not spread his arms like wings and float down with a hawk's graceful swoop. Before he could run to the street by the serpentine paths, she would be far away, and the steps of other pedestrians would be rumbling on the bridge. He would not find her.

Grace. Would he miss her? Would he have swept her away to Budapest? He smiled at the thought of disrupting the wedding, of asserting that the girl was unwilling to go through with it. What could he say, what reasons supported his case? A kiss, a few words clouded with ambiguity? They would look at him as if he were a lunatic or worse: a fool. They would say, That Hungarian has a weak head. Take him out quietly. And his friends would lead him to the veranda and slip a glass of full-strength grapefruit juice into his hand. Who knows if here, amid all this sumptuousness, this music and these festoons of lights, something violent might not happen? And Grace would not be grateful; she would deny everything. They are among their own, these Hindus, he thought wryly, and the case law is on their side. The will of both families is being carried out, and the young will be obedient. Today the girl is still chafing at the bit, but tomorrow she will acquiesce, and in a year she will be adjusted to it.

He felt a warm hand slide under his arm as it rested on the railing. He whirled violently around.

"You ran away? I wanted you to enjoy yourself. I called the girls over; you could have had your choice. The rest depends on you, and you know how to turn someone's head."

"Why are you bullying me, Grace?"

"You must find them pleasing. Only don't say that you would have preferred me. I'm getting married. They are free. Beautiful as flowers, and just as passive. Perhaps you could direct your attentions to Dorothy? Or Savitri Dalmia? She is a little like me," she said in a half-whisper, breathing unevenly, obviously excited. "I would like you to have each of them, all of them—"

He gazed at her in astonishment.

"—because then it would not be that one I already hate," she breathed into his face. Her breath smelled of alcohol and half-chewed grains of anise. Her eyes flashed in the twilight like a cat's. Clearly she had had too much to drink.

What does she want from me? he thought, assaulted by uncertainties. She's playing a hard game, but for what?

Suddenly she pulled away her hand, then stood erect, altered, imperious. Her very posture jolted him into alertness and he turned around. Men were coming; he saw the lighted ends of cigarettes. At once he recognized the figure of old Vijayaveda and the bald, nut-brown crown of his head in its garland of gray hair. Now he felt that he and Grace were confederates. But no one drew attention to the private conversation they had been carrying on. It seemed a matter of course that they were walking back to meet those who were approaching.

"Father, the brahmins have arrived," Grace said. "I made a place for them in your study." When the old man gave an angry snort, she said placatingly, "Uncle and the boys are with them. I ordered that they be served rice and fruit. Everything has been seen to."

"Very well, daughter. I will look in directly. You still have time; it is just ten. You ought to lie down. The wedding rites begin at midnight."

"Yes, papa."

"You should look well. You will not sleep tonight. Some rest now, perhaps?"

Istvan looked at her out of the corner of his eye. The dialogue went on harmoniously, the solicitous father and the obedient daughter, a good actress. Was she also playing with him, pretending, deceiving?

They moved toward the palace, which glowed orange and gold in the lamplight. They passed the crowd of guests that milled about on the lawn as servants carrying trays of tumblers and shot glasses circulated among them. The singer, with closed eyes, not heeding the noise, whined to himself as the accompaniment flailed in an uneven rhythm. Perhaps they did not even hear each other; an improvised concert was going forward, in harmony with the spirit of the wedding night.

Istvan walked beside the old manufacturer. "Grace will be happy," he said in a low voice, as if he wanted to assure himself of it.

The Hindu reached up and put a hand on his shoulder in a gesture of good-natured familiarity. "She will be rich—very rich," he said chattily. "Our families can do more than government ministers in your country. But Grace must bear him a son."

Beams of light near the ground jarred the eyes. Beside the black evening trousers of the European guests the short, narrow, crumpled white pants of the servants, their untucked shirts and their dhotis carelessly wound around their hips, made them look as though they had come in their underclothes by mistake.

A swarm of insects danced like a blizzard against the glass reflectors. Moths and beetles perished at once, sizzling against the hot tin. Others, lured by a glaring white spot on the wall, beat blindly against it and slid down with a crunching of open shells and a furious buzzing. Stunned, they fluttered onto the paving tiles; the plated scarabs crackled under the feet of passing guests. It seemed to Istvan that the crisp bodies of dead insects at the source of light gave off a stench like burnt horn.

The shadows of people walking played over the wall: slender legs and distended torsos with enormous heads. They reminded him of the figures in Ram Kanval's painting. Now he was sorry that he had not bought it.

A tranquil dimness filled the spacious hall. A few lamps with ornate shades, mounted low, threw warm circles of light on the carpets. The rajah, extending his legs, reclined in a chair. The stripes on his trousers blazed emerald green. All the light from a little lamp set in a copper pitcher fell on varnished boots and on the picture the tipsy painter held in his outstretched hands.

"What does this picture represent?" the rajah mused contemptuously. "There is nothing to see. What sort of people are these? A child could have painted better! Indeed, you finished school, Ram Kanval; could you not have taken to some respectable profession? Why lie? You haven't a modicum of talent. I will not pay for your flight to Paris. A waste of money! Whenever you want to begin working for me or my father-in-law—" he noticed Vijayaveda approaching—"we are ready to accept you for training."

"And I like this picture," Terey said perversely. "The people are carrying bundles on their heads. They are returning after a day's work in the heat."

"Those are the launderers from beside the river bank. The washers with dirty linen," the painter explained impatiently. "The picture represents worry, futile toil."

"And you really like it?" Grace asked incredulously. "You would hang it in your house?"

"Of course."

"It's sad."

"That's what the painter meant."

"Launderers! What kind of subject is that?" the gray-haired Vijayaveda jeered. "I see enough of them in the kitchen! Do I have to look at them on the dining room wall? No eyes—no noses—heads like bundles of wash. That isn't painting. The background all one color, flat—did you have a shortage of paints?"

"Come." Mercifully, Grace drew her father after her. Istvan had the impression that she was doing it for him. "Thank you, Mr. Ram Kanval. Perhaps it is good. One only needs to grow accustomed to it." She held the picture up and a servant took it from her.

"Oh! Miss Grace is very cultured," Kanval said, leaning toward the rajah, but the compliment had an equivocal ring. Fearing that the painter would offend their hosts, Istvan led him toward the doorway to the garden.

"Have something to eat, Ram. They are serving very good filled dumplings."

The artist waded waist-high in a white glare that played like limelight on his tall, lean figure. The rajah followed him with his eyes and said, "The conniver! He wanted to cadge a ticket to Paris out of me. He said so convincingly that I would share in his fame that I demanded that he show me how he paints. And after all that, there was no skill, simply—nothing."

"He was not lying. He deserves support. He is no copyist or photographer. He wants to be himself. If he persists, he will be famous."

"I will wait," the rajah drawled patronizingly. "How much does he want for his pictures?"

"Two hundred rupees."

"And how much does he really get?"

"A hundred, a hundred and twenty."

"And he sells two a year, one to some embassy or American tourist, another they buy out of pity at the annual exhibition. The price itself shows that the pictures are worth nothing. I have a pair of Impressionists at my place in Cannes, for taking them out of France is not allowed; my agent paid a couple of thousand pounds apiece for them. Those are painters."

"Were."

"So much the better! They don't lower the market price with new pictures. If your protégé were dead, it might be worth the risk to buy one or two canvases. Boy!" he called. "Pour us some cognac. No, not that. From the bulgy bottle, the Larsen. All the old French cognacs had false labels; not one cellar could hold out against the pressure of the liberating armies. Nothing was saved but the cognac the Swedes bought before '39. I believe in Larsen—a solid firm, cognac aged more than forty years."

The servant approached, knelt, and handed around bulbous snifters. He tilted the bottle, peeping at the rajah's raised little finger; at a flick of that finger he pulled up the neck without spilling a drop. They warmed the snifters with their palms, shaking them lightly, watching approvingly as the trickling unctuous liquid left its tracery on the little crystal walls. The rajah put his fleshy nose to the glass and sniffed.

"What an aroma."

Terey drank the cognac down. It rolled around his tongue with a stinging savor. He tested it on his palate. It had a rich, complex bouquet. It was a noble liqueur, a drink for connoisseurs.

"Another hour of this torment." The rajah exhaled heavily and spread his legs. "We must say goodbye to our guests. You will stay, of course, to see the traditional ceremony? Now we may drink to my future obligations! After midnight, not a drop."

"You want so much to be with Grace?"

"If I had liked, I could have had her long ago." The rajah waved a careless hand. "I was thinking of something else. I dream of giving up the uniform. Feel—" he took Istvan's hand and shoved it under his red shirt. Terey felt the swelling of an elasticized corset.

"They say that I am fat, though I engage in sports. I have a good appetite, they serve me the dishes; must I deny myself? Some do not eat because they have no food. Should I starve myself when I can afford anything? A thin rajah is a sick rajah. My position demands that I look impressive. In our country they say, fat, because he has plenty of everything, fat—that means rich, and rich, because he has the knack of making money, because he is smart. A logical chain of reasoning! I would like to be free of this frippery, to be at ease in a loose dhoti."

Terey looked with growing aversion at the short, corpulent man with his face gleaming like a bronze cast from the alcohol he was sweating out. The rajah parted his dark lips and panted, nearly stifled by the tight uniform he wore as captain of the lancers of the president's guard. His words about Grace had struck a nerve with

Istvan. He blinked and, peering through his upraised glass at the rajah's face, saw it distended as in a warped mirror. It was repulsive to him. He swallowed the cognac, drinking, in fact, with antagonism toward his host. But the rajah interpreted the gesture differently.

"You are a likable fellow." He clapped Terey on the knee. "You have the knack of being quiet in a friendly way. It is a rare virtue in a communist, for you must be continually moralizing, as if you yourselves had not properly digested the knowledge you gained, and then, right away, you brazenly reverse yourselves. Well, do not be angry because I say it."

Then he reached for the bottle and poured for himself.

"More?"

Istvan declined with a motion of his hand.

"Why did you rush the wedding?" he asked cautiously.

"Do you ask for personal reasons, or professional?" The rajah roused himself. "Have you heard about our law? It will make life more difficult for you, too." He stopped speaking, still holding the snifter against his lip.

"Don't speak of it if you'd rather not," Istvan shrugged.

"It is the end of free transfer of pounds abroad. Half a year earlier than we foresaw, the law will come into effect. For a couple of years now, old Vijayaveda has invested capital in Australian weaving mills. He had the privilege thanks to influences in the Congress Party. He got special permission.

"The government took over my copper mines. Part of the damages it paid me I would like to entrust to my father-in-law. A worthy family! He helped Gandhi; they were in jail together. That counts for something. It's worth it to remind a few ministers of it at the right times. The lawyers were vetting our financial standing. They vouched for the probity of 'both the distinguished parties,'" he laughed. "The families held councils. The benefits and a certain risk were weighed—well, and marriage is like a guarantee of long-term credit, which I gave my father-in-law. I had to hurry. I don't want them to freeze my capital here. I dare say the details would not concern you."

"And Grace?" Terey rotated his glass and the golden liquid swirled inside it.

"She is a good daughter. The family council made its decision. That is enough. She could have objected, but what for? Could she have been sure of a better match?"

"She loves you?"

"Only with you in Europe is that a great issue. Love is a device of the literati, filmmakers, and journalists, who batten on marital scandals, and they do well financially by keeping up that myth. With us one approaches marriage seriously. It can be big business, especially in our sphere, when it involves real money. Does Grace love me?" he repeated, and his vigor revived. "And why would she not? I am rich, healthy, educated. I can ensure her welfare and her position in society. She will remain not only in the upper ten thousand, but in the thousand of the supremely influential." He dabbed with his fingertips at drops of sweat on his upper lip and eyebrows, and wiped them on the arm of his chair. His eyelids were almost black—from fatigue, obviously, and too much alcohol.

"Is such an arrangement really necessary?" Terey leaned forward and offered him a cigarette. A servant who had been waiting almost invisibly in the shadows hurried forward with a light. They smoked. Muffled music whimpered beyond the veranda doors, which stood wide open.

"You have forced me to it. Well, perhaps not you"—he exonerated Terey—"but it was easier for us to get rid of the English than to control what you set in motion. You entice people with talk of paradise on earth. That is your advantage, and your weakness. You continually move the time appointed for this happiness up by five years, but people still believe. The first stage surely is yours by right: to take from the rich and give to the poor. But that does not suffice for long, and the hardships become severe, because those who rebel acquire a taste for change. They grow vociferous, they make demands, they exert pressure.

"My land was taken. Well, not all of it. I still have enough. The government pays me rent for my lifetime, every year a tidy sum in pounds. Something must be done with it. Sometimes there are businesses which are risky but yield quick profits, and are easily dissolved; even the air transport partnership Ikar. We have airplanes from the demobilization, Dakotas, still in fair condition.

We buy them at auction. I see to it that they are not made available to our competitors, but to people we trust. The money must be put to work, every rupee must triple," he nodded with unctuous gravity.

He paused and seemed to doze off for a moment, then roused and spoke with animation, "I did not ask the astrologers about my marriage, only the economists, lawyers, those who know the international markets, copper and wool futures. I talked with politicians—not from the representative side, but those in control. We are receiving signals from all Asia: there is a downturn, a stubborn one. It is possible, by taking action, to retard it or pass through, as in wartime communiqués, 'to positions designated in advance,' but the pressure on us persists. I am a modern man. I must have a strategy to deal with all this. I will not be content to sell the family jewels." He leaned forward and blew out a plume of smoke. "I carry on sufficiently extensive financial operations that, should one business fall through, the surplus on five others will make up for the losses. I consider marriage one of the best."

In the course of these reflections the rajah lapsed now and then into anxiety that cut him to the quick. He had to unbosom himself, and to him Terey was a harmless poet, even a friend. He spoke more candidly to him than he would have to one of his countrymen; he felt no constraint.

The guests were beginning to disperse in pairs, quietly, avoiding goodbyes. The men's patent leather shoes and the women's silver sandals gleamed in the low light of the lamps. A crackling like gunfire floated in from the veranda, then voices full of delight. The fireworks had begun.

"You do not expect a revolution?"

"Not in India. Our peace is assured for a long time. Listen, Istvan, are Hungarians good soldiers? Good as the Germans?"

In spite of bitter memories, Istvan answered objectively, "I would say so. Hard fighters. But we are a small country. Keep that in mind."

"I understand. We have more holy men than you have people. Here ten million of the devout mill about on the roads in search of eternal truth, but each walks alone; that saves us. And communism is crammed down your throats."

"And what about the example of China, which is literally next door?" Istvan goaded.

"A beautiful boundary, the Himalayas. They barged in there and they have been looking down at us ever since. Here people don't like them. They call the Chinese corpse-eaters because they eat meat."

"They would organize your life. They would teach you to work."

"No need! I understand that the poor, in a mob, will always crush the rich because they aren't risking much. They don't value life. And the rich man doesn't like to stick his neck out or take chances with his fortune. Revolution takes hold easily in poor countries. Take the Russians. Take the Chinese."

"In India there is no lack of the destitute."

"Just so, the destitute—too weak to raise a stone, let alone a rifle. They are proud of their own powerlessness. Think: there are four hundred million of us. Ants. Conquer us and we will assimilate the conquerors, and go on being ourselves. No, there will be peace here for a long time."

From the park came the booming of rockets. Bursting projectiles sprayed festoons of sparks. The whistle of the shooting fireworks set Istvan on edge. It reminded him of the war. "Come," he suggested, putting down his glass. "The illumination will be worth a look."

"Leave me in peace. Go yourself," the rajah demurred. "I know precisely what the show is like. I signed the bill." He sat resting his head on his hand with both knees drawn up onto the chair, like a pampered only child who did not go to sleep when he should have and is petulant toward the whole world.

Terey stood in the doorway. Deep darkness bore in on him. The cables were disconnected; the reflectors and the garlands of colored bulbs gave no light. The guests, densely clustered together, looked with upturned heads at what was going on above them. Luminous streaks crossed each other, and arcs of green, as if someone had hurled emerald rings into the sky. Chrysanthemums of fire blossomed and softly trickled down. Then stars heavy with gold soared upward, riveting the watchers' eyes, and the fiery flowers fainted imperceptibly and went out, swallowed up by the night.

The lawn that had been cordoned off—where the wedding gifts were displayed—had been taken over by the master of the fireworks, a Chinese. Two assistants had driven bamboo rods with pointed tips, full of compressed energy, into the grass. With a wand tipped with a small flame the master lighted the fuses until they sprayed sparks. The missiles full of stars glided into the sky with a bloodcurdling whistle, bursting apart in flashes of color.

Istvan leaned against the door frame, smoking a cigarette. A warm hand touched his back. He was certain that it was the rajah coming out to his guests. He was watching a shooting star when the fragrance of a familiar perfume reached him. He spun around. Grace was standing behind him.

"A few hours yet, Istvan, and I will no longer be myself," she lamented in a low voice. "He bought me like a piece of furniture. No one asked my opinion. I was simply informed that it was going to be this way."

"You knew for a year, after all, why he was courting you."

"I didn't think it would come on so quickly. I will only be a Hindu," she said with a despair he found incomprehensible.

"The Englishwoman in you is struggling." He stroked her hand. Their fingers pressed each other.

"The Englishwoman in me is dying," she whispered.

"You wanted this . . ."

"I wanted to be with you. Only with you."

Flakes of trembling light floated around her face, mingling with the sparkle of her eyes. Suddenly he was seized with bitter regret that she had slipped away from him—that she would be inaccessible, enclosed by marriage, hedged about by the watchfulness of a wealthy family, shadowed by servants.

"Indeed, you could not have married me."

"You never spoke of marriage, even as a joke." She seized his hand with unexpected force. "Have you never heard of predestination?" she asked.

"It's easy enough to write everything off to fate."

"I will convince you that it exists. Come. Have courage. I have it."

He did not speak. Tenderness swept over him. She must have known it, for she turned away slowly and walked along the edge of the shadows through the hall, then toward the stairs that led to the inner rooms on the second floor.

He walked a step behind her. She was on the opposite side of the wide room where the rajah lay dozing in his chair with his legs tucked up. In his mind Istvan heard the man's self-important prating, and again felt an angry aversion. Grace was standing on the stairs with one hand on the banister. She beckoned to him. The small white purse she wore on her wrist swung like a pendulum, as if it were measuring time. Istvan passed through the hall with determined steps and hurried to her. They started up the stairs together as if everything had been foreseen long ago.

The house was empty; all the guests and servants had turned out to admire the spectacle in the park. Inside, the roars of exploding rockets resounded as a dull echo. The two moved silently, quickly. They stopped before a dark door.

"Where are you taking me?"

"Here." She was leaning down, plucking a small key from the purse.

Inside the room, only one lamp was burning, its form like a flower on a tall stem. Tables and sofas were piled high with boxes artistically bound with ribbons. Stacks of folded bridal lingerie and silk saris lay on the floor.

"Here are the presents I received. I will take this room for myself."

Knowing what she risked from the moment he heard the rattle of the lock, he held her close. He cared nothing for the consequences to himself. If they were found, there would be no explanations.

"And those others?"

"Don't worry. Those are the doors to my bedroom. They are also locked," she whispered, touching his neck with her lips. He plunged his lips into her fragrant hair. She hung in his arms. She slid down, pressing her body to his, and knelt. In a voice full of tenderness she whispered, "My dearest, my only love . . . my husband . . ." Her eyes were wide as she looked at him, without defense.

"You're mad." He buried his fingers in her hair and shook her head.

"Yes, yes," she affirmed passionately, clinging to him. Her gown rolled up, pulled by her feverish hand. He saw her dark, slender thighs; she wore nothing under her long skirt.

"You have me," she breathed.

He bent over her. He saw her tawny hips and a triangle of dark, curling hair. Like a wave rolling onto a shore she came against him, striking at him impatiently. He took her with angry delight as she entwined him forcefully in her legs, drew him into herself; she captured him, clamped him in hot fetters. He felt her burning and slippery inside. She gave herself to him with desperate passion until he wrenched free, pulled away—escaped.

She lay with parted lips, exposing her teeth as in a grimace of pain. She crossed her hands defensively on her breast and clenched her fists.

"What is it, darling?"

"Nothing, nothing . . . don't look." She turned her head away and, with a moan, wrung her fingers. Her unplaited dark hair drifted in a wide round mass; her small face seemed to be drowning in it. Her legs were parted, open, like a gate forced by an assailant. He saw how she trembled, how her belly pulsed. At last her eyes met his. She fixed him with a tense stare. He stroked her, quieted her, soothed her. Huge tears rolled down her hot cheeks. Her presence of mind and judgment returned. Seeing him kneeling over her, she handed him the hem of her wide, lacy, foam-like skirt.

"I won't be needing it."

He wiped himself with her wedding gown. It began to dawn on him that, for that moment of raging desire, a time of reckoning would come. His heart contracted violently. The fires went out; he felt only shame, uneasiness, and a growing wish to be gone. He wanted to disappear, to awaken as if from a dream.

Suddenly they heard applause like thunder. The guests were thanking the Chinese man for the show. The din of conversation, the clatter of steps on the tiles, grew louder. Without warning the reflectors outside the windows lit up, illuminating the palace walls. The glare hit the windows like a fist, spurting into the room, cutting the naked thighs with yellow streaks.

Grace sprang up and swept her hand through her hair. "Go," she pleaded. "Get out."

"When will I see you?"

"Never." He knew what was occupying her thoughts. "In an hour I will be saying my vows . . . and I will keep them. A Hindu woman does not betray her husband." She disengaged herself from his arms. "Go. Go. Go." She pushed him toward the door. She turned the key and peeped out.

"Now." She grazed him with her fingertips as if to apologize, and the door swung shut.

Stunned, he walked downstairs to the wide hall. The rajah's chair was empty. He poured himself a large whiskey and dropped in a pair of ice cubes. Without waiting for the drink to chill, he took a swallow.

More and more guests gathered at the bar, jostling him, pressing against him, and he wanted so to be alone. He was afraid they would scrutinize him too closely. Lightly swinging his glass, he went up to a tall mirror. He did not see his reflection clearly, but he grew calmer. "She was mad," he whispered in wonder, feeling a wave of sudden gratitude. "The poor thing!"

"Is what you see in the mirror more interesting than what is going on here?" Terey heard Dr. Kapur's voice behind him.

"No," he said with emphasis. "I only wanted to look at myself. But perhaps you will tell my fortune, doctor?" He thrust out his palm with a challenging air.

Kapur took it as if he were testing whether it were made of sufficiently resistant matter. Without looking at the lines on it he said, "You are fortunate; even your mistakes will be turned to your advantage. That which should harm you will bring you gifts beyond measure. The punishment meted out to you will be your salvation." The words flowed with the distasteful glibness of the professional chiromancer. "Miss Vijayaveda . . ."

Terey gave a start and wrenched his hand away. Then he understood that this was no reading of omens, that Grace was really coming down the stairs, veiled in red, attended by two elderly Hindu women, as if she were under guard. She did not respond to the greetings of her European guests, who were already beginning to leave the palace. She advanced with short steps, like a mental patient. When she was immersed in bright light, he made out the dark oval of her face, the lines of her eyebrows and the darkish tint of her lowered eyelids. Her grave aloofness and concentration wounded him. He belonged to the past, and it was behind her; it was closed once and for all.

The rajah, in white and gold, walked toward her. In the hush one could hear the shuffling of his slipper-like shoes, with tips turned up like new moons. The young couple bowed to each other. The rajah moved first toward the canopy with its hanging clusters of bananas. She followed him meekly, three steps behind, as befitted a wife. They sat with crossed legs on leather cushions.

Now the priests made their appearance. In singsong accents they recited verses and called the guests to witness that the pair here present, of their own free will and consent, were swearing to be faithful to each other until death, solemnizing the act of marriage.

"Not true! Not true!" he repeated inwardly. But beneath it all lay the bitter certainty that he no longer mattered. She was another woman, a woman he did not know.

The rite progressed slowly. The guests had lost their curiosity; they settled onto the lawn, men and women separately. Conversations were carried on in undertones; Istvan could not understand them. He felt conspicuous, out of place in his evening clothes. He was the only European who had outstayed the hour stipulated on the gilded invitation.

On the other side of a whispering circle of women, he noticed a copper cap of smoothly combed hair; someone had just given Miss Ward a chair, assuming that she could not sit comfortably on the ground for long. She looked in his direction, so he raised his hand and made a sign of greeting. She answered with a nod.

The ceremony dragged on. Under her red veil, Grace glittered with jewels; she was immobile, curtained off. The rajah's plump hands had fallen onto his knees. His swollen eyelids, which gleamed as if he had rubbed them with oil, were half shut. He seemed to be dozing. There was a sleepiness in the air. The lights were dimming as if they had been stifled with a bluish dust that had been sprinkled about without anyone's noticing. The nasal voice of the brahmin rose and broke off, only to rise again, supported by the murmur of the acolytes. Terey leaned toward Dr. Kapur, who was sitting by him, and the doctor held out an open cigarette case of gold. They smoked furtively like schoolboys, blowing smoke in various directions and waving it away to keep from being noticed.

And so, he decided, it is over. At least one of us should have a little common sense. Grace—she is helpless, hemmed in. But I? He imagined the rumors, the whispers; the effects of a widely circulated scandal; the spurious sympathy of his colleagues; the helpless gesticulations, with hands spread in the air, of the ambassador, "You understand, comrade counselor, that one must disappear on the quiet. I have sent Budapest a code dispatch with your request for immediate recall. Of course I signed off on it, I wanted no harm done. I understand: too much to drink, a beautiful girl, the heat. You were carried beyond yourself. Pity to end a career this way."

The darkness lowered and grew denser. Crickets chimed in the grass as if they were attracted by the lights. He heard the distant noise of passing cars, the irritable squeal of brakes, the impatient horns. Some still waited like a herd of sleepy animals in front of the palace.

No one saw us, he thought with inexpressible relief. Then he despised himself for the cowardliness of the thought and the implied repudiation of Grace.

Gigantic trays loaded with glasses of lemonade were brought from the kitchen. A waiter knelt to serve those sitting on the lawn. Kapur handed one to Terey. He took a swallow and immediately put it down. A sickening tinge of cane syrup was on his lips—a sticky-sweet taste—and a fuzzy mint leaf. He glanced in Miss Ward's direction. She had evidently just finished the same experiment, for her nose was wrinkled and she was quivering with revulsion.

"Do you wish me to tell you more?" the doctor began, stroking his beard, which was tightly rolled and secured with ribbon. "What fate has ordained for you, what is imprinted in the lines?"

"Thank you."

"It is not permitted to read that one, because that brings on changes."

"I'm afraid it is the whiskey that speaks and not your intuition."

"If I like, I can keep the whiskey from affecting me," the Sikh insisted. "I draw this sign"—he made a zigzag motion in the air above his glass—"and I can even drink poison."

"I shouldn't advise drinking this lemonade, though."

The first circle of witnesses to the rite sat rigidly, but around the perimeter of the crowd people had risen. Men stretched, walked not far away into the bushes and returned after a moment, adjusting their robes. Terey went over to Miss Ward, who, like him, was a stranger at this gathering.

"Do you like weddings?"

"This one has gone on too long. And it's a strangely sad ceremony," she reflected. "The end seems nowhere in sight. I believe I'll slip out."

"Where are you staying?"

"Here. I would have preferred a hotel, but they insisted that I stay with them."

"Nothing more is going to happen. The brahmin will utter precepts and bless the young couple."

"Will you stay?"

"No. I will escape as well."

They left. No one tried to stop them; no one said goodbye.

The shadow of the priest fell on the bride and groom; the three rings of those seated shimmered white in the diffuse light. Dark heads grew faint against the background of greenery. They looked like bundles of linen carelessly done up and thrown on the grass—a picture from a bad dream.

"Are you in India for the first time?"

"Yes. I came to the UNESCO center. I am an ophthalmologist."

"The best place for an apprenticeship." Kapur's voice could be heard just behind them. "Even as you gouge a patient's eye out here, he will bless you out of gratitude that at last someone is showing him some attention."

"You are a doctor?" she asked, bridling.

"That is how I live; I cannot afford philanthropy. I take those who pay. The more I charge, the more they believe in the effectiveness of my advice and treatment, and the more highly they value their health."

"And the poor?"

"They remain at your disposition." He spread his hands in a courtly gesture. "You may experiment. One must be firm with them, however, and keep the riffraff at a distance. I would advise that you begin by engaging two strong watchmen to keep order. Otherwise the dregs of society will invade you like lice."

A tumult broke out near the house. They heard the tinkle of broken glasses. Ram Kanval appeared in the doorway of the veranda, propped up by a servant.

"Let me go." He tried to shake the man off. "I can walk by myself. Oh, counselor!" he called, pleased, as if he could have Terey as a witness. "I put an empty glass down and it tilted the whole tray, and everything went flying."

"Where glass breaks, success comes in a hurry. A good sign," Kapur nodded. "With us clay pots are thrown near the bride's feet, and she crushes the potsherds on the threshold to bring happiness on the house."

Gently but with determination the servant pushed the slender painter in front of him, saying something in Hindi. "'Time to sleep. He should go home,'" the doctor translated.

"Good advice," Terey concurred. "Let's not wait until they order us out. Good night, Miss Ward."

She gave him her hand, and he put it to his lips involuntarily. He smelled the disinfectant that permeated her skin, and at once he understood: beware, Kapur has a good sense of smell, and no talent for palmistry.

"We will see each other again. India is not as large as it seems."

"That would be a pleasure," she answered smoothly.

He took the painter by the arm and waved a hand to the doctor. They went out to the front of the palace. Again the fragrance of the subtropical night met them in a rush. No one was near. Large moths fluttered in figure eights around the lamps. Drivers slept in the dark, silent automobiles, their thin legs propped against the seat backs. Others sat with their cars open, smoking cigarettes and chatting about their employers.

"I have a great favor to ask you," the painter ventured. Vodka had made him bold; he was becoming aggressive, but he halted every few seconds. "I cannot return home empty-handed. Lend me twenty rupees."

"Forty, even," Terey agreed readily.

"As soon as I sell a picture I will repay it, I swear."

The car was empty. The counselor blew the horn, and the mechanical blare, out of place amid the muted night sounds, roused the chauffeurs, who yawned shamelessly. Finally Krishan appeared.

"The rajah is supposed to be a great man, but he gave us rice, as if we were sparrows." He displayed his belly, which was flat as a board. "So empty it rumbles."

He drove the car out onto the road. The headlights splashed glare on the tree trunks. They hurtled along, but Terey did not try to slow them down. He wanted to be alone as quickly as possible. Insects lashed against the headlights like rain.

When they pulled up near the house, the watchman got up from the veranda. By the glow of the bulb that hung in the convoluted greenery under the ceiling, the old soldier had been knitting a wool sock. "All's well," he announced, beating on the ground with a bamboo stick as though it were a rifle butt.

"Krishan, drive Mr. Ram Kanval to Old Delhi."

"Very good, sir."

The painter said his effusive goodbyes. His hand was sticky from cane syrup. Istvan waited until the car moved away, as courtesy required. On the ceiling of the veranda, around the light bulb, whitish lizards crouched; they had a fine hunting ground there. As he passed, Terey always craned his neck and looked distrustfully to see if one of them was going to fall on the back of his neck. But they held themselves fast to the ceiling.

"Good night, sahib." The watchman stood at attention.

"Good night."

His "good night" was unnecessary. They had to offer him the appropriate good wishes; he should have accepted that and remained silent as custom dictated.

As he closed the door, he saw the lights of his car. It was already returning. Krishan had not wanted to take Ram Kanval home, and had put him out on the next corner. But Istvan did not have the strength to call the driver over and give him a tongue-lashing. He knew how Krishan would explain it: Kanval himself had not wanted to be driven further. He liked to walk, it was warm, a fine night, it would damage the car to hurry over that rag of a road. Let him walk. He would sober up more quickly.

Chapter II

The big cooling machine gave out a measured drone. Terey was sitting behind his desk, which was swamped with stacks of weekly magazines and documents. The clutter reminded him of the editorial office in Budapest, where he could hardly make room on the table for his typewriter as he plowed through heaps of off-scourings from the presses while the clatter of the linotype machines flew up from below like hail on an iron balcony. Men in aprons shiny with grime dropped in and tossed damp strips of galley proof with a sharp smell of ink on his desk. Furious that they hindered his writing, he pushed them onto the floor. Then, distracted from his train of thought, he sprang up, smoked a cigarette, and paced around the crumpled proofs. A moment later he picked them up, spread them out, and read them with an editor's alert, expert eye.

He was irritated when the cleaning woman tidied up. He was exquisitely conscious of where he had put articles that had to be critiqued, of whose photograph he had hidden in the fat dictionary. In Delhi he tried to carry these habits over. In this respect his conception of his work was quite to the liking of the ambassador, who asserted that he alone could allow himself a clear desk.

No one knocked, but the door opened a crack, and the gentle face of Judit Kele appeared. He pretended that he did not see her, that he was lost in admiration of the bald head of the dignitary in the portrait, so she tapped on the door frame with a pencil.

"Wake up, Istvan."

"You fly around as quietly as if you were on a broom. Come in. What's happened?"

"I'm sorry for you. You will surely die young, in obscurity. The envoy extraordinaire, the plenipotentiary, has summoned you."

He rose lethargically.

"Perhaps you should wait a little. I let an Indian visitor in to see him."

Istvan liked the ambassador's secretary. She was warm and genial. Her job as keeper of the ambassador's threshold gave her certain prerogatives. People attached weight to her remarks; it was whispered in corners that she had confidential assignments now and then, that she threw light on issues and gave opinions about the staff. When Istvan had asked her straight out about these things, she had replied:

"Have I done anything to you? No? Be quiet and don't meddle in things that don't concern you. In any case I will not rebut these rumors. It is better for them to be afraid of me."

She gave him a comradely pat, the kind one gives a horse before it runs toward a hurdle. "Keep your chin up."

"Is it that bad?" He inclined his head in astonishment.

He stood up and raked two documents into a paper portfolio, for he wanted to take the occasion to secure Kalman Bajcsy's approval for the screening of a film about rice communes by the Danube. Anyway, the boss liked to be asked for advice. It made him feel important, even indispensable.

The ambassador greeted the counselor with an upward tilt of his heavy chin. Tall, stocky, with small eyes and thin, graying hair that bristled slightly where it was parted, he gave the impression of being a strong man. Once in a rush of candor he had explained to Terey why he had left the management of great institutions named for Stalin and gone into diplomacy.

"I am a man with a heavy hand," he confessed, "and there were other heavy hands there than my own, so it became necessary to get out of people's way for a while. You know yourself that with us it is not enough to shout to make the horses go. One must reach for the whip."

At the embassy he made an effort to win the good will of the staff, to show a fatherly interest in them now and then. He inquired as to the health of wives and children. A few times he promised

Terey to have his family brought over, but the issuance of passports was somehow delayed. Ilona had not insisted. Both boys had begun their studies, and there was of course no Hungarian school in New Delhi. They did not know English; before they acquired the rudiments, it would be time to go back, especially with the constant hints of changes to come, the couriers who were awaited with a sense of something like disaster.

"Sit down, comrade." The ambassador motioned Terey to a seat at a small table, where a lean Hindu was sitting hunched over. He wore glasses; his comb had left ridges in his greasy sheaf of hair. "This is our counselor for cultural affairs. You will arrange the rest with him."

Terey pressed the chilly palm; its long fingers were stained with violet ink spots. Neither man let it be known that they had already talked. The counselor had not considered it necessary to inform the ministry or even the ambassador of the man's intention, it seemed so senseless to him.

"Mr. Jay Motal is a well-known man of letters and wants to write a book about us, to give Indian readers a view of the new Hungary of the people—our achievements, our social gains. In fact, he has already acquainted himself with our brochures, but that is not enough for him; he wishes to conduct interviews with dignitaries, to observe our life at close range. You will take his information. A coded message must be sent to the ministry to determine the conditions under which they can accept him."

He spoke grandiloquently, inclining his head toward the visitor, who nodded in turn, sensing victory at hand.

"How do you envision your stay in our country, sir? What would you like to see?"

"I would like to write a full-length book, so I would have to travel around Hungary for about three months. Surely you would pay for the sightseeing, hotels, necessary expenditures."

"And your journey?"

"The most direct route would be by Air India to Prague. If it proved too costly, I could return by way of Poland and East Germany. I have made inquiries at those embassies and help was promised."

"Do you want to write a full-length book about them as well?" Terey asked blandly.

"If I take such a long excursion, it seems to me that I could do it all while I am about it." The man twirled his palm in a dancer's gesture. "They are ready to accept me, but they make it conditional upon the payment for a ticket."

"In what language do you write?"

"In Malayalam. I fled from Ceylon. I was for its incorporation into India."

"How many books have you written?" the counselor queried.

"Three, not long . . ."

"With press runs of what size?"

"They did not appear in print. It is hard to find a publisher in our country, and in any case I had to flee. I was being hunted. The English wanted to put me in prison."

The ambassador, who was listening closely, asked, "How do you support yourself, sir? Not by literature, surely."

"My father-in-law owns a rice mill. Apart from that, we have been putting out money at a respectable rate of interest."

"Your clients didn't repay it?"

"They had to." The man smiled at the counselor's naivete. "We took jewelry as security. Strongboxes stood in the office with the deposits."

"So in fact you have published nothing?" Insistently the counselor returned to the subject.

"I have published a great deal." He pointed to yellowed newspaper clippings painstakingly glued to cardboard, worn from often being shown, smudged by greasy fingers, like sheets of paper card sharks use at fairs. "Here is an article about Poland, this one is about Czechoslovakia, and this is about you, printed in English. You can see for yourself that I write with warm feelings about Hungary."

The counselor inclined his head and at a glance recognized whole phrases lifted from a brochure about Hungary's new education system that had been distributed at a UNESCO convention.

"How do you think information about Hungary might gain a large audience in India? Who will publish this book?"

"It can be published without risk in Madras in an edition of a thousand copies. Because the embassy will distribute them, surely it will buy eight hundred in advance, and pay me an honorarium? Then I could easily find a publisher, for they would not risk anything."

"How many people speak Malayalam?" the ambassador asked with interest.

"Well—over twelve million. We have a splendid literature. Great poets; a history encompassing two thousand years."

"Would it not be better to publish in English? Then the intelligentsia of all India . . ." the counselor reflected.

"I can also write in English," the man agreed hastily.

"An attractive proposition." The ambassador tapped the edge of an ashtray with his cigarette. "How much would your honorarium amount to?"

"Two rupees—" Motal looked narrowly at the heavy, bloated face and hesitated, "well, one and a half for each volume sold."

"Are you counting the copies the embassy would take?"

"Of course."

"We must get the ministry's agreement," the ambassador declared. "I believe, however, that there will be no resistance."

"So I am going? When could that occur?"

"Your journey around the country must be planned. You will need an interpreter—better yet, a female interpreter," the ambassador smiled. "Women put more heart into this business. Call on us in a month; perhaps we will know something concrete. Thank you for your readiness to cooperate."

The young man wanted to say something more, but the counselor was already standing up, extending his hand. Ceremoniously he conducted him to the secretary's office. He exchanged knowing winks with Judit, who was busy at her typewriter.

The writer from Ceylon was not easy to get rid of, however. Mustering his courage, he asked Terey for a packet of Hungarian cigarettes, for his daughter collected the boxes, it was a fad.

"Here you are." Judit offered a box. "Take mine. It's almost empty."

"No, thank you, madam," Motal said almost rebukingly. "It must be an undamaged packet. As with postage stamps, one little tear and the most valuable specimen is rubbish."

"Very well; I will give you one." She reached into a drawer. "Or perhaps you would like a variety? I will give you several kinds of cigarettes."

"You understand what a joy it will be to the child." He pushed the boxes into his pockets. "The other girls will envy her."

In the hall he asked if he might take a few of the illustrated publications that were laid out on a table; he wanted to add to his store of material about Hungary. Terey ordered the office caretaker to prepare a file of magazines.

Just as he thought he had finally finished with the petitioner, Motal returned in a wave of heat that rushed in through the open entrance door and asked with a resentful air, "You will have someone drive me to Connaught Place, will you not? They always do that at the Russian embassy. I got a whole basket of jellies and wines from them for the Diwali festival, and my wife got a shawl, and my daughter was given a big box of all sorts of cigarettes; they remembered our whole family. I like the Russians very much; Russia is a great nation. I like you, too. Be so kind and try to get me a car."

The counselor summoned Krishan.

The heat was unbearable. The white light was like a load on the shoulders; even as he re-entered the dim interior of the embassy Terey felt the heated fabric of his jacket on his back, as if he had leaned against a tiled stove.

"Until the one o'clock break," he whispered to Judit. "Keep your fingers crossed."

He knocked at the door, heard a friendly rumble, and went in. The ambassador looked at him with the eye of a raging bull; he was speaking with someone on the telephone—someone at home, no doubt, for he was speaking Hungarian. At last he hung up the receiver, carefully, as if he were afraid of smashing it with his heavy hand.

"What more do you have to say, counselor?" He began applying pressure to Terey with a long silence. "He came to complain that you have been misleading him."

Terey listened calmly, not hurrying to defend himself. He took a cigarette and placed it in an ivory holder.

"May I?"

"Of course, smoke. That's what they're there for. I'm afraid it's only in matters like that that you ask my permission, that you remember my existence. If it's a question of forming friendships or sitting around in clubs at night, my opinion is of no importance. Well—why are you looking at me that way? Say something."

Terey blew out a stream of smoke slowly. In order to remain unruffled, he had to know first what he would be blamed for; a justification offered too soon might expose a weakness on his side of the argument.

"I think, comrade ambassador, that you are a good psychologist."

The other man drew himself up behind his desk and looked at Terey suspiciously. But his curiosity came to the fore; he could not restrain it.

"You must have something on your conscience, since you begin by flattering me so coolly. As it is, I know quite a few things. Speak up! Delhi is just an oversized village. Rumors fly around faster than pigeons."

"You recognized at once, comrade minister, the true value of this hack. He wants, like everyone, to go away, to escape. He makes the rounds of the embassies and begs. The long and short of it is he does not know how to write."

"And what of the article he showed us?"

"The content is from the promotional brochures."

"But they print his work."

"I understood the entire process. Nagar told me. He brings in a text culled from other writings; he shows it to the journalists, promising to cut them in on his earnings. Then he races over here with a clipping and demands an honorarium for shaping public opinion favorably for us, gets thirty rupees, and keeps ten for himself. He is content with the scraps. One thought captivates and consumes him: to go to Europe at our expense, to forget about hardship, about the inquisitive looks of his wife and daughters, the frugal dinner, the carefully counted cigarettes, the embarrassing emptiness in the pocket. You saw through him at once, comrade ambassador, for you asked how many books he had published, and how many copies of each."

Would he accept the compliment or rebuff it? He ought to remember who asked those questions. Bajcsy frowned and remained silent.

"Poor fellow. But he is useful in some way to the Russians."

"They give him articles already prepared, which he places under his own name. They pay him, so the firm that publishes the articles gets them free of charge, and the Russians' stake in the situation remains secret. A rumor without authority. So he himself crosses out the most pointed phrases, and says that the censor expurgated the article."

"He was an activist for freedom, all the same. The English wanted to arrest him. He fled from Ceylon."

"I have heard the general opinion on that. It is always necessary to question people from another quarter of the Hindu community; they loathe each other. He went to jail for usury and embezzling security deposits. He himself was not guilty, but his family made him the scapegoat. He escaped, and they blamed everything on him. They had to send him some money to tide him over, but lately those dribs and drabs come very seldom."

"How do you know all this? Do you have it from credible sources?"

"I wouldn't stake my life on it, but various small facts confirm it. For example, to let it be known in one embassy that he has connections in another, he takes out foreign cigarettes like those he cadged here, and in this way arouses generosity. It was brilliant, comrade ambassador, how you saw through him. We have gained a month without antagonizing the fellow.

"The hope of an excursion to Europe is a powerful engine. Tomorrow half of Delhi will be talking about it, and he will begin waiting for what he is boasting of to come true. They will sympathize with us a little for allowing ourselves to be duped, or perhaps, conversely, a rival will be miffed and send him so as to get ahead of us—Poles, or East Germans? He has a beat, like a beggar who circulates through his town not too often, trying to milk the inhabitants even-handedly."

"Why didn't you put me on my guard? I would not have received him."

"He announced himself at the secretary's desk; everything happened over my head. He had had enough of me. He wanted to knock at the door of someone higher up. I didn't even mention him because—what for? After all, my job is to filter out the truth about people and the country and spare you difficulty."

The ambassador took his face in his hand. His plump fingers were tufted with dark hair; the folds of his fat jowl oozed between them. His look was saturnine and disapproving.

"Tell me one thing: must you sit around at the club until all hours? I have been told that at Khaterpalia's wedding as well, everyone had gone and you stayed because the bar was still open. Aren't you drinking too much?"

"It depends on the circumstances." Istvan spread his hands.

Bajcsy huffed.

"Give me just one piece of evidence that you are not pulling my leg."

Terey thought coolly: don't hurry. Don't give way. Someone must have been telling tales.

"During that wedding I found out that the law prohibiting the transfer of pounds will go into effect half a year earlier than expected. That will have a serious effect on importing, and will limit the scope of our activities as well," he flung out as if he were reluctant to speak.

"That is information of the first order of importance," the ambassador said, raising himself in his chair. "And you only tell me about it now? Is it certain? I don't ask the name."

"I looked into it. I sought confirmation. Only as of yesterday am I certain. It checks out. They are barring the doors. My original information came from an officer of the president's guard. He himself was an interested party. He wanted to get some capital out of the country."

"Terey, write me a memorandum about this."

"I have it with me as we speak, but, comrade ambassador, you have not let me get a word in edgewise." He put a sheet of paper with a few sentences in typescript on the desk.

Bajcsy read slowly, moving his thick lips. Then he looked suspicious, as if it had just occurred to him that he had been drawn into a game against his will. But Terey calmly closed his briefcase and sat unassumingly in his chair, smoking a cigarette.

Exiting, he met Judit's glance. It was full of camaraderie. He raised a thumb to signal that all was well. She had been waiting behind the door like an anxious mother when her son is taking a test.

"The ambassador asks that you send in the cryptographer."

"Did he give you a dressing down?" Her tone was solicitous.

"For what? I live modestly, I do my work. You see me like a goldfish in a bowl. What do I have to hide?"

"You know very well." She wagged a cautionary finger. "Be careful not to get yourself in trouble."

In spite of the wheezing of the big fans, agonizing moans made their way in through the windows. His face contorted as he heard them.

"Who is wailing so?"

"Krishan's wife. Go through to Ferenc's office. It's enough to break your heart, the way that woman is wearing herself down."

"What's happened? Is she sick?"

"I don't know. Krishan only laughs and shows his teeth. A bad lot, that one."

"Perhaps we could look in? We can't let her suffer like that."

"What do you want to drag me along for? I'm afraid of sickness. To my taste, life is too short here. I detest the way fourteen-year-old girls become mothers. Children bearing children." She shuddered. "Every smell here carries a waft of something putrid, a stench of burning bodies. No, I will not go."

He stepped out of the embassy and was immersed in a thick suspension of dust and sunlight. At once his skin was covered with sweat. He blinked: the air was filled with rainbow-tinted sequins. They rose and pulsed as if in rhythm with the contractions of a breaking heart.

He walked around the corner house with its clumps of trees brandishing vermilion torches; their dark green leaves held sprays of blossoms garish as flames. A large lizard, covered with iridescent scales, stood on his hind legs, gazing at Terey with a sharp, unfriendly yellow eye. The spikes on its back bristled at every breath.

It looked like an antediluvian monster in miniature. The old gardener, in an unbuttoned shirt, threw a clod of earth at it. It only hissed and disappeared up a tree.

"It spits, sir," he warned. "You can go blind."

The light cut through his mesh shirt, glancing off his ribs and the back of his wrinkled neck. His legs were black and covered with clots of dried mud like rusty iron.

"Sir goes there?" He motioned toward a building in which the ground floor rooms had been made over into quarters for the servants. "She calls for death—such a pretty, plump woman," he mumbled. "For the second day she prays to Durga."

"But what is the matter with her?"

"Who can know?"

"Has a doctor been here?"

The old man leaned on his hoe. The edge, worn to silver, threw specks of bright light onto his lean, knotted calves. He looked at Terey; his dull, cloudy eyes were full of sorrow.

"And why a doctor? A yogi was here. He broke the spell, but now he does not want to look in. He only gave her an herb, and then she slept all night. Death alone will help in this case."

"Blithering nonsense! We have to make sure Krishan takes her to the hospital."

"She has been there, sir. They were going to cut her. But she doesn't want to be burned bit by bit, but all at once. For then where would she look for the next birth?"

The moaning could be heard more and more distinctly; Terey could distinguish pleading, singsong cries of prayer. The white walls in the house blinded him; the masonry trapped the sultry air. The door had been taken off its hinges and carried away to the garage. In its place hung only a muslin curtain, tied back.

On a bed a stout woman dressed in a sari lay with her legs spread. He saw her feet, which were painted red. A roll of fat was exposed at the waistline above her distended belly. The navel, with a small piece of colored glass set into it, peeped out impudently. A little girl was sitting beside her, waving a fan of peacock feathers to chase away the flies that crawled insistently into her eyes and nose and pushed themselves between the lips open in moaning.

"To die!" the woman howled.

"But where does it hurt you?"

"Here—" she touched her abdomen "—and my head, my head is splitting."

"You must go to the hospital," he urged. "To a proper doctor. The embassy will pay."

"No. I want to die or give birth."

She raised her flushed face. The dyed mark on her forehead was dissolving in perspiration and running into her eyebrows like blood. The parting of her hair, which was colored red according to the custom of married women, looked like an open wound.

Istvan recalled dying people, shot in the head by snipers, but they had not screamed with such despair; they expired quietly. At first he had been relieved to come in under a roof, but now he was unable to breathe. He was choking on the sour smell of smoldering manure under the little clay stove, on stifling perfumes and the odor of sweat.

Feeling himself at his wits' end, he went back to the embassy. He knew the customs here; nothing could be done by force. The sick woman did not want to take his advice—that was her right, to make her own determination. No physician would touch her; he had no right to. Probably the woman would lose consciousness, and even then her will was binding if it had been clearly expressed.

Krishan was squatting beside the car, smoking a cigarette. He was having a rest; the cries from the house did not disturb his siesta. The sun glinted on his frizzy, greased hair. On his hand he had a tattooed monkey that was covering its eyes. (May they not see what I do, ran the illustrated prayer.) On his fingers he wore a heavy gold signet ring, a gift from his wife. It was hard to think of him as one of the poor.

"Krishan, is your wife giving birth?"

He lifted his triangular face. His little catlike teeth showed from under his mustache in a smile like a grimace.

"Don't trouble yourself, sir. She gives birth this way every month. The spoiled blood does not want to come out of her, and it hits inside her head. She has a tumor, but if it is cut out she will not be able to bear a child, and what do I want with such a wife?"

"Krishan—she is exhausting herself!"

"And I am not? For the second day I have not had a moment to breathe. Let her die or get well; then this will not be a hindrance to life or to work. She knows that, so she doesn't want an operation. She loves me; the fortunetellers said that she would have a child. Perhaps this will pass and she will heal? My uncle had a tumor, and then the holy man came and pierced the place that hurt with a fork. It made a little wound that ran for three weeks, and that was the end of the tumor. It depends on what a person's fate is. My horoscope commands me to avoid sweets. I don't eat them."

Terey went to the secretary's desk to drink tea from a thermos. He bathed his hands in the stream of air from the large fan. Judit listened to his report.

"Beast," she said, referring to Krishan.

She drew a flat bottle from the medicine chest and poured half a glass of cognac.

"I'll give her a swallow."

"You will kill her. Her husband will charge you."

"It's the old English way. When I was in London—"

"Or in Siberia?" he broke in.

"There as well. If someone's period was late—for no cause of her own making—she took a glass of something strong and—to the bath! Here we all have a bath, but without the liquid incentive. It will work; you'll see."

She walked through the corridor with a firm step.

"I must pour it in myself. She loves Krishan so, she would leave the cognac for him."

She went down the corridor slightly hunched, looking at the surface of the golden liquid in the little glass.

Istvan was left to his own thoughts; he sat down and, feeling relieved, lit a cigarette. He relived his conversation with Bajcsy, thinking of more adroit responses, more resourceful ways of making his case.

"Calm down; quit thinking like a second-rate actor," he scolded himself and began looking over the mail. Invitations to lectures had arrived, and letters asking when an exhibit of Hungarian handicrafts was coming to Kampur, and several notifications of receptions, including one from the vice minister of agriculture.

Among the magazines lay a long brown envelope that Judit had brought him. He shook out photographs and spread them fanwise on the table.

They were all there—beautiful girls seized by the unexpected, ruthless glare of the flash. In the slender, flexible bodies, the dancing gestures, he discovered again the joy of that evening hour. Light bulbs in the background appeared as luminous flecks, like stars too near. What would be the fates of those blooming young women? What awaited them? The flash appeared to hold them in suspension, to fix them, to shield them from the liberating, destructive force of time. But how briefly! These photographs will still have meaning for me, will evoke the sultriness of Delhi at night, he thought—but for my sons?

If his boys were to exhume from a drawer the file of glossy thick papers with images of exotically dressed beauties, they would lean forward eagerly, they would snatch them out. Perhaps they would allude to him with some vulgar, boyish word of admiration that would suit their notion of man-to-man complicity. Dad: he knew how to get the girls! They would consider Grace's beauty with detachment; they would look at the wide Hindu eyes, the full lips. How much of what he had experienced was it possible to transmit? How could the surging of the breath and the nails clawing on the carpet, the fragrance of the hair his face was buried in, be preserved in words? How to capture that excitement which even now made the heart pound? He wrote poetry. He had published two volumes that had received measured praise, that were not easily understood. Perhaps, then, that wedding night, which had not been his wedding night, would be revived in verse.

Toward Grace, however, he felt a thankfulness slightly tinged with aversion. He was even gratified that she had gone with her husband to Jaipur to be introduced to the rest of his family and shown her new estate. Though it had the ring of a romance from a century ago, she had to receive homage from the subjects to whom the young rajah was not only a master, a figure of authority, but an object of affection. They spoke of him with concern and respect; they had known him since he was a child. Istvan was relieved at not having to meet the rajah, to look him in the eye, to smile, to press his hand—at being spared all that. Though, of course, he could have managed to lie, if one could describe as lying the resumption of the friendly gestures that had passed between them before the event he would have preferred to erase from his memory.

He was grateful to Grace that she was not in Delhi. He felt the cowardly satisfaction of an accomplice who sees his partner in crime and does not feel their act as a betrayal, but thinks indulgently of himself, feels his guilt mitigated, and absolves them both.

A past to hide, to bury. Would that mad, reckless act not be punished some day? Would not justice demand that it be reflected on once again, apart from the violent spasms of the flesh and the singing of the blood?

He shuddered. He began to listen intently. The cries outside the window, so monotonously repeated that he had almost become accustomed to them, suddenly stopped. She died, he thought with a mixture of sorrow, relief, and disgust at the imbecility of Krishan's wife. But did he have a right to judge her? What could she have done? Krishan had long since squandered her dowry. To be barren is to be cursed. He would send her back to her parents in the village to be a laughingstock. Perhaps it was better, instead of letting oneself be spayed, to accept the verdict of death.

When he left the embassy after work, he met Judit returning from the servants' quarters. Her face glistened with sweat, but she was smiling triumphantly.

"It went well. It flows," she whispered in his ear. "She had never touched alcohol before; that is the Hindu religion. The cognac worked a miracle."

"Not for long."

"No miracle exempts one from death," she said soberly. "In any case, she is not suffering now. We have a month to get her to a surgeon."

Terey looked into her dark, somber eyes, now, in the glare of the sun, lighted from inside like amber. He could see that she was moved.

"You don't allow yourself a show of emotion."

"Do you want me to cry over her? I hate pious stupidity. If she will not listen to us, too bad, let her die. I'm afraid a month will seem terribly long to her. She has so much time yet. The day after tomorrow she will forget that she was calling for death to free her from suffering. When I know people better, even when I look at you, it seems to me that each is to himself both hangman and victim. There is no salvation."

"It will be a hollow victory for you that you predicted the course of events. You need only be patient and wait a little."

"Yes, Istvan," she nodded, "but surprises happen sometimes. A couple of times I was so fortunate as to happen upon—a man."

"Well, and what about it? Were you happier?"

"This is not the time to talk about it. You are coaxing confidences about lost love from me. Believe me, for those few people, and I can count them on the fingers of one hand, it was worth it to live."

Out of the embassy walked Lajos Ferenc, still immaculate and fresh after a day's work, with the bow tie between the points of his starched collar perfectly straight. His long, wavy hair was slightly tinged with silver. He had the good looks of a mannequin in a clothing store window.

"Will one of you be in town today? I have a little work to do, I must be at home, and I have films to pick up."

He would never have admitted that he wanted to lie down, to look through the magazines or play bridge with his wife and neighbors. No—he always had to sit down to work, to attend to something, broaden his knowledge; he never broke free of work, but he achieved his goals.

He avoided meetings with friends; when everyone agreed to meet at Volga just for ice cream, he turned up as well, but ate ice cream at a different table, on the watch for an interesting contact that would add to his understanding of the political situation in the country to which he had been posted.

"I will be at an exhibition of children's painting. Old Shankar invited me to be on the jury. I can pick up the films," Istvan spoke up.

Ferenc handed him the receipts for the films and thanked him effusively. He walked with perfectly erect posture down the path toward his house.

"I'll take you, Judit. Wait." Istvan drove the car out of the slightly shaded parking space. "Oh, what an oven!"

Even through its linen cover, the plastic seat was hot on his back. He slowed down as he passed Ferenc and with a gesture invited him to get in the car. But the secretary only thanked him, slightly raising his Panama hat. It occurred to Terey that they wore hats like that at the Russian embassy.

"Do you know what he said today when I asked him if he weren't bored sometimes?" Judit began. "'A man who works with integrity has no time to experience loneliness.' I tell you, he will go far."

"And he will not get on anyone's bad side," Terey agreed, "not because he has no opinions—but why should he express them, since one can simply repeat the ambassador's weighty pronouncements?"

"Confess: do you envy him?"

"No. I prefer to be myself and have time to experience loneliness."

"And I prefer you that way. Well, goodbye. If you go to the cinema this week, think of me—an hour's kindness to an aging woman," she joked cheerlessly, tapping his hand.

He didn't drive away in a hurry. He watched her as she went down a path under enormous trees with leaves that seem to be lacquered.

I know very little about her, he thought. And she also covers over the lacunae in her biography. If she learned languages before the war, she could not have been from the proletariat. Who is she, really? She says that kindness is a form of weakness . . .

In front of Terey's house stood a two-wheeled cart with a pony harnessed to it. The cart was loaded with rolled carpets; a fat trader was sleeping on them. The hiss of the braking tires woke him. He started up like a spider emerging from its hole when its web twitches, nudged by its prey.

"Babuji," the man called, "I have brought carpets."

"Not today," Terey said roughly as he passed him. "Another time."

"A week ago sir also promised. After all, I want nothing. I only ask you let me show you my treasures from Kashmir."

"I will not buy."

"Who said buy? Sir don't have time to look at the whole collection. I brought only one carpet I chose special for you. We don't talk about money. I have one dream; I want to spread it out for you in a room. You like it, it stay. If no—in a week I bring another one until we find the right one. No. Not a word about money. Is important my little joy when sir pick out something. All right? Please, do me favor," he begged, holding out his hands.

The watchman blocked his way, holding a thick bamboo stick crosswise.

"Not today. I don't have time," Terey rebuffed him.

"That is bad for sir. Americans take the best, but do they know carpets? And I was so happy. Let me spread under feet one rust color, short pile, flower pattern. A true treasure. I saved special for sahib."

The clusters of climbing plants were parted by dark hands and the vulturine head of the cook in his starched blue turban appeared.

"Sir," he advised, "it costs nothing. His rugs are beautiful, old. Let him spread it out."

Istvan suddenly felt tired. So the trader had suborned the cook to aid in the entrapment! The watchman, too, was looking around, making a barrier, with a theatrical gesture, of the bamboo stick. The trader had a pained expression on his face such as one rarely saw even at a funeral. The pony gave a quick shake of its close-clipped mane; horseflies stung him and he stamped the cracked red clay until clods spattered. They were waiting. Can I disappoint them all? he thought. In a couple of days I will tell him to take the carpet away. I am under no obligation because he unrolls it today.

"All right. Show it." He waved assent. "But quickly. I have no time."

Then something inconceivable happened. The diffident merchant shouted imperiously; the watchman leaned his stick on the low wall and jumped to lift a thick roll of carpet on his shoulder. The cook disappeared into the house; his commands floated out as he prodded the sweeper, and together, with scraping noises, they pushed a table out of the way, dragged chairs about and cleared a place.

"Who of us has time to lose, sahib?" sighed the merchant. "But worth it to look a moment at this carpet. I go away. Sahib look at it today, tomorrow sit in chair, smoke cigarette, and think why this carpet now the nicest place in the room. Not only nice for the eyes, needs bare feet. Take time and decide. I don't push. I go away."

Heavy, sweaty, his puffy, starched white trousers rustling, he walked to the gate as if the outcome of the inspection were of no concern to him.

"Sir—" he turned around as if making a confession with tenderly half-shut, lachrymose eyes "—I cannot make profit off sir. I know sir's soul. It hungry for beauty."

Soul? What can he know of me? Istvan wondered. He questioned the neighbors, he got some opinions, he made sure I can pay. He has nothing to lose. He promised the servants a handful of change, he drew them into the scheme. They worked out the tactics and the timing.

He went inside. In that short instant, when he opened the screen door, a little swarm of flies squeezed in and glided around, following the alluring aromas from the kitchen.

The cook and the sweeper stood chatting with their heads hung down like two parrots in a cage, admiring the carpet. It was handsome: rust and brownish-green, with a small, bluish motif of a tree and yellow-green blossoms. The tones were soft, harmonious, the pattern the work of no common artist. The rug pleased Terey, and that exasperated him. The trader must have been a good psychologist, or perhaps they had let him in on the sly, and he had glanced around the walls, spied out Terey's favorite combination of colors in the pictures.

The sweeper squatted and with a gnarled hand stroked the short nap of the carpet, as if he were afraid he would wake the dyes from sleep.

"The merchant admitted," Terey said on a hunch, "that he gave you five rupees each to show him the house."

"He is lying, sahib," the cook said indignantly. "He only promised me half a rupee. He had to give the watchman twenty naye paise at once or he wouldn't let him in at the gate. I have still gotten nothing." His speech had a reproachful ring as he looked with his black eyes from under bristling, grizzled eyebrows.

"So you only have to be promised half a rupee to betray my trust and intrude on my privacy? Aren't you getting enough?"

"Sahib, I wanted to do the best for myself. We will take out the carpet in two days."

"Serve the dinner. If you don't like working for me, you can quit any time and be that merchant's helper, since you know so much about rugs."

The cook stood as if stricken by a thunderbolt. His jaw dropped at the thought of leaving the house. There were tears in his eyes. Istvan was sorry for him.

The sweeper had vanished some time before; on hearing angry words, he preferred to disappear.

Terey pulled off his shirt, which was clinging to his back, and removed his sandals. With relief he immersed himself to the neck in the water that was waiting for him in the tub, and relaxed. A few minutes had hardly passed when Pereira was scratching discreetly at the frosted glass in the bathroom door.

"Sahib, dinner is on the table," he said coaxingly. "Today we have chicken with rice and raisins."

WHEN HE DROVE THE CAR toward the center of New Delhi at six, the heat had subsided in a golden dust; the softened asphalt smacked under the wheels. He passed slow-moving two-wheeled arbas pulled by docile white oxen. Birds sat on their pale necks and combed through their coats with their beaks, searching for ticks. The drivers, nearly naked, dozed squatting on the shafts. Half asleep, they emitted cries and made disjointed motions, prodding the animals' hindquarters with sharp sticks. At the sound of the horn they woke and tugged at the strings attached to copper rings in the beasts' wet nostrils. But before he had passed the arbas their heads had already fallen onto their meager chests, which gleamed with trickles of sweat.

The bare, stony hills around the city looked as if there had been fires on them not long ago, with their dark red, glowing rocks and ashy white bristles of dry grass. The wind raised columns of reddish dust; it powdered the foreheads of pilgrims shrouded in white who moved with small, determined steps as their hands rested on shepherds' staffs.

Figures like those in Doré's copperplate etchings in the old Bible, Istvan thought. The world of a thousand years ago.

Huge trucks, with raised coops on their flatbeds, wobbled as they moved along, loaded with sacks of cotton. The hoods painted with stars and flowers reminded Terey of the tops of boxes made by peasants from the region around Debrecen. They passed each other, exchanging joyful blasts of their horns. Some drivers had fastened copper trumpets with red rubber bulbs, two or even three, to their vehicles. They drove the trucks with one hand and with the other played the whole scale of squeals and whines. Passengers casually picked up, sprawling as best they could on the freight, raised lean, twiggy hands in friendly salutes.

In a flutter of dhotis like great skeins of white unrolling, breathless cyclists came riding up in swarms, a little dazzled by the glare, their dark knees moving up and down like levers on a machine. Their unlaced boots dangled from their bare, callused feet. At this time of day the streets were a pulsing mass of bodies; the return from work had begun.

Terey made his way under the viaduct, with difficulty passing the tramways plastered with clusters of people hanging on, and turned into Connaught Place. Motionless clumps of trees and blossoming branches gave off a smell of blighted greenery and dust. The silence startled him. Bicycle bells in the distance chirped like cicadas. Cows, sacred to Hindus, slept in the shade; beside them were whole families of peasants seeking a semblance of coolness and relaxation.

He put on the brakes.

The colonnade of Central Delhi spread in a wide arc of separate shops which even had glass windows. It was possible to walk all the way around it in the shade, under arches supported by light-colored columns. Here sat sellers of souvenirs hammered out of heated horn into the shapes of chalices and lamp shades; a potbellied fellow hawked a stack of sandals; the colorful covers of cheap

American detective novels were displayed on a piece of plastic. A peddler discreetly pushed forward a collection of pictures of sensuously entwined couples—an imitation of a frieze from the Black Pagoda, produced somewhere among the bordellos of Calcutta or Hong Kong.

From a little stove under a pillar came the smell of roasted peanuts. A hand studded with rings was extended, offering the nuts in a horn formed by twisting a large leaf. He looked with pleasure into the woman's beautiful eyes, but shook his head.

"Not today," he said, so as not to leave her without hope.

He collected Ferenc's films and was driving to Volga for iced coffee when he caught sight of Miss Ward—her slim figure, her graceful legs. Her chestnut hair glistened red in a streak of sunlight. She was so absorbed in examining some homespun cotton printed with little horses, buffalo heads, and dancing goddesses that he overtook her without her noticing. He stood close behind her, watching the hands through which a cascade of linen poured, before saying in a laughing voice:

"Hello, Margit."

"Hello," she flung back. But no sooner had she thrown him a sharp glance with her blue eyes than her face lighted in a friendly smile. "Ah, it's you."

"You have forgotten my name? Istvan. Why have you given no sign of life? I thought you were stuck in Agra."

"For the time being they are keeping me in Delhi. I have four hours' work at a clinic. I'm learning the language, the indispensable phrases, 'Be calm,' 'This won't hurt,' 'Look to the left, to the right,' 'Don't move,' 'Everything will be all right.'"

"Are you staying long?"

"Till the end of the month."

"What do you do by yourself?"

"How do you know that I am by myself? Do you think I'm bored?" the girl laughed. "True, Grace is in Jaipur. I was counting on her to initiate me into this world, but now I see that I can take care of myself very well. I make the rounds of the shops, I see more than I buy. Folk crafts cost nothing here! Embroidery, peasant prints like this"—she shook out a strip of material printed with galloping horses. "Sandalwood figurines. I must take something home to each of my women friends to prove that I thought of them even in India."

"Don't buy them here." He took the fabric printed with blue and vermilion out of her hand. "I will show you real peasant saris. Have you been to Old Delhi?"

"No. I go around the neighborhoods I know. Mr. Vijayaveda advised me not to venture there. Would you have time to go with me some day?"

"It would be a pleasure to take someone there for the first time, to hear their cries of rapture and admiration—to look at India again through other eyes."

"Do you have your car? I sent away the one from UNESCO. I wanted to walk around a bit when the heat let up."

Angular rays of sunlight invaded the tiled passage under the arcade. Motes of dust sailed in the glare. The seller of fabric unfastened his shirt to the navel to cool his bulging, shaggy chest with a palm leaf fan.

"How do you feel—being here?" Terey took the young woman by the hand.

"Well, even very well. Look how I've tanned." She showed him a supple arm. Her skin had a golden tint. There were freckles on it, which made him smile.

"Shall we begin with coffee and ice cream? Or go on a souvenir hunt first?"

"Can one risk eating anything here? So many times they've frightened me with talk of amoebae, dysentery, typhus."

"Look—they all eat, and they are still alive." He pointed to peasant women in orange skirts who were camping under the trees.

"But there are such multitudes of them, and only one of me," she laughed.

"One must eat what they eat," he explained when they were sitting in the coffee shop. In its dim interior, electric lights created an artificial night. In spite of the fragrances of strong coffees set out in containers attached to stands, and the breeze from cooling machines, hardly any buzz of conversation could be heard.

Glum Hindus sat at the tables, resting their heads on their hands. Women with lovely eyes toyed with flowers or crumbled cake with their spoons. A Chinese musician beat out jazzy rhythms. He noticed Istvan and, inclining his head, played part of a march by Radetzky—the only melody he associated with Hungary.

"Start with this cake," Terey suggested, pouring them coffee.

"What is sprinkled on it?" Her finger hung over the tray of cakes.

"Real silver. It was hammered so long that it broke into flakes. They dissolve and the system absorbs them. People here consider silver a supplement essential for emotional well-being."

She put some on the end of her spoon with comic distrust, and with an air of concentration took a bite. She had luminous eyes, as dolls have sometimes. She wrinkled her little freckled nose with humorous charm. She was certainly not a beauty in the classic sense, but she attracted attention; he saw glances aimed at her, he heard whispers, and they gave him pleasure. A new face, a woman about whom everything was not yet known.

"I don't feel the silver," she exulted. "It is utterly delicious. And the green at the bottom is edible as well?"

"Pistachio paste."

"You will have me on your conscience—I've forgotten your name again!"

"Istvan."

"It's hard."

"You will remember it if you repeat it often. Especially just before you go to sleep."

"Istvan. Ist-van," she said, pronouncing it with an English inflection, like a polite little girl learning a lesson. "Couldn't I change it to Terry? I had a dog by that name."

"I will accept whatever name you give me."

"Grace was right to put me on my guard against you. You like to trifle with people's hearts."

"No!" he contradicted her with zeal. "You said yourself that you have been left on your own. It's no particular sacrifice on my part to share your solitude. I'll give you my home telephone number. Perhaps one day we can go to the cinema? Or I'll take you to a hunt? We can take a trip by car and I will show you an authentic village. The country people are good, hospitable. There's nothing to be afraid of. As long as you're here."

"So many ideas, Istvan! I'll hold you to your word." She looked at him warmly. "You must be bored if you find even a lady doctor's company diverting. But perhaps you have me confused with Grace?"

He looked at her through bluish cigarette smoke, at her graceful head, her candid, unpainted lips—nude, he thought jocularly—and her eyes, so crystalline and full of blue lights that they were disturbing.

"I certainly do not have you confused with Grace."

He felt a great friendliness toward her. It was pleasant to appear in public with a woman who was good-looking, well dressed, and young.

"You don't even know what I'm like. Perhaps after one stroll you'll have had enough of me."

"No." He shook his head; he was certain of that. She smiled perversely, emphasizing the dimples in her cheeks. She looked a little arch, as if she knew a good deal about him. He grew uneasy: had Grace whispered something to her?

"Let's get out of here." He rose suddenly, touching her hand, for the double curtains that served as doors had parted, and in the unforgiving blaze of the sun he spied Judit with two acquaintances from Bulgaria.

They rose and exchanged greetings with the new arrivals, motioning them to their vacant table, for which a bearded Sikh had been lurking in wait. Terey did not fail to notice that Judit discreetly raised a thumb, a sign that she endorsed his choice. They went out into the sun, blinking.

The Austin exploded with heat. They rolled down the windows frantically. The blast of air scorched their faces.

"Why did you take fright when that woman came in?" Margit adjusted her dress, which had been pulled askew by the wind.

"She is the ambassador's secretary. They'll be talking straight away. And what concern is it of theirs?"

"Oh, Terry, Terry, you must have gotten into a lot of mischief here. I already know whom to ask about your past if you don't tell me yourself: Dr. Kapur lives not far from us."

"No doubt he will charge you like a patient coming for consultation. Only you must remember that he is a clairvoyant. He will tell you of future matters, things that have not occurred yet."

"You are afraid of Kapur?" She clapped her hands. "A fine how-do-you-do! Grace has gone away and I am thrown back on your evasions, with no defense! Who will reveal to me what you really are?"

On the road, climbing up a bare hill, stretched a caravan of wagons pulled by oxen and camels. The big wheels, made of boards nailed together, creaked loudly. The drivers shouted. The great horns of the oxen drooped with weariness in the red sun; the camels moved in stately procession, their heads swaying.

A girl in a green sari, with a bulbous vessel on her head, knelt in the middle of the road and elevated her hands in a movement full of grace. Her bracelets threw off fire; bells fastened around her ankles chimed. Terey blew the horn. She looked around, startled, and fluttered to the edge of the road.

"Stop. I'd like to photograph her," Margit requested. "She danced so beautifully."

"I'd rather you looked at her from a distance, but try approaching her. See what she does."

He stopped the car beside the road and watched with roguish satisfaction as Margit made her way to the girl, showing by signs that she wanted to take a picture. The girl resisted, covering her face with fierce determination; the pot fell and dark shards scattered over the road.

"I warned you." He opened the door. "You'd be better off listening to your elders."

"She was gathering ox dung with her hands. She packed it into the pot on her head. Yet she seems like a princess in a fairy tale, she has so many jewels."

"Bamboo hoops studded with sequins and colored glass. She was gathering fuel. She will mold it into cakes and stick them to the wall to dry in the sun. Who would want to cut these bushes with those tough branches full of thorns? Manure mixed with straw burns well. Look: there they are carrying away whole bags of dry manure."

Low mud huts clustered densely along the road. On roofs covered with pieces of rusty tin, pigeons walked. Women squatted next to smoking bonfires, frying cakes in pans. Naked children with large eyes ran along behind automobiles that flew humming down the road, or sleepily sucked bits of sugar cane. Streaks of bluish smoke hung in the air, violet against the scarlet sky.

"Remember that pungent smell," he told her. "It's the smell of India at supper time."

They turned off the road. The Great Mosque, an enormous red building, seemed to menace the sky with its toothed walls. Vultures dozed above the gate, each on its turret, like adornments cast in bronze. Innumerable market stalls huddled by the steps leading to the fortified entrances.

A crowd surrounded them. Itinerant barbers, cleaners of ears, sellers of vegetable soup, and swindlers with monkeys dressed as soldiers, all shouted. Leaning on the horn, Terey cut his way with difficulty through the mass of people. They stepped aside reluctantly and peeped eagerly into the car, beating their fingers on the windows. All around rose the racket of voices hawking merchandise—old pots, wires, screws, spread out on newspaper. Every kind of rubbish thrown away in a European neighborhood was looked over three times here; anything might come in handy. Some objects could be sold, others bartered, if the buyer lacked the small change to pay for them. Homeless loiterers, gawkers, moved along the stalls among the odds and ends, hoping that if they spoke favorably of someone's wares, they could add their voices to the bargaining, be useful as intermediaries, and perhaps by flattery cadge a few paise.

Terey cleared a path through the crowd and parked the Austin. So many people gathered around the car that Margit hesitated about getting out.

"Well, brave it," he prodded. "They will make way for you, they will move back. You wanted to see real life, after all."

Half-naked boys jumped forward, raising their hands like diligent pupils.

"I will mind the car!" they called. "I will be watchman!"

He appointed two so they could keep each other company; they would guard both sides of the car. They shouted to passersby, proud of their employment.

Margit seized Istvan's hand tightly, as if she were afraid the crowd would separate them—that it would pull them into the narrow, crooked little streets and they would never find each other.

The odor of drains, of rotting peelings and steaming urine, beat into the nostrils. The three-story houses, solidly built below but with casually knocked together upper floors, pulsed with life. Lamplight leaked through chinks in the walls, along with the sounds of gramophones and sewing machines run by impatient hands, singing, and the crying of babies. Smells of heated coconut oil and smoldering sticks of incense, placed in clusters in vessels filled with votive ash, rode on the air.

On roofs barely secured with railings made from poles, children chased each other, squealing. Terey and Margit squeezed slowly through the crowd that breathed in their faces, reeking of spices, sweaty clothing, and pomade. Gaunt, perspiring peasants tried to catch up with Istvan. They touched him familiarly, saw that he was a European, and hastily pulled away. In front of the white-skinned pair the crowd was sparser; behind them came a growing mass of those who would not retreat but went on staring, discussing Margit's beauty at the tops of their voices, admiring her dress and high heels.

"Goldsmiths' shops. Look!" He pressed her hand.

A peasant woman in an elaborately gathered orange skirt and a tight green bodice pulled a scarf from her black hair, wound it around her hands, and stood with one foot on a stair. With caressing gestures an apprentice placed a heavy ring of silver around her ankle. An acetylene torch hummed with a clear flame. The silver ornaments shimmered. Delight showed on the woman's face; she must have coveted the anklet for a long time. Leaning on a counter, a master craftsman with a fat, almost female chest shouted to a young man, who quickly heated a thin silver wire and with light strokes of a hammer secured the anklet so it could not be removed. Two mustachioed peasants with very dark skin, wearing sun-bleached robes unfastened and dangling loose, picked coins out of a red kerchief and stacked them on the counter. Touching them with their fingers, they counted them several times. Chains, necklaces, and buckles, hanging on wires from a ceiling invisible in the dimness, revolved slowly, alluringly. Flashes from the torch threw darting shadows; the glow from little lights trickled as if in drops around the ornaments.

"How beautiful she is," Margit whispered. The crowd pressed in on them; they felt its warm, spicy breath on their necks. The peasant woman was alarmed. She tried to pull her skirt around her slender calf, but the blows from the hammer went on ringing.

"That can't come off, can it?"

"No. She will be the guardian of the treasure she wears. When they run short of money, she will come to this street and put her foot on the step, and the goldsmith will hammer the wire apart or saw through the anklet. He will throw it onto the scale and then he will repay her—only for the silver by weight, not for the anklet as an ornament, a work of art. That is his profit."

The woman gazed around with huge, splendid eyes that were clearly troubled. The craftsmen had made a mistake in their reckoning. One of them wiped the tip of his beak-like nose with his thumb. The goldsmith raised his bloated body and in the flute-like voice of the castrated invited the foreigners, if they would be pleased to come in, to look at his wares. He lifted the lid of an encrusted box and, like one who feeds poultry, sprinkled a fistful of unset stones on the counter.

"Perhaps you will go in and choose something for yourself? I warn you, they are not worth much. The real jewels are hiding deep inside the house. He would show them escorted by assistants, would do the honors, would tell the histories: how he acquired them, in whose hands they had been previously, and what luck they had brought their owners. Apart from their value, stones are highly esteemed for their magical properties."

But Margit was already moving down the street, her sights fixed on a tall Hindu with a black mane of greased hair. On his forehead was a yellow and white three-toothed sign. He walked aloof, as if he saw no one. The crowd parted before him. He was naked; his muscular body gleamed warm bronze. A sheath embroidered with beads covered his maleness, rather defining than concealing it.

He passed them, looking over people's heads into the red sky full of the fire of evening.

"A holy man. A devotee of Vishnu."

"I don't understand."

"A saint. For him the world is an illusion, as dreams are for you. He is awakened to eternity."

She shook her head, signaling that she did not comprehend, until her hair shone like copper.

A little girl lifted a baby who had been straddling her hip and blocked their way, watching Margit with rapt attention. She asked for nothing; she did not notice when the crowd pushed her toward a wall. She only went on looking greedily, astonished at the color of Margit's hair, her blue eyes, and her clothes.

A cow with a floppy, lopsided hump on the back of its neck made the road impassable. The faithful, smearing their hands with red lead, pressed their fingerprints on its flaxen-colored back. Beaded rosaries rattled around the animal's creased neck; a glass ring stuck on its horn gave off a greenish shimmer. It poked its friendly muzzle, wet with saliva, into a vegetable seller's basket and plucked a carrot from a bunch. The weak, emaciated man did not cry out, was not angry, did not strike. He only folded his hands as if begging a favor and tried to persuade it to walk a step farther, to move toward the other stalls.

The cow's muzzle worked sluggishly; it seemed to be cogitating deeply. The carrot vanished between its dark lips. Its black eyes, like those of the Hindus, were full of melancholy.

Suddenly it stood with legs wide apart, raised its tail, and pissed voluminously. Margit looked on astonished as an old woman in a sapphire-blue sari pressed her palms together and caught the stream. Piously she washed out the eyes of a girl who was keeping her company.

"A sacred cow," he explained, "so magical forces are latent in everything that comes from it."

The human river flowed by until they were dazed by the gaudy turbans, fiery scarves, saris edged with gold, faces of piercing beauty, full lips, and deep looks from artfully made-up eyes.

"Does their gorgeousness affect you, Terry?" she asked. "I feel terribly commonplace here."

A smile played on his face. He leaned toward her ear.

"There are no eyes like yours. Only now, against the background of this crowd, have I seen you. Is that what you wanted to hear?"

"You console me a little." As if struck by a sudden discovery, she added quickly, "Did you see how many here have diseases of the eye? Painted—and running with pus. Beautiful—and threatened with blindness."

"You suffer from occupational fatigue. I see only their shape and luster. Fortunately, I am not an oculist."

They turned onto a side street that was still more crowded; it was full of little silk shops. Whole sheaves of orange and yellow shawls hung from rods, like banners of the hot summer. Sellers, sitting cross-legged at tables, poured through their bare hands limp veils, diaphanous as mist, with glittering gold and silver threads.

"Shawls from Benares for the most beautiful . . . blessed shawls," they called patiently.

On the upper floors behind gratings made of flimsy wooden slats appeared a multitude of rouged faces. They were strangely cheerful. This sudden atmosphere of pleasure, the provocative cries, the laughter like the gurgling of pigeons and the jangle of music Margit found disquieting. She looked around the clusters of heads on the porches. Women pointed fingers at her, emitting birdlike cries of astonishment. She raised a hand to them and fluttered it in greeting. A roar of merriment answered her.

"Is that a school?"

"No. A brothel."

She looked down the street. Gramophones were playing; radio speakers blared. Girls who seemed identical, all with jewels in their hair, leaned out of innumerable windows.

"How is it possible? All those houses?" She could not conceive of it. "The whole street? There must be hundreds here."

"Thousands," he corrected her. "They don't have an easy life. Every Saturday the father comes from the country to collect money for rice for the family."

"Have you ever been here?"

"The very poorest come here, those who cannot afford a wife. This is not for a European."

The noise in the alley mingled with the strumming of music. Someone called from a roof and clapped his hands to attract their attention. There was a pungent smell of incense.

They walked one behind the other like straying children, holding hands. The paving was uneven and slippery from dishwater and fermenting peelings.

"Oh, wait"—she caught hold of his arm—"something's wrong. I've broken a heel."

"Go barefoot—I don't care," he laughed. "Half the people here do."

"Let's go back to the car. Really, I don't know what you find so amusing." She was limping.

"You're hopping like a sparrow."

Suddenly it seemed to Margit that from all the houses, from roofs and porches, they were looking at her and laughing. Even the throng moving about in the street seemed to have become a mob of scoffers. Her whole body was covered with perspiration. What concern are they of mine, she scolded herself. I'll get into the car, I'll go away, disappear. It will be as if I died. I am from another world.

"Good evening," someone behind them said in English.

They stopped. Ram Kanval had overtaken them. Nothing distinguished him from other men in this neighborhood: not the unfastened shirt over a slender chest glistening with sweat, the sandals on feet without socks, or the black eyes with the somnolent, hungry look.

"Perhaps you would like to visit me?" he suggested. "I live not far away, by the Ajmeri Gate. I will show you my new pictures."

"That would be nice, but not today. Miss Ward has broken a heel. She must buy some sandals."

"My acquaintance has a shoe shop not far from here. I will take you there."

Through a murky yard littered with barrels, beside a little restaurant where strips of cake were being fried in an enormous pan, they squeezed past a gate and came out on another street.

The red reflection in the sky was not enough; the interiors of the shops burned with glittering lights. Thousands of colored bulbs blinked.

When chairs had been pulled up and they were seated, the painter disappeared for a moment into the labyrinth of rooms and partitions from which the rattle of a machine and the noise of hammering issued.

The owner had put a jacket on over his untucked shirt. He was a bearded Sikh with a fleshy nose. He ordered coffee to be served. They sensed that their presence had aroused his hopes and that large purchases were surely expected.

Two men knelt by Margit. They took off her shoes. A low lamp placed on the ground beside her threw a bright beam on her narrow bare feet. Bundles of varicolored sandals were brought. A large finger unfastened a strap and grasped her instep obliquely. In full light Istvan saw her legs, slender, graceful, exposed. The motions of the kneeling men, whose shadows played on the ceiling, seemed to transform the measuring of the shoes into a mysterious ritual.

"The shop is a real discovery!" Margit was elated as she walked out with three pairs of sandals. "I feel different already!"

On the street, night was falling. The air was still and heavy, choked with scents. "Just a moment—please wait—I will accompany you in a moment," the painter said, then edged his way back into the interior of the shop.

"What are they quarreling about?" Margit was listening intently. "Did the Sikh cheat us?"

"Don't pry," Terey said. "You were not supposed to notice this scene. The painter is pressing his claim for a percentage because he brought them customers, and good ones, who didn't haggle over prices. Understand: this is not greed. He is struggling to live. To live—that means to eat, and where does the money come from?"

"I had no intention of injuring his self-respect. Look—now the street is like a scene from an opera."

In spite of the host of lights and winking neon signs, figures swathed in garments like sheets swarmed about in the golden dusk. They had embroidered openings for their eyes, like specters. The Muslim women were returning from the mosque. The slender figures in saris, with their beautiful eyes, moved with stately grace. Flashes of colored light dotted the men's white shirts. An intoxicating aroma came from inside the shops: the smell of spices, insecticide, and incense. Bands of carefree, giggling children raced about in the crowd.

Ram Kanval returned with a boy who took the parcel of sandals from Margit. "I had to see to it that your purchases were put away in the car," he said.

The little watchmen raised a joyful clamor on receiving half a rupee. The painter said his goodbyes, inviting them to come again and look at his pictures.

The walls of the Great Mosque reached the nearer stars. The minarets were like spears thrust into the sky. "Are you satisfied?" Terey turned to Margit as the beams from their headlights sent the white figures scampering.

"I felt that I was a drop in that relentless river of life, imperceptible, insignificant. We, white people, consider ourselves very important, as if the world would collapse without us. Newspapers, films, and our limited range of acquaintance feed that sense of superiority. Here I felt how terribly full of living things this country is. They multiply, they teem, they are on the march. One would like to know, where is this march going?"

Terey listened with an indulgent smile: the enchantment with India! She is still carried away with the spiritual life, the philosophy of renunciation. And then she will notice the effects. She will understand.

"I will show you where that river ends."

He grew somber. They passed the last homestead. They drove down along the Yamuna. Its water flowed through a slimy bed and wove itself into a riffling current under a railroad bridge. A guard with a rifle paced up and down, whistling a doleful tune.

Dozens of fires blazed on the bank. Some were overgrown with bristling heaps of stone; others simply glowed red when light breezes from the water drifted over them.

"Why have you brought me here?"

From a clump of trees, cicadas strummed so gratingly that it was like a drill in the ears.

"Do they burn the dead here?" she whispered.

"And there is the cemetery." He pointed to the water spotted with starlight. Streaks of smoke wandered above its surface. Over the bridge rumbled a line of tiny lighted squares: the windows of the southbound train to Bombay.

He took Margit's hand and guided her among the burning pyres. A dry crackling came from the flames. Two fire tenders covered the stones sparingly with kindling, forming a meager bed of sinewy sticks for a body shrouded in a white cloth. A woman in white brought a small brass vessel and poured a little melted butter on the remains. The pyre, kindled with a torch, burned laboriously, reluctantly.

There was no singing, no funeral speech, only the dry snapping of the swaying flames, the smell of butter and another smell that evoked dread in Terey—the odor, well known to him from wartime, of burned, bombarded cities, of charred corpses.

The writhing bed of fire—the pyre beside which they were standing—moved from inside, as if the dead body were trying to rise. Among the flaming branches a blackened hand thrust itself out, its palm open as if in pleading. Tatters of linen were burning on it.

"What's that?" Margit huddled close to Terey.

"The spasm of a muscle in the fire."

One of the funeral attendants pushed the protruding hand with a pole and held it in the thick of the flames until it blackened and fell down.

"This is where the course of the river that so delighted you ends. Without seeing this place you could understand very little about India."

Up to their waists in thick smoke, they started back to the car. The dead were being carried down on flimsy palls.

"Where do you want to go now?"

"Home, Terry, home," she whispered submissively. "You teach me humility."

"Not I. They." He pointed to the long, flickering fires as if they were warning signs.

Chapter III

"Tell me, Istvan, what has been happening with you? You used to find time for me," Judit reproached him. "Yesterday you were very unkind. You didn't want to go to the cinema with me. You said you had urgent work."

"I really did." He looked worriedly at her.

"Don't lie, at least. You're no good at it. I went by myself."

"To what film?" Suddenly he showed an interest.

"To the same one." Then came the home thrust: "I sat two rows behind you."

"I didn't see you."

"No wonder; you were so preoccupied with her. A pleasant girl, but you're seen together a little too often. And then the way you hop around her—be careful that you don't turn into a kangaroo."

She smiled, but her eyes looked troubled. She rotated a fan and put her face into the stream of air. The scorching sun made a yellow glow on the curtain.

"Infernal heat—"

"Don't blather. I've seen a lot and I've lived through a lot. You ought to take account of people a little, you know. You live in a bubble."

"I can swear to you that there is nothing between her and me." He looked her straight in the eye. "She is just a nice girl—and it gives me an occasion to speak English."

"You poor thing—is there a shortage of people here for you to speak to in English?" she said with a sympathetic grimace. "You could have kept from giving yourself away. I'm sure you will enrich your vocabulary, but in an area far removed from the professional."

"You're buzzing like a fly. Upon my word, with Miss Ward it's quite a different story."

"Are you—involved?"

"What put that into your head? Believe me, it is not serious."

"So much the worse. Istvan, you belong to the corps of our embassy, and she is from the enemy camp. Both sides will be suspicious of her. You will do her harm. At least, my lad, you ought to remember that. You ought to use a little judgment."

"Stop. You're being a bore." He pretended to turn back to his work, but Judit settled in for a long stay and lit a cigarette.

"Don't let me disturb you. Work. I came to look at you because I had almost forgotten how you look."

"After all, we see each other at the embassy," he said in self-defense.

"What kind of seeing is that?" she waved dismissively. "You used to come for a Coca-Cola and talk like a close friend."

They were silent for a moment. A cicada in the climbing plants behind the tightly closed window jangled monotonously; the sound was like a mowing. The insect was intoxicated with the surfeit of sunlight.

Istvan looked at Judit's mild face in profile: the capricious lips, the heavy wave of dyed hair. She must have been a very handsome woman. She had been through a great deal; she was wise and self-possessed. By now she only wanted peace, the companionship of well-wishers, a few comforts.

"After all, we didn't meet just yesterday," she said to soothe his irritation. "If I caution you, I do it for your own good, not to nag you. You surely don't suspect me of jealousy?"

"Certainly not," he rejoined warmly, not noticing that he was causing her pain.

"Istvan, Istvan! You do not see the woman in me at all!"

"I am so sorry!" He raised her hand to his lips.

"Well, as compensation you may tell me what your Australian is like." She gave a conspiratorial wink. "Out with it—yes, as you boys would talk among yourselves. What sort of person is she?"

"A doctor. An oculist. She works for UNESCO. Her father has some woolen factories; rather a wealthy family. They have a yacht.

Her mother died, her father married again, but she thinks highly of her stepmother."

Judit folded her arms and nodded sympathetically.

"You speak of her as if she were one of the Hindu girls: money, factories, yacht. What do I care about all that? Tell me about her, about what she is. What do you see in her?"

"Nothing. Really, nothing." He wriggled like a boy whose mother has caught him with his first cigarette. "I take her around and show her things about India—sometimes frightening things. She came here to work for at least a year at the Ophthalmological Institute to spite her family. Do you understand?" he said, almost pleading.

"More than you think."

The door opened cautiously, and Ferenc stood in it.

"Don't you hear the telephone in that room? It has been ringing and ringing."

"We hear it," she answered lightheartedly.

"Why don't you pick it up?"

"You only have to hurry if you want to catch fleas. It will ring and it will stop. Do you have more serious worries? If it's really something important, they'll ring back."

But the secretary leaned forward and whispered, "The ambassador has called a briefing at eleven. At five to eleven there will be a meeting in my office."

The breeze from the large fan blew into the painstakingly arranged waves of his hair. He smoothed them down immediately.

"Terey," he said with a disapproving look, "here you are again without your tie. You are introducing bohemian habits."

"Don't you know what the boss has on his mind? He usually notifies his captive audience about these conclaves at least a day in advance. I have a tie in the drawer. I will make a dignified appearance."

"Hurry up, then." Ferenc tapped a fingernail on the crystal of his flat gold Doxa watch.

"Do you know what he's going to talk about?"

"I know." He raised his eyebrows and, seeing that their curiosity was aroused, withdrew, closing the door.

"They are certainly beginning to treat me like a schoolboy again," Istvan sighed. "I've had enough of this sermonizing."

"No. You will come into your own when the time is right, when everything is ripe. I know what is on the boss's mind, too."

"Everyone knows but me. I am not worthy of confidence." He strode around the room, pulling on his tie with an expression of dread, as if it were a noose.

"It's the best evidence that you have distanced yourself. Istvan, you cannot think only of that woman. If you had come over to say a stupid 'Good morning' to me before the beginning of work, I would have whispered, 'Glance into the garage. Have a chat with Krishan.'"

"What the devil for?"

"Let's go. It's time." She crushed her cigarette in an earthenware ashtray. "We are at the mercy of Bajcsy's watch, even when it's a quarter of an hour fast."

She took him by the hand and pulled him along with a jocular air.

"To know does not mean to understand, and even less to spread something around. What you know, keep to yourself, and be glad that you are privy to it. Remember, old Judit tells you so, and beware. Sometimes your knowledge may be turned against you."

The ambassador had the appearance of a man whose energies have suddenly been roused—who has encountered defiance and must enforce obedience ruthlessly, must administer the matter as he has determined beforehand. He was rather like a predatory animal who puts its heavy head on its limp, tucked-up paws and blinks its yellow eyes, while now and then a spasm darts through its muscles and its claws thrust themselves out, ready to rip open a living body.

They sat in a half circle, in armchairs. Ferenc occupied a smaller chair, looking very proper, his head tilted forward in a way that signaled concentration and readiness to serve, provided the expected services did not affront his dignity. Judit had a notepad on her knee in case some decisions needed to be recorded. The cryptographer, a short, sturdy fellow, drew in his legs, hardly hiding his boredom, for after all, how could these instructions concern him? His duty was to change words to numbers, to read dispatches, to painstakingly destroy notations and guard the key to the safe in which copies of reports were hidden, together with Ministry of Foreign Affairs directives and codes. The ambassador carried the other key in his wallet. It was the emblem of the highest level of initiation. The members of the trade mission waited on a sofa, treating each other to cigarettes. Only the caretaker Karoly was missing.

Several bottles of Coca-Cola and siphons of soda water glinted on a table covered with green baize, rather ominously presaging a long meeting.

"Dear comrades," Bajcsy began, "do you recall the recent incident involving the Turkish ambassador, who went on a hunt for peacocks? A peacock is a sacred bird here. In fact, the devil only knows what isn't sacred here. The monkey is, too, and the snake, and the cow. The meat of the peacock is a delicacy"—he seemed to be remembering the savor; he closed his puffy eyelids—"especially from the female. They went out at dawn and killed a few birds. The driver shoved them into a bag. He was a good Muslim, he didn't find the blood revolting. But the ambassador's wife wanted a fan of peacock feathers for the wall, so instead of tearing off the tails, crumpling them up, and throwing them in the bushes, they left them on, sticking out of the bag like feather dusters.

"As luck would have it, two tires went flat. The chauffeur had no spare, and the tubes had to be patched. They stopped in the village. A crowd gathered, staring. In a place like that anything is worth gaping at, let alone taking tires off and looking for holes. The villagers helpfully brought a tub of water and assisted en masse. Unfortunately, the chauffeur opened the trunk, and out flashed a tuft of peacock feathers. The crowd hooted and began throwing stones.

"The ambassador didn't wait to catch a thrashing, but took off on foot. The driver tried to defend the car; he has a broken hand. The peasants turned the car over and set it afire so as to ensure a worthy funeral for the sacred fowl. And that was not the end of this unlucky diplomat's troubles, for the affair was bruited about and got into the papers. Though there's no official ban on hunting peacock, custom ought to be observed. As a matter of fact, the Indian Ministry of Foreign Affairs apologized to the ambassador, but such a climate of opinion grew up around him that he had to ask to be recalled—to say nothing of the fact that the Hindus never made restitution for the demolished car."

Bajcsy suddenly exploded with fervor. He stared into the faces from which no glimmer of interest was rising and delivered his blow:

"Why, you must be wondering, does the chief blither about this? Yesterday I had an accident. That idiot Krishan rammed the car into a cow."

Everyone shifted in their chairs and looked him nervously in the eye.

"A sacred cow?" Ferenc asked with a hint of a laugh in his voice.

"Is there any other kind of cow in this country?" Bajcsy, incensed, puffed out a thick lip. "Fortunately the hood was only a little bashed, and a headlight was broken. We were able to escape before they beat us to a pulp. I assure you, they would have liked to. They were flying around with sticks and gathering up stones, and the cow lay on the highway with a broken spine, roaring like a siren. An old, mangy cow. Krishan, that hysteric, went to pieces, covered his eyes and bellowed. I had to drive the car myself."

"Did you manage to protect yourself on the legal side, comrade minister?" asked the counselor for trade in a voice full of concern, as if for the chief's health.

"Absolutely. We went to the governor of the province and I told him everything. He summoned the commandant of police and they took down statements, particularly the statement of that blithering imbecile, Krishan. The worst of it was that there is no other road back from Dehradun, and we had to go scurrying through that same village . . . and the car so easy to recognize with that shattered headlight. I didn't want to be driving at night with one light, and they could only do the repair here in Delhi. So the governor gave us a truck as an escort, a platoon of police with billy clubs. What are you taking notes on, comrade?" He looked uneasily at the pad Judit was holding. "What I am saying is to be kept in strict confidence."

"I'm just scribbling." She held up the pad, which sported a geometrical design.

"Imagine: the villagers were waiting for us, the road was cordoned off. But the police made quick work of them. They beat them over the head with their sticks like farmers at their threshing." He shut his eyes approvingly. "In three minutes it was all over. I saw how they drove them away so they could clear the highway. At once the people returned to the way we know them every day: slow, feeble, very quiet. They only wiped their snotty noses, which were dribbling blood because the police had given them a pretty good drubbing. And everything was calm again.

"Would you like to know what happened next? The sacred cow lay under a baldachin crowned with flowers. It only groaned with its muzzle open. They had put a myriad of little lamps in front of it. But to bring a bucket of water and give the expiring beast a drink—no one thought of that! It's not their sense of how things should be done. The vultures had gathered on a meadow nearby; they came jumping up to see if the victim was in the last stages. If it had not been for the wailing villagers, they would have taken the entrails out of the living cow. I preferred to tell you about the accident myself, comrades, in order to show you by my own example the dangers that lie in wait here."

He rested both hands on his desk. "The conclusion? I would ask that you remember what I have communicated. They make mountains out of molehills here. I remind you that this is a highly confidential matter. Though my position and diplomatic immunity protect me in the final analysis, please keep conversation on the subject to a minimum; I appeal to your good judgment. In particular I do not wish it to reach people who are not well disposed toward us"—he looked significantly at Terey—"people from outside our camp, for they can bring harm, not on me, but on us as a whole. Is that clear? Any questions?"

"No," they answered. "No."

"You had quite an adventure, comrade ambassador." The counselor for trade shook his head. "But it could have been much worse."

"I hope this will be the end of it," Ferenc mused. "If only Krishan, that fool, won't babble too much!"

Leaning on one elbow, the ambassador lifted his upper eyelid with a finger. They saw the dark tufts of curly hair on the back of his hand.

"What do you advise, then?"

"I would let him go—but not right away. There are reasons enough. He damaged the automobile. He drives like a madman." Ferenc looked Bajcsy in the eye.

"He has a sick wife," Terey ventured.

"Oh, yes!" Ferenc seized on the mention of the ailing woman. "His relations with his wife are detestable. Instead of sending her to the hospital—"

"And I would slip him a few rupees to keep him quiet," the counselor for trade put in, looking at the cryptographer, who did not speak but drummed with his fingers on the arm of his chair, as if he were sending something in Morse code.

"No. No money. That's the worst way to go about it." The ambassador beat the air with his hand. "He would never leave us alone after that. In any case you agree with me that he is not a good driver, and, worse, not a good man. We have to put up with him for the time being. But, Comrade Ferenc, warn Krishan that if there is the slightest infraction I will be ruthless, I will chuck him out! We must have order here, and, believe me, I know how to keep it."

He looked at them grimly, malevolently, as if he were trying to tell which of them would be first to show himself an enemy. He turned to the cryptographer, whose mouth was half open.

"There will be no notification of this matter to our country. The repair is minimal: to beat out the dents, restore the finish, install a new light. I will cover it myself. And now, dear comrades, in such heat—since our meeting is coming to an end"—he spoke in a paternal tone—"perhaps Judit would break out a bottle of Tokay for us. Well, they are small bottles; perhaps two. Three. Why make two trips?"

Everyone began to move around, gratified. Only the counselor for trade asked to be excused, for he had an appointment with someone who wanted to buy a dozen buses and open his own transport line to Agra.

When the others had dispersed, the ambassador detained Terey, opened a drawer, and gave him a letter. At once he recognized the diminutive letters joined as in chain stitch: his wife's handwriting.

"It must have come here by mistake when the morning post was handed around," he said by way of explanation.

Istvan took it in his fingers and pressed: the letter had been cut open. Several other letters of his had gone astray recently. Was the ambassador involved in the inspection of correspondence? Were letters being confiscated as evidence for personal attacks?

Bajcsy's heavy figure hung over him. The ambassador inclined his head and looked out from under bristling eyebrows. "Well—what has you so mystified?"

"It could at least have been steamed open and given back with no clue that it had been breached. Any jealous wife would do it better than this."

"Calm down, Terey. Calm down. I opened this letter by mistake. Involuntarily. First I ripped it open, then I was taken aback when I saw it was not to me. My apologies."

"But there is a pattern in these mistakes that happen to me. Why has my wife not gotten a passport to this day?" He held the opened envelope with its ragged edges as if it were repugnant to him.

"I have sent a notice of urgency concerning that matter. It seems that the arrival of your wife would be most expedient here. As to this letter, I have offered my apologies, and that should be sufficient. Goodbye now. This heat is unbearable, it wears on everyone's nerves."

When he had closed the office door and thick oilcloth cushions had shifted with a smacking sound, Judit raised inquiring eyebrows.

"Well?"

He showed her the torn envelope. "This is what I got. I told him what I thought of it."

"I assure you, he was not the one." She shook her head.

"But who?"

"I don't know for sure. Ask the caretaker. That letter was not in the mail that passed through my hands. I would have set it aside."

"God repay you, Judit!"

She looked ruminatively at him.

"When I hear that, I get an ominous feeling."

"Because you know only the Father, and I the Son," he answered soberly. "I was not calling down vengeance on your head."

He walked out to the hall. He was in no hurry to read the letter. He felt as if he were reaching for an apple someone else had gnawed from the other side. Only when he was sitting behind his desk and had finished smoking a cigarette did he shake out the sheets of paper and photographs of his sons. They were holding a sheepdog by the collar; they were looking with keen, wise eyes toward the camera. They were small and slender, with hair clipped short. This was their grandfather's work. And there was friendly Tibi, the great shaggy dog, who let himself be mounted like a pony.

Ilona did not raise his hopes that she would appear in India soon; she was encountering resistance. She asked him not to worry, for they were well. The boys were doing well enough in school, and she was managing. They had spent Easter with her parents; hence the photograph with Tibi.

Since you have been away, visitors have stopped coming. A delightful peace fills the house, yet it gives me a strange feeling. Only Bela, who is so kind, thinks of us. I see only now that without you I am not necessary to anyone except the boys. They ask that you put many stamps on your letters, and of various kinds, for they exchange them with their friends. We long for you, we kiss you—Your own Ilona.

And then the scrawled postscripts from his sons:—*And I as well—Geza*. And with a fanciful flourish: *Sandor.*

The letter was two weeks old. What had happened during that time? Nothing. Obviously, nothing. He would have gotten a telegram. She could even have called. Every day there was a designated hour for a connection with Budapest, or a cable through London, a roundabout way. He remembered only one telephone conversation, which had concerned a sudden decision on proposals by the counselor for trade. The telephone connection existed, it represented a possibility, but a call would consist of sentences spoken in the hearing of many witnesses, like a meeting in the visiting room of a prison.

The letter exuded sadness. Reproaching himself for thinking of home so little, Istvan ran his eyes over it once more. No—he found nothing to disturb him. Yet it left a residue of something like pain in his heart. Ilona had stopped believing that they would be together here; she had decided to wait out his tour of duty, she thought the solitary stay in India was for his good. The care of their sons filled her life. It was easy for her to adjust to this long separation, and rightly so. Doesn't she need me, he wondered. Feelings remained, after all, not just the bonds of marriage. If Bajcsy had really sent that notice of urgency . . .

He heard the throb of an engine. He looked out the window lit by the fiery sun with instinctive aversion. Clear weather: he was sick to death of clear weather. Krishan had arrived. He must ask him about the business with the cow.

The dry air smelled of baking leaves and dust. The tiles of the walk that led around the building sent heat through the soles of his sandals. He peered into the dim garage and saw only concrete with a greasy oil stain. He bent over and touched it with his finger. It was sticky: the spot was fresh. Krishan must have hit the cow hard, since oil was leaking, he thought; the results could have been worse.

"What are you doing here?" He heard Ferenc's voice at his ear. He gave a start. He had not heard the man's light step.

"I thought Krishan had come."

The secretary looked at him truculently.

"I wanted to ask him—" Terey floundered.

"And I came at the ambassador's direction to order him to keep quiet. I advise you to mind your own business. No private inquiries. You are from the cultural division. There is no need for you to become intimate with the driver by chewing the fat about everything. Every Hindu must file reports about us, even the silly sweeper. The oversight system here works very efficiently; they want to keep an eye on our affairs. When you go out on some escapade, not to mention personal meetings, it's always better to drive the car yourself. It's more secure. And don't talk with Krishan about the accident. What's to be gained by alerting him to its significance?"

"Very well." Terey nodded.

They went out into the sunlight. Terey had a bad taste in his mouth because he had let himself be caught in an indefensible position.

Mihaly, the cryptographer's son, walked up to them in unbuttoned pajamas and a hat of plaited reeds, pulling a tin box on a string. Deprived of companions his own age, the child devised odd amusements for himself. He helped the chauffeur with chores in the garage. Four hours each morning he spent in a school conducted by nuns. There he had quickly learned to chatter in English, and, from Hindu children, in Hindi. Often his mother took him to the marketplace as her interpreter, for he could express himself better than she. He had the head for it, and she enjoyed showing him off. What was said in front of him he remembered at once, so that one had to be careful.

"*Namaste ji*," the boy greeted them respectfully.

"What have you got there, Mihaly?" Istvan drew the boy to him. The little fellow raised his head, rubbing it against Istvan. The brim of his big hat rustled.

"A bus. I'm taking little birds to the shade."

"You cut them out of paper?"

"No. Live birds." He held the box up and handed it to Terey.

"Put it to your ear, Uncle Istvan. You'll hear how they peck. And you, too"—he turned to Ferenc—"only don't open it or they will fly out."

Istvan, torn with longing for his own sons, was moved by Mihaly's confiding behavior. The shadow of the hat, which was painted with red zigzags, fell on the warm little face.

He heard a tapping sound in the box when he held it to his ear. Ferenc did not restrain himself; he raised the lid and big grasshoppers shot out, opened their rust-colored wings and flew into the glare with a loud whirring. They landed high among the climbing plants that swayed when a breath of wind grazed them. Mihaly did not seem at all aggrieved, but rather amused at the secretary's surprise.

"I told you they would fly out."

"They are grasshoppers."

"No, birds," he insisted. "Isn't that right, uncle?" He seized Istvan's hand.

"Of course they are birds. Mr. Ferenc doesn't have his glasses, so he didn't see."

"It is that way with God," the boy said gravely. "My sisters say He exists, but Daddy says He doesn't. He must not have glasses, either."

"They are muddling the youngster's thinking," Ferenc said angrily. "Of course there is no God," he added, speaking as one who imparts a fundamental precept to a child.

"You always like to play the devil's advocate," Terey laughed. "Of course there is. Only not everyone sees Him, and even to one who does, it may be more convenient to take the view that He does not exist."

Ferenc sighed and let his hands drop in a gesture of helplessness. "Carry on this theological debate without me. It's too hot. And when you have arrived at an understanding, look in on me, Istvan. I would like a word with you in private."

He walked away with a quiet step. The sun beat down; even his shadow dwindled in the heat.

"And now we will let out the rest of the grasshoppers or they will roast in this sweltering—"

"Birds," Mihaly corrected him. "After all, you see."

Istvan took them in his palm. He was amused by the long legs that kicked hard and then flitted into the air, by the little red wings that flashed in the sun and suddenly sank, falling into the leaves like pieces of a brown branch. They faded into the background without a trace until they began to hiss and ring.

"Show me those glasses, Uncle Istvan," the boy begged sweetly.

"What glasses?"

"The ones to see God with."

"I cannot show you those because each person must have his own. They are called faith," he whispered confidentially to the child, who looked at him with wide eyes. He felt a quick spasm of grief: who is speaking of this to my boys?

"And will I have them too, when I am big?"

"If you want them, you will surely get them. Many grownups have them. They just don't want to admit it."

"So no one else will take them away?"

From around a corner Krishan appeared. In a white shirt with sleeves rolled up unevenly, in wide linen pants, he looked like thousands of other men on the streets of New Delhi. It struck Istvan that although he was thin, gnarly muscles could be seen under the light covering of his skin. He was a strong, agile fellow. His watch and a heavy gold signet ring were reminders that he earned a good living. He walked with a light stoop; one could see from his expressive face that he was dejected.

"Krishan, Comrade Ferenc wanted to talk to you."

"I have just come from him, sir, but what am I going to do when the police summon me again?"

"You have given your deposition already. And signed it."

"Yes." He looked dolefully at Terey.

"Stick to what you said then."

"You know everything, sir?"

Terey nodded.

"The car will be ready for the evening."

"Don't worry, then. They will forget it. But you must be discreet. Don't talk too much."

"I know, sir. The secretary ordered me."

Krishan turned back with a heavy step and walked toward his quarters in the outbuilding. Istvan felt that the driver was expecting sympathy, understanding, rescue. But he remembered Ferenc's instructions and shrugged his shoulders. Krishan had been in the war in Africa; he had experience, he was not a child. He ought to know what he was doing. After all, was this Terey's concern? He had a wife. Let her cheer him up.

Mihaly looked after the driver.

"Krishan is sad. Why, Uncle Istvan?"

"Because his car is wrecked."

The boy walked behind him. The tin box rattled as he dragged it over the tiles. "Uncle—" he seized Istvan's hand in his hot, moist palm, "is it true that you have a kangaroo?"

Terey stopped where he stood, stunned. The rumor-ridden atmosphere had begun to exasperate him, but it had its amusing side.

"Mama said she saw you at Jantar Mantar with your kangaroo. I would so terribly like to see it. Will you show it to me?"

"I will show you, but don't tell anyone. It will be our secret."

He twitched the brim of Mihaly's hat and pushed the hat onto the boy's nose, then walked into the stuffy interior of the embassy.

What to do, then, he thought. Go into hiding? How, exactly? The very idea was funny. They might stop paying so much attention to me. Now, fortunately, they have the accident to talk about. Perhaps they will let me have a little peace. He felt almost grateful to the ambassador for concentrating the attention of their little world on himself. But his impatience was growing. If Ferenc tries to play the teacher with me, I'll give him a talking-to he'll not soon forget.

Having to explain his acquaintance with Margit, to endure conversations about her, to anticipate gently mocking smiles, seemed odious to him. He wanted to pass by Ferenc's office, but the door was partly open and the secretary said invitingly, "Come in. As it happens, I need you very much."

He got up from behind his desk and closed the door. As if wanting to make the most of their time together, he offered cigarettes. Istvan bristled inside.

"Have you ordered many cases of whiskey from Gupta?" the secretary began.

"What concern is that of yours? Would that give me bad marks in your book?"

"This heat! Everyone jumps at each other's throats, and you are on edge as well. But I wanted you to put twelve dozen for me on your account. It's just that I have ordered too many lately, and I don't want customs to notice."

"I haven't ordered any in the last month."

"So I surmised when I filled out the order card. Just sign it and I'll take care of the rest with Gupta. Don't worry about a thing."

"Why so much vodka?" Terey marveled, reaching for the card.

"The case has a dozen bottles. I have been here two whole years longer than you, I know many, many people, and everyone wants to take some. Whiskey is the best gift, especially when they raise the duty. You understand?"

"Now I do," Terey smiled. "After all, I'd have bet that you didn't drink alone."

Ferenc laughed, and they parted in good humor.

Istvan returned to his rooms to write a letter to the *Times of India* correcting some malicious information about Hungary reprinted from an American agency. Such a letter might be published under the heading "Conversations with Readers," but it would be better if it were signed by someone who was not from the embassy. Ram Kanval, perhaps? Or Vijayaveda himself? He did not want to draw Margit into political imbroglios.

The cook announced with some perturbation that there had been two very important telephone calls.

"I wrote them down." He pulled his glasses in their wire rims down from his forehead and faltered out the words he himself had scribbled, "Sir . . . Vijayaveda reminds you of the . . . party . . . to celebrate the return of the young couple . . . and Madam—that is, Miss—" he corrected himself, straining his great gloomy eyes—"I have it written here . . . 'also asked if sir will be there.'"

"But—Miss who?"

"I must have made a mistake here. I can't read it." He straightened the crumpled paper. "But it was an important call. In English."

Perhaps Grace had wanted to be sure that he would come? It would be better not to appear at all. Shame and apprehension engulfed him at the thought of such a meeting. How to talk to her so as not to touch her? To pass over everything in silence? She would decide, would set the terms of their new relationship with a coloring of her voice, a glance, a way of extending her hand. He would prefer to avoid meetings, but at the same time he felt that suddenly to change his behavior toward them would be harder still—in a word, stupid. He would have to find a way of explaining it to the rajah and Vijayaveda.

No sooner had he sat down at the table, which was set with a linen place mat, and Pereira taken a grapefruit from the refrigerator, than he sensed that something in the room had changed.

He hesitated for the twinkling of an eye before he noticed that a blue and white carpet lay on the floor, downy as moss in a beech forest.

"Where is the other carpet?"

"The merchant was here and exchanged it for this one. I myself chose it."

"But who told you to?"

"Sahib never said a word about whether the red one was suitable."

"Find the merchant and tell him to leave it for me," Terey stormed, as if the rug they had disposed of were his property. "I want that carpet returned to me."

"And if he has found a buyer?"

"I was first." He removed a seed with his spoon.

The cook's face brightened as if a beam of sunlight had passed over it. He was already calculating the tip he would haggle from the vendor.

"Sahib wants to keep the red carpet?" he queried, pressing for confirmation. His hair rattled dryly as he scratched above his ear with a bent finger. "It will be expensive. It is real cashmere."

"If he thinks he's going to fleece me, let him not bring it at all. I don't want to look at him or at rugs. And you, instead of doing business of your own out of this, attend to the kitchen."

A strong smell of burnt cake wafted from the half-open door. Pereira went pattering out in beaten-up slippers, shaped like the boats boys whittle from pine bark, that were never cleaned. In a moment he was back, passing a lump of something black and smoking from one hand to the other.

"The teacakes burned," he announced, as if it were a great achievement.

The dining room was stuffy in spite of the large ceiling fan that whisked the air into motion. The cooling machine hummed like the roar of the sea in a shell. At the thought of the oppressive sun, which was out of eyeshot here but now and then crossed the threshold and fell like a weight on his shoulders, Istvan felt a pressure in his head and a sudden faintness swept over him.

He lay down and was beginning to read *The Naked and the Dead* when the open book fell onto his forehead. He let it fall and sank into sleep.

He awoke dazed and uneasy, with a dew of perspiration on his chest. He had dreamed that he came in by a narrow wooden stairway, roughly hewn with an ax like cottagers' staircases, to a cramped loft. Dried sheepskins were hanging there, with their fleecy sides toward the center, smelling of rancid fat and an herb to keep away maggots. Ilona would be waiting there. In the darkness he reached out and touched a snugly wrapped baby sleeping in a wicker trough. Groping with his fingertips, he felt the moist, open lips. They smacked and the infant slept on.

In the bathtub, he chuckled as he remembered his grandfather, who had a knack for explaining dreams, "A child—that's trouble. It sleeps all wrapped up, and everything is fine, but be careful not to wake it up." His cheerfulness returned; he seemed to hear that voice, grumbling but full of warmth, just behind him. But his grandfather had died before the war, before Horthy . . . Oh, foolishness! He swatted his shoulders with a rolled towel and instead of rubbing himself with it, let the air dry his skin. He wanted to preserve the fleeting illusion of coolness that lingered after his bath.

He drove out to the gardener's plot behind the European cemetery, where patches of snapdragon and gladiolus grew, and baby's breath with tiny, silvery blooms that created a mist over the dense cluster of color—the indispensable finishing touch to a bouquet.

He bought flowers for Grace.

The rajah greeted him with sincere delight, handing him a tall glass of whiskey in which ice cubes gleamed like chunks of topaz. A slender man in immaculately pressed trousers, noticing the familiarity between them, gave Istvan his seat. The leather chair sighed like a human being as it accepted its new burden. When the man was introduced, the counselor did not hear his name distinctly. The skin lying firm and tight across his cheeks made it hard to determine his age, but he must have been over forty, for the neatly trimmed hair at his temples was streaked with silver.

"Who is that?" Terey asked in an undertone.

"Another one looking for credit. No one so important that you have to remember him," the rajah said dismissively. "I don't ask what he wants money for. What's important is that he return it at term and pay the interest. But what he does with it—"

The conversation went on this way, as if the thin Hindu did not exist for either of them. But he, without antagonism, stood in obedient readiness a step away so as to be able to join in at any moment.

The rajah settled in to dwell at length on the splendid homage that had been done him at Jaipur, the hundred elephants that had come out to meet him and his bride. They had ridden into their estate on an elephant wearing a caparison of gold. Merchants had brought presents in spite of the fact that legal subjugation to the ruling family had ceased a few years before. But the merchants themselves kept up the tradition in order to signify that they enjoyed favorable relations with the wealthy of Rajasthan.

Miss Ward was not at the reception, so Grace must have called. Pereira couldn't manage to repeat anything. Terey writhed, listening with one ear to the rajah's boastings.

Grace was hidden in a bevy of sleek women who passed their lives lounging about and gorging on pastry and gossip. Each year they gave birth and wheedled jewels from their husbands as rewards, then used them to pique the envy of their friends.

Grace's face was full of soft brightness, but impenetrable, like still water in temple ponds; it hid a mystery. Could marriage have changed her so?

He took the earliest opportunity to escape the rajah and attach himself to Vijayaveda, Dr. Kapur, and a tall, hunched man wearing a white shirt gathered into innumerable creases and drawn together with a band under the neck. The man wore a dhoti and held the ends of it in his fingers like a dancer's skirt, fanning his bare calves.

"War is not so terrible when one is our age." Vijayaveda beat his chest. "We are talking of events in Tibet—a minor revolt of the lamas, the slaughter of some Chinese advisers," he explained to Terey. "Even if the Americans took up the cause of the Dalai Lama—"

"You speak of something you have never experienced, sir," the Hungarian countered. "I have seen war at close range. One must have vast patience and great intelligence to hold in check an arrogant opponent who is cocksure of his technology. Even if it takes enormous concessions, peace must be preserved."

"You repeat it like an incantation, sir: peace, peace," Kapur attacked him, "because the communist strategy demands it. You put the world in fear of nuclear annihilation, then you yourselves foment small wars, which are just, you say, because they are fought for freedom."

"War is not so bad," the manufacturer insisted. "It brought freedom to India, it dislodged foreign capital. And it all happened at little cost."

"Little? If you disregard several million who died of hunger. In spite of catastrophic droughts, with your help the English pumped rice through to the African front. The passive death of Indians was also an ingredient in this war," said the tall man in the dhoti.

"There are enough of us left." Vijayaveda shrugged off the point. "I would rather see a war in Europe. There would be movement here straight away: orders for factories, turnover of goods, technical advances. War is not terrible so long as you maintain neutrality."

"Easy to say, but who can guarantee that?" The tall Hindu spread his hands and raised the edge of his dhoti, uncovering half his lean thigh.

"The politics of Gandhi, Nehru," Kapur put in. "As long as the Congress Party, the party of former prisoners, persecuted and struggling for freedom, is in power—"

"You know very well that the whole Congress is like one of our joint families, a family partnership. You were honest as long as you were behind bars; when you got your hands on power, you began to change overnight. I don't deny that Nehru, Prasad, Radhakrishnan are noble people, leaders without self-interest. But the rest? Behind their backs the rest find ways to profit, to suck the people like horseflies on an ox's neck. The money goes to a common pot, and they hand off funds to the Congress for propaganda and for the police, who are the guardians of their shady businesses. 'Joint family': one set of faces from the outside, another from the inside," the Hindu said vehemently, his dhoti flapping like a sail. "And no sooner are they caught than they invoke the memory of their past merits, which were even in many cases quite genuine, because in those days they took no account of danger. They also like to point to other people's scars, and to cluck, 'Oh, Gandhi, Gandhi,' thinking that that shibboleth will anesthetize the agitated public. It is time for us to have a proper role in the running of this country. Socialism!"

"Another shibboleth." Vijayaveda shrugged. "An antiquated nineteenth-century economic theory elevated to the dignity of a philosophy."

"Professor Dass, as you have just witnessed, is already infected by you. He dreams of revolution," Dr. Kapur whispered to Terey. "And those humanists who extol revolution are the first to have their necks wrung by it."

"You will never take over governments in India." Vijayaveda struck his palm with the other fist. "You are compromised once and for all. When we called for boycotts during the war, when we haggled with the English for our freedom so blood would not have been shed for nothing, the communists directed the laborers to work loyally for the English. You condemned the strikes and demonstrations. And why? Why so loyal all of a sudden? Because Moscow was in danger, and you listen to her. What concern of yours are the interests of that nation? Chandra Bose was better."

"Not Moscow, but humanity, was in mortal danger. That is why we agreed to make concessions," the professor retorted. "The enemies of our enemies were our natural allies . . . for the time being, of course, for the time being. And if Chandra Bose had been successful, we would have had a Japanese occupation. Ask them in Singapore how they liked that! To drive the English out with help of the Japanese is to chase one devil away and let all hell in. Madness!"

"And what actually happened to him?" Istvan asked, recalling a snatch of an old newsreel and a crowd of moviegoers, not given to being demonstrative in public, rising in the darkness to pay homage.

"He died near the end of the war," Vijayaveda said.

"When the campaign for the subjugation of India did not succeed," Professor Dass said with a sneer, "the powers summoned him to Tokyo to explain why no uprising had broken out here. But on the way it appeared that the verdict had come down. They swung him by his hands and feet and threw him out of the plane."

"He was a man of integrity," Kapur said.

"Where would he have led us?" hissed Dass. "Perhaps he dreamed of a great India, but at what price? The people felt the tyrant in him and did not support him."

"Stop hiding behind 'the people.' 'The people, this,' 'the people, that,'" Vijayaveda shouted. "The people is a great mute. First of all, it doesn't speak because it doesn't know, and you shout on its behalf. And then, when you take power, it cannot speak even if it wanted, for you hold your paw over its mouth."

Jumping as if on a spring, raising its rump high, a gray monkey ran in from the garden. Its long tail hung in an arc over its senile, ugly head. Its eyes, pale green like gooseberries, had a mocking look. In its paw it dragged an open bag that belonged to one of the ladies, dropping a handkerchief, lipstick in a golden case, and a bunch of jingling keys along the way.

A servant lunged to the rescue and tried to snatch away the booty, but the monkey tittered, shrieked hysterically, and with its back bristling, leaped over onto Grace. Complaining like a child, it cried and buried its little face under its arm.

"Let the monkey play with that," called the owner of the purse. "She will grow bored and give it up of her own accord. There is no point in annoying her."

The Hindu ladies resumed their conversation. The monkey, now soothed, jumped onto the back of a sofa and began to pluck sheets of paper from a little red notebook as if to put it in order.

"Delightful!" gushed the victim. "Grace, did you raise her?"

The monkey tousled her hair, making a shambles of her coiffure. It pulled out jasmine blossoms that had been threaded into her hair and began chewing them and spitting them out. Then it went back to separating the tangled strands of hair.

"Careful, that hurts!" the Hindu woman bridled, offering the little animal a mango. "She behaves just like my husband. My hair bothers him in his sleep. He says that it gets in his face, that it suffocates him. He wrestles with it. In the morning he can't get his fingers untangled."

The monkey sat on the back of the sofa, above their heads.

"My husband gets his ring tangled," the rajah's sister-in-law chimed in, shielding herself with a napkin from the drops of juice that leaked from the darting black paws of the monkey. Kapur, who was watching this amusing little contest, winked at Terey.

"I met the ambassador in Amritsar."

"I know. He told us about the Golden Temple of the Sikhs and the extraordinary success of the speech. Reportedly the hall was so crowded no one could breathe."

"We found around thirty persons: officials, intellectuals, members of the Hungarian-Indian Friendship Society."

"Those people also belong to the Czech and Bulgarian societies."

"Socialist sympathizers," Professor Dass interposed.

"Not necessarily. Snobs—and some are simply there under orders, but many reports confirm that the activities of the Society do not escape surveillance," the manufacturer added. "Perhaps this is painful to you, Mr. Terey, but so it must be. Self-defense."

"Allow me to finish," Kapur insisted, distending his hairy cheeks with a smothered simper. "It was after the ceremonial greeting, when the crowd pressed into the hall with wives and children. Not only were all the seats occupied, but people were even sitting on the floor and the windowsills. The ambassador expressed his thanks with elation, because he thought he himself had aroused such interest. No one disabused him. In the meantime, it was a rabid monkey that had driven listeners into the hall where he was speaking. It was jumping from a tree onto the necks of passersby and biting them. It was attacking cyclists in particular; no doubt their torpid pedaling irritated it."

"I read in the newspaper that some Sikh killed the monkey," Terey recalled. "And he didn't even claim the reward."

"Very wise. If the monkey in question hadn't been mad, he would have been accused of sacrilege," Kapur explained. "He shot it with a bow and arrow. The whistle of the arrow attracted no attention. Those who had been bitten were summoned to be inoculated against rabies. About three hundred people reported, but none had bite marks. People simply like to be treated. The shot is free; they must take advantage of it."

"Did anyone seek out those who really were bitten?" Istvan asked worriedly.

"Have you no more pressing concerns?" The doctor shrugged. "They will fall ill, they will die out and the circle of exposure will eliminate itself. We trust in the wisdom of nature."

"You say that," Dass said angrily, "as if you meant, let us leave it to the gods."

No; Kapur enjoyed treating people. Even his ritualistic questions about health resonated with the secret hope that he would hear some guarded admission of sickness, spy out its first symptoms. He was a surgeon for the love of it; he had a deft hand, and even in this accursed heat, wounds closed easily and pus stopped running. He delighted in injections; as often as he could he applied those he received free of charge from pharmaceutical houses, each in a package with its advertising prospectus. He divided patients into two classes, the chronically ill and the incurable. During the time of treatment he did not spare expensive measures, especially when the medicines were nearly out of date and needed to be used up quickly. For the rest, under his tender care any sickness could take on the character of a chronic condition. The dark prognoses that surrounded his patients lent drama to the success of the ensuing treatment.

The members of the diplomatic corps knew him and even liked him, for he assured them from the first that all sicknesses reside in each body, that what mattered was only to discover modes of coexistence. In that enterprise a double whiskey with ice was remarkably helpful, taken after sunset, of course.

The dosage of whiskey he prescribed linked the number of years the patient had spent in the tropics to the height of a box of matches. In the first year he laid it flat beside the glass, in the second he put it on its side, in the third he stood it on end. After that, one could push out the center of the matchbox with a finger as one saw fit, and fill the glass to the prescribed level. "For if three years in India does not make you my patient for life, whiskey will certainly do you no harm," he jokingly assured the embassy staff.

"I must come and see you, doctor," Terey began. "It has been eight months since I was inoculated against smallpox, and there are many new cases."

"There is nothing to be perturbed about. We always have smallpox among us, someone always falls ill with it, but they don't put it into the newspapers because it bores readers. If there is a large outbreak—several hundred dead—in the vicinity of Delhi, then they set up an alarm. The team goes out, they inoculate people, they burn the victims' belongings, they sprinkle the lodgings with creosote and it's all over. Call me and I will get some vaccine from the hospital cooler."

The man who was sitting on the edge of his chair, leaning toward the rajah—almost kneeling like a penitent—suddenly rose to his feet and walked away with his head down, as if he had been granted absolution. His rapt eyes slowly began to focus on what was around him; he smiled apologetically at Istvan. He pulled aside the lapel of his jacket; from the inside pocket, where the wallet is usually carried, protruded a row of metal holders.

"Perhaps you smoke? These are healthier than cigarettes," he urged, opening an aluminum case. He shook a thick brown cigar with a little crimson and gold band out onto his palm and involuntarily pushed it under his twitching nostrils, savoring the aroma.

"Havana. Havana," he said elatedly. "The whole secret of the perfection of those cigars is in the hand work. Girls roll the leaves on their bare thighs. The hand moist with spit, the perspiring thigh, create the variable fermentation which decides the flavor of each cigar—not chemists, not machines. Please feel free. I have more of them." He pulled aside the other flap of his jacket with the gesture of a man being searched under a warrant. The cigars stood in their holders like cartridges in the dress uniform of a Cossack. "Americans bring me any number of them. I get them straight from the embassy, duty free."

He took out a little cigar cutter and trimmed the end.

"Wait—" he raised a match and held it in midair. "Do not spoil the taste with sulfur. Now there is a red flame; we may light it," he said imperiously, then pressed for encomiums, "Well—how is it? Was it worth it?"

They inhaled for a moment, concentrating deeply on the smoke. Finally Istvan raised the cigar, which exuded thick, aromatic fumes.

"Excellent," he had to confess.

"Please take a couple more, for later. Give me the pleasure." He thrust his pocket forward, but Terey mistrusted the sudden cordiality. Instinctively he felt that it concealed a desire to put him under some undefined obligation.

"Do you go to Pakistan sometimes? Above all, I mean to Karachi."

"No. I have no reason; we have an embassy there as well." After a pause Terey added, "And I can hardly afford it."

"Or to Hong Kong?"

"Not there either. It is beyond the range of my posting."

The Hindu seemed to be turning something over in his mind. He moved the end of the cigar around his thin purplish lips.

"But might you not have reason to go there? The means could be found. It is very easy to get money. If the occasion arose, would you think of me? I am in need of a favor." He looked at Istvan gently, as if he were an uncomprehending child. "Why are you always so resistant? They are strict with you. It is easier to communicate with the Americans."

"What do you have in mind?" Istvan inquired. The man smiled, his lips forming an indulgent, slightly disgusted grimace.

"Don't worry; not intelligence. Ordinary business. I am, like Rajah Khaterpalia, a businessman. But since you are not going, for the time being there is nothing to talk about," he snorted superciliously. "Don't rack your brain about it. Here is my card. If you go, please let me know. I do not think you will regret it."

He handed him a cream-colored card and suddenly, as if he had lost all interest in Istvan, went into the part of room where the rich ladies in varicolored saris sat on the couch and in leather chairs.

"A. M. Chandra," the counselor read. There were multitudes of Chandras; it was a common name. Beneath it was written in small letters, "Philanthropist." And in the corner an address, Kashmir Gate, office of legal counsel, the telephone number. Yes; Old Delhi. Istvan had to smile, it struck him as such a highflown designation. Philanthropist: it reminded him of the card they printed as a joke on the birthday of one of the editors, who was always sitting around in a coffeehouse nearby, with the name in large type—"Founder"—and below, in nonpareil, "and Chairman of the Bored." But here the eccentric designation "philanthropist" must have a particular significance—to establish a position, to attract certain persons, to arouse respect?

Since Vijayaveda and his son-in-law had been left alone, Terey took the opportunity to ask confidentially what Chandra's occupation really was.

"Everything that is not allowed. He is an excellent lawyer, he knows thousands of gambits. He can call on precedents from fifty years back. He handles cases that are impossible to make disposition of, that drag on for years. He pulls witnesses out of hell. A man drowned in a swamp—well, a very rich owner of a copper mine—and because there were no remains, no one could take possession of the inheritance. Chandra managed to produce remains. It was said that gold fillings were put into another dead man so the dentist could identify him as his patient. He is a careful fellow: he never leaves his fingerprints on anything. He knows how much to give someone to move the case along, to obtain the indispensable signature and seal on the decision," the rajah said reflectively. "Everyone is ready to take, but they are not so eager to work. He knows who gets things done, he knows people," he added approvingly. "Such knowledge is invaluable. Did he propose anything to you?"

"Yes—rather vaguely," Istvan said hesitantly.

"He is worth taking seriously," the rajah said reassuringly. "I have lent him large sums and he has always paid them back on time. He inspires confidence. One never knows when such a man might be useful, and for what. If I were in your place, I should keep up the acquaintance."

Through the pleasantly shaded room Grace sailed toward them. She walked with short steps, carried forward with a slight movement of her hips, her head tilted as if under the weight of her luxuriant black hair. On her neck she wore a gold chain in the form of leaves and lotus flowers, set with rubies. A servant with a tray of glasses walked behind her.

"Are you happy, Grace, to be receiving guests in the old home?" the rajah asked.

"My home is where you are," she answered, lowering her dark-tinted eyelids.

This expression in the presence of a listener pleased her husband. Istvan thought with relief that that was the end of it, that it was as if the incident had not taken place. Suddenly he felt as though he were choking: he stood still for a moment with the cigar, now extinguished, in his uplifted hand, looking around at the faces, studying the movements of hands and bodies, the rippling of white dhotis, the impeccable cadences of sentences spoken in English. The large fan whirled above him, scattering ashes from the cigar.

He had had enough. What had he expected? What had he found here? Nasal, languid voices, enormous, flashing eyes, theatrical gestures. He bowed to Grace and the rajah, pointing to his wrist watch, and walked out without a word. The bored monkey hobbled along behind him. They stood, he and the little animal, at the top of the stairs, surveying the abyss of sunlight. Dry, twisted leaves drifted from the trees; the tobacco-like aroma of dying greenery rode on the air. A lone cicada chattered on a leafless acacia. He could see its lucent wings like trembling slivers of mica.

Hot breezes sprang up, driving the shriveled leaves around the asphalt. Tires ground them to a dust that was wafted through the air and into the faces of passersby. Istvan had just driven to the gate when a taxi with an unkempt Sikh at the wheel stopped, its tires screeching. He put his head out and was ready to berate the man when he noticed the passenger. Miss Ward alighted, holding a raffia basket full of peaches.

"Why didn't you let me know you would be here?" she reproached him. "And I waited and waited at Volga. After all, you could have called."

Her sudden fit of pique gave him pleasure. He liked her with tight lips and a threatening flash in her eye.

"I've had a rotten day. Since morning nothing has gone right. I needed you very much—needed a shoulder to cry on—and of course you weren't there. Go on!" She dismissed the taxi driver with a gesture of her hand in a green nylon glove; her suntanned fingers were half silhouetted as if seen through water.

"Madam has not paid yet." The Sikh thrust out his hairy lips and, gratified by her discomfiture, scratched himself under his arm.

"Oh, sorry!" She hurriedly retrieved her purse from the bottom of the basket. Two peaches rolled out and vanished under the taxi.

"Why this anger? I am not Dr. Kapur; I cannot marshal my powers of concentration and divine that you are sitting in Volga. I can only envy you. Strong coffee, ice cream." He tucked some money into the driver's hand. The man started up his rattletrap sluggishly.

"Where are you rushing off to?" He stopped Margit. "The at-home is still going on."

"I wanted to wash. I'm sticky all over. And so tired! I'm sorry that you got the brunt of that"—her lips trembled like those of a child who can hardly keep from crying—"but if you knew what I've had to contend with, you wouldn't wonder at it."

He took the basket out of her hand and put it down beside him. Before she noticed, they were moving down the avenue.

"I must look horrid!" She peeped at the mirror. "Where are you taking me? I can't be seen anywhere in this rumpled dress."

He said nothing; he only looked far down the road. The air, veined with tremors of heat, threw a haze over the trunks of trees near the pavement and blurred the brown leaves at the tops. A pool of blue gleamed like spilled water on the asphalt. Around them stretched empty fields full of soil of a vermilion hue; the stubble was not plowed. Only patches of sugar cane stood like a green wall. In a ditch a pair of storks walked about, irritably snapping up brittle grasshoppers. In the blank sky a vulture glided like a black cross on invisible currents of air, reconnoitering.

"You won't bother to talk to me? Have I annoyed you?"

"I'm taking you out of the city. We'll sit in the shade, by water. You'll rest a little. You don't mind my abducting you?"

He drove with his left hand, putting his right out the window. The air whipping against the car was refreshing as it flowed over his body, ruffling his shirt.

"I had about thirty patients today, almost all of them children. Why do they deserve to suffer like this? Swollen eyelids oozing pus.

Pupils that can't bear bright light . . . the sun jabs them like a needle. Do you know, tears have made furrows on these tykes' cheeks. Over and over I perform the same treatment: put the hook in place, pull away the eyelid, scrape, remove ingrown eyelashes, which are irritants; they lacerate the eyeball. The nurse holds the child's head, and the mother sinks to the floor and embraces my legs as if to plead with me not to hurt the little one." She flung the words out angrily, not looking at Istvan, only at the vacuousness of the parching fields and the bluish sky that seemed full of hot ash. "But maybe this disgusts you? Have you already had enough?"

"I am happy to hear about the Dr. Margit Ward who is unknown to me." He leaned on the horn, for a flock of peacocks was crossing the road, their iridescent green and gold tails sweeping the dust and leaves like brooms. "Until now I have only known Miss Margit."

"Every mother loves her child, but here love injures, blinds, sometimes kills. I rub the inside of the eyelid with ointment, I put in drops—and later I see through the window how the mother rubs the child's eye with the border of her skirt, spits on her finger and wets the inflamed edge of the eyelid. And she will take the sadhu into her house and let him intone spells, she will apply amulets from sacks with dirt caked on them, or cow piss. I could show her what to do a hundred times, but she will not do it. She will repeat my instructions as if she were in a trance, and I will see in her eyes that she is promising in order to placate me, but when she is on her own again, she will not carry them out. She will get her friends together and tell them what it was like in the clinic, and when they have finished their oohing and aahing, she will take to painting the child's eyelids with that disgusting grease of coconut oil and soot.

"Oh, it's my fault, because I washed the child's eye and it has eyelids white as a vulture's, and it is supposed to be beautiful! You know, I would like to take the sick children from their mothers by force, because the whole treatment is all for nothing! It's enough that the eyelid heals over a little; right away they stop taking the treatments seriously; they even stop coming. Now and then I'm overtaken by a rage like this one today. And I've taken it out on you. I apologize."

"It's nothing. Nothing," he soothed her. "Go on."

"Yesterday a girl was brought in. Believe me, I truly wanted to help, but I'd treated thirty patients and my hands were shaky. I gave an order for her to come with her mother this morning. I wanted to take her first, while I was still full of confidence that I could save her sight. I waited. I sent away other mothers. There was no trace of her! She didn't come. You can't even imagine how I reproached myself for letting her go yesterday, until I questioned the nurse.

"The nurse, who was trained in an English school, knows what hygiene is. She calmly explained to me that the mother bought a black goat, made an incision in its throat and walked it around the altar of Kali. The blood flowed out, and the pus. Now that whole cataract will come out of the child's eye. And if not, why treat it, since the goddess wants it that way?

"Until then I had looked at the nurse as someone who was on my side, as an ally. Then she said with a sweet smile, which I would have liked to wipe off her face"—she bent the fingers of both hands down to the trimmed, unpolished nails—"'Yes, I advised her to do it myself, for why should madam doctor wear herself out for that dark peasant girl?'"

"Do you understand? She put her up to it—so how can I count on the mothers to follow my directions? It's hopeless!" she cried in despair. "Worse, it's foolish. And I believed that I could help them."

"You want too much too soon. You will see; you will adjust, you will get used to it."

"I've already been here two months. Istvan, I can't work without having faith that there is some sense in what I'm doing."

They were quiet for a moment, listening to the even hum of the motor. Then he turned his face toward her with a truculent gesture.

"Have you saved even one child's sight?"

"Of course!" she burst out.

But he went on without heeding her indignation.

"That child will be able to distinguish colors, shapes. You have given him the whole world. Is that a small thing? Wasn't it worth it to come here even for the happiness of one child?"

"Don't let my bitterness upset you. Something has come over me today. I'm mad as a hornet."

"Look." He pointed to the silvery-white sky. "Sand clouds, charged with electricity. A dry storm is on the way. The birds are taking cover, the cicadas are quiet, and we feel the tension, but we have lost touch with our instincts and don't know what's threatening us. We only feel an uneasiness."

They turned between the spreading trees. Wagons were standing there, and motorcycle rickshaws with blue-striped canopies. Drivers in unbuttoned shirts dozed in the shifting shade. Horses with yellow teeth tore at the dry, dusty leaves of bushes and switched their tails over hindquarters stung by horseflies.

"Entry prohibited." She pointed to a road sign.

"Not for us. For the Community Development vehicle." He steered over the crunching gravel under the ruins of the palace of the Grand Mogul. Flies like bullets that had been blown into the moving car and battered against the rear windshield now took flight with a loud, desperate buzzing, beating against their faces and foundering in Margit's hair.

"Dreadful!" She shuddered as she combed them out with her fingers.

The hot, listless hour had emptied the park. They stood at the foot of the reddish thirty-story tower, which seemed to reel among the silvery streaks that were spreading through the sky—to totter as if it might fall on them.

In the dark gateway a half-naked beggar slept with his head on his chest. His bony black hands had fallen between his parted thighs. His toenails were as long as a dog's. He did not wake when they walked through the little passage leading to a winding stone stairway worn by innumerable footsteps.

Nebulae of whitish light shone through the narrow guard windows. They climbed the stairs, almost groping their way. In the tiny flame of a match, greasy streaks of dirt could be seen on the wall. Hundreds of thousands of sightseers had leaned on it with their hands and moved sweaty fingers over it, lending a patina to the plaster. The interior reeked with the musky smell of bats and urine passed stealthily by pilgrims. From the higher flights of stairs came the squeals of young girls, amplified by the echo.

"Shall we go all the way up?" he asked. "Eight hundred and sixty-two steps."

"I would never forgive myself if we didn't go up." She quickened her steps. "I must reach the top."

A line of girls in loose pantaloons, colorful tunics, and light scarves with ends hanging down their backs passed them on the stairs. Their shrieks and titters and the clatter of their sandals could be heard long afterward.

They paused more and more often, out of breath. Margit put a hand on her heart.

"It's pounding."

They startled a couple in white who were embracing. Pouting, the young people joined hands and began to descend, but the sound of their footsteps died away quickly; they were in no hurry to leave their stony retreat.

"Did you see? They were kissing," he said, amused. "The censors cut scenes like that from the movies."

"It's remarkable to me, as well, that men here show greater feeling, that they walk around embracing each other, they hold each other's hands, they plait flowers into their hair. I haven't seen a boy and girl walking hand in hand. And if that does happen, they are marching in the company of the whole family. Oh, it's not far!" She was elated by the light from the summit of the tower.

They saw an arid plain with strips of smoldering thorny brushwood and clumps of yellowing trees. Under the turbid sky, like streaks of distant rain, veils of dust were carried on the air along with the rhythmic mutter of thunder. In the copses the domes of old graves darkened, like the shells of gigantic turtles, stripped by a sacrilegious hand of their ceramic scales. Nearer the tower, a few white mud cottages caught the light in a banana grove, and in a pond, like boulders come to life, the black bodies of buffalo wallowed.

Istvan held Margit by the waist as she pulled herself from the brick shaft. Over the smooth, steep wall, one could look straight down, past two small balconies with white figures of men, to the ground, the stone tiles and reddish dirt sprinkled with gravel. Then came a tingling under the skin, and the thought that a person could fall with a scream of despair which would summon no one until the dull collision of body and earth silenced it forever.

"Careful, please," warned a guard in a military uniform and creaking hobnailed boots. "Two days ago a girl threw herself off here. The marks are still here—" he showed them dried black spatters on the steep slope of the wall. "When they lifted her, she was like a bag of wet wool; all her bones were broken. Just after the feast of Diwali, as well, a couple jumped. They were holding hands. It was love, and the parents would not permit it, for he was a Brahmin and she was from a village. It is strange how this tower attracts suicides. It is better not to lean out: the earth lures, it draws, one feels dizzy, and before you know it—tragedy!"

The guard shot Margit a look full of suspicious concern.

"They posted me to watch over this place," he added. "But when someone makes up his mind to jump . . . I turn my back, and he is somersaulting in the air."

The wind grew stronger; the narrow windows of the tower whistled like flutes. A cloud of dust, torn grasses, and dry leaves was rising below them. A gust of wind tugged at their hair and they felt a warm stream of air flow over them. Margit huddled down, pressing her swelling skirt around her knees.

"There is going to be a powerful storm," the guard warned. "It is better to go down."

"No," she insisted. "A moment more."

There was a roaring in the trees below. Their tops lashed in the wind; handfuls of leaves flew off them. A red smoke rose from the parched fields.

"Don't be afraid, sir. There will be no trouble with me," Margit assured the guard. She was drinking in the sky, as violently, like a hallucination, it went gray, with swellings dark as ink. A rose and yellow flash kindled on clouds pulsing with light; the lightning heralded dry weather hot as brimstone.

She tried to smooth the hair that had blown about her forehead with a comb, but it was charged with electricity and rose on the air, giving off sparks.

"And it will hit like a thunderbolt." Suddenly she was frightened. "I have no desire to perish at the hands of the gods. I have outgrown the years when one thinks of death without fear."

She was silent. After a moment she spoke with an unnatural calm:

"There was a time when I wanted to kill myself."

She looked him in the face. "I was very young then, and very silly."

He said nothing. The stale taste of the desert was on his lips. A loud hum and a flapping noise rose around them. Grains of sand hit their cheeks, pricking like pins.

"I loved a cousin. We kissed in corners, like that couple. A splendid fellow. It was pure joy. He went as a volunteer. I vowed I'd wait for him. He was going to write. I never got a single letter. It was 1943. Burma. He died on that hellish road to Mandalay. The Japanese murdered him."

She moved nearer to him because the wind was carrying her words away. She stood so close that her skirt fluttered around his knees. He caught the smell of her overheated body.

"I wanted somehow to be with those who were fighting. I was working then in a hospital in Melbourne. I still knew nothing about the war. We didn't have many of the wounded. Neither the ocean nor the jungle were sending back victims," she said in a passion of remembered grief.

The wind whined loudly. They heard the hum below them. At moments Terey lost her words and caught only the harsh tone of her voice.

"When someone told me, 'Sister Margaret, someone from the army is waiting for you down below,' I was sure it was Stanley. I ran down the hall. I can still hear my heels clattering. It was as if I had wings. But a strange man was standing there. He said with a heartiness that appalled me, 'Be brave, madam. Stanley is dead.'

"I had nothing to remember him by. Nothing. If that man had had any heart at all, he would have given me even a button of his own and said it was Stanley's. A good lad, but without imagination. And the same evening I gave myself to that man. With Stanley I hadn't. And the man went back there. All the time he was kissing me, I thought, after all, it means nothing. Stanley is gone, gone, and I don't want to live.

"I knew the flesh could defend itself, could rebel. Perhaps they would bring me back to life. I remembered one thing: if I got poison into my muscles with a syringe, nothing could help. I had easy access to the ampule. But I didn't do it immediately after the man left, and I wasn't able to do it a week later. Perhaps that first one, even unwittingly, saved me? My lover—" she laughed mockingly. "He didn't even take account of the fact that he was the first; he regaled me with hideous stories of what the Japanese did to prisoners. The next day he telephoned to say goodbye. Perhaps I should have sent him flowers?"

The whole sky trembled above them. Dry lightning flashed three or four bolts at a time. Breathing was difficult; the storm gathered force. Sand lashed them.

"Go down, please." The guard came up to them again. "It may be dangerous here," he warned.

They could not see the ground. Below them brownish-red dust gathered in clouds, blotting out the trees. Flurries of dust surged above the ruins of the palace.

"We must listen to him, after all," Terey urged. "It's becoming unpleasant. My eyes are full of sand."

"All right. And I'm sorry I brought this up. You must have thought, she's a hysteric. Time soothes everything, and life is too short. One shouldn't throw it away. We must have the courage to see it through to the end; so I think today, at least."

The guard was grappling with the door, which the wind was jerking about. With difficulty he pushed the bolts into place. Istvan and Margit stood beside each other in the darkness. A white stain of lantern light slid around the wall.

"Why have you not married?" he asked suddenly. "You are pretty, well educated, and, well, you have money."

"It gives me independence. I don't have to work. I exercise my profession because I want to be of some use."

"That explains nothing," he persisted, taking her arm. The wind keened inside the tower; it forced puffs of dust through the narrow windows.

"I am not yet intimidated by the word 'alone.' To marry—there is still time for that. Understand: I have not yet renounced love."

"I didn't mean to force you into confessions," he said quickly.

"I am saying only as much as I want to. You are a person one can be friends with. You are not demanding. Are you disappointed that we haven't slept together? You probably understand that that first man was not the only one. After him there were a couple more, equally unimportant—I mean, not worth remembering. I noticed soon enough that though it wasn't difficult to have my choice of men, I didn't feel happy, even satisfied, the next day. I'm telling you frankly how it is so as not to spoil this comradeship between us."

They started down the stairs in silence. He saw her graceful legs, bare in the light of the guard's lantern; the corridor cut its spiral down the thick wall of the tower. They made their way down the monotonous curve until their heads were spinning.

"Surely you aren't put off by my frankness?" she asked in a breathless voice as they stood at the bottom.

"It was your courage that took me by surprise. Women don't talk that way about such matters. At least I never knew one who did."

"Perhaps you never knew women at all." She laughed in the darkness. "Except as companions in the bedroom."

The force of the wind drove it through the narrow passage like a draft in a chimney. The hot, dry air had a coppery taste. The old beggar sat stoically with his back turned to the entrance. His arms encircled his legs; his forehead rested on his knees. The wind tousled his hair and showered his bare back with dust.

Istvan was worried about the car. Squinting, he looked at the palace yard. The Austin stood nearby like a faithful animal. It seemed to quiver before the hoofbeats of the charging storm. He was thinking that even if they didn't drive away, it would be best to wait out the storm in its comfortable seats.

He ran over and unlocked the door. It pushed back against him violently. He struggled until Margit sank into a seat, then settled in beside her.

"The clouds are boiling around us. It's like being in the cockpit of an airplane." He rolled down the window and dust poured in. In the wild torrent of sand they saw a green parrot. The wind was bowling it along by its outspread wings, breaking its long flight feathers.

"Poor bird."

"Poor people! Think of the huts the wind will pummel to bits—the sheets of tin ripped away, the cane supports—the sand that will be strewn through the roofs the wind pries open, and into pots of rice and babies' mouths. It whips the face."

The storm droned around the car. Thick grains of sand rang on the roof like a pelting rainstorm. A yellow glare pierced the undulating grayness. The wind flung up a disc of fire, large as a soccer ball and spraying sparks. It made three great jumps and struck the trunk of a tree. Malignant zigzags of white light flashed, then grounded themselves in the earth with a roar like a cannon shot. It seemed to Istvan and Margit that the whole world trembled. Terrified, she seized his hand.

"What was that?"

"It must have been globular lightning." He saw her green-clad figure indistinctly; he was half-blinded by the lightning.

"Let's get out of here. If you can drive." Her voice broke. "The tower attracts lightning."

He started the engine and released the hand brake, but before he could put the car in gear it began to roll lightly, pushed by the gale. In front of them something dark was being flung about in the clouds of dust. The wind was dragging a severed branch, inflating its thick clusters of leaves as if they had been a sail.

"There's no sense in this, Istvan," she pleaded. "The highway will be blocked by broken trees. Let's take cover in the ruins of the palace."

The thick walls offered shelter. He turned off the engine and put on the brake. His forehead was sticky with sweat. There was not enough air in the car.

"Were you afraid? It was very unpleasant to me, too—the way that ball of lightning flew toward us."

"Give me a cigarette," she answered tersely. "Let's open the window a little." They smoked in silence, watching the wind rush over the tiles in the palace courtyard, welter among the enormous dry leaves, and split the cherry-red pods, long as sword blades, that had been blown from the thorn trees.

"I know that moment must come. Yet that invitation to the darkness alarms me," she said reflectively, quietly, as if it did not matter whether he heard.

Only after a moment did he understand, to his great astonishment, that she was speaking of death. A wave of shame swept over him; he had seen in her only an Australian with a pretty face, unseasoned to life, bored and amusing herself a little by treating Hindus. Now it seemed to him that with these confessions she had exposed herself—more than if she had flung off her dress and invited him to touch her breasts.

"For can one still be oneself there, and remember?" She sat musing, her eyes following the streaks of dust that seemed to swirl like smoke among stone tiles rubbed to a sheen by the feet of generations. Her head was tilted down a little and her lips were tight as if with some suffering not expressed. He wanted to help, to comfort her, if only by showing that he understood her feelings.

"The war affected both of us. I had my bad times as well. They drafted me from the university; I couldn't get a deferment even for a couple of months, so I could take the examinations and have my year's work count. They sent me to Ukraine, to the front, and in 1944 fighting was going on by the Danube, on Hungarian soil. Today it's easy to say: the capitulation of an ally of the fascists. That's not the way we felt then."

He took a deep pull on his cigarette and exhaled the smoke, startling the flies that were creeping around the windowpane.

"You fought the Russians?" Her small face with its heavy wave of chestnut hair turned toward him.

"Yes. I knew then that the Germans were losing. I was full of rage and despair that we had been drawn in. But we fought to the last ditch. For the Germans, Hungary was only a point of retreat—to me, this was the end of my homeland. I wanted you to know: I was your enemy then."

She nodded.

"I saw when the Germans fired at the withdrawing Hungarian divisions, though the position was impossible to hold and they themselves were retreating. I hated them. But I was afraid of the Russians. When Budapest fell, I wanted to kill myself. I thought it was the end of Hungary, that we were a lost nation. By chance I came upon a family—I was wounded and hungry, my strength was gone—and they gave me clothing, they took me in. I left after a couple of weeks to finish my studies, as if none of it had happened. There is always time for death. And it will come without being invited. It appeared that we had to begin all over again. There was work for all. At that time they didn't ask many questions about who you were. They didn't rummage through your past like a policeman going through your pockets."

She nodded again and he spoke on.

"Naturally you don't know much about my country. How would you? We are a small nation, surrounded by a Slavic sea. It seemed that we would never raise our heads again, that we had to resign ourselves to the outrage perpetrated by history, which would enter the fact in its dry record. I thought that that was the verdict and that we would be quartered, divided among those whom we had invaded. That we would cease to exist as a state. But it happened otherwise. We have a republic."

Before them the arcades of Akbar's palace came into view: broken columns in a rain of sand, their outlines unclear as in a worn-out film.

"And how is it now in Hungary?" She put out her cigarette.

"It is possible to live."

She brooded a moment before gathering her courage to ask, "So things are not good there?"

"No. You are thinking that it is our fault. It certainly is. The Russians came, bringing people who had lived among us at some time or other—people who were model Hungarians to them, but not to us. They said they came to teach us, to mold us in the spirit of equality and freedom. Some had gotten out of jail through the good graces of Stalin. Others, even if they had managed to avoid prison, were morally stunted, were easy tools. They knew very well how to intimidate the resistance.

"Prisons! They were eager to build them. The shadow of prison walls fell on everything we undertook. They had very little in common with our country. They knew nothing about it. They frightened people even with their pronunciation of words, their strange accents, the clumsy idioms that reminded everyone of where they had come from and who was behind them.

"Unjust verdicts, coercion, hardships beyond people's strength—they were so careless that they counted all that as part of the cost of building. They didn't imagine that it could be any other way, that they shouldn't be the leaders, speak from the rostrums, have their faces on busts and portraits. They! They! But then something arose that was a people's republic after all. Workers came to understand the mechanism of politics. Laborers in the countryside began to read. New forces came into being, forces they had to deal with."

She looked at him with heightened curiosity. What was he driving at?

"What kind of achievement is this—to assure oneself a comfortable situation, to placate the more powerful, to beat down the weaker with impunity so as to enhance one's sense of well-being? To write so as not to interfere with anyone, to win approval? I want to live, but I want a life worth living—to influence things, not to flatter the powers that be.

"I love Hungary. Time mixes us as a baker mixes a cake. I search for leaven, for what is good for the nation; I want justice and freedom. They exist, and notwithstanding those plaster busts, they force changes, since socialism is what it is. And these changes are irreversible. Have no illusions: this would not have been the Hungary that was my homeland."

"So you give them bricks when they build the prison walls," she said with an indulgent smile, looking at the tips of her dusty shoes. "You serve those you don't consider worthy of respect."

"Only if I plant my hands in my pockets and say: No, I will change nothing, not even myself. There was a time when I thought it was enough for me only to write in Hungarian, a beautiful language. Now I know that that is not enough. Many forces lie dormant in the nation. Socialism awakens them; that's not just a platitude. Often those people themselves are not aware of what they have unleashed.

"The time will come when the intermediaries must be gone. The changes began in Russia, from Khrushchev's time. We still have the old, proven system: suspicion, informing, fear. They already think differently in Poland. A thaw, a breaking of the ice; the politicians speak so euphemistically, it's as if they had all become poets. A storm is coming. It must come to us. It must. And the struggle must not go on without me. Otherwise I would have to blame myself—to despise myself."

She looked at him; in her blue eyes was a stubbornness that seemed to match his own. "So you don't see a life without politics," she whispered bitterly.

He shook his head.

The sky cleared and suddenly they felt the low sun, now a bright blur in the triple curve of a rainbow, as it looked out from beyond the horizon. The wind stopped. It had become unbearably hot; warmth radiated from the desert sand the storm had showered on the roads and the trees.

A sympathetic silence fell between them. He drove the car out onto the road. Sand, swept into waves as if by the current of a brook, covered the asphalt. Shattered branches and piles of leaves parched by drought lay on the road.

"When I shake my head I feel sand falling on my neck. I must have a bath. Take me home."

"All right. As you wish."

He turned the car toward the suburban villas. A few minutes later he was being informed by the watchman that a window was broken in the hall. Led by some mysterious instinct, the cook appeared.

"Where have you brought me?" Margit asked, wiping her dirty face.

"Home, as you ordered. I'll give you a towel in a minute, and a bathrobe. I warn you: the tap marked cold is actually hot. Well, why are you looking at me like that? First you say so much about friendship, and then you seem taken aback."

She went into the living room and her eyes fell on the rust and dark green carpet as it glowed in the western light. She stood still.

"Beautiful colors!" She nodded with approval. "I like it."

"So do I. It reminds me of you."

She looked askance at him.

He showed her the bathroom and threw her a fleecy towel. "If you'd like me to soap your back—" he offered facetiously.

"When I want that, I'll call, but then don't you be taken aback," she interrupted, locking the door.

"Pereira!" He summoned the cook. "What do you have for dinner that's good?"

"Rice with sauce and a piece of chicken in the ice box." He threw out a furtive, helpless glance, but seeing that Terey was impatient, added hastily, "We have Hungarian salami and plum vodka. I will run to the market right away and buy something else. You gave us no notice that we were having a guest."

"Do you have green pepper? Onion, tomatoes?"

"We have!" he cried joyfully.

"And bacon and eggs?"

"Those also."

"Good. You are free. I will cook a Hungarian dish myself."

"I understand." The dark eyelids were lowered knowingly.

"You understand nothing!" Terey's anger kindled suddenly. "That lady is an eye doctor. We were caught in a sandstorm outside the city. She came to get cleaned up."

"I understand," the Hindu repeated, wiping his hands on the hem of his untucked shirt.

"Set the table. Don't forget flowers."

He was exasperated at having made excuses to the cook.

Pereira disappeared. Shouts floated back from the kitchen, and the patter of running feet. Istvan peered into the corridor. Pilgrims' canes and bundles were lying there. When the cook returned with a tablecloth and silverware, he asked abruptly, "What is that crowd in the kitchen?"

"My relatives arrived from the country. They are in the city for the first time. They wanted to see how richly we live, sahib and I. They are not disturbing anything, and they can sleep in the barsati. There is enough room on the roof."

"Istvan, come here." He heard Margit's voice from behind the door.

She was sitting in a chair, her skin clean and golden, her freshly brushed hair a silken river.

"It went very well without your help. Take a shower; you'll revive immediately. I heard how you gave the cook his orders. I was hungry at once. Well, jump into the tub. I won't sit at the table with a dirty man."

The cook brought in a brass tray on which tall glasses clinked, flanked by a bottle of whiskey, ice cubes, a blue siphon, and two glasses of Coca-Cola.

"I can help myself," she said, motioning him away. "Go."

The warm shower was a relief. The streams of water ran red from the desert dust; his skin began to breathe. He dried himself, deliberately leaving a little of the delicious moisture. He put on a clean shirt. He looked in the mirror and saw a face with cheerless eyes and set lips. One short hair still stuck up, forming a cowlick.

He was unexpectedly moved at seeing a strange comb lying beside his shaving kit. What whim of mine is this? he thought. He shook his finger at his reflection; a wave of warm feeling came over him.

"Here's your lost property." He dropped the comb into the girl's lap. With a glass in her hand, she looked at the picture on his desk of a woman and two boys with a dog.

"My sons. My wife."

"You've never spoken of them." She took the photograph in her hand and looked at it closely. "A beautiful woman," she said thoughtfully.

"You didn't ask. I must leave you for a while. You're probably not hankering for Indian cuisine?"

"All right. I can wait now until midnight. Drink up." She handed him a cool glass. "You remember—that's how our acquaintance began."

He took her hand and kissed it. They were quiet for a moment. See, you have her, he thought. You drew her out of the crowd of guests the night of that wedding; you got to know her, you are happy together. What more do you want?

"I'll be right back." He put the glass down.

The smells of spices and perspiring bodies hovered in the kitchen. Pereira had spread tomatoes, white globes of peeled sweet onion, and strips of pepper like green icicles on the table. He looked around with knife in hand, as if waiting for the command to attack.

Istvan took bacon from the refrigerator, sliced it, and threw it into the frying pan. Before the fat melted he cut the center out of the pepper, shook off the seeds, and chopped it fine. The cook followed his lead; the work progressed as adroitly as a piano duet. The green chopped pepper was covered with brick-red slices of tomato, then overlaid with white onion, which was topped with round cuts of bacon. Juice oozed from the vegetables and the pan bubbled pleasantly. He added salt and a pinch of hot pepper. Then he waited until the vegetables were tender.

"But don't you dare let the onions turn brown," he warned the cook. "Keep the cover on. Before you serve it, beat in two eggs and mix it well. Be careful not to burn it. Serve red wine."

All the time he thought he was hearing throaty whispers from behind the thick window screen, but he could not make out the cook's kinsfolk in the darkness that had descended all at once.

"I wasn't long, was I, Margit? You weren't bored?"

"No. I was thinking." She raised her eyes to his. "I'm never bored. I don't have to be amused. What were you making?"

"*Lecso.* Our simplest dish. If you take up with a Hungarian, you have to try it."

"You got me to eat cake with silver sprinkles. I might as well take another chance."

"And then we have Bull's Blood." He was amused when she made a face. "Never fear. It's a red wine."

Outside the window lights in the villas went on, and yellowish street lamps still dusty from the storm.

"Is one lamp enough for us? Shall I turn on the higher one?"

"Let it be. I like low light."

"You're not angry with me for bringing you here?"

"I am not angry at all. I don't know myself how it came to this, that I am perfectly happy to wander around Delhi with you. You are kind. Sometimes at the hospital it occurs to me: I must tell Istvan about this!"

There was a knock at the door.

"Well, what is it?"

But the cook discreetly declined to enter. Istvan had to open the door to hear his whisper, "Sir, everything is ready."

"Good. Serve it." He saw that Pereira had put on a white linen jacket and white gloves; he was appearing in full regalia.

"Come. Now you will see my better side," he invited her. "No more whiskey. We will move on to wine."

The table was covered with an embroidered cloth. Fruit in a straw basket gleamed in the ray from the hanging lamp. The cook had put a branch with curly masses of orange-colored blossoms into an earthenware pitcher. They had hardly seated themselves when Pereira brought in a tray with the steaming frying pan and placed it in front of Margit.

"Oh, it smells lovely!"

"Be brave. Take some and try it. You may compliment me."

The cork popped loudly. He took the bottle from the cook and filled the glasses. He felt Margit looking at him with inexpressible astonishment.

"What is it? The dish is not good? Did he manage to botch it just then?"

"Look around."

He turned his head. Behind him, next to the wall, four men in white and a young girl sat with their legs folded under them, staring with wide eyes. They saluted the couple with folded hands. At a sign from the cook they came closer, walking barefoot without a sound.

"What are they doing here, Pereira? Take them to the kitchen and let them have something to eat. Have you gone mad?"

The cook stood his ground, full of dignity, holding the tray with the frying pan as if it were a sacred relic.

"They have already eaten. They would not put this to their lips. They are believing Hindus and there is meat in it. I promised to show them how sahib eats; they have never seen such a thing. To them it is a true art. They say that indeed we have fingers to mix everything, to knead it and to eat it, as people eat. But sir and madam eat altogether differently, with knife and fork. That is an art which I promised to show them."

"Did you hear?" He turned to Margit. "He is making a sideshow of us. I have to chase them away."

"Leave them alone," she laughed, carried away with the humor of it. "You shouldn't disappoint them. What's the harm? And the cook counted on you so! He is anxious, like a theater director before a premiere. Don't be angry, don't mind them." She raised her glass and a little red flame flitted over the tablecloth. "Your health. Remember, we are in India."

"We are in India. We must amaze and excite them."

"Do you speak English?" she asked, looking toward the figures in white.

"No, madam," the cook answered. "These are dark peasants, and that little girl is my youngest son's fiancee. Sahib has seen him."

"How old is your son? Eight?"

"Ten, and she is fifteen. She is already mature. She will care for him, work like a slave for him. It is a great honor for them to be connected with such a man as I."

The *lecso* was a success; the dry wine brought out the pungent flavor of the dish. Nevertheless the conversation foundered. They felt the eyes of their mute audience watchfully trained on their faces and hands. The dinner became a torture.

"I will give him a piece of my mind." In his thoughts Istvan was already threatening the cook. "His head will spin."

Pereira switched on the device that connected the rotors of both ceiling fans. The peasant family was enchanted, impressed by his technical skill. Margit finished her coffee. She lit a cigarette and choked restlessly.

"Take me home," she requested. "I'm beginning to feel tired."

When they were sitting in the car, she took his hand.

"Don't be angry. Think what pleasure we have given them. The cook has gained new authority. They will have something to tell: they have been where they are normally not received, they have seen something they have not seen before. Surely you will invite me again? I thought the *lecso* was delicious."

The watchman's upraised truncheon flashed in the glare of a headlight. He called to the neighbors' guard in Hindi:

"My sahib is driving out—with the woman."

That much at least Istvan heard. He gripped the steering wheel hard. Rage swept over him. Quite an event! Sahib drives out with the woman who was with him in his house.

Chapter IV

"The meeting took place in a warm atmosphere full of mutual understanding; it became yet another proof that cultural relations are solidifying." Istvan put down his pen and sighed deeply. Just such orotund, almost meaningless sentences were expected in the reports of all ministries of foreign affairs.

The curtain was not completely drawn; the sun beat through the chink with a white glare that made the eyelids blink and forced the face into a tired grimace. The drone of the cooling machine did not drown out the measured tapping of the drops that gathered at the end of the pipe and splashed into the little tin drip pan, then dried without a trace. The slow spattering measured the time. He raised his eyes irritably to assure himself that the next drop that clung to the copper pipe would swell and lazily detach itself. He urged it on with a look; he almost begged it to fall.

The telephone rang jarringly.

"Be so kind as to bestir yourself and come here. Comrade Ambassador summons you." It was Judit's voice.

"Must I come right away? I have just begun—"

"I'd advise you to come. Ferenc is already here."

"But what for?" He tried for another moment's delay. His trousers were sticking to his sweaty legs; the leather on his chair was unbearably hot. He didn't want to get up, to go out into the stifling heat of the hall, to carry on a conversation with an artificial smile.

"Agra," she said, and hung up.

He rose so quickly that a lizard that had been dozing on the ceiling scampered into a distant corner.

The ambassador stood with his hands in his pockets, resting his broad backside on the edge of his desk and stooping forward with raised eyebrows, like a bull ready to charge. Ferenc, sporting a sheaf of black curly hair and the affability of the leader of a gypsy orchestra, opened his briefcase.

"An invitation to a congress in honor of Rabindranath Tagore has arrived," he began, as if he were serving a tennis ball.

"How do you feel, comrade?" the ambassador asked Terey solicitously. "The heat has not overcome you?"

"No. I like dry weather."

"He likes it," Kalman Bajcsy repeated morosely. "So you will go to Agra. Tagore—that's your department: a writer, a Nobel laureate. You will represent Hungary!" he added grandiloquently.

"I thought we could pass this up. Tagore is not published in our country. We would escape troublesome questions," Istvan said as if in self-defense.

"I count on your astuteness. Speak, impress them, but don't commit us to anything. In personal conversations, unofficially, don't spare the praise, it costs nothing," the ambassador coached him. "Who doesn't like to bask in approval?"

"Comrade Ferenc hasn't been to Agra yet. He could take the occasion to see the historic landmarks. The Taj Mahal is one of the seven wonders of the world," Istvan offered. "He could take the car and Krishan, he would be at his own disposal."

"I will not send Krishan anywhere," the ambassador bristled. "He is an utter fool. I must keep an eye on him. His behavior is so erratic that it is time to look for a new driver. The accident taught him nothing. You have a car. Drive yourself there. You like the weather so much," he said ironically. "Run over to Agra for three days."

"So you are assigning me to do this?" he asked, secretly gratified. "So our presence there is really necessary?"

"I wish you to go," Bajcsy said emphatically.

"Something is wrong with my eyes." Ferenc adjusted his sunglasses, which reflected like mirrors and made him look like an exasperated bumblebee. "The sun hurts them. I would gladly go, but there isn't enough time. Work is pressing. We've had word that the couriers will be here in a couple of days. We must prepare the mail, compile the reports. Everything is coming down on me."

"Very well. I'll go."

"The congress begins tomorrow," the ambassador reminded him, producing an ornate invitation card. "As occasion arises, you will serve as our correspondent. You are really a poet, but that needn't hinder you from drafting statements in prose. So—acquit yourself well for my sake." He clapped a heavy hand on the counselor's shoulder. It was rather like the comradely gesture a commander makes to encourage an officer sent on a dangerous mission.

How naive they are, he thought, rolling up the window as the big gadflies swooped blindly and rattled against the windshield. They thought they were forcing this down my throat, while I was only looking for a chance to dash over to Agra.

The wish to see her is getting the best of me, he thought, finding himself surprised. How I have missed her lately! It's good to talk with her. She is excellent company on evening walks to Old Delhi and the cinema. Somehow she has inserted herself into the dull rhythm of my life.

The breezes stirred reddish streaks like smoke from the parched, empty fields. Packs of vultures slept fitfully in the bare tops of lonely trees. Nothing was vivid green except the wings of parrots feeding in the road, tottering clumsily as they pecked at dry camel droppings. They darted away just in front of the car; some hit the fender lightly and flew away screeching, but none fell under the wheels.

What do I really want? What am I expecting? he thought. Without answering his own question he smiled, for he saw her as she came up to him—slender, lithe, with a coppery sheen to her hair as it swung with the rhythm of her walk—and caught him in the glance of blue eyes shining like water in a mountain stream in the spring, when the snow melts. Surely she would be waiting. She must have gotten his telegram the day before.

He found himself in villages built of clay, and now empty. Scrawny hens ran away startled, stretching their necks, which were bare of feathers. Only by the well were there women, women in green and orange saris who beat the wet linen with sticks, gossiping cheerfully. At the sight of the car they stopped their work and shielded their eyes with their hands, watching for the bus. Their necklaces and bracelets glittered as if they were wealthy.

As he approached the city itself, he had to slow down. In the shade of the trees around the temple, arbas stood in a circle with their shafts raised. The oxen lay together, lazily munching dry grass. A crowd of the faithful were singing and beating gongs. For the last few minutes he had to steer through the spellbound crowd; it left him tired and irritated.

When he pulled up in front of the hotel—a one-story building replete with shady verandas and pergolas, its horseshoe shape set in a park—he was certain that Margit would immediately emerge from the shade. He even loitered for a moment, raising the hood, checking the oil, glancing at the overheated tires.

His room was reserved.

"Is Miss Ward staying here?"

"Yes," answered the clerk, shooing a cat from a table. The cat stretched and yawned widely, showing the pale pink interior of its mouth. "Yes, sir, in number eleven, on the right."

As he signed the register he saw a telegram tucked into the frame of a large photograph of Gandhi. He could read the address: it was his telegram to Margit. He was a little troubled.

"Miss Ward is in?"

The clerk spread his hands helplessly.

"I do not know, sir. The key is not here—" he checked the pigeonhole in a drawer. "Miss Ward is not a tourist. I do not know her schedule. Tourists get guides from us, from the hotel. Perhaps you—"

"I know Agra. I'd be a pretty good guide myself. Thank you."

Two porters in turbans with gold piping were lurking about, ready to carry his suitcase.

"Number fifteen, the third room past Miss Ward's. We have no room thirteen; tourists don't like the devil's dozen."

He drove the car into the shade. The metal body was unbearably hot. He followed the porter through a pergola overgrown with a dense screen of wisteria.

The door of number eleven was ajar. He went in without knocking, pleased that he would surprise Margit. The white room felt cool. He looked around: a bed, a table, two armchairs, a wardrobe, a fireplace without adornment. There was no trace of a woman's presence: no photographs, no flowers. He was thinking that the attendant had made a mistake when he noticed a few pairs of shoes next to the wall; he recognized the sandals they had bought on that first evening together.

He heard the drumming sound of running water in the bathroom.

"Margit," he called, tapping on the door with his fingers.

The door opened instantly. An old Hindu woman who was on her knees scouring the bathtub, and was obviously startled, answered that Miss Ward had gone out in the car that morning with the gentleman who usually came for her. That pained him as if it had been an insult.

"When will she return?"

"She took a bag of bedding with her. Perhaps she is spending the night away," the maid said in a languid drawl, tilting her head with a bewildered look.

On the desk lay stationery and envelopes with a little image of the Taj Mahal, which drew multitudes of visitors to Agra. He had pulled out the chair with the thought of writing a few words when suddenly, with unreasoning vehemence, he whispered, "No. No." He went to his own room, his steps pounding on the brick pavement. He sighed like a dog that has lost the scent.

Where has she been taken? Who comes for her? It seemed odd to him that he felt such acute jealousy at the first suspicion that he might have a rival. Perhaps it was simply a doctor, a colleague from the center.

He washed his hands and face and knotted his tie with abrupt motions. The room smelled of insecticide and fresh paint. He felt a premonition that this first setback was a sign of more to come. Everything to do with the congress became distasteful to him.

He sat behind the wheel and tried to find his way through the streets. They all led to the riverfront, where peasants brought cattle to wade and dead bodies were burned. Through trails of bluish smoke he saw the rhythmic gestures of herders leaning forward with palms cupped, splashing water on the backs of the oxen. White terns flew over the water and, meowing like cats, collided with their own reflections. They shook off the drops and flapped their wings, disappointed that the water was only water and not an abyss of light that would bring them more reflections glistening with silver.

The little map outlined on the invitation was not enough for him. He had to ask directions from passersby, who looked at him and then at the car with great black eyes as if regretting that they did not understand. Here, away from the center of the city, it was hard to find people who spoke English. Suddenly he spied the Peugeot that belonged to the French correspondent and followed it to a large park.

Under the trunks of huge mangroves groups of Hindus stood, engaging in lively discussions. The university—as it was rather pompously called—resembled a Greek temple of harmonious proportions with tympana resting on columns. He had hardly parked the Austin when its representatives came up and welcomed him effusively. They fastened a golden badge to his jacket. On it were a lotus flower and a red ribbon on which he read "Tagore: knowledge, truth, God."

They spoke with gaudy rhetorical flourishes of the weather, the charming features of the journey, the attractions of the country. When they learned that he was the delegate from Hungary, they tried to determine exactly where that country was. Of course they had a general idea that it was somewhere in Europe.

They conducted him to a building where he was introduced to the director of the institution, who could have posed for a monument to Tolstoy, with his majestic mane of gray hair and luxuriant beard.

There was the ceremonial opening of an exhibit of translations of Tagore. He noticed with pleasure that there were several in Hungarian. He showed them to the director, discreetly declining to mention that they had been issued before the war. Later, infuriated critics had branded Tagore a naive idealist and a woolgathering mystic, making a revival of enthusiasm for his work impossible.

"Is our great writer popular in your country?" asked the director, who had the face of a prophet—a dark face of saintly gauntness framed with white wisps of disheveled hair, and a fiery eye that seemed to pierce Istvan straight through.

Famous? Before the war his books had enjoyed small press runs; the elite read him, chiefly women. Popular? His name was dropped in conversation in salons but rarely mentioned by critics. Certainly he was no less famous there than here, where ninety percent of the people did not have his books within easy reach.

"Of course," he said warmly. "Tagore is excellently translated. He is numbered among the classic poets. It is impossible to be a cultured person and not know what he was to India."

"Splendid!" the prophet exulted, and began to recount how some under these old trees had walked with the master, and what he had studied. From that peaceloving, self-abnegating theory that the world could be changed slowly by persuasion and personal example had come the strength to resist British imperialism. Here the core of the Congress Party had formed; here Gandhi had spoken. And it had all begun as friendly meetings, strolls in the shade of old trees, the sharing of views on beauty, progress, and creativity.

The hall was empty at first, and rather cool. Istvan was called to the platform. When his turn came, he was supposed to give a welcoming speech and assure his listeners that Tagore's thoughts were alive and bearing fruit in Hungary. There were not chairs for all who were gathering in the room; some sat on carpets. The organizers, in untucked shirts, brought in a microphone and tested its sound. Boys with sashes over their chests, wearing floppy sandals, were enjoying themselves under the pretense of keeping order. There were necklaces of strung flowers for the honored guests, but too many had been prepared; the boys searched out beautiful women in the crowd and threw the extra garlands onto their necks.

The ceremonies began with the singing of a hymn to the Mother of India, the words of which had been written by the master himself.

A little girl came running in with a tray. Bowing, she anointed people's foreheads so their thoughts would turn without distraction to the highest matters. A man spoke with exaggerated fervor in Bengali, sometimes reverting to a few sentences of English to sum up his exposition for the small number of Europeans in the audience. White draped robes and dark upraised arms created an effect like gestures from classical theater, recalling the ancient Greeks or Romans.

"This blather doesn't bore you?" asked Maurice Nagar, a short, very fragrant man with a neatly trimmed mustache.

"Not yet," Istvan said with unguarded candor. A Russian professor sitting nearby must have known several Indian languages, for he reveled in the discussion that broke out when the speaker asserted that the finest Indian literature originated in Bengal, and that only because of that had Tagore's genius found the perfect medium and been able to express itself so freely.

His statement evoked an instant rebuttal from the Tamil quarter and an unofficial denial from supporters of Hindi, which as the national language was going to displace English. The dispute grew hot in spite of efforts at mediation by the director himself, whose head seemed to rise above the agitated audience like an apparition at a seance. He raised and lowered his hands like a conductor unable to keep pace with a storm of instruments outshouting each other.

Istvan made notes for a report and a press release. The Frenchman looked at him skeptically; he knew that, true to good English custom, they would be handed a release before the end of the session. It would only be necessary to alter it a little, depending on the country to which it would be sent and the typescript of that country. But that was merely cosmetic.

When an intermission was announced, Nagar caught Terey by his sleeve.

"Surely you are experienced enough to know what will come next. Let's stay here," he coaxed. "We can have a chat, a smoke."

They pulled lawn chairs up to a tree with a thick, knotted trunk that looked as if it had not grown out of the ground, but built itself by trickling down and hardening. Clusters of aerated roots hung from its branches. The two men stood in what looked like an unfinished cage.

"What does this remind you of?" Nagar pointed to the motionless ropes of roots. "It looks to me, quite simply, like a noose."

"And to me, like the ropes in a belfry. I always have an urge to pull on them, to rock the whole tree. I used to envy the altar boys because they could hang onto those ropes and fly up over the floorboards when the bell tilted, and set it ringing through the whole neighborhood." He nudged the thick, woven mass of whitish roots with the toe of his shoe.

"Be careful." Nagar's small, boyish face wrinkled with loathing. "I tried that once and shook a hundred beetles, caterpillars, and red ants onto my head. They stung even though I crushed them with my fingers. It felt as if someone had set me on fire with a match."

From a distance they heard the voice of the next speaker, assisted by a megaphone. Parrots, shrouded in the leafy arch, quarreled. Huge white branches like gnawed mammoth bones seemed to dissolve into the deep shade.

A two-wheeled tonga rolled down the street. The drowsy gray oxen ambled along; on the heavy shaft between their hindquarters, like a bundle in a soiled bag, a squatting Hindu dozed. The heat seemed to congeal; the air trembled like a vitreous jelly.

"One might think that nothing happens in this country," Nagar said, motioning to the distant landscape: the empty fields, the clumps of trees with bleached trunks and almost black shocks of leaves blurred by a ripple of hot air. "However, since my arrival—and I am in my ninth year here—there have been enormous changes. They occurred imperceptibly, as if through no one's volition. The awakening revealed itself in collective action that surprised those who were put off guard by the apparent passiveness of the Hindus.

"A consciousness of rights is growing in the depths of that mass of people, and not even the rights of class, but human rights. If they would go further and take the view that they only live once, that each is unique, that in any case they should act quickly . . . If that crude definition of religion as an opiate applies anywhere, it applies above all here in India. They suffer calmly as oxen; they accept the yoke of predestination; they trust that for that humility and submission, that lack of rebellion, they will be rewarded in the next incarnation. You know, I would wish for a bloody revolution in this country—if they were at all able to pull it off."

"You say that?" Terey looked at Nagar's ruddy, creased face. "I thought you were here to find peace above all else. Your country has had enough to live through: defeat, painful capitulation. Struggles of generals for power, struggles for influence with the Americans and the English, for benevolent patronage. The breakup of your empire: Vietnam, then Morocco and Algeria. When it comes to the point, you've had enough of unstable governments, ministerial intrigue, corrupt police and collaborators in high places."

Nagar rocked back and forth and smiled indulgently, with a hint of irony.

"Peace. There are these years to appreciate it"—he began toying with a cigarette—"and just a little more perseverance to hold out here at my observation post while new forces, still unknown to themselves, try to take power. You are astonished that I love India. A splendid country! Money is worth more here than in Europe; I can get everything for centimes. Where would I find such deferential servants, such lovers—" he winked knowingly. He did not hide his weakness and often let himself be seen in the company of supple young men with crimped hair reeking of brilliantine. "Where would they entertain me so regally, so sumptuously? I am on a first-name basis with the heads of all the government departments, and with people rich as monarchs. What magnificent hunts! And yet I would wish this country and those grass-eating sheep a bloodbath. War . . . though not many Indians died for England in Africa, Burma, and Italy, war opened their eyes and showed them that England is weak, that the British lion will roar, will behave menacingly, but when one waves the firebrand in front of him, he will back away."

Nagar was in his element. He had snagged himself a patient listener; he perorated with the gestures of a populist politician. Istvan lit a cigarette and thought of Margit.

"War? It hastened India's independence. Though the present state of things is very convenient for me, I would be glad to see the next stage: revolution. For just this reason, that in my own way I love these people. You, Istvan, ought to understand me. Quite simply, I feel better when I admit this thought—when I accept internally the changes that the India of today will inflict on me."

It's easy for you to talk of being resigned, Terey thought, since you only see the arrival of that moment in the distant future. You are almost certain that it will not affect you.

The cigarette smoke drifted away in the sunlight. The parrots screeched. The rattle of casual applause reached them: the gracious acceptance of the conclusion of someone's speech.

"Doesn't it seem to you that there is an unhealthy momentum in business these days, a driven quality? The papers are full of sensational headlines; the country teems with shady transactions. Pity that they are of no interest to anyone outside India. We would have an easy life; I'm thinking of us—" Nagar pointed a thumb at his tight blue striped shirt and the big sapphire bow tie that fluttered like a startled butterfly—"of us, correspondents. Those who have money want to turn it around as soon as possible, to take the profit, hide the income, withdraw the capital. The ground shakes under one's feet. A foul smell is in the air. One grasps, one wrests what one can, as long as one can. I am not thinking of foreign capital under Indian names, only of no less rapacious Indian nabobs—the workings of instinct," he reflected, crushing a Gauloise between his fingers, "as with flies, which are the most vexing in autumn, the day before the first chill, which exterminates them."

"You're in a good humor," Terey said, nodding. "You're galloping on our horse! The threat of revolution—that's the prerogative of the communists."

"I could settle for war," Nagar conceded. "The impulses that unite a nation are needed here. They might equally well come from within as from outside."

"But who would want to fight them?" Terey said doubtfully. "Winning such a war might be more troublesome than losing. What could be done with those hundreds of millions? How could they be fed and clothed and goaded into rational activity?"

Nagar brooded. "Pakistan could attack them, with the tacit approval of the Americans, if they move too far to the left. Or China, if the Americans instead of the English became overly involved with them. Perhaps war would bring a sudden assumption of power by the army, as happens in newly formed democracies. That was the case in Egypt and Turkey, and not long ago in South Korea.

I wouldn't be at all surprised if momentous developments set in before our stay in India is over."

"But the Congress Party and Nehru—"

"Tradition still keeps the party going; they wrap themselves in their achievements in the time of the struggle for independence. But by now that is history, a defense of the power the nation bestowed on them, and they know how to make the most of it. Nehru is an old man. He can only ask, like Gandhi, that they respect his gray hair. But every plea, every appeal for restraint and deliberation, may be drowned out tomorrow by an uproar from the impatient crowd."

They heard the whistle of a locomotive from beyond the river: a long shriek on two notes, like shepherds' pipes. Maurice listened with his head tilted.

"You take me for a drunken soothsayer, and my throat is dry as pepper. I can't drink alone. I'd like to get you to slip off with me to the hotel bar. If we take a whole bottle, we can be sure they won't dupe us with watered-down whiskey, as my valet tried to do. I warn you, they will pour tea into it."

"That hasn't happened to me so far," Istvan laughed. "Maybe it's because when my friends get together and we start a bottle, we don't stop until we can see the bottom."

"Good principle, but it only works at your age. I drink for taste, and more for memory's sake than for new excitements. Well, let's go; it was only a sense of obligation that brought us here." He sprang up and pressed forward jauntily, with the exaggerated sprightliness of old men who pretend when others are watching that they have preserved their youthfulness.

Terey looked around at the pale columns of the building; inside it, voices ascended with a singsong lilt. They felt the mischievous delight of schoolboys playing hooky. Maurice drove out first in his Peugeot and Terey glided quickly after him. They passed peasant carts and squeezed between wagons loaded with young timber. Their cars chased each other like two dogs.

On the narrow road, bursts of wind stirred up red dust full of golden flecks of chaff—the dried, matted straw ground by arba wheels heavy as the vicissitudes of peasant life.

When the drivers of the wagons cringed at the blast of the horn, he imagined that they must take the vehicles speeding by in flashes of glass and nickel, with Europeans lolling on the cushions, for demons in flight. They emerged from a cloud of dust, they hooted, they threatened to smash the carts. They slowed their tires with a moaning noise, almost touching the carts with their gleaming hoods. When an opening appeared for a moment between the ponderous arbas, they jumped unexpectedly, their tires spinning out sand and gravel. They were not automobiles, but monsters from hell, spreading fear.

He smiled as it struck him that to the peasants, the oxen with swarms of flies grazing on their ragged necks, the flat, creaking wheels, the palm tree that had reluctantly fallen off, were part of nature, of the everyday order of things. Those half-naked, dozing wagoners were surely thinking, Where and why are the white men going so fast, to what are they racing? Do they not know that what they acquire they must relinquish, and what they possess they will abandon?

Istvan tried to keep up with the Frenchman, but Maurice drove like a virtuoso. He calculated unerringly the position and speed of a wagon and managed to slip past without snagging his car on the protruding copper-clad axles of the arbas, while Terey became mired in traffic and lost speed. He wanted to pick up the telephone and call the hospital, call Margit, or beat on her door. Perhaps she had returned at last? Although she did not know of his arrival, the very strength of his longing, the returning thought insistent as a cry, ought to draw her back, to impel her to come to him.

As soon as they had parked the cars in the shade of the pergola, Terey told Nagar with apologies that he had to leave him for a moment.

"I'm going to take a piss as well," the other said with a matey air.

"And I—to the telephone." The Frenchman's easygoing ways grated on him, especially when he alluded in raw detail to the young men he consorted with, speaking without braggadocio, like old people confiding in each other about intestinal disorders.

He found the number of the hospital at once; it was underlined several times with colored ink marks. The numbers for UNESCO's center for ophthalmological examinations were there. Immediately after he heard the ring, a nasal voice spoke in an unknown language. It rose, repeating something emphatically, as if hoping the European would understand somehow.

"Ask for someone who speaks English," Terey exclaimed edgily. "Doctor. Doctor. Give me a doctor. English!" he barked, with heavy stress on the crucial words.

Worried gasps came from the receiver. The guard or attendant knew only the language of his village.

"Call a doctor," Terey shouted, but the other man, out of patience and wishing to avoid bother, hung up.

"He didn't understand, the stupid peasant," the Hindu clerk said with a flattering smile. "They keep the most awful riffraff there, absolute savages. Perhaps I can help. I will be the translator. Whom am I calling?"

"Miss Ward," he said in a tone that implied that the desk attendant should have known all the time whose room he had inquired about that morning. He was exasperated by the sight of the dark, slender finger slowly inserting itself into the holes on the dial and carefully guiding its rotations. There was a conversation, then a pause during which the clerk glanced knowingly at Istvan.

"He knows nothing. He went to ask," he explained. "They are having lunch now. Beggars from all over India are crowding to the hospital."

The wait was excruciating. The clerk felt no need for constraint; he did not use his hand to cover the receiver, that greedy funnel that seized the sound. The man on the other end of the line did not understand the situation in any case, while the clerk felt a bond with his foreign guests. Even every weakness of theirs that he detected and slyly stored away in his memory was like an initiation. They could allow themselves a great deal, refuse to acknowledge restrictions and laws divine or human, because they had so much money. He would have liked to use his knowledge of English to display his readiness to perform intimate services. A lackey intoxicated with the condescension of the powerful, Istvan thought.

A cat lay on its back, watching a large moth that was fluttering around a cluster of violet wisteria blossoms under a roof of greenery. Terey caught himself inwardly urging the cat to jump, to seize the moth between its jaws, for the insect's heavy body was breaking off the petals.

"Very well, sir. You may speak." The clerk bowed. Before he handed Terey the receiver, he rubbed it on his sleeve. "The head physician is there."

They introduced themselves. Now he knew: he could not count on seeing Margit today. He might not see her at all. She had gone for an audit with the entire team. Where? The doctor could not say; everything depended on the volume of established cases. They had gone into the back country, they would travel around the villages, a hundred miles or more. The doctor was an Englishman, so he measured in miles. He invited Istvan to visit him at the hospital. Istvan laid a rupee on the desk for the clerk and scratched the cat on its fluffy throat. The little Adam's apple trembled under his fingers in a rhythmic purr of satisfaction.

He did not have to hurry anywhere. He heard the jingling of insects in the blossoming roof of the pergola, the plaintive call of the seller of nuts, and the rattle of the magician who stood near the entrance gate with shallow baskets of reptiles, looking longingly for someone to summon him with a motion of the hand. That he could step through the wide-open gate never crossed his mind. The training of the English sahibs was still in his blood. The fakir lifted the rattle high above his head; the harsh noise shattered into an echo that rang from the wall of the hotel. Terey waved dismissively. No, he had no desire for this spectacle. Not now. Not today.

If my boys were here, he thought with a sudden longing for his sons, it would be worth it to show them the snakes' dances. I think too little about the children; I imagine them as though they had not changed, not grown, as though when I return I will find them exactly the same as when I told them goodbye. Ilona? The delay with the passport was an indignity—yet another proof that I am viewed as suspect, untrustworthy, and they are holding the stakes. Or are they? One of the most trusted, when he defected and it was thrown up to him that he had left his family in the country, answered insolently, "I have taken my family out with me. I will never be separated from them," and insinuatingly patted his crotch.

Without a sound Terey walked along the thick carpet, which brought him straight to the bar. The long paddles of the ceiling fan turned idly. The Frenchman crouched on a high stool with his knees bent. The whiskey in the glasses had a golden glint.

"Well, at last!"

"You should have begun alone."

"You know very well that I get no pleasure from alcohol. It's a conversation starter. I like having a listener. Loneliness? It's possible to feel it only in Asia, in the human sea, the indifferent mass. We melt into oblivion here. We are lost atoms, utterly alien and dispensable."

Terey sat on a stool and raised his glass invitingly. They drank under the solicitous eye of the bartender, who with obliging readiness brought forward a square bottle and a silver jigger for measuring the liquor.

"But you feel more at ease here."

"Yes, for my income, in the face of the universal poverty, is worth twice as much. I can even allow myself the luxury of extolling the merits of revolution, of thinking seriously about improving the lot of human beings, and about the rights of citizens. Those, however, are purely theoretical reflections. In my country, the lower echelons have grown bitter; they are exerting pressure. The working classes feathered their nests and nothing would quiet them down. You turned their heads, they got a hankering to take over governments. That is to say, they wanted to gain ground, to liberate themselves from the complexes of their class. At my expense, obviously."

"If I were in your place, I shouldn't trust India too much."

"Well, there are changes. I myself haven't spoken of them except when it was necessary. I'll wager that when we meet ten years from now, the greatest difference will be in the price of whiskey; of course it will go up," he prophesied, leaning comfortably on his elbow and looking into his glass as he swirled it gently. "The Americans are no more adept than the English. Even their help causes offense."

"Your French don't go about things very wisely, either," the counselor baited him. "Remember Dien Bien Phu and the Organisation Armée Secrète in Algeria."

"Say what you please. Apart from a liking for true culture, and that I only find in the cuisine, nothing much connects me to France."

"You speak as if you didn't consider yourself a Frenchman."

"I am a Frenchman. I am. Only before that I was an Austrian, and I was born in Sosnowiec—"

"Where is that?"

"In what was Russia, then Poland, then Germany, and now Poland again. My birthplace also changed national allegiance."

Terey looked stealthily in the mirror at the small, wizened face of the journalist, which was covered now and again by the white blotch that was the bartender's back. It seemed to him that he saw in Nagar the embodiment of the most harassed nation to which providence never gave a respite. He thought with sympathy of the perpetual rootlessness, the flight from death.

"Is your family still alive?"

"Father? Mother? That was so long ago and so terrible that sometimes I think my life began from the time I supported myself. I don't delve farther back into my memory. I feel as if I gave birth to myself. Do you think I didn't take a look there just after the war? There was no one. Even the wooden house painted the color of gingerbread, the beams full of housebugs—" he smiled, but his eyes were full of grief. "Above the window, to indulge the artistic sense, wooden cutouts such as you find all over Russia as far as Vladivostok. Don't correct me: in czarist Russia."

"The Germans burned the house?"

"That would have been too great an honor. They simply ordered the Jews to clear it out. It was demolished and a street was built there."

"No one was saved?"

"Not even memories of them. Now there is another neighborhood. Other people live there."

"Do you still speak Polish?"

"A little. We are clever. We have to be in order to live. I would even have learned Hungarian in nothing flat. By now I manage fairly well in Hindi. I don't like to stand out. I want peace. Nature endowed us abundantly; we always find ways to prosper. We have to learn more; we have to work at night. We want to consolidate our position, but they only let us have money. If you have acquired that, people don't forgive you. That's why I prefer Asia. Here no one points the finger at me because I am Jewish. Perhaps they don't even notice. If they hate me, it's because they hate all Europeans. That's a relief. I can breathe."

"When did you go to France?"

"Just in time. I went to Algiers for six months before the defeat. I waited there for the Americans and de Gaulle to arrive. Then I was on the radio with de Gaulle once. Among the Americans there were a fair number of us. If you asked in Yiddish they would be irritated, but they helped on the quiet, arranging things, furnishing contacts. They would put you on the right track, they would whisper in your ear. And what is a journalist? A fellow who knows where to look for information, how to get access, and then writes something else entirely. I was no star; I just sent the usual dispatches, but they valued me. What Nagar sent was sacred. And I rather like you."

He leaned forward and clinked their glasses with friendly solicitude.

"If you're in a jam, come straight to me; don't hesitate. Nagar has a head, not a big one, but it holds much, and much of value. Oy, many would pay well to shake everything out of it, like money out of a strongbox."

He looked at Istvan and winked wearily.

"I have a soft spot for you. Take advantage of it. My grandfather used to plant his thumbs in his vest pockets and say, 'Well, Maurice, the good hour has struck. Speak, perhaps you'll get something. Ask, only ask wisely.' And sometimes he gave me twenty kopecks. That was money. Nothing to laugh at. And sometimes he took me by the hair on the side of my head, wrapped it around his fingers, and pushed my head back and forth until it hurt. 'You, you crazy boy, you mischief-maker, what do you fancy?' For I had cadged five kopecks out of him to go to the peep show and see the big world. Oh, my luck! Now I sniff out what stinks from Rio de Janeiro to Hong Kong, and nothing surprises me. What I take a liking to I can have, and I don't feel pleasure. There is no one to impress. In our business you hardly open your mouth to speak before everyone interrupts: they were there, they saw, they know better. They don't let you get a word in."

They drained their glasses. Other participants from the congress began to come in; a crowd was gathering at the bar. "Off we go," Nagar said. "We should do some work. You listen to those, I'll listen to the others. We'll sit together at lunch and exchange information."

He clutched Terey's hand in his hot, dry paw and shook it as if he were giving him a signal.

"Thank you for the chat," he whispered, "though I was the one who went in for confidential disclosures. If I were a little more honest, I would say: Thank you for your silence, for being willing to listen to a garrulous old man."

Terey looked at him as he squeezed between the tables. Everyone here knew him, and greeted him in a friendly way. Why did he feel isolated? Did he see everyone else as more powerful than himself? Was he trying to win over everyone in his environment? He pretended that he was someone else, he played the sybarite, the gourmand, the affluent Frenchman exchanging pleasantries with a lady reporter, for it created the illusion that he had his place in the churning mill of events. If he himself had no influence on them, at least he knew about them. But that knowledge rarely proved useful. It was a burden—and it could easily bring ruin on him.

Better not to know. And if by chance you were a witness to something, don't be complacent and say, I know the truth, for that is an indictment. Nagar certainly knows a great deal, knows much too much. It would be better for him to shout from the housetops: I have grown so accustomed to India that I want to stay here.

The luncheon, with English dishes, was intimidating. From the kitchen came the cloying aroma of mint sauce; the flat black slices of lamb had been drenched with it. A Yugoslavian journalist, a tall mountaineer with a scar on his forehead, beckoned to him with an upraised hand. One of the uniformed waiters, who looked like barefoot generals from an operetta, pulled out a chair.

"Do you have Indian dishes?" Terey asked hopefully.

"Yes, sir, but vegetarian only."

"With curry?"

"With hot curry or mild?" The waiter had a black mustache rakishly twirled up and a starched white turban with notched ends that stuck out like tufts of feathers. "Mineral water? Coca-Cola? Orange juice? Perhaps a beer from the can?" He concluded the ritual, "We have it fresh from Germany."

"Water, please."

It was more expensive than the other drinks: real Vichy, brought in crates from France. The foggy bottle, the dewy little glass of sparkling water, aroused thirst.

"Will you drink some of this?" he asked the Yugoslavian.

"Yes, indeed. It reminds me of the springs in our caves, unforgettable water. Especially when I swigged it down after running for my life from the Germans, it tasted like life itself."

"What were they talking about at the congress?"

"Rabindranath Tagore as a watercolorist."

"What was their assessment?"

The journalist shrugged. He reached for a radish; it had been disinfected in a potash solution, and left violet spots on the plate.

"When someone is counted a saint, everything about him is seen as perfection, even the shirt he wore. The faithful call for relics."

"But according to you?"

"It's enough to cite other opinions. There is no shortage of authorities."

"It's as bad as that?"

"He dabbled in painting, and now they are trying to build a cult around it. I will give it a paragraph and let it rest. There is a party this evening—dry, unfortunately. Too spiritual a crowd."

The Yugoslavian's grimace when he spoke of the party was amusing to Terey. The room hummed with tired voices. A burly Italian journalist was extolling the beauty of Indian women with such delight that he might have been scanning the verses of d'Annunzio. A black-skinned man dressed in European style sat down near them, attracted by the Italian dishes.

"I am the delegate from Ceylon." He introduced himself without extending his hand. "It will not annoy you gentlemen if I eat according to our custom?"

He kneaded the rice with his right hand. As he squeezed a handful, the yellow sauce leaked from between his fingers. He licked it with childish enjoyment, unashamed. His thick bluish lips parted in a greedy smile.

"Try it. Rice with curry should be eaten as nature intended. In the hand one can savor the thick paste it makes. And how do you gnaw the chicken? The fun of it is to hold it in the fist, like our forefathers. And crabs? Without hands and teeth, applying all your arsenal of pincers, chisels and hooks, eating was transformed into a gynecological operation and lost its primordial beauty. At every party in London I horrify people, but I am immovable on this point. I will not deprive myself of the delight of traditional eating. They can scowl, they can pretend to be disgusted, but I know that they envy me, for I am utterly myself, while they are imitations of others." Again he vigorously sopped the sauce from his plate with his forefinger and absorbed it eagerly with his thick lips.

"I also have eaten with my hands, when I had to," the Yugoslavian shrugged. "I was not impressed, but it did not bother me much. It was in the partisan battles in the oak forests of Velebit."

Istvan was not even listening. He remembered corn roasted in the campfire, the smell of smoke in the stalk, chunks of meat charred on the surface and half raw in the center, rubbed with gray cattle salt and garlic—all washed down with sour red wine drunk breathlessly in great swallows from a round bottle.

"You didn't wait for me." Suddenly he felt Maurice Nagar's hand on his shoulder. "And rightly, for they wouldn't let go of me there. I say, could you send my dispatch when you send your own? I'd like to doze off for a while. I feel tired. The racket is making me sleepy."

"I'd be most happy to." He took the papers, which were covered with writing in a perfectly even hand. "I was just going to the post office."

They made their way among bowing servants toward the exit. In the shadow of the pergola a hot breath of air brushed their faces, carrying dry leaves, dust, and the fragrance of blossoming vines.

"I like you," Nagar said unexpectedly. "And I worry about you a little."

"I know." Istvan pressed the man's small, dry hand. He looked down at the journalist's balding crown, which was tanned and gleaming. "What clouds are gathering over me?"

"No. It's bird flutters. A premonition. Too many times I've had to throw everything over and run away because I didn't heed the signals. Something bad is in the air." He raised the regretful eyes of a Pierrot and smiled slightly.

"Until this evening. I'm going to have a rest."

He walked with short, prim steps down the brick path toward the guest rooms. Istvan went to his car. The shade was gone; the metal surface blazed with heat and reeked of gasoline. He opened the doors on both sides before he was ready to sit down. At once a light sweat covered his back as in an attack of malaria. He knows something, he thought, but he doesn't want to tell me. Surely this was a warning. But what was it about? Margit? Has some gossip from the embassy reached him?

The Frenchman's act of entrusting him with the text to be sent off was evidence of his confidence and kindness; he could take advantage of it, select from Nagar's piece what seemed useful for his own dispatch about the congress. To be sure, his mission placed him outside the circle of professional journalists. He was not really a competitor, so the friendly gesture had not cost Nagar much.

The guests had already left the dining room. He wanted to be alone. He turned on the engine and slowly drove toward the open gate.

THE AFTERNOON SESSION was devoted to Tagore's metaphors. He could hardly wait to escape, if only to the Taj Mahal. The perfection of the mausoleum, the dome like a peeled onion, and four minarets like spears of white asparagus against a background of powder blue sky, made him think of a cheap Air India poster. The immaculate beauty of it was tedious.

"Ah, so the emperor's love created this," exclaimed a slender Englishwoman, looking at the tomb with wry admiration. "I wonder—was she beautiful?"

"She had nine children," said her companion, reading from a red-bound guidebook. "I hardly see how she could have preserved her beauty after such an output."

"Perhaps that is why she preferred to die."

Terey watched as the sightseers made their way, awestruck, over the level stones. The pools, unruffled by fountains, reflected the harmonious façade of the mosque like mirrors. Cypresses and arbor vitae stood against the white walls like moulded iron. Into the polished marble the hand of the sculptor had hammered the ninety-nine names of Allah in a black zigzag, honoring him and praising his might. From a distance the inscriptions looked like a fanciful piece of fretwork.

The sky was growing red; weightless veils drifted across it at various depths. The dome of the mausoleum shone with a violet luster. The landscape reminded Istvan of Persian miniatures; only riders on white chargers were missing, draped in scarlet cloaks, brandishing golden bows as they chased the nimble spotted panther.

Enveloped in the falling twilight, forced into the role of a mute spectator, he felt cut off from the world and intensely lonely.

I came to India because I imagined a completely different country. I thought I would tell them about my homeland—after all, we have a common past: my people came out of Asia. But how can one establish friendship here when they have no desire for it? Europe for them is only England. Technological progress does not impress them, only tradition, established social norms, the observance of segregation even in the pub—well, and the queen.

Why should we be of interest to them? To the contrary: revolution fills them with fear and disgust. Violent changes, a need to act, even the business of choosing a course of action, urgency—no, that is not for them. How much better it is to be swathed in tulle and sit on a warm stone bench, to gaze at changing lights on smooth slabs of marble, to plunge oneself in somnolent dreams of things that have vanished—not to hear the hoarse cry of the beggar, not to see the leper's stumps raised beseechingly, not to think about hunger and the undeserved suffering of children. To float away, to drown in delight at the beauty of evening, to reconcile oneself completely to what is and what will be, to whisper submissively: Fate, do as you must, as the condemned man, unresisting, bends his head under the executioner's ax.

No; he shuddered at the thought. I am from another world, a world differently constituted. To live—that means not simply to adapt to the world as it is, but to hasten change, throw out those in power, and build. I would lead those famished people, that staggering mass of shadows, to full shops, I would let them be satiated for once. I would push weapons into their hands and strike the dry ground like a drum with my heel, calling on them to fight for the rights of man. But they would look at me with mild cows' eyes, not comprehending what I was calling them to. The knife would fall from their apathetic fingers, clanging like a false note on the stone steps of the temple. They would take me for a madman, perhaps for one of the demons that Ganesh, the god with the head of an elephant, rammed with his body in the depths of hell.

The sky was streaming with scarlet; his eyes were riveted to it. A painter who imitated it would have been criticized for his lack of restraint. Only nature could allow itself this lavishness, this delirium of achingly vivid color.

"Wonderful! That is really exciting." Behind him he heard the voices of Englishwomen. He turned his head, but saw little; the fire in the heavens still filled his eyes. Slowly he accustomed himself to the duskiness of the fortified tower.

In the spacious passage, four naphtha lamps shone with a yellow glow. By their light he could see something like a stage: a frayed mat spread on stones. An animal was jumping. It looked like a marten. In the center an enraged cobra lifted its distended flat head. Its eyes, glittering in the lamplight like drops of molten copper, were fixed on the dancing predator. It hissed; its head like a broad spear it held level, ready to strike.

Istvan went nearer and nudged the fakir, who pushed a flat basket toward him. "Give me five rupees, sir," the man said in English.

Just this sort of duel takes place in reality, only much faster, he thought. Pity my boys can't see this; in any case they would have read *The Jungle Book*.

The reptile leaned forward, poised to glide from the lighted arena into the friendly darkness. The two tourists retreated with cries of fear.

He threw two rupees into the basket.

"Is this real?" asked the thin Englishwoman.

"I don't understand what you mean," he answered. "Obviously it is a live cobra."

"But does it have venom? Is the bite fatal? It's said that they pull out snakes' teeth and extract the poison glands."

"Put it to the test, madam," the fakir challenged her. "Please give me your hand."

"Oh, no! No!" She recoiled. "I thought it was all an act, a spectacle for tourists."

The mongoose, which had numbed the snake with its monotonous hopping, suddenly broke the rhythm of its hunting dance, leaped onto the back of the cobra's neck, and shoved it to the ground with its muzzle, squealing. Its white teeth gnawed into the scaly skin like a tiny saw. It held its victim like the winner of a wrestling match who wants not only the judge but the spectators to acknowledge his supremacy. Then it jumped away, stretched itself, and lay down in the basket. The cobra shook with revolting spasms of powerless rage. It hissed and with wide open mouth moved toward the viewers. Then the bare black arm of the fakir emerged from the darkness and seized it adroitly by the head.

"Why didn't he let the mongoose bite it to death?" the Englishwoman asked. "He duped us!"

"Thirty rupees for biting to death," said the snake tamer gravely. "This is an exceptionally cunning reptile."

"I will pay." She dug nervously in her handbag. "I want to be certain that it will be killed. Here is the money!"

The Hindu, eagerly taking what she offered, let a smaller snake out of a bag. It was more venomous than the cobra, he boasted, yet the mongoose made quick work of it, biting it into three parts and then, in revulsion, scratching with its hind feet.

"It's a swindle!" The Englishwoman pouted. "I paid for the cobra."

The Hindu was displeased.

"I am honest," he cried. "It had to be a poisonous snake, bitten to death, and it lies on the mat. There had to be death, and there is death."

"If everyone paid them for a cobra killed, they would catch them and exterminate them themselves," the tourist muttered, "and India would soon be a pleasanter place."

"No one demands that the animal tamer in the circus shoot his lion," Terey said in the man's defense. But the Englishwoman persisted rigidly:

"I paid for the cobra."

"The cobra is a holy serpent." The Hindu spread his hands. "To kill it for amusement is not permitted."

"With you everything is holy—monkeys, cows, snakes," she stormed, working herself into a rage. "That's why a human being meets the fate of the beasts."

The gaunt Hindu gazed at her as if he understood, though he hardly knew even the words he needed to gather an audience. His dry, shriveled face glistened like old ivory. He crouched behind the departing woman as if he wanted to leap onto the back of her neck.

Something could be done with these people yet—Istvan clenched his fist—only there would have to be powerful incitements. They fear the loss of dignity more than the loss of life. That is their strength.

He walked between the huge trees. Thick leaves, curled and crackling, rustled under his feet. The sky was sprinkled with stars. He looked at the glowing hands on his watch: it was time to change into his dinner jacket and put in his appearance at the reception.

THE TIME DRAGGED BY. He waited, half unconsciously deluding himself that he would meet her, that she would appear unexpectedly among the chatting groups of guests. Margit . . . There was a moment when he thought he saw her reddish hair. He was moving across the withered lawn when suddenly the woman turned her head and he saw an elderly, violet face and flabby dewlaps like a turkey's.

He was surprised to see Chandra, the lawyer, at this evening party. The modest title on the man's business card—"philanthropist"—had lodged in his memory. They greeted each other and again Chandra made Istvan a present of a cigar.

"Are you wondering what I am doing here? Tagore is my real passion," the Hindu mocked unblushingly. "Only on this occasion can I meet people who adore him as I do, exchange opinions, enrich my intellect. Well, don't flinch. Of course I am here on business. But it is a rallying cry: Tagore!"

He abandoned Istvan for a magnate in a long white shirt and tight, creased knee-length pants, who wore so many rings that his hands seemed to hang helplessly under their weight.

"My dear fellow," said Nagar, who knew almost everyone, "don't demand too much of your friends. Chandra is a dangerous man, for he is clever and without conscience. He really did come to deliver a paper on Tagore. He will be rewarded for it. In Delhi it is possible to underestimate by a hundredfold the value of a meeting with the elite here—in Delhi, or in the rest of India—yes, perhaps in the rest of the world."

"But how?"

"Don't be naive," Maurice scolded. "A first impression is important. So is the place of meeting, and the people who keep company with him. Later he will allude to the acquaintance formed here, discreetly emphasizing its intimate character, and it will be difficult not to receive him, to refuse him a favor, since he commented so beautifully on Tagore's prose. The name of the dead writer can be used like a master key."

"What door will it open for him? I would give a lot to know."

"What for? If you know about wrongdoing, you ought to denounce it. If you don't, you become complicit. Why the devil be involved with him against your inclination unless you have something in particular to gain? Better to keep your distance. Let it be enough that I know him, and I don't vouch for him."

"Exactly where and for whom does he work?"

"Work?" Nagar reflected, frowning playfully. "Not the most apt way of putting it. Chandra is an artist at business. He must find it entertaining. He likes risk. If I were looking for the dominant trait in his character, I would say: pride. He undertakes things that seem hopeless out of perversity, to show himself and the world that he can bring them off, that he can win. Of course he doesn't do it for free; rest assured of that."

Their eyes followed him until he was lost in the crowd.

MOCKING HIMSELF A LITTLE, Istvan began the next morning by strolling through the pergola and knocking on Miss Ward's door. He listened outside, feeling like a boy on a date. He looked around furtively to see whether anyone from the staff had noticed him.

At the morning session he wrote letters under the guise of making notes on the speeches. He drew, spitefully, a gallery of portraits, knowing they would amuse his crony in Budapest. A letter to Bela would be read aloud to their colleagues in the editorial office.

He wrote his sons in a mysteriously macabre tone about cobras and fakirs and the white tomb of the empress. He thought with satisfaction of the pleasure such stories would give them. They would see the India he had come to this embassy to see, and had not found: the India of tales from a bygone age.

When he dropped in for lunch at the hotel and noticed a jeep with a red cross painted on it, he knew Margit was there. Immediately the clerk hurried up to him from the doorkeeper's lodge and announced:

"Miss Ward has returned. She is in her room."

He walked with a quick step through the shady tunnel of blossoming vines. Branches moved, stirred by jumping lizards. A maid in a whitish sari met him, touching her inclined head with folded hands.

"Miss Ward is having a bath," she whispered.

He gave her a tip, but the fact that many people were aware of his impatience to see Margit was disturbing to him.

Margit had already bathed, for as he stood before her door, feeling an inexplicable agitation, he did not hear the sound of water, only a Bartok concerto. The rapid tempo of the orchestra seemed to urge him on, to accelerate the rhythm of his heart. The music stopped; it seemed to him that the girl felt him there, that she would hurry to him. But after a moment he heard the melody again. She had only turned the record over. He was in no rush now.

He had her near him, just a step away. They were only separated by a flimsy door painted brown, with peeling varnish. He was happy, and he wanted this state of joyous certainty to continue, to be fixed in time. He knocked lightly.

She did not answer. He was seized with a fear that he had appeared too late—that she was not alone, that he had been supplanted, displaced by someone who was here, in this place, at hand. She did not love the other man, he could swear it, and the other man could not love her—he only wanted her, desired her, was seducing her, taking possession of her with his hands and lips.

He pressed the latch and the door opened quietly. The music goaded him.

Margit lay on her back with her head tilted sideways, resting on her hands. Her rust-colored hair streamed in a luxuriant wave. From inside her open bathrobe, he saw her bare legs, saw the skin above her knees, all golden from the tropical sun. A sandal dangled from one foot as it hung off the bed; the other sandal lay on the floor, its upturned sole smooth and gleaming. The record turned over quickly and the melody gushed like a fountain. He felt her coolness and his throat contracted. She was alone.

He understood that he had slipped in like an intruder, had caught her at a moment when she was unaware, undefended, exposed to his eyes. He knew he should knock with his fingers, even on the open door, offer the usual greetings, perhaps a little more loudly, to hide his emotion. He wanted time to stop. He drank in the slow movement of the upraised arm, the palm, the fingers entwined in her hair. She sifted it sleepily. He heard the plaintive notes of the piano. She must have felt the glare from the open door, for she shook off the sandal that hung from her big toe and immersed her foot in the sunlight as if it were a stream of golden water.

The record whirled too fast; the sounds of the orchestra broke, wailed mournfully, then died away. The girl leaned over to turn off the gramophone. In this catlike, lazy stretching that nearly caused her to tumble from the bed there was so much beauty that he advanced two steps and caught her by the ankles in a strong grip.

Suddenly the squawking of frightened parrots could be heard in the room.

The girl coiled herself with a movement like a lizard. Her blue eyes flashed with fright.

"It's I, Margit," he whispered. "It's I . . . it was open."

She raised herself a little, still crouching, covering her knees with the edges of her robe. Its dark green pattern, now splashed with sunshine, shimmered with color.

"Terry—" she extended her hand. When he bent to kiss it, she shook his collegially and rose briskly from the bed.

"You've caught me in a lazy moment, but I'm entitled to a little rest. I just got back from the villages; we did an absolutely punishing statistical survey. After that misery, even a bath isn't enough. I loathed myself for having spent so many years living well, for being healthy and strong. I had to key my ear to a different music. They only whine to the sky. They beg for mercy. Their flutes and their slow song are a complaint without hope."

She spoke hurriedly as if she wanted to hide something, not letting him put in a word, avoiding questions. With a movement almost like a dancer's she pulled a dress from a chair and disappeared through the bathroom door.

"I'll be there in a minute, literally," she called. "I didn't expect you. When did you arrive?"

"I've been here two days." Reflexively, as if they had been partners in some misbehavior, he adjusted the blanket on the disheveled bed linen. "Were you expecting someone?" He barely restrained himself from adding: someone for whom you didn't have to dress?

"Why, no! At most, friends who were out knocking around the countryside with me might drop in. You must meet them. That would certainly be great fun for you; they believe that they are reforming India. You have already infected me with self-distrust. Well, I'm ready. I feel like a different woman."

She walked out of the dim light in a simple dress of peasant cotton in an uneven print. She sat down near him and looked warmly into his dark eyes.

"Are you staying here overnight? Will you be here for another couple of days? You don't even know how glad I am. Sometimes I missed you so—"

"But you didn't manage to write."

"It's the way I was brought up. If you have to write a letter, better to send a telegram: you're less likely to say something stupid. If you intend to send a telegram, better to call; and if you're going to call, be brave enough to meet and speak face to face."

"I would have had to wait a long time," he sighed. He found her extremely alluring, stretched out in a wicker chair and smoking a cigarette.

"Something has come up: a chance to pop back to Delhi for a few days. If you hadn't come here, I'd have been with you sometime this week."

"Surely my arrival didn't prompt this change in your plans."

"Certainly not. I've been longing to see you. I have so much to tell you." She pursed her lips as if for a kiss; he understood that she had become accustomed to those evening rambles around Old Delhi during which they talked, sought each other's advice, exchanged confidences, and he felt himself favored.

There was a knock at the door.

"Come in," she called, but no one hurried to open the door. Margit started to get up, but Istvan reached the door first. An elderly chambermaid with dark skin beneath her gray hair bowed against the light of the sinking sun.

"Excuse me, miss—" she folded her hands as if in prayer "—but the clerk told me to come and take your dresses to the laundry. He did not know you had a guest."

Under the old woman's lowered eyelids her dark eyes were rolling, scanning the bed, the room. She knew perfectly well about me, he thought, but they wanted to check, to see what sort of bond we have, friendship or deeper intimacy; this hotel is known as a hideaway for lovers.

"Go on, take them. I threw everything into the basket in the bathroom."

"Perhaps tomorrow. I do not want to disturb you."

Istvan looked at Margit. They understood each other without words.

"No, take them now. Count them and write it down. You are not disturbing us at all."

In reality they were both more at ease because the maid was standing in front of the half-open door. Her presence changed the atmosphere of their meeting, freeing them from the necessity for intimate gestures, words, perhaps even confessions, that might cause them regret. At last she left with the bundle, carrying it on her head after she had crossed the threshold.

They felt an urge to escape. It was too early for dinner. Terey decided to surprise the girl and take her to the city of spirits, Fatehpur Sikri.

LARGE TREES WITH LEAVES that might have been cut from leather stood tall and motionless, like theater decorations. Vacant fields, yellow and red, dozed in the sun. In spite of the glare, the sky was pallid and hostile, oppressive to the sight. They were relieved to see a gentle knoll and the toothed line of red stone that was the city wall.

As he drove up under the great gate, which stood partly open, walls appeared above them, exhaling fire, enclosing a haunting emptiness. The city and its palaces slept, bearing no traces of human inhabitants, undamaged by any siege. Swarms of monkeys had taken them over. They sat on ledges between statues, looking like statues themselves; sometimes they climbed indolently, shaking their silver crests and showing their yellow teeth in grimaces of disgust. The silence was still more arresting, for not even a cicada chattered within the walls. There was something malevolent in the air; it lurked, it waited. So Margit felt, at least. An echo multiplied their footsteps and mimicked their voices. In spite of themselves they walked lightly and spoke softly.

Suddenly they heard a melodious cry. They saw a slender black silhouette on top of the wall. A man was standing there. He wore a red sash that seemed to cut him in two; from that distance he looked like a phantom.

He took a step and stretched out a hand toward them as if he wanted to stop them, then leaned out awkwardly and, with legs drawn up, fell. They heard a howl of despair, then a splatter, as if a body had struck the ground.

"My God," Margit moaned. "He's killed himself!"

A low wall with statues concealed the place where he had fallen. They ran, their echoing steps clattering as if an unseen crowd were hurrying along with them.

They could not see a body.

"He jumped when he saw us. Why?"

"He wanted an audience," he said, enjoying her fright.

"You really are dreadful," she sniffed. "Oh, God!" She stopped, horror-struck. "He fell into the well!"

Clutching Istvan's hand, she looked into the shaft. The stone casing was dark with spattered water. She stirred the mossy green coating of plants below them, which had been torn in the center by the falling body.

"He drowned," she whispered. "Horrible. He hit the water from three stories without bracing himself—that's enough."

Then from under the ragged layer of water plants, something emerged: the round shape of a head, pushing apart the tattered greenery that covered its eyes. It grinned, showing white teeth, and shouted joyfully.

After a moment the man crawled out. He came toward them exuberantly, making wet tracks on the red stone and pressing water from his slender body with his hands.

"That was a jump in honor of this respected lady, to entertain her!" he exclaimed. "Only five rupees, sahib. I can repeat it so madam can take a photo."

When he had gone, Margit stood in front of Istvan with clenched fists.

"You knew all the time. Why didn't you tell me?"

"I didn't want to spoil it for you. He is the guardian of the dead city. You give him great pleasure if you experience his death. That's his theatrical stunt. You remember how he fell? It looked like a real accident. A good acrobat! He deserves his payment. He might have missed the well, and if he had turned in the air, he would have broken his neck on the shaft and been dead as a rabbit."

"Stop!" She put her hands over her ears. "I don't even want to listen to this. You're appalling."

They walked side by side. The echo marred the rhythm of their steps. Shadows fell on the red walls. Shriveled lizards, turning up their tails, ran in a grayish-green stream over the stones. A bright sky, clear as if it had been swept, lighted a palatial room from end to end. How she charms me, he thought. How pretty she is when she is provoked. She reminds me of an angry cat, though she would certainly not claw, only beat like a little boy with her fists. Her hair is a little stiff; it will blow freely in the hot wind, and the reddish gleams will show. The magnitude of these empty buildings quiets these thoughts, inspires brooding, feeds the heart with sadness.

They went in by the stairs to the galleries. They passed spacious rooms where the radiance of the low sun lay on the floors like golden carpets. The air smelled of arid rock and dried bird droppings, though their movements did not start up a single bird. At moments they heard the voices of monkeys and a sound like the patter of bare feet. But when they went out to the terrace, monkeys with long coats like silver tippets were sitting on the neighboring roof, just across a narrow street, observing them with mischievous yellow eyes—attending them from a distance, like guards in disguise.

"From this porch the emperor surveyed his provisions. There was his harem. Counting only one wife per apartment, which is doubtful, for they were probably domiciled by twos or threes, it would amount to something modest: thirty women. You see those paved squares in the courtyard—the giant chessboard on which he played with living people as chessmen. Legend has it that he always won from the time he beheaded one of the rajahs who dared to play with him as with an equal, and might therefore have become a political rival."

They went into the dooryard and stood still, overcome with delight. Against a red wall, three cupolas in the shape of lotus buds rose from a small temple of white marble. Their walls—marble leaves and branches—gleamed in the rose-tinted sunset, rubbed smooth by the hands of the sculptors and of the faithful, who prayed clinging to the stone plaitwork, begging favors from the saint buried inside under an unpolished block of white stone. The little shrine was reflected in a shallow pool used by pilgrims for the ritual washing of the feet before they went in by the steps.

"Tell me; why did the people go away from this place?" She turned her bright eyes toward him. "It is beautiful here, after all."

"Shall I tell you the truth or the legend?"

"I prefer the legend, so you don't spoil the charm. We have the city in the palms of our hands." She took off her sandals and carefully, gathering her skirt up, walked into the water.

"It's hot!" She nearly whistled. "Surely this is allowed? I'm not committing some sacrilege?"

Her legs were dappled with light as she waded toward the steps, disturbing the white reflection of the three cone-shaped roofs.

He sat on the polished flagstones of the yard, his arms around his knees, and looked at her with undisguised yearning. It is not just because of the heat, he thought, nor the sensuous sigh of India, nor my own isolation, that I desire her. I could peel her dress from her here, in the middle of this courtyard, and have her on these stones that are exuding heat. But he did not move or call her to him. He was lost in contemplation of the musical lines of her neck when she shook the wave of her hair impatiently, her straight back, the curve of her hips. She raised both hands and lodged them in the woven stone work; she tried to look into the shadowed temple. She looks like a Hindu woman at prayer, he thought, and perhaps she is asking for something, not only for herself, but for us.

"Listen! It's full of red strings, all attached." She plucked at the yarn that was wound around the sculpted shoots and leaves and unraveled it.

"Don't disturb it—those are pleas for a child," he exclaimed in a warning tone. She bent down and replaited the yarn, tying up the ends. Like a terrified little girl she came back to where he was, leaving wet footprints.

"Why didn't you tell me before?"

"You didn't wait. The emperor was the ruler of a great state, the most beautiful women from the remotest part of Asia were brought to his harem, but he had no offspring. He tried various medicines and spells, but to no effect. Then he turned for help to a saintly old man. The old man ordered him to fast in solitude for twenty days, then fed him lavishly and sent for his favorite wife. That night she conceived. The emperor was then twenty-two years old. He wanted to thank the elder for this firstborn, this heir, so he asked him what he desired. The holy man replied, 'I want peace, for that is more precious than anything in your treasury; I want silence.' And the emperor, so the saint's meditations would not be disrupted, ordered the people to leave the city and went away himself, with all his court. Three years later he died, wounded by a poisoned arrow."

"That's rather far-fetched."

"Of course," he conceded lightly. "But the man who jumped into the well is a descendant of the old wizard. Only that one family lives in Fatehpur Sikri. It guards not only the walls but the abandoned palaces. It opens the gates at dawn and closes them at dusk. At night the town is under the sway of the spirits."

"I'd like to spend the night here," she whispered. "When the moon is full, it must be exquisite."

"Just as it was among the movie sets during the shooting of *The Indian Tomb.* Unfortunately they haven't allowed anyone to stay here since some American tried to break off the statues and lower them on a line down the wall."

"You've said so many times that everything is allowed here if only one pays well."

"Because it is. But what do you want to find here? Haven't you had enough thrills? I will tell the man to jump into the well again for you, if you like."

"No. No." Her hands fluttered as if to repel the suggestion.

"The legend of the healing of the impotent king lures infertile women. They come, they whisper beseechingly through the plaited marble, and then they tie in a red thread."

"What for?"

"So they will not bleed. And you know how effective that is."

"You're terrible. You manage to spoil everything." She sprang to her feet and picked up her sandals. "Why did they really go away from here?"

"Look at your feet. Touch them. They are rough from salt. Beds of it are underneath us. The water is not fit for drinking or for crops. The place is easy to defend, beautifully situated—but treeless, with only desert plants. It is simply impossible to sustain life here. Come. You have completed your pilgrimage, you have attached a red thread. Let's go home."

The western light kindled on the battlements at the tops of the walls. Long shadows fell from the towers. The first bats trembled in the air, squeaking, blackening the light, and scattering again into the dimness of the city's interior, where they wheeled in the air as if to summon the night.

Margit stood in the sun, at a loss, embarrassed. She was ready to shake off her sandals, run to the pool, and tear away the thread. But she saw that Istvan was teasing her and, feeling annoyed, made her way to the gate.

"Silly superstitions," she shrugged. "I'm a doctor, I appreciate the influence of desire and expectation on biological processes. That may interfere with a woman's rhythms, but it will not give her a child."

A trumpet could be heard in the distance: we are closing—like the signal that tells people strolling in city parks that they must leave.

"Because of that custom, there are descendants of the saintly old man." He took the girl by her arm. "Thanks to their very simple practices, tradition endures, and instances of women receiving the gift of children increase. And women make journeys to this grave."

"You're a monster."

"After the first child, a wife makes a pilgrimage of thanks, performs her acts of devotion here, and is blessed with the next offspring. This is a miraculous place, haunted by spirits extremely well disposed toward women."

Before they walked into the deep shadows of the tower, they looked around them. The black contours of palaces and temples loomed against a fiery sky. A cry of despair seemed to come from the light; the night rose from the ground like a vast silence.

The guard waited at the half-open gate, squatting above a myriad of small elephants, monkeys, buffalo, and tigers carved from camphor wood. Margit squatted, too, and set about choosing some animals. When he leaned down to advise her, he smelled the warm exhalation of her body, the aroma of camphor and the odor of slime from the acrobat's turban, which was still not dry.

The Hindu packed the statues into a bag of woven palm leaves and handed it to Margit with his compliments. Istvan held out money, but the girl nudged his hand away.

When they had gone down from the knoll, he had to turn on the headlights, though there was still a glow in the sky. Night was rising in the east; stars swarmed overhead, first large, then blinking, as if the sky had been sown with golden sand.

"Are you satisfied?"

"With this excursion? Yes. Thank you very much."

"And with me?"

"Don't talk so much. Look out—don't let us run into an arba. I'll be grateful to you if you get me back in one piece."

As he stood in the dusky pergola in front of her door, he was sure they would go to dinner together. The sound of people bustling about, the jangle of glass and silverware, could be heard distinctly from the dining room. The buzzing of cicadas made his ears ring. Leaves rustled. Lizards, not yet sated, were feeding on them. The red ends of burning cigarettes flashed far away in the twilight; evidently the participants had returned from the conference. Margit felt for his hand in the darkness and tucked the bag with the carvings into it. He thought she was looking for her key, but the door was open, for the pungent smell of insecticide blew in his face.

"I'm tired. Forgive me—I'm not coming to the restaurant."

"Eat in my room. You will drink whiskey on the rocks and get a second wind."

"I'm half asleep."

Their hands met. Their fingers entwined.

"Go yourself. Drink to my health. I know you'd like to see your friends." She spoke in an undertone, a little sleepily. "I got the animals for your boys. But perhaps you've already sent them some?"

"No," he admitted, feeling ashamed.

"Ah, you see. I've taken up too much of your time."

They were silent for a moment. The cicadas were like drills in his ears.

"When will I see you?"

"Not anymore today."

"Till tomorrow, then. Good night."

"I'll show you the hospital. You will meet our doctors. Good night."

Her fingers slid from his palm. In the heavy dusk he did not see, but felt, that she disappeared, and when he reached out, he touched a closed door.

He shrugged. He was thrown back on himself, and he felt exasperated. What had happened to her so suddenly? Did I offend her in some way? He recalled every word, but he could find nothing for which to blame himself. With closed eyes he saw her, graceful, leaning over in the sunlight, her neck golden brown, her hair bright with copper glints. Her blue eyes, brilliant to their depths, blinking in the glare. Freckles around her nose, winsome as a little girl's freckles. The full, sensitive lips that called his name.

He threw the bag on the neatly made bed. The mosquito netting, bound into a knot, fluttered in the twilight like the mushroom cloud they painted on posters exploiting the fear of war.

"A woman. Yes, a woman," he repeated with relief—as if that discovery cleared up all disquieting uncertainties.

Like a lighthouse the reception desk, with its obtrusively bright glass panes, marked out a path. He passed Margit's room, keeping himself under tight rein. One must have a little dignity, he admonished himself. She said no. If she had wanted, we would have been together, so don't force yourself on her. How can I know what happened during the time we were separated? A beautiful, dangerously smart and self-aware woman: such a woman cannot be alone for long. She reminded me clearly enough where my place is: buying toys for my children. Could anyone say more forcefully, Don't cry, you have your own life.

A group of his acquaintances stood by the bar, which at that moment had few other customers. Little Nagar was gesticulating animatedly, while Chandra, the philanthropist, received praise with ingratiating modesty.

"You should be sorry that you didn't hear that speech. Everyone here toots his own horn, after all; Rabindranath Tagore is only the pretext. They clamber up his monument to be seen better themselves. But here was a surprise: subtle analysis, dreamlike motifs in his watercolors, the subconscious, the faiths of childhood, things heard of, unclear, but accepted as one's own, incarnated in art. A case study in the observation of genius from inside."

"Why, I only know a little about the texts, and I have studied the watercolors that are on exhibit," Chandra parried, inclining his head. "Anyone who wants to think properly about the writer would stop in and have a look at them."

"That is precisely the point," Nagar said, clapping and shifting about on a tall chair. "What I appreciate most in you is your ability to think boldly, to make associations. You know how to look at things."

"What is your pleasure, gentlemen?" The bartender leaned forward. He wore an enormous white turban stiff as meringue. Nagar's clapping had lured him to the group.

"Nothing for me," Nagar demurred. "Pardon me for the sake of my age—the hoary head, you know," he added, coquettishly stroking his raven-black, sleek but thinning hair. "Where have you been? I don't dare ask with whom."

"With a beautiful woman," Chandra interposed.

"You saw?" Terey found the rejoinder disturbing; suddenly it seemed quite probable that the omniscient philanthropist might have been moving furtively among the ruins, observing them from palace windows. "Were you also at Fatehpur Sikri?"

"You passed me when you got out of the Austin. I was standing not far away, smoking a cigarette. You talked a moment longer and I tried to imagine who the lady might be."

"You also were not alone," he retorted in a knowing tone.

"Oh, no—" and he laughed abruptly. "I didn't mean to be inquisitive. Fatehpur Sikri is in the style of socialist urban design: a whole city all at once, a tour de force, handsome façades—and uninhabitable, because they forgot to investigate whether there was water. Humanity hasn't learned much. There is truly no progress except in killing. And it doesn't do to nurse any particular bias against that occupation; it is so universal and so well accounted for by science that it is even difficult to discern who is guilty. Knowledge of the law and clean hands: that is my maxim."

"Well, come clean: whom were you with?" Nagar leaned toward Istvan with an insinuating wink. "You can be sure I won't be jealous where a woman is concerned."

"I was with Miss Ward. Surely you know her: a doctor. She is fighting to eliminate blindness," he answered casually.

"A very risky business," Chandra said with a crooked smile. "Life in India is easier for the blind than for those who see. Why open their eyes? I knew of a couple of cases in which blind men whose sight was restored committed suicide. One became convinced that his brothers were cheating him; the other found that his beloved wife, who was quite devoted to him, had skin that was speckled like a panther's. Loss of pigment: to this day we don't know the cause of this illness."

The gong was vibrating languidly, so they finished their whiskey and passed through the double row of bowing servants into the dining room.

During the conversation the thought of Margit returned to Istvan time after time, like a bad toothache, until he was exasperated. He expected to see her enter the room with some man whose company she preferred. He was dispirited and impatient; he left early to go to his room.

If she had a light on, I would still drop in for a moment, he told himself to avoid admitting defeat.

The cone-shaped tent of mosquito netting reminded him of a snow-covered mountain peak. He began to undress lethargically. Through the thick wire screen that covered the bathroom window he heard what was taking place in the neighboring room; someone wheezed and snorted in the shower, and then he heard a call like the meowing of a cat:

"Darling"—he heard the English word—"how long do I have to wait?"

The voices irritated him. He didn't want to hear them, and not only was he hearing them, but in his imagination he saw the indistinct outlines of bodies tumbling under the wavy netting.

Mosquitoes stabbed his bare feet; it was like a fire. He remembered something Chandra had said: "Since they built a swimming pool here for the Americans, which they don't use anyway because it is overgrown with algae, the hotel has had mosquitoes."

He crawled under the netting and pushed hard to secure the ends of it under the mattress. His pillow reeked of camphor; beside it the bag of carved animals lay where he had tossed it. An attendant had spread blankets on the bed, but he had not dared to rearrange anything.

He did not want to get out of bed. He scratched his ankles with satisfaction. He licked a finger and moistened the swollen bites. He thought of Margit, then of his boys; he wanted to show them the ruins of a temple, but they were not listening to him. A herd of horses, black and bay, came running up in a cloud of dust, panting from their warm muzzles. But that was already a dream, and he looked for Sandor and Geza in the shaggy hair on the horses' necks, in the forelocks, in the flying legs and beating hooves; horses, he saw in his dream, were trouble.

He woke early, rested and calm. All trace of disquieting dreams he seemed to rinse away in the shower, and he was whistling as he shaved, when he heard a tearful feminine voice unexpectedly near:

"Darling, there is someone in our bathroom—"

He smiled at the traitorous screen in the little window under the ceiling and called affably:

"It's me. Good morning!"

He heard shuffling steps, then the sound of a man relieving himself. A gravelly bass voice assured the woman that the bathroom was empty, that its only door led to their bedroom.

The day sparkled with sunshine. The dew-sprinkled grass and the vines on the pergola blazed with rainbow-tinted fire. The greenery beguiled the eye with a freshness which in an hour would be sullied by brick-red dust rising from under the wheels of automobiles.

Istvan was delighted with the sky, which was not yet discolored—with the vast reaches of pure air. Though the door to Margit's room was open and the familiar cat from the reception desk was sitting on the threshold, he walked from the brick path into the still-benign sun and busied himself with the car. He had hardly raised the hood and glanced at the motor when he found two young men beside him. Curious, they touched the nuts, ready to help, willing and friendly.

The motor hummed quietly. The freshly wiped windshield gave him a view of the white columns of the pergola, clusters of orange flowers tinged with gold, and the red road with barely visible ruts.

"Hello! Have you already eaten breakfast, Terry?"

Margit stood near him, exuding a freshness like spring. Her eyes as she looked at him were frank and warm.

"I'm getting the car ready for the road."

"When are you leaving?"

He heard a slight dismay in her voice.

"The congress ends at noon. There is no need for me to be at the farewell reception. I'm leaving as early as possible. A mountain of work is waiting for me at the embassy."

"Isn't it better to travel at night? It's cooler, and the road is freer."

"I agreed to be here for three days. They have places reserved for a Cook's tour. I wanted to vacate the room for them."

"Bring your things to my room instead of cramming them into a suitcase," she said simply. "In the evening you will leave. I haven't yet been able to make the most of your being here."

"It isn't my fault," he pointed out, a little aggrieved. "You were tired yesterday."

"I really was tired yesterday. But what were you imagining? Stop spending time with the car and spend time with me. Let's go to breakfast. Then you'll drive me to the hospital. The congress begins at ten; there's enough time for me to show you what I'm doing."

"Go. Take a table. Only don't order the sickening porridge for me. I'll wash my hands and be right there."

Standing in front of the mirror in the bathroom, looking himself in the eye, he thought with a hint of impatience: Is she trying to patch things up with this proposal? Yesterday she pushed me away, today she holds me. Is it a trick to entice me, a game? Or perhaps she is simply saying what she thinks, without subterfuge or calculation.

He gathered his shaving gear, threw his rumpled pajamas into his suitcase, and carried his jacket on a hanger to Margit's room.

As he hung it in the closet, he found himself stroking her dresses so tenderly that he was frightened.

"I am checking out," he told the clerk at the reception desk. The young man wore an immaculate white shirt; his starched linen made crunching noises. On his swarthy, boyish neck was poised a handsome head. Nagar would have been enchanted with him. But the young Hindu did not understand, was not conscious of these priceless gifts—youth, beauty, a slightly effeminate grace—or what they could do for him, since he believed that he would return in innumerable incarnations. We must whip them into impatience, into a frenzy of desire. We must act quickly, we live only once, and our life is terribly short.

He put a tip on the desk and pressed the clerk's hand, which must have pleased the young man even more, for a joyous smile brightened his face.

"I hope you will come to us again soon, sir."

"I hope so, too," Istvan affirmed, and made his way to Margit's table.

In a warm camaraderie, bantering like the best of friends, they drove up in front of the sprawling two-story building that was the hospital. Under its walls, on the tin-roofed verandas, where peasant women in green and beet-colored saris had settled in for long stays, it was colorful and buzzing with voices. When he had parked the car, stifling odors blew into his face: disinfectants, pus, blood, and the sweat suffering wrings from human bodies.

He followed Margit. He had to step over the thin black legs of the village women. Their heavy silver anklets clinked on the concrete floor.

Margit was well liked here. Women greeted her, folding prayerful hands and wailing blessings. Half-naked little boys clung to her hands and raised their faces to her trustingly, looking at her with one eye while the other was covered with a wad of soiled gauze fastened with a pink bandage, like a broken window boarded up crosswise.

"It's worse inside," she said, anticipating his thought as she made, with difficulty, a path for them. "We have no room for all the sick. They're lying in the corridors on nothing but mats. We don't want anyone who's dragged himself here to leave without our being able to assess whether the treatment is working. That's why there's such a crowd. Even in hopeless cases when the sight can't be saved, it is possible to provide some relief. We try to teach them how they should care for the eyes."

"Are all these people sick?" Shocked, he pointed to groups of villagers with wives and children who were making their way toward the hospital.

"No. Those are families visiting our patients. They are bringing them food. It is difficult for members of each sect to provide themselves with the obligatory ritual cuisine. We allow the close relatives of the sick to feed them. They come with children, with kinsfolk; such an expedition to the hospital is an event. Some of the sick have never lain on a bed before they came to the hospital, never in their lives eaten until they were full. They believe in spells more than in medicines. Their systems are not accustomed to the pills we take without thinking; here every day something as commonplace as aspirin or pyramidon can work miracles, to say nothing of the signs the head physician himself makes on their chests with a gentian solution."

"He uses spells? Suggestion?"

"Suggestion doesn't help much with trachoma," she answered sadly. "He marks them with their initials and writes a case identification number."

They went into a ward where, though the windows were open, the sticky-sweet smell of decomposing pus nearly choked him. The chatter, the weeping, the moaning of prayers stopped and a swell of greeting started up. He was moved by the sight of children who, in spite of the dressings on their eyes, played contentedly with little clay pots, rag dolls, and coconut shells. It was enough that they felt no pain and had already forgotten about the disease that threatened them. They picked the gauze away with their fingers and looked at the people moving around the room from under inflamed eyelids, with glassy, clouded eyeballs.

"Put on a gown. You don't have to fasten it—just throw it over your shoulders. I want to show you the outpatient department."

Two doctors came toward them, one tall, balding, and with nearly white hair, the other young, energetic, and sporting a crew cut.

"Professor Salminen, I would like to introduce Mr. Terey, a poet from Hungary. He is here for the Tagore congress."

"Dr. Connoly, from the Ford Foundation." The young American shook his hand vigorously.

"Do you want to write about us, sir?" the professor asked anxiously. "Dr. Ward is not conversant with all the hospital's affairs. Perhaps Connoly will tell you more."

I am not going to write about the confounded hospital, Istvan vowed to himself. Margit is already being pulled away from me, and I won't be able to get out of here.

They went to the outpatient department. A young woman was sitting by the door, holding a bowl in her hands. An orderly was standing over her. Pulling out her swollen eyelid, he plucked out her lashes, which were heavy with pus and plastered together with it, as calmly as if he were pulling feathers from a slaughtered chicken. If the eyelid bled, he reached wearily for a tuft of cotton, wet it with an acrid-smelling liquid, and dried the eye. In the bowl, which the woman was holding with great care, lay bloody tatters of cotton and eyelashes sticking to the edge like fish bones pushed to the edge of a plate. Big flies crawled around the dish and beat against the window screens. Two sheets of flypaper dangled from the ceiling, black with insects. Istvan heard their long, desperate buzzes.

"I am preparing the case for madam doctor." The orderly opened the peasant woman's swollen eye. "I did not know madam was here already."

Margit washed her hands, rinsed them in a bowl that was lavender from permanganate, and put on a pair of rubber gloves that were floating in it. Over her forehead she wore a round mirror that looked like a silver star. When she was leaning over the woman and peering into the diseased eye, Istvan saw a reddish-blue tangle of veins and yellow grains of encysted pus like boiled barley. The skewed reflection of them, magnified in the mirror, hung above Margit's lips as she pursed them in concentration. It was repugnant; somehow he wanted to protest.

"Go, Terry," she said tenderly. "Connoly will tell you about our base of operations. You see, they've already caught up with me. Don't be angry."

"Good luck," he half-whispered, as if the wish were for himself, not for her.

"Good luck." She raised a hand; it looked alien and dead in its rubber glove. "We'll meet this evening. Wait for me."

"If you need statistical data," the doctor said invitingly, "we'll go to the records room."

The nauseating smell of the hospital was on Istvan's lips.

"Perhaps I will seem rude," he began cautiously, "if I speak frankly: no. Let's go out to the yard. I'd like to smoke."

"But here we can—" then, noticing beads of sweat on Terey's forehead, Connoly added quickly, "You're right. A cigarette doesn't taste right in here. Let's go into the open air. The senses can be numbed in here—and you are a poet!" he concluded with a mock frown.

With relief they walked out to the open verandas and on to the dry grass of the yard. Terey exhaled deeply, as if he wanted to dispel the stench of something foul from his lungs. He looked at the women's clothing, at the copper vessels they used to wet their hands as they washed them symbolically before eating. He asked anxiously:

"Are these diseases contagious?"

"Very," Connoly muttered without taking his cigarette from his lips.

"Why let in this mob of visitors?"

"At home in their villages they are also in contaminated places. The resistance of the organism is the crucial factor; after all, there is no hygiene. They might as well at least watch, learn the rudiments of changing the dressings, treating the eye—that much, anyway. We don't want to think too much. We treat them, we send them away to their homes, to the villages, into the same conditions, where they are sure to be reinfected. We're ladling out water with a sieve to put out a fire."

"How to save them, then?"

Blowing smoke from his lips, the doctor looked at the crowds camped in the shade of the veranda.

"Are you an expatriate, or are you from here?"

"I am from Hungary."

"I tell you, another six months here and I will go mad. I will be a communist. There must either be enormous, immediate reforms here, or revolution. Those in power must either give, give as they would to themselves or their own, munificently, without counting, or the people themselves must take. Otherwise all our treatment, no matter how dedicated we are, is just stirring the water in a flood—philanthropy for the fun of it. Only it is not an issue for doctors, but for you."

"For us?" Istvan said quizzically. "You want to leave it all to the communists?"

"No. To those who can set the imagination on fire, move hearts. I'm thinking of writers."

They went toward the car; the dry grass crumbled under their feet. It was painful to Terey that he had not managed to show the admiration their work deserved.

"You are a true enthusiast."

"Me?" Connoly said in amazement. "I think I understand now the futile, heroic labors of the saints who want to convert sinners. I simply treat people, because that's what I was trained to do. I try to help the suffering. They're so docile and defenseless that it drives you into a rage. Certainly they are more deeply grounded in moral principle than people in our society; they are like plants subject to the laws of vegetation, very good, very tractable."

"Have you been in India long?"

"I signed a contract for a year. Hardly anyone sticks it out longer. One begins to rebel, and then comes the desire to escape. Then desertion."

"Will Doctor Ward stay here long?"

"Ah, Margit!" Connoly said with visible delight. "There's a doctor with a true vocation. She loves the sick—not, like Professor Salminen, just the complicated cases of trachoma."

"It is not too solitary for her here?" Istvan asked, stung that the other man had spoken of her intimately, by name.

"We do our best." Connoly spoke with the cockiness of a soldier stepping out three paces ahead of his line—as if he were certain of his importance to Margit. "But there's not much time to get away from this place. There's a fleabitten cinema here; there are lizards on the screen. There's one decent hotel bar. They fleece tourists there, but at least they serve real whiskey. You have to find yourself a hobby. One person collects bronze statuettes of gods, another wooden masks, another snake skins, but after a month they've had enough. They lose the passion. Only work is left, and exhaustion. I fall onto the bed and lie there in a stupor. I'm supposed to play bridge and I don't go. I know a shower is all I need, but I don't have the strength to drag myself to the bathroom."

"There is still coffee," Terey smiled. "It gives the heart a jolt."

"Or the ampule with morphine. That has to be guarded. I saw how people died in the war only because there was no control and they had too ready access to the medicine box, where the narcotics were kept."

"You must run over to Delhi now and then. Look me up. Margit knows the address." He could not resist this reference to their relationship.

"With pleasure. We'll be happy to come when time permits." Looking him keenly in the eye, Connoly gripped his hand too hard; there was something challenging in their handshake, and both knew why.

WITH DEFT MOVEMENTS of the steering wheel he passed wagons drawn by oxen. The rank smell of the animals' sweat and dried manure was in his face. The responsiveness of the automobile delighted him; it was as if he and the Austin were one.

Is he pursuing her? he reflected coolly. I am really going mad. Perhaps nothing has happened yet. She herself said, after all, that she has had lovers. She told me to stay. She is a sensible woman. I shouldn't complicate matters. Perhaps today it will be settled.

Gravel crunched under the wheels. He parked the car beside the others, shrewdly calculating which way the shade would move. Tangled gray roots hung like stalactites from the enormous trees; some roots had grown into the red earth, creating still more trunks, which supported masses of branches.

The congress was easing toward its close. The attendees were going out for cigarettes and, notwithstanding efforts to summon them back by the bearded moderator in the tunic of Biblical cut, were in no hurry to return to the hall.

A large group drove out to visit a model collective farm, the strong point of which was not only agriculture and dyed fabrics, but, as Nagar informed him, that its workers had even managed, without coercion, thanks to four years' persuasion and patient advocacy, to divert to a field a stream of liquid manure that for ages had flowed straight to the well. The drinking water was no longer fouled and fewer people fell ill with typhus—a genuine achievement, he concluded satirically.

Only a few dozen white figures in academic headdress could be seen in the hall. A poet with splendid eyes and hair curly as a woman's falling to his shoulders recited verse to the accompaniment of three-stringed violins. He wore a wide-sleeved shirt fastened with a scarlet ribbon in front, and black and gold slippers with turned-up tips.

"A good poet," attorney Chandra, sitting by Istvan, whispered in his ear. "Pity they don't print his work."

"The police prohibit it?"

"No. There is no money for printing. And there are no people keen to purchase; they do not yet know how to read."

"What about records? Every little shop has a gramophone. What do you say to that—as a philanthropist?"

"Not a bad idea," Chandra admitted, raising his hand as a sign that he wanted to listen to the musical intonations of the poet.

"What is he talking about?"

"He is speaking of the joy of knowledge, of bathing in the sun of truth," Chandra whispered.

"Aha!" Istvan nodded with feigned approval. "I understand."

He took advantage of the ovation to slip toward the door, culling publications from a table on the way. He settled into a wicker chair under a tree and smoked a cigarette, gazing into the dome of leaves drenched with light.

This is nice; I'm suspended in heat like an insect in amber. I completely forgot about Delhi and the embassy. I sent a dispatch, and I feel like a man in a boat with the ropes cut, drifting with the current. I loathe my own passiveness and acquiescence. I've become like the Hindus: let it be as it must be—he laughed and threw away the cigarette butt, then thought of Margit—provided it is as I desire!

At four he called the hospital. Again he could not get a connection, so he sat in the bar and chatted lazily with guests waiting for a bus before he summoned the clerk. Margit called to tell him to eat dinner alone—not to delay it, for she would be coming later. He should get the key to her room, not stand on ceremony, rest.

"I'll get the car right away and come out for you."

"No. It's not necessary. I don't want you to wait here. Fred will drive me."

"Perhaps I should go back to Delhi. Perhaps something has changed?" He was angry, and still angrier at the few seconds of silence that passed before she answered:

"No. Stay. Then you will do as you like." She threw in the last phrase with a smile, as if she realized that she had promised too much. "I still want to see you, Terry, so much."

He hung up the receiver heavily and left, followed by the clerk's watchful glance.

A wasted afternoon; why is she keeping me here? An angry obstinacy rose in him, and an urge to assert his independence. He did not reach for the key, though to the staff the very permission to take possession of her room was evidence that they enjoyed a close relationship, and he could have savored a moment of easy triumph in her confirmation of it. He bided his time in a corner of the bar, slowly sipping whiskey. He waited it out, stiffening internally with resentment and vowing to even the score with her for leading him on.

But it was enough that finally she appeared, simply herself, her hair almost dark in the dim light, and affectionately extended her strong hand. It was reddened from its recent scrubbing and from the disinfectants. He was disarmed.

"Why didn't you take the key? You didn't want to compromise me? And what do I care about all of them? I see that you've been drinking a little. Well, why are you sitting here in such a mood? I had to perform treatments, then write my notes on them while it was all fresh. Order a double for me. I won't spoil your dinner with tales of my cases. Cheer up—" she raised her glass with its goldish liquid. "I made Fred hurry, and when I knocked on my door, I thought you were asleep. Then I got the key. I was sure you were angry at me, and had left. I turned on the light, I waited a while, and finally I came over here, as befits a doctor, to enjoy a glass of something. Then I saw your car and I wasn't worried anymore."

With wide eyes she took a swallow from her glass, then looked at him with great tenderness, or so he thought. They went together to the dining room, which was almost empty. They were immediately surrounded by waiters in red and gold who set out huge trays of sliced meat and a profusion of vegetables cut with masterful precision, some sculpted into flowers. There were toothed spirals of turnip, radish roses, red starfish made of carrots, frizzly lettuce.

"You're not afraid of amoebae?" She munched a cool spear of white radish.

"They're washed in a potash solution. Anyway, a drunken amoeba can't hurt you."

He looked at her with delight. "If only you knew how beautiful I find you!"

"Perhaps I know. I had proof of that today, when you cleared out of the hospital. But now, after the whiskey, I can even believe it—" she chaffed him, touching his hand. "You like me, a person who does not exist. The Margit invented by you. For what do you know about me? You haven't even looked at my passport. Perhaps I have a husband, children."

"No. After all, you said—" he went steely all over.

"How old are you? Do you still believe what women say? They create themselves all over again for every new man. Well, don't look at me like that. I'm not lying. Why did I keep you here? I don't know myself. Perhaps you mean something to me and that's why I wanted you to stay."

"But yesterday—"

"Maybe I was afraid. Today at least I'm certain that you're capable of going away. And probably you should. That would be better."

She spoke in an undertone, rather as if she were lost in thought and talking to herself. Suddenly she slapped his hand and demanded, smiling, "Put down that cigarette. Eat." She herself set about eating fried fish with such an appetite that he found it infectious. After a while they were chatting like a pair of students skipping their lectures.

"Shall we have coffee in my room?" she asked simply.

He followed her, gazing at her hair, which was swept up and fastened high on her head. He wanted to plunge his fingers in it, to seize her, turn her toward him and kiss her.

"You've done your hair differently."

"Oh, you noticed." She turned her head. "You must be in love."

When they were immersed in the deep twilight of the pergola and the leafy roof curtained them from the star-strewn sky, he felt every accidental touch of her body. There was something furtive in his step, like an animal ready to spring onto its prey. In front of her door he put his arms around her and kissed her on the lips. Inside the room he tried to kiss her again, and she yielded without passion. The fragrance of her skin, her hair, disturbed and inflamed him.

"Let me go," she whispered.

He felt that she was resisting. He still held her in his arms; he touched her, not with his lips, but with his breath.

"I asked you," she reminded him, so he let her go.

She turned on a little lamp.

"Sit down."

He saw the rippling hem of her skirt, the graceful legs, almost bare, in Indian sandals. She went into the bathroom; he heard the rushing of water from the tap. He breathed uneasily. He imagined that she was pulling her dress over her head, washing, perhaps dabbing on perfume. He felt a stinging disappointment when she returned, not in the least altered, with a mug in her hand, and turned on the electric machine. She checked with a circular motion of her hand to be certain it was warm and put it on a tile. Then she sat hardly two steps away—but terribly far—pulled up her knees and clasped her hands around them.

"Do you feel very disappointed?"

"No." After a moment he ventured, "There was no joy in your kisses."

"You felt that. I invited you for coffee and a moment's conversation, an important conversation," she said with emphasis, "at least to me."

"But you let yourself be kissed."

"I'm not made of wood. And I didn't want to hurt you."

They looked at each other wordlessly. Fear swept over Istvan. Where is this leading? What does she want from me?

"Istvan, I love you. That's all," she said heavily. "Perhaps you've heard that many times from other women, but to me it's—rather a revelation."

He breathed deeply.

He knelt by her, held her with his hands and put his head on her breast. He heard the beating of her heart. She stroked him gently, with a motherly motion.

"Oh, that's good," he said in a voice so full of relief that he was ashamed.

"I'm not sure of that."

She pushed him away lightly, not with aversion, but very tenderly.

"Well, sit still. Listen."

"That's not all?"

"No."

He kissed her eyelids and sat obediently in an armchair. He watched as she busied herself with the coffee, for the water had just heated. She sprinkled Nesca into the cup and mixed it with sugar.

"Let me have it." He took the cup, holding the handle in a handkerchief, and poured in boiling water. He was calm; he had time. He knew that he had won her. She would be his. There was no need to hurry. He looked at her legs as she shifted and stretched them, at the rising and falling of her bosom, which was only lightly covered by the thin fabric of her dress, at the outline of her face in a stream of lamplight as she turned it toward him. So a general would have looked at a city in a valley that he would take in battle.

"Drink some coffee. It will do you good. You will be driving at night, and you have a little alcohol in your blood."

He looked at her attentively. She had gone silent; it was as though she had forgotten him. She was distant—or perhaps she was only pretending to be indifferent.

"I had a fiance," she began, speaking very low, looking straight ahead with her head slightly raised.

"I know. The Japanese killed him."

"You know nothing," she interrupted calmly, almost dreamily. "Let me finish. They sent him on patrol. The regiment was in retreat; everything was in disarray. The men were utterly exhausted. Stanley volunteered. Seven went with him; they didn't want to be outdone. They went through a swamp, and they cursed him. Every step forward made it less likely that they would return. It was night. It was real jungle, not like the thorny underbrush here. You know how darkness chatters, how it frightens you?

"They were caught in an ambush. The Japanese wounded two of them and, to save themselves trouble, finished them off at their officer's command. He ordered Stanley to point out the regiment's location on a map. The soldiers said, as he had instructed them, that they were from a division that had wandered away from the regiment, and only the leader of the patrol knew where he was taking them. Stanley refused to tell them what they wanted to know. He was always stubborn. From the time he was little he did as he liked." She brooded as if she were searching in her own childhood for that young man.

"They tortured him?" he asked, wishing to make it easier for her to omit the worst, which he had already guessed.

"Yes. They bound the soldiers' hands behind their backs and set them in a row so they would see what awaited them. They tore Stanley's shirt off and tied him by his feet to two young trees that were bent to the ground. When the trees sprang back up, he hung with his head down. His hands were tied and touched the grass. The Japanese lighted a fire and with one kick the officer set that living pendulum swinging. Do you understand? They roasted him alive. He tried to shield his face, and then to scatter the flames with his bound hands. His hair caught fire—" she spoke with a terrible calm. "He howled with pain, but he never said a word. The officer deliberated a long time before he shot him."

Istvan could hear the dripping of water in the bathroom, the nagging rattle of the cicadas outside the window. The poor girl. He felt enormous pity for her, and he was like an empty vessel. All the haze of alcohol vanished as if he were under a spell. What can I give her, he thought. What words can console her?

"Stanley never betrayed the regiment. The ones who watched him in torment revealed everything. Each tried to speak before the next."

"How do you know?"

"The one who brought me the information—my first," she sniffed contemptuously, "was looking for absolution from me. He didn't do badly out of it. Well, you know already."

She sat hunched over, bent with pain. Her hands, resting on her lap, looked as if they had been cut off.

What can I do? he thought in despair. Caress her, cuddle her like a puppy whose paw someone stepped on? Why did this have to happen to me? He felt aggrieved and resentful. Why did she tell me this now?

"Margit," he began hesitantly, "that was thirteen years ago."

"Thirteen years ago you stood by those Japanese. You were the enemy."

He tried to defend himself. "That was long, long ago. Don't you see, we were forced into that! Hungarians didn't want it. Margit," he pleaded, "forget that. I love you!"

"Don't lie. You want me. You can have me. Today. Tomorrow. Any day you like. Don't speak now. That way you won't regret anything. For I truly love you. It's terrible. I know you have a wife, sons. I accept that. Though I will fight for you if I believe you love me. So think about it, you have time. I'll certainly not run away from you." There was desperation in her voice. "I'm not looking for easy comfort from you. Understand: you are my life."

He was silent, shaken, stunned as if by a blow.

"Go," she whispered. "This isn't easy for me, either. You understand why I'm defending myself from you."

He felt utterly helpless. Instinct warned him not to say anything equivocal; every word would ring hollow.

"Well, I will go," he muttered, taking her limp hand and kissing it with dry lips.

She nodded. She did not raise her eyes when he closed the door behind him noiselessly, raising his suitcase like a thief.

He started up the engine and drove away. For a moment he imagined that she would open the door and look after him, but the pergola was still black; no light flashed.

As he passed Agra, he turned on his headlights. He sped away like a man escaping something.

"Margit. Margit," he moaned. "What can I do—"

He knew that she grasped the truth. If he loved her, he would be able to throw off the past, to erase his memories. They would be shadows, perishable shadows. Her prescience told her that. That virginal love was precious to her. It revived the hope that she could experience transcending joy, that she could lose herself in happiness. It would not be enough, after that, to satisfy the restless flesh, to sleep in a man's embrace. She is honest. She is warning me.

His mind was clear. He remembered his own behavior; he thought of himself with anger and contempt. He saw the girl curled up in the chair and, again, the other man thirteen years ago, a living body with bound hands clawing at the embers of a fire until the sparks fluttered onto the squatting prisoners and each waited until at last he died—to join in betraying the regiment.

In the glare that streamed from the headlights, innumerable insects flew like sparks. He had to slow down. He blew the horn. A column of wagons drawn by white oxen with horns like lyres moved slowly down the middle of the road. The huge, mild eyes of the animals burned with violet fire. The drivers, burrowed in between sacks of cotton, slept heavily.

Chapter V

A chalky sky, vacant as far as the eye could see, teemed with glittering dust. Tremors in the air created the appearance of motion, but the yellow, withered leaves and tattered palm fronds, weighed down by the burden of the heat, did not even sway. Together with the glare, which assaulted the eye like fragments of a broken mirror, the nagging rattle of cicadas floated from all directions, rising and falling like the sound of drilling. The insects were rasping furiously; all space seemed to throb with their noise. One could hate this malign aridity which had not changed for months. It made unshaded walls breathe fire. It lay heavily on people, incapacitating them, setting them on edge, making it impossible to work or rest.

In vain Istvan circled the embassy, looking for shade. Finally he parked the Austin by the garage wall with the front end buried in a curtain of vines. Terrified lizards trickled from the colorless leaves.

He was returning from the studio of an Indian radio station, where he had succeeded in arranging for fifteen minutes of Hungarian violin music and folk songs to be played on the air. No doubt it was at least partly because of the gift he had placed on the desk of the silk-clad program director. Good thing she didn't open the box while I was there. The chocolates must certainly have melted and gone sticky, he thought, smiling maliciously. They had described the music as akin to their own; he had hardly taken it as a compliment, given his familiarity with the whining of the Hindu instruments, the songs like laments with their undercurrents of sadness and pain.

Near the garages he heard a rhythmic chopping. Mihaly was squatting on his heels, almost hidden behind empty crates. With a cleaver from his mother's kitchen he was cutting boards into long slivers, helping himself by pushing the end of his tongue out of his mouth, not even looking around as the car pulled in. Only when Terey stood over him did he raise his flushed face and rub a drop of perspiration off his nose.

"It's not too hot for you?"

"No. I have to help, because wood costs so much."

"And you want to sell it?"

"I'm going to give it to Krishan. I like him very much."

"Be careful—don't cut yourself."

"I am, uncle," he answered gravely. "Is this enough?"

"For the kitchen, for kindling, that's enough."

"I'm chopping wood for a Hindu funeral," he said, doing squat jumps like a frog.

"A silly game," Istvan scolded him. "Please stop. Run along home, sit in the shade, take a rest."

"It's not a game. I'm really helping," the child insisted, hitching his crisscrossed suspenders up on his tanned, slender arms. "Will it hurt her?"

"Who?"

"Krishan's wife. She is completely dead. The old women came and put their fingers on her eyes," he informed Terey, as if there were nothing unexpected about it. "They will burn her this evening."

He looked at the boy in consternation. He saw lustrous eyes shaded by the light hat, and brown hands clutching the wooden handle of the cleaver. Its blade cut into a beam of sunlight, scattering sparks. The cicadas jingled as if they had gone mad.

"Is she here?" Terey pointed to the boxlike building where Krishan lived.

"No. They've wrapped her in blue cellophane with the ends trimmed, as if she were a sweet, and carried her on a bamboo rack. The musicians came with a drum and fifes. And her younger sister was chasing away the spirits all the time with a bunch of peacock feathers. They carried her to the river. They burn the dead there."

"Poor Krishan."

"He was awfully worried that the funeral would cost too much," Mihaly explained, "so I wanted to help him."

"You are a good boy." Terey stroked him on the back of his slender, perspiring neck. "The rest of us will think about how to make it easier for him as well. Now be off home. That's enough of this chopping."

The boy straightened up reluctantly, with a deep sigh. The wall exuded heat. Big flies hit it with a metallic banging and spattered off, buzzing furiously. Istvan raised the cleaver to strike at one, but it disappeared into the glare before the blade jabbed the wall.

"It's sly," the boy whispered almost admiringly. "The mourners drove them away because they are spirits. There were never flies like that here. They like to squeeze into the ears or the mouth, and then the body moves. And do you know, uncle, that Krishan already has a new wife?"

"Oh, you're talking foolishness."

"I give you my word, uncle. I saw him give her bracelets of the dead lady's and she tried them on in front of the mirror."

"Mihaly, wipe your forehead. You're sweaty all over."

"She came from a village. Mama says a man can't hold out for three nights without a woman. I heard her. When papa stays in the embassy a long time, mama climbs a ladder and looks through a window to see if he is alone."

He spoke cheerfully; evidently he did not understand the real meaning of his mother's grumblings. Istvan felt that he was abusing the child's trust, but he yielded to temptation and said, "What about me? I have a wife and sons in Budapest, and I am alone so much of the time here."

"Oh, you talk that way, uncle"—the boy smiled like a little fox—"but I heard that, though you don't have a wife here, you have a kangaroo. Will you show it to me?"

All right, he thought spitefully, that's what they wanted, that's what they'll have. I live in India; too many eyes. It's enough to be seen once with a woman and already they know about you. But he drew the boy close to him and whispered:

"I don't have a kangaroo, sweetheart."

"It ran away?"

"It is a long way from here."

Mihaly clung to his hand with his warm, sweaty little fingers.

"Don't worry, uncle. Maybe it will come back."

"If it doesn't come back for a long time, I'll go and find it," he said, and suddenly he knew that he would. All he needed was an opportunity. He was overcome with affection for the little fellow who devised pastimes for himself and mimicked adults. He must help him find some enjoyment—take him out for ice cream or to the theater for a Disney film.

He heard a rumbling above his head. Someone was knocking on a windowpane. The sun blinded him; he only saw a curtain pushed aside and a figure summoning him with a gesticulating hand.

"Run along. Give your mama the chopper," he reminded the boy, and walked into the embassy.

For an instant he felt relief. The nagging jangle of the insects died away, the hall was cool and shadowy. But soon the building felt stuffy. The odors of mosquito repellent, polish, toxic dye from the coconut matting, and smoldering cigarettes were stifling.

He found the staff gathered in Ferenc's office. Judit's high chestnut bun was bent above her typewriter and she tapped away doggedly while the secretary dictated, pacing around the room. The short, bald telegrapher-cryptographer sat in a small chair, calling as little attention to himself as possible.

"Well, here you are at last. You must have cut short a chat with your friend," Ferenc remarked sarcastically. "Talking of ultimate concerns again?"

"As a matter of fact, yes," Terey admitted. "Mihaly was telling me about death. A clever boy. I always learn something when I talk with him."

He noticed that the cryptographer was looking tense, uncertain whether this was praise or mockery.

"Something must be done for Krishan," the counselor began. "It was said, it was hinted that his wife would die, but no one really believed it. Surely we will make a contribution for the funeral."

"Why? If we cared to be involved in the funeral of every Hindu who wanted to change his fate, we would go naked and barefoot, and there would be no embassy here, only a crematorium," Ferenc cut in acidly. "He has rupees enough. I paid him two months' compensation."

"At last something sensible has been done," Istvan said, gratified. "I endorse that decision heartily."

"And you said that Terey would be of a different opinion," Ferenc turned to Judit, "though that's the boss's wish, and talk changes nothing. Krishan is dismissed as of the first of the month. We part ways and—adieu!" He spread his hands expressively.

"He is a good chauffeur, in any case. Perhaps it was all a little too much for him. Can't we wait?"

"Comrade counselor," Ferenc broke in. It's no good, Istvan thought, their turning to me this way; it means that they want something, they are inviting me to be one of the trusted few, they are banding together and making me a party to a decision taken without my advice. He stood with his head down, thrusting his hands into his pockets. "He was the ambassador's driver," Ferenc went on. "He had a bad reputation. The recent accident involving the cow entirely confirms it. We waited too long. But he had a sick wife; it was appropriate to exhibit patience."

"You waited like vultures until she was finished."

"The comparison is offensive." Ferenc delivered his censure in his usual unctuous tone. He surveyed the others and the cryptographer signaled his agreement, as if he had swallowed something that had been sticking in his throat. "We proposed that she go to our hospital, we said that an operation was urgently needed, but he didn't want to hear that, Comrade Terey. He didn't want to hear that. Remember that we are in India, a capitalist country. We are, so to speak, under fire. We were not free to barge into a household with a troubled history and drag the woman onto the table by force. We cannot violate their cardinal rule: nonviolence. We did what was proper.

"I at least have nothing for which to reproach myself. It was Krishan who abused his own wife; his treatment of her was inhuman. He simply wanted her to die. She herself often said so, in tears. So we have no reason to sentimentalize him. Krishan is dismissed.

The month has hardly begun. We are paying him for two, and even that is too much."

"Krishan is a good driver. The accident could have happened to anyone, especially when cows are ambling all over the streets."

"If he is really so good, it will be easy for him to find work, so we are doing him no harm."

The cryptographer's face brightened, and he nodded. Evidently that point of view suited him; he seemed pacified.

"You are dismissing him," Istvan pointed out. "It is your affair. Why do you need me?"

"Because I speak too sharply. You, Terey, have the knack for chatting with people, explaining things, seeing a subject from every side. People trust you. Krishan is prepared for this. He already knows. The important thing is only that he not leave here with information about our confidential affairs."

Seeing Terey's astonishment, he added, stroking the air with his hands:

"He must not talk about where he drove and with whom. Why should they know who our contacts are and keep lists of those who are friendly to us? Do you understand?"

"Not very well." Istvan hesitated. "And I wouldn't believe him even if he swore by Kali."

"You must convince him that we are well disposed toward him—" Ferenc locked his fingers together "—that after a time he may be able to return to his job here."

"I don't grasp this. Then why let him go?"

"You have a strange way of becoming less intelligent when there is something to be done. The ambassador directed you to speak frankly with Krishan. Understand: in India a dead cow amounts to sacrilege. It's a serious matter. No shadow must fall on the embassy. Talk with him, sound him out, and then the three of us, you and I and the ambassador, will take further steps. It may be necessary to have recourse to a lawyer."

"When should I speak to him?"

"Well—not today," Ferenc eased off. "Tomorrow or the day after will be soon enough. In any case, before he begins to look for a new job. I would prefer that he not turn a profit from information about us."

"These are mysteries to me," Terey said dismissively.

"But suppose he went to the Americans. They are enlarging their center. Or to the Germans from the Federal Republic. They have modernized their industry and they are pushing their way in here, ready to open branch offices. Look at their information bureau on Connaught Place. They remind everyone that a few of their marks are already equal to a dollar. Whose currency is stronger? Hindus are sensitive to that. Such a driver could suit the Germans' purposes very well. He would be a credible witness. Two facts will be true and five fictions added, and then a matter is difficult to interpret."

"Wouldn't it be better to keep him?"

"Evidently not, since the boss ordered that he be let go. He knows what he is doing. He has drawn up an evaluation of Krishan—a favorable one, but before anyone takes him, they will call us to verify it. Then it will be possible to allude lightly to our reservations if his new employer is not to our liking. People have stopped blindly trusting written references. We can influence the outcome of his search from a distance."

He spoke casually, as if motivated only by friendliness. He glanced at his oval face in the windowpane and ran a comb through his thick, crimped hair.

"The couriers will be here tomorrow. Don't forget about the reports," he warned Terey. As he was going out, the cryptographer rose from his chair and made his way to the door as well.

"Has anything of interest come in the dispatches?" Istvan asked.

"Oh, nothing. I'm the type who, once I have decoded the dispatches, writes them out clean and right away forgets what was in them. No, there was nothing important. Certainly this much, that Rajk was innocent. Though they hanged him, he will be vindicated now."

"Thank God!" Istvan stopped where he stood and exchanged a look with Judit. "Changes may come in the government. Well—what else?"

"I really don't remember. I gave them to the ambassador. If he likes, he will call a meeting and inform us. If he has received other instructions, in any case we can read the details on the front page of the *Times of India*."

"Well, there will be a stir in our country," Judit said.

"Won't there just! And whom will it benefit?" The cryptographer gave a quick nod of his close-cropped head. "It won't bring Rajk back to life, and it won't be easier for us, either, because everyone remembers what the papers said, the procurator's statement, 'Sentenced according to the law.' And whom should we believe? Once those graves were tamped down, I'd have left them untouched."

"But where is justice, man?" Terey cried. "We can't give him his life back, but we can at least restore his good name. He was no traitor. He was a true Hungarian and communist."

"You speak as though it was other people who condemned him." The cryptographer raised a pale, bloated face. He did not immerse it in the glare of the Indian sun; he only sat in his dim room behind armored doors. "I am a simple cryptographer. They took me from the army and sent me out here. I mind my own business. But I see, counselor, that everything we read about, even what is clear and completely visible to the eye, is also a code, and only our children will read it right. It's too bad a man can't live to see that. Well, I'm going to my den. When the couriers fly in, they will tell us what the moods are in our country."

The door had hardly closed behind him when Istvan sat down heavily on the other side of the desk. He looked at Judit's darkened eyelids. The fan hummed unbearably; it grated on him.

"You've heard the voice of a simple man. He has to trust authority in order to hear what it says. And here the effect of everything is to undermine respect."

"Are you for treading on those graves, Judit?"

"No. And I understand very well what you mean, but I long for a few years of peace and order after what we lived through during the war. And later. Surely my demands are not excessive?"

"Judit, the restoration of honor to a man murdered under the majesty of the law will accomplish nothing in itself. That is hardly the beginning. People will ask: What of the judges, who now appear as assassins? And the comrades who disowned him and the others, who, moreover, condemned him and applauded the false verdicts? I ask, which of them knew that when he cast his vote he was consenting to a crime? Shadows that boded no good for us hid the bloodshed; by now you don't ask questions, the responsibility is spread around. Even carrying an investigation to the limit would not be any good. We all bear a burden of guilt. In the end, those who would show themselves to be innocent would have had to stand under the gallows back then, as a sign of protest. And who is capable of doing that? I know Hungarians; the nation demands heads, and if it doesn't get them, it reaches for them itself. You know what can happen then."

"You speak as if you were in the party." He heard a ring of approval in her voice. "I saw many things and I know people who lived like saints but knew what was concealed in that last apartment, though they pretended that it did not exist. They would have hated anyone who spoke openly about what they knew, forced them to take a position, to make a pronouncement. It is very difficult to blurt out a statement: I erred, I was deceived—to reverse decades of one's life.

"They lived with socialism, come hell or high water. They endured labor camps, betrayal, torture. They believed that was the inevitable price of laying the foundations. And now it's clear that it could have been managed without that. Why is the boss shut up in his office? He understands: it's not a matter of a career, of joining a new group that might take over the management of things; it's a bitter time of squaring accounts with oneself. The detection of the first concession, that deviation, still in the hope that one could easily put the lapse behind one, that eventually it would no longer matter when one consented to the betrayal of the party—of something that aroused our passion when we were young, and still today is a great aspiration fulfilled, and unfulfilled, before us."

He looked at her uplifted face. It was full of passion. He had never seen her like this.

"Ferenc, though he is young, doesn't understand the signal he received today. But the ambassador is an old party man. I know because I was there. I know those scarred, anguished families who choked back their curses with shouts in honor of Stalin. They thought that it was necessary, that that sacrifice would call forth new strengths, hasten the future, assure the greatness of their country. What is left for them now?"

"And so—silence impenetrable as a concrete slab?"

"No. Only I would not rush to judgment. If we have borne with so much, must we burst open like fish from the deep in the glare of the sun? Time is an unbribable judge. It weeds out ruthlessly all false quantities. Patience is not a virtue of revolutionaries, but I am afraid of reckonings, of random blows of the ax." She dabbed at her eyebrows with the ends of her fingers. "We ought not to be carrying on such conversations, even though we trust each other, for you know how it is here. Every word may come back to harm us."

"Are you afraid?" He patted her affectionately. "We are far away, after all. I have people to worry about: my wife, my boys—but you have no family in Hungary, have you?"

"Someone might come in, and we will be sitting together and working out who the guilty one is among us," she whispered fretfully. "And it will certainly not be either Kalman Bajcsy or Ferenc or that other one. I can vouch for that. I'm afraid I will have to disavow our friendship."

"That won't be so bad," he said comfortingly. "Perhaps I exaggerated the mood at home, though I got a few letters from Budapest that gave me plenty to think about."

The telephone chattered. She picked up the receiver and looked significantly at Istvan.

"Yes, comrade minister, the reference for the driver has been written and counselor Terey will present it to him. Yes, he already knows, he understands your concern."

She hung up wearily and raised a hand, as if she were afraid of hearing another directive.

"Take this. It's yours." She handed him a paper with the embassy's overprint. "Try to get this business over with."

"Though it's not part of my responsibility." He shrugged as he glanced over the smoothly turned phrases of banal praise that had gone into the evaluation of Krishan's work. "Why didn't Ferenc do this? He likes to be grave and magnanimous."

She looked at Istvan so solicitously that he smiled at her. "Well, don't be so worried. I can handle myself."

But she did not smile in answer. He saw that she was preoccupied with something. Her skin, in the cut-out triangle on the front of her dress, glittered with perspiration. The curtained window glowed yellow; the yard would be an inferno.

WHEN HE WENT IN under the tent of climbing plants that grew over the veranda, he heard the pitapat of bare, callused feet in the house, and shrieks.

"Sahib! Sahib has come!"

The cook opened the door—a tall figure in a darned shirt which he wore untucked. He had on half-boots which had never had the benefit of brushing or polishing, and for the sake of comfort he had removed the laces. The boots fell away from his legs with delightful ease; that was why Pereira never quite walked but only moved with a dignified shuffle.

"A letter arrived," he announced. "There were two telephone calls from that painter. He will call again."

He didn't even have to ask; the letter lay on the table near his place setting, leaning against a vase that held a flowering branch. It must be from Budapest, from Ilona, he thought, but he was surprised to see that it had an Indian stamp.

Another invitation or request? The letter fell from his fingers onto the table. He went to have a bath first.

Only as he was eating, unhurriedly, the sticky, yellow-green dish of yams, rice, and onion sauce, did he reach for the envelope and open it with a knife. The cook was describing at great length a dispute with the Sikhs next door. They had scattered garbage onto the yard from their roof, and pissed on the freshly planted flower beds.

"And that burns the flowers, sir!" He was ready to send the sweeper for a few limp, spotted phlox as evidence.

Istvan, my dear,

I have set your picture in the old silver frame that I got from Connoly. In the hall of our hotel the passage is flanked by two screens with numbered photos from your congress. There must be a hundred. I found you in a dozen pictures. But "mine" is the best; you are smiling, you look interested. You will not be angry with me for cutting off the lovely Hindu woman who was standing beside you? To tell you the truth, I cut her to pieces. The Tagore congress. You didn't even tell me what you did at it, or who it was that drew so many pretty women to the event.

Agra is growing on me; I am adopting the local customs. I've burned pastilles in front of your photograph; they glow, and give off a fragrance. I put on a record, the Bartok concerto. Every day when I return, the same music, played several times, brings you near. It's as well that the rooms nearby are empty; my obsession doesn't startle anyone.

Indeed, I'm moved that a Hungarian speaks so that I can understand him. I thought about this—that I would not understand a word if you spoke to me in your language. When I asked you for a couple of sentences, I wanted to hear the ring of it, the rhythm. You looked me in the eye, you smiled, then you spoke, and it sounded so beautiful. I thought, He is saying something very loving about me . . . or perhaps it is one of his verses? I didn't ask. At this moment I think of that again.

You went away suddenly. Did I do badly telling you what happened? But you had to know. It is important to you as well.

He saw Margit curled up in her chair, saw her long legs in the beam of the lamp that stood on the stone floor. He held the limp paper, but the even lines of painstaking writing disappeared before his eyes as a wave of tenderness washed over him.

"At noon today they threw down an old basket and the whole yard was littered with banana peels. They stood on the roof. They did not even hide. How I cursed them!" Pereira jabbered. "When one of those fellows passes by, I will be lurking behind the door and I will thrash him—if sahib will defend me afterward from the older ones."

"Go away," Terey said calmly. "Leave me in peace for a while."

He waited until the door closed, then turned back to his letter.

I am not writing clearly. Everything will depend on the mood in which you read.

The heat is wearing. At night the pillow sticks to my back. I turn it over but that gives no relief. The sheet is thick and scratchy. I can't sleep. My hair sticks to the back of my wet neck; it's disgusting. I set the fan to blow straight in my face, but it is impossible to breathe. It's like a hothouse. My colleagues come to work sleepless and on edge, the sick people are quarrelsome, the help tire us out with complaints. We search the newspapers frantically for the bulletin about the monsoons. The Hindus say, to comfort us, that they will come before long. May those winds drive you to Agra—though I know you are chained to the embassy, you have obligations, as I have to this flock of the blind and those who are becoming blind.

Grace wrote, but I have not mentioned you to her, not a word. How good to have you, to think of you, to wait. If you keep me waiting too long, I will come to Delhi. Don't be surprised if you find me there one day.

Then you left me. I know you were right to, but . . . it was enough, that you . . .

The words were written on the very edge of the sheet. They broke off and he looked for what came after, but found only a signature on the side:

Margit

The envelope was postmarked three days earlier. His first impulse was to take the car and go; then he remembered that he had an appointment. He read the letter a second time, brooding over every sentence. The mention of Grace disturbed him. But he was at a loss as to how to warn Margit, for he wanted to avoid a confession about that wedding night. Grace was like a receding vision, fading, diminishing. Perhaps he had dislodged her from his memory. That evening he must call Agra.

The taste of dust was in the air. At moments the windows quivered from top to bottom and a dull moan came from the panes as the noon heat advanced in a wide wave. He went to his bedroom and slumped into a chair.

Margit—he saw her crown of red hair, remembered its light warm fragrance in the sun; the radiance of her great blue eyes pierced him with sudden delight. She has tasted suffering, she distinguishes the perpetually unappeased hunger of the body from love that leaves one a slave. With what joy we accept its bonds! With secret pride we subject ourselves to the longed-for tyranny. What happiness, to give ourselves with no thought for our own interests and to be assured that submission and lamb-like defenselessness will not be turned against us, for the other also loves.

Is it possible to love two women at the same time, each in a different way? he thought with his head thrown backward, feeling the frame of the chair warming and sticking to his back. It is not difficult to accept the possibility when the other one is a thousand kilometers away. My wife, my children: indeed, I am not going to disown them. Ilona in a simple dress with rose-colored stripes, dark as a gypsy; her heavy chignon which took unbearably long to undo; he saw her head crisscrossed by her fingers as if it were in a golden frame, heard the clink of hairpins on the stone floor. It was cool in the old house, and bright; the walls were a good, gleaming white from the painting that had been done for the holidays. The meadow smelled of freshly mown hay which they had been spreading with rakes, for fun, since the dewy sunrise.

"Well, why do you love me?" He looked deep into her eyes.

"Because you chose me." The shadow of a smile flitted over her opulent lips, the full lips he had smothered in kisses. It was as if she had said, "Because you awoke me; there was a readiness in me, an expectation, but I did not know it yet." And in that she was like the earth: she belonged to her conquerors, then she took possession of them, lavished herself on them. They were certain of their dominion over her. Earth; earth. When they went away, they carried her image before their eyes. They dreamed of her at night. Even dying, they dreamed of resting in her.

Ilona's swarthy body was steeped in the beauty of the great steppe. He had even told her, "I would like to live in the twilight of your hair." He slept—after he had run half naked until he was gasping, when the tall herbs grazed his chest; he still remembered the touch of the moist buds—and woke to her kiss, feeling the precious burden of her head, and then they fell on each other with their lips as the thick, dusky wing came down. Their faces immersed themselves in her hair as in a tent that shut out all the world. "I will be with you always, always, for better and for worse," she whispered, and it had the ring of a vow. His own voice spoke clearly, "And I will not leave you until death."

Bees crept over the stems of the spring catkins, with which vases on the altar were filled, until he was sprinkled with dust gold as honey in the sunlight. He did not say that to her when she was bent under a veil as if under the remains of winter hoarfrost, which melts instantly in a breath of warm air. He did not say it to the priests or the witnesses; their mustaches glittered like beetles' shells and their cheeks were flushed dark from fruit brandy. In those companions of pleasure in the pasture, there was a deepening impatience: they wanted dancing, wine, perhaps even a brawl, which would give vent to pent-up energies, and then an occasion for making up, calling it even, embracing and getting enormously drunk. "And I will not leave you until . . ." he said, taking God as witness.

Margit did not want to be nothing more than an adventure; she had been honest enough to warn Istvan of that. He felt rather like a man who has usurped someone else's rights. Her fiance had died as a soldier. But who could know what might have been hidden behind his death? What did he think of in his last moments? Perhaps he blamed himself, wanted to live, whimpered for mercy. Where did his pride end? For to the last he had had his audience before him—his own soldiers, who failed to honor his heroism. But was it decent to suspect him of pride when he had been burned alive? Perhaps he had only tested himself to the limit, discovered strength he had hardly suspected he had.

That was how they remembered him. That is how she remembers him.

And what if some Japanese had cut him down in time? What if he had fallen, scattering sparks, into the hot ashes, dragged himself on to escape the pain that tormented him? What if he had survived, his face scalding and glistening with scars? Margit would have stayed by him. But, seeing himself in the mirror one morning, would he not have shot himself in the head to free her and end all her self-abnegation, devotion, and sacrifice? For that would not have been the old love that they had pledged . . . Yet it might have been a love unlike what is usually called love, though to those looking on from outside it would have seemed a perpetual hospital duty, a charity.

How dare I accuse him of pride, Istvan thought. Only because I want to take what belongs to him? Am I afraid she might think me inferior, less worthy, greedy for spoils, like a jackal? She writes, "I wanted you to know about him; it is important to you as well." To know that I come into someone else's entitlement, into privileges the other man could not enjoy? That I have a chance to show myself a worthy successor? Hero, martyr. Would too much be demanded of me?

He sprang up and rubbed behind his ear; a drop of sweat was crawling like an ant. I want to love her and not to suffer. I must have her, I must—he shook off the thoughts that vexed him—then I will see. Life itself will sort things out.

He wanted to drink. The cook opened the door slightly and glanced in through the chink with one eye to assure himself that his master was sleeping. Taken aback on seeing that Istvan was lounging in the chair and looking him in the face, he shut the door and waited for his summons.

"Well, what is it?"

"The telephone, sir. I didn't want to wake you, but he was so insistent."

"Who is calling?"

"The painter who comes here sometimes."

Istvan rose wearily, stretched, and yawned. Through the receiver he heard Ram Kanval's low, pleasant voice. He wanted to know if the counselor had left the capital, like most people in their right minds, who had escaped to Dehradun or Shimla, in the foothills of the Himalayas, to wait out the harshest season.

Kanval himself was being allowed, free of charge, to exhibit his paintings in a hall in one of the clubs. He was overjoyed at this, and, since the counselor had been such a staunch well-wisher, warmly invited him to visit him and with his critical eye assist first with the choice of pictures that might please Europeans, and then with the varnishing. The fact that members of the embassy corps were in the city had led him to hope that someone would buy a painting. Diplomats were people of importance. Many had gone away on holidays. That was why Istvan's presence had taken on special significance.

Finally he assured him that he remembered his debt and would repay it, if not with cash, then with a picture. He would not dare make that decision on his own, however, and so he would expect a visit.

"Good. I understand. Yes, certainly, I will be there," Terey murmured into the receiver. Pereira stood in the doorway to the kitchen, trying to divine from the sound of the words whether he had done well in calling his master to the telephone. In his black hands he held a cup of strong tea. Terey was anticipating it; he smelled the pungency of it, felt already its reviving action, its clearing of the mind. So he beckoned with a hand and listened to exuberant plans for the conquest of New Delhi by innovative art, sipping his tea and inhaling its aromatic vapor. The cook, with a bright face, stood by him like a mannequin, slipping him a saucer on which he finally set his empty cup.

"One more?"

"No. Thank you."

Those were the words, as friendly Hindus had taught him, that it was not proper to use with the servants. The master's satisfaction, after all, was thanks beyond measure.

HE HAD HARDLY SPREAD OUT his papers at the embassy when Kalman Bajcsy summoned him. He stood, heavy, lumpish, blinking his swollen eyelids, looking out at the courtyard from behind the parted curtains. Involuntarily Terey looked to see what had caught the ambassador's attention, but apart from trees shriveled by the sun and the road from which red dust rose in columns, he could discern nothing.

"Well, you see." Kalman Bajcsy clapped him on the shoulder with a white palm and fingers covered with curly black hair. "Here under us, on the roof—"

Terey saw two brown starlings standing motionless with gaping beaks. The feathers on their necks bristled. Their wings hung half spread.

"The heat is exhausting them?"

"No, this is a moment's pause. Soon they will begin mauling each other again. One will try to catch the other by the throat, choke him and peck out his tongue," he said gloomily. "Little singing birds! Which one do you bet on? I'll wager the smaller one on the right will win. Well, bestir yourselves!" he urged them on.

As if at a signal the birds hopped toward each other, pecking, clawing, each beating the resilience out of his opponent. Ripped-out feathers protruded from their beaks. Locked together, they pushed each other into the withering vines with their wings. It was clear that the battle had not stopped, for startled lizards fled from the hot wall.

"Pity we won't see the end—" the ambassador thrust out his lip—"but I called you in about another matter, as you would have guessed."

He pushed Terey in front of him a little paternally, steering him with a disdainful motion toward the chairs reserved for guests.

"Let's sit down. Cigarette? No? Good for you. Heat like this makes everyone feel that his heart is short of oxygen, that his lungs are boiling."

He sat resting his elbows on the arms of his chair. His hands dangled wearily. His eyelids drooped; his mouth was partly open. Tiny lines of sweat glittered on his thick neck. He looked like a tired old man. Only his dark eyes, full of life, forestalled signs of sympathy, for he might not receive them well—might feel that those who showed them perceived him as prematurely weak.

How old is he? Istvan wondered. Fifty-four, fifty-five—not old, only spent, burned out. He wore himself out in the struggle.

"I had to dismiss the chauffeur," the ambassador began dispassionately, "even though I like him. A good driver—" he was looking up carefully to gauge the effect of an objective assessment on the counselor, but concluded quickly, "Only he is unstable. Hysterical. Nerves just under the skin, like most people's in this country. It pains me a little, for the dismissal coincides with his wife's death, though they attach less weight to death here. So I'd like you to see to it that he gets an extra hundred rupees, but discreetly: don't say it came from me. I don't care about gratitude. Have a chat with him, then drop in and see me. I have a premonition that there might be trouble with him. Well, tell me now, what is going on? Have you any news?"

"Nothing in particular. It's the dead season."

"Perhaps you will unearth something. What's good at the cinema? You're flagging, counselor. Have all the ladies you know left town? Have a word with the cook, he'll bring you back to life. But in such heat—" he exhaled deeply—"oh, young people, young people, you don't know how to take care of yourselves."

He seemed to say it, not reproachfully, but with envy.

"*House of Wax* starts today at the Splendid. It's an English film about grave robbers."

The ambassador looked at him, propping up one thick eyelid with a nicotine-stained finger, as if there might be some hidden meaning in what he had said.

"I know. I saw it five years ago in Geneva. It is sad when more and more is behind you, when you have weighed it in your hands, felt it, explored it, let it go. There are fewer and fewer faces that I would wish to meet, fewer landscapes to see. Those one saw in youth, even on an empty stomach, were more beautiful. The whole world had more vivid colors. Now it is exhausted—stale, like out-of-date merchandise. You say: it's the heat, the boss is bracing himself to reveal something—now, now, I know you call me that. No, dear counselor, it is the years. I speak of the age I feel myself to be, not the age on my birth certificate. Death holds no strangeness for me. We will meet as acquaintances who have already exchanged salutations. From darkness into darkness. Happy Hindus! He was—" he muttered, compressing his thoughts—"there is not even a dent in the air. He was. Oh, we don't like to think of that moment."

As if remembering Istvan's presence, he opened his eyes wide and rumbled:

"So you have nothing to tell me?"

"Except for the Rajk affair," Terey ventured.

"And how do you know about that?" the ambassador bristled. "That is strictly confidential."

"From the journalists. Nagar had the information. Tomorrow all the world will be trumpeting it. But this is only the beginning."

"You are brave enough to think that way? Well, you had better keep those hopes to yourself. Power always demands victims, and governing is not a parlor game but an exercise in force . . . though I don't know what people have been saying . . . if, of course, one wants to accomplish anything. Certainly it is force to which the nation consents, to which in the end it is reconciled, if it is to have significance in today's world."

He breathed heavily for a moment, looked at Istvan morosely, then added, "I don't like people who dig up graves, poke their noses into prisons, walk around the back walls of buildings, and wail that they smell a stench. There must be a stench. All power, the best power, has its muck. There is no need to ask what's in the garbage heap, only what was possible for a man, what was done, if there is some guarantee that everything won't go to the devil, that no one will demolish Budapest as you would plow an anthill under with your boot. And the panic begins, and the running about, and the general helplessness. And perhaps you are one of those who can't stand to listen to anyone and haven't the knack of giving commands themselves; such people are the worst! I can smell them a kilometer away.

"So you say Nagar had this information? One can believe him. The worst of it is that what comes to us only in snatches rebounds a hundredfold in echoes from the world, and creates confusion for us. And I would so have liked to live out the days I spend in Hungary, when I return every few years, in peace—to see how things progress, how much has been built. That gives me great relief, for in the foundation are my labor and anguish and sleepless nights. And I beg you," he changed the subject, resting his belly on the tabletop, "speak a few warm words to Krishan. It's always better that we part as friends. I count on your tact."

He sank into a chair as if he were breaking down. He slouched and covered his face with his hand; his fingers crept down around his fleshy nose. He grimaced and began fussing with the hair that protruded from his nostrils. Terey saw that his presence was superfluous. He slipped silently out of the room.

THE ARRIVAL OF THE COURIERS enlivened the torpid atmosphere. Typewriters rattled more vigorously; footsteps quickened in the corridor. The Hindu workers shuffled documents and rustled creased carbon paper like birds cleaning their wings with their beaks. As usual it appeared that, though reports had to be completed, under the watchful eyes of the ambassador some expressions took on equivocal shades of meaning. He set Ferenc and Terey to the urgent task of executing together the final stylistic amendments.

The couriers were alike as brothers: tall, with a military habit of standing at attention. Their faces were frank and open, full of a mindless sincerity that inspired confidence. Their wide eyes were not devoid of a spark of shrewdness. One could tell at once from which school they had come, could discern the stamp of the office in which, until recently, they had worked.

As they themselves had hinted in a rush of unthinking candor, behind their promotions to the foreign service were hidden some unnamed offenses to which they never alluded, though they were attributed to them as merits. The authorities simply thought it expedient to keep the two out of the public eye. Such journeys as these, taken regularly—although they always came as a pair, like gypsies or nuns guarding each other from mishap or temptation—furnished opportunities for a little business, for profits on the side, became an overt reward for blind obedience previously demonstrated. Even full exposure to foreign cultures, infusions of the magnificence of Paris or Rome, could not sow doubt in these minds, but rather awakened their contempt and a kind of pride that, in spite of renunciation and poverty, they were faithful, they were among the elite who moved between both worlds.

They tossed salami onto Istvan's desk. In its white coating it was thick as a man's arm, and smelled of home. He had to invite them to his residence, though it was not proper for a counselor to maintain social relations with them because of their low rank. They both came, wearing their navy blue suits as though they were uniforms. They answered questions briefly, in generalities, each looking at the other to assure himself that his statement was the correct one and did not deviate from the obligatory formulas Istvan knew from the first page of *Szabad Nep.*

But the whiskey they downed as they munched salted peanuts took the edge off their alertness. Lulled by Istvan's permissiveness, they took off their jackets, loosened their ties and unfastened their limp collars.

They vied with each other to assure him that all was peaceful in Budapest. "People work, earn their money, enjoy themselves. The outlook for the harvest is not bad. No particular shortages are felt. There is enough meat. Perhaps earnings are a little too low. But when has a man not wanted more cash?"

"And the mood?"

"Rather good. Discipline is a little on the decline; a degree of apathy has set in since Stalin's death. People aren't as committed as before."

"You know our country, counselor; it needs the whip," the other added eagerly, plucking at his mustache, which was clipped short like a small brush. "Now our leaders want to ingratiate themselves, to loosen the reins. When there is a temporary shortage of something, right away people say that the Russians took it, that for the good of the partnership it is necessary to make sacrifices."

"And when we were in Moscow, I heard again that it was necessary to tighten the belt to give something to us and the Czechs and the Poles, to keep everyone in the camp. Such talk is bound to rankle."

"Do you see dissatisfaction, then, or not?" Istvan persisted.

"There is the expectation of change, the hope that there will be new appointments, even in the government itself. But which direction change will take, or where the new people will come from, no one knows."

"A thaw," he offered.

"So they call it in Moscow. But what does that mean in practice? Everyone points to the Soviet example, and indeed Rakosi and

Gerő studied government there. They won't do anything foolish, they won't agree to any compromises."

"Well, and what will happen with regard to the Rajk affair? What about those who were innocently sentenced to death?"

They were troubled. They looked questioningly at each other. They raised their glasses and dawdled between sips of the amber liquid. The sunset flamed in the sky, full of fierce blood red and coagulating violet. The colors were disturbing. They riveted the eye; they threw a copper-tinted reflection on the walls and the faces, with their altering expressions.

"Well, perhaps sometimes we have been hasty in branding someone an enemy. But one must remember what the situation was, what forces were closing in on us. When the Russians left Austria, we found ourselves in the forefront," the older one pointed out. "All the pressure from the West was bearing down on us."

"And enemy propaganda? And Szabad Europa radio, which abused the government unrelentingly? I don't even find it surprising that there were those few verdicts. Not for nothing is it said that the ideological front, like the front itself, can't do without cannon fire. Was there a lack of victims from our side?"

"Perhaps when you return home," Terey began, "you will find changes."

"Perhaps. Perhaps," they assented, but the thought did not seem to please them. They were, after all, from the bureau that efficiently furnished documentation on every charge. I had to ask someone; they will inform on me again, they will throw their own light on our conversation, Ferenc will make notes eagerly, and there will be another document in my file. There must be control, but they should know what they are after—he shrugged—they should at least manage to repeat accurately what they heard from me.

They left one after the other, warmly pressing his hand. They said they wanted to run out to Old Delhi to find presents for their girls. He offered to take them. Visibly uncomfortable, they thanked him, begging him not to fatigue himself; perhaps they did not want a witness while they made their purchases. With relief they left him behind the curtain of vines on the veranda. He heard them send the watchman for a taxi. It drove up immediately, coughing and kicking up a cloud of dust.

The room was growing dark. Beyond the screens loomed the yellow glow of streetlights. Sadness came over him, a bitter feeling of being lost. The drone of the cooling machine was tiresome. He heard the lagging shuffle of the cook in the hall. He guessed what the servant was doing: crouching and peering through the keyhole. There was no light in the room, so he is not sure whether I have gone out or am napping. He will go and ask the watchman if sahib left with the guests.

But the door opened violently and a dazzling light flashed.

"Put that out," he said a little too loudly. "What do you want?"

"Excuse me, sir—I did not know that you were here." The cook moved in the darkness, shaking cigarette butts into his hand, for he liked to crumble the tobacco into his pipe. "May I serve the meal?"

"What do you have for dinner?"

"Vegetables and eggs. Meat—no. Fish—no. Before I bring it from the market, it already stinks. I have also a mango on ice, very good. I have papayas. They are very healthy; they cleanse the kidneys. In such heat there is pure salt in the kidneys, because all water is excreted through the skin."

"Good. Set the table," he said without enthusiasm.

He turned on the lamp that stood on his desk. A rumpled newspaper lay there, and an open novel by Forster: *A Passage to India*. He picked up the book, then closed it. He saw a bulging letter hidden under it. At once he recognized his friend Bela's somewhat childish handwriting.

There were no stamps on the envelope; the couriers must have put it there. Why had they not put it into his hand? They were not supposed to carry private mail, but who would attach any importance to this? Were they afraid of each other? The letter was not sealed. Well, no, so they could examine what was inside, see if Bela was smuggling dollars to me. He smiled wryly, drawing out sheets of ugly paper covered with slanted lines of nervous handwriting and folded twice, so they could be crammed into an envelope that was too small.

He leaned forward, straightened out the sheets and began reading greedily:

Dear Istvan,

When I snatch up the telephone and call you and Ilona answers, I no longer feel panic, thinking it is another wrong number. Yet it is you I want—you, for whom else should I talk to? To the devil with India! Every day now there are events here that I would run to tell you about; I would drag you out for coffee and at last we would chat to our hearts' content. You will say I could write a letter. Not true. I would have to have time, to have the paper spread in front of me, to be in the mood to write—well, and to be sure the letter would get into your hand.

So many borders; so many prying eyes. A letter will reach you in a week. And everything I have written will be invalid, for there will be new developments. How to register them, as a seismograph registers tremors of the earth's crust?

Things are abuzz everywhere; there is a feeling of excitement and tension. Suddenly everyone believes that there will be changes. No—not the kind you are thinking of now, smiling skeptically. It was not an idea that was at fault, only the smallness of people who learned to listen to what came to them by fiat; they do not give commands themselves, but for years have repeated the commands of others. They are afraid of freedom, for they would not know how to deal with it. They do not trust the nation, so they spy on it. And we sense that, like a horse whose skin quivers when it spies the whip hidden behind the driver's back. For it has tasted the lash, it is accustomed to it.

In whispers we used to mention the names of those recently arrested; what the offense was was always decided afterward. We would be drinking coffee and everyone would look around to be sure that no one from the next table was overhearing—that the waitress did not come running over too early with the check, for she might be an informer, and she knew the regular customers.

You remember Tibor M.? We were astonished, wondering why he was arrested. A communist, a staff officer, a patriot. Clean; not intoxicated with power. Universally liked. Perhaps that was the heaviest strike against him. He went down like a stone into water. After two years he floated up at the trial of foreign minister Rajk, charged with treason, with spying for the imperialists, with organizing a coup d'etat. He refused to testify. He said not a word before the court. He behaved with dignity. He was demoted and sentenced to death. He has been released now, and I have talked with him.

He was innocent. He was a lucky devil; they postponed his execution because he was supposed to serve as a witness in trials yet to come. You would not recognize him. He is gray. He speaks as if chewing his words, looking you doggedly in the eye with his hands on his lap, for so he was trained. His lips are pursed; he hardly opens them. His teeth are gone. Yes—what pains him most is that he was beaten by his own, by people wearing the same uniform but lower in rank. And though they spoke the same language, though they were Hungarians, they understood none of what he was trying to explain. No logical argument had any effect. That horrified him, even aroused his pity for them. They were automatons who had to wring from him confessions of crimes he had not committed. They had received their orders and they had listened blindly.

"They were more afraid than I," he told me with a lifeless smile, "and that gave me strength. They were trembling for the approval of their masters, for promotions, for their careers. I understood how transient those things were in relation to the values they had lost. They had ceased to be Hungarians, perhaps even repudiated their humanity."

He told how they interrogated him for four days without stopping. He fainted, tortured by lack of sleep and by the lamps that seem to blaze in the brain even when you close your eyes. They beat him in inventive ways and made him drink castor oil to humiliate him, to show him how even his own body was betraying him, weakening, stinking. They told him his friends had turned him in and even then were testifying against him. They shoved prepared depositions under his nose, but Tibor only shrugged his shoulders and hissed through his tight lips, "I always took them for a band of swine. This is no news to me."

They told him next that they had set a trap in his flat, but the men on guard were not bored waiting for unexpected visitors, because his wife was so very accommodating. They dragged in nauseating details: how she pleased them in bed, what she whispered. "That crackpot—I haven't lived with her for ages. You can have her. Enjoy yourselves, boys," he answered. You know yourself how he loved her. But he silenced them with repartee, divining instinctively that it was a pack of lies, that they were only probing for a weak spot. If he had let them see that any insinuation affected him, they would have bored deeper into the open wound.

Then he had one interrogator—the one with the longest assignment to his case: a year and a half of investigation, if you could call it that. A year and a half of writing biographical data that achieved the scale of a novel, full of subtexts, implications, suspicions, of threats and pleas to induce him to denounce his partners. Depositions had been prepared long before. This investigator waited for a moment of weakness to obtain his signature, his confession of guilt.

"After several hours of fruitless effort, the investigating officer looked at me with such exasperation and disappointment that I was sorry for him," Tibor told me in his throaty whisper, "because he must have been in such anguish, since he knew as well as I did that I was innocent. After all, they could have hanged me without my confession, but the appearance of justice was less important to them than breaking me down, destroying me psychologically. The investigator tore up the deposition papers without reading them and said in an impassive voice, 'You are lying. You are lying. We know the whole truth. You are a traitor.' He put a file of documents and a pencil in front of me and commanded, 'Write from the beginning,' and he himself broke into English, from time to time repeating the words mindlessly and looking at me with a face full of misery.

"'Friend,' he begged as dawn broke, 'I must have your depositions. My future hangs on it. Look how my temples have gone gray. I do not sleep. I have disorders of the stomach.'

"'And I?' I ran my fingers over my whitened temples; my hair had not been cut for a long time and was coarse and brittle. 'And

I?' I pulled aside my lip and showed my colorless, toothless gums. 'What have you made of me? If I resist, it is only for your good, so you will know that not all men are worthless. So you will finally catch a glimpse of that unattainable level of development: human dignity.'"

The interrogator was not offended. In fact, an intimacy ensued between them. They knew each other so well, reached such a level of familiarity, that the officer asked the prisoner to quiz him when he was practicing his English.

Suddenly one day Tibor reached the end of his endurance; he had had enough. "I have made up my mind," he declared to the astonished officer. "Call the clerk. I will give my deposition."

"You will testify against your partners at last?" he asked incredulously.

"I will give one name. I will not be tormented any longer."

"One—that is good," the investigator said with zeal. "What is that name?"

"Yours. What are you gaping at? You are a traitor. I'm going to squeal on you." Tibor jabbed him with a finger.

"But that is nonsense!"

"Not at all, because as I sat here, I recruited you into the intelligence service. You were getting five hundred dollars a month, and that tempted you. You were paid for the same set of interlocking investigations. And you were in contact with workers at the American embassy. You yourself handed the report over to me, did you not?"

"This is an insane lie!"

"Certainly not," Tibor continued, maintaining his composure. "And what were you doing five months ago, November fourteenth, at seven in the evening?"

"How should I remember? Perhaps I was at the cinema. Perhaps I was working here."

"Then I must remember. Because you told me that you were at the Beke cinema, at the last showing, and that you gave a box of matches to a strange man who asked you for a light. He gave you another box, because a warning was hidden in yours—a warning that someone was going to escape—and an excerpt from the documents in my case."

"It's all a fabrication. I wasn't in any cinema. I never gave anyone a light."

"You will remember. You will have time enough in a cell. And I will remind you of certain details you told me. You carried out everything according to my instructions. And perhaps you aren't hiding a wad of dollars at home?"

"I have no dollars!"

"Your wife has already managed to clear them away? She will have to be grilled; she will let the cat out of the bag. Anything to give the investigators a start. We'll see what she has to say about you."

"But you have no evidence against me. Not a shred of evidence—" he beat his fist on the table. It seemed that he would collapse with a heart attack.

"You're wrong. I have." Tibor clutched a notebook with English words written in it to his chest. The officer leaped like a man demented. He was the stronger of the two; he snatched the glossary away.

And at that moment he understood the depths to which he had sunk. Indeed, he was at the prisoner's mercy. This weak, ill-treated rag of a man could destroy him. It would be enough to give the deposition he had threatened. The investigator knew well that he had rivals who were only waiting for him to make a slip. He saw that he was trapped. Tibor could get revenge, take the officer down with him. Then he wept—a terrible sobbing without tears. He explained that he had a wife and child. He begged Tibor not to bring ruin on them.

"And I?" Tibor asked.

Then the man was forced to feel the cruelty of the machine in which he had been one of the cogs.

When Tibor declared that it had been a joke, that he was not thinking of giving a deposition in order to frame him—that it was only an object lesson—something in the other man gave way. He said that if Tibor would only hold out longer, they would not do anything to him. He even called Tibor's wife and gave her the first information she had received about his health, ensuring anonym-

ity by using a pay telephone on the street. Something in him had broken, and the interrogations became a mere formality.

Tibor was transferred to another prison where there were several others in his cell. His glasses were returned to him; he could read books. Then one day they heard the scream of factory sirens and the clanging of bells, and they thought that it was the alarm, that war had broken out. Only that night did the soldier patrolling the corridor—one of the chosen, the most worthy of trust—strike the metal-clad door with his fist to wake them and call, "Be brave; endure. Stalin has died. Soon Rakosi will go to the devil." He wasn't afraid to shout at the top of his voice, though there might have been an informer in the cell.

"Then," Tibor said, "I felt a wave of love for that soldier from whom I was separated by that door with its metal fittings, for my prison guard. I was ready to die for him. The unity of the nation filled me with ecstasy. I was truly happy."

A month later he was given teeth. He was force-fed. He even got a sun lamp; his skin was no longer the color of plaster. He thought they were grooming him for another trial. Meanwhile he was called to headquarters. They gave him a uniform, shook his hand, and sent him home. A member of the security police was occupying two rooms in his flat; he is still there, in fact, though he promised to leave. He asked Tibor to put in a word to help him get a flat, for they have to do something to oblige the one "unjustly sentenced." This man, from the most powerful office, is looking to the former prisoner for patronage.

And Tibor remains in the army. He was given back his party card, which had been confiscated and attached to the indictment. It is on such people as Tibor that the kind of socialism we will have depends. Imagine: He said to me, "How fortunate that we still have comrades who have stood the test, faithful to the cause and to our people. Remember Janos Kádár; he is still in prison." We talked openly in a coffee shop about his ordeals, feeling quite secure. Tibor mentioned you as well; your name was dropped during the investigation. He set you up as an example of loyalty, reliability, cooperation. He asked me if it were true that you had filed a deposition against him. I hotly denied it. He was very glad, for he is starving for people to trust.

Istvan swallowed hard. Yes, he reflected bitterly, our behavior, the motives of which we ourselves do not understand clearly, can be turned against us when they want to bring charges. Tibor has the advantage because he has passed through hardships and I have not. He felt a rush of fear. Tibor has it behind him by now. Pray God I don't have to—

A dark hand, almost violet in the harsh lamplight and cut by a white shirtsleeve, crept over the table. "Sahib, dinner was served long ago," Pereira said coaxingly. "I beg and remind, and sahib sleeps."

"I am not sleeping."

"Sahib was so far away that I was afraid. The son of a babu in our village fell ill at his studies in Calcutta and the father worried himself sick about him. Then he, too, went out of himself. Though he was in his body, you could stick pins in him and he sat like a dead man."

"You're being tiresome. I was reading a letter and was lost in thought. I will eat very soon. You may leave."

"When I tell you the real truth. He returned to himself and cried. And then he said that his son had died, and the next day a telegram came—"

"Go."

He raised his eyes to the uncovered window. Yellow and greenish beams from the distant streetlights marked out the square. He longed so for Budapest that it gnawed him like a physical pain. He took up the last page of the letter, eagerly absorbing the words in uneven rows.

. . . for he is starving for people to trust . . . That I read. *We spoke of his ordeals with complete freedom. We did not concern ourselves about who might be there, though the coffee shop was full of customers. Tibor has crossed the boundary; he has stopped being afraid. One cannot tighten a screw into infinity, for it bores through and instead of holding, loosens. Something of that sort has*

happened with us. "Thou shalt have no other gods before Me": for whole years we didn't think of that. Suddenly the scales fell from everyone's eyes; now they talk of changes as if they had already occurred. And indeed the security police are here. Agents are writing reports. Surely card indexes are full to bursting. But we don't hear of new arrests. It is as if all this gathering of information had lost its effectiveness, even its meaning. So far no one has said that Rakosi should step down, but he is already looking for successors, as if he had been buried with Stalin.

Every day fresh evidence of cruelty comes to light, of criminal mindlessness and folly. An eighty-six-year-old peasant woman was freed from one of the security police's cellars. She was confined there because she had not delivered the milk on schedule! The old woman had written Horthy to ask for a pardon; she didn't even know who was ruling Hungary now. She had been accused of economic sabotage and the matter became a political case.

You should be sorry that you are not with us. It is a momentous time. The atmosphere is charged, yet full of gravity—I would even say grandeur. There is an Eastern proverb: When a wronged man sighs, hardly a leaf stirs, but when a nation in anguish sighs, a gale springs up that sweeps the powerful away. I feel its sigh. You hear—this is not literary affectation, in which you suspect me of indulging. I wanted you to be able to understand a little of what is happening in our Budapest.

Affectionately—Bela

Istvan sat at the table, listlessly eating the rice Pereira put before him. He drank cool tomato juice; he scraped the mango halves on ice with his spoon. The mushy fruit dissolved on the tongue with a bland taste rather like carrot.

One of the couriers must have concealed the letter. The envelope was open; no doubt he had not been able to resist reading it in some hotel in Austria, Italy, Turkey, Pakistan. Yet he had delivered it. So those most dedicated also had their uncertainties? Did they feel a solidarity with the people from whom they had been culled, and to whom they had been taught to feel superior? Were they, too, amenable to new leadership? A decent fellow, Bela; he pressed his clasped hands together angrily. He must have had access, he had regained their trust, or they would have taken it straight to the embassy and handed it over. No, they did not want to risk it. Private mail? Who knows what significance this information could have? And perhaps Ferenc has already read the letter, and therefore the ambassador as well, and it was planted here as a test, to see what he would do next? Loathing crept over him.

"It's impossible to live this way." He clenched his fist. "Impossible."

Pereira regarded him anxiously. It seemed to him that the counselor had a fever. When Terey went out to the bathroom, the cook strained his ears suspiciously, then raised the whiskey flask to the light and critically estimated how much was gone. He evidently determined that only a little was missing, because he poured together what remained in the couriers' glasses, topped it off from the bottle and lapped it up, blinking as he tasted it full strength, then slipped noiselessly away to the kitchen.

Istvan paced around the room, too restless to sit down. A stray cricket had gotten into the house and was chiming timidly in a corner of the room. The motor in the cooling machine whirred. The full glare of the lamp fell on the rumpled sheets of letter paper covered with green handwriting.

What the letter communicated was staggering. He wanted to share the news, and his homesickness, with someone. He walked to and fro, wondering to whom he could go so late in the evening. There were two people who would receive him at any hour, friendly people but distant enough that he did not have to be on guard with them. One was Nagar; the other was Judit. Agitation burned in him like a torch passed from the homeland on another continent. He was hungry for conversation, eager to share thoughts, calculations, predictions.

The folds of the letter, like the pleats of an accordion, caught the lamplight. He read the first sentence once more and put it down. The gentle semicircular glow warmed to brilliance the green and rust motifs of the blossoming trees in the carpet. He remembered how he had resisted being pushed into purchasing it. An exquisite rug. It reminded him of Margit. He would have liked to see her on it, nude, as she waited, leaning on her elbow, smoking a cigarette, the white of her flesh lightly touched with violet—to see her tawny hands, long legs, and rust-colored, tumultuous hair. A boyish dream of a woman from a Matisse illustration he had come across somewhere. He gave a self-pitying shrug. The refrain of a Hindu song crossed his mind: "Everything we desired and possessed was taken from us. Everything for which we do not stretch out our hands, yet is worthy of pursuit, lures. Do not wrest things from the world, and the world will give itself to you. Do not seize greedily, and you will have. You will realize."

No; he would not resign himself to that. A wolflike rapacity was growing in him, an urge to lay hands on, to grip, to bite open, to devour. Even to tear to pieces. To have, in order to feel release.

He opened the door to the hall. He heard the cook shouting at the sweeper and the cadenced knocking of the brush on the flagstone floor. They were scrubbing the kitchen.

He lifted the receiver and dialed the operator's number. A girl answered; her speech was full of excessively proper Anglicisms, like a recording from a language course. He asked for Agra, for the Taj Mahal hotel. He stood there, catching the distant static, the traces of voices on the line. He wanted a cigarette, but he was afraid to step away and search on his desk, for the hotel receptionist might answer just then.

The uproar from the kitchen was unbearable—the slopping of water, the nasal commands of the cook, who lorded it over the other servants because he was the only one with a fair knowledge of English and could invoke, in his statements to the rest of them, the authority of the master. I must correct his behavior, Istvan mused. His head has been turned completely. Moreover, he allows himself familiarities.

But he did not hush the servants because it would have drawn their attention. They would be quiet soon, and they would overhear his conversation. Yet perhaps he would manage to exchange a few warm words with Margit, to catch a change in the tone of her voice. He might even find out when she would come to Delhi or invite him to Agra.

He knew there were no telephones in the hotel rooms, yet his face contorted with impatience when the clerk, hemming and hawing, said that he would call Miss Ward to the telephone right away. As he scratched the wall mechanically with his fingernail, drawing slanted lines that resolved themselves into her initials, he seemed to hear the rasping of the cicadas hidden in the dusty festoons of blossoms on the pergola.

The time it took to summon her was unendurably long, a sickening void. He really had little to say to her apart from the one word which would explain his worry and longing. But he knew that he would not say that word, that the sentences would be as dead as plaster moldings. He thought of the multitude of ears that would be listening in on their conversation, the mute witnesses, bored but inquisitive. He saw girls with jingling necklaces and receivers clinging to their hair, which would be moist from sweat and fragrant oil; they would be on the line to assist the callers, and by accident.

He heard Margit's voice, unfamiliar, distorted by the distance.

"Hello! Hello," and then with a hearty note of recognition, "Is that you, Grace?"

"This is Istvan. You weren't expecting—"

"No. Not you. Oh, how wonderful that you've called! Thank you."

He said nothing. She offered, "Perhaps you are coming? When will I see you?"

"Saturday evening."

"Four more days? That's awfully long. May I call you?"

He did not answer. He still wanted to hide his relationship with her, to shield it from view like a miser, to keep it to himself. He saw obstacles mounting, saw avalanches hanging over him which could easily be sent thundering down.

"I got your letter."

"Ah, that prompted you to call. And I thought that you yourself—that you really missed me." He felt rather than heard a trace of disappointment in her reply.

"It's true." He licked his sticky, suddenly taut lips.

"What's true?"

"I miss you, Margit."

"If that were true, you wouldn't be calling. You would be with me."

"I can't just now."

"Evidently you don't miss me enough."

He was stricken. He did not speak; he could not contradict her.

"I'm sorry," she said hastily. "I'm a capricious only child. I'm used to having what I want. You know that even waiting gives me joy I've never known until now. Istvan, are you there?" she asked, suddenly anxious. "Hello—can you hear me?"

"Yes," he answered fervently. "I hear everything." He seemed to be saying: You touch my heart, I understand, I am hanging on your words. Speak on.

But men's voices were coming through the receiver, calling Margit impatiently, nagging her. It pained him; for an instant he even imagined that their exchange had been a clever sham.

"Wait. I'll be right back." Then he heard her say to those in the room, "This is Grace, my friend from Delhi." Picking up the telephone again, she explained a bit defensively, "I'm having a little party. It's too hot to go anywhere, so we're sitting here, listening to Bartok. We'll drink, but only a little. It's just our group. Don't be jealous. The professor is here, and Dr. Connoly, whom I promise to bring to you, since you invited him.

"I would so terribly like to see you," she said in a completely different tone. "And now, quickly, tell me something pleasant that I can remember just before I fall asleep."

He hesitated, then, amazed at the strength of his own emotion, whispered, "I'll be there Saturday evening."

"I already heard that. Say something more . . ."

"That's all," he said, turning around suddenly, for he had spied the cook's long shadow on the wall, and the sweeper's head hung down just over the threshold. They had been watching and listening.

He was furious. But then words that pacified him flowed from far away: "I understand. Thank you very, very much. Until Saturday." There was a rattle as she hung up the receiver. The next instant the impersonal voice of the operator came on.

"Will you speak longer, sir?"

"No. I've finished."

"Thank you," she breathed, and the telephone jingled briefly, just once, as if there were a tremor of the heart in its bell.

He caught his breath like a swimmer emerging from deep water. He wiped the sweat from his forehead with his hand. Instinct warned that he was in the power of an element the strength of which he did not know. He would have to dislodge the other man she had loved, to push him into the dark. Where would the contest take place? Certainly not amid the disheveled bedclothes, where subduing the shadow would be easy.

"Finish your work," he said to the cook.

"Yes, sahib—but we would not have wanted to make noise," Pereira answered earnestly. On the wall Terey could see the shadow of the cook's thin foot nudging the sweeper. A second later he could hear the rhythmic scraping of the brush as it made its way in circles around the kitchen floor.

He went into the living room and sat down in an armchair. When he lit a cigarette, his fingers trembled. Lamplight glowed on the sheets covered with green writing. A sudden pain pierced him, for he was certain that Margit would never understand all that Bela's letter conveyed, and what it meant to him. Though she loved and was loved, she would not be one of them.

Late the next afternoon, as dust gathered in the air and hovered just above an earth that exhaled fire; as the dry, yellow grass crumbled even when the grasshoppers trampled it; as the clamor of the cicadas in almost leafless treetops rang in the air like a great complaint, Terey drove up to the embassy garage. One of his directional signals had gone out, and even after the bulb was changed it refused to light up. Instead of the stocky Premchand he found only Krishan, whose clothing made a blotch of bright white as he sat on his heels by the wall, like an ordinary peasant resting at dusk. His hand, holding a smoking cigarette, almost touched the red ground. He seemed to be napping with his head down.

He did not move a muscle when the Austin pulled in not far from him and the counselor got out. The yellow glare reflected from the sun, which was now buried behind the houses, streamed over the white of Krishan's narrow trousers, his dark, dangling hands, and the long lines of his fingers crossed by a white cigarette. He did not raise his dark head with its waves of greased hair even when he heard Terey's greeting.

"Good evening, Krishan."

"Good evening, sir," a gentle, girlish voice answered from the dim interior of the garage.

Though she was too abashed to walk out, Istvan, seeing the outline of her figure, could tell that she was young and pretty. She must have clasped her hands in front of her chest, for he heard the jingle of silver sliding over her wrists. He sensed that there was something between them, though the driver did not turn his face toward her, and the girl did not assert her right to his attention. She only looked out with large, solicitous eyes, which gleamed with a moist luster in the dusky garage.

"Krishan, what is it?"

"Nothing, sir. I do not work at the embassy anymore."

Terey was sorry for him; he remembered the ambassador's instructions. He leaned against the hood and lit a cigarette. He heard the sigh of the cooling motor, the bell-like chirp of crickets, and the dry whisper of leaves from the plants that grew on the embassy walls.

"I'm very sorry, Krishan," he began. "We all sympathize with you."

Krishan raised his forehead. In his dark, narrow face, white, even teeth gleamed in a catlike grimace under his short mustache. He laughed without a sound until his shoulders shook.

"That is why you are letting me go."

"We know what you have lost—"

"No. She went out because she wanted to. She told me to marry her younger sister because they are poor and there was no money for another dowry. Nothing has changed with me. There was a wife and there is a wife. She even asked me to call her by the dead one's name, because she loved her. Only where will I find work now?"

With an effort, Terey understood how different the custom of this country was—that death loses its fang of despair when one dies only to return, that the passage beyond the black curtain hardly alarms one. He felt clumsy. He was left with nothing to say, no comfort to offer. He could not muster the ideas he needed; he could not revive their old camaraderie.

"You had expenses connected with the funeral. You see, we do appreciate you. I am going to give you some money. You ought to rest. You ought not to sit behind the wheel right away."

"How much?" He clutched at the banknote with the ends of his fingers, held it in his left hand as if he were going to let it fall to the ground out of disgust, and took a deep pull on his cigarette, inhaling the smoke. In its red glow his eye glinted as he blinked derisively. "Only a hundred?"

"That's more than a little, Krishan," the counselor said hotly.

"Sir, I have one question: If I am summoned before the court, will you give a statement as a witness?"

"I was not with you then," Istvan reminded him.

"I also ask only if you would like to testify as to who gave me a hundred rupees. Nothing more." Now he rose nimbly; he was slender and graceful. He tossed away the cigarette butt and stamped on it, raising a little spray of sparks. "And perhaps there will be no hearing in court. Then you will pay me more, much more."

"I don't understand, Krishan."

"If you had understood, you would not have come to me with this paltry hundred rupees. If the ambassador thinks that I am stupid and that any trifle will be enough to shut me up, he is very wrong."

"But who will bring a case against you? Even the insurance company was not informed. The embassy paid for the repairs."

He went silent again, then raised a finger toward the sky, where ever-larger stars were shimmering and sinking.

"Kali," he whispered. "Repeat it to him. Kali and I are thinking of him." He put his narrow, dusky hand on his chest. Suddenly, in a completely normal voice, the voice of an obliging servant, he asked, "Your car is damaged? Shall I repair it?"

Istvan hesitated to accept this proposition, but decided that he personally would pay him for that service. He wanted to reestablish their old relationship; he had a vague feeling that he had allowed himself to be drawn into something unsavory. The drilling of the cicadas wore on him, intensifying his watchfulness, like a warning. The girl standing in the shadows pressed her hands together; her bracelets jangled dully.

"The left-hand signal doesn't light up. Perhaps you could check the installation and then drive the car up to my house. All right?"

Krishan seized Terey's hand with his damp fingers, raised it, and pressed it to his chest. Through the man's shirt, near his ribs, Terey felt the hammering of his heart and sensed an answering tension in himself.

"Sir, if I am bad, I will be very bad. It is impossible to stop in the middle of the road. The mountain of lies grows even if I do not open my mouth. Tell him that."

Terey pulled his hand away—pulled far too hard, for Krishan let it go so easily that he was ashamed of the violence of his motion.

"I will check that signal right away." Krishan almost shouted. "This minute." But when he took a step toward the automobile, he seemed to grow weak. He propped himself awkwardly against the hood; he slipped, and his nails scratched against it. Then the girl came out of the darkness and with surprising strength, for she was of slight build, took him in her arms and led him, unresisting, into the garage.

"Is he ill?" Istvan asked in an undertone.

"He is weak," she answered tenderly. "He was smoking."

At once everything was clear: the strange, uneasy movements, the florid sentences. He was smoking hashish. All the sympathy Istvan had lavished on the driver in the past dissipated. Now he understood the ambassador's decision. Indeed, they all should be relieved that a genuine disaster had not occurred. Once again it appeared that he had been wrong. Naive goodheartedness could easily have placed them in the hands of a blackmailer. It had been right to let the driver go, to seize the first occasion to sever his tie to the embassy.

It seemed to him that in spite of the light vapors of gasoline and lubricants, he smelled the harsh aroma of cannabis. But everything was masked by the raw animal odor of the girl's perfume as she came fluttering up through the dimness.

"Forgive him, sir. We have met with great misfortune," she pleaded, her bracelets clinking. "He is full of sorrow."

"Is there a way to help him?"

"No. He must have a long sleep."

He turned on the headlights and drove out onto the road. When he heard the even hum of the motor, he felt relief. He stepped on the gas as if he were running away from something. One curtained window glowed in the embassy, behind a grating. The cryptographer was still working. The directional signal was repaired at the Shell station when he filled the fuel tank.

Connoly felt shunted aside by their reflexive affability, which seemed conspiratorial, though they had induced him to stay for coffee. He gathered up his shaggy tobacco pouch made of deer scrotum and tucked his pipe into its flannel bunting with a cherishing gesture, like a mother fondling her baby. He wrinkled his forehead suspiciously, like a dog that has lost the scent in a chase and now sees the cat stretched flat on a branch too high to reach. He understood intuitively the awkwardness of the situation.

Margit, in a simple ivory dress cut so low that her breasts showed white as they rose with her breathing, was speaking with an unnatural vivacity, as if she were hiding something under the cadence of her brightly turned, empty sentences—sentences which would have been suitable for an official reception but were off key in a conversation between people meeting as friends. From time to time István turned his head in her direction, and neither man could have failed to notice the light that filled her eyes as they met his.

Connoly realized that he was superfluous, though they both held him there as if they were afraid to be alone in the deepening twilight on the spacious veranda of the hotel. He felt, though somewhat vaguely, the bitterness of defeat; in the end it had been the girl, not he, who had made a choice. He had not had a chance, in spite of the will he had mustered. He could not turn back or stop the course of things, he could only slow it down, and because it seemed that they both wanted that, he rose to spite them, rubbed his thinning stubble of hair, said a jaunty "Goodbye," and left, tall, broad-shouldered. Blotches of light from holes the drought had bitten out of the leafy roof of the pergola flowed over his back. For as long as they could see him, he walked with an exaggerated vigor that belied the effects of a tiring day's work, the heat, and the elaborate late lunch they had forced on him.

They sat in the rapidly lengthening shadows, so close that their hands could freely have touched, clasped, entwined, but neither made the slightest gesture. If the witness had remained, then they might have done it sooner, out of audacity, out of a kind of defiance, simply as a sign that they were lovers, though that was not yet true.

The dust above the trees was rapidly turning blue; Margit's hair looked almost black. Far beyond the gate, with a sound of ungreased axles like cats' meowing, the thick, bare wooden wheels of tongas rolled along. The white coats of the oxen in their harnesses gave off a violet shimmer.

I must remember—it returned to Istvan like a soothing melody—remember the smell of dry leaves, dust, and straw matting. Voices: the singing calls of drivers squatting on the shafts in enormous turbans, swaying like wilting poppies. The light of a few lamps, not yet a glare, but daubs of yellow between the trees, marked the advance of night. Its first breezes rippled through the air, bringing relief. A moment more and, like the quick blow of an ax, the semitropical darkness would fall.

She was also looking at Agra. The town was transformed by garlands of colored lights—the evening illumination calculated to entice tourists to the little shops full of ivory and sandalwood, embroidery, lace, and scarves of batiste with drawn-work delicate as frost, though frost had never been seen here.

He glanced stealthily over her neck, her flawless profile, her lips, slightly parted and a little swollen from the heat. She looked for a long time without blinking, as if the sudden onset of night like the rising of a river were disturbing to her. In that moment of quiet brooding she seemed captivating to him. He wanted her, wanted to feel the burden of her head in his hands, to feel her hair flowing in coppery streams through his fingers. To hang over her lips, not to kiss, only to mingle his breath with hers, to prolong the moment of yielding. She also felt no hurry. The silence of the receding day was accompanied by a peaceful certainty that they belonged to each other, that before long they would be together, not by virtue of predestination or indefinable fate, which might deprive them of their rebellious joy—that they had chosen each other and each would take the other as a gift, because they truly desired each other.

Large beetles droning in bass voices flew over the disheveled festoons of climbing plants, then suddenly lost their balance and fell with a dry crackle, as if someone in hiding were trying to break the silence by throwing pebbles. They heard an angry snorting, and both turned their heads. The cat from the reception desk beat with an outstretched paw at a fallen beetle, crunched its shell with her teeth, and shook the crushed insect out of her muzzle with revulsion.

The summer night had settled in. The darkness seemed to engulf the girl. He reached out and put his hand on hers in order to feel the joyful certainty that he had that privilege. When he felt her warm touch, he thought he also smelled the delicate fragrance of her perfume, or perhaps it was only that she had turned her head and he was catching the scent of her warm hair.

"Come," she said, and their fingers linked.

He stood up in a passion of readiness, like an obedient pupil. She did not steer them under the arcades of the pergola, however, but into the depths of the park, to a pool half dried up by the heat. Lawn chairs stood propped against the wall of an empty bathhouse; they found them easily and sat down beside each other. By now the pergola was twinkling with lights. They had escaped just in time, for a waiter wearing a starched napkin like a crest atop his red turban was already beginning to gather up cups, and the servers were moving about in the yellow light of grottos dripping with leaf-covered stalactites.

They sat side by side without a word. The water gave off a breath like the air in a swamp. A handful of stars in a shimmering, fluttering tissue like a dragonfly's wing seemed to fly toward the earth. In the pool, where no one was swimming, in thick, turbid water that seemed to be covered with a soggy clotted mass, other stars trembled, now and then nearly blotted out, violently shaken by drowning insects that had fallen splattering into the water.

In the bushes little lights soft as a fine rain twinkled. They flew about unsteadily, leaving shiny streaks behind them. All space, from the sky to the earth, was full of movement and instability. A small green flame floated calmly in the air and spiraled down; opposite that one another swam out, reflected in the viscid mirror. They seemed to run toward each other, drawn by an irresistible force, to join for a moment as if in a kiss and then disappear—to drop into the darkness or separate because of some perceived error, one soaring up, the other falling deep into the black water.

"You see?" she asked in a voice not like her own, low and a bit fearful. "The birth and death of worlds. An eerie night."

He was silent, at one with nature, profoundly calm.

"What are you thinking about? It seems that you have left me, that you are very far away."

His first impulse was to deny it, to seize her hand, cover it with his own and whisper, "I am thinking of you." But he told the truth, caught off guard by her intuition.

"I was recalling a night like this in my childhood."

"Everything that is and will be between us reminds you of something? And I wanted us to . . . You don't understand that you have become a whole world for me, still undiscovered. I envy those who were with you when you took your first steps, the first girl you kissed, the friends you told who you wanted to be when you were still in the making. I even envy the dogs who walked by your feet, put their muzzles on your knees, and looked into your eyes attentively, intelligently.

"If you think I'm mad, you're not mistaken. I am mad, mad—" she repeated rapturously, more and more loudly, as if even now she were not quite sure of herself. "You must tell me everything, so I can recover the parts of your life that I've missed. Tell me about your parents, your country, the books you loved, your dreams. When I've thought about you, I've had to tell myself every minute: I don't know, I don't know, and what joy the little word 'yet' brought me! I felt like a little girl in front of the locked door of a room in which nice surprises were being arranged. I told myself: He will tell me. He will let me into his life. What joys and discoveries I have to look forward to . . ."

He said nothing. He breathed deeply, passively observing the nuptial dances of the fireflies in the half-empty pool and the stars low in the sky. They seemed to fly toward the earth, for they dilated enormously in eyes that brimmed with tears from the strain.

"Tell me what you were thinking about," she begged him. "I want to be your companion even in the things that were only yours."

"Why did you bring me here?"

"I wanted us to be alone, completely alone. Dinner will be served soon. The staff will disappear, the guests will sit down, and then we can go. The whole wing of the hotel is empty because of the end-of-season painting. I looked out for myself. Moving wasn't necessary; they refurbished the room while I was out in the villages. We must wait."

The duality of her thinking took him by surprise—the shrewd calculation, the avoidance of risk, the adaptation to local customs, then this sudden outburst of pent-up feeling, the predatory acquisitiveness, the desire to possess him with all his past, for she must already have taken the future for granted.

"We'll go soon," she whispered, enjoying the impatience with which he waited for her; at least that was how she had understood his question. She reached out and put her hand on his temple, outlining the edge of his ear with her fingertips until he trembled all over with desire. She bent over and the frames of their chairs tapped each other; she wanted to say something or to kiss him, but they heard the crunching of gravel nearby. Two men emerged from behind a corner of the building and came toward the edge of the pool, their footsteps tapping loudly on the tiled walk. They stopped for a moment, watching the fireflies at their frolics. One threw away a cigarette; its red fire, crudely material and inharmonious, made an arc in the air and went out. The other twice dug up a fistful of gravel and dashed the reflections of the stars to bits. They seemed to be speaking Italian, which here in India had a familiar ring for Istvan, though he did not understand it. They walked away unhurried. They did not see the pair lounging in the chairs.

The fingers Margit had put on his lips Istvan held lightly in his teeth. He moved his head and cradled it in her hand; he smelled the faint odors of medicine and nicotine and the fragrance of her skin.

In front of them velvety greenish lights rose and fell, making illegible signs in the air. The image of wide pastures returned:

the grass, the barely perceptible smell of smoke, or rather of white ashes from burnt stalks, for the campfire had gone out long ago.

"Very well. I will tell you," he began, deliberating over his words. She embraced him warmly and removed her hand. She pressed her fingers under his arm and rested her cheek against his shoulder.

"I lay on the ground—not on the grass, for it had been trampled away to nothing. Only on the ground. It was not hard at all. It was like a body, like flesh. I felt at one with it, as if it were a dog's belly and I her puppy. Around me the grass that was not pressed down by my weight bristled like an animal's coat, a pelt smelling lightly of the earth's perspiration and giving off a vapor under my warm hand. The dew had fallen. The herdsman was dozing not far away, but was so cut off from the world by his peaceful sleep, so oblivious to a call, that it was as if he were not there. In the deep dusk I heard only the steps of horses, the dry clicking as their teeth cut the grass, their snorting and sighing. At moments they pressed so near that I felt the turf tremble as their hooves struck it. I smelled their odor, wild, bracing as the lash of the willow switch on our naked calves and thighs when we rode bareback, driving the galloping herds to bathe in the river."

He turned his head toward her and spoke into her dry, fragrant hair. Only now, with his lips, did he feel its firmness and buoyancy.

"Aren't you afraid of the stars? Raise your head and look. They hang over us in the vastness of the sky, in space the mind can hardly encompass. They may have already gone dark, but the blue fire of their light will flow toward us for centuries. During the day they retreat. At night they take advantage of the time when we sleep and are not watching to come closer to the earth.

"Everyone has his own star. It waits for him. Everyone—and you, and I. Its wings flutter like a crystal hawk's and give off sparks. When someone dies, his star falls like a spider down its thread somewhere on the horizon. They threaten, they warn. They spin their beams into the eye, into the heart, which feels the omen and beats with agitation.

"To travel between them, to climb with the eye, higher and higher . . . Don't you feel the earth under you fall away as you hang like dandelion fluff tossed about on a light breeze? How hard it is to return from those intoxicating heights, from that dizzying flight toward the earth, into cramped, sleepy, torpid flesh!

"I looked for a star that would give me a sign, stand out from the rest, wink as if to greet me. I looked until the tears came. I felt the rotation of the earth, the circulation of my blood, the sap in the plants. Sometimes it seemed that I would fly up, weightless, drawn by them with irresistible force, and never return. The earth would awake and forget about me as if I had only been a dream. I clutched at the grass. I clung to the sod with my arms spread. Under my back I felt every node, every lithe stem. The trampling of horses close by, striking the ground as if it were a drum, and the dull pulse of the prairie soothed me. I slept with a feeling that I had been rescued—not that day, but it would surely come, surely . . ."

She trembled and clung to him, pressing with her fingers, burying them in his arm. All around them the fireflies' little green flames moved in their puckish orbits, and on the surface of the pool below, the reflections of drowned stars quivered.

"I don't want," she said like a small child, "do you hear, I don't want—"

He took her in his arms and kissed her hungrily, avidly. She did not resist. He nestled his face in the hollow of her shoulder and pressed his cheek to her neck. He absorbed her with every breath; he satiated himself with the fragrance of her skin, which immediately went moist and clung to his as if there were no boundary between their bodies. Their breaths mingled. Their mouths opened deeply; their tongues met.

Through the dusky park, now outlined with pulsating lights, rolled the boom of a gong. It throbbed with a hard, painful note. Suddenly she pushed against Istvan's chest and struggled free of his arm.

"Please—let me go."

Reluctantly he obeyed. They lay beside each other like swimmers carried onto a shoal washed by waves. They knew that the next tide would engulf it, and that night was before them; that in this joining, long and splendid as a battle for life, they would draw near each other, deepen their intimacy and, finally, be one. The night was warm and thick as a black fleece in which they would be hidden until dawn came like a silver mirror, full of light, color, and twittering hubbub.

They heard the voices of guests hurrying to dinner. Figures in white moved about in the glow of lights half hidden among sprays of leaves. They lay with hands barely touching, every nerve vibrating.

At last the bustle at the hotel died away completely, and such a silence ensued that they could hear the jingling tick of the watch on the hand that cushioned her head.

"I was afraid," she accused herself. "You are forgetting that this is India and they can hear us."

"Who?"

"The dancing gods who jeer, mock, revel in tormenting their adherents, and are extremely jealous of human happiness." She raised herself a little and leaned over. Suddenly, to his consternation, he felt her warm, moist lips pressed to his hand.

"What are you doing?" he bridled. He would have been less startled if she had put out a lighted cigarette on his skin.

"Istvan, I'm happy." She rolled her head over his hand, sweeping it with her hair, warming it with her breathing. "You'll never understand. I've found myself—"

His heart beat violently. Its pounding, not in his chest but in his throat and ears and through his body, and the dull muted roar of the surging blood, were like the blows of a hammer.

They started away, unhurried, keeping even more than a normal distance between them. Walking on the dry lawn, they passed the illuminated pergola and the doorkeeper's lodge, which was shining like a lighthouse. They made their way straight into the darkness of the long veranda and toward the door of her room. As she groped for her key, Margit felt his hot hand on her fingers. He had remembered that the lock was stubborn, and that gesture of readiness to help open the door revealed his tension and impatience.

Inside, a little lamp had been lighted by a maid. Its low beam fell on the neatly made bed. The coiled mosquito netting hung over it like a white turban.

"Wait," she said in an undertone, restraining him with a hand that he pressed to his cheek and touched with his lips. She looked at him with immeasurable tenderness. She was filled with a peaceful joy; I have him. He is mine.

"Shall I turn it out?"

"No. For you I would undress in the middle of Delhi." She tossed her head provocatively. Her hair rippled onto her shoulders.

He followed her with his eyes to the door of the bathroom. He heard the light rasp of a zipper, the hiss and flutter of silk pulled quickly down. He undid the knot of mosquito netting; it uncoiled with sudden force and its white wisps lashed him in the face, releasing a smell of mouldering fabric, dust, and insecticide. The netting dropped, and veiled the whole bed; in the low light it looked like a transparent tent that had fallen to the earth.

He began to hurry. He threw off his sandals and tore away his shirt. His tie lay twisted like an injured snake. He heard the changeful hum of water as it beat on flesh and on the stone floor. He reached under his arm and noticed the pungent smell of sweat. Accursed India; he shook his head with a wry look. I must rinse off.

He waited. He lifted the thick white mesh and knelt on the bed, which gave under his weight. He waited, resting his hands on his thighs. His breathing was labored. It seemed to him that he filled the tent with the heat his body exuded through his bronze skin and black hair.

After all, this had happened once before—had certainly happened—he had been through it already. He had come to this room just as certain as he was tonight that Margit would be his, but he had left chastened. She had returned in his dreams, and he had had her, had taken her with all his might. And when he had raised his head in delight, it had seemed that their time was measured by a great pendulum sizzling in a fire. He knew that pendulum, knew it so that it filled him with pain and loathing. Don't call him back, forget, a voice admonished. Life belongs to the living. Hating himself, he triumphed over that other man. He was alive with male force: his torso glinted with veins of sweat, a different sweat than torture had drawn from that man's body.

He did not hear her step; she was barefoot. Only when she appeared leaning on the drooping net did he see that she was naked and wet. The partition bent at the touch of her hand and fell away.

He looked through the netting and saw the rising of her breasts, the lines of her hips and the dark triangle between her thighs. He moved toward her on his knees and rested his hands on hers. She was his already; only the dusty froth of white netting separated them. He wanted to kiss her, but the trace of mustiness and insecticide in the air put him off. He wanted to have her leaning on his chest, to press her until she lost her breath, until it hurt, and she would leap and toss in the circle of his arms like a fish caught by the gills. He raised the netting and saw her uncovered. Knees. Thighs. The eternal tremor that fills a man when he brings womanflesh out of hiding—familiar and mysterious, worthy of scorn, yet desired. The dream of boys. The lust of the eyes.

He threw off the netting above her head with one tug so that it flew behind his back, and then he encircled her, caught her in his arms, settled her on the sheet and explored her body with his lips, learning its parts by memory. He found her breasts docile to his hands; he took possession of her flat belly, nipped at her knees with his teeth as if they were apples. He divided her into sections with his looks: she was there—and then in an instant he forgot about her, lost in delight at her cool, refreshing skin, where perfect beads of water lingered, at the taste of that skin, which he knew now for the first time.

With his cheek he caressed the insides of her thighs, which were far smoother than the lips of a foal. He felt an overpowering joy in this voyage of discovery when she gave herself to him as if she were running out impulsively to meet him, then clung to him and trembled. He was, consciously, making his appeal to her body, not to her, and she was participating. He had bought off the resistance with caresses, by conspiring with the crew in spite of the commander, who might still be ready to mount a defense. The understanding between eager lips and the summits of her breasts; the absorption in her body, which did not annihilate but restored him; the shape of the ear remembered by the mouth; the fingers combing the flame of hair, the plucking of the fruit . . .

He stole a glance at her eyes, glowing with points of light, at her lips, half open in defenseless receptiveness and altered, unfamiliar, swollen with delight. She did not see him. She closed her eyes, she forgot him, though he felt her hands playing over him, grazing him, stroking him timidly, like swallows' wings stirring sparkles from the smooth blue surface of a pond. Almost sleepily she drew up her knees and opened them with a movement like a butterfly; in that unashamed, desirous yielding he saw a beauty that choked him. His arms to the elbow were under her back. His face was tangled in her crisp, fragrant hair. The coolness of her skin, pressed against his chest, vanished, and by now he did not know, could not feel, where his body ended and hers began as he passed beyond the boundary he had abolished with such joy. He enclosed her, he drew her into himself, and she was entwined with him; he was under her, on her, and in her.

"I want you so, Margit," he said, reeling as if something had struck him.

"You have me." He heard the words as if from a distance, from the depths of drowsiness, and he thought that he would never conquer her, never possess her heart, her imagination. That is why he had sought to reach an understanding with the inner secrets of her body, the interior of smooth moist satin, the sweet shell, as he whispered to her—true to the custom of conquerors naming each part of the new land as they please—in the mysterious language, like incantations, of the rites of love.

Unceasing entry: flight into clouds. And she understands, feeling the weight of him, seeing his uplifted head, his tanned neck bent outward, she knows that in this moment, though she is the cause of all his exultation, he has almost forgotten her, he has soared and is far away. Margit rocks wildly, like a wave in a boat's wake, squeezes and curls.

She moans—a moan that is the delight of a man, like the last voice of an expiring enemy. Her teeth are parted, her lips thick, her eyes swimming, too clouded to receive the light. It is as if she were in agony, and her face should frighten but only delights him. At last he has what he so doggedly pursued, has it, though he wishes this flight would go on forever. And by now she is conscious of him again, making certain that he is there, blushing as if caught sleeping, ashamed that she abandoned him for a moment to be enclosed in herself, happy now that she could have made him such a gift.

Suddenly, as he wrings his tense hands and falls on her breasts with his warm lips wide open and creeps toward her neck, Margit whispers in his ear, "Ay-ker." She pronounces it in English, "Ay-ker," and after a long moment of mild stupefaction, he comprehends: Icarus. He only smiles.

They lie beside each other under the white cone of mosquito netting, their bodies, slippery with sweat, resting like animals herded into a shelter, animals who know and trust each other. Margit's fingers wander around his chest. Her lips touch it lightly and brush his arm. He takes her hand, puts the ends of her fingers to his lips and whispers:

"Thank you."

Chapter VI

"Repeat his exact words to me again." The ambassador's face was porous, like a cheese sprinkled with cattle salt. A fold of puffy razor-scraped cheek drooped above his fist as he patiently calculated the level of threat. Malevolent intent showed in his dark eyes, which were swollen with sleeplessness. His thinning black hair was streaked with bristling gray like pale lichen on a dry branch.

"So Krishan shows himself ungrateful," he mumbled. "I expected this. People like that always take kind gestures for signs of weakness. We will have to protect ourselves from his greed and stupidity, which could harm us. Yes—above all, he is stupid. Don't deny it: stupid, for he doesn't know that I have him in the palm of my hand." Kalman Bajcsy stretched out a bloated paw with glistening lines of sweat and slowly squeezed it into a fist. "He hasn't a chance of shaking us down. But a good lawyer might come in handy."

Istvan thought immediately of the "philanthropist": Attorney Chandra of the ageless face and diminutive, almost boyish figure, the Hindu who liked difficult cases. He did not hasten to offer advice, however, since the ambassador not only had not asked for it, but had not even confided to him the true cause of the dispute with the dismissed chauffeur.

Bajcsy's light, airy clothing of black alpaca, long forgotten in Europe, still passed as stylish here. The edge of his collar had a greasy gleam, and when Bajcsy raised his hand to rub his balding crown, Terey spied a white salt stain under his arm.

The ambassador nodded his head and blinked. "Thank you," he said in an easygoing tone that proceeded from a sense of his own dignity and his strength, which could destroy his opponents.

That "thank you," which seemed to admit him to partnership, filled Terey with aversion, vague uneasiness, and a feeling of guilt. It seemed to him that he had abused the driver's trust—that he had sold him out and received nothing in exchange, not even one piece of silver.

He walked down the hall, brooding. The secretary's door was open, as if he had expected the counselor to pass by.

"Look in for a moment," Ferenc called, springing up from behind his desk. "It's getting infernally hot. The boss is going to Shimla in two days. Things will be quiet."

"About time. He isn't looking especially well." Terey frowned. "The heat is hard on him."

He did not admit that Bajcsy had not even mentioned to him that he intended to take a holiday. A sudden cheerfulness overtook him, for the ambassador's leaving was a sign that the vacation season was beginning for all of them, or in any case an easing of the strict observance of schedules, the long stints at paperwork, the obligatory rituals. He saw opening before him the exciting prospect of freedom, an opportunity to vanish from his colleagues' eyes. No one would object even if he took a few days away; among the staff there was a mutual understanding about such things.

"He has reasons." Ferenc looked him in the eye. "A ridiculous affair. And he is not in the bloom of youth. Look—" he pushed aside the shade and blinding white light poured through the window—"a sky like sheet metal. It's enough to overheat the motor of a car, let alone his old, worn-out heart. The sooner he goes to the mountains the better. We will breathe more easily."

He let go of the shade and the scorching glare dimmed. It was a relief.

The secretary's appearance was impeccable: his figure was trim, his collar unwilted, his tie flawlessly knotted. He was the model of the trusted civil servant who, whatever his own ambitions, is too loyal, controlled, and good-natured, even if his superior is no longer secure in his position, to give away any of his secrets, or to indulge in witticisms or gossip at his expense. He knows that such behavior might cement his popularity for the moment, but that in the hands of alert competitors it could become a hindrance, however slight, to his advancement in the bureaucratic hierarchy. For him, to know means adroitly to revise his way of proceeding, not to lapse into familiarity, to distance himself discreetly from some people while striving for the regard of others. To know, to be cognizant, above all for his own purposes, not for social display. He does not parade the fact that he is privy to inside information, of no interest to the general public, about political actions—probative measures involving discreet requital for services, or honorable removal from the scene for a time—and to secrets about the patronage that governs postings to diplomatic missions abroad. Of course, the most coveted postings were to the "dollar zone," not within the "peace camp."

"I have a favor to ask you, Terey," Ferenc began, moistening the wrapper of a dried-out cigarette with the tip of his tongue. "Are you ordering very much whiskey from Gupta this month?"

"No. I have enough for a while."

"Could you buy me two dozen? Better yet, to save yourself the bother, simply sign the form and I will do it myself." He had already taken a printed slip from a drawer and put it in front of Istvan. "Don't forget your identification number. It isn't valid without that."

"Are you planning a party?"

"The ambassador is leaving, and you will be away yourself," he said with an understanding smile, "for certainly you want to go here and there. India lures you. All the social obligations connected with the embassy will fall on my wife and me. With the new customs barriers, alcohol has become a luxury. The Hindus gravitate to us like flies to honey. The thirst grows as the prices rise. It's a good thing we are not obliged to pay additional duty."

Terey, standing in front of the secretary's desk, signed the order form.

"The identification number is easy to remember: four, two twos, and three."

"Four, two twos, and three," Ferenc repeated automatically. "Yes, that is easy. It is better that the boss is going away. It is healthier for us all." He led Terey toward the door. "A ridiculous affair, but it may be the end of him. Anyhow, best not to speak of it."

"Indeed, best not to talk freely about the matter." He nodded, not wishing to confess that he was still in the dark about things that were evidently known to others. In the embassy, only Judit operated on the principle that she knew nothing, that each new piece of information was a surprise to her. Only the slight corrections she inserted when one shared secrets with her attested that she had known the sequence of events perfectly well, and probably much earlier. But her vocal signs of gratitude and sincere elation preserved her visitors' agreeable illusions that she had been caught unaware and dazzled by the news they conveyed.

Curious and a little disquieted, Istvan took refuge in his office and decided to ask her some artful questions, or at least promised himself to do so. He was anticipating a busy day; a visit from Jay Motal, with his nagging pleas for an expense-paid trip to Hungary, would not be the most agreeable part of it. Fortunately he remembered Ferenc's look of mocking gravity and his quiet, calming observation:

"Do not refuse him. Only say that the matter is being considered by several of us in turn, that we make decisions as a collegial body, and that the petitioner is notified of them at the appropriate time. The use of the plural deflects the blame and resentment. You will meet him in company; why offend him? We will let him go on expecting a miracle."

As he looked over the letters waiting to be answered, his eyes fell on Ilona's handwriting. He was saddened by the dull account, the detailed recital of everyday doings, the praise of their younger son's drawings, and the complaints about the neighbor on the floor above, who had beaten a carpet on her balcony and sent dust flying into their open window at dinnertime. He could more easily imagine that roll of coconut matting falling down and blotting out the light in the room than Ilona, who would hurry to shut the window, clenching her teeth; indeed, she would never lower herself to brawl with the neighbor. It was hard for him to admit to himself that with the cooling of his feelings, every word of this letter, rather than connecting him to his distant home and embodying their affection, seemed annoying, even distasteful. He would not put in so many words the bitter thought: it is of no concern to me.

The letter fell from his fingers and lay among the other papers, the unfulfilled requests, the bulletins printed on the duplicating machine, the newspapers with circled headlines—lay in the heap of litter, mute, dispensable. It was impossible that he had erred when he took her in his arms for the first time . . . when he had happily put his hand on her swelling abdomen, taut as a ripe fruit, and felt the helpless drumming of tiny heels on the walls of their fleshy prison. No. No, he answered himself as he drew a zigzag with his finger in the dust that had drifted through the chinks. The sun was burning outside the window; the bluish-gray trunk of a palm slashed the sky, a metallic geyser of motionless fronds. A green fly was battering itself against the mesh, buzzing in distress. Its lament had summoned white lizards, who scurried over the wall from three sides.

"Margit." His lips parted and his face softened as if her very name, uttered like a call for help, had the power of an incantation.

Two nights with Margit. So it was possible to have women, and then a wife and children, and finally one day discover that one had not known what love could be. With astonishment he understood how the significance of every word, gesture, look had been transformed. He felt again the rhythm of accelerated breathing, the fragrance of hair and skin, and one's own smell, all intensified by the nearness of bodies and the warmth of the Indian night that swayed on the ghostly sail of mosquito netting.

And then that sudden sinking into sleep with his face nestled in her arm—sleep, which made him feel ashamed. A half-conscious existence, when from nebulous memories of earliest childhood the sheltering nearness of a woman's body exuded peace. He saw the rust-tinted sheen of Margit's hair, the blue of her wide-open eyes, the curve of her inclined head resting on her elbow.

"Didn't you sleep?" he asked, feeling guilty and hoping that she had awakened only a moment before.

"Why, no. It would be too bad to take my eyes off you," she whispered tenderly. "I can sleep all those nights when you won't be with me. Those empty nights."

And then he truly woke up. Under the wings of mosquito netting a blue remnant of darkness lingered. The yellow light of a lamp standing on the floor was fading. Not trusting his watch, he pushed aside the shade and saw the sky like a bowl of mercury, the grass without a trace of dew. He heard the cries of birds flying in pairs toward the pools around the Taj Mahal; their pipings were telling him that the approaching day would be a torrid one. He slipped the curtain into place, trying to lengthen the soothing shadow, but the glare was already squeezing through every chink, and kindling on the floor. So he sprang back and embraced Margit hungrily, as if these were their last moments.

"What, then? What happened? You see, I'm here." She was moved; she held him close.

Then the quick, light movement of hands, the shower, the warmth of the palm sliding over the bare back in the spray from the copper sieve, so chilly it brought on a shiver. It was bracing; with faces raised they gave themselves over to its cool crystalline lash. The water smelled of the pond and mildew. It washed away the torpor of the night. Without drying himself he hastily pulled on a shirt. It stuck to his chest, but the wet spots dried quickly. By the time he raised his clenched fingers to Margit's lips and slipped out under the vine-covered reticulated roof, it was broad daylight.

In front of the fishbowl that was the doorman's lodge a short servant with thin legs like a crane was sprinkling the gravel drive from a watering can, deluding himself that he was protecting it from the haze of dust that had settled on the leaves. The doorman slept with his forehead on his hand; his hair hung in glistening coils on the back of his bent neck. A cat licked its back paw and outspread toes and blinked its yellow eyes in an almost roguish grin. Terey exhaled deeply: the air smelled of hay, the bitter breath of leaves, and tar. As he opened the door of his room he looked around him like a man pursued, but the servant went on sprinkling the drive with a circular motion, absorbed in his work. He did not notice that someone had passed by in the shade of the pergola. The time for waking had not come yet and the hotel guests slept heavily. He could be certain that no one had seen him.

"COUNSELOR, SIR"—HE HEARD the discreet voice of the Indian clerk—"are you ready to see Jay Motal? He says he has an appointment. He is waiting below."

"I'll be right down," he answered. But when the clerk had quietly shut the door, he sat for a moment more, rubbing his eyelids with his fingertips as if he had been wakened from sleep.

In the dim hallway, under the watchful eye of the caretaker, the lanky Hindu sat with his legs, in wide blue trousers, drawn back under his seat. His hands, dark against the background of his white shirt, were adjusting the flat, grease-stained knot of his tie. There was a watchful readiness in his eyes, which looked out keenly from behind hornrimmed glasses. He had an air that was at once servile and insolent. He was familiar with the etiquette of greeting; he was forming conjectures about what considerations would be brought to bear on his case and if the conversation about it would take place in the hall, among the dusty palm leaf fans in wooden boxes, or if he would be invited upstairs to the counselor's office. Determined to steer the meeting toward a conclusion favorable to his interests, he rose obligingly, picked up his portfolio, which was made of torn paper mended with tape, and stepped up to meet Terey.

"Most sincere greetings," he began, bowing his head, "and very best regards from Attorney Chandra—who would like very much to meet with you," he added significantly, leaving Terey to conclude that the lawyer had mentioned nothing in particular and that Jay Motal, boasting of his acquaintance with officials at the Hungarian embassy, had simply been eager to affirm his willingness to convey greetings.

"Thank you. How nice to see you. We have not yet received a disposition of your case from the ministry, but I think that no news is good news—that you may hope for a favorable outcome." He saw a glint of misgiving in the Hindu's eyes, but the man seized the offensive.

"All ministries are alike. In ours as well it is easier for them to order an article than to tap discretionary funds for payment. I am prepared, if it helps my cause, to wait long and patiently. For the time being I am gathering materials and acquainting myself with the history of your country, especially with the issues of recent years. It is not at all easy to gain an understanding of the political forces that determined how the republic would arise. I have my own ideas, which might awaken your interest, counselor, and induce you to support my plan to write a book on Hungary. But surely we will not talk here; perhaps we will take refuge in the quiet of your office." He took Terey by the elbow as if they were intimates and led him toward the stairs, politely cocking his head, ready to take fright at the first gesture of impatience, to withdraw into the posture of humble petitioner.

Terey allowed himself to be steered, however. He acquiesced easily to these tactics, knowing what their results would be. He only wanted to guide the discussion to a figure that would not seriously unbalance his budget.

When they were sitting at a small table, Jay Motal with quick fingers pulled a box of cigarettes toward him and placed one in a yellowed ivory holder. He waited for Terey to give him a light, taking the courteous gesture as a point in his own favor, and began to expound his theory.

"Your country is different from those that surround it. You were always a kingdom," he began, looking the counselor doggedly in the eye. "You have many gypsies among you."

Intrigued, Terey listened, wondering where the impertinent foolishness of this windbag would lead. The writer, forgetting about the smoldering cigarette, unfolded his vision of the formation of the Hungarian state. As gypsies unquestionably descended from inhabitants of Rajasthan attested, it must have come from India and—after centuries of migration and conquest—eventually reached the fertile Danubian plains. Acknowledgment of blood kinship was the greatest compliment, and there were proofs: the predilection for raising oxen, for violin music, for dancing, with the hand beating the rhythm on the heel of knee-high boots . . . though here in India, high boots had been replaced by wide leather straps over the ankle, hung with bells and rattles. And the long observed and respected division into aristocracy and peasants was a distinct reflection of the caste system.

The tone of this recital, which was supposed to dazzle the counselor, changed imperceptibly. Now the man was saying that his services were much sought after by the Germans, and that they would be delighted for him to write about the Federal Republic, rebutting the stubborn calumnies it had suffered from nations genuinely harmed by the late war, but unsophisticated in their thinking, incapable of a proper appreciation of Germany's historic mission and the magnitude of the sacrifice that heroic nation had made to save a free—what an expressive accent he placed on the word!—a free Europe from the onslaught of Bolshevik barbarism.

He described the difficulties of extracting the truth from conflicting analyses, from the sources that were eagerly pushed forward. He implied discreetly that he was ready at any moment to hear the enlightened counsel of qualified people, but that the memoirs of such distinguished personalities as Churchill certainly provided material for reflection, especially the cutting designation "Rakosi and his gang." It would pain him if his lack of knowledge were used to the disadvantage of Hungary, with which he felt such kinship. But the Germans had shown great interest in his creative projects and were prepared to support him financially, and he must unfortunately take that into consideration.

"How much better it would be"—he spread his hands as if in benediction—"if the embassy would arrange a journey to Hungary for me and pay for a three-month stay. If I could see the changes resulting from the revolution at close range, I could form my own opinion and marshal unassailable arguments which, when published in the Indian press, could promote friendship between the two nations and spread progressive socialist thought."

His sing-song speech, naive inventiveness, and timorous faith that he was charming the counselor, securing support and perhaps even money, aroused pity. He knew how to use his gift of expression; his politeness and readiness to concede a point were ingratiating; he was inclined, like a bird, to be satisfied with a seed graciously thrown, providing the stooping to retrieve it did not require too great an effort. He had already stayed much longer than he had intended, watchfully observing the counselor's varying moods. The coffee served by the caretaker bolstered his certainty that this was his lucky day.

The sun burned behind the curtains. The cicadas stirred the sultry air with the fluttering of their wings until the silvery jingle became anesthetizing.

Jay Motal, playing with a pack of cigarettes, was just signaling his intention to force the question of a small advance when the telephone shattered the drowsy atmosphere. It was Pereira. He had never called the embassy before.

Terey was gripped by a fear that something had gone wrong at his house. He thought a servant must have gotten into a brawl with the Sikh neighbor. He had often been told of the bearded warriors' fits of rage, set off by the very raising of a finger toward the sky, which signifies noon. At that time their wits wander as the sun goes to their heads, which are overheated by topknots of hair, untouched by scissors, and thickly pleated turbans. He saw a blackening corpse on the concrete yard and a silent circle of figures draped in sheets. Meanwhile Pereira's languid voice apologized interminably for his boldness in disturbing sahib at work.

He wanted to put an abrupt end to the polite verbiage that trailed like a peacock's tail when he noticed that his visitor was watching him closely, trying to gather whether the telephone call was undercutting his case, influencing the counselor's treatment of his request.

At last the cook, as if unwrapping a gift from a flowery scarf, lowered his voice and said, "That lady is in the bathroom. She asked not to speak to anyone, only to leave her things and come back in the afternoon. I ask, should I keep her here? Serve tea? I considered it my most pleasant duty, in spite of her stipulations, to let you know."

His tension dissolved; Margit had arrived. He wanted to run. He was filled with joyous impatience. Let the devil take the whole embassy! He could disappear for an hour. There were no problems requiring immediate solutions. There was only this would-be freeloader. He would have to get rid of him.

"Of course, keep her there. Receive her as I would do. I'll be right home," he told Pereira. He hung up and looked around for a cigarette. Jay Motal grudgingly pushed him a pack he had marked for his own.

"Please submit your ideas—which, by the way, are most interesting—to me in written form. Please provide a clear conspectus of your work, point by point, without dwelling on details. That will expedite the decision."

He saw the Hindu's face turn to stone. Jay Motal sensed that his labor was wasted, that an agreement about the journey he dreamed of would be put off yet again—his flight from India to the gentleman's country, to England. Hungary was a stage in that exodus. If only he could reach Europe! That was not a vast continent like Asia: from Budapest, from Prague, he would be so close to London. He knew that it was much easier to create the yet-unwritten book with the ring of the voice, the wheeling gesture of the hand outlining its structure in trails of cigarette smoke, than to hammer out an outline of it. He feared the sardonic winks the embassy staff would trade behind his back as they ruffled through the papers on which would be written the synopsis of the future book. He fell from the height to which he had soared—the limit of his hopes—like a bird shot down, and the wings of his eloquence fluttered despairingly.

"That will require additional reading and the exclusive concentration of my attention on Hungarian affairs. It will occupy a great deal of my time," he began.

It was clear from the counselor's approving smile that that delay precisely suited his convenience—that in fact he was counting on it.

"It is only that work on the conspectus would limit my freelance earnings. I must refuse all orders for articles and perhaps even alienate my friends at the ministry with that refusal."

Yes—but that way lay defeat. Despising himself, he wondered what madness had induced him to expound on the yet imaginary book in such detail, to show the opponent his cards. He had lost. He must grovel, must beg. But he was spared that, for the counselor was in a hurry.

"Dear Mr. Jay Motal, I was perfectly aware of that," he said with businesslike gravity, "and for that reason we are of a mind to give you an advance—a modest one, for it is a question of an outline, only a few pages long, of a work not yet written, for which we will probably remunerate you as it progresses. Well, for this we will give—" he saw the Hindu's hungry look, saw as his eyes seemed to ooze through glasses smudged with greasy fingerprints. Motal moved his lips like a dog when a tasty bit of food is shaken in front of its nose. Terey was sorry for him. Thirty rupees; well, fifty.

But the Hindu was a good sport. He swallowed the unexpected promise of an advance without flinching. He saw the coming months as a row of rooms full of lights, where across every threshold a hand waited to count out bank notes. His childish joy mingled with calculation and a complacency that impelled him first to take what was offered, and only then to ponder how to extricate himself from his obligations.

Terey did not unleash a new torrent of talk, but only reached for his wallet and counted out the money. He asked for a receipt. Those simple actions brought a natural end to the conversation. As he was conducted to the hall, Jay Motal thanked him profusely for understanding that he was acting from the best intentions, and for his support. Istvan stood without smiling, imagining what it would be like if with one nudge of his knee he could kick the man out of the embassy into the blistering glare.

He did not return to his office. He only telephoned to apprise the secretary that he had an appointment in the city and was going out.

"For long?" Ferenc asked.

He wanted to shout, "Forever!" But he mastered himself and assured him that he would either be back after an hour or call to inform him if he had to prolong the interview. As he climbed into the car, he glanced at his watch. Not even ten minutes had passed since the cook called; only to him did it seem much longer.

When Istvan put on the brakes in front of his gate the watchman, in a floppy linen hat, locked his knees with their pink scars, beat on the cracked ground with his bamboo stick, and announced with menacing movements of his jauntily twirled-up mustache, "Milady is here."

He had hardly pushed aside the vines when the cook, who had been watching the door, appeared like a specter and whispered, "Milady is drinking tea."

They were handing him off one to the other, making signs like partners. Both announcements had the ring of bandits' speech: we have her. Istvan did not fail to notice that the cook appreciated the significance of this visit: he was wearing an unpatched shirt of immaculate, gleaming white.

"Will madam be here for dinner? Should I buy something good?"

"I don't know. But best to buy something. How much shall I give you?"

"Nothing, sir. I will take my money and bring back the bill." There was indulgent compassion in his look, as if he were a mother and Terey an only child who had just broken a vase. "That is a real lady."

Seeing him come in, Margit rose and extended both hands. There was an enchanting freshness and simplicity about her. Her modest dress in a vermilion pattern was pleasing to him. He remembered that they had chosen the material together under the arcades at Connaught Place. Her tawny complexion and heavy plaits of hair, so easy to arrange in becoming ways, were alluring.

A sudden radiance lit her blue eyes, and her mouth seemed to invite a kiss. He embraced her, rocked her lightly in his arms and caressed her with his lips. She rested her temple against his cheek and clung to him with her whole body.

"Oh, Istvan, Istvan, it's been so long since I've seen you," she lamented, nipping softly at the end of his ear with her teeth. "When the professor said he was coming to Delhi, I asked, I pestered him. Connoly, decent fellow that he is, promised to stand in for me."

They sat down beside each other. She held his hand tightly, as if she were afraid he would leave her. She told him of the arrival of a UNESCO commission which she was going to meet at the airport the next day. The program was limited to official ceremonies at which she should appear, maintain a presence, and offer to help entertain the visitors. Afterward she could disappear before she was caught up in the rituals of hospitality, the customary sightseeing of the city arranged by the hosts. She was only certain of having a free afternoon and night; she spoke of that openly, as if it were of equal importance to both of them.

"You will stay with me," he said, looking her in the eye. Her irises were crystalline as fruit drops; he remembered the rattle of the tin scoop in the glass jar as the shopkeeper spooned them out.

He had looked at them regretfully as they dropped onto the scale, for there were always so few in the little horn twisted from torn-off paper.

"Would that be wise?"

"Pity we're not Hindus. We could write everything off to predestination. I want you to stay."

"And I want to. You see that I came straight here. But won't it cause you trouble at the embassy? Won't everyone know?"

"If I know India, no. As things are, they had better get used to your being in my home, and without this smack of secrecy. You will be here, quite simply, as if it were your own house. That's the way it's going to be."

"You don't know what you're saying. After all, you have a wife. She may be far away, but she is your wife. People who have a regard for her will tell her. The situation will be painful."

"So what do you advise?"

"You mustn't change your schedule in the least. I can wait here or come at dusk. You can pay the servants for their silence. It's easy to make sure you are in their good graces."

"Confess: have you done that already? The cook called you a real lady."

"I gave him two rupees for carrying in the suitcase."

"And the watchman got something for opening the gate? Now I understand everything. You walked in here like a princess."

"Did I do badly? It's so easy to give them a little happiness. I wanted them to feel my joy."

He looked at her and was delighted: the straight nose, the light arch of the eyebrows, the darkened eyelids. How he loved her!

"Don't go to sleep." She took both his hands and, pressing them with her fingers, drew him toward her.

"No." He shook his head. "I was thinking how to force them to keep quiet. Probably I will frighten them a little so they will keep each other in check."

"Will that help? We have a battle ahead of us, and we can only count on ourselves."

Her fingers were moist from clasping his hands. When he bowed his head and touched them with his lips, he noticed that they smelled of medicine and nicotine. She smoothed a tuft of his hair—as one strokes a horse, he thought. He caught the subtle fragrance of her dress, of linen heated from the sun, which reached through the window like a white ingot. He felt the warmth of her thigh as he leaned against it, and a tingling swept over him.

"If you feel like it—only for a little while, even a moment—lie down with me."

"I do," she answered with such a jubilant readiness that he felt a catch in his throat. "But is it worth it for a moment?"

He laughed happily and helped her unfasten the back of her dress.

"Perhaps you'd at least lock the door. It's still daytime." She nestled against him.

"No one comes in here," he murmured with his lips pressed between her breasts, though he was not certain of that at all, for he knew how stupid the servants could be. He thought of the car, which he should have driven into the garage, of the key, which could be turned to open the door, yet he could not tear himself away from her. He drank her in like a man wandering in the desert who finally finds a spring and falls on it with open lips. He saw that her eyes were open wide, filled with delight and receptiveness.

They rested, lulled by the double echo of the toy peddler's fife and the shrieks of children in his wake. Silence returned; there was only the seller of ice cream crooning his song of praise, "Frozen cream, very good, sweet like honey, vanilla, pistachio."

The watchman brandished his cudgel and with a hoarse cry drove some boys away from the Austin. The splash of water from an opened hydrant formed a counterpoint to the jingle of crickets. The young banana trees were drooping from the heat; evidently the gardener was trying to revive them.

They felt a profound release. They were not hurrying anywhere; they were not even clinging to each other. They knew they were comfortable, ready. Their breaths could mingle, their lips touch, their eyelashes brush. "That was good," she said drowsily, putting her knee on him and stroking him lazily with her foot.

The telephone rang for a long time, but neither picked it up. They wanted nothing but each other. The world flowed by in soft notes that penetrated the walls of the house and died away, to repeat themselves in the mind again after a while.

Margit was still combing her hair when he went out to the dining room. He saw the table set, the tea kettle swathed in a towel, and fresh flowers: snapdragons of rust and yellow. There was no one in the kitchen. Through the window he saw the servants sitting crosslegged in the shade, resting against the wall, amusing themselves by throwing a knife. The old soldier—the watchman—hit a matchbox set several paces away on the trampled path. He saw Terey through the windowpane and made a sign to the cook, who ran up full of reproaches.

"Why did sahib not ring for me?" he exclaimed accusingly. "I would have waited. But everything is ready for tea. The painter Ram Kanval telephoned to ask if you were coming. I did not know how to answer. He insisted that he would wait on the street corner. It is not easy to find his house."

Terey looked at the forehead creased with care, the gray stubble of hair, the eyes dimmed as if with fog.

"Listen," he began gravely. "Do you like being in my house?"

Pereira folded his hands prayerfully and beat them against his scrawny black chest until it rumbled.

"Sir, you know that you are my father and my mother. I and my family live in your shadow."

"What happens in this house remains between you and me. It is enough that the two of us know. I have a diamond ring, and you should be happy that you have a rich master. Do you understand?"

The black eyes glittered from under raised eyelids. He understood.

"But not everyone must know of it, for there are many who are jealous and greedy."

"Oh, yes, sir, there are many bad people."

"So if I hear from my friends, who hear from their servants and they from you, that you are talking about my ring, the price of which you do not know, you may not return to the kitchen again, even if the door is open. I will take another cook who will work for me and be silent. Do you understand?"

The cook looked at him attentively, broodingly.

"And if the sweeper—for he is able to enter the rooms—and the watchman—he walks around the house at night and sleeps on the threshold like a dog—if they let the cat out the bag?"

"Warn them that I will dismiss everyone, for I like peace and quiet. And you know, cook, that I do not speak for the pleasure of hearing my own voice."

"Yes, sir," he said worriedly. "What time should dinner be?"

"At nine. Make the bed in the spare room. Milady is my guest and will spend the night here," he said with quiet emphasis. "You are a wise man, not young. Remember what you said after you welcomed her: 'That is a real lady.' That is what I want you to say even when she leaves this house in the morning."

He saw beads of sweat on Pereira's forehead. A diagonal shadow slashed the blind yellow wall of the yard. Large tin bins gave off the bitter smell of fermenting peelings; big winged cockroaches whirred under the lids.

The concrete had been wetted down and was drying unevenly. Istvan smelled the sickening sweet odor of manure from open sewage ditches. Languid, throaty voices came from beyond the wall, and, from farther away, the tinkling of bicycle bells. The hour was approaching when people would swarm out of work and the road would be overrun with packs of cyclists, arms round each other, pedaling lazily.

"Should I serve dinner at the table?"

"Yes. Only wash your hands. You've been leaning on the ground," he commanded, and went to his room for Margit. She greeted him with a conspiratorial lowering of the eyelids and parted her lips as he poised above them like a hawk.

"Come: a 'very aromatic cup of tea' awaits you," he said invitingly, mimicking the cook. "You can even spoil the taste with a spoonful of fresh cream."

"Don't let my unexpected arrival disrupt your schedule for the day," she said, munching toast with orange marmalade over melting butter. "I'll gladly wait for you here. But I'd be happy if you could take me with you, so we wouldn't be separated, if only—"

"I was supposed to visit the painter—Ram Kanval—but I can call that off at a moment's notice. You know him. He was at Grace's wedding. He helped us buy the sandals."

She looked at him with eyes alight.

"It would be nice to pay Grace a visit. After all, you are friends."

"I don't know if the rajah has taken her off somewhere," he said, wishing to defer such a meeting. "They are always traveling."

"Find out. Call. She would be hurt if she knew I was in Delhi and didn't look in on her. I wonder if marriage agrees with her. Has she changed much? She's really an Englishwoman, not a Hindu."

"So I thought, but you will not know her now. She is an orthodox Hindu. From the very day of her wedding I've lost contact with her," he hedged. "With him as well. He stopped spending time at the club."

"Confess." She wagged a finger. "You were a little in love with her. Nothing strange about it; she's lovely. If I were a man . . ."

"I didn't know you then," he said, seizing on a sincere justification.

"If her marriage pained you that much, we mustn't go there," she agreed easily. "Only take me with you now. Will that painter tell the whole city about our visit?"

"I don't think so." Better an excursion to old Delhi than an evening at the rajah's, he thought. He was afraid for Grace and Margit to meet, afraid of the sparkle of happiness in Margit's eyes and the little, impulsive gestures of intimacy that a jealous woman understands at once. "Good. We'll go to Kanval's studio."

All the servants were sitting by the blind wall of the yard, carefully observing their departure. So they saw at a glance what was happening, and cleared out of the house after finishing their duties to leave us at our own disposal, he thought, and was pleased. Well, we will see; if he manages to make them the guardians of our secret, I know how to reward their silence.

As he drove the Austin, passing cyclists hurtling along in fluttering white pyjamas with a swinging motion like butterflies in flight, he saw Margit's hands in a patch of sunlight shining through the windshield. They lay so near that he could hardly keep from taking a hand off the steering wheel and stroking them. He had to slow down on the old stretch of road; the car floundered among the tongas, whose drivers did not give way, though the blare of the horn disturbed them. They rose and looked around helplessly but had nowhere to move, so they huddled down again on the stout shafts between the withers of the slow-moving long-horned oxen. The odor of laboring beasts seeped into the car together with the smell of manure and the acrid smoke from the fires burning in front of clay huts.

Then the real houses began, four- and even five-story houses, and a few trees, which in spite of the long drought had not lost their leaves. A new neighborhood was growing up, its streets as yet unnamed, but, as usual in India, all the inhabitants knew each other, knew even too much about each other.

He spotted Ram Kanval from a distance, standing on the curb—tall, slender, turning his head like a hen who has lost her chick. He shouted imperiously at the tongas that were bearing down blindly on the braking car, converging with a creaking of axles and lowing of oxen. The painter settled into the back seat with relief, pushed his head between Istvan and Margit, and showed Istvan how to maneuver the car to his house. The road had been dug up in a few places for the laying of water pipes and cable.

Groups of children were playing on the road; the car attracted their attention. They ran behind it, gathered around it, and stroked its heated metal body as if it were a cat. The painter appointed two boys from the neighborhood to guard it. They shouted at the girls not to smudge the fenders with their fingers.

"We live on the third floor, Miss Ward," he explained as he walked across the threshold. "We have four rooms. My studio, however, is on the roof, in the barsati. I have more light on the roof. Perhaps you will come in for coffee?"

The doors of all the apartments opened onto the staircase. Children ran in, calling to their elders, who looked with curiosity at the Europeans.

"They are envious of such a visit," Kanval explained, obviously flattered. "I must whisper a word to them about whom they have the honor of seeing. I really had lost hope that you were coming.

Diplomats are so quick to promise, and then they disappoint. I am a painter, not a merchant or an official. I do not count in the scheme of things. I am not important to anyone."

The cramped stairs, splattered with chewed betel nuts as if with clotted blood, led them toward the aromas of kitchen spices and scalded coconut oil. Children clung to the banisters, hoping to brush against the European clothing, which was a novelty to them.

"My youngest sister." Kanval introduced a petite girl in a cherry-red sari, who bowed demurely. "Will you have some cake? I did not send for cakes while I was still uncertain that you were coming. They are only good if they are fresh."

Terey knew what this really meant: the painter had not been able to afford to arrange a party. If the guests had failed to appear, his family would have reproached him bitterly for wasting their money.

"No, thank you," he answered for himself and Margit. "We have just had our tea."

"But you will not refuse coffee? It is just heating," Kanval said, catching the aroma. "Allow me to introduce a few members of my family." They were clustered in the doorway of the apartment as if they not only had no intention of inviting the visitors in, but were unwilling even to let a curious glance get past them.

"My father, the mayor emeritus." He presented a grizzled elderly man. "My brother-in-law is a real estate broker; he sells building lots. Oh, he makes money!" he added proudly, though the tired wisp of a man in a sport coat and a dhoti with rumpled skirts, from which spindly legs protruded above his sandals, did not look wealthy. There were two sisters, both married—as the two brunette heads bent, the partings of the hair blazed red with dye—and "my younger brother, a translator, who is working just now on a commissioned translation of *Crime and Punishment*. The author is Dostoevsky," he said, happy to display his knowledge.

The brother wore wire-rimmed glasses. He had the pale complexion of a man shut up in darkness for a long time and a thin mustache that grew in tufts near the ends of his lips.

"Do you know Russian, sir?" the counselor asked, grasping his soft, sticky hand.

"No. My brother translates from Bengali to Hindi," the painter interposed.

"With the help of an English version," the translator explained in a surprisingly deep bass. "I also cast horoscopes, but only for pleasure. Perhaps one of you would like—"

But Ram Kanval forestalled their responses.

"Another brother-in-law. A merchant, the owner of a large shop in Old Delhi. He could have one at Connaught Place, but there is less turnover there."

The powerfully built man moved majestically, as if to make others feel his wealth and importance. He pressed their hands and rebuked his wife, who was tittering, pointing to Margit's red hair, and whispering something to her sister.

"We will go up. There is a beautiful view from there," Kanval said to his family, as if he were a little disappointed by the turn the visit had taken. "Send us coffee."

"Is that the whole family?"

"Oh, no," he laughed, as if he had heard a good joke. "There are still my wife's parents, my wife, and too many children to weary you with counting. I have four myself, three sons and a daughter."

They climbed the steep stairs. They were relieved to emerge onto the flat roof, into the sun.

For economy's sake two buildings had been constructed together. Only parapets separated the roofs, forming enclosures like coops in which children were chasing each other. The barsati, a small room without a front wall that had been added onto the building like an unfinished toy, was intended to serve as a bedroom for servants in the summer. The painter had fitted it out as a studio. In place of a door he had nailed up a roll of matting. Apart from easels and bundles of pasteboard leaning against the wall, the only furnishings were a broken wicker chair strewn with a few magazines and a bed frame covered with a net of string. They walked to the edge of the roof and looked into the smoky space beyond it. The warren of buildings that was Old Delhi was darkening unevenly like a great rubbish heap. Beyond it they saw the red stony hill and the withered foliage of parks, through which the widely overflowing Yamuna glimmered with a shifting brilliance that was disconcerting.

On the flat roofs of the six-story buildings around them groups of women sat, inquiring intently about their neighbors' lives and commenting on events like a Greek chorus. A crowd of children sat on the parapet, pointing to the extraordinary visitors. As the painter approached they fled as lightly as startled sparrows.

"Those little imps," he said ruefully. "They have to sleep here. I am preparing for an exhibition, and they climb onto the roof and turn everything over, steal my brushes and paints and start painting themselves! I find traces of their frolics not only on the walls of the barsati, but on my own canvases."

"Can't you press them into service, use them as models?" Margit suggested. "Draw them into your work."

"I have tried. The whippersnappers are indefatigable with their tricks. They spy on me, they mimic me. Neighbors complained that two sheets had gone missing, that someone had cut them up and put them on a canvas. Inevitably I was suspected. It was hell for me, for of course the little devils had hidden them among my pictures."

He threw an old bathrobe onto the chair. It was streaked with paint; brushes had been wiped on it.

Margit, seated by the barsati wall, was finding it difficult to keep her attention focused on the paintings as he showed them; her eyes wandered over the rose and yellow walls of the distant houses, the clumps of trees, the palms with their arcing, jagged fronds lazily brushing a washed-out sky in which a few vultures hung motionless.

Terey sat by her on a pile of English magazines and old albums with ornate covers. The painter brought out paintings two at a time, leaning against the railing and looking uneasily at his guests, trying to read their responses in their faces before hearing their trite expressions of praise. The small fry crowded on the low wall between the roofs greeted each new painting with a chorus of laughter and applause, which must have irritated him greatly, for he turned toward them several times, pleading and threatening—or so at least it seemed to Istvan after the tension in the man's voice reached a nearly hysterical pitch. Only the presence of foreign guests, a rare occurrence, restrained Kanval from chasing the mischievous little rabble away.

The pictures, in a serene spectrum of gray and rose or vivid juxtapositions of ocher, yellow, and white, contained distorted outlines of houses and human figures, or perhaps only masses of human forms draped in gray sheeting. From them came the moan of warm earth devoured by drought, and the melancholy of sudden twilight.

"He doesn't know how to draw," a little girl squealed in English, hopping about on the wall. The little bells around her ankles jingled like sardonic laughter.

The viewing of the pictures, the choice of some for the upcoming exhibit, seemed a torment for the painter. He switched the canvases more and more quickly, astonished when Terey stopped him. This was real painting, perhaps more genuine because it had no market in the city. Even among the artist's own kindred and acquaintance it was seen as a wasteful obsession. To his overworked brothers-in-law, who were forced to chase every business opportunity that could bring in a few coins, the artist himself seemed an offensive idler maintained by their charity, and they were quick to make him feel it. Once in a gloomy moment he had confided to Terey that they had also turned his wife against him: she had refused to give him a carefully hoarded rupee for paints and paper.

"What do you think of this?" Margit asked in a whisper when Kanval had disappeared into the barsati. "It's good, isn't it? It would be cruel to praise it if you don't believe in his art."

"It is very good," he answered sincerely. "This one, for example, with a girl in a green sari, covered to her eyes, and the pairs of slender figures leaning toward each other, almost transformed into a pattern of plants—everything lighted from below by the fading orange fire that always burns in this country. I'd like to buy this picture."

"Unfortunately, I cannot sell it," the painter said, leaning out, "but I would gladly paint madam's portrait. I warn you in advance, so you will not be disappointed, that it will not look exactly like her; for that there are photographs. Your coloring appeals to me, the copper of your hair, the yellow dress, the violet tints in the flesh. If you find the time."

He looked at the girl as if he were recreating her as an arrangement of lines, a heap of geometric forms painted in one dimension. There was such delight in his eyes that Istvan thought sympathetically, Yes, he would need help, but perhaps he could manage to mount an exhibit in Budapest, especially if the one in Delhi brought favorable reviews.

"And would you not sell me that grayish-blue landscape?" Margit rose, pulling a painting from a stack of canvases that faced away from her. Their backs were covered with greasy stains that shone in the glow of the sinking sun.

"With the greatest pleasure. You have chosen well. If you will allow me, madam, I will make you a present of it after the exhibition. My paintings are deteriorating here. They have no purchasers among our people. I tell myself that we have not yet grown up. Nineteenth-century realism forms our tastes, and the English, or printers' calligraphy, imitations of decorative folk arts, superficiality—"

"No! I can guess how much this is worth. I cannot accept such gifts. Tell me, how much."

He hesitated, fearing to name too high a price, yet already feeling his triumph over his brothers-in-law when he should shove a coil of banknotes in their faces. Or perhaps better to say nothing, to save the money for canvas and paint, for a frame, which enhances a picture as a gown enhances the graces of a woman. At the same time he wanted to show his gratitude for Terey's favorable regard.

"Would one hundred rupees be too much?" he stammered at last.

"No. It is worth more."

"To a lover of art, in Europe, perhaps, but not here. Will you take it now, or may I still show it? I would place a card on it to say that it is sold, perhaps even with the price. That is how it is done: the picture will gain credence with snobs for whom the rupee is the measure of everything. It will be more attractive; it will serve as bait."

"You might put a higher price on the card." She shot him a conspiratorial look. "I will say that I have paid that much."

"Provided it's not too high," Istvan warned, "for then it begins to have the opposite effect: he came across a gullible foreigner, he succeeded in duping him, but we are wise to such tricks."

"You are right. Moderation is always best. Let's go inside," he said invitingly, seeing that Miss Ward was opening her bag and searching for money. "Why should they all be looking at us?"

He drew up a chair for her, pulled the cardboard and drawings down from the bed, and tugged at a string. The roll of matting over the entrance clattered down in a cloud of dust. Margit was already taking out bills; she paid in tens, so there was a thick wad of them. He took them, wrapped them in a handkerchief and put them in his trouser pocket.

On the hanging mat they saw outlined the figure of a woman leaning lower and lower. Through a chink filled with harsh glare they could just see sandaled feet and rings on bare toes. The palms of her hands were a garish red as she set a tray with cups of coffee on the concrete. She waited a moment, stooping, but the painter did not raise the mat until she had gone away.

Handing around coffee which he had liberally sprinkled with sugar, he explained in an undertone, "That was my wife. I did not introduce you because she does not know English. She is from a village and was brought up according to the old custom. She would be ill at ease in our company.

"No. I am not ashamed of her. She is good; she would like to help me change and be like others, help me earn. She cries at night because she was given as a wife to a madman: what kind of business is this, smearing canvas with brushes? And from it arise pictures which do not resemble the world she sees. Her family married her to me. They were wealthy; it seemed that they could help me. But I have been a burden to them all these years." Pensively he stirred a thick residue of coffee grounds and sugar. "You have no idea, madam, what it means to me to sell a painting. It is not only the money, though thanks to that my wife may believe that I really do work, and that what I do is worth something."

Descending from the flat roof, escorted by a band of children, they found themselves immersed in pungent aromas from the kitchens on the landings. They took the steep stairs cautiously, one or two at a time. The painter unexpectedly decided that he must leave with them, for an opportunity had arisen for him to attend to urgent business. Again they met his family in a cramped huddle on the staircase, and pressed their sagging slender or plump hands. They returned greetings and murmured goodbyes. The painter's parents and brothers-in-law must have been drawn out of their apartment by the shrieks of the children, the patter of feet, the jumping about and squeals of laughter. The little ones raced out, pushing and shoving each other to get to the car before it could be driven away. Below, the boys on guard stood erect as soldiers and reported on the events of their watch. Ram Kanval served as interpreter.

"The automobile survived unscathed, though one of the guards even squatted on the roof!" Then he said reassuringly, "Do not worry because I am coming with you. I will not squander the money, though it has fallen from the sky. Whatever I did with it, the family would be dissatisfied, for they pay for me to live. Suddenly it occurred to me that I should go and buy something for my wife. A ring or a sari? She has not had a present from me for years. After all, my paintings count for nothing; she has no capacity to enjoy them, and when she puts them back in the barsati for me, she tries to avoid being seen. Today I can give her something that will be a genuine gift, something that at last her sisters will envy."

"How nice!" Margit said with elation, turning her head. "You are a typical husband: you want to make your wife happy, but surely you don't know what she fancies or what she really needs. Perhaps it's better to give her money. She could choose for herself. And perhaps she has some expenses which she hasn't dared to mention."

"She has too many of them," he shrugged. "Of course she would prefer money, but the family would soon fleece her of it. Whether she needs it or not, my present will be for her alone, and it will come from my hand."

Istvan listened with a feeling of guilt. He should have thought of Margit long ago and surprised her with a gift.

The Austin glided through the streets of New Delhi among loaded trucks, tooting its horn to scatter the dilatory cyclists, whose bells chirped like crickets.

"Where shall I take you?" Istvan asked.

"No matter where, only to the center. Do not take any trouble on my account. The boulevards are best, around Parliament and at Connaught Place. Surely that will not be far out of your way."

It was sunset; the domes of pagodas were drenched with rose. The toothed wall flared red under the empty sky, which was rapidly taking on layers of darkest blue. Peasant women in wrinkled orange skirts and dark jackets sauntered along a path. On her back each carried a bundle of grass raked from the park. Bare sickles with broad blades like scythes gave off red gleams.

A tall girl with bushy black hair walked with a dancing step in spite of her burden. Her long, full skirt rippled; silver anklets shone below it. She sang in a strong voice and the others repeated the lines in rhythm. The melody, leaping brightly from note to note, seemed familiar to Istvan, as if the girl were singing in Hungarian. The painter laughed and put his arm out the window, catching the light on his open palm. The girls were startled and hid their faces behind their bent arms, but above their elbows their large, dark, gentle eyes with garishly painted lids could be seen.

"What was she singing?"

"That her bodice is tight and there is no friendly hand to loosen it, so I offered my help."

"Well, well! I didn't think you had such songs." Margit shook her head. "Your customs are strict: the family exercises discipline and a girl goes meekly into the bed of the man who is the family council's designee."

"That is not a real song," the painter countered. "She made it up herself. She is hot from her work, her bodice is squeezing her, and she finds relief in singing. She thought no one could hear but others like herself. How could she know that someone else was listening? Well, well, such girlish banter!"

The radiance from the west hovered under the trees among heaps of fallen leaves. The lavender earth gleamed through the trampled grass. The shirts of men walking along the paths were dazzling white.

"It's amusing to overhear such a request," Terey laughed.

"Don't forget that the singing was not meant for our ears. I overheard and translated it," the painter said defensively.

They were heading into a traffic jam. Police in red turbans were standing by, their bare legs dark, their sleeves rolled up; in their sinewy hands they held long bamboo sticks.

"The road is closed," Istvan said, taken by surprise. "Something must have happened."

"Full speed ahead. Have no fear," Ram Kanval urged. "They will not dare to stop you."

Indeed, when they turned aside and drove toward the cordon with one wheel on the grass, an officer—a black-bearded Sikh with a pompom on his cherry-colored beret—saw the insignia of the diplomatic corps on the car and ordered the police to stand aside.

"Some important person must have arrived," Kanval mused, leaning out through the open window and staring curiously in every direction.

"They would have sent me an invitation to an official meeting," Terey said a little huffily. "No, this is some parade. A big crowd is standing around the Parliament. Probably we won't get through."

They had to stop. Three trucks with police were blocking the street. They could have walked farther by taking the shortcut across the grass, but everyone was doing that. Istvan saw the journalists; the fiery sunset flashed in the lenses of carefully aimed cameras. He spotted Nagar's slight, nimble figure in the crowd, but before he decided to try and overtake him, Nagar was swallowed by a wave of rushing women. They were being chased by the police, who seized them and menaced them with uplifted clubs but hit no one. The light caught the shifting greens and yellows of the women's saris. The crowd gave way, squealing, then formed a circle with all eyes on a group of people who were shouting in rhythm. In these chases, or attempts by the police to disperse the crowd, there was something almost like fun, almost comic, yet grave, for a hymn or recitative was rising from the square.

"Shall we go closer?" He took Margit by the arm, afraid that she would be swept away in the whirlpools and waves of human particles and he would lose sight of her.

"This is curious." She pulled him into the dense mass of people who were chanting in the square. "What is it about?"

Women were moving all around them. Not only did they hear the soft rustle of silk and the clinking of bracelets; they were caught in a stifling wave of fragrance, the mixed odors of strong perfumes, powders, spices, sweat, and heated bodies. They saw young faces and wasted ones, flamboyantly painted, eyes glowing feverishly, hair ingeniously piled high on the head, plaited with garlands of flowers and covered with misty veils from Benares. Supple bodies gave way to them reluctantly, but eyes watched importunately, provocatively. Thick lips parted in enticing smiles. It struck Istvan that he had really never met Hindu women of this sort on the streets or in fashionable coffee houses. They were conscious of their beauty, of their full, warm bosoms as they nudged him. An atmosphere of animal tension was forming, of lurking readiness to bite and claw, and, it seemed, a great despairing sob. Istvan and Margit felt the agitation.

"What is this strange demonstration?" she asked. "Where did these women come from? Look, they're dancing."

A tremor ran through the crowd on the square. The dry earth rumbled. Light dust rose and floated toward the sunset in a red cloud. Flutes and three-stringed fiddles struck up; drums purred like cats and small bells twittered. Half-naked men, old and gray or very young, stamped in place in front of them, blowing fifes. With wooden fingers like partially burnt roots they tapped, they scraped, they stroked the skins of drums that chatted in bass voices. Istvan shuddered; he had just noticed the sunken eyelids, the empty eye sockets, or eyes wide open looking straight into the savage glare of the sun, eyes with white, dead irises.

"Look!" He pulled Margit closer. "Blind—the whole crowd, as far as those trees. They are all blind."

"What's going on here?" she asked in a frightened whisper.

"Nothing alarming." Ram Kanval had just come up behind them. "The prostitutes came to present a petition against the implementation of a decree that would resettle them outside the capital. They are not allowed now to practice their profession closer than twenty-five miles from New Delhi. It is amusing"—he pointed to the steps of the Parliament—"they call the delegates by name. Several they know well. No, not as clients, but they own the streets, the houses in which they live. They are calling out—" he translated, "'Must I return to the village, where people dry up like the earth?' 'Does my body, which gives pleasure to so many, have to wither away?' 'I support an entire family. They live because of me. Condemning me to hunger, you condemn them as well.'"

The calls became more and more anguished and despairing. The high, senile whine from the choir was filling the square.

"Why are those older men shouting?" Istvan tugged at Kanval's arm.

"They are afraid of what will happen to them. The blind—they will starve as well. Till now they have had work. They earned money honestly."

"How?"

"They played for the dancing in the bordellos. They accompanied the singers. They made time pass pleasantly for the guests. They are blind, so their presence does not interfere with the diversions. Living music boxes, human nickelodeons. What will they do? Where will they go? They can only beg, condemned to slow death."

"How many of them can there be here?"

"Well, about a thousand. There is an economic problem that cannot be assuaged by talking. The deputies will think long and hard before making a decision. At any rate, pressures will be felt from all sides. It will take away income from the owners of the houses, shopkeepers, tradesmen. Astrologers, drafters of love letters, they all earned money. And doctors and charlatans. Hordes of people lived off those girls. The resettlement decree could ruin tens of thousands of families whose livings are indirectly connected to that trade, its supplies and services. It is a more important matter than you think."

The exhalation of the crowd was in their faces, the smell of sweat, attars, powders. A great lament resounded from the square. Two women carried a petition encircled with garlands of orange flowers toward a group that stood, cordoned off by the police, on the stairs of the Parliament. They did not dare hand it directly to the deputies, but, according to an old custom, laid it on the steps, bowing to the feet of the officials standing a few steps above them and putting their fingertips to their lips in an act of humility and obeisance ("I kiss the dust of your sandals"). One of the police brought the rolled paper to his officer, who handed it to the deputies.

Then someone leaped through the cordon—a young man in a loosely wound dhoti and a shirt hanging from under a European sport coat. Dark, slender legs moved piston-like in shoes that were too large. He shouted something to the crowd, but was drowned out by commands issuing from a megaphone. The crowd swayed and began to flow, peacefully forming itself into a procession.

"I know him. He is a communist delegate," the painter said. "He has given them his pledge of support."

It seemed to Istvan that he saw a familiar face among the deputies—sallow, ageless, the face of Chandra, the attorney. Others, talking and debating, were gathered around him. Slowly the large building of rose-colored stone swallowed them all.

The philanthropist, Terey thought with a bitter smile. He will take care of them.

A haphazard, iridescent river of women drifted along. Songs started up here and there and mingled; the melodies drowned each other out. The noise and the twanging of instruments grew louder. The pleading calls repeated themselves in the twilight with a hollow sonorousness, but could not penetrate the thick walls behind which the decision would be made.

They walked down to the grass. In front of them the blind moved in rows with short steps, shuffling. Those on either end of each row held onto long bamboo rods that served as fences on both sides of the marchers. Little boys led them, shaking tambourines, hitting them against their close-clipped heads and jumping cheerfully about, unaware of the seriousness of the demonstration. A pale memory of sunset shone in the sky.

"A Breughel painting, indeed!" Margit shuddered.

"A hundred times over—for that is India," said the painter, not without pride. "The government must deliberate well before it extricates itself from this ruling. It is easy to pass a law, but how can it be implemented sensibly, without adverse effects? What the women were shouting is the truth: resettlement is a sentence to death by starvation. They have nowhere to go back to. They earn what they can to maintain their families, they put up dowries for their sisters, the younger ones for whom they find husbands—the affianced virgins, submissive, resigned. The one knows only the arts of the bed, the thousand-year-old prescriptions and recommended methods of lovemaking, but love itself she will never know. The other is ready to love anyone her family designates, or fate or the matchmaker presents."

They looked at the procession streaming slowly between the huge trees. Behind them, like sheepdogs driving their flocks along, the policemen walked unhurried, their red turbans glowing in the rapidly falling darkness. Others climbed into the covered backs of trucks. The bluish smoke of the first cigarettes, well earned after a long stint without them, floated out from under tarpaulins and formed a mist against an apricot-colored patch of sky.

The odor of musk and the spicy smell of heated bodies lingered in the air, but cars were already moving. They forced their way through the traffic, trumpeting angrily, flashing their yellow headlights, demanding the right-of-way with long blinks. Streaks of dust and exhaust bleared the stream of lights. This was the scented twilight of a city in the tropics.

"There is a cruel curiosity in the human being," Margit whispered. "One forgets that they also desire and suffer. One would like to lay bare their secrets, learn how they live, what makes them happy. Though I know that knowledge is no good, since I can't help them."

"What they have they value very much. They even think that fate singled them out: they have enough to eat, they wear silk saris, they bask in adoration and desire. Some find permanent admirers. Not only do they receive gifts, they share them with their own families," the painter shrugged. "The rules of your world, which you would try to impose on them as if for their good, they would not consider liberating. We cannot better their condition, and, worse, we do not want to share with them, to give up wealth. The deputies only institute demands, judge and contemptuously condemn these women's way of life and of earning a living, the only one available to them."

"Have you ever been—with them?" she asked, moved by the anger in his voice.

"Certainly. There is nothing shameful in that. In our world, matters of the body are hedged around with so many prohibitions that they continually distract and disturb us. Even those little boys who are running around near the women—though they are kissed and petted because they remind the women of the brothers and sisters they left behind—see nothing that would corrupt them. What we see there is what we are told in a poem about gods' struggles for love, or by statues in temples—entwined bodies, which for those accustomed to look at them from childhood become almost like the linear motif of a frieze. Certainly I have been there. This is not like prostitution in your world—the debasing purchase of a body, which because of that is only a body, for someone demands it, so it must dehumanize itself. Here there are not prostitutes exclusively, but dancers, singers, tellers of magical tales whose art involves physical movement. True artists are found among them, artists whose way to the stage was blocked by poverty and peasant origins.

"In front of a crowd of men sitting on the floor, they dance to the birdlike whistle of the flute and the dove's cooing of the drum, expressing the love of the earth goddess for the sun god. They bend the naked torso, part the thighs, tremble, surrender to an unseen lover. The dance is like a primordial prayer, like a compressed history of the world, a creation of what is alive.

"Everyone sees what he desires: one sees poetry, grace of movement, and the traditional school of sacral gesture; another is fascinated only by the pretty young girl who taps the floor with her bare feet dyed red as her bells clink like hail. And she is inaccessible, though everyone present is panting with lust, his mouth hanging open with delight. They have forgotten about their cigarettes, which are burning their fingers. One man alone will have her that night. The others can only envy him.

"That one takes out a banknote, moistens it with saliva, and sticks it on his forehead. The dancer has already seen him; she approaches him with catlike steps, her hips swaying. She sits by him, exuding warmth and scents, for we have special methods of enhancing the effects of perfume—the temples, underarms, and nipples are all moistened differently, and the knees, and the insides of the thighs. So she bends, she leans over her admirer like a branch heavy with fruit, she gives off the scent of a body heated from the dance. She brushes against him lightly, like a moth against the reflection of a lamp in a mirror. She is not permitted to reach for the banknote with her fingers, only with her lips, for he is supposed to press it to her bosom, which is gleaming with sweat. When she removes it, that is consent. So—you did not know this—the woman has a right to choose. She conquers in order to be bought. With this one lover she goes to an alcove, and the remaining men return home. They are aroused; they will take their own wives, still seeing in their minds the other woman with her serpentine movements, the woman who was coveted, desired."

"How dreadful!" Margit clenched her fists in front of her chest as if to defend herself. "Don't you understand that?"

He smiled at her indulgently.

"I would not say so. It is the pursuit of the unattainable, for quite a few of those men were poor, were street vendors. Each could pay for entrance, but not for the woman. But sometimes she rewards a man's perseverance, responsiveness, and strength of feeling. Why kill dreams? Why should people not have longings? For all those men whose decision to marry was dictated by the family council in order to increase their capital, unite clans, gain patronage and influence—who married women they did not desire, women chosen for them by others—here is a temporary escape, a change from the everyday tedium. With their wives they will have children; the families demand nothing more. There they can seek fulfillment, delight, beauty, I dare say even cleansing from the sins marriage perpetrates against love. But you cannot understand that . . ."

"Istvan, say that he is lying," she pleaded, clutching his hand. "After all, this is not true. Everything that can be bought there is filthy, filthy! It is repugnant."

"Let them think in their own way."

The painter looked at them impatiently, irritably. He was displeased by what lay at the heart of the quarrel: the impotent pity that the women of the bordellos could not even have understood. Or perhaps he saw only colors—the play of lights and tints, the copper helmet of hair, the dark blue eyes fiery and beautiful in anger, the simple dress of thin linen that revealed the outlines of the tanned, womanly body.

The square was quiet. The whines and murmurs of automobiles—as if they had been exasperated by the unexpected halting of traffic—had died away long since. The ground shone with a red afterglow. A garland of white flowers lay spread out and trampled on the gravel a few steps from them.

Two cows, tinted rose in the evening light, ambled lazily across the square. Car horns blew warningly and headlights flashed, but they plodded on, unconscious of danger, as if the whole world did not exist for them, or was merely a wavering illusion looming in their great dark eyes. One veered slowly from the direction in which she had been walking and stood above the wreath, nosing it, or rather lowering her head and exhaling, for red dust was rising from the ground. The fragrance of the flowers must have irritated her; she stepped over the garland and moved forward as if in a dream, with the last radiance from the sky on her back. The other trailed behind her, repeating the same movements, as if they were part of some eternal ritual.

The shirts of cyclists still glowed rose in the fading sun. Spire-like palms cut the sky like long brush strokes. The night hovered low among the houses, full of gaudy lamps, the noise of radios, the chiming of bicycle bells, and boisterous hallooings. Vehicles flew by, murmuring like bumblebees. Their burning headlights hardly brightened the anxious dark.

"Oh, the devil!" said Istvan, looking at the sky half-covered by a lead-colored cloud with fire flashing around the edges. "A storm is coming."

"Only a bluff," Kanval said dismissively. "There has been no bulletin forecasting rain in Delhi today."

"At all events, let's go," Margit begged. "Remember how it was around Qutub Minar that time. The wind nearly blew us away."

Inside the Austin the strong odors of gasoline and heated plastic were suspended in sweltering air. Only as the car gathered speed did the breeze bring an illusory relief. They dropped the painter off at Connaught Place. At once he was lost in the chattering throng that moved about under the arcades—among the luminous white shirts, the dark faces over which the fragrance of brilliantine drifted. Young, slender men clung to each other with indolent sensuousness. The whole city seemed to have boiled out onto the street; the human stream hummed with voices and rustled with women's silks as bodies jostled and gave off heat as evening came on. In these hoarse, tittering noises and fitful snatches of song there was an undertone of expectation and anxiety.

Margit's hand groped for Istvan's in the dark. Its warm touch transfixed him with desire. The girl seemed to sense it and withdrew, startled.

"Shall we go into Volga for ice cream?" he asked. "Pereira doesn't make it."

"No," she whispered languidly. "Let's go. I want to be with you."

He thought it was just a pretext, but she surprised him by leaning over and resting her head heavily on his shoulder. Tenderness and peace swept over him.

After he drove the car into the garage, she helped him close the blinds. She turned out the lights, for the watchman had gone to the kitchen for the evening portion of chapati. He felt as if they had been married for a long time and were returning home—as if his life were only now assuming its rightful, tranquil rhythm.

Heat radiated from the walls of the villa. The earth gave off the dry, famished scent of things that wither and die. The darkness trembled with the long drill-like clanging of insects. Pereira, who had heard the car approaching, had already opened the front door for them. He was still rubbing his lips with the back of his hand and smacking his lips, as if he were savoring the aftertaste of rice fragrant with cloves.

Istvan was moved by the calm assurance with which Margit made her way around his house. She navigated gracefully among the furnishings. She knew where to find the electrical outlets.

"Saaa-hib!" He heard the cook's plaintive whisper.

"If everything is ready, serve dinner. Remember the ice cubes."

"Oh, yes, everything is here," Pereira answered with zeal. "Krishan has turned up again. He wants . . . he asks for the embassy to vouch for him so he can buy a motorcycle on time."

As if horrified by the audacity of the demand he had dared to repeat, he blinked with dark, membranous eyelids like a bird's.

"He's mad." Istvan shrugged.

"Yes, sir, he is a lunatic." The cook wagged his head. "He knows the ambassador is going to Shimla, and before that he would like to give the American firm the guarantee. He wants a very strong engine. He is afraid of nothing."

Irritated that this conversation was drawing itself out, Istvan ordered tersely, "Serve the food."

He went into the bathroom to wash his hands. Warm water trickled dully from the tap. He saw his sunburned face in the mirror. His eyes looked dogged and cheerless.

"Terry, come quickly. The drinks will get warm." Margit's calm voice gave him joy. He opened the door and looked at her affectionately. She held out a glass with ice cubes and Coca-Cola.

"Try it. It's a coca libre."

He took the glass, holding her cool hand to his cheek and lips by way of thanks.

"What have you put into it? It smells very nice."

"A little rum. Lemon juice and one slice for aroma. The Coca-Cola isn't cloying. It loses its sticky sweetness right away."

He caught himself listening to her voice so as to hear the altered tone in which she spoke to him, only to him. It lent the simplest words a tinge of passion.

"My father mixed it this way at our house in Melbourne. It was the only alcoholic drink I enjoyed."

The room had filled imperceptibly with her presence, with the subtle fragrances of her dress and warm skin. Or perhaps he was only beguiled by the delicate aromas of rum and lemon peel from the glass he was holding to his lips.

"Do you miss Australia?"

"I wouldn't say so. You forget that it's a continent." She blinked indulgently. "There are a very few places that I'm familiar with.

The rest of the country is unknown to me. It's waiting for us. We'll discover it together. If you want to."

She was assigning him a part in her life. That was disturbing; it put him on guard. Was he being dishonest in wishing to preserve his own freedom? But passion dictated that he fulfill all her desires. He wanted her to be happy.

The door creaked. The cook gave the sign that he was putting dinner on the table. His olive face with lowered eyelids seemed to say that he would not offend by allowing himself even a glance at a woman who interested his master. Istvan could have blessed the man when he told him that he was going to the roof, to the barsati, and murmured something about an approaching storm. Yellow lightning was flashing outside the windows, as often happened in summer during dry weather. He closed the curtains and set the wings of the large ceiling fan in motion.

"And now let's eat," he said encouragingly, pouring the red Egri.

She needed no urging. He liked her freedom, her frank displays of feeling, her lack of calculation and refusal to play the games of coquetry. She helped herself to large portions. She was becoming accustomed to Indian spices.

"I don't know much about wines," she confessed, raising her glass and looking with delight at the red fire in the delicate crystal, "but this is nice after that devilishly hot sauce."

"When you come to Hungary," he began, but his words lacked the confident ring of her invitation to Australia. He broke off, embarrassed.

She rotated the glass in her hand, enjoying the play of red lights on the tablecloth. Suddenly the lamp went out.

"What the devil—" He stopped the clatter of the ceiling fan. "Don't move. I'll check."

He pushed aside the curtains. The long, vivid flash against the walls of the neighboring villa startled him; only when the darkness returned like a thick curtain falling outside the windows did he understand that it was the reflection of lightning. The windowpanes jingled faintly and a mutter as of a bass voice jarred the walls.

"What are you doing?" he asked, unnerved by her silence.

"Nothing. Drinking wine," she answered nonchalantly. "We had already finished, and to tell the truth, we don't need the light."

Outside the uncovered window a shifting flame pulsed, though not the slightest breeze stirred the leaves of the banana trees. Reeling shadows rolled over the blind wall of the villa opposite. In the black sky, light flared in several places at the same instant. When a bolt of lightning illuminated the room, he found a flashlight in a drawer.

"Aren't you afraid?" he asked. The room was bathed in undulating green. The windows, shaken by the rumble of distant thunder, began to chime.

"No. A splendid show!"

They finished the wine. When she rose, he kissed her on the mouth and led her to his room. He saw with satisfaction that Pereira, before he left, had made the bed.

"And where is my suitcase?"

"In your bedroom." He handed her the flashlight. "I checked. Everything is ready."

"Where shall we sleep? Here, or in my room?"

"Wherever you prefer."

"Wait."

He did not want to be in her way. He listened: the sky murmured in a deep bass register, but those were not thunderbolts, only a dull, vibrating rumble that the walls took up. Then a silence fell—such a dead quiet that the watch on his wrist seemed to emit a metallic chirp. Not one cicada jingled. Insects were silent, terrified by the night full of growling flame without heat.

He had to wait for Margit too long. He grew uneasy. He began to look for her. The door of the other bedroom was open. Margit stood before the uncurtained window with the darting fire that had erupted in the sky rippling over her. Her hair was blackish-green, her arms yellow as brass. The light poured over her bare body. He remembered the tales he had heard as a child of enchantresses who, beaten down by a storm in drum rolls of hail, fell among shepherds curled up on haystacks under straw hats. They chose the young, innocent boys, they smothered them with kisses and made captives of them. Their lips had the taste of herbs and the freshness of rain.

In self-defense the boys surrendered to the mad onslaught of opulent female bodies, then slept with their faces immersed in their lovers' hair, fragrant with damp meadow flowers. They awoke, lonely, lethargic, and weak, on a dim morning, in a cloud of fog. Stallions, barely visible, with dark backs like boats, seemed to float in the mist; their mournful whinnying drifted over the river. From that time on, no woman could give them the delight they had known then. They searched among the girls for wives, they married at last, but they were never happy in love.

He watched as the glare from the lightning flowed over her arms like a glittering shawl. She turned suddenly, sensing his presence, and saw that he was still dressed. In a timeless gesture of embarrassment at her own nudity, she crossed her hands to cover her breasts. But a second later she was laughing without shame and running her fingers through her disheveled hair, which was standing on end because she had pulled her dress off over her head. She came to Istvan and embraced him, hiding her face on his chest.

"It's not very nice of you to look at me that way," she whispered.

"Enchantress," he breathed into her hair.

"I'd like to be one of those. I would change you into a jewel and wear you on a bracelet, and in the evening, when I was alone, you would be yourself again. And all the time, even when people were around, I could touch you with my lips and caress you. We would not be apart even for a minute. Do you want me to do that?"

"I want it. I want it so." He held her close. They stood in each other's arms as the window burned with lurid green and yellow, the colors seeming to flail the sky with brooms of fire. Lightning leaped in the distance, striking, flashing. The earth seemed to quiver like a drumhead.

Their bodies, now familiar and intimate, sought each other, discovered accommodating movements, shared rhythms. Each felt the other's breathing. They dissolved into each other; his moist skin clung to hers. He took possession of her as if she belonged to him. He bent like a bow and her eager yielding filled him with joy. In the rumbling glare the walls of the house seemed to sway. It was as if the distant roar had summoned an unknown, enormous beast that hovered over the city, ready to devour it. He wanted to remember the metaphor; already he had preserved in unfinished tropes the mood of the night, the curve of lips kissed and kissed, dark in the shimmering downpour.

"Tell me a story," she begged. "I love it when you do."

They lay quiet, listening. It seemed as though the crackle of the lightning could be heard in the room, but they only heard a large fly, invisible in the shadows, strike the ceiling with a doleful moan. Its lament must have aroused the appetites of lizards, for they smacked greedily with their tongues.

"I can't hear anything but you. After all, you know that I am happy."

"I don't know. I don't." She shook her head. Their fingers entwined and they felt the pulsing of the blood subside. In the closed room the smell of bodies slippery with sweat mingled with the odors of insecticide and camphor wood.

He looked with wide-open eyes at the ceiling, which was flooded with flickering green. He saw the lizards gliding, converging; somewhere among them there must be a fly dumb with fright. In a moment he would hear its desperate buzz. He breathed in the fragrance of Margit's hair and her moist body. Her passive fingers pulsed in his hand. She was tired; had she fallen asleep? He was immersed in the peaceful certainty that at last he had met the woman whose existence he had foreseen, and whom he had always desired. He was not thinking of the body's cravings, the delights that would be her gifts to him. He knew that he could spend all his life with her, that here was a friend who would not leave him until the last darkness, which he would have to traverse alone.

Overcome with thankfulness, moving carefully so as not to waken her, he lowered his head and touched her with his lips, tasting her skin with the end of his tongue. It had a saltiness like blood. He thought she breathed more deeply; her arm fell across his chest and, as if reassured by his presence, lay still.

For that first conversation at Qutub Minar during the sandstorm—one of the most important ones—he kept a special place in his memory. She had spoken with disarming frankness about herself and matters of the body. Women, knowing the self-conceit of men, prefer to be silent about their experiences. Each man wants to be the only one, exceptional, unforgettable, since by now it is too late to have the troublesome privilege of being the first. At the time her revelations had disturbed him, drawn him toward her like challenges to battle. That strict sincerity persisted in her behavior. Margit pursued her goal honestly, with a courage rarely seen even in men. Was it a way of measuring his love?

"I am happy": the words were too simple. The poverty of the phrase struck him painfully when he tried to find a name for this state of joy beyond joy, to fix it, to lock it into the core of memory.

What will happen to us when Margit's contract expires? And my continued residence in India is uncertain as well; it depends on my personal rapport with the ambassador and the whims of some official far away in Budapest. Not on long-term projects, only on unspecified initiatives.

Be glad that you have her near you, within reach. Don't provoke the jealous fates, he counseled himself. Under this timorous silence he harbored the instinctive certainty that when he stood face to face with the ultimate choice, he could make it, even if he had to defy everyone: friends and enemies. But what a price he would pay for Margit!

The soft burden of her hand rested on his chest. He put away his misgivings and fell asleep unawares, though he would never have admitted it, for he was determined to satiate himself with the joy of this evening hour. Through his closed eyes he still felt lightning flashing over the city, as if some enormous stranger were running to the window with a lamp to peer at their figures as they nestled together like fallen statues, not even covered by a sheet, defiantly naked.

The walls quaked from the distant thunderbolts. His joy was mingled with apprehension: for a moment he felt as if they were snuggled together on a berth in a train hurtling toward an unknown coast, while light from the stations they were passing in the night was glaring into the half-open window. They would travel that way over the ocean to immense beaches, he was sure, beaches the dawn had just reached. He already felt the nearness of those measureless waters in the bracing wind and distant roar of the waves that died with hisses on the sandy curve of a bay like an arena.

They were roused by a rumbling outside the house and the mournful rattling of the windowpanes.

"Istvan."

"It's the ocean," he answered, half conscious but filled with satisfaction that he could reassure her. "Sleep."

Her laugh banished his sleep. He saw what was amusing her: rain was battering the windows. It washed over the walls in great spurts, pummeling the vines on the veranda. The ground could not absorb the water, which covered it in a widening tide. Green lights blazed on the flooded square.

"The monsoon!" she cried. She leaped to the window and threw it wide open. Through the wire mesh a cool draft rushed toward them, together with the frenzied splashing of water flooding the ground and the splendid fragrance of the awakened earth as it began to quench its thirst. Heaven and earth reeled in the swaying light. They seemed to hear the distant booming of a drum; they saw flares surrounded by swords of fire. Hindus, hunched over and wrapped in sheets of linen, ran through the streets seeking shelter. Thin bare legs pounded through puddles full of glare. They looked like corpses from cruel legends, running around fiery meadows in search of their severed heads.

"At last one can breathe," she said, kneeling over him. Her body itself exuded the freshness of the cleansed air. "I'd like to run out now into this downpour full of fire and drink those cool sparks the wind is sprinkling. I'd like to dance for you. If you could only understand how beautiful the world is when someone loves you! Get up and come to the window, anyway."

He encircled her with his arms, put his lips on hers and pushed her down into the sheet.

"I will give all the world for you," he said as if it were a vow. "I will give everything. Everything. Margit!"

The afterglare from the lightning was coming through the window, and distant thunder like a cannon salvo. A strong scent of vines, soaked hay, and wet masonry rode on gusts of wind that careened over the flat roof. Huge banana leaves flapped like half-furled sails in the green and yellow glare.

"Tomorrow is ours," she said happily. "In weather like this they will have to cancel flights. There will be no delegation."

How had she managed to think of that at such a moment? He imprisoned her in his arms. Having seen that the sky was going pale and the rain quieting down, she was already rising.

"I'm going to my room. They will check to see if I have slept there. You may laugh at my silly deviousness; they know we spent the night together. But we must care a little for appearances."

He stroked her back. She sat hesitantly on the edge of the bed.

"Surely you won't leave me alone? But perhaps by now you want to sleep. Are you glad to be rid of me at last? The whole bed to yourself: really, how delightful." She taunted him on her way out until he sprang after her. Bare feet beat on the stone floor.

When he had caught her and clasped her to him, she commanded, "Go back and close the window. The rain is blowing in." She nestled close to him and whispered in his ear, "And then come. But only for a little while."

The storm was regaining force. In its heavy muted roar they slept profoundly, satisfied.

Chapter VII

A short, violent rain chopped at the riotous greenery of the trees and rattled among the wide, wobbling banana leaves, then suddenly stopped. The sun blazed in myriads of puddles. Starlings dived into the beaten-down grass, whistling impertinently and gorging themselves on waterlogged insects unable to escape. The earth emitted the cloying odor of teeming life breeding in a layer of fermenting decay—a sweet smell as from a vase when no one has changed the water for a long time.

Istvan shuddered when the branches of the climbing plants he jostled with his head sprinkled him with water. He could not bear being in the house; an angry restlessness forced him out among people. He needed company, though he knew he could open his heart to no one. He did not expect to find relief, to free himself from oppressive thoughts. A moment before he had flung down the receiver because the mild voice of the receptionist had told him that Miss Ward had gone away from Agra.

He had not seen Margit for three weeks. To be precise, it was the twenty-third day she had eluded him, perhaps even deliberately avoided him.

Without thinking he flicked large beads of water from his pale jacket, where they had left dark spots. From the garden and from the overgrown lawn on the square came the smell of drenched plants, a musty smell that subsided into a haze of moisture.

What could be simpler than to take the car and dash over to Agra? Again?—he mocked himself. After all, he had been there and not found her; he had loitered around all the familiar corners of the city with a bitter, lost feeling, as if he had happened on the wrong address. In the hospital the old Swedish professor had looked at him as though he were an insect fluttering on a pin as the sick people droned monotonously. They seemed to hover in the overheated air along with the soiled bandages, the whiffs of stinking sweat, pus, and the souring milk their families were giving them to drink.

"Miss Margit is conducting surveys with Dr. Connoly out in the neighboring villages." With his hand the professor described an arc on the horizon. "It is difficult to say exactly where they are, for a sudden downpour could wash out the road in a couple of minutes and turn it into a red swamp. The all-terrain vehicle would hardly get through. Many times they got oxen from a village to help. They laid branches under the wheels. With the Austin it would be impassable. When Dr. Ward returns, I will tell her you were here. Perhaps you will leave a note?"

He looked at the narrow, red-veined face and wanted to hit the man, though he had in no way injured him. The professor was looking at him with pale eyes and blinking with white eyelashes. His failure to supply information was irritating, but how could he guess that Istvan had a right to ask about Margit, that he was not just a casual acquaintance?

She had let two letters and a telegram go without answering. She must have received them, since they had not been returned. His masculine pride had hardened into a determination not to beg; he was not one of those who whimper. But by now he knew, he had resolved in spite of himself, that at the first sign he would be ready to run to her, to apologize, to plead. After all, one of us must be wiser than the other; this was his rather weak justification for his willingness to give way.

But what happened? Why is she determined to evade me, to shun me like this? What have I done? He ransacked his conscience. How have I hurt her? But she would have laid the whole bitter truth out in the open, demanded explanations. Perhaps someone told her something reprehensible about me. But she should come to me with it. Why would she be afraid to? Damned female nonsense—he clenched his fists. Entice me and then run away. She wants to worry me, to demonstrate her power over me.

But that was not like her. And indeed he felt that he knew her, for out of their nights together had grown conversations as unreserved as the intimacy of bodies hidden in the dark, under the pile of luminous white netting.

The tiresome, wavering but incessant lament of the sick crowded behind the screens of the vacuously staring windows, the waves of stinking disinfectant and feces, were carried on the stiff breeze. Stunned flies fled before the downpour and hit the men's faces like shriveled seeds. Rain in heavy spurts clattered on the corrugated tin roof. The professor jumped aside, holding down the edges of his apron, which was flapping in the wind. Istvan took refuge in his car. He lowered the windows and would have gone on chatting, but the rain fell in sheets, so he only waved and they parted. The wipers could not clear the streaming windshield; he drove at a snail's pace. Oxen in harness stood still, resigned. The peasants squatted naked, even without headbands. The rain beat on bony, bent backs. And then the sky was wide and clear; the partly formed arches of a triple rainbow glowed high above them.

Remembering that long, lonely ride in the torrential rain of the tropics, he turned his face toward the invisible sun and raised his hands to shield his eyes. Puddles stood on the square, their smooth surfaces giving off a glare that made him squint.

As he was driving the Austin out of the garage, the watchman suddenly appeared. Awkwardly holding up a long knife which he had taken from behind his belt, and a ball of yarn with knitting needles stuck into it, he helped Istvan maneuver the car by signaling with his finger.

"Sahib," he announced breathlessly, leaning toward the open window, "I am going to be married. Krishan's wife has a friend. Perhaps you will raise my salary by a few rupees?"

"I will see. And where will she live?"

"In the barsati. It is warm now. Oh, thank you for rewarding me for faithful service. I keep watch on the threshold of the house. I do not sleep."

"And how will it be now?"

"I will sleep even less," he smiled, happy that the master had assented to his request and was joking graciously.

He was touched by the servants' trust. Not only do I feed and clothe them; I am the foundation of their futures, they cobble nests together around me. They look for happiness and believe that I can ensure it for them. Then one letter from Bajcsy could have me recalled and everything would fall apart. They do not take that into account, as we, Europeans, do not take death into account. They all have a right to happiness except me. Or perhaps they are simply satisfied with less, with what is more easily available.

In his festering resentment it seemed to him that he would rather see Margit dead than give her up to another. He felt robbed, as if the most precious thing he possessed had been torn from him. Though she had said so many times that she belonged to him, she was not his property; she had given herself. Now she had changed her mind. She did not want to be with him. She was rebelling. He must have the courage to acknowledge it. In a helpless rage he muttered a vow to get her back. But then, if she were standing before him, he would take her by the arms and shake her until his fingers bruised her. "Answer me: why have you had enough of me? What has separated us?" And afterward he would kiss her, kiss her.

He drove out beyond the cemetery, where in exemplary harmony, on a square divided into sections, Christians, Jews, and Muslims slept beside each other, though they had been brought there through gates marked with a cross, a star, or a sickle. The asphalt smelled of tar; the puddles splashed under his tires, which dried instantly. Vapor hovered over the road—a whitish smoke, swelling and quivering.

And what if Margit had simply fallen into a wayward frame of mind—needed a man and jumped into bed with him, and now, he thought vengefully, is ashamed to come back to me? Perhaps it would be better to indulge her . . . The miserable tramp. What a joy it would be to beat her, what a relief to humiliate her. I won't meet you halfway, not even one step. You put up the wall; I'll put in a few bricks from my side. He decided to drop in on Judit in the evening. She was a person who deserved his regard. Seeing her would cheer him up. For a while he would be able to forget Margit's withering silence.

Margit. Margit. He repeated her name as if he were tugging at the bell by a locked gate. Why are you punishing me so?

Only now did he begin to feel the full extent of his loneliness, to fathom how much his life had changed. He had distanced himself from his friends. He had stopped spending time at the club. Margit had been enough; she was his world. He had forgotten the days of impatient expectation, when she put her head on his shoulder or stretched out beside him on the bed, shaking off her sandals. He had lived for the gift of those hours; they were the only ones that counted.

But I must see her, he said through clenched teeth as he plunged into the sultry shade of the boulevard. I must talk with her. I really have not gone mad. There is surely some logical reason for her behavior. She is too good to walk away without a word.

Yet the thought recurred like an echo: she is a woman.

So many times she said that she loved me, he reminded himself firmly, gripping the steering wheel harder. And the last time, too, she repeated it as if she were praying, when as we said goodbye I lifted her head with my fingers in her hair and kissed her until it hurt.

Her frankness was cruel sometimes. She did not conceal the past. When he had said tersely, "It is of no concern to me," she had answered, "I want you to know everything about me." With a sudden pressure at his heart he remembered that when he had asked her if she compared him to the others, she had shaken her head until her hair fell onto her shoulders, and slapped him on his bare chest.

"How silly you are," she had laughed. "They are gone. I don't remember anyone, anything. Nothing. I told you about those things because they happened in my life, but they meant nothing. It's as if I wiped the slate utterly clean. Tabula rasa. You are only you, and only you matter."

What if now it had been just as easy for her to rid herself of him? To wipe the slate clean? I am thirty-six years old now; half my life is behind me, and I still take women at their word. Yet he rebuked himself: be fair, she is not here to defend herself.

He saw his gloomy sunburned face in the mirror. Botflies darted in through the windows of the car, buzzing and creeping around the windshield until he squashed them with the chamois. Women in orange skirts held an unrolled strip of freshly printed fabric in their hands; it had come from a workshop under a tree, where a man was transferring designs to the material from blocks of wood treated with dye. The printing had to dry quickly; the women spread the fabric out like a sail swelling in the sun so the patterns would not blur. The air clung to the skin like oil as smoke from wet wood and smoldering stalks drifted from clay cottages, and heavy steam from laundered clothing, drying rags, and lye.

After all, he assured himself, true love could not end in such a ridiculous way.

Yes, it had been just here—there was even the tumbledown house patched together with dung and clay. He knew the worn path into the sugar cane fields and the old tomb, the shrine with the domed top, the old stone overgrown with lichen.

They had driven away from Istvan's house when Mihaly came up to them unbidden.

"Take me, uncle," he begged, pressing his lips together drolly.

"Let him come," Margit took the boy's part, "he won't bother us."

The little fellow slid into the car.

The fringes of the suburbs, overgrown with thorny shrubs, adjoined old cemeteries and the ruins of ancient temples. As they were speeding along, Istvan saw the massive gray hulk of an elephant. It was leaning against the remains of a wall, rubbing the back of its neck until the crumbling bricks fell down. Margit insisted on photographing it. He stopped the car and the three of them got out. Peasants hidden behind trees shouted something in husky voices and waved lean hands like withered branches, but no one paid any attention to them.

Mihaly found a half-crushed stalk of sugar cane on the road and picked it up for "our elephant." Margit hovered at a distance; the elephant was too large to be photographed at close range, so Istvan stood beside her as Mihaly moved fearlessly, carrying the broken stalk in his outstretched hand, where it dangled like a whip.

The shouts stopped. The silence was broken only by the piercing squawks of parrots.

Instinctively the boy slowed down; he seemed to grow smaller as he drew near the ponderously advancing giant, which relentlessly rubbed its neck against the rough wall. They could hear the scraping of the thick folds of skin and the clatter of falling stones. Suddenly the elephant stood still and spread its ears wide; only their edges fluttered lightly. It turned its head. Its eye in its yellow ring looked toward the approaching child with a tormented, furious glare. The elephant took a few steps, crushing weeds and raising a cloud of dust. Just then Istvan noticed that with every movement the animal was sweeping the ground with a broken length of thick chain that was fastened to one hind leg.

"Mihaly, stop!" he cried, and lunged for the boy.

With incredible lightness the elephant turned where he stood and, grunting, broke into a gallop, trampling the bushes. He ran straight for the huddled cottages. The Hindus shrieked and ran like frightened hens, grabbing naked children and trying to hide. Under the stomping of his powerful legs the huts shattered like pottery. Dry thatch and wisps of straw must have fallen onto a cooking fire, for a pale flame burst out unexpectedly. The elephant moved at a lumbering canter, tearing his way through the brush. They heard his trumpeting and the cracking of branches; then nothing remained but the noise of crying and the smoke from the fire.

Istvan seized the boy and ran to the car. "Come on," he said to Margit. She stood pale and breathless with the camera pressed to her chest.

"Why was he so frightened of me?" Mihaly asked.

Half-naked figures were swarming about. People crept out of ditches and from behind large trees and clustered around the Europeans.

"That is a mad elephant, sahib," a tall villager wearing a shirt explained in English. "He has killed two people. We warned you."

"Are there injured people in those ruined houses?" he asked.

"No. But there are heavy losses: burned beds and saris. Give a few rupees, honored sir, madam," they begged, extending their hands.

Margit shook out all the contents of her bag into their hands. They grabbed eagerly at the ten-rupee notes. On all fours they clapped their hands on the coins that rolled around on the road and fished them up. A clutch of bodies scuffled in the dust.

"You must have gone mad, too," he scolded her when she clung to his arm. Then he saw that her eyes were wide with fear. "What are you afraid of? He is far away," he said comfortingly.

"You could have been killed," she whispered. "He could have trampled you. I was so terribly afraid for you when you ran like that. Istvan, what were you thinking? What were you counting on? That the elephant would be frightened?"

"I don't know," he said, and it was the truth. "I wanted to stop the child. It was a reflex."

"But he isn't important. Only you!" she cried accusingly, as if she were delivering a verdict on the boy.

"Would you have wanted me to leave him to the elephant?"

"Oh, no, Istvan. No. That's not what I was thinking. I love you so for what you did. That's right: it was a reflex."

"Anyone would have done it. Nothing happened, after all." He backed the car up and turned it around.

"Nothing at all," Mihaly declared. "I won't tell anybody about the trampled houses because my dad would give me a spanking."

He drove the boy, who by now was drowsy, gorged with cake, to the embassy. Margit stayed in the house; she preferred not to be seen. In the night they clung to each other through long, sleepless hours.

"I got you back. He gave you back to me when He could have taken you."

"Who?"

"He," she whispered gravely. "You believe that He exists."

Then he remembered the elephant as it turned with unimaginable lightness, and its fluid gallop, which made the earth groan.

"I think he was unnerved by the broken sugar cane in the boy's hand. It reminded him of a whip," he explained.

"No, they don't use whips on elephants. You know that very well," she insisted. "It was a sign."

They lay in silence for a moment. His heart beat its measured rhythm under her hand.

"It beats," she whispered almost reverently. "It beats for me."

"You're becoming as superstitious as a Hindu woman. It doesn't know who it's beating for. And if it does, it beats for itself, as it was formed to do in my mother's womb," he said to ease her tension.

But she did not quarrel with him. She kissed him on the mouth so he would say nothing that could cause her pain.

The next day the cryptographer showed him a notice in a newspaper and thanked him effusively, for Mihaly had blurted out the whole story. The counselor read that before soldiers shot the crazed elephant, he had wreaked havoc at a bazaar and trampled two people.

He stopped the car behind the large trunks of trees that were growing beside the road. Behind a stone pillar marking the sacred trail of King Ashoka, grayish-brown cottages stood among the thorn bushes, their walls patched with great clots of clay and dung. Women were cutting dry grass with sickles and using it to fill out the sparse sheaves of thatch on the roofs. Children were shouting in the ruined temple and running around under long strips of fabric—freshly laundered saris—that had been hung over the shrubbery.

"What am I searching for in this place?" he asked himself, looking at the vapor that rose from the thorny, matted vegetation. He knew: he wanted to remember Margit's eyes half mad with fright, the eyes of a woman who loves.

He walked around the Hotel Ashoka, a modern building like a castle of red stone. He heard the tinkle of music; beach umbrellas pulsed in the breeze like blue and green jellyfish. Excited cries and the din of childish voices rose and fell around the pool when the dark figure of a diver vaulted from the board to flash in the sun and disappear behind the wall. He had no desire to meet strangers; there was too much glare and excitement, and it grated on him. He preferred the dim, expansive interior of the Dinghana Club, with its deep leather chairs and splendidly appointed bar. The smells of insecticide, dust, and cigars drifted together; the breeze drew in the robust odor of horse manure from the stables nearby.

The bartender greeted him as if he were the prodigal son, and, seeing two upraised fingers, poured a double whiskey from a silver jigger and tossed in some ice. He rocked it for a minute in his dark palm, testing the temperature, before handing it to Istvan with a genial smile.

"Your friend the rajah is out riding today, sir. He also had not been here for a long time."

"Justifiably. He has a young wife."

"And that does not help: he is fat again," the old barman said solicitously, stealthily pouring himself a little whiskey and sniffing rather than drinking it.

They think of me as one of them, Istvan thought. They do not stand on ceremony with me. He would not dare drink in the presence of an Englishman, even if the English were buying for him. He would thank them politely and pour it into a cup, assuring them that he would take a sip for their health, but only when he was off duty.

A diffuse yellow glow from fly-specked bulbs hovered high up under the ceiling, which was ribbed like the ceiling of a hangar. Large fans milled the stagnant air; he felt no breeze. He took his glass and had just settled in among the creased, agreeably cool cushions of a chair when he spotted Major Stowne, with his narrow head like a bird of prey's, in another corner of the room, apparently napping. His head was thrown back; from under his lowered, lashless eyelids he was actually observing the exit to the riding course. He greeted Terey with a dilatory raising of his open hand. The gesture and the downward movement of the protruding Adam's apple on the lean neck amounted not only to a salutation, but an invitation to keep him company.

Stowne belonged to the old cadre; he was one of the British who could only be comfortable in India, for the changes that were taking place in England aroused their revulsion. They felt almost like foreigners on the island, or newcomers who had wandered in from an earlier epoch in which the social hierarchy was respected. In India he was still shown deference; he moved in the best society, among ministers and diplomats. Rajahs invited him to hunts, and his protégés glittered with generals' gold braid. He could honor, could add splendor to parties with his presence, could revive the prestige of the former guard of the Empire.

The story that was told about him Istvan could hardly believe. It was said that he had been enamored of a wealthy Hindu woman, or even been her lover. At first it seemed incredible; it was enough to look at his stark profile, which seemed carved from red wood. Then, too, the sternness long ingrained in him would have appeared to render it impossible. There were allusions to a Hindu beauty with enormous eyes and dead-black hair, the furled sail of nights of love. She concealed her left hand in a lace glove and never removed it. Even the servants, from whom inquisitive women friends tried to wrest the truth, never saw their mistress's hand uncovered. It was whispered that she had a birth mark or eczema, but her beauty could not have been significantly marred, for the deep tone of her skin glistened through the eyelets in the lace.

The Hindu must have had a fortune if she had allowed herself to defy convention and appear openly with her English friend. Then, unexpectedly, she disappeared. Stowne, even in his cups, never answered questions about the absent woman. He turned his back and left the room, then smoked a cigar and paced pensively around the park long enough to be sure the conversation had moved on to some other subject: the price of emeralds, the value of horses, the trustworthiness and devotion of servants.

But then vague rumors arose that the Hindu lady had gone mad, that they had been forced to lock her up, that she had been sedated with a brew of herbs and conveyed to the vicinity of Shimla, or that she had renounced the world and become an initiated yogini in one of the mountain retreats.

The major had not married in spite of many determined overtures from dowried women. He remained alone with his legend.

When Istvan had risen from his restful leather chair and its cushions had regained their shape, wheezing as if with relief, he made his way slowly to the major, uncertain whether he had read his gesture of permission correctly. Stowne waved his forefinger as if he were shaking the ashes from an invisible cigar, so Istvan sat down beside him, reassured. They had still not spoken, were not even looking at each other.

"Have some more?" The major said at last, showing him a bottle and siphon nestled close to his brown chair. He himself took a generous swallow from a glass.

"Yes, indeed."

"Pour for yourself." When the hiss of the siphon stopped, he whispered, "Hard, eh?"

Istvan nodded.

"Playing hard to get," the major sighed. "Resisting."

"How did you—" Terey turned away abruptly.

"There isn't much that I don't notice." He winked with thickly creased eyelids. "It's not only hard to find true feeling these days, but one doesn't meet real women."

"Oh!"

"You think I don't know about anything but lances and horses: stupid retired old Stowne." With strength from some unknown inner source he sat upright and his watery, somnolent eyes took on a gleam. "She could have had me—indeed, I begged—and she wouldn't, though she could have so easily—" he lapsed into an alcoholic daze.

"She didn't love you enough," Istvan said, not sparing the major or himself.

"She loved me for sure, you foolish boy. She held my lip with her teeth and closed her eyes and trembled. 'I want to be with you! I'll throw over the service and the uniform and I'll go where you go,' I said. 'No,' she replied, 'I can't. I love you too much.' It was enough to make her press harder with her teeth."

He looked down at Istvan as if he wanted to peck him. Red veins showed in his face and his inebriated eye flashed from under a bristling white eyebrow.

"The only woman who was capable of loving that much. You see? That's why she renounced me. And we could still have been happy for years. There was always time for that. I had a revolver, I wouldn't have hesitated. If she had said so, we'd have gone away together. Understand?"

He shook his head.

"Leprosy. The nursemaid took the girl to the cave to be blessed. The sadhu scratched her with a dead hand."

Istvan looked spellbound at the man's bluish lips: Stowne's secret had been revealed to him. Before he understood what had prompted the major's confession, he heard a whisper:

"Go to the veranda. She is there. She came with him, but I know she is waiting for you. Go, then, and behave unwisely. I tell you this, I, Major Stowne. It is worth it to behave unwisely."

He was willing Margit to appear so insistently that he already saw her with Connoly. He shook the major's dry, bony hand, put down his glass, and moved toward the door. His steps beat dully on the walkway of thick coconut matting.

On one of the lounge chairs that were scattered about in the shade of the veranda Grace was resting, wrapped in silk. She turned her head reluctantly from the level course, drenched with gold in the sun, with its bright white horse pens, posts, and stakes. The riders bustled about, flashing in shimmering colors like doves in the cloud of dust that rose from under the horses' hooves. From behind the shrubbery came the joyful calls of children; a little girl burst into happy, intoxicating laughter when a groom ran out into the light leading a trotting pony.

"Oh, it's you." Grace smiled gently. "You were lost; we have not seen you for years, Istvan."

She must have noticed his surprise, which was slightly tinged with dismay, for she turned her face away and let her eyes escape to the wide pastures and the riding course as if to assure herself that her husband was there—as if only he were important. Only when Istvan was standing over her did she seize his hand convulsively. Here was no great lady, only a poor, groping, uncertain woman.

"I didn't expect to find you here."

"Why did you come? You pass my house and all the places we used to frequent—"

He cut her short. "I want to forget."

"You have forgotten already. I am a handful of ashes. But others remember. They do not need the lights of Diwali to find their way to my door. On Tuesday Margit came with her boyfriend, an amusing American. His hair bristles like a colt's mane when it's cut."

"Margit visited you!" The news stung him. "How was I to know that you had returned to Delhi?"

"There is the telephone. Don't lie—you haven't called. I instructed the staff to record every name. Yours is not on the list, and they know you."

She laid her narrow palm on his hands.

"Sit down. You see—my husband is out there testing a new horse." She motioned with her head.

The stout figure of a rider swayed on the back of a light dapple-gray Arabian with dark legs and mane. His cork helmet gleamed like brass in the sun.

"And you aren't riding? You liked it so much."

She removed her hand as if she were closing into herself. Her gold bracelets jingled.

"I can't just now. Doctor's orders."

She was not looking at her husband, but at the children on ponies who were breaking into short trots. The hubbub, the laughter, and the whinnying of the horses could be heard distinctly; it was like a gleeful picnic. Both her hands were resting protectively on her lap. With a sudden spasm of the heart he remembered her wedding night and the spoils he had taken. Perhaps it is mine? A rebuke shadowed by alarm flashed through his mind: Why had he not waited, not denied himself that night's pleasure, in order to gain the deeper, more ardently desired love of the woman he had lost? I am paying for Grace now.

"You are expecting a child?"

"A son," she answered with such certainty that it seemed a foregone conclusion. "The rajah wants a son. I do, too."

She gazed at Terey with huge, sparkling eyes full of longing. Perhaps she wanted to lock the precious features in her memory and transfer them to the unborn child. I never loved her, after all, he thought, and was appalled. I was only under her spell. I was practicing, like a dog that hones its teeth before moving out on a new scent. He felt an aversion: she was pregnant, filled with the child. He so wanted it not to be his that he disowned it at once; he conceded paternity to the rajah without contest. Margit: her name rang like the whimper of a dog scratching against a door shut and bolted. Margit, only Margit.

They heard hoofbeats very near and the rajah trotted up. The horse looked white in the harsh light; it swept its hindquarters with a lash of its darker tail and tossed its head, chomping at the detested bit. Istvan saw only knee-high boots, the glint of a lowered spur and gloved hands pulling up the reins. The rajah's head was obliterated by a low awning that waved in the breeze.

"Hello, Terey." The rajah was panting after his gallop. "I'm glad to see you; you've been avoiding us lately. I know I stick in your craw a bit, but I have nothing against your looking at Grace the way you used to, especially now." He nearly choked with triumphant laughter.

"You're pestering me," she said, taking the offensive to dispel suspicion.

"I have no intention of depriving you of admirers," he parried. The horse under him danced and executed a half turn, then under a slight pressure of his rider's calf returned to the spot that bore the indentation of its hooves.

Istvan bolted from under the ruffle of the flapping blue awning. With his head raised challengingly he looked into the rajah's fat, sweaty, affably smiling face. He breathed deeply and rested a hand on the back of the horse's neck. A tremor ran through its skin and he stroked its smooth coat.

"A good horse," the rajah said. "Do you want to ride? Look: everything I have is at your disposal." He flung his outstretched hands wide open as if he wanted to clasp Istvan to his chest like a brother. "And you sulk—"

"Thank you. I'll stay with Grace."

"Only do not take her away; wait for me. We will drink Coca-Cola. Well, do not frown. I said that so as not to annoy Grace. We will get something stronger."

Only then did Terey notice that the crepe formerly displayed on the left lapel of the red frock coat the rajah wore as a member of the club was missing.

"Since you married you have removed your mourning," he said comprehendingly.

"I removed it because my older brother is alive." His face tightened into a bitter grimace. "He died, he was burned, his ashes were thrown into the Ganges, and now he has risen from the dead and is threatening to take me to court. His advocate came to see me—the celebrated Mr. Chandra."

"He is your partner, after all. Surely you can arrive at an understanding with him. He rose from the dead?" Terey shrugged. "That's lunacy."

"You forget that we are in India." The rajah combed out the horse's mane with his fingers as if he were toying with the fringe of a napkin at an unpleasant party. The cries of children jogging on ponies were disturbing the horse; it pricked up its ears and raised its lean head. "Chandra is not my partner, though I loaned him a large sum on security. I am afraid he wants to show his gratitude by fleecing me."

Before he pricked the mare's side with his spur, she broke into a smooth gallop, lowering her ears and thrusting her muzzle forward as if she wanted to bite at something.

The rajah sat her well. He knew how to ride, Istvan had to admit, watching the buoyant gait of the horse and the rhythmic springing movements of its legs until the animal and its rider disappeared between the hedge and the white stables.

"What's going on here, Grace?"

She sat with the face of a drowsy madonna, intent, as if she were hearing something. Pregnancy had not marred her beauty, only lent it gravity and a quiet ripeness—the charm of an orchard before the harvest.

"It's kicking." Her lips parted in a shy smile and she pressed her hands to her belly. "I felt its first movements on the left side, under my heart. It will be a boy."

He looked at her with a feeling of guilt, dismay, and a slight impatience, as one looks at a dog that fails to understand a command, though it stiffens in friendly readiness to retrieve.

"I asked—"

"Oh, don't bore me. When he comes back he will tell you all about it. He will be delighted to have someone to listen. When will you come to us?" She raised her eyes, large eyes that seemed to draw everything into them. "I thought I was free of you, but it only takes—and it comes back as hidden tears, a tightening in the throat at the thought of what might have been, what I cast aside through no wish of my own. When will I see you? Must I wait for a lucky accident?"

"What point is there in meeting? You have your own life."

"Before long there will be his life, too." She laid her hand tenderly on her swelling abdomen. "A little visitor will appear and must be guided through the world. So many stars fell that night." She spoke as though only to herself, sleepily, slowly.

He did not understand her. He saw a rocket making flashing arcs. Glistening tears slid down. A shudder ran through him when he thought of the insane audacity of his behavior.

"One star fell onto me. It is here, I feel it shining. I would tell no one but you. You will understand."

They sat motionless, leaning forward like people half asleep, incapable of any gesture. In the distance the noise of the galloping ponies died away; they could hear the boastful squeals of the small riders and the scolding of the mothers who sat on blankets in the shade of an acacia, never taking their eyes off the mischievous youngsters. Leather boots creaked, then came the light silvery jingle of a spur.

"I am waking you," the rajah whispered, leaning over the musing pair. "Enough of this tête-à-tête. Get up. Let's go. Istvan, come with us."

"I have my car." He was still resisting.

"Go first. I want to be sure you come to us." The rajah laid a hot hand on his shoulder. Grace had already risen and seemed to have regained her enthusiasm for life, for she took both their arms and drew them toward the door.

When they had passed through the middle of the lobby, not acknowledging the bartender's obsequious bow, it seemed to Istvan that Major Stowne, still dozing in the corner, lifted a hand from the arm of his chair to signal his delight that harmony was restored and that he had assisted fate by steering the lovers toward each other.

Before they reached the exit door the sky went gray and a heavy rain set in. The gleaming curtain of water stopped them. The downpour sang, twittering in streams from the roof, from teeming gutters overgrown with young grass sown by the wind. A barefoot servant hurried up noiselessly and handed them a big black umbrella.

The rajah let go of his wife's elbow. Uncertain if this were a gesture of courtesy, of favor, or if the other man were simply leaving him to perform the function of a retainer, Terey took the umbrella with the name of a London firm stamped in metal and held it over the woman. She nestled close to him and her fingers wound themselves around his hand—No! No! he cried inwardly, we are walking close together because of the umbrella. He led her down the streaming steps to the automobile, which was standing among the trees. The driver jumped out to open the doors and tried to take the umbrella from Istvan, who was shaking like a wet dog, for the leaves were soaked and streaming.

"Thank you," Grace whispered, gathering her sari around her. She pushed off her sandals and stamped her spattered bare feet. Her cherry-colored toenails gleamed garishly.

Now Istvan brought the rajah down under the umbrella. It's shabby on my part, he thought, this show of being meek and obliging. Was she worth no more than this to me? Margit, Margit: the name throbbed with grief like a funeral bell. He barely restrained himself from starting his car and driving until the abyss of rain swallowed him. He closed the umbrella and threw it from the open door of the Austin to the servant, who caught it in flight.

For a moment he looked at the blue fumes that belched from under the rajah's wide green car. Behind the rear windshield Grace's dark hair loomed; she was waving. With warning blasts on his horn he moved out in front of the rajah's limousine. The Austin rolled forward softly on the asphalt road, which was spattered white with rain.

The avenue was darkening. The large leaves of the trees, bent under spurting water, spread and drank in the steaming moisture. He almost heard the ravenous burble of plants, leaves, and grass as they sucked in the warm torrent. They seemed to swell. The very air took on a green cast.

The balding elderly man was nearly bouncing on his chair with impatience. He was eager to break in ahead of the rajah's easygoing narrative, but an admonitory look from his son-in-law silenced him. His bulging eyes shot angry glances and he drank his coffee with loud slurps. Istvan let himself feel the familiar atmosphere of the house: the smells of dampness and extinguished cigars, of spices, of a clump of narcissus, cloyingly fragrant as a field of blossoming potatoes, in a glass vase on the floor.

"After the death of my older brother, the entire estate passed to me," the rajah was explaining.

"And before that you had enough," the father-in-law put in.

"Yes, but if only for courtesy's sake, I had to submit information about financial operations for my brother's approval. So when he died, probably from heart failure—he was always sickly—the whole estate fell to me. There were bequests, but then jewels, currency, safety deposit boxes one doesn't take account of. Those are family matters."

"Good customs," Terey interposed. "Discretion ensures lower inheritance fees."

Vijayaveda nodded in agreement.

"His body was taken to the river in the evening. The pyre was quite grand; we don't spare the camphorwood for our dead." The rajah spoke with emphasis. "The body rested as if in a small house. It was covered with aromatic chips. Melted butter was poured from pitchers. When the priest touched the four corners of it with the torch, all the sky began to rumble and rain fell in sheets.

"The pyre smoked, but it caught fire. It poured, so there was nothing to wait for. I ordered the servants to attend to the burning of the remains and we took shelter in the automobile. Later we went out to the castle." He lowered his head and brooded, then after a long pause added, "The next day it was reported to me that the remains were consumed by the fire and the ashes thrown into the river. And now he turns up, and claims his rights." He struck his heavy parted thighs passionately with his fist.

"Now, now. A moment—" the counselor quieted him. "Did you recognize him? Is he really your brother?"

The rajah turned his head toward the window, which was washed by the pelting rain. His eyes were sad.

"I recognized him and I did not recognize him. He is so terribly burned. All over him are scars unevenly healed."

"But he must remember at least a few things that no one knows but you. Can you catch him in some inaccuracy when he alludes to childhood events—an old nurse, a dog, toys?"

"It is not that simple. He remembers some things. Others he seems not to remember. He blames the fire for eating the past out of his head. He is surely suffering. You know, I would like him to be my brother, but I am afraid there is some trickery."

"The servants are dark peasants. They long so for miracles that they accepted him as their master at once," old Vijayaveda fumed. "They try to persuade us that this is the true rajah, and they want it to be him so much that they constantly feed the person who was not burned up new details, and he begins to live his role. Another month or two and he will feel himself to be the older brother. He will demand shares in the businesses, request rigorous accounts. He will be different from the dead man, for he will know what he wants."

"Well, very good, but what do the attendants at the place of cremation say?" Terey inquired. "Is there the slightest chance that he could have survived? What does the doctor say? Surely you brought in a doctor."

"Attorney Chandra heard statements from everyone. Confronted with this blatant miracle, they admitted that the pyre was not consumed, that the rain extinguished the flames. They threw the remains into the Ganges so they would be carried downstream. The wood they sold; it could be used for other funerals, for new dead were being brought to the place. They swear that the remains were half charred, as the terrible scars and disfigurement confirm. No one would voluntarily allow himself to be so savagely injured, even to acquire a fortune like this.

"The man says that he felt how the flames gnawed and bored into his body, but he could not move or call for help. Only when they threw away the smoking pyre and pushed him into the water did he return to consciousness. The goddess Durga ordered the waters to carry him. They licked his wounds and assuaged his suffering." In the voice of old Vijayaveda there was a note of irony; he looked to his daughter for support, but she was silent.

"In the morning it seems that he regained consciousness, having been laid gently on the sand. He scooped up water and quenched his thirst. Women were caring for him as they did their washing on the river bank. He did not know who he was, but in his dreams, by degrees, heavenly powers restored his past to him. Do you understand?" He nodded at Terey. "It is all miraculous, out of the ordinary, exciting—but it is about money, a great deal of money." He shifted restlessly until his spoon fell on the stone floor with a jingle like glass.

"Incredible," Terey sighed. "And how did he get back here?"

"Attorney Chandra brought him. He found him in a cave on the shore, surrounded by worshipers, people doing him honor. The villagers fed him, brought offerings. He was, after all, visible proof that it is possible to die and return by the grace of the gods."

"And how did Chandra come to be there?" Istvan asked suspiciously. "Aren't there too many of these coincidences?"

"Chandra is a devout Hindu and came to wash away his sins in the holy waters. He heard of this new sadhu, so he came to ask for a blessing. They began talking and Chandra suggested that he abandon his retreat and return to his former life. He promised to appear before the court and defend his just cause—to force me to return the inheritance I had improperly taken possession of."

The rajah exhaled deeply and pondered for a moment how best to explain his troubles.

"The trial took place. The court had to decide who that grossly disfigured person really was. Only the court had the right to return him to life," he explained for Terey's benefit. "The judge asked me if I wanted to acknowledge him as my brother. Well—what would you have done in my place? If I had said no, right away they would have had evidence that he is indeed my brother, because I would have been defending my rights of possession: I would not have wanted to return what I took as my inheritance from him, and they are not trivial sums. I would have had everyone against me—"

"Who is 'everyone'?" Istvan interrupted.

"The attendants at the cemetery. The women from the village who found him. Even my own wife. Yes, even Grace, who is simply afraid he will put a curse on her child. Well, what was I to do? I acknowledged him. He was in the castle, and I took Grace away, so she would not be staring at that terrible face that looked as if it had been flayed, and I came here—to arrive at terms with Chandra. Yes, for in fact it was he who called that specter to life. And he hints that he would be able to convince the man to sign an act of relinquishment and go away to his retreat to perfect his inner life. To all appearances the rajah would die and a sadhu would be born."

"So, damn it, I'm asking you: Is he your brother or not?" Terey almost snarled.

"I do not know. I truly do not know. When I look into his tortured eyes through the slits in those eyelids scarred by the flames, it seems to me that I recognize him. When I hear his voice, I think: he is a stranger."

"Because it is a fraud!" His father-in-law sprang up and ran around the office, kicking the red cashmere carpet until it lay in folds. "They threw the corpse into the river and it drifted for a hundred miles. At least that was where the washerwomen found him."

"Oh, do not wear me out." The rajah raised his hands as if to shield himself. "I would rather give up money than repudiate my brother. There is so much that is miraculous about this business that no one will marvel at this hundred miles. You know very well what the judges said: that he must have floated on the wood as on a raft. After all, the pyre did not burn up."

"How much will Chandra get in the end?"

The rajah looked from under his eyelids at his father-in-law. They exchanged gestures of helplessness.

"If I do not pay him, my brother will, for he is a puppet in his hands. His trust knows no bounds. He is ready to turn over half his fortune to him. And he would be within his rights. Chandra brought him into the castle, gave him clothing, servants, a fortune, a good name. He made him my brother."

"Well, decide, then: He made him your brother, or he is your brother?" Istvan persisted. "Everything that happens from now on depends on this."

"You must protect yourself from this corpse that survived the flames!" Vijayaveda shouted. "It concerns not only you but Grace, and the one not yet born. Why must you allow yourself to be robbed? It is all Chandra's fault—Chandra, that demon whose appetite for gold and influence is never satiated. Can you conceive of it? He is obviously amusing himself with this whole affair, in which even the gods are implicated."

"And your sister-in-law? Did she recognize her husband?"

"She recognized him. She recognized him." The rajah spread his hands like one who is at his wits' end. "Understand: it is not possible to expect good judgment from women. She pities him."

"She even commends him," snorted the father-in-law. "He exercises his marital rights and is more adept at it than your deceased brother."

"So what can be done?"

"Things could be arranged with Chandra." The rajah inclined his head. "You know him. It seemed to me that he liked you. Talk with him. Cross-examine him. Perhaps he will show his hand. He has one weakness: he likes to brag. About everything, from his excellent cigars to his intimacy with ministers."

"Oh, he is proud as the devil himself," the older man concurred, pacing impatiently around the carpet, which lay diagonally across the floor. "But when he wants to make money, he can be"—he lowered his hands to knee height—"such a dear little thing."

"But after he humbles himself, he does not forget it. He is vindictive as a wounded elephant," the rajah added in his easygoing way. "No one would want to have him for an enemy. For the rest, he is a past master at law. He can unearth examples from old laws to settle contentious cases, examples that support his conclusions. You know that with us, as in England, legal precedents are binding. The judge must take them into consideration. I regret now that I engaged in business dealings with him. I yielded to the inducement of high interest and the impunity which he guaranteed me."

"And I warned you," his father-in-law said testily. "I didn't hide what they were saying about him—"

"None of which kept you from availing yourself of his services, father," the rajah cut in. "Who executed the transfer via Ceylon to Australia, to the Ward account?"

"Once, much, quickly, and an end to it." With a gesture of his hand the older man cut an unseen bond. "Was I going to dissolve the estate here, to let them squander it on their scheduled investments? It is possible to take risks, but good sense dictates that the future be secured—not for me, only for you and your children. I want nothing from life by now; I must think of your happiness." He spoke a little mawkishly, and the rajah caught the false note, for he rested both hands on his knees, leaned forward and looked at his father-in-law with a hint of mockery.

"Well, well. Let us say no more about it. I got myself into this and I will find my own way out." His face clouded over and he looked toward the door, where the portieres swelled in a light gust of wind as if something sinister were entering the room, breathing into their faces a cool dampness with the rotting odor of greenery run rampant.

"You must remember," Vijayaveda began gravely.

"I remember. I also remember our guest, whom we ought not to bore," the rajah said, discreetly signifying that Terey had been made privy to family secrets—real secrets, because they had to do with financial operations

A cart rolled out of the premature dusk. A servant, his sandals pattering, squatted beside the chairs and collected the emptied cups that stood on the bare floor and on the carpet. He put them on the cart with such a clatter that they might have been made of iron. He was announcing, with this rather unnecessary commotion, that he was working zealously. He could have gathered the dishes on a tray and cleared them away, but he preferred to roll out the tea cart in order to show that this was a modern house, a house of the highest class.

None of this was of any concern to Grace. She had changed her sari, which was sprinkled with rain, for a dark blue one, and was sitting in the shadows. Shifting gleams of light played only on the slippery silk that streamed over her knees. The gold of her sandals flashed, and the ruby red of her nails.

"Istvan—" she raised her head as if she were impeded by the burden of her artistically wound hair—"It is good to see you. I think we could renew our old friendship. I know I have become heavy and ugly, but that will pass. We will go riding again. I know I am not attractive to you just now."

He shook his head and said nothing. He saw her uplifted face, her doe's eyes open wide, her lips full and unresisting, parted in a wistful sigh. He was not certain if it was for him or for the girlish freedom, the joyous possession of a body free as it had been before marriage. Or perhaps she already felt pain and apprehension about the fate of the one who was growing inside her.

"Something has changed, Istvan." She spoke like a capricious child. "Margit is not the same, either. When I took her hand and put it here, so that she felt how he moves, she cried suddenly. You have all disowned me, even my father, though you heard him say he does everything for my good, and I don't even want to think that he sacrificed me for his business interests. They are his only true passion: to have, to possess. Indeed, he does not manage to use even a fraction of what he owns. My husband is like him. They call it prudence, sensible provision for the future, but it is a sickness. The goal is millions of pounds, tens of millions of rupees. Money be damned."

"But without it—you know how it is. You know life." The rajah rose and stretched. "You, my love, can allow yourself to disparage money because for us wealth is as much a matter of course as the air he breathes is to a poor man. Do not believe her, Istvan. She flatters you; she dreams of some utopian justice. Well, ask him what his colleagues do in that red hutch of an embassy. Everyone wants to skim off something. No one would say that he has enough, let his friend get a raise, a promotion. The increase of wealth is the very essence of life. You will get everything for money: dignity, honors, justice, and power. No one is immune. True, they will say no, but it is enough to bargain with them and they set their real price. They change their minds."

She smiled tolerantly, as if her mind were fixed on a different truth. She seized Istvan's hand and turned toward the rajah.

"And what do you have to reproach Terey with? That he seeks contacts and information, that he wants to earn a living? Perhaps he is immune to your sickness."

"I? Nothing." He spread his hands in a gracious gesture of powerlessness. "You forget that he is a poet." His tone seemed to say: an idler, a person with an impairment, even a cripple. "Istvan, beware—indeed, that is almost a confession of love. I will have to separate you, for she will bring up my son as a communist yet! Don't frown; after all, every revolution beginning with the French was fomented by jaded sons of aristocrats, bankers, and manufacturers."

"And the people?" Istvan asked truculently.

"The revolutions need their blood, and their voices, to legitimize the power that is taken over. I can have that power by paying for it with good money, not the false coin of slogans and illusory hopes. You will not convince me that you have equality, and where equality is achieved, it is like a freshly trimmed hedge: mutinous, ready to explode with wild growth."

"The law of the people is sanctioned lawlessness," his father-in-law asserted. "He was born a rajah; he must defend his own privileges and those of his children. True equality is in the hands of the gods. They decide where one is born. Perhaps it is just one of the despised, the suffering, the hungry, the cleansed from sin and after death incarnated into a noble race, who now absorbs our blood into his freshly formed heart—"

"No, I won't have that!" cried Grace, curling up and clasping her hands protectively over her rounded abdomen. "This is no stranger. He began from us."

"Yes—he is no stranger," her father affirmed. "He is from here, from India."

"Don't believe it, Grace," Istvan said comfortingly. "We only live once. You are very much a Hindu, Mr. Vijayaveda."

"What the devil else should I be?"

"You are very comfortable with it, sir," Terey concluded, raising Grace's hand to his lips ceremoniously as if apologizing for the words that must have hurt her. "It's time for me to go."

"When will we see you?" The rajah walked him toward the door with a friendly clap on the back. "You must not wait for a special invitation. You know we are both fond of you."

The car stood gleaming wet in the twilight. The fragrance of blossoming trees permeated the early evening air. The luxuriant greenery perspired, full of rustlings, the ticking of heavy drops of water, the sizzling sound of trickling rivulets. The light of lamps with overgrown branches pressing on them seemed to sing with the passionate tremolo of insects. Into this cloud, as it moaned with delight, bats fell like slivers of the deepening night, pricking holes in a drizzling horde of dancing moths, grasshoppers, botflies, and winged vermin that swarmed from under soaked foliage, from puddles, hollow trunks, steaming dung, chinks in old walls, and leaves delicately curled into tiny sheaths.

He breathed in the narcotic aromas of burgeoning plant life, listening to the throbbing of insects and the saucy rattle of large beetles, which shouted straight into his ears and tumbled like pebbles over the body of the car. The glare of the headlights caught a man in white with outspread arms. The watchman was hanging on the wrought iron gate, trying to open both sides of it with one tug.

Margit must be ill or she would not have let it be seen that something bothered her. Why had she been crying? Was she jealous? This meeting with Grace had held no importance for him; he was ashamed of that. Margit had stung him when she had spoken with brutal frankness of "wiping the slate clean," but now he had plumbed the meaning of the phrase. Grace had only attracted him because of her beauty; she had aroused desire. And now he was immersed in the element of love, which would either save or ruin him.

He did not have the strength to return to his house, to listen to the grumbling of the cook and the insipid effusions of the guard, who would speak of his future with such paeans of gratitude that it would be necessary to lay out a handsome sum for the wedding expenses. That was inescapable. To shut himself into the bedroom with a book, smoke a cigarette and chafe, to review the developments of the last few weeks . . . Why was she so stubbornly silent? She had been in Delhi several times, after all, and he could swear she had given no sign that she wanted to distance him. He could still hear her warm whisper close to his ear as her hair lightly brushed his cheek: "I am so happy with you."

They had visited Ram Kanval's exhibition together. In the dark hall of the club, in spite of the burning lights, the pictures lost their vividness; they looked gray. Potbellied Hindus, turbaned Sikhs with beards shining with pomade, streamed by indolently. Their untucked shirts and creased white trousers created an impression of torpor and slovenliness. They stood before the canvases exchanging malicious comments in whispers, tittering into their hands and fanning themselves with the printed programs. Professors of the Academy gathered around the artist with troubled faces like guests at a funeral.

The greatest interest was aroused by the cards with the inscription "Sold," and the price named. Until the counselor came with Miss Ward, and, when called as witnesses, they vouched for the painter, the little signs were taken for a shrewd advertising gambit. Hardly any diplomats attended; it was the wrong season, it was too hot. Whoever could had decamped to the mountains. And the exhibit was not to the taste of the Russians, though they had painters of their own who were searching for something novel. Only the Yugoslavians bought two pictures, and the Academy took one large canvas for thirty rupees to keep for a future museum of contemporary art, promising that for the time being it would be hung in a corridor.

Margit, full of joy and ready to share her happiness with everyone, then induced Connoly to pose for a portrait by Kanval, making sure that he paid the artist an advance. These successes, to all appearances minor but minutely observed by his competitors, reinforced the painter's cachet, and after the opening day flattering notices appeared in the press—except for a newspaper of the extreme right which called Kanval a subversive, an enemy of the national landscape, and, worse, of the beauty of Hindu women.

Margit had been in the capital twice more, and once on a Saturday night he had gone to Agra. Nothing had suggested that she would suddenly stop answering his letters, that she would not pick up the telephone.

He drove through the streets of Delhi, which were empty after the recent rain. A jackal fleeting past loomed yellow in the light; it looked like a little fox. Istvan saw two farther on, jumping nimbly as cats from crates full of garbage and ash. He heard their whining, like the crying of lost children, until it wrung his heart.

Kanval. He wanted, sincerely, to help him. Simply by using his scissors he had been able to alter slightly the tone of the reviews he had sent to the ministry to press a request that the painter be invited to Hungary. There was a chance that he could wheedle a stipend out of them and open the way for him to travel to Hungary and other parts of Europe, where they ought to understand his work and appreciate his originality. From their conversations, from the tone of Kanval's impassioned requests and sudden rushes of hope, he had gathered that such a journey would be not only the ultimate test, but an escape, a rising to the surface, an extrication from life in the anthill—from the struggle for daily rice, for a shirt for one's back, for favorable notice for art with a value not measurable in rupees.

Near the ruins of Jantar Mantar, where the enormous stone curves of the royal astrolabe bent into the sky over the tops of palm trees, he was too distracted to notice that a light-colored Citroen was blocking his way until he was forced to stop by the curb. A small man popped out of it, spread his hands in a gesture of welcome, and leaped straight into the glare of his headlights.

"I dreamed of meeting you," cried Nagar, hugging him suddenly and hard. He clapped him on the back and held him with restless hands, as if Istvan were the trunk of a tree he wanted to climb. "Great news: I predicted it! I smelled it!" he gloated. "I followed my nose."

"And I am looking for—"

"Everything will be there"—Istvan could not get a word in edgewise as Nagar held him by his sleeve and dragged him after him—"and news, splen-did news," he reveled in the weight of the words, "and a modest little bachelor dinner. Wait, for this is no less important, the aperitif: a martini with lemon and a drop of gin, but literally only for aftertaste. Perhaps Dubonnet. A cup of turtle broth, from a little turtle, it must be, not those great flat carrion eaters, I know, I know"—he forestalled doubts and reservations—"then quail and a heavy red. I can sniff the wine, and you will give me pleasure by emptying the bottle slowly, very slowly. Nothing is to be left for the servers; they don't understand wine. The English are boors in the matter of cuisine. Stinking whiskey is enough for them. So who is going to teach the Indians?"

In spite of this stream of chatter and the other man's quick, clumsy movements, Istvan pulled out a vinyl briefcase and locked the car. The wet branches along the boulevard brushed against their hands. The open house blazed with yellow light. A spotted setter was sitting on the threshold. She had not run up to meet her master; she only gave a wide yawn and casually wagged her tail.

"How are you, Trompette?" Nagar pulled a drooping ear. "A big old mutt, and still stupid. She thinks she will catch a jackal. When they begin to run close to the house at twilight and wail and prowl around the rubbish heap, the bitch goes into a frenzy. She nudges me with her nose, paws at me, and leads me to the gun rack. Straight away she tries to incite me to murder, and when I explain to her that one does not shoot at jackals, she looks at me reproachfully, even a bit contemptuously, for when she walks away she scratches the floor with her hind feet as if she were burying something."

The small, brightly lit hallway was filled with the aroma of wood burning on a hearth. Nagar squatted and thrust in his hands. His outspread fingers fluttered over the flame.

"I can't abide dampness." He pointed to the buffalo and antelope skins that hung on the wall. Between bunches of spears with tufts of horse hair dyed red he had displayed, as if its neck were built into the wall, the horned, majestically ugly head of the Indian rhinoceros. "I bought him," he confessed. "Isn't he a fine one? Nature's tank. I would not have shot him. Fewer of them remain than of us." He nodded for emphasis.

Two servants with languid movements and liquid glances—men of feminine aspect, flaunting their beauty—took bottles from a carved box. Listening with rapt expressions to the orders their master was issuing in Hindi, they poured the contents of the bottles into glasses and whittled thin slices of lemon, releasing the aroma of the peel. Nagar himself poured in a little gin, counting out the drops with the painstaking care of an apothecary. He tested the drink by sniffing and almost dipped the tip of his nose into the glass. He adjusted the proportions like a connoisseur. The very sight of these rituals aroused not thirst but craving.

The reddish cockscomb of flame trembled deep in the fireplace. As they were holding generous glasses that smelled of herbs and the forest and were garnished with tilted moons of lemon, Istvan heard the chirp of the teletype machine through the dark hall and said diffidently, "You were going to tell me—"

"In a moment. You are insatiable. Is nothing enough for you? You still want anxiety from the world to spice things up?" He cocked his head like a bird who wonders from which side to peck apart a crust of bread. "Only after the twentieth congress did he comprehend," he mocked, affecting the sober, expository voice of a radio announcer. "'I understood that the gravity and consequences of the errors are worse than I had thought . . . The damage caused by our party is significantly greater than I could have predicted.' Who is saying this? Something for you, Istvan, especially for you. Matyas Rakosi himself, and with beads of sweat on his bald head. For he knows it is his own funeral oration. And he is not sure if they will let him walk away or if they will demand an accounting for those he pushed to the wall. Everyone in the hall knows that those he murdered were true communists. He looks around and sees faces like clenched fists, and though he still sits in the presidium, he is wondering if the guard at the door among the oleanders will protect him or is already waiting to apprehend him. Or so it is said among you in Budapest.

"Rakosi has fallen, the secretary is Gerő, and his deputy is a former prisoner indicted under the imprimatur of Stalin—Kádár. Say now, what am I glad about? You should be glad! Your people at the embassy will only learn about this tomorrow from the newspapers, but in three days, when all the rejoicing is over and you get the official coded message that there are changes, you will see how your Bajcsy begins to realign himself, to set his sails handily for the new wind. But you have the news from me while it is still hot. Take advantage of it: you know how the cards have been dealt. Do you even understand what has happened there? There is another Hungary—you are a representative of a different country than the one that sent you here." His small face twitched into violent grimaces, like the face of a monkey struggling with a woman's handbag and its delightful contents, the value of which it feels though it knows nothing about how to make use of them.

So Bela signaled the temper of things correctly, Istvan thought with elation. Changes are going forward, great changes . . .

"Well? Well, what do you say?" The old reporter waited to hear Istvan's transports of joy. "Still not enough for you? Comrade Number One has no more cards up his sleeve, and people still living, because they suffered, don't feel the ache in anyone's back except their own." He beat his thin, sunken chest with a clenched paw, as if he himself had been in prison, been beaten by interrogators. "It's a healthy pain, a blessed pain, because it reenfranchises those on the bottom, who are forgotten. He can't see them through the memoranda on the production of steel, aluminum, corn. They disappeared because a black swarm of statistics effaced them."

"I knew that there was a congress. I had some sense of the mood—" The counselor tried to catch his breath.

"And you thought it would be a meeting of old apparatchiks, a row of plaster busts against a background of four profiles, the last of which veils those older ones as violence muffles the hopes of philosophers. And today they are separated from their natural constituency by a triple cordon, inaccessible. They listen graciously to applause and watchfully measure the volume of it.

"They have told me about it. I know as if I were there. They had a separate smoking room; each had his own coffee, which was examined by a doctor and heated by the trembling hands of the colonel himself. Instead of conversations with the nation for whose benefit they were trying to make decisions, out of those rooms came arrangements made in fear of the inevitable cleaning out of that—heroic, I don't deny—room full of dusty junk by young, prudent professionals. By engineers, economists, who have the courage to ask how much this will really cost, whose interest it will really serve. If young people begin making decisions about the future, people who are not encumbered by their pasts, who have no grievances, who are passionate in their fields of study—people who are not for sale and who see an opponent as someone who can be persuaded rather than having to be bought off—then Hungary can move forward."

He gazed into the fire, sipped his cocktail carefully and licked his lips, savoring it. He chewed the lemon peel for a moment, and when it became too bitter, spat the rest deep into the hearth, where it sizzled.

"The race with capitalism. Why should I be happy for you? How does it concern me? I don't want to race, I want to live"—he smacked his lips twice—"no more poorly than I do today, but I will refuse no one the right to such a life. By all means, strive like Nagar and you will have . . ."

Istvan had just grasped the significance of this new information. Rakosi's exit marked the beginning of an avalanche. His heart pounded. He foresaw enormous change: in Moscow, Khrushchev; in Warsaw, Gomulka; in Budapest . . . Who would have the courage to stand before a roaring crowd, tell the truth, and shoulder the burden of leadership without a feeling of contemptuous superiority toward workers, the indigent, the stubborn farmers? It must be someone free of the pride of the initiated, someone inured to every humiliation and to the fickleness of those who chanted his name, ready to lift him higher than their heads today, to serve him self-effacingly, as ready as they had been yesterday to tread him down with the vengeful rumblings of a thwarted herd of animals.

Trompette gave a sudden leap and squeal in the dusk of the garden and began to bark, romping under the bushes. They heard a machine clacking in the large room, striking its lever. A long tape filled with information unrolled in spirals, then stopped.

Like a miller awakened from dozing by the scraping of the sluice gate, Nagar rose briskly, put down his glass, and ran, shoulders hunched, down the corridor. Istvan saw him crouch by a machine and pass strips of type through his hands, then throw them around his neck like a snake charmer.

Just then he noticed that a young Hindu in a white shirt with a blue-speckled bow tie handed Nagar more tapes, and scissors, which the older man pushed away impatiently and then tore off the crisp paper with his fingers. With one determined smear he glued the printed strips together; he was doing his night's work.

Istvan would willingly have helped him, would have hovered beside him, seized the finish printouts of the news and read them greedily over his shoulder. As it was, courtesy dictated that he wait. Nagar knew both sides of the divided world; he had been forced to coexist, to survive concurrent tests of humanity's capacity for survival, but he belonged to the other side.

He returned with a long strip of paper hanging around his neck to his knees, perspiring lightly and wearing the complacent smile of the tailor who has conducted a successful fitting and knows that the client should be satisfied.

"A 'bloodless revolution,'" he mocked, reaching for his glass. "Gerő is already boasting that there was, fortunately, no Poznań there, though some writings in the West—" he drummed on the glass with his fingers until it rang jarringly—"our writings, ours, tried to describe some incidents in the Petofi club by calling it 'little Poznań.'"

"Agents of Western imperialism must have been at work in Poznań!" Terey bridled.

"And in the Petofi club were old comrades, even some from the Spanish underground, and Rajk's widow cried out to them to be brave enough to demand that the honor of her murdered husband be restored." He prodded him with his finger. "No doubt imperialist agents were there as well, yelling in the hall, 'Stalin sent us hangmen. Court martial for Rakosi!' 'Those people of Stalin's sow suspicion of treason and hate among us, comrades—whatever will keep them in power.' 'The struggle for freedom is the struggle for socialism.' Yes, those are certainly the voices of agents provocateurs. One hears the crackle of the dollar in them," he said sardonically.

"My dear fellow, unity of authority in the nation—that is no easy matter, and reports are no substitute for knowledge of the collective fate. Well, ask them: When was the last time they walked the streets of Budapest like normal people, drank a glass of wine in a tavern, not at a party, under the eye of the plainclothes police? When did they themselves buy something? You can mock the queen of the Netherlands because she rides a bicycle, but, well," he laughed unaffectedly, "I'm a bit of a demagogue myself. Holland to me is a great country. I imagined Khrushchev on a bicycle, as if he were already gone. Of course he must use that jet that is the bane of the continent whose fate is being decided."

Two servants took turns coming in and setting plates and little porcelain dishes with covers on the table. The smell of roasted meat mingled with the scents of wine and smoke from the fireplace. From the open door came the hum of rain. The dog ran in, wet and out of breath, shaking herself irritably. Flushed from under the trees by the downpour and lured by the light, moths flew in, whirring around the lamps, and lay on the white tablecloth like fuzzy buds broken off by a child.

"Justice, Istvan, is best left to God. At least I, an old Jew—or Frenchman, if you like, for that's more elegant—prefer to leave it to Him. Only sometimes He loses patience, He also becomes fed up, and entrusts the execution of it to people. He does not return life to the dead; broken human beings cannot be repaired like broken pots. So the guilty must pay. And if they are all shielded by the new leaders in whom people are now vesting power in order to secure, at last, this justice of theirs, there can be trouble if it takes too long." He spoke passionately until the light, throat-tickling, mouth-watering fragrance of turtle soup reached him. Then he rose from the stool by the hearth, bumped into the dog, who looked at him reproachfully, and sat down at the table. He lifted the lid of one of the cups without handles and sighed with relief.

"It is there—and I was so on edge because I thought they had forgotten to sprinkle a little chopped herb on top. Without parsley it's as insipid as," he hesitated, then brightened, "as reformation without justice. Tasteless; send it back to the kitchen. Let it cook longer."

When they were seated at the table and the dog had put her heavy head on Nagar's knees, he asked with a smile of childish cunning:

"Do you know why one sprinkles parsley on that broth? So it will keep you from eating too fast, so you will not swill it down but savor it, just as you tuck a tuft of hay into a bucket for an overheated horse before you water him after a run, so he can strain it through his teeth. It's healthier. It prolongs the pleasure. But what am I telling you this for? You are a Hungarian, you come of herdsmen and horse thieves. Hungary is not a stupid nation; when we were wandering around the wilderness on foot, you were riding from Asia on horseback like dukes."

But they could not finish dinner in peace, for messengers from the Delhi newsrooms, swathed in capes streaming with water, came to the house on bicycles, clamoring for bulletins, not from Hungary, but from Yugoslavia.

A little perplexed, Nagar rushed to the room with the teletype machines, sniffing like a bloodhound. He rifled through the coils of printed tape and tossed them behind him, cursing at his Hindu assistant. Trompette shook her muzzle, which was full of rustling ribbons of paper. Joined by the serpentine white loops, they looked like the modern figures in the satirical Laocoon of Salvador Dali.

"Here it is. I have it at last!" he shouted, hopping about as the dog tried to seize the twisted ends of the tape that fluttered just beyond her mouth. "She knows. She understands already that this is important information, and you, you sleepy scarecrow, missed it," he said abusively to the Hindu, who was not very much affected but put on a mawkish expression and set his lips as if he were about to cry. It was a bit overdone, but Nagar went silent, stroked the dark hand, and kissed the cheek comfortingly. Istvan saw how the young man smiled complacently behind his employer's back and lit a cigarette.

"I have to attend to everything myself," Nagar complained. "Look, a very important dispatch: a declaration by Tito, Nasser, and Nehru on the island of Brioni. Here, of course, we change the order of the names; Nehru will go first. They support the aims of the Algerian liberation movement. Now I understand why Sherif, a true Riffian from the Atlas Mountains, was hanging around here seeking admittance to the diplomatic corps. The representative of the state that is still a French province, and a member of a regime that does not even allow itself to be photographed—what times these are!" He rubbed his hands together. "Most eventful; even to be the dispatch agent is stimulating."

The telephone barked urgently and Terey, feeling that he was in the way, began taking his leave.

"Pandemonium! All my life it's been shouted over my head that the world is on fire"—Nagar pulled him back to the table—"but you must still drink this glass of burgundy. A good vintage; I got it from Ambassador Strovski. His family is from Poland, like mine, but that count from Galicia who became an ambassador only knows perhaps two words of Polish, both filthy, and meanwhile we are to believe in sentiment, in inheritance through blood. Well, how is the quail?" He picked it with his fork, using his fingers to help tear a slice of meat from the breast. He dipped it in the golden sauce and chewed it with relish.

"The Indian quail becomes tender quickly. It lies half the day in shallow swamp water before it catches the wind." He used the hunting imagery with obvious delight. "Eat, Istvan, don't stare at me. Your cook can't make you anything like this."

He paced around the room. The small gnawed bones he flung into the fire on the hearth. He gave the dog his fingers to lick, then wiped them on a printed tape that had stuck to his shoe and been dragged into the dining room.

"Cheese? Coffee and cognac? Ah, barbarian, barbarian! It's as if you had dressed in a frock coat and forgotten the socks for your patent leather shoes. Well, since you must, be off—" he patted him affectionately. "I know what's driving you. Make good use of your few hours' advantage over the embassy. And remember that you have someone here; true, Trompette?"

But the dog, with a furious whine, once again leaped out among the trees, which were drenched by the diagonally lashing rain.

HE WAS SO OVERWROUGHT that he could not think of going home.

Long sprays of rain shone in the headlights. The outlines of trees, and the villas hidden behind greenery from which banana leaves burst like geysers, flew by like an old, torn film. He drove up near Judit's door but did not get out, did not turn off the engine.

The curtain in the window was drawn aside and yellow light poured over the hood of the Austin. Thinking he had been recognized, he raised a hand in greeting and got out of the car. But instead of Judit, Ferenc opened the door, with a motion that seemed to say that Istvan was expected.

"You have heard already?" he asked confidentially. "It is certain. It came through London."

"Good. You've come." Judit sailed through the room, touching up her hair and giving them their chance to admire her full, shapely bosom. "What will they do with him? Do you think they will let him make a quiet exit? Even in retirement he would not be content. He is eaten up with ambition. He might become a source of trouble—a thorn in the side of his more successful competitors."

"He will take a side track. They will hide him away," Terey said vehemently.

"So I thought. Surely this is not an earthquake, only a cosmetic change." Ferenc looked him in the eye. "Others were also at the helm with Stalin—"

"But they must have preserved their humanity, since they are pressing for change. Democracy doesn't mean that it is permissible to arrest anyone, to condemn them for crimes not committed, to shove them into camps for years, or shoot them." Istvan's voice rang with passion. "Any government may find itself compelled to resort to force, especially revolutionary force. The difference is, and this is fundamental, that force cannot be the only form of contact with the citizens. It's the same with lying, for you must admit that every government has to lie, or at least be silent, about many things that are of pressing concern to people."

"Istvan, I find your analysis objectionable," Ferenc said worriedly. "To whose side have you slipped over? Are you edging too close to the capitalists?"

"I? That's just what you are doing. They pay us miserably at the ministry. Everyone lives in hope of getting abroad and grabbing a little hard currency—feathering his nest, fitting himself out, putting a little something by, perhaps even developing a couple of little businesses on the side. I'm not thinking of systematic abuses, only of what happens when the masters turn a blind eye."

"I don't understand what you're driving at," Ferenc said as if to distance himself.

"You understand. You understand perfectly well," Judit whispered with a wink, as if to say, the game is up.

"Your fears are well founded. There will be changes. There must be a democratization of this system which calls itself the most democratic, but how much we paid only the historians will tell us half a century from now. The stupid must go—that has just begun, and best if they are not pushed to the wall, for they will defend themselves. They will resist desperately; they will unite. They must be sent into retirement, to well-earned rest. They put themselves to great exertions; now let them set about writing memoirs in which they can exculpate themselves and bring the truth about their friends to light. Let us give them time to exhume what is in their consciences, perhaps even to sentimentalize their own misery."

"You think this is the avalanche?"

"I think the same way you think." He looked him hard in the eye. "You know that the boss, too—"

"Do not be quick to condemn, Istvan."

"You hope to outlast the ambassador, and, it follows, me," Ferenc said slowly, incredulously, his face contorting. "Oh, you poet! Poet!" he hissed.

"No quarreling. You two are standing rigid as a pair of roosters," Judit said soothingly, "and in the end, we are all of the same opinion."

"Not all." Ferenc turned aside unexpectedly. "I will not trouble you anymore. Do the agreeing yourselves." He bowed and walked out.

"You were carried away and you chose your confidant." Judit shrugged and sat down on the couch, looking worried. "You cannot just stir up the hornet's nest with that kind of talk. You know what he is like."

Istvan shrugged indifferently. "He's afraid for his skin."

"And I for yours," she said warmly. "You are a true hotheaded Hungarian. Silence is not always treason, and deliberation is not subjugation. You want to fight your way through everything. Before Kalman Bajcsy leaves—and he has connections and influence at home—you can create a great deal of bad blood. Do not be deceived by his indolent manner; he knows how to hit. Even if they recalled him, his opinion would carry great weight for a long time. They used to say that a man is composed of soul and body, then given a passport. Today he gets a whole file marked Confidential. You know how people love to speak ill of others." She tilted her head and moistened her lips with the end of her tongue, smiling as if to say, what can one do? "Even I," she added.

"No." He shook his head. "We've known each other too long. You are good. You have a heart."

"Don't count on anything. I have been through too much to be able take risks, even in the name of friendship. I tell you in all sincerity, I want to live in peace. Enough of those romantic gestures, one-day coalitions, capitulations on the eve of the scheduled attack. Enough whispered warnings, small betrayals. I want peace; surely you'll admit that I am entitled to it. I know everything." She thrust out her full lips with bitter assurance. "Well—why don't you ask me what?"

Her warm brown eyes looked at him invitingly. She sat hunched over, her locked fingers gripping one upraised knee.

"I fled Hitler and went to Russia. I wanted to be as far from him as I could. And I was. I was taken to the mouth of the Obi. Oh, to be sure I understand that they could not trust deserters. With a terrible effort that enormous country fought against the invasion! I remember to this day those browned clusters of log houses, those appalling tree trunks like dead columns, the clogged chimneys, the forest cut to a height of three meters. I beat my brains: who inflicted this senseless difficulty on themselves? And without further ado three meters of snow fell. Loggers were out standing on skis and cutting in a minus-forty-degree frost that made the beams in the cottages crack as if you were battering them with axes.

"There were plenty of trees. You couldn't chop through the wall of entwined trunks. The healthy cedar held up the weak birch, which crumbled at the touch like decayed fungus.

"I didn't meet my quotas. I had lice, impetigo, bumps on my face from gnats, those tiny midges that cut the skin. I had bites from the ticks that dropped from the leaves—but I still aroused desire. They did their business on plank beds in the bathhouse; I got a hunk of bread. Do you despise me? Istvan, I wanted to live. I took to sewing. The dress I'm wearing I made myself. Then they stopped taking me for a German spy. I got my own corner, set off with a large slab of wood, and the officers stood in line, competed for my regard, gave me boxes of fish paste, bottles of homemade liquor, cigarettes. Sometimes I see the tundra in my dreams and I wake up with my heart pounding. I breathe easily now because that is all over for me. I returned to Budapest. I worked for the military prosecutor. Don't look at me that way. And don't demand too much."

He looked at her with profound pity. He seemed to see her from a great distance, as if through the eyepieces of a lorgnette turned backward. She has foreseen the thunderbolts that will fall on my head. Are things really that bad for me? His breathing grew labored.

"My dear," he began gently, "I came to you because I was looking for my own, for Hungarians. When great developments are occurring in Budapest, surely we ought to be together. The embassy, after all, is a piece of the homeland, or at least it should be. And both of you—and you yourself—Judit, I knew I was alone, but I did not think I was so very alone." With a savage motion he snuffed out his cigarette. "No. Don't be afraid. I'll not cause you any trouble."

"Terey," she ventured timidly. "Istvan," she corrected herself, "I didn't want to hurt you."

"It's I who am apologizing. Well, all right, then. There is nothing more to talk about. Goodbye."

He walked with a heavy stride through the living room, in which every piece of furniture seemed to have been put in place only temporarily, as on a stage—even the flowers, enormous lavender bouquets of gladioli. Nothing, not one picture, tapestry, or piece of earthenware, was from Hungary. She could have gone out of that room with a suitcase and someone else could have moved in, and nothing would have been changed. He raised her hand to his lips. Suddenly he felt her warm, ample arms around his head. She kissed him maternally on the forehead and pushed him away lightly.

"Go now," she whispered.

He stopped on the threshold.

"No one yet has seen how I cry," she said with her head erect, and suddenly he noticed the unnatural flash in her eyes. They were brimming with great tears which she did not wipe away but which rolled slowly down her cheeks.

"Until tomorrow," he said warmly, his fingers on the door handle.

When he had slammed the door of the Austin, the light in the window went out and the house seemed to retreat behind a heavy veil of rain that had waited just for that moment. The windshield wipers, purring monotonously, slid over the glass. He forgot about the weeping woman; he was forced to concentrate on the road. Glimmering reflections lit up in front of him and the half-obliterated landscape loomed like a bad dream.

In the morning—a morning full of cheerful flutterings, starlings' cries, leaves rinsed and sparkling clean—he had hardly driven up to the embassy and heard the friendly crunching of gravel under his tires when Ferenc came out to meet him, greeting him as if they had not seen each other for a long time.

"Everything is confirmed. Headlines in bold type," he announced triumphantly. "The ambassador is here already." He leaned forward. "Someone must have let him know, because he called during the night and asked what Budapest had sent over. He directed the cryptographer to get the dispatches to him immediately."

They looked at each other.

"It is only a bulletin. Less information than in the newspapers."

"You know already?" Terey asked tauntingly.

"The cryptographer gave me a copy before he burned it." Ferenc was not in the least troubled by the admission; it was as though he and the ambassador, only they, had the right to read the coded dispatches.

"How is the boss?"

"Hard hit, not showing it. A diehard."

"He is well schooled," Terey admitted. "As if he were going to show anything! Dissatisfaction? Now he must turn all his ingenuity to making allies of his recent opponents, just as if they had been waiting for that all the time. He can manage it."

"It is not known yet if the changes will be permanent." Ferenc hesitated as if he were not certain whether to confide everything to Istvan. "The boss crumpled a dispatch, threw it on the table, and said to the cryptographer, 'They changed the hat for the time being, but the head remained the same. Get those papers away. They are littering up the place.' Apparently he believes that everything may still reverse itself."

They went in and walked up the stairs to the second floor, each to his own office. Stacks of local newspapers lay on Istvan's desk. He read the large headlines, inhaling the familiar odor of printer's ink. Above the news of the changes in the central committee in Hungary he saw the proud words about freedom for African nations: the declaration from the Brioni islands on the issue of freedom for Algeria. Nehru, Nasser, Tito; the order of the names was just as Nagar had predicted.

He waited until noon, expecting that the ambassador would call them in and give an account of the situation in Hungary. The matter was becoming urgent, for journalists they knew were calling, asking for what they politely called "background" comment. But the embassy staff had no details, no sense of the atmosphere of the congress, no authoritative information from the home country, he thought, writhing.

Outside the window the heat was intensifying. The cooling machine wheezed air sticky as vapors from a laundry. Rakosi gazed at him from the wall with a roguish sneer. I didn't hang him there. Let Ferenc take him down, he sighed, rubbing the sweat from his face. The caretaker had just brought him coffee when someone knocked lightly at the door.

"Come in," Terey said in Hungarian. He was not expecting any calls from "contacts," the term used by embassy staff for Indian visitors from the city. But no one entered.

Then the caretaker opened the door. Behind it stood a stocky man, an importer who numbered the embassy among his customers. He pressed his hands together in front of his chest and inclined his head, which appeared distended in a turban painstakingly done up in small pleats. His face had a greasy gleam.

"Greetings, sir." He approached the desk. "I have a small matter."

"Are you taking orders, Mr. Gupta? I asked for half a dozen cases of whiskey."

"I have just brought them. They are waiting below in the automobile. As you ordered. The servant will bring them directly. Or perhaps we will simply leave them at your home?"

The caretaker waited to see if the counselor would tell him to bring more coffee. Terey paid no attention to his questioning look.

"And what about payment? Check or cash?"

The merchant threw a meaningful glance at the caretaker. Obviously he found the presence of a witness bothersome.

"Well, then, Mr. Gupta?"

"Cash." Reluctantly he drew a thick envelope from the pocket of his wide, baggy, rumpled trousers. "Mr. Ferenc doesn't like checks." He tried discreetly to hand the counselor the envelope, which was stained with grease and bulging with a roll of banknotes.

"What is this money?" he asked in amazement.

"It is for the whiskey." The Sikh thrust out a thick lip under an oiled mustache. "They have raised the duty so that my countrymen will only drink at embassy receptions." Suddenly comprehending that the counselor was not going to take the proffered envelope, he snatched his hand away and began to explain that the secretary was not in his office, though he had called from the city and arranged a meeting.

At that moment the door opened and Ferenc came in. He greeted Gupta.

"I went out for a moment. The ambassador summoned me. Have you brought the vodka?"

"Yes, and I cannot find out how much I am paying for it now, because they have raised the duty."

"For Indians, not for us. Diplomatic status. True, Mr. Gupta?"

"Yes," he affirmed warmly. "For me, a poor merchant, it is a loss; for you gentlemen it is a profit. They locked my warehouse. I can sell only what I brought in at the earlier price."

"Well, how much must I pay?" Terey demanded.

"Nothing. It is a gift from a friend," said the Sikh, twisting his puffy face into a grimace.

"That is not possible."

"But it is possible. It is." Ferenc took the merchant by the arm and pushed him toward the door.

"Take it as they give it, Istvan. As you drink it, you will have time to think about why you got it."

"Take it, counselor, sir," whispered the caretaker. "Perhaps you will have a bottle to spare for me?"

"One always has to pay three times over for this free whiskey," the counselor retorted. "What does he want from me?"

"I am waiting for a new order," the merchant said, bowing. "I even have one written out here."

"Come to me. We will consider this in a calmer moment." An impatient Ferenc waved the man out. "How hot it is!"

When they had gone, the caretaker looked at Istvan approvingly.

"May I have a bottle? Why not a little something for me, too?"

"Take it," Terey waved a hand, "and be off."

"Right you are." He drew himself up in soldierly style. "I have not been here at all, counselor."

The telephone rang shrilly. The ambassador was calling him to a briefing. Istvan rose, stretched, and adjusted his loosened tie. As he closed the door, he looked again at the portrait, at the bold, conical head of the man who had bullied Hungarians for years.

"I HAVE READ YOU the bulletin." The ambassador rested both hands on his desk and, straightening his heavy trunk, looked out from under lowered eyelids. "Well—this you already know. De-Stalinization has taken over our country. It is a complex process—the consequence of errors, perversions, and a quite complicated situation in our camp. It must be embraced with great caution, since the very process that carries within itself the possibility of favorable changes, if unleashed without restraint, may lead to internal upheaval and drastically weaken the resiliency of the party machine, and its enemies are just waiting for that."

They stood in a huddle, a little dismayed by the paucity of words, the absence of a feeling of relationship to recent events.

"He is biding his time," Istvan whispered to Judit. But she only pressed his fingertips to silence him.

"Go back to work. Are there any questions?"

"Journalists are on our doorstep, wanting details," Terey began.

"They must be pacified. Tell them the truth—Hungarian radio does not reach us, and we have received no official commentary as yet. Do not rush to the fore with any statements. Send them to me, and I will get rid of them . . . as many as manage to catch me, for I intend to leave Delhi for a couple days just now." He grinned, showing crooked teeth yellowed from nicotine. "There is no need to rush into some folly. There is always time for that. True, Comrade Terey?"

It seemed to Istvan that he was only now about to hear a truthful remark. He took the bait.

"'To err is human,'" he said.

"But an official, especially when he is attached to the embassy, ought to avoid it. Remember, Terey, that you are not here as a poet. Do not let your imagination have its head too soon."

"This mentoring is rather astonishing to me."

"To me as well. You are not a young colt, Terey, to go kicking over the traces here. It should be time to think seriously of the future."

"That is just what I am doing," he said obdurately. He turned and walked out. But he felt that the ambassador had not let him out of his sight, and was barely restraining himself from calling him back.

Nothing has happened. It is just the way he is, he reassured himself as he smoked a cigarette in his office. He shouts at one person to single him out from the group and force him into some capitulation, taking the occasion to throw fear into the others. He spoke quite sensibly; there is nothing worth worrying over, though the schoolmasterly tone was grating.

The caretaker came in quietly, set a small chair in place, and took down the portrait.

"Pish! Away with the vermin," he shuddered. "I mean the lizards that lived behind the photograph. I have loathed reptiles since I was a child."

He peered at Rakosi at close range, as neighbors gaze with undignified curiosity at the face of someone who has died.

"Comrade secretary ordered that the portraits be stored in the library. He said that in a few days we may be hanging them again." He lingered, wiping away smudges of dust. "But you, counselor, stand up to them all. You will not swallow that."

Terey did not engage him in conversation. The anger he was stifling smoldered in him. He was annoyed with Ferenc over the matter of Gupta. I'm not the prosecutor, he thought, biting his lip. I don't care how much he makes from it, but I won't be played for a fool. Does he think I don't remember what he asked for?

He was so irate that he rose impetuously, shoving his chair aside. For a moment he plunged his hands in the stream of cool air from the machine. Then he made up his mind to have a talk with Ferenc.

The secretary put a calm face on the issue. He invited Istvan to have a seat, to smoke a cigarette—or perhaps he would prefer a sip of orange juice with ice?

"What is on your mind, Istvan? My little flair for business? Really, the money comes of itself. If you want me to, I will give you half. I swear to you, I saw that Sikh in person for the first time today. Gupta Brothers—and that must be the stupidest of them. Take this." He pushed a wad of banknotes across the desk as if foreseeing that Terey would reproach himself for signing the orders. That Ferenc had five hundred rupees already counted out exasperated Istvan most of all.

"You know where you can put that cash," he snarled. "You'll have no partner in me."

"You feel disgust? So much the better. Just remember that your signature is on the orders, and you cannot deny it, and you cannot justify it. So be careful," he warned coolly. "If you become annoying, I have ways of dealing with you. Bajcsy will be on my side. Would it not be better to part amicably and forget about the whole business? It is a bore in any case."

"It's rotten, do you understand?" Terey shouted. The other man smiled as if it were a compliment, full of the sense that he had the upper hand.

"Do you want it to be war between us?" He blew out a stream of smoke. "Comrade Terey, think well: you have no chance. You will lose. Well, I extend the hand of friendship."

Istvan ran out of the room and slammed the door. He summoned the caretaker and told him he could take the remaining five bottles of whiskey.

"Oh, counselor, sir! That really is too many. I asked for one because when the sun dries a man out in the daytime, he likes a nip of something wet at night."

"If you don't want them, give him back to Gupta when he shows up here."

"Ah! I am not so stupid. He gave what he gave. They will not be wasted on me. Thank you very much." He bowed in the doorway. "And if you think better of it, counselor, sir, why, as long as they are with me, they are, let us say, on deposit. Perhaps I will crack one a week."

"Go now."

"Everyone is irritable today. Things seem to have become a little less difficult at home, after all, and Rakosi is not your kin or mine. What is there to regret?"

When he was alone he began to make notes, to answer messages from Indian officials. A feeling of powerlessness weighed on him. He was in trouble; he had to be courageous enough to admit it. He would have to pay for his obtuseness. He heard Ferenc passing through the hall: his footsteps stopped in front of his door, but after a moment he moved on. The engine of the ambassador's large car growled in its familiar bass. Through the window he saw one figure lolling in the back seat. So they didn't go together, he thought with relief.

It would be enough to tabulate and produce a checklist of the casually signed forms to ensure that evidence that the counselor was speculating in imported vodka would find its way into a report to the ministry—evidence that he was exploiting his diplomatic status to avoid paying duty. "This kind of hole-and-corner profit-taking is unworthy of a diplomat and may lead to intervention by the Indian authorities. We defer the decision . . ." Or a simpler accusation: "Counselor Terey has been drinking heavily, as the enclosed invoices with his orders for alcohol attest. In recent months the value of his orders has amounted to three-quarters of his salary. We are of the opinion that, before a scandal results, it would be advisable . . ."

Then they remind themselves that he is a poet, and the officials only nod their heads: these are the effects of experimentation with unsuitable personnel, of making a poet a civil servant. Complaisantly, with untroubled consciences, they present his recall from his posting to the minister for his signature.

A desperate longing to see Margit came over him again. The fear that he might have to leave without seeing her assaulted him with the sense of the power of this clandestine relationship. Margit. Margit. He had no claim on her apart from the one she had given him out of generosity. He had no opportunity in the course of the next two weeks to go to Agra again. He was ready to humble himself, to offer explanations, to plead; anything to ward off a final rejection. He swallowed and opened his mouth as if he were gasping for the steamy air. To have Margit back, nothing else, nothing, only to hold her in his arms, to breathe the fragrance of her hair, to feel her thighs pressing against him, her belly, her breasts, warm breath on a bare neck. The thought of his loss was bitter as gall. He ached; a great hunger cried out in him, a hunger for tenderness.

He looked through the dusty window screens to the fringed tops of palms waving in the sun and the brilliance of the sky washed with torrents of rain. He was overcome by the desire for movement and space—to escape from this stifling room, from the odors of damp, creased papers covered with writing and cigarette ashes shaken onto the carpet, from the the nauseating smell of DDT.

One more letter and he ran to the car.

The shaggy greenery of the climbing plants rippled. The embassy seemed to be sighing in the broiling noon heat.

"Uncle, wait!" He heard Mihaly's plaintive voice. "Uncle, take me with you."

"Where do you want to go?"

"I don't care. Where you go." He looked Istvan in the eye, pushing his pale blond hair aside.

Terey sensed the boy's wish and announced without hesitation, "I'm going a long way. I will tell you where, but don't tell anyone."

"I won't. Word of honor." The boy blinked in the glare.

The counselor leaned forward and whispered in his ear, "For ice cream."

The little fellow did not believe this. He fixed him with a crest-fallen smile and said, "You are always joking, uncle."

"No. I was afraid you wouldn't want to go."

For answer the boy got into the car. They rode along the avenue, where warm gusts of wind blew up great sprays of fallen, withered blossoms. Motorcycle rickshaws passed them—small, crowded vehicles. Under their heavily fringed canopies, Hindu women's shawls fluttered, blue, cherry-red, and light as mist. The drivers' downy cheeks bulged with wide smiles as they honked, squeezing big pear-shaped rubber horns as gleefully as if they had been the full breasts of girls.

"You know, uncle," Mihaly confided, "I have a friend, a mongoose. He is not afraid of me at all. He comes to my hand. He lets me pet him. I feed him every evening."

"What do you feed him?"

The child faltered. He rubbed his nose with his hand, turned his head away and mumbled, "Different things, but he likes raw eggs best."

A wide perspective on the avenue leading to the India Gate opened in front of them. Space bursting with light streamed toward the car.

"And what does your mother say about this?"

"Nothing." He shrugged his small shoulders. "Mama doesn't know about it."

Under trees with succulent foliage growing wild stood an odd building with the appearance of an enormous tub, covered by an undulating blue pavilion. They could hear the noise of an engine, like the roar of an enraged tiger, rising to a whine as the motor raced. The planks beneath the flying motorcycle rattled like loose timbers under a bridge.

"Have you been here, uncle?"

"No."

"But I have. He told them to let me in. His wife sits there all day and prays to the king of monkeys for his success."

"Who are you talking about?"

"Krishan," the boy said indignantly. "He is the death rider. He rides just like this"—he turned his hand flat—"until it's frightful to see. When he comes flying by everyone huddles behind the barrier, and it hurts their ears."

"That daredevil!"

"Krishan says he likes it. Sometimes he lies on the grass and smokes a cigarette and I run to the cashier to see how many tickets they sold, because when there are fifty, they tell him to do the show."

Light and shadow played over their faces. They sped along beneath the overhanging boughs of old trees.

"Listen, Mihaly. What do you want to be?"

"I?" His eyes opened wide. "I want to be a real Hungarian. Like you, uncle."

Through his linen shirt Istvan felt a warm little hand resting against him.

"Because I love you very, very much."

"You certainly know how to get ice cream!" He put on the brakes at Connaught Place. "Well, get out."

But Mihaly sat still and stared him in the eye.

"Go by yourself. I will wait. Because you said that I know how—"

"You'll be sorry."

"Yes . . . but if you want, you can bring me a little bit on a waffle," he said, relenting.

"Get out. Don't be annoying," the counselor said, feigning impatience. "Indeed, you know that I am very fond of you and that I could not eat ice cream knowing that you were waiting in the car."

"Oh, uncle," the boy sighed and clasped him around his neck. Istvan felt each of his limber knuckles and the eager quivering of the heart.

He kissed the little lad with dry lips, reproaching himself inwardly because he had not answered his sons' letters for two weeks. He held Mihaly's hand and led him through the arcades. A slender boy with a sash around his hips moved along behind them, playing a simple melody full of lamentation on a flute. A monkey dressed in Scotch style with a plaid kilt, caftan, and beret darted ahead of them and blocked their way, then struck a tambourine and threw furtive glances from bulging eyes brimming with a human hunger.

Chapter VIII

Swollen drops of moisture falling here and there from the trees made rainbow-tinted etchings on air washed clean by the downpour. Greenish light fell through the wide, unfurled leaves. A Tibetan woman who had spread out her wares on the sidewalk cast a leery eye at the sky and rolled up the yellow sheet of plastic that had been covering bowls of old coins, round and octagonal, worn smooth from centuries of use, with holes so they could be strung on leather strips; wooden demons' masks with grinning teeth; little bronze figures green with verdigris; old knives; boxes full of beads roughly shaped from semiprecious stones; turquoise buttons; and little pellets of nephrite that seemed to be filled with gold shavings: tiger's eye.

The woman, with her flat, ageless face, with her hair in a mass of braids and silver reliquaries on her necklace, sluiced shining rainwater from the recesses of the plastic covering. Squatting in voluminous red and blue skirts, she arranged figurines and votive censers in even rows.

Istvan walked out of his stifling office, where the fan was stirring the cigarette smoke. It was a relief to breathe in the fragrance of wet earth and fresh leaves. The censors, or rather the Bureau of Film Appraisal, as it was discreetly called here—a commission of lethargic old bureaucrats carelessly dressed—had given him permission for the release to the public of several short informational films about Hungary and two amusing folk tales. They had demanded that one frame showing a playing field with girls in gymnastic costumes be excised as immodest. Every gesture of intimacy on the parts of embracing couples was eliminated; kisses evoked outraged mutters. "Throw it out, get rid of it!" "Scandalous!" the chief of the commission exclaimed, belching garlic into Istvan's ear as he leaned forward in the dark projection room pierced by a cone of hazy light. No extenuation was of any use; the scissors chattered and with a dry crackle, as when one steps on a centipede, the cuttings of film fell in curls under the editing table.

Yet Istvan had been gratified when nine boxes, each containing three meters of film, were returned to him with the official inscription: Released for distribution in India and Kashmir by the Bureau of Film Appraisal. In his briefcase he had a special memorandum, a photocopy of which was to be sent with the films to the Hungarian-Indian Friendship Society.

Its members had come primarily for lectures, after which a poster announced the film and a cartoon. Papers were read in unctuous voices over the monotonous whir of fans boring through air thick as tallow; from the opening sentence the notables dozed, sprawling in armchairs. When the film came on, the hall revived and no harm was done if the boxes had been packed incorrectly and the reels were out of order; the incongruity between the commentary and the action on the screen set off a strident discussion. Each had understood what he saw in his own way. Yet even out of these dissonances a sense of his country arose—associations and images that would spring to mind when they read about the Republic of Hungary in the newspapers.

He walked along the pavement over wet flagstones the rain had littered with leaves and the remains of flowers. The square of dry red clay that had been covered with plastic glowed in the light; the crowd of oddly shaped figurines intrigued him. The bowls, boxes, and tin cans seemed to conceal unknown treasures. The Tibetan woman smiled with eyes that were narrow slits and beckoned with both hands until her tight braids bounced on her shoulders.

"Cheap, very cheap, sahib," she cried in a croaking voice like a parrot's. "Precious stones, beautiful stones, necklaces, earrings, bracelets, rings. And gods of bronze, stone, wood, clay . . ."

He leaned over and picked up a figure of the goddess Lakshmi, which was as sinuous as if she were dancing. Spots of verdigris and dried blotches of mud attested that the little statue had been dug out of the ground.

"Very old. Sahib knows to find what I have most precious." She clicked her tongue approvingly. "Only fifty rupees."

"What are you looking for, Mr. Terey?" A shadow fell on the little cluster of divinities. Istvan whirled around like someone caught in wrongdoing. Attorney Chandra was standing behind him, smiling indulgently.

"You prefer gods of stone and silver—"

"I can't resist temptation. I must dig through this garbage heap." He handed the figurine to the lawyer. "I'm always hoping to unearth a true work of art."

"Do you like this?" Chandra moved the figurine to and fro casually on his open palm. The woman scowled at him.

"Nice lines, very graceful—and surely old."

"Smell it." Chandra pushed the little goddess under his nose. "Notice the odor of hydrochloric acid, the artificial patina. They may even have ancient forms, but the casting is fresh, done for tourists. They rub it with acid to make it green. They smear it with clay. The vendor is so shrewd that she will swear every trifle you choose is a true treasure. Give that back to her. It is a waste of money."

Istvan put the figure down gingerly.

"You are a man of good judgment," Chandra commended him. "You know how to profit from good advice, so you will be rewarded. If you wish to buy, and cheaply, a genuine work of art, a few centuries old, take that stone head the peddler woman uses to weigh down the plastic. It has a chipped ear and a dented nose—we can bargain for it—but it is the only piece worth anything. Do not look at it so eagerly. I will buy it for you."

Chandra asked about a heavy silver necklace, haggled for a moment, then, as if resigned to defeat, reached for a copper lamp that he also rejected as too expensive. Just as he seemed on the point of leaving, he pointed the end of his shoe carelessly at the battered head.

"And how much for that?"

The Tibetan woman did not want to antagonize him by naming too high a price. She was afraid they would go away without buying anything. So she raised both hands and spread her fingers:

"Only ten."

"Good!" said Chandra. "Take five and be glad of it. This rubbish is not worth that much."

He did not even bend over, but waited for her to kneel and hand it to him. He frowned as he passed a finger over the nicks in the stone.

"Very well, sahib," she said. "My loss. Please take for luck. Today I almost give away, tomorrow I make profit. It is from a temple. Very, very old."

"In that case I will not take it. Do you know that carrying away old sculptures is not permitted? And still you say that you are losing. And I wanted you to sell something, at least. It would have been useful as a paperweight, but I can use any stone for that. No, I will not take it."

"Sahib will buy—"

"No, for you ought to know that you may be able to swindle someone, but not me. Look: a chip. A dent . . ."

"Sahib, three rupees." She held up three fingers on her left hand.

"No. I have changed my mind. Let's go—" he turned to the counselor.

"Two rupees. One—" she begged. "Take without money, as gift. Do me great favor."

They stopped and turned back. Chandra took the head with an indifferent air.

"Heavy," he sighed as if disenchanted, and handed it to Terey. Nevertheless he groped in his pocket, took out two rupees and tossed them to the bowing peddler.

"Gift for gift." He glanced at her as if with reluctance.

"I am happy." She bent over, pressing her fists to her chest in Chinese style.

They left. Istvan was delighted as he looked at his prize: the heavy lips in a somnolent smile, the eyes with their tolerant, complacent gaze, the impeccable lines of the elegantly secured hair. The flaws only heightened the charm of the old sculpture. He touched it delicately with his fingertips, as if its wounds could feel pain. A raindrop from a tree fell onto the stone and flowed over one smooth cheek like a tear, leaving a trace of wetness. A beautiful head! Suddenly he felt grateful to Chandra, who was saying in a low, melodious voice:

"There is a great deal of the child in you; you are capable of taking pleasure in anything. Really—do not give me back the two rupees. Rather it is I who should be embarrassed that I took the liberty of offering you such a trifle."

"You know that the delight this bit of sculpture evokes is beyond price."

"Some herdsman must have broken it from a temple frieze," Chandra mused. "He pried at it with a crowbar and chipped the ear. The head fell off and rolled down from the upper floors of the pagoda. It hit the stones and dented the nose. I suspect that the peddler did not pay a penny for it, but received it as a makeweight or gratuity. She did someone a favor by taking it. The thought of buying such a piece of sculpture would never even have crossed my mind. What would I buy it for? So my eyes would always be lighting on that head—that head, which came into being a couple of hundred years before me and will still be here when I am gone, when my ashes mingle with the Ganges slime."

"But you believe, you should find comfort in it . . ." Istvan looked at him in amazement.

"Comfort—that beauty can be destroyed by nothing more than a little stupidity and greed? He was not even thinking of the possibility of selling it; he tended goats and he was bored. He climbed onto the temple wall to grapple with the stone figures. He did not even know that he had knocked off a god's head. Do I believe?" he said meditatively. "In what? That there is something indestructible in me, a breath of immortality, a spark which will return to life, grown over with new and ever-varying flesh? If that will not be myself, Chandra, what concern is it of mine? If I lose the memory of my own acts, merits, and faults, how can they influence my fate?

"The return of the reincarnated," he mused, "greeting the world with tears and cries, the despair of the infant who has lost its knowledge of itself and must begin all over creating its personality. I tell you, I do not believe, and the moment of fear when the thought of eternal existence rears its head I consider a weakness unworthy of a man. One must have the courage to say to oneself: I am condemned and there is no salvation. Every day gently but relentlessly brings me closer to the threshold of night, the darkness which will finally close over me. That is scientific truth, after all, and you are taught it in school. And you yourself—"

They walked through cascades of sunlight that gushed between the treetops, through the succulent smells of greenery and earth that steamed as if from the breath of an unclean animal above them. Istvan tasted fear. He saw the wise smile of the stone head he was cradling in his hands, and Chandra's hungry eyes.

"No," he contradicted the lawyer passionately. "I believe."

"Certainly." Chandra was letting him dodge the issue, was offering him a way out. He need do nothing but be quiet and enjoy the gift. "You are a poet. You believe in the immortality of gracefully ordered words."

"I believe in God." He was amazed himself at the gravity with which he made the pronouncement. Chandra paused.

"You are right. Each of us can be a god. But that takes courage. That god of yours as well was only a man. You see—I am a god without disciples, for if they are submissive, they are boring. I leave behind those I have won over; I am only attracted by those who resist. I test them, I fulfill their dreams. I try to ascertain whether they truly possess what I could not buy or obtain by request. And what contempt I feel for them when they surrender to me, giving themselves over with the trust of chickens who peck up grain, lured to the feet of the cook even when he does not hide his knife!"

"But you went to Benares seeking purification."

"So our babbling friend the rajah said. I went because a tale was going around about a pious man who returned from beyond the threshold," he said pointedly. "I wanted to verify it, and I recognized the deceased." He laughed silently. "I reminded him of his past, and the liberated one returned with alacrity to his abandoned assets."

"So he is really the rajah's brother?"

"If you do not trust the verdict of the court, you must believe God. After all, I myself resurrected him. I. I. I called him out of darkness and if I like, I can push him back into it. That is the cruelty of resurrection: the one who receives the gift of life is also under sentence. He does not want to remember that, but I know the day of his demise and that amuses me."

"And yet you demand to be paid."

"But why not, since I rid people of difficulties? I do not need money for myself, but to secure the happiness of others. I enjoy fulfilling their requests, their dreams, and I watch as they stand troubled and helpless with the longed-for gifts of fate, not knowing what to do or where to turn."

"You are in a very unhappy state, Mr. Chandra." Istvan looked at him compassionately. "Do you despise everyone? Have you met with nothing worth loving?"

"Nothing exists that I could not buy, obtain, possess, and since I have it, it must not be worth very much. One must be occupied with something. So I decided to be a god on whose will human fate depends, if only some want to believe in me. I serve them, I grant their requests more quickly than that god to whom you must sometimes turn. After all, you want him at your service; you look to him for help and protection. You have no right to pity me. You want to be richer that I am, better than I am." His smooth, slightly gaunt face constricted suddenly with spite. "You are simply misguided and foolish. You will never be rich."

Istvan, passing the heavy sphere that was the severed head from one hand to another, thought the lawyer was offended. He considered the entire conversation an oratorical display not to be taken seriously. But Chandra did not go away. He looked in front of him, listening to the bicycle bells and the bleating of motorcycle rickshaw horns. He was ruminating about something, pursing his narrow violet lips.

"I lost my temper unnecessarily, and anger belongs only to God. You are so sure of yourself, then?" He looked sideways at Terey. "I could easily create a small earthquake around you and look on as you reach out and call for help. And, stranger still, you could rely on me, because . . . No, no, only youth and naivete produce such feelings of power. And health," he threw out after a pause, as if he had found yet another gate to storm. "You wish to be a poet? A real poet, one of those who count? You must suffer, and suffer a great deal."

They stood in the shade. A step farther on the air crackled with heat and green parrots crept over the roadway on short legs, picking through dry lumps of horse dung.

"Now I know why I like talking with you." He looked around with eyes wide open, as if the light could not hurt them. "You are aware of what makes you different, of your little illusions. I found it pleasant to chat with you."

"So we do not part as enemies." Istvan sighed with relief.

"Indeed. And in enmity there is the hope that we will be won over, united, embraced, or thrown to our knees. Do you really think it is possible to be an enemy of God? Even those who struggle against Him render Him a service; even hating Him, they seem to confirm His existence. It is enough to do as I do. To feel oneself to be a god. And so it is in the lives of the majority of people, though they do not always have the courage to be consistent."

He gave Istvan a dry, bony hand. It was cool in spite of the heat.

"May I give you a lift?" The counselor opened the door of the Austin.

"No. Thank you. I have an automobile, one that is even too good. I prefer the rickshaw. I do not like to attract attention."

Istvan put the stone head on the back seat. He rolled the window down so the heat inside would abate a little. Chandra, in spite of all his cunning, his astute financial manipulations and his legal ruses, seemed to him an urbane madman. He wants to open me to the world with suffering as with jabs of a knife, he thought; or it may be that he noticed my sadness and irritability. My wound is Margit.

He flicked away a locust that had flown through the window with a loud rattle and lodged in his hair. He drove along, tooting the horn and squeezing between groups of cyclists in white or striped linen. When he put the brake on hard, the stone head rolled onto the floor with a loud thump. Obstructed by its chipped ear, it rocked continuously, beating like a bass drum.

He was overtaken by a violent impulse to turn back, pick out the slender figure of the lawyer in the crowd on the street and ask for his help to get Margit back. Yet instinctively he preferred to search out the truth on his own. Chandra seemed a doubtful ally, though Istvan did not believe he could do him harm.

"THE AMBASSADOR WAS LOOKING for you," Ferenc announced with malicious satisfaction. He was hurrying down the corridor with a fistful of documents and a lost expression, as if he were in pursuit of the solution to a problem and it was eluding him.

"But you knew where I was."

"Yes—there is always a reason to escape the office." He nodded indulgently. "Go and face him. The weather is stormy in that quarter. What do you have there?"

"An old sculpture." He turned it in his hand.

"You have too little kitsch in your house? How much did you give for that?"

"Not an anna. It was a gift."

"Never fear. You'll pay. They give here in order to gain something, not out of friendship."

"Don't worry."

"I forgot: you have the ambassador's storeroom at your disposal. There are bins enough there."

Terey made sure that the caretaker carried the boxes with the films into the storeroom and put them on a shelf under lock and key. He turned the big fan on at full speed, and when the annotated papers on his desk bristled, he placed the stone head on them. It rested there sideways, and he found something disturbing in its open eyes, its lips full as if satiated with delight. So we lie in the dark sometimes, listening to the pounding of our hearts, full of expectation and fear.

The telephone rattled.

"It is I," came the deep voice of Kalman Bajcsy. "Where have you been off to?"

He had hardly told him about the films when the ambassador broke in:

"How is your car? Running nicely? Get yourself home, pack your grip, and run over to Agra. Give a talk for me at eight tonight. You must leave in plenty of time, for there may be detours; remember, this is the monsoon season. Now there is a road and now there is none, only a raging river. Do not lapse into detailed assessments of our situation. Do not play the prophet when you answer questions; no long-range predictions. I depend"—he hesitated—"I must rely on your good judgment."

"What about Comrade Ferenc?"

"He is needed at trade talks. And I am flying to Bombay for three days. The deputy minister for trade is coming in. We will return together to sign an agreement. It is an urgent situation."

"I understand."

"Well, get moving."

"Right away, sir, and on that subject—had you announced a theme?"

"Only a general one: Hungary today. But you can take up some issue you're familiar with. Something from literature, perhaps. Speak freely, enjoy yourself. Give a critique of your fellow writers; they have no specialists in Hungarian culture here, and nothing you say will have repercussions. Between us, the thing is to bore them for an hour so they will not feel that they have been treated disrespectfully."

"I could talk about painting. I have a color film that isn't bad."

"If you feel up to it. That is even better. The talk will begin later. They have arranged an outdoor party and the film will shorten the discussion. Do not criticize socialist realism—that is my only injunction, because what if someone from our sister embassies happens to be there and begins to protest? Why make a spectacle of a quarrel in our camp? Well—good luck! Give me a report on Saturday."

Terey stuffed his letters and documents into a drawer in his desk and locked it. He looked in the storeroom for the box with the film, checking a few cages in the glare of the light—for the Indian employees often packed borrowed short-feature films in boxes with incorrect stickers—and, his spirits rising, hurried to the car. Even the heat did not seem so oppressive now. The air surging through the open windows of the Austin hummed a high note like wind in a storm, and time after time the saw-like voices of cicadas pierced his ears.

His servants welcomed the announcement of his journey with unconcealed satisfaction, just as he had welcomed the ambassador's departure. The cook, scratching himself under the arms through his shirt sleeves with their ripped seams, assured him that he would take care of everything. He even wanted to prepare a dish especially suited to the heat. But Istvan only ordered him to sew a missing button on a shirt he had chosen in addition to others more casual and colorful. His thoughts were fixed on Margit. No: this time she would not elude him. He had to learn the truth.

At a gasoline station with a border of cannabis, its purplish-red flowers fleshy as a rooster's comb, he filled the tank. Glassy streaks in the air over the large fuel pump, now switched off, showed how rapidly the gasoline was vaporizing. The grease-stained bodies of working men glittered with trickling sweat. They moved with maddening sluggishness, with open lips and dull-witted, pained expressions. Istvan's shirt clung to his back; the sun caught his legs above the knees, burning through his pants. A pair of little clouds scudded over a sullen turquoise sky; how unjust it was that there, high above them, a wind was blowing, while scorching air hovered stubbornly over the earth. The big tin gasoline sign with the yellow-painted Shell emblem emitted a metallic moan under the onslaught of the sun.

He drove out onto the highway. The trucks in front of him churned up red dust; he had to close the windows as he passed them. Barefoot drivers with wet towels on their heads steered trucks piled high with cargo with one hand as they hung out of the windows to their waists, cooling themselves in the rush of air. Even the trees were turning red from the dust, which was soft as talc. Only the sugar cane, which was flourishing after the rain, stood like a wall of dark green. A crowd of monkeys presided over it, breaking off and chewing the stalks that oozed sticky sweetness; the old males ran up to the road itself, shamelessly thrusting out their molting rumps.

Could the British embassy have forbidden her to see me, he wondered. There is nothing secret in the surveys she conducts. She signed a contract; she is a free agent. Apart from her medical duties, she is at her own disposal. Even if they had cast me as a spy and a dangerous subversive, if all she said to me is true, she would have come straight to me and demanded an explanation.

It's no matter what women whisper—his lips curled with contempt—the electrifying touch of the hand, the yielding lips, the body sweetly accessible, say more than vows. Are other assurances needed? Words mean nothing by comparison with the clear signs of the joy of our being together, breathing the same air, seeing the same landscape. The union of bodies that have no secrets, the smells of skin, of sweat and warm hair, from which arises desire. Assurances of love under the sail of mosquito netting were not necessary. Of course she could tell herself, Enough. No. I will not be there. She could enjoin silence. But her hands are empty, in her sleep she gropes around a rumpled sheet in search of his arms, her breast longs to be pressed down by his, crushed, aching, her breath taken away as delightful expectation surges through her body. Only to run to her again, to have her before me. She will not resist. She must come back.

Shadows of trees and flashes of sunlight played over the hood of the car, beating his eyes numb. The heat was draining. Caravans of tongas rested in the bushes. The drivers had crawled under the wagons and were sleeping with their legs spread in a patch of shade. The white backs of the buffalo were streaked with red dust. Only camels worked their cleft lips with threads of green saliva tirelessly, like rabbits, plucking little leaves from the smaller thorn trees. They reminded Istvan of the plaster figurines in the crèches set on little nests of hay in churches at Christmastime. The warning signal from the horn aroused no tremor from them. They dozed in stone-like repose, utterly still in the fiery air full of the hissing of insects.

The smells of burning, of chicken dung and dried mud hovered among the clay-walled cottages with flat roofs. Collectors for rainwater gleamed as if wax had been poured over them; glare leaped from the surface of the road. The horned heads of buffalo rose like tree trunks out of a flood, smeared with slime. A flock of peacocks bustled across the road, trailing their long, iridescent tails and scolding in screeching voices.

Time seemed to be compressed. Not believing what the hands of his watch told him, Terey pressed it to his ear. Its gears made biting sounds like a bark beetle gnawing the old wooden bed in the alcove in his parents' blue house. The minutes passed imperceptibly, like a slow leak.

The road fell away behind him.

Tense in every nerve, he turned in at the park gate, where peddlers and snake charmers with baskets full of reptiles had taken up residence, and drove up to the glass-encased reception desk. Looking over the young clerk's shoulder, he saw the key to Margit's room hanging on a hook. The Hindu smiled as if Istvan were a good friend: rooms would be vacant later; a few people would be leaving after the siesta, but he was willing to give him the key to Miss Ward's room. She had been away again for a few days. She had gone to the vicinity of Dehradun. There were many blind people in the villages there. She had gone with orderlies; it was not known when she would return. When she had established an intake point, no doubt.

It began to grate on Istvan that the young man knew so much about Margit. He took the key from his yellowish hand and moved away with an ease that was partly feigned; his heels beat on the brick pavement of the pergola. Feeling as if he were committing a crime, he opened the door and, like a burglar, reconnoitered the room with his eyes. His heart raced as if he were doing something against her wishes and was afraid of being detected by witnesses. Despising himself, he opened a drawer and saw a little frame of hammered silver lying face down at the bottom. He seized it eagerly. If he were not going to meet Margit here, he wanted to assert his presence in her room by setting out his photograph, which she had once mentioned in a letter. But the frame was empty. He clenched his fists as anger swept over him.

Now he must pry, must know for certain who his successor was. He peered into the cabinet, he looked on the shelf and on the little table by the cot under the springy mushroom-like coil of mosquito netting. He found an opened letter but put it aside, for it bore Australian stamps. On top of other papers was a telegram from him, and with a paid reply; he wanted all the more to insult her, to wound her. This, he knew, was petty malice. He stood resting his knees against the bed, confused and uncertain, like a dog that has lost the master's scent. In the bathroom, water dripped more and more loudly; large drops with an oily sheen spattered on the wet stones.

He knelt and pressed his face into the placid smoothness of the bedspread. He was pained by a barely perceptible fragrance, or perhaps it was only his imagination. There was an odor of insecticide in the air, and a mustiness—the smell, quite simply, of an empty room.

A sense of injury rose in him, a bitterness such as children feel when adults do not keep their promises. Feeling a tightening in his throat, and angry at himself for disturbing the contents of her room—silence, after all, had the force of interdiction—he went through to the bathroom and looked in the mirror. His own face, clouded by uncertainty, exasperated him. He washed his hands like a man who wants to erase the evidence that he has broken into a house. The towel was immaculate, freshly ironed. Obviously it had been changed during the occupant's absence.

Water dribbled from the rusty showerhead in beads that swelled with maddening sluggishness. As they fell he did not see them, only the rainbow-tinted glimmers into which they shattered in the sunlight, wetting a spot on the slippery concrete that was overgrown with fleecy mildew. The tamping sound sent a shiver of dread through him.

He went out, startling the lizards, which flitted in zigzags from the walls to the ceiling. I understand nothing, he thought, like a man who has lost his wits. Now I truly understand nothing.

He informed his hosts of his arrival and handed them the round box containing the film. The meeting would take place in a garden under mango trees covered with fruit like old pear trees. Perhaps a hundred people were expected.

"It is an official agreement," the old Hindu in the field cap of the Congress Party exulted unabashedly. "The event can be considered absolutely private and no one can intrude, but the family is gathering, and guests will come."

Because the counselor admired the yellow fruit sprinkled with red, he was given a whole basket for the car so he could suck the mangoes when he was thirsty.

The ophthalmological hospital reeked even at a distance with iodoform and pus, as if the sudden rainstorms had accelerated the rotting process. He held a heart-shaped mango in his hand and sniffed it to counteract the stench. He wanted to talk to Connoly, to ask about Margit. But he found only the tall, slender professor from Sweden.

"You are out of luck." He distorted his face into a pained expression meant to be taken for a smile. "Dr. Ward is stuck in the very heart of the epidemic. It appears that we will find one more cause for the spread of the sickness, and a classic one: quartz dust."

"Is it far away?"

"About a hundred kilometers. It is possible to reach the place in a couple of hours, but everything depends on the rains." He raised a long, bony finger and waved it dismissively. "Do not even attempt it with your car. It will bog down at the first washed-out river ford."

"I would like very much to see what she is doing there."

"The fight against trachoma interests you?" He scratched the back of his neck. "If you have time, come with me. I am going there tomorrow morning in our Land Rover."

"Professor—you would take me?" Istvan blurted out. "What time should I be here?"

"Five in the morning, if it does not pour during the night. But you must be ready for a two days' stay, for when the rivers rise . . . We will form an inspection team and surprise Miss Margit. Are you staying at the Taj Mahal? I will come to the hotel for you."

"I was not prepared for such an excursion," he said more reflectively, driving away the large, loathsome flies whose nimble legs were tickling his face.

"I can take a mattress and sheets from here, and we can share food if you are not particularly squeamish."

"I was a soldier. I can eat what I am given. But I doubt that I will have much appetite when you have shown me your sick."

"If you want to write about our work"—the scholar moved cautiously toward him—"we can only be grateful. Perhaps you will be interested in methods of combating trachoma. Are there many cases among you?"

"Before the war there were—a few cases in the mountain villages, where there was the greatest poverty. Now even medical students rarely have the luck, so to speak, to observe an instance at close range. There is no trachoma in Hungary. Conditions have changed: people earn more, housing is better, doctors are on call. People listen to the radio, they see educational films. They know by now that they must not dab at their eyes, or treat them with old wives' remedies, or wait for the ailment to pass, but go to the doctor at once."

"You have hit on the heart of the matter." The professor spoke animatedly. "Altered conditions. But for changes to occur, people must truly want something, must do something, not simply wait."

The damp odor of the hospital and the stench of putrefying bandages, wads of bloody gauze, and papers burning in a fire wafted toward them.

"Hellish climate. It's disabling. It puts them in a stupor," Istvan said agreeably.

"And those various faiths . . ."

"Would it be of any importance to you if an article on the UNESCO team appeared in the Hungarian press?"

"Send me two copies. Publication is important not only because of the statistics, but because someone has written about us in one more language. You have been in India long enough not to be surprised at anything. And thanks to your acquaintance with Dr. Ward, you understand something of the magnitude of our work. I like to talk, only take careful notes, for I will look like an imbecile in the reporting if you garble the technical terms."

"I will give Miss Ward the English text for her perusal." He pressed the professor's hand, full of joy that he had uncovered the man's vanity and hunger for recognition. To be sure, he was a first-rate doctor, but when he shut himself in his office, it was with the greatest delight that he turned the pages of the thick album in which he had painstakingly pasted all the notices concerning himself, his mission, and the activities of UNESCO. It was his vice.

"Wash your hands now, please," the doctor instructed, turning on a little tap from an enameled basin on the wall. A violet stream of water mixed with permanganate trickled from it. When he rubbed his cheek as he drove to the evening meeting, he seemed to catch the familiar, barely perceptible scent of Margit's hands.

The hope that he would see her the next day transformed him. His sense of humor returned; he was playful and witty. The showing of the film went off successfully, though the faces of the actors bulged on the unevenly stretched screen, and time after time moths made darting black spots on the picture as they flew into the white eye of the projector.

The night came on, warm and close. The guests did not want to leave. The fragrance of the flowers in the women's hair was intoxicating; their silks rustled. The crowd broke up into small groups. People sat on cane chairs or leather cushions or blankets spread on the grass. When conversation died away they disappeared, sinking into the darkness. Only the high trill of cicadas sprinkled down from the tops of the mango trees.

The house observed tradition: instead of alcohol the servants carried around glasses of lemonade, sweetened with cane syrup, garnished with a pair of mint leaves or a jasmine blossom.

The heirs to the property gathered around Terey. Extensive tracts of land belonged to them; they were leased to peasants in return for half their yield. In the humid dusk their clothing gleamed white—shirts, narrow trousers creased in the crotch, dhotis like skirts. They look like spectres without heads or hands. Sometimes a face appeared when a cigarette was lit, hidden by a curved hand to keep a moth lured by the flash from sizzling in the flame.

"How is it possible that you did not know what your security service was doing in Hungary? Today you denounce the abuses, you vindicate those who were hanged. Was there some mechanism for control in your country? Must it not have given signals that there was malfeasance?" they asked in gentle voices. "Mistakes, errors may always be made, but here a fundamental principle was violated. In the *Hindustan Times* it was written that there were thousands of groundless arrests. Can everything be blamed on Stalin? What of your law guaranteeing freedom to citizens?"

"It was known that there were abuses. It must have been known," he answered spiritedly. "But it was not easy to live with that knowledge. No one wanted to believe; criticism was taken as having come from our enemies. The stomach produces digestive juices; if it gets no food, it eats itself. It was the same way here. The enormously overgrown investigative apparatus, well paid, privileged, had to make its existence felt. It not only pursued adversaries but created them, to have someone to hunt."

"And the law? And the courts, which mete out justice?" they pressed him, clasping their knees with warm hands and gazing into his invisible face.

"You forget that there had been a revolution in our country. That is the inevitable price of great transformations."

"Just so—and were they not too great?" Someone spoke up in a voice smooth as velvet. "For perhaps it is a revolt of the root against the flowers and the fruit. A great extermination of culture and beauty that centuries labored to produce."

"The gardener prunes the tree so it will bear fruit more abundantly," he countered, exploiting their love of metaphor.

"He prunes, but he does not cut at random from the most reckless impulses," someone else retorted. "From a well-judged pruning come laws and codes."

"All the world is moving toward socialism. The state takes over the very large industries; it limits incomes. You will say that in Western Europe industrialists themselves share their profits with their workers voluntarily. It is because they see that among us the workers also share in the power, in the governance of the state. They must make concessions, must give something in order to delay, for a little, the inevitable process of history," he explained fervently. "Look how it is with you. Look how much unwarranted harm came to you as a legacy from the English. Great tasks lie before your generation. You have just crossed the threshold: independence."

"We are a technologically backward country," they admitted. "We have not yet taken inventory of our own natural wealth."

"Enormous means are needed, and who will supply them? The Americans, or Russia? And if they help, how will they demand to be repaid?" These voices were full of doubt. "We are afraid of changes that are too rapid."

"We are used to tradition, religion, old customs." A bass voice sounded in the twilight, without sarcasm. "We love peace."

"People are good in our country. They do not want what belongs to others," intoned a womanly alto, mild and warm.

"If we argue with you, it is not because we are averse to reforms"—they offered him cigarettes—"only in order to know what awaits us."

"For socialism is coming to us."

"The Chinese," hissed the voice of an aged person.

"That is still far away, fortunately. Our peasants are patient."

"But they demand land," Terey said tersely.

"To them, land means full bellies, life itself," someone said, unexpectedly supporting his point.

"And a great deal of land is being given them."

"And a great deal has already been given them."

"Peacefully, without violence. Do not sow unease and hate among us. Why awaken hungers which cannot be satisfied, even at the price of blood?"

The sudden flash as lamps were lit behind the white columns of the porch startled the gathering; people turned their heads, shielding their dilated eyes. The light was understood to be a signal that the meeting was ending. Istvan was surprised to see how many listeners streamed toward him from the park. He pressed their outstretched hands and thanked them for their patience and receptiveness. The girls said goodbye to him by bowing their heads deeply and folding their hands as if in prayer.

"We are very grateful." The host, clad in white as if undressed for bed, shook his hand. "A successful evening."

Inside the house, as if for a group photograph, the large family clustered together: a diffident band of uncles, aunts, children, grandchildren, and gray-haired residents who had been pushed into the extensive service wing and were eager now for contact with the wider world.

In his hotel room, when he had rinsed off in the shower and shoved the edges of the mosquito netting under the mattress, he reached for a mango, breathed in its fragrance and held the smooth coolness to his cheek. Margit's knees: the recollection pained him. He did not have long to sleep. Mosquitoes whined and bumped against the soft curves of the netting.

"Two months. Two by now," he fretted in an undertone, as if he could not trust his own count. "She captured me, she took me as her property. I became rooted in her and now that I am torn away, I suffer."

The jangling of the mosquitoes blended into a mournful music. He lay half covered by the rough sheet with its fresh, airy smell. An alarming thought came to him: Surely not. No. That last night, when he had bent over her, she had whispered, "You may. It isn't my time . . ."

Though he trusted her utterly, a shadow of uneasiness remained. But if something had happened, she would have let him know, after all. And what then? He would have been in Delhi just as she was, with no recourse, both of them thrown on the mercy of the Hindus.

By the pool where they had been sitting that first night, a toad croaked, as if someone were stubbornly shaking an empty gourd with a few pebbles in it—a dull, wooden voice in the distance.

If we had a child—the thought left him unable to breathe—it would mark the beginning of another life. He had simply never taken the possibility into account. No, no—he could not foist off all the responsibility on her, could not say, She knew what she was doing.

No, it is surely not that. He sighed with relief. The embassy must have ordered her not to see me. An Australian woman is under the protection of the English. Perhaps they find our relationship disturbing. In their books I am persona non grata.

He slept, pressing to his cheek the aromatic fruit, which gently absorbed the heat from his body. The mosquitoes' dirge was like twanging strings, as if the netting itself were growing taut.

A shadow slid slowly from behind the corner of the cottage warmed by the sun. Istvan recognized the figure at once. He waited breathlessly until Margit emerged; he lay in wait to catch her in his arms and surprise her with kisses. But she stood still, as if she suspected an ambush. He raised his eyes and saw with great astonishment the tuft of cut grass on a stick that stood in the hallway—the redtop grass, wrapped in a rag, that was dampened in a barrel and used to sweep out the bread ovens. I didn't know they had those in India as well. How could I have been wrong?

Suddenly he saw that Margit, dressed in a sari like a Hindu woman, was making her way down to the river. Pyres were burning low on the bank and greasy smoke hovered near the ground. He wanted to warn her. He knew that she was going to bathe—not in that place, the ashes of the dead are sprinkled there!—and he tried to call to her, but a nameless dread constricted his throat. He overtook her when she was standing knee-deep in water with her back to him. She did not turn toward him, though he touched her arm. Then, filled with terror, he saw that her face was not reflected in the water, and he realized only then that Margit was not there. She had immersed herself in the water and was dissolving slowly in the dark gray current full of funnels, streams, and eddies, and some foul life as yet without distinct form.

He seized her hand. Her fist was clenched. He tried to separate her fingers as if everything depended on that, as if that could save her. But his hands were so weak, as happens sometimes in dreams, that he bit his lips with rage. To his despair, she sank. She vanished. He could not understand why only she met this fate, since he, too, had offered himself up to the malign powers. But her hand rose unexpectedly like a plucked flower, cool and moist. He pressed it to his lips and whispered an unfamiliar word he had never uttered before: my love, my *cradle*. His breath warmed her cold, tight fist and her fingers opened like petals; in the center he saw a tiny round red object. He shook it out onto his own outstretched hand; to his amazement it was a button, sculpted in coral, from a mandarin cap—exactly like one he had seen in a cracked bowl between the Tibetan woman's rows of figurines on the walk in front of the Janpath Hotel.

He knew that it was beyond price, that he had acquired it in exchange for Margit, and that he had paid for it with the grief that was choking him with unshed tears, with a stifled cry of anguish. All because of Chandra; at last he had found the guilty one. He must be killed, before . . . and, full of this resolve, he woke.

He gasped for air and slowly came to himself, remembered where he was. He held the mango in his limp hands. What am I going to kill him for?—he exonerated Chandra—he is not my enemy. It is the rajah who has a dispute with him. Perhaps Chandra does envy him his wealth. Of course; he likes to feel himself the dominant one. A silly dream—he rubbed his damp face with the sheet, but could not rid himself of a gloomy premonition that Margit was ill and he should hurry to rescue her.

He remembered an old milkmaid who interpreted dreams; she covered her mouth with her hands and whispered straight into the ear of a girl who blushed fiery red and shut her eyes with alarm at the sinister prophecy. He recalled the signs that were keys to the dream's meaning: bathing in a muddy river—illness; picking flowers—loss, final separation, death. But the coral button, polished and pulsing with light? He could not intuit its meaning, and perhaps in the old woman's book of signs there was no such symbol, so it should not have appeared.

Outside the window, through the dense greenery of the pergola, came a dawn the color of mud. He jerked away the mosquito netting, frightening the drowsy mosquitoes, and turned on a lamp. It was a few minutes past four. At once the thought of the upcoming expedition roused him to full wakefulness. He lay for another minute wondering uncomfortably how Margit would receive him—lay at full length, nude, with his fingers locked under his neck. Now the mosquitoes were gathering around the globe of the lamp, warming themselves on the glass, which was yellow as a ripe melon.

He stretched and felt all the strength of his healthy, athletic body. He breathed deeply.

"A senseless bad dream," he murmured.

Afraid of growing too comfortable and falling fast asleep, he pulled the basket of fruit under the netting and with increasing relish sucked one mango after another. The tangy flavor restored his alertness. He smeared the drops of juice onto his bare chest and thighs so as not to stain the sheet. His hands were so sticky that he pushed the netting aside with his foot. Mango pits big as fists, covered with spongy fibrous pulp, struck dully against the stone floor. A handful of mosquitoes flitted through the rift between the curtains; their bites on his neck stung and itched. Now he was sure he would not sleep again

Bending back the whitish netting with his elbow, he slipped into the shower. The water, warmed in the daytime, smelled like the pond from his childhood—the never-to-be forgotten water, green and gold, with the smell of sweet flag, that left a smoothness as of a fine oil on the boy's slender arms.

Beyond the window the gray daybreak hovered tremulously. Large morning stars, those least able to fly away, still fluttered unsteadily. He packed an airline bag and opened the door on a black pergola with leaves like wrought-iron garlands in the style of the Vienna Secession. He took his suitcase out of the Austin and pushed his finger over the dew-spattered car, tracing his own initials. He bustled about, drinking tea from a thermos, pacing around the room as if there were not much time—as if he had only begun to understand the significance of the day which was just beginning, and which would reveal a secret he had already begun to guess. Holding the warm top of the thermos in his fingers, he brooded. He looked through the rectangle of the opened door at the awakening greenery on the lawn. The stars were disappearing; large drops of dew began to sparkle on the ends of the supple leaves, and the clinging tendrils twisted into spirals. He felt as if he were detached and floating. He thought he ought to hold his breath and listen to the ardent voices of the starlings and the ripple of leaves swaying in the first breeze, as he would listen to the rustle of the gown of someone passing by who loved him.

The glare of unnerving intensity, the trees and the grass, were a clamorous chorus of immaculate green. The flower bed with its enormous chalice-shaped red cannas seemed to be spurting fire. The whistle of starlings, the tender trills, were lavished on the air like bells set ringing by the earnest, fervent hand of a little boy who knows whose coming they announce, and gives the order to bend the knees and humbly bow the head.

It seemed to him that if he were single-minded in his reverence for this hour, he would discover a simple truth like the truth affirmed by the last trembling tear on the eyelid of a dying man.

But he was startled when the Land Rover, perched high on six thick tires and with its top still down, drove up in the yard and the professor in a soft linen hat began to shift his thin legs over bundles done up with straps. He sprang up as if he had been suddenly awakened and hurried out to the vehicle.

"Don't disturb yourself, professor," he called, throwing his bag onto the seat. "I will turn in the key and we can be off."

"Good morning," said the Swede. "Oh, good. This is the time appointed, and you are ready."

"Good morning, boys." The counselor shook hands with both the Hindus, the mustachioed driver in his faded army uniform and the orderly, whose sunglasses of arsenic green and spotted turban suggested a fortuneteller or sorcerer from an operetta. Both were more dismayed than gratified by this friendly gesture.

The Land Rover looked like a metal trough with four seats. It was very roomy, with small benches with mattresses at the sides. Shovels and axes were strapped to the walls, and boards, fastened together with wire like a heavy rope ladder, to put under the wheels if they should be mired down.

Istvan tumbled onto the back seat next to the professor. The automobile leaped forward; the breeze grazed his hair.

"If only the weather will hold." Salminen's eyes swept the vacant sky. "We have a two-hour ride on the highway, and then through the bush along the tonga tracks. Then the fun is only beginning. I have brought a shotgun with me to shoot pigeons. Do you like to hunt?"

"No. I've done too much shooting."

"The war fortunately passed us by," the professor admitted. "I shoot sometimes to test my reflexes. For sport."

"Roast pigeon is very tasty," the driver put in.

Level fields stretched out around them, planted in soy and peanuts. Sugar cane with violet tassels rose in dark green squares. A well replenished with rainwater hid in a clump of massive trees and white oxen wearing blindfolds turned a treadmill. A naked boy in a great blue turban squatted on a pole like a sparrow and shouted dolefully as he jabbed them with a prod. From a wheel to which reddish clay pots were attached with a cord, a stream of water flowed with a green glimmer into a ditch that irrigated the nearby fields.

"I prefer to hunt for images like that." Istvan pointed with a hand.

"I do, too. I have a movie camera"—the professor tapped a leather box—"but I only collect oddities. Interesting that a man trusts his eyes most of all, yet so many times they deceive him. When I write to friends in Malmö, they think I have fallen to telling tall tales. But it is enough to show them a film and they are enormously impressed."

"I send pictures to my sons."

"You are married? I saw no ring."

"I took it off. It was too tight."

"From which year of marriage has it been too tight?"

"My fingers swell in the heat, so I took it off. Do you think I am misleading women?"

"No. They like to be led astray. At least it furnishes them justification for their errors. Some do not even need that."

His faded blue eyes flashed knowingly.

They passed villages—the chunky gray clay cottages, the blind walls plastered symmetrically with daubs of cow dung dried to opal in the sun; the streets, which were deserted, for the villagers had gone to the fields to hill up the sweet potato patches and feed water into the cleverly contrived system of canals. Only by a well could they see two women in yellow and pale green saris carrying round clay jugs on their heads.

Flies and horseflies swarmed from the trees by the road. Carried on the breeze created by the moving vehicle, they hit the passengers' faces like pebbles. "Slow down," the professor ordered, seeing that dogs with mangy, thinning coats lay where they had fallen in the dust, unable even to raise their muzzles to see what was flying toward them with its horn blaring. Even the fleas did not goad them into moving.

They had hardly passed the last cottages when a sickening stench of decay blew over them. In a grassy field they saw a dark mound of vultures pressing against each other, battering each other with outspread wings.

The professor ordered the driver to stop. Aiming his camera lens at the feeding birds, he walked toward them. They moved apart as if something had disturbed them, hissing as purple strips of entrail dangled from their beaks. Their long necks, naked as if their feathers had been freshly plucked, writhed like enormous worms. They jumped about fitfully; their thrashing wings drove the stench of rotting carrion in waves toward the men.

"They look like rugby players in a scrum," cried the elated professor. "I must see what they are pulling to pieces. A dead swine!" he exclaimed triumphantly, kneeling and jostling the camera against the ripped belly, the spattered skin with stubbly black bristles. "Superb footage for my guests!"

He moved the camera in a curve around the huddle of waiting vultures. The birds turned their heads to look at it. He had just stepped back a little when they began to move slowly, then faster, hopping like children in a sack race. Spreading their wings wide, they raced to block others who tried to approach the kill.

"First a good dinner, a cigar, cognac, and then a sight that reminds us of the sort of world we live in." The professor's long, weathered face creased into a sardonic smile. "Why so pale? And you were in combat?"

The carrion stank.

"Let's be on our way," Istvan suggested. When they were moving again, he bathed himself in the stream of air until it filled his shirt like a balloon. "A hideous sight!"

"Hideous," the professor agreed. "That is why I filmed it. You could not work with us. You are too soft."

"No. No." He remembered his first autumn after the war: the yellowish-brown fields scarred by tank tracks, with corn stalks broken and in some places burnt out. Bela invited him to visit his father and hunt partridge. The covey they had shot circled as if on a tether and fell among the dry stalks with a loud rattle of wings. His bullet found its mark, and the grayish-brown feathers grazed off by the shot whirled above the rustling twigs. The empty stalks crackled underfoot.

He waded through the bare cornfields. In a thicket, as though under a ragged tent, lay a dead German in high boots. Horseshoes and nails gleamed red in the low beams of the sun. He lay on his weapon with his teeth embedded in clods of clay, in a greenish coat with a black belt that was peeling from exposure to foul weather. Istvan took him by the arm—he felt the loose flesh under the coarse clothing—and turned him over. From under his helmet grinned a grayish face without features, teeming with maggots, and the same stench had burst from that body that now covered Istvan's forehead with sweat. Beyond the iron barrel of the gun, which lay at a slant, he saw freshly scratched earth and white traces of bird droppings. The partridges were coming here to feed, to peck at the swarming maggots. He let go of the dead man, who settled down as if with relief; one hand fell onto the sparse grass as if he wanted to remember its cushioning softness. And then Istvan heard the fluttering wings of a partridge that had been shot, heard how its body shattered, yet there was still a scratching in the corn. He found the bird and administered the coup de grace, striking its head with the butt of his shotgun.

They informed the administrator of the village and the fallen German was buried under the name given on his military document, which dampness had left curled and swollen. A few days later Istvan ate the partridge with gusto.

"No, I feel no repugnance for your work. Even Margit—"

"Ah, Miss Ward is Australian. That is like a different race," the professor forestalled him. "They still behave with the hardiness of pioneers. She is quite amazing: she works like a man, and indeed, it is not as though she is compelled to—a wealthy woman, an only child."

"You are mistaken. She has to work," Istvan said vehemently. "She would not be herself otherwise."

"A woman of character, alarmingly intelligent. It will not be easy for her to find a husband. I would be afraid of her in everyday life. She would be closed into herself. A despot."

"Oh, Dr. Ward is very hard to please," the orderly declared, clutching his turban as the blast of air struck it. "She works like a machine herself, and does not let the other person take a breath."

"Yes," the driver put in, "she is like a young officer. She cannot bear for people to sit still."

"She has been especially on edge lately." The professor leaned toward Istvan, displeased that the others were overhearing their conversation. "It is no wonder; the heat and humidity are dreadful for women. This murderous climate breaks them physically and psychically. I was against bringing a female physician here at first.

Even the men have sudden attacks of rage that must be alleviated with meprobamate. Or they begin drinking. But she copes. I did not do badly, taking her on. A diehard."

How little you know her, Istvan exulted internally. Only I can tell how much warmth and tenderness is hidden inside her, how good and accommodating she is. But then the thought of her sudden disappearance cast its shadow—the unanswered letters, the telephone calls, the twittering in the receiver as if the space measured out by the wires were moaning—all ending when the clerk croaked in broken English, "Miss Ward gone out."

He had asked to be notified if a call came from New Delhi. The man had made a note of the carefully spelled-out name; again there had been long days with no word. No, it was not easy to penetrate Margit's thoughts; she had secrets, a past that put its badge of black crepe on her life. But today he would meet her face to face. He would demand explanations. Yet, properly speaking, what right did he have to demand anything of her? What could he offer in exchange? He had said, I love you, I love you, but the feeling did not justify his behavior. How egotistical he had been to want to have her as his property, to possess her, to ravage her with desire.

Was it possible to settle accounts in love, to establish conditions like those governing commercial transactions? Is it not subjection, though voluntary, to a bondage not perceived as such? How assign a value to the discovery of joy inaccessible to others, incomprehensible, unfathomable in the unreserved giving of oneself for better or for worse—for even pain inflicted by that hand is only a kind of shock, an awe that we have submitted so deeply to love.

Fields partitioned by clumps of shrubbery stretched to a horizon whitened by small, luminous silver clouds. The slender dark figures of farm laborers bent and straightened rhythmically, partly obscured by the flashing of their wide hoes. Backs the color of brass gleamed with sweat.

"They work hard," Istvan said.

"Very hard—and not very productively," the professor added. "They lack fertilizer, tractors, and good seed. It is hard for them to scratch enough from the earth to keep body and soul together."

"What could help them? They build the simplest machines themselves. They whittle them out of wood. They are proud of their windlasses, which are held together with pegs, without one nail. They are so proud that they put the *Ashoka Chakra*—Gandhi's spinning wheel, a form of windlass—on the flag as a symbol of progress. Labor is cheap; life is cheaper yet. Plagues have stopped. The government tries to rescue them from the disasters of drought and locusts, so they reproduce, they multiply with mindless exuberance—"

"Family planning? Here?" the professor exclaimed disdainfully, seizing on Istvan's point. "The women listen, they assent with gratitude to what they are told, they look at you with good, cow-like eyes—and nothing changes. They have nothing to feed six children and already the womb is swelling with the seventh. All around is the dry clay, baked by the sun. The grass is so depleted it cannot even serve as forage. Only the vultures shift from one leg to the other on flayed treetops. The mother gives herself to the child; the embryo is relentless. Such are the laws of nature. It robs her body. It leeches calcium from her bones. A generation of the sickly. Then there are the precepts of religion, vegetarianism. I have nothing against their refusing to eat meat, as long as they eat something. It is madness to be finicky about food when one is continually on the brink of fainting from hunger. After all, they have cattle enough. Whole herds go roaming around, destroying crops. Insane—this respect for life as an element of the divine. It is not permitted to slaughter them, but to drive a herd into a fenced-in square to die of hunger—that is allowed, and then the conscience is clear."

The exasperated professor raised his big, bony hands toward the sun, throttled it with fingers yellowed by nicotine, and jerked as if at invisible curtains.

"It is known that they buy no contraceptives. They haven't enough money for a pot to piss in," he went on. "They do not use what is distributed for free because they do not believe in it, because it is contrary to their religion, because children are a blessing from the gods. They press on toward self-destruction with no more thought than insects. They were given necklaces with beads marking out the rhythm of the menstrual cycle and the infertile days. Do you think that helped at all? They pushed the beads around as if they were talismen, happy, eager to conceive—which only puts them at the mercy of the mechanisms of natural selection. The weak must perish, and they do. Mothers carry to the riverbank little skeletons in withered skin, to be covered with wood and incinerated. A frenzy of childbearing, for what? For death."

"Perhaps you must turn to the men," Terey offered.

"They lie on a ramshackle hammocks in front of their houses, wrapped in sheets and smoking hookahs. They gorge on the smoke in a mindless state of euphoria, drawing energy from the sun," he said sarcastically, "so as to execute these dozen or so simple movements in the nighttime and beget a new life. They are also happy to be fathers, and then they fly into despair, they scream and cry at the moment of their child's death. But they do not associate causes with effects. They remain fixed in a fairy-tale world of predestination written as if in stone ages before, of ineluctable fate. So what can be done with them?"

"Wish them a revolution," he said harshly.

"They have too little vitality and muscle. They do not bear arms." As he shook his head with a frown of disgust he reminded Istvan of a wire-haired terrier who has choked a rat and does not know what to do with it, where to throw it. "They only know how to achieve unanimity by saying no, to sit and let themselves be cudgeled: passive resistance. Their watchword, No violence, arouses respect. In practice it means no action, or, worse, not even the thought of it."

"Yet you are profoundly dedicated to their treatment. You instruct them. You work hard to help them. It is not possible to demand too much from one generation, professor."

"I work because I am interested in the opponent, trachoma. I have genuinely interesting cases here which I would not be able to find in Europe. I heal them, I teach them, and they go out into the same murderous conditions, only to be infected again. I am fully aware that I do not help them very much. But we work for the future. We look for new, easily adaptable methods, simple methods that appeal to common sense—practical antidotes. Someday they will awaken, and then our experience will be useful to them. Perhaps they will even build a temple to us and burn incense."

"No one can help a man if he doesn't want to be helped," Istvan concurred. "Of all the gifts one can give another, free will is the most difficult."

They sped on, bouncing over the washed-out asphalt in the dusty glare. The honeylike fragrance of blossoming grasses and grain blew toward them from the fields.

"Christianity formed the European character. It instilled the sense that others are our neighbors. We feel a common responsibility for the fate of the other man." The Swede sneered as if he were chewing something bitter. "We want to defend him if he suffers harm. Marxism dealt with that in a pragmatic way, for no one likes to give up what belongs to him voluntarily, even to give of his excess. I subscribe to the view that sometimes it is necessary to take, to demand, to extort one's fair share of bread."

"But one must understand the indignation of people of good will in the West who respond to appeals for assistance when they are presented with images of poverty, hunger, sickness, and ignorance. They give generously, but as they do they wonder, they investigate, they analyze: 'Why do we in Europe restrain ourselves, limit our birth rates, when those people in Asia indulge themselves, breed, multiply beyond all reason?'" Istvan interjected. "'Why do we have to pay with renunciation for their unthinking folly elevated to the status of sacred principle?' That is a problem in Africa and South America as well." He rubbed his forehead wearily. "In the end this pernicious thought returns—I heard it once from an old peasant: 'There must be war, for people have propagated too much. For flies there is the frosty autumn night, for people, war.'"

"That is amusingly put, except that now we can disappear, and with us all progress—rockets, penicillin, Picasso and Brigitte Bardot—and by chance these grass eaters may survive, mild as sheep, quiet, multiplying like the herbs of the field and as uncomplaining as herbs when they fall under the scythe. Or locusts," he amended the comparison. "Locusts in human form, governed by their alimentary systems and their sex organs. By hunger and libido."

The Land Rover braked hard.

"What is it?"

"Probably we should turn here," the driver said worriedly. "The road goes off to the north. Check the map, sir."

The professor spread the green-veined sheet of paper on his knees and ran his finger over the red dashes.

"Yes. We should be able to turn."

The vehicle tilted violently, pushed its way into an eroding ditch, and climbed onto a road that led through the fields. They were shaken and thrown about so that they had to hold desperately to the grips. The bundles migrated slowly over the floor, pressing against their legs although their feet were tucked back.

"That was only the beginning. Not bad so far," the Swede said comfortingly.

"Are you sure we turned at the right place, sir?"

The professor leaned aside suddenly so as not to bump Terey with his head and whispered with childish cunning:

"You cannot find roads on this map. Except for first-class highways, nothing corresponds to the terrain. I am sure they have a sense of direction like jackals; they know instinctively where to turn. They only wait for my permission in order to foist off responsibility. This way we will get there in the end."

The road disappeared in a fan-shaped maze of deep wheel ruts, so they drove cross-country, passing pits full of water that were overgrown with clumps of small flat-topped trees like giant mushrooms. They rolled on, startling flocks of parrots that hovered over them with legs tucked in, like a handful of yellow-green leaves. Then they were on a road again. The motor whined as it jerked the wheels from the deep ruts, spattering water.

Thorny branches scratched and snagged the equipment fastened to the outside walls. Red ants were shaken out of them, and stung the men hard. Whiskered scarab beetles crept over Istvan's legs and began to buzz on his knees. He shuddered. The professor held out a pill in his open hand and shook it gently.

"It is for seasickness. Too much shaking."

"Thank you. I'm all right."

But a moment later he felt a spasm when the orderly hung over the side of the car and threw up, snipping off a crystalline thread of saliva with his hand. The man turned away his face, which was the color of an unripe lemon, and apologized, rolling his enormous dark eyes.

They drove into a ravine with furrowed violet banks. Its bottom was washed with water which, milled by the wheels, splashed high and trickled from the talus.

"Be careful not to let us bog down," the professor warned.

"I see the end of the trap." The driver grinned, showing white teeth under his dark mustache. "I will push hard on the gas so it does not suck us down."

The vehicle scrambled out onto the bank, its body streaming with watery mud. A plain overgrown with dense bushes lay before them. A flock of sheep scurried away down a dark gray rivulet. The shepherd, sheltered from the sun by a large sack, held a spear under his arm and clasped the base of a water pipe in both hands. Its smoke spiraled around him in a blue cloud. The driver and then the orderly shouted to him, but he only sucked the mouthpiece and looked distrustfully from under his three-cornered hood. They passed so close to him that he stretched out a hand and touched the mud-streaked vehicle as if he could not believe his eyes.

"A dark peasant," the driver said contemptuously. "He does not understand what is said to him."

"Perhaps he was afraid of us?" Istvan suggested.

"He?" The chauffeur laughed. "He did not move back one step. That kind, when they get angry, may even kill. They throw a spear and run away. They fear nothing but spirits. Stupid peasants."

The car began to quake rhythmically. It was as if they were riding over a washboard. They shook until their teeth shattered.

"Damned roadless backwater!" the counselor complained.

"We are coming to a village or watering place. The buffalo stamp out ruts like these," the professor said. "Stop." He nudged the driver's arm. "Turn off the engine."

With unexpected alacrity for his age he jumped out, holding up a shotgun. He pointed to a pair of coffee-colored birds.

"Pigeons."

The driver fastened on a revolver in a holster made of sacking and moved out behind him. They vanished into the bushes between clumps of cane and grass. When the motor had quieted down they heard the voices of the bush: the whistle of birds, the deep-throated cooing of pigeons, the jingle of innumerable crickets.

Istvan got out to stretch his legs, and suddenly stood as if he had turned to stone. From the grass, which was knee-high, rose a flat head covered with scales. Narrow, shrewd eyes looked doggedly at him. He glanced around for a stick; he was ready to run away. The unknown creature stood on its hind legs and tail like an antediluvian reptile, its forelegs resting on the springy grass. It stared at him angrily.

"That is a lizard, sir." He heard the orderly's voice. "A mud lizard. Not poisonous."

"That large?"

"There are even larger ones. They do not bite. Their skin is good for handbags and shoes."

He snatched a spade from its mounts and handed it to Istvan.

"Hit it, sir! Stun it!"

But the amphibian understood the danger it was in and took a long leap, bending the tufts of grass and then gliding into them until it was lost to view. Only the zigzag waving of the rushes showed which way it was darting. The grass, which rose taller and taller until it was waist-high, hobbled the men's feet as they ran, and the spongy, quaggy ground brimmed with water.

"It got away. Careful! It's a bog." The orderly grabbed at some branches. "Best go back."

They heard faint blasts of gunfire muffled by the incessant, piercing jangle of insects. They counted: two, and after a moment two more.

"Four, perhaps even five pigeons." The orderly puffed out his lips and pushed wisps of hair back under his turban.

He was not mistaken. Wading through the bubbling, miry meadow, they saw the professor with his shotgun on his shoulder and the driver, who triumphantly brandished a shock of freshly killed birds.

"Congratulations!" Terey clasped his hands above his head and waved them.

"It is nothing. They are so trusting; it is like aiming in a shooting gallery. A slaughter, not a hunt," the professor demurred. "I wanted us to have them for this evening—if they do not go bad. The heat is unbearable."

They wiped their perspiring faces with handkerchiefs to remove the tiny midges that were creeping over them. They ripped away clinging spider webs, nearly invisible but elastic and sticky, and daubed at the yellow dust from the blossoming grasses.

Satisfied with the results of the shooting, they fell onto the hot oilcloth seats. They welcomed the bass whirring of the engine with relief. It slightly dulled the numbing rasp of the cicadas and the hissing of grasshoppers—annoying sounds whose shifting timbre made them impossible to ignore.

The vehicle tore itself out of the bushes and grass that had become entangled in its axles. They rode up the slope of a gentle hill toward two oblique red ruts that crossed the grassy ridge. Again they came to a road.

The orderly pulled open the wings of the pigeons Salminen had shot and peeled away bird ticks as big as peas from between the feathers. Istvan saw how the breeze inflated the shirt on the professor's hunched back, and how it clung again until dark stains of sweat appeared. There was a ringing in his ears; he swallowed thick saliva. He dreamed of a thermos of strong tea with slices of lemon and lumps of half-melted ice, of the first sip that would run down his throat as he felt the cool breath of the roomy interior of the jug on his face.

"I do not like those clouds." The professor pointed to the sky, blinking in the glare. "Too many clouds like that have given us a drenching."

"Let us go over to the old bed of the Yamuna," the driver urged. "The sands begin farther on, and the rain will not be so dangerous."

Air sticky as oil, carrying the stifling smell of the swampy meadows, brushed their faces. Large, sunny fields were still opening around them when with a dull humming, a lashing of leaves, and a tumult in the sky, the first spears of rain cut through the air. The Hindus leaped to put up the roof, but the professor commanded, "Drive on! A momentary shower. We will press forward."

But when water splashed them, when their shirts were wet and their trousers clung to their legs, he himself raised the steel frame that supported the canvas roof and put the catches in place. The rain rattled on the canvas as if it were a drum.

"Well—we are having an adventure," the professor scowled. "From the beginning that sun today looked too bright to me. The proverb rightly says, 'In the season of monsoons, do not lose sight of home.'"

They did not ride so much as dive into the water that poured from blue sluices. Innumerable flies and tiny moths with unerring instinct sought shelter with them under the moving roof. They attached themselves to the canvas or, frightened by the patter of the rain, flew about, beating against the men's foreheads or clinging with their wings to their sticky skin.

The Land Rover rolled on at a slant. One side lodged in a deep rut, churning up and driving before it a red wave of rain water. Below them a village appeared: a dozen or so scattered cottages plastered together with clay. Their flat roofs with high railings had openings at the corners, and on each roof a kind of gutter had been made from the halves of a split stick of bamboo. Streams of water fell from them in full, foaming arcs, with loud splashes. The few trees bent and shuddered under the burden of the rain.

"Drive on." The professor tapped the driver on the back. "Perhaps we will still make it through to the other bank."

The village was deserted. Only a pair of black buffalo with enormous horns raised their wide muzzles joyfully toward the waves of rain that lashed their backs.

On one side of the road the cottages were shut up tight, the wood already darkening from the splashing water. On the other they saw squatting figures in an unlit room, colorful skirts and feet stained by clay now washed away. Smoke purled above inquisitive faces and dispersed below them in a sour whiff of smoldering cow dung.

They rolled on, sliding about in a bumpy stream the color of blood that was washing along the roadbed. Even before they reached the bank, they knew it was too late. Below it, a swollen, turbulent river full of swirling currents and eddies was advancing at menacing speed. Purplish red water, thick and silty, with scraps of foam like pieces of ripped-out lung, pushed steadily forward.

The roof of the car was streaming, and sagging under the weight of the rainwater. Without leaning out from under it, they measured the rumbling river with their eyes, roughly calculating its velocity and force and the distance to the far bank, which they saw blurred, even half obliterated by spurting water. The deluge was bearing down; where meadows had been moments before, the current was spilling greedily, stirring up and scrambling the underlayers of soil and depositing rose-tinted foam. The deluge moved on. Rivulets ran noisily on the road, dislodging hunks of clay. Tufts of uprooted grass floated about. Broken branches seemed to creep sluggishly but with dogged persistence toward the river, as if predestined to find their way there.

"We can forget about crossing for today," sighed the driver. His wet turban was coming undone; water trickled from the untucked end.

"We must stop for the night," the professor decided. "Though we are not far away now."

"Do you think we will be there tomorrow?" Terey asked worriedly.

"If it doesn't pour." Salminen shrugged. "The river rose in a quarter of an hour. We will see when it will fall. We must find a cottage with enough space for us. We will turn back."

It was easier said than done. The automobile surged forward; the ground beneath it was covered with water in which the wheels spun. The engine whined at high speed. The Land Rover shuddered, tilted, and began to crawl up the sloping shoulder of the road.

They drove up to the open door of a cottage that stood apart from the others. Above them stood the village, a scattering of houses sheltered by a low hill, and a dense thicket of acacia with thorns as long as a man's finger. The familiar domestic smell of smoke mingled with the odors of wet straw, milk, and a trace of dung. They jumped from the vehicle one by one and walked into the dim interior, calling out words of greeting. In the haze of a smoldering fire Terey spied a cluster of children sitting cross-legged, a woman who covered her face—only her eyes flashed curiously in his direction—and an old man. His bare thighs, thin and gnarled, and his knees covered with scars gleamed as if he were a bronze statue. On the bed, covered with a large cloth, lay a form like a cocoon, coughing and quivering.

There was nothing to sit on, so they settled down on the floor. Unlike the old man, who remained motionless with the gravity of the very weary, the children were poking at each other, chatting in squeals and bursting into titters like birds on a branch before they fall asleep. Through the open door the hum and clatter of the frothing water made the quiet house feel snug and sheltering. In the other half of the room, separated by a small gutter, two cows rested, chewing tranquilly.

"Will we stay here?" Terey looked around blankly.

"It would be the same anywhere. There are a few children too many, but we will sleep well enough through the night. Anyway, they will leave the house to us; you will see. They are, quite simply, afraid of us. We are beings from another world from which they expect no good," Salminen assured him. "Who is lying there?" He pointed to the bed. "Ask," he ordered the chauffeur. "A sick person?"

A few sentences were exchanged and the driver translated, "Not a sick person. A very old woman. His grandmother." He pointed to the dejected peasant.

They tried to overcome the dour distrust of their hosts. Terey offered the men cigarettes. The peasant reached for one slowly, looked it over, sniffed it, and put it on the ground by his bare feet. The whole family looked at Terey closely, with wonder.

Salminen opened a tin box of biscuits. They smelled of vanilla and bore the imprint of a smiling face. He held them out to the woman and the children. They took them and held them in their hands; their eyes were round with suspense, so he began to munch one, showing them by this pantomime what to do with them. One scraped it with his teeth and, shamefaced, burst into giggles. Others held the little discs and regarded them from both sides like pictures, obviously grieved at the thought of eating them.

"I told you they were afraid of us," the Swede said in a low voice. "We have certainly come the wrong way. If our team had passed this way, they would have behaved differently toward us. Ask him." He nudged the orderly.

"No. They have not seen an automobile, nor any English people, or so he said," the orderly translated proudly. "Stupid peasants. He has never stuck his nose out of his fields. Even on pilgrimage he only went to the temple near the river."

"Tell him who we are."

"I told him," the orderly smiled, "but here, doctor means witch doctor. He asked if we had come with the police who are in the village."

"Tell him no."

"I told him."

"Why have the police come?"

"He says he does not know. He heard shots before the rain."

"Perhaps it was when you were shooting pigeons?" Istvan asked. "But could they be holy birds?"

"No," the driver rejoined, and moved closer to the old man in order to hear more. "They wanted to catch a *dacoit*. They shot rifles," he explained. "That is why the peasants are so frightened. A *dacoit* is a bandit, a robber. He comes from this village, but he has done no harm to anyone here. He went far away for his plunder. Often he disappeared for half a year. He knows him because they are related. It is good that they did not catch him."

"Do you understand any of this?" the Swede asked, rolling the empty tin biscuit box over the floor of straw and clay toward the children. A little girl pushed it back, laughing. The professor repeated the maneuver and then they rolled the box back and forth to each other. They were too absorbed in the game to notice that the rain had stopped. It only trickled from the roof. The sky cleared and brightened and the earth began to steam heavily.

It seemed to Istvan that the silly game with the box had broken the ice. The atmosphere changed and the woman brought an earthenware vessel with cool sour milk.

"Are you going to drink this?" Terey asked the professor uneasily. "Aren't you afraid of brucellosis?"

"They give it, we drink it, and then take sulfaguanidine."

He swallowed the cool, clotted liquid with relish, and Terey and the driver followed his example. Only the orderly waved his hands as if to say, No, thank you.

"He knows there are such things as bacteria and viruses," the professor said sympathetically. "Yet he does not recognize the simple truth that what is crucial is to maintain a balance in the organism, to keep up its ability to fight off infectious agents. Excessive sterilization, inordinate hygiene, take away our resistance. And one must live amid contagion, one must breathe, eat, touch. Do not look at me that way. I guarantee that if the expectation of sickness itself does not bring on aches and pains, nothing will happen to you. Well, little ones, eat."

He encouraged the children with gestures, and at once they began scraping the biscuits with their teeth like squirrels, looking intently at him.

The professor took a small box from his pocket, pushed aside a leather flap, and ran his finger over its contents until a shrill, breathless jazz rhythm erupted. The children gazed at him as if they were bewitched. Even the prone figure raised itself on one elbow and a gleaming bronze head with a few wisps of grizzled hair looked out from under the gray sheet.

"A Japanese transistor radio. They have better ones than we have. I bought it in Hong Kong."

Shadows darkened the doorway and two policemen came in. They wore shorts, shirts with sleeves rolled up, and red turbans, and stooped slightly as they crossed the threshold. Then they stood erect, one leaning on his rifle. The other, wearing sunglasses and with thumbs thrust into his burlap belt, which had twisted under the weight of his Colt revolver, was trying to understand whom he was dealing with and what attitude to assume. Should he treat the unannounced arrivals as intruders, take a hard line from the start, or—since, after all, they were white foreigners—be polite to them? The professor was still amusing the children by rolling the box. The police did not speak the ceremonial words of greeting, so no one welcomed them.

The officer squatted with a reflective air and when the box rolled near his feet, pushed it adroitly. "Who are you, gentlemen?" he began. "What do you want here?"

"I am with the UNESCO mission from Agra. We want to wait out the rain."

"But why here?"

"Because fate willed it," the professor smiled, and the policeman nodded comprehendingly.

"Is one of you a doctor?"

"I am."

"We have two wounded. Are you willing to treat them?"

"I am an eye doctor, but I will do what can be done. Where are they?"

"Not far from here, but we will not go in the automobile. We are on horseback."

"I am well able to walk." The professor rose and directed the orderly to take his medical bag. To the disappointment of the others in the room, he put the radio, which was still playing, into his pocket and went out in front of the cottage.

"You will go with me? Do you want to go in such mud? You are not obliged to," he pointed out.

"Certainly we will go together. This is interesting."

He bent down and stepped across the threshold, where the box of biscuits had come to a stop. They walked in a stream of noisy music that lured the curious from the neighboring cottages. Istvan surveyed the havoc the rain had caused. The water was washing over the shoulder of the road, cheerful, coffee-colored, gleaming. They passed brimming floodplains fringed with bristling sticks, tufts of torn-up grass, and leaves as thick as if they had been cut from linoleum. Inebriating smells rose from the fiercely steaming earth. Clouds trailed over the sky like rapid chalk strokes. The storm had swept by; its traces were barely visible. The sun blazed and the angry roar of the swollen river could be heard, though only distantly.

"Where was he wounded?" the professor asked.

"In a tree," the officer answered gravely.

"But I am asking, where is the wound?" He pointed his open hand toward his chest.

"In his head. He is unconscious. But he speaks continuously, so surely his condition is not very bad."

"And the other man?"

"A peasant, stabbed with a knife. Not serious."

Outside the village they waded into the tall, streaming grass. Quail darted from under their feet with a loud sputtering of wet wings.

"Pity I did not bring my shotgun." The Swede's eyes followed the birds gliding among the bushes.

"When were they wounded?" Istvan asked.

The orderly translated. "In the evening and later at night."

"And why were people still shooting this morning?"

The policeman looked gloomily at the counselor, then shrugged.

"We did not know how many of them there were. Best to be careful."

"And he was alone?"

"Alone."

"You have him?"

The policeman walked quickly. The legs of his short pants, wet from the grass, brushed loudly against each other. The mud on the path made sucking noises under their feet.

Finally the officer spoke. "No." He almost spat out the word. "He got away."

"Does he have a weapon?"

"Only a knife. We will get him and take him before the court. He will be sentenced to hard labor. It is worse than death."

Clouds of droning mosquitoes hovered over a swamp overgrown with reeds and rushes. They saw a few horses with coats darkened by the recent downpour and saddles covered with transparent plastic that sparkled in the sun. A dark gray cottage with a flat roof surrounded by a thick, low wall of flax looked from a distance like a bunker among banana trees with young leaves in a luminous green glow. Farther on they could see a mango tree, tall and spreading, with a white trunk and roots like ropes growing into the earth.

Beside the horses stood a policeman with a rifle slung on his shoulder, barrel down. A man sat against a wall as though he were a puppet, with bare legs wide apart and straight out. In the middle of his chest a bandage was held in place by a cross of adhesive. An old woman crouched beside him, holding up a copper vessel from which she poured a stream of water onto her hand and lapped at it, then after a moment sprayed it from her mouth into the wounded man's face. Wet hair hung on his forehead; his eyes were closed in a lassitude like death.

"Not even bloody," the officer said belittlingly, passing the man on his way to the door. A policeman lay on a piece of oilcloth; two more sat by him. Squeezed into a corner, hunched over with her arms around her knees, sat a young girl with fiery, wrathful eyes. Her hair was thick and disheveled; her deep bosom, hardly lighter than her arms, could be glimpsed through her torn bodice. It was clear that she had been working nude to the waist in the fields.

The professor bent over the man lying on the oilcloth. His head was wrapped in a thick bandage black with congealed blood. The doctor raised one eyelid, looked into the eye, then lifted a limp hand. He felt the pulse and, as if dismayed, let go. The hand fell onto the clay floor with a muted bumping sound.

"He is beginning to stiffen."

The orderly set about fastening the flaps of the bag with the sign of the Red Cross.

They left the house with its smell of a cooling fireplace and wet clay. Bristling clusters of dried red pepper pods hung by the doorway, rattling lightly at each breath of wind.

"He has already died?" the officer asked incredulously.

"A couple of hours ago."

"That is impossible! A moment ago he was still warm."

"When you lay him on the fire, he will even be hot. But that is a corpse. It can be burned."

Then he went to the wall where the half-naked peasant sat wounded in the chest. He took out the twisted tubes of his phonendoscope and listened to the man's heartbeat.

"How did this happen?" he asked the elderly woman who was clutching the copper jug.

"How did this happen?" the orderly repeated. "Tell the truth."

She began rapidly; his translation could hardly keep pace. From time to time he stopped to search for a word, but when the professor urged him forward with a wave of the hand, he persevered.

"He was with us for two days. He ate and drank. My son received him like a brother. It all happened because of that she-devil." She pointed to the young woman, who by then had crept near the threshold and was leaning on it with both elbows. Her wrists glittered with bracelets of silver wire, and she sniffed like a dog as she looked at the distant clumps of shrubbery.

"He wanted vodka. He sent my son to the village—not to this one, to the one farther away, by the river. He gave him a few bracelets to sell. He said he would repay us. My son had to go, for the man had a gun and a knife. He boasted that he had killed two policemen and cut off the nose of a spy who was hunting him down. He was a terrible man, worse than a demon, but she liked him. My son had hardly left when she climbed up to the roof where he was, for he had called her. I know what they were doing. I strained my ears. I know every sound. I heard something different: she was beating her heels into that swine's backside. I called to her to come down, but she would not. She only shouted, 'Mother, come here,' so I would see that she had him and the accursed girl could laugh at me."

"It is not true!" the girl shrieked from behind the threshold. "I called to you for help! He was raping me!"

"And my son learned at the silver merchant's that they were already looking for that bandit, that the police were abroad in the villages, and that he might descend on us. He was afraid they would charge him. When he met the patrol, he told him who was in our house."

"The reward tempted him!" the girl shouted. "He sold out a friend, though he paid him back for every handful of rice!"

The man sat motionless, his head propped against the steaming wall on which Istvan saw bulletholes. His eyes were half closed, as if the world were of no interest to him. He seemed conscious only of what was happening inside him.

"The police approached the house very quietly," the old woman went on.

"Because the betrayer was leading them. But the horses snorted and jostled each other in the dark," the girl said. "And on the roof we did not sleep. We were stargazing."

"Quiet, bitch! They rolled around the whole roof. She lured him on and played fast and loose with him. She gave him no rest. She was insatiable. I heard everything. If I had had his gun down below, I would have shot, but he took it up with him, the coward—"

"Because he is nobody's fool," the girl cut in.

"When they began to close in, he fired from the roof. The police stopped and began firing as well. Then my son shouted for us to run away, and the police would kill that other one. But they came down from the roof and tied me up and gagged me. She helped him."

"How do you know that I did that? It was dark."

"It was very dark, and one policemen climbed a tree so he could see all over the roof, and shot over and over until he wounded that bandit in the leg."

"He did not wound him!" The girl beat her fist on the doorsill.

"Then why did he scream?" The old woman craned her lean neck toward the door.

"For joy. He shot the policeman in the tree and heard him drop his rifle and fall through the branches."

"The bandit was happy!"

"There were many of them and one of him. He was the bravest."

The policemen smoked cigarettes, looking indifferently at one woman and then at the other. Only the scrawny chest of the wounded man quivered as he sighed briefly.

"Another policeman went into the tree and shot again and again, until they had to hide inside. Then other officers came running up to the house and gouged out holes in the walls—with sticks, for the clay crumbled easily. They pushed their gun barrels in and shot. He was lying with her under the place where the barrels pushed through, and he paid no heed to the shooting."

"He pushed you aside, too, because he did not want you to die!" the girl cried. "Mother, you traitor! You are ungrateful!"

"And when they started to make holes from the other side, she began shouting to them not to shoot because she was coming out."

"Because he was afraid for me. He did not want them to kill me," the girl corrected her angrily.

"And then she gave him her skirt and shawl. She lay there just as she is doing now. She shouted, she howled on the threshold like a dog, 'Don't shoot, it is I, Lakshmi.' And that one, that wicked creature, went running out. My son thought it was she and leaped out to meet her, and he stabbed him with the knife and got away . . . got away, though they shot at him. The police waited until morning before they had the courage to go in. And that one never told them they could; she only cried and cried. I could not tell them. I had a rag over my mouth and I was tied up."

"It is not true! I did not cry! I laughed. I thanked Kali that he was saved."

"And my son will not live."

"He will live—translate that—" the professor said to the orderly—"if there is no damage to the trachea. The lung is pierced but the heart is whole. He should live."

"Better if he had died," the young woman said with calm cruelty. "For my Mandhur will come and kill him as punishment. He must kill him for betraying him. It would be better if he had died."

The mother could not endure this. She raked the earth with her nails and leaped up. She sprinkled a handful of mud in the girl's face, blinding her, struck her in the head with all her might, then kicked her where she lay.

Istvan moved toward the girl, but the professor stopped him.

"Best not to interfere." He pointed to the police, who had watched the entire incident with complete detachment. Cigarette smoke swirled tremulously and horseshoes clicked on the soaked ground. The horses whisked their hindquarters with their tails.

"I will go to the council of elders. They will punish you!" shouted the mother-in-law, flailing aimlessly like a drowning swimmer.

"Mother," the son said suddenly.

The hoarse voice restored her presence of mind. She fell on him and, kneeling, stroked his temple with its high hairline and caressed his ear. He raised a hand from his thigh and pointed to the door. He shook his head lightly as if to say, No. No.

Then the young woman darted from the shadowy interior and ran with her bare feet pattering toward a sugar cane field next to a clump of thornbushes. The police rushed out in pursuit, but the girl, in full flight like a frightened animal, was nimbler than they. One officer tore the plastic from his saddle and leaped onto his horse, but as he plunged into the thornbushes, he saw that the barbed mesh was impenetrable.

"Stop! Stop or I will shoot!" he called, rising in his stirrups and aiming into the thicket, from which they could hear the crackling of branches; she must have been creeping along the bottom like a lizard.

But he did not shoot. The police returned to their commander, who gave them orders as to how to redeploy themselves.

"Let her be. She will guide us to him," he said. "Surely they have agreed on a meeting place. She has lost her husband and now she will lose the object of her infatuation," he added calmly. "She is crazed with love."

Crazed with love: the words sank into Istvan's mind. He too was insane, evading obligations and trying to find Margit against her will. Love . . . with equal ease it creates and destroys.

It was well that the policeman had not fired. Terey knew he would have had to throw himself on the man. He breathed deeply and slowly recovered his equanimity. Would I so passionately have taken the part of the girl who had trodden on all the bonds of family? She was following a voice that I know. She is wild—he thought, but the word took on an unaccustomed meaning: genuine. She had the courage to be herself.

"What will you do with him?" He pointed to the wounded man whose mother was holding him up. "He ought to go to a hospital."

"Travel on horseback, and even more by tonga, would be bad for him. In any case, we need to question him," the officer said, leaning toward the man. "Would you like for us to take you away?"

"Yes!" the mother replied vehemently. "Save him!"

"No, I will wait here."

"You want to wait for her?" cried the outraged old woman. "She will be back, but with him. She ran away to him. Do you hear? She will be back to watch while he kills you. Do you want that?"

"Yes," he whispered. He moved his limp fingers, which were half-buried in the wet ground.

"We cannot take him, then," the officer sighed with relief. "He does not want that, so he does not go."

"I will let you have the vehicle if it is needed," said the professor.

Fear seized Istvan: would this be the end of the expedition? Would they go back without his ever seeing Margit again? If only the officer would end the haggling! Let the wounded man stay where he was.

"After all, he has hardly any blood on him," the officer persisted.

"The blood collects inside, in the pleura." The professor swung his phonendoscope. "There may be complications."

"There may, but there may not," Istvan said so eagerly that he was embarrassed at the sound of his own voice, which showed no regard for the injured man. "What could you do for him in a hospital?"

"I might try pressure to slow the movements of the lung. But the clots that form there themselves stop up the wound and create pressure." He reached for the orderly's bag and Terey, certain now that they would travel on, drew a long breath. "I will leave him a little codeine." He dug out a small bottle. "Tell her to give him a couple of drops with water if he begins to cough. He must not lie down. He must sit just so."

The mother squeezed the bottle in her hand and looked distractedly at them. She had one arm around her son, who seemed to be dozing with his head drooping helplessly.

"Shall I show you the way back, gentlemen?" the officer asked.

A policeman held two horses, which were stamping and jerking at their reins. The departure of the rest of the patrol had made them restless.

"Thank you. We will find it ourselves."

The officer wrestled with the horse for a moment with one foot in the stirrup before he jumped into the saddle and, with a casual salute, rode off at a trot.

When they came to the wet meadows, Istvan turned around, casting a farewell look at the pair huddled by the reddish wall of the cottage. The mother crouching by the limp body of her son he could imagine to be a cruel mockery of a Gothic Pieta.

The professor reached into his pocket and reflexively turned on his radio. But the boisterous voice of the saxophone blared like sacrilege in the vastness of the open landscape—among the tall grasses and thorn trees, the swelling choir of dissonant voices, the ringing and rasping of millions of insects with drying shells, now saved from the flood and praising the sun. He turned it off.

"Do you think she will return to her husband?" Terey mused. "What is he hoping for?"

"That his wound and his defenseless condition will arouse her caretaking instinct. That in the end she will come to the one who most needs her help. He calculates wrongly, for his mother is with him. That is enough to soothe her conscience. She went after the other man because he is lonelier. The whole world is against him. So he will prize her all the more, and they will cling to each other all the more tightly in the night. They are condemned to be together. As long as he lives, until they shoot him, she will have him exclusively to herself as she could have no other man."

"And apart from that, he is a man," Istvan laughed, "at least judging from what the old woman said. No ox was ever so numbed from work as her husband."

"Must a loving, faithful husband always arouse compassion?" The professor lit a cigarette. "Somehow I cannot sympathize with him."

"He betrayed the other man, and from greed. You could find a hundred justifications, but neither you nor I have any sympathy for him, because we approve of honest struggle and, like all the world, we don't like informers. Say what you like, he was tempted by the bounty on the head of a boyhood friend. Sometimes it's necessary to use the services of Judas. Then one pays him, but doesn't shake his hand or sit at the table with him."

"Are you trying to convince me, then, that we are both on the side of that robber?" the professor asked reprovingly.

"No. But we do not approve of the axiom that the end justifies the means. Though it may achieve results, it destroys those who apply it."

"Do you prefer knightly gestures? Do you believe in the duel between the transgressor and the noble policeman who must put himself at risk, as in Graham Greene's novels?" the professor teased him through a nimbus of cigarette smoke. "And could you dare to say, I never betrayed anyone? I do not say for money, but for position, to avoid a conflict, for peace and quiet? Have you never contradicted the truth? I am old now and I can claim the privilege of being candid. In another sense, of course, I am not much better than that Hindu whom fate so promptly repaid. He can be happy that his account with himself is settled; our sins still cry out for justice."

"I hate such conversations," Istvan flared, "because they absolve all wickedness. I may seem a boor to you, but I am on that woman's side. She has the courage to be herself, to be guided by passion, by her heart."

"She is carried away by her physical longings." The Swede threw his cigarette into the grass. "She is thinking from below the belt."

"She is a woman."

They walked through the steaming grass without speaking. Large grasshoppers fluttered from under their feet with a rustle of bright red wings; then they fell like dried pods and jangled triumphantly as they sank from sight into the underbrush.

Above the trees the sky blushed rose and the clouds, weightless tulle spread high above them, began to be suffused from below with the deepening colors of the sunset.

"I am hungry," the professor said at last, in a conciliatory voice. "We must bestir ourselves and cook something."

"We have the pigeons," the orderly reminded them.

When they emerged onto the road between the cottages, where groups of half-naked children were dabbling in mud and building a dam, the professor turned on his radio. They heard music, then an English bulletin from New Delhi. They listened curiously. The children did not move away at their approach, but clustered around them and looked importunately into their faces, astonished by the music no less than by the voice from the professor's pocket.

Suddenly, at the conclusion of the newscast describing the meeting of Premier Nehru with a delegation of Sikhs demanding autonomy; a fight against rampant tigers in northern Vietnam; and a fire on a cotton boat in Calcutta, Istvan heard an announcement from Europe, pushed to the end of the program and condensed to one sentence. Budapest: The government has declared amnesty for political prisoners, claiming abuses by the security service; authoritative sources estimate that approximately four thousand will be freed. Istvan clenched his fists; he wanted to learn more, to hear some commentary. But he was in the middle of Asia and the attention of the listeners was absorbed by Asian affairs, not by what had happened on the other side of the globe in a small country of nine million: Hungary.

"Did you hear? Amnesty in Hungary!"

The professor had been too preoccupied to have any attention to spare for the news. "I was waiting for a weather report," he confessed. "I did not even hear the dispatches. Is it important?"

How to explain it to him?

The driver announced that he had arranged for beds, taken linen from the vehicle, and hung mosquito netting. The owners of the cottage had voluntarily vacated it and moved in with neighbors, as Salminen had predicted.

The orderly reached for the pigeons. The feathers yielded softly to the plucking; the skin was torn away. The fingers stuck to the spongy meat as if it were clay.

"Throw them away," the professor ordered. "They stink. Take the tinned meat and make tea. We will go to the shore to see if the river has fallen."

The street was swarming with people. Flutes chirped; measured slapping brought moanings from a drum. They looked out from the cottage. The body of the policeman, wrapped in a sheet, was being carried to the shore for burning.

Terey lay covered with mosquito netting, feeling under his back the thick plaited ropes stretched across the frame of the peasant bed. Time after time a reeling flash of distant lightning could be seen through the open door.

"There will surely be good weather," the driver said to reassure the professor before mumbling "Good night" and beginning to chuff and whistle in his sleep.

They left the door open to create an illusion of moving air. The night noises were disturbing. Istvan heard a loud tread: something passed by with a slow step and scraped against the door frame until flakes of dried clay fell off. In the fitful glare of lightning he made out the long black snout of a pig scratching itself. It moved on a step and took a long piss, snorting with satisfaction. The voices of cicadas pealed, piercing as alarm bells. The villager singled out to be the guard walked around the Land Rover, coughing and muttering. The river hummed below them. Mosquitoes on the screen sang their threnody of hunger, begging for a drop of blood.

The white-draped form that had made its mournful way to the river bank haunted him. Trailed by shrill dirges, it had taken the shape of a phantom. In the evening, when they had gone down to the water, the pyre was already going out. The black, rushing river was swallowing the shining red scales of fire. Two peasants, hunched over, were raking up the unburned branches with rods; a handful of sparks flew toward the low sky.

A policeman. Yesterday he had ridden out on his horse, swaggering, certain of his power, with a gun, with comrades, and in a moment his ashes would whiten the muddy current. He had been, and now he was no more. And his wife still did not know that she was a widow. She was putting the children to sleep, squabbling with her neighbors, perhaps daubing the edge of her ear with perfume or buying a prosperous future from a traveling fortuneteller.

The wounded man was sitting in front of his cottage, resting against the wall. An oil lamp standing on the ground threw a wavering yellow glow on the bottom of his face and the cross of adhesive tape on his gaunt chest. It seemed to be marking out the target for a bullet. He did not feel the mosquitoes that bit him and then, satiated, sizzled in the flame of the lamp. The policemen converged on the village for the night. Their horses whinnied close at hand: it was a homelike, familiar sound. "Do you know"—the driver, an old soldier with an affinity for weapons, had mulled over the day's events that evening—"that when that bitch escaped, she took the *dacoit*'s gun?" There had been more wonder in his voice than condemnation.

And I am running away to Margit. I am living, I am breathing in the hope of meeting her. If the river falls . . . Not Ilona, not the children; the one I would will to come to me is the red-haired girl. A few months ago I did not know her; if she had been in Australia, I would not even have known of her existence. In India, too, we might not have met. He felt a stabbing pain at the thought. How has it happened that she is closer to me than anyone else? Not to know her—it would be as if she had died, or as if she had never been. He felt despair in this wandering on the brink of sleep, then smiled as he thought, If I had not known her, I could not have longed or suffered. The bulletin from Budapest repeated itself: the freed prisoners took their rumpled clothes, sprinkled with shining flakes of camphor, out of bags and looked doggedly, inquisitorially at their troubled guards: "Well—and who defended socialism, you or we?"

And into the well that was the prison yard, with its sharp odor of tar and privies, the intoxicating aroma of summer was bursting. The whizzing of automobiles, the grating of tramways, the hallooing of children, was beating against the wall topped with barbed wire, into the windows covered with rusting tin baffles, through the chinks open to a sky full of twittering tongues. The breath of free life filled the air. One could walk, not only three paces from the next man, but as many as one liked. A scraping of the gates and one's vision reached to the bridges over the Danube, the burnt castle on the high bank of Buda, the innumerable lights spread wide, wide as arms that want to embrace the recovered capital, and more: the homeland.

Whom will they set free? Everyone? He thought of the journalists and writers he knew who had been arrested. He was saddened at the thought that he would not be there to share their joy. No doubt someone would telephone, and Ilona would answer, "Istvan has been at the mission in India for a year."

Tomorrow I will see Margit. No: there is nothing more important. I am not a good husband; a feeling of guilt suffused his heart, and the words took on a new tenor, as if someone standing by had said, He is not a good Hungarian, he cannot be trusted. With relief he recognized Ferenc's voice, with its tone of obliging readiness.

He breathed deeply, and in spite of his remorse and rancor peace returned, for he knew he had only been dreaming.

Morning began with the plodding of buffalo, the groanings of a herd streaming with watery mud. The peasants were driving the animals from the miry, flooded river banks to the meadows.

Istvan shaved with his head at a slant so as to see the edge of his cheek in the mirror, which gave off such a glare that the sun itself, the source of the brilliant weather, seemed to pulse from it. The little band of children would not leave him. Thin girls dandled big-bellied tots, bracing them on their hips. They chattered like sparrows and flicked away the flies that crawled on their parted lips and wide eyes. The villagers brought the men cheese and milk; they were too dignified to accept payment.

The river had receded visibly, leaving a bright silver strip of thin silt more than a dozen kilometers long. Two boys in water up to their knees were sounding the stream in front of them with poles, shouting to keep up their courage. Their reflections were chopped by a murky wave and snatched away by the rapid current.

Inserting plucked branches with tufts of quivering leaves into the river bottom, they marked out a new ford. A lane as wide as the Land Rover appeared behind them, lined by the branches, which swayed with the current. The vehicle would have to roll down onto the river bed, turn upstream almost in the center of the freshly deposited, hard-packed sandbar in order to reach the shale sill a hundred meters on, and travel over the shale to the other bank. The chauffeur, wading in the turbid water, scrutinized the route.

"I will try to drive through."

But the professor preferred to wait until noon, and ordered that two pairs of oxen be prepared in case the engine died. The villagers had already transferred the baggage to the other bank, pulling it from each other's hands, making a game of moving the vehicle's contents. Terey entrusted a bundle of clothing to a little boy, and he himself swam with the current. Two young fellows set off after him, pounding the water, but could not catch up. The river had a yellowish sheen; the bathing was refreshing.

Sliding into muck greasy as lard, he scrambled out onto the shore. His legs seemed to be covered with red lacquer. He washed them for a long time, cursing. Finally he agreed that six Hindus should carry him onto the grass. There they were happy to smoke the cigarettes he offered them as treats.

All the village came down to watch the expedition. They cheered the driver on by shouting rhythmically, in chorus. The Land Rover rolled along slowly, accompanied by a pack of boys who clung to its sides. In an excess of zeal they even waded ahead of the hood, showing that the bottom was even.

They managed the fording without incident. It appeared that the oxen waiting at the ready had not been needed.

"As of today I pronounce you captain," Istvan said to the professor as he climbed into his seat in the Land Rover. "You cut a splendid figure in the automobile in the middle of the river, just as if you had been on the bridge of a sinking ship."

"Thank you. We made it," Salminen muttered. "You know, I loathe rivers. They always remind me of cemeteries. And custom, to say nothing of parsimoniousness, leaves some remains unburned."

On the other bank, as if a new journey had begun, they rode along with no difficulty. After an hour they came upon a column of tongas loaded with sacks. The wheels, hewn from thick boards, whined mournfully.

"What are they carrying?" Istvan asked the orderly.

"Sand. They are swindlers. They are making good money."

The heads of the swaying oxen hung low; the animals breathed heavily. The drivers shouted rather from habit than from hope that they would move faster.

"Sand from the old river bed. The funeral company sends it in small bags to devout emigres so they can mix the ashes of their dead with it before they scatter them into strange African rivers. There are a couple of firms in this business," the orderly explained matter-of-factly. "This sand is whiter and more beautiful than sand from the Ganges. The living like it better, it reminds them of their old dreams, and the dead do not complain. It is all the same to them."

The hot breath of the desert blew into their faces. A sparkling white ocean of sand ran in delicate ripples to the horizon. The glare from the dunes hurt the eye. Grains of sand spun about on the wind, as if a light smoke were rising from the tops of the dunes, then scattering onto the perpetually shifting ridges. The desert, in spite of its lifelessness, seemed full of sinister motion.

They had to wait their turn. A line of tongas stretched ahead of them, moving in the opposite direction, and a horn tooted from a stray truck painted with flowers and elephants.

Istvan saw that the wheels of the Land Rover were rolling over black strips sprinkled with sand—two iron tracks laid in the very heart of the desert.

"During the war the English built this railroad," the driver explained. "The tongas will make way for us and we will cut over to the village. To our Dr. Ward."

"I feel as though we have come terribly far from Delhi," Terey said reflectively, "and hardly a day has passed."

"We are around a hundred and twenty kilometers from Agra." The professor measured the distance with his fingers on the outspread map. "Under normal conditions, on a good highway, it is a two-hour trip."

Above the blinding white dunes they saw a pole with a long, writhing tatter of orange fabric. Low cottages appeared, and a large water tank painted white. A windmill, flashing in the sun, pumped water without stopping. Mats were stretched over the entrances to the cottages to provide what shade they could. Women draped in red and blue went with jugs for water. Suddenly they caught the smell of smoke and a nauseating odor of human excrement. This was the village they had labored to reach.

Istvan thought his heart would burst with anxiety. He moistened his dry lips. He did not know how he would be received. What would he hear? He was like a prisoner awaiting a verdict.

"I see them!" the driver cried suddenly. "Madam Doctor!"

He began honking the horn like a man possessed, forgetting that from that distance no one in the village would hear.

They sat erect; searing heat blew into their faces, drying their sweat. With blinking eyes they gazed at two small figures in white as they passed between the cottages, blurring in the light, flashing in the shadows, then disappearing.

"How much longer will she be here?" Istvan asked the professor.

"A week. Ten days. But I would like to look over the results, glance at the bacteria culture, and start back—to get away, for if high winds set in, we are trapped."

Like the black skeletons of unknown beasts or the bold outlines of modern sculptures, half-buried tree trunks with a few branches chopped off protruded from the ground, polished by the sand to a shining ebony.

They drew near the low cottages and sheds knocked together from pieces of tin barrels and crates. There were more than a dozen houses, clustered like shrewd hens alarmed by a hawk. White, glassy sand trickled through the wattled fences.

The vehicle drove up and stopped near a jeep covered with oil-stained canvas strapped to pegs. Istvan jumped out, landing up to his ankles in a pile of gravel that scorched him through his shoes like ash from a smoldering fire. A low breeze made the canvas flap and blew the odor of gasoline vapor, lubricants, and overheated iron into their faces. The drivers were chatting, tracing a route in the sand with their fingers. It appeared that if they had gone thirty kilometers farther and turned onto a road through the fields, then toward the river, there would have been not only a ford but even a ferry.

"The professor ordered, above all, that we find the tracks," the chauffeur told his colleague to justify himself, "and we arrived here successfully."

Istvan had already seen the white flag with the red cross on one of the sheds. He walked toward it first, then slowed down so the professor could catch up to him. The desert heat surged toward them in an unbroken burning wave. He saw Hindus lying inside the cottages, almost naked and wet with perspiration, arms outspread. Two dogs with dingy coats pawed through a rubbish heap, raising clouds of ash. As the men approached the sheds, Istvan spied the three-cornered muzzles of jackals. They scurried away one after the other, moving in their own shadows along the dazzling white slope of a dune.

A girl came out of one of the buildings, led by her mother in a voluminous skirt and unfastened caftan. The woman's long, heavily suckled breasts looked like dying tumors. They greeted the men diffidently as they passed. Istvan noticed the child's swollen, oozing eyelids and the streaks tears and pus had left on her cheeks. Enormous desert flies sat on her face, crawling and grazing with legs hairy as spiders'. She did not even try to whisk them away.

"Hello, Miss Ward!" the professor called impatiently. "At last we have waded through to this hell."

He saw Margit. She was a little slumped as she walked out, but immediately held herself upright as an old campaigner at the sight of his general.

"Salve dux." She raised a hand with forced cheerfulness. "So you have exhumed me from the sand!"

Asserting the privilege of his age, the professor took her in his arms and kissed her cheek.

"Hello, Margit," Istvan said, timidly reminding her of his presence.

"Istvan!" She held a hand out to him joyfully, as if there had not been almost two months' ominous silence between them. He pressed her hot, slightly sticky fingers and his heart contracted with emotion.

"I couldn't wait," he whispered. He wanted to look at her. He raised his dark glasses but the sun streamed into his eyes, unexpectedly blinding him.

"We have arrived!" Salminen was infused with new life. "But after such adventures! A real *dacoit* and a full-blown murder with a fresh corpse. Give us something to drink and we will tell you everything."

"I only have tea in a thermos. The water is foul here. It's ghastly even for washing."

"Give us tea at least. And I was dreaming of a glass of whiskey with ice," he sighed.

"Where would ice come from? From this blast furnace? Here even I want to cry for myself and my stupidity," she said with rueful jocularity. She led them between the cottages into a tent that glowed inside with a honey-colored shimmer. Its walls were distended like the gills of fish thrown up on shore.

She walked in front of them. It seemed to Istvan that she carried herself like a more mature woman. She had lost weight. Only the hair he so loved, covered with a light, flat cap woven of straw, seemed more richly alive, took on a fiery sheen against the white of her apron. She was beautiful in this lassitude; even her loose apron of starched linen could not hide the contours of her body. He knew that body—knew it intimately—and now it seemed distant, unattainable.

"As you predicted, professor," she said as she poured the tea into mugs that had been set into the sand and covered with a napkin, "the course of the disease is different here, and much more aggressive. The mechanical irritation caused by grains of sand accelerates the formation of pus. Everyone here is infected."

"By what path?" The professor looked around, but saw only one chair and a box serving as table. He huffed resignedly and seated himself on the ground. "As usual, their own fingers?"

"Fingers. The edges of mothers' skirts. They rub their own eyes with them when they cry as well as the children's. Well, and the big flies. I think the strain of bacteria may also have a more active mutation. It must be checked in the hospital. For the time being I'm teaching a few willing villagers how to assuage the symptoms; I can't call it treatment."

"And how are you feeling?" He inclined his head, fanning himself with his crumpled linen hat as if it were a succulent leaf.

"Well," she murmured coolly. "Very well by now."

"Do you have specimens?"

"I have some prepared. I rather thought you would be coming."

"I will tell you now what happened to us on the way. First a deluge. Surely it rained here?"

"Yes, but the rain evaporated before it touched the ground."

I will not find a moment to talk with her if she does not want to help me. How to get rid of this jabbering old man, Istvan thought. He was close to despair. Stealthily he intercepted a glance and asked her, begged her with his eyes.

"Where should I bring the things?" the driver called from the road.

"Here. Will you stay overnight?" she asked.

"That depends on the weather." The professor shifted, rose, brushed off his sandy hands, and turned on the radio. "I must show them what to unload or the simpletons will not bring in the cases that are most important to me." He went out reluctantly into the sun, slowly pulling on his droopy hat. Now, Istvan thought. Before the music draws gawkers.

"I must talk with you."

"Good. Later," she said almost unwillingly.

"Surely I have a right to know."

"Indeed you have." She smiled bitterly. "If you care to."

"Why were you avoiding me?"

She sat with her darkly tanned legs and sandaled feet extended, burrowed deeply into the white sand that glittered like shattered glass. She hung her head and said nothing.

"I telephoned. You were never there. Did you get my letters and telegrams?"

"I got them."

"What does this mean? What has separated us? Speak to me. Please."

She raised her dark glasses wearily. Now he could see that her eyes were very pale and ringed with deep shadows.

"A child. Yours." She hastily corrected herself: "Ours."

The voices of those carrying the cases and the professor's remonstrations could be heard close to the tent. Istvan was stunned and silent.

"How did that happen? After all, you said yourself . . ." he whispered helplessly after a moment.

Music—the chirp of the flute and the moaning of two-stringed violins—filled the tent and, echoing off the canvas, wandered around the village. The driver carried in a long box; fortunately he backed into the tent, for Terey's face, like a mirror, reflected his shock and despair.

The professor was kneeling, searching for keys to the padlocks. "I have a surprise for you here," he began. The radio standing beside him wailed plaintively.

Terey rose from the ground suddenly and made his way toward the doorway. He felt the force of the sun with all his body, as if he had been drenched with boiling water. He moved forward, squinting. He took a quick breath and smelled the fusty odor of the open cottages, the smoke of fires burning low. He passed little shops with jars of colorful sweets and hanging bunches of dusty red pepper strips. Two boards propped on empty gasoline drums, and there was a market stall; a leaky roof of stalks had been patched together to cover it. Grains of sand rode on the wind, tumbled from roofs, beat him in the face, and roamed around his skin like ants.

I've taken a hit . . . he dragged his pain behind him as a wounded animal, fleeing, carries the bullet that has struck him. He had been appalled when he saw her defenseless in the ruthlessly denuding Indian sun. Nothing could be hidden here; she would be given away. They would not be able to keep silent. She must be taken from here, she must go to Bombay or Calcutta. Already you want to be rid of her, he accused himself, and you have not even gotten her back. No, no, he defended himself as he waded in the soft, sinking sand, his feet swollen and burning from the heat. Get rid of it while it is still possible, the coward in him whined. But that, he remembered, was against the law. A doctor who agreed to perform the procedure would be a criminal. They must be prepared for everything, even for blackmail. All at once he was terrified as he saw images of curettes not disinfected, specula wiped with pocket handkerchiefs, turbans, hairy faces, unwashed hands, and self-confident dilettantes who bought not only their practices but often their diplomas as well.

You would be risking her health if not her life. It is wrong; you have no right to push her into this. Be brave enough to see her through it. She has demanded nothing from you, after all, and you are already looking for faults in her, accusing her. Speak now, blurt out what you have to say: I love you, I love you . . .

He drew himself erect. His face was tight with anger. He felt as if he had been slapped in the face. No! No! I have the courage to repeat to all the world what I whispered with my face in your hair, when we enfolded each other in the darkness and I was one with you: Margit, I love you. It will be as you wish.

The sand was grinding under his feet with a dry, unpleasant biting sound. The entire plain was gradually shifting, alive with dust, enveloped in a fine drizzle of grains flying on the wind.

"She must feel that I am beside her," he whispered. "But why did she say nothing? Why did she hide it from me?"

When in the evening he managed to get Margit out for a walk among the dunes, under a sky full of fire like the mouth of a gigantic furnace, he repeated the question. She turned her face toward him; it was covered by her black glasses.

"And what would you have thought of me?" she said bitterly, even a little contemptuously. "A doctor, and I didn't know? Those would have been your first words. I'm an adult. I know what I'm doing. I had to deal with it myself. I didn't want to involve you."

She went on a few steps and he heard the mournful sizzle of the scattering sand, the glassy music of the desert. They walked side by side, but far apart.

"You shouldn't speak that way. I really didn't deserve it. I'm asking you honestly: What shall I do? What do you expect from me? Surely you know—" his voice broke like a child's, as if he were about to shout at her and threaten her. Only with difficulty did he control himself.

He took her in his arms. He kissed her lips, which were dry and salty and dear, dear, dearer than anything.

"Let me go. They will see us."

"Let them!"

"Let me go. I'm dirty and sweaty. You can't even wash properly out here."

He held her close and rocked her as if she were a small child. "That's nothing. Nothing. I couldn't care less. I only want to know: Do you love me?"

She raised her face toward him and moaned with parted lips, "This is terribly hard for me, Istvan." She kissed him on the neck. "I'm sorry. I shouldn't have—"

When he was holding her, now yielding and his once more, the caressing word from his dream returned to him. "My darling, my—*cradle*," he whispered into her ear, "remember, we're together."

"You see, Istvan, it was bad of me not to tell you at once. But you came with the professor in that blinding sun, so strong and sure of yourself. You came for me as for something of your own. I must have . . . so cruelly . . . I am bad, bad. Istvan," she whispered with her lips on his chest so that he had to strain to hear the words, "for almost two months I have been living with this: that I will have a child. Only for three days . . . I still tremble at the very thought that . . . I could not kill your child. I knew that. I ran away. You might have thought that I wanted to use the child to bind you to me, and that that was why I told you."

"But what was the reason?"

"I don't know, though I have a dozen explanations by now, all plausible: change of climate, a different type of work, full of tension, and you. Well, yes: you. Inhibition caused by the fear of passing time, for that affects one: fear paralyzes. Days passed and I was frightened when I counted them.

"I was in torment. I ordered the pregnancy test to be done. I gave another name, a Hindu name. They were not careful in the laboratory. They bungled it. It takes six weeks to be sure." She gripped his hand. "And I had to go away without knowing the result. I wanted to preserve appearances, to act as if nothing were happening. Nothing. Istvan, forgive me. A few hours have been enough for you, and I lived through two months of this. So many days and nights. Now you understand me better."

"This has happened for the best," he said, looking into the frenzy of color that was deepening in the sky, tinting the waving sands cherry-red that languished to violet. "It is a reminder that we ought to decide what we really want. We are not Hindus."

In the distance they heard the professor calling, then the blare of the Land Rover's horn. "Coming!" Istvan shouted back. "We must be on our way. He is obviously possessive about you."

"Be serious." He heard such a happy new lilt in her voice that it moved him.

Two jackals scampered among the dunes, sweeping the sand with their fluffy tails. In the sheds fires winked red and from far away they heard the professor's radio as it spewed Hindu music full of complaint and resignation. A drum rumbled as if beads of lead were falling on the tightly stretched skin, measuring time.

"I thought you two had gotten lost," the professor said crossly, "or that the jackals had eaten you. There are plenty of them running around here."

"Now, now. We were standing on top of the dunes and you saw us all the time."

"True. I did not let you out of my sight," he admitted. "Well, you will have something to write about."

Istvan lowered his head.

"And in the meantime we must load. The bulletin is warning of rain again. Before night we will go along those iron rails, by another and, I promise, nearer road. I called you, however, so we can eat something before our departure. And perhaps have a drop to drink."

"That won't hurt," Terey murmured.

"When I look at these people wearing themselves out here, I cannot fathom why they insist on living in the middle of this frying pan."

"They were always here," Margit pointed out. "The desert came to them. It engulfed them."

Chapter IX

The high-walled corridor in the ministry, inlaid with stone, was alive with the soft chiming of bracelets. Slender Hindu women draped in silk moved about with short, restrained steps. Preparations were underway for a convention of the World Women's Congress. Under orders from Budapest, Istvan had to acquaint himself with the composition of the Congress's slate of officers and its positions and statements. It was feared that right-wing elements would stage a demonstration; in that case it would be better for Hungary not to send delegates, to limit its involvement to blandly worded telegrams with greetings and wishes for fruitful deliberations, than to be forced into statements of protest and end by having its representatives leave the hall.

A few ladies, however—including the vice-minister's wife—were insisting on seeing India. That had led to a lively exchange of telegrams with the embassy and a demand for detailed information. The convention was scheduled for the middle of October, only six weeks away. The ladies had asked if it would be appropriate, at least at the opening, to appear in Hungarian folk costume.

Miss Shankar, gently smiling and pressing her heavily braceleted wrists to her bosom, had assured him that she was working with the organizers and had not noticed any efforts to turn the convention into a rally. Of course there might always be an unexpected development; and then someone from the South American delegation might bring forward a troublesome resolution. But it could be suppressed, mired down in procedural disputes, so that the audience would be wearied and the final action on the matter delegated to the officers—with the hearty agreement of those in attendance. The issues to be discussed would be equal rights and higher wages for women. If equally qualified, they should not earn less than men.

"So there will be nothing of a sensational nature?"

"There will be." She raised her almond-shaped eyelids and fluttered her long lashes. "We are preparing a pronouncement against the traffic in women."

"They sell themselves, after all. How can you forbid them to do it?" he laughed.

"I am speaking of slaves—little girls kidnapped here and in Pakistan and carried away into harems in Arab countries. And to Africa. Entire criminal organizations work almost openly. It is difficult to ascertain the number of young captives, for if their parents themselves sell them, they certainly do not boast about it. Oh, Rajah Khaterpalia"—she motioned with a hand lithe as a flower—"you know, his brother died, the one who had been miraculously returned to life."

The rajah had just spied them. The corner of his lapel was wound with crepe once more. He received expressions of sympathy with dignified satisfaction.

"What happened to him?" Istvan asked.

"Nothing. His heart simply weakened as it had previously, and he died. This time we stayed to the end, until his ashes were scattered to the Ganges." His face had taken on an unhealthy puffiness, and greenish shadows ringed his glittering eyes. "Only then did I truly feel grief for him. That terrible scarred face frightened me, but it was my older brother."

"You think that he really was your brother? After our conversation I also had begun to have doubts."

"No. That was certainly my brother. I could swear to it now. We are completely different in character. He was meek, a dreamer. He was easily moved; you know, such a—" he groped for a term—"a poet."

Miss Shankar tittered and looked Istvan in the eye with an unaffected, childlike smile.

"Oh, I beg your pardon." The rajah put a hand on Istvan's shoulder. "I didn't mean to offend you. Anyway, what kind of poet are you, when you are sticking it out at this remote post? You are a good embassy official, and that means something."

"Thank you for that endorsement." Terey bowed and the beautiful young woman laughed again, covering the bottom of her face with a silk shawl of iridescent peacock blue. "At least one person appreciates me. In the embassy I still have a reputation for being a poet."

Still chatting, they went out to the wide stone stairs.

"Won't you stop in and see us? Grace has been complaining because you do not come."

"I can't. I have some work, and I must be worthy of your compliment. Don't forget: I am an official. May I take either of you anywhere?"

"I have a car." Miss Shankar placidly gave Istvan her hand. "Thank you."

"My chauffeur is waiting. Do not forget about us. Come—even tomorrow night. There will be a few people, acquaintances from the club. You ought to look in. People are beginning to say that India has changed you."

"Yes." Istvan seized on the point. "Tell them that I have taken up yoga and I concentrate for hours in silence."

"Really?" the girl marveled, covering her bare arms with the shawl so as not to tan like a peasant woman.

"Yes. Doesn't it show?" He looked out at the wide square around which cyclists swarmed in colorful wide trousers and untucked shirts, and into the air that quivered with veins of sunlight. He breathed in the smell of dust and heated stone and the light fragrances of girls' perfumes. For an instant he forgot about his companions and was absorbed in the summer afternoon.

"You really have changed," she whispered timidly. "And we thought you were in love."

"No," the rajah smiled triumphantly. "He was faithful to Grace; he must trust to future incarnations. Well—goodbye!"

He hurried to the large green car. A driver in white leaped out to open the door for him.

In the Austin Mihaly sat with his hands on the steering wheel, wearing an expression of enormous gravity. Three Hindu boys were peeping through the lowered windows. At their request the little fellow solemnly blew the horn. He had learned Hindi in preschool, whole phrases together, and it gave him pleasure when, as he talked with Krishan in the garage, his impatient father asked, "What are you two running on about in there?"

He raised the big, pensive eyes beneath his parted bangs to the counselor, brushed the bangs off his forehead and said:

"Uncle, they don't know where Hungary is. They think it is so small that there is no point in learning about us."

"And what did you tell them?"

Sulkily he confessed, "I told them they were stupid. They wanted me to start up the motor, but I didn't have the key. So I only told them I would toot the horn if they would shout, 'Hungarians are the smartest nation on earth!' They shouted and I blew the horn until a lot of people came around."

They rode along the wide avenue, dazzled by the glare from the glass and nickel of automobiles passing them on the right. Above the fresh dark green of the trees rose clusters of the red flower "Flame of the Forest." The thin white haze in the sky promised more sunny weather.

"Uncle," whimpered the little boy, "let's go to Krishan's for a little while. I haven't seen him for four days, for I get a scolding right away if I go away from the embassy. Papa is always in a bad humor now. He says I have to stay home."

"In a bad humor about what?"

"Because the ambassador comes even at night and shouts at him because there is no answer to his dispatches. Now papa sleeps in his room with the iron door, and mama is angry, too."

They drove up in front of a building like a gigantic wooden barrel, covered with a bulging striped awning. The stammering, rising roar of a motor had already reached them, and a babel of voices full of delight tinged with fear. A band of children stood in an enclosure formed by a net of ropes secured to steel stakes beaten into the turf. Amid a cluster of bicycles leaning on each other and guarded by a bearded Sikh, vendors squatted with shallow baskets of peanuts, mangoes, and small, candy-sweet seedless grapes on which swarms of flies grazed when they were not waved away with a fan made of horsehair.

"I don't need a ticket," Mihaly informed Istvan. "Here is how I will get in." He said something to an attendant in a white uniform with a wide green sash and scampered upstairs to the gallery.

"What did you say to him?" the counselor asked when they were leaning on the railing and looking into the black pit of worn boards.

"That Krishan is my uncle!" he said impatiently. "Look, he is coming up. He saw us!" The little boy jumped up and down, clapping. "Krishan! Krishan!"

"Be quiet." Istvan put a hand on the back of the child's neck, though he knew that Krishan could not hear him over the thundering of the motor.

Krishan, fastened into a suit of gleaming black leather and wearing a silver helmet and rectangular goggles, spun his wheels in the arena, trailing a fleeting blue streak of gasoline fumes. Strips of greenish leather a meter long hung from his arms like a tippet that rose as he gathered speed. The roar intensified. The motorcycle moved faster and faster, in wider and wider circles, until it reached the walls. The vibrating whine grew louder and the machine carried the rider onto the wooden casing of the barrel. The big boards throbbed in a dull bass as he flew around them with greenish wings growing out of his arms. There was a spine-tingling metallic whistle as he rocketed forward. Istvan's jaw tightened as he remembered the screeching of airborne bombs.

Krishan sped by so quickly that they felt the onlookers' heads turn to watch him. He leaned far to the side, defying the law of gravity, ever climbing in a spiral toward the edge of the wooden pit. He was already so close that they jerked back their heads when fumes of gasoline exhaust and scalded oil struck them in the face. The whistling leather wings almost lashed them.

Krishan bounced like a pea in a bottle someone was shaking with both hands. It seemed that he would reach the edge and shoot out between the ropes into the fluttering treetops, into the glare, into the sky like a stray comet. Mihaly squealed excitedly, caught up in the madness of the stunt.

Suddenly Krishan jerked his right hand from the handlebars and raised it toward the people as if to salute them. Then he took away the other hand. The motorcycle was hardly touching the ground. From the crowd leaning through the railing came a rapturous howl. Istvan's throat tightened at the needless bravura; after all, the least tremor—the slightest skipping of the wheels on the boards—and the machine would go out of control. In this situation, at this speed, that would mean certain death.

But Krishan lowered his hands, seized the handlebars as if he were curbing a vicious stallion, and, they saw with relief, began riding down. Applause broke out. People leaned over and shouted into the wooden well, which amplified their voices. They clapped with all their might when he spread his legs, planted himself in the very center of the arena, and raised his head toward them as if surveying with disbelief the height to which he had soared a moment before.

"Krishan! Krishan!" Ecstatic viewers standing in the circular gallery like foliage on a wreath leaned down, shouting rhythmically. He stripped off one black glove and brandished his swarthy open hand amid the blue fumes.

"Come on!" Mihaly tugged at Istvan. "He will come to us."

They began pushing through the crowd in which sellers of golden-brown potato chips sparkling with salt crystals moved about. From a box of ice that hung on a vendor's belly they took slender bottles of Coca-Cola. The caps rolled, clinking, around the corrugated gangway.

The boy led the counselor behind the gigantic wooden tub to a clump of spreading trees. A kind of tent, flimsy and airy, had been set up there. An Indian bed with a pair of flat pillows in a red and yellow flower pattern stood inside it. A woman, hunched over and half kneeling, gazed at the entrance.

A group of young men, beside themselves with delight, pushed the motorcycle over the heavily trodden lawn. Krishan strode behind them issuing commands, his leather costume creaking to the tempo of his buoyant step. The girl rose and at once Istvan recognized the sister of Krishan's dead wife—the same languid grace, rather like an animal, the same wide mouth with two points on the upper lip, challenging and childish. Krishan oversaw the placement of the motorcycle and the boys clustered around him for a moment more, holding out photographs of his flight with streaming leather wings—photographs which had been sold in front of the entrance—for his autograph. The picture must have been taken from below, by the furled roof, for the figure of the frenzied rider was seen against a background of clouds.

"Ah, sir, it's you!" He held his hand out to the counselor without his former air of deference. "Please sit down."

With one shout he frightened the boys away from the enclosure. He unzipped the costume that sheathed him like black armor and peeled it off, exposing a dirty, oil-stained tricot shirt. His lean chest heaved beneath it. He was perspiring profusely.

"I must stretch out for a moment." He sat on the bed and the leather of his narrow pants squeaked. "I have a few more appearances."

Only now did Istvan notice that pent-up tears thick with sweat were gathering in the red furrows Krishan's goggles had made on his cheeks.

"Will you smoke?" He held out an open pack of cigarettes.

"No." Krishan shook his head. "The ventilation in there is no good, and I inhaled fumes until my head was spinning."

The woman knelt by him, poured boiling water from a thermos onto a towel, and with great tenderness rubbed his face. He yielded to her touch as to a caress, closing his eyes. She must love him a great deal, Istvan thought.

"You came to see the show?"

"Yes. I see that you are very successful."

"The ambassador was here also. I knew what he wished for me. But he can kiss my—"

"You're taking too great a risk. You shouldn't let go of the handlebars."

"They pay extra for that." A small, bitter smile played over his tightly compressed lips. "After all, everyone hopes they will see me break my neck. What a sight it would be! It would give them something to chatter about for a year."

The wall of the tent bent in the breeze. The machine twittered as the motor cooled. The rising hum of the leaves seemed to shift with a circular motion above their heads.

"That's no good, Krishan. It's nerves. Do you think that way often?"

"Lately, yes."

"Are you afraid?"

He raised himself on one elbow and looked so contemptuous that the counselor lowered his eyes.

"I would like to see something that could frighten me! And you?"

Smiling, Istvan shook his head.

"It comes over me when I am in the pit and I see where I was, how high I had gone. I feel a numbing pain in my thighs, as if someone were squeezing me with pincers. Then I say, Enough. This is the last time. Take the cash and say goodbye to the managers, those old thieves. Turn the motorcycle into a rickshaw. You will earn a living that way as well."

"A sound idea."

They heard boisterous music from megaphones and the deep voice of the barker, who was promoting Krishan's next show through a bullhorn: "Neck-breaking! Your blood will run cold!"

The girl sat on her heels, gazing at Krishan like a guard dog.

"When I begin riding into the circle, I really want to climb to the top as fast as I can and get out of that smoke pit. It chokes me."

"The motor burns oil?"

"No. The fuel is specially formulated for effect. The management demands it."

"You can't trust that machine, Krishan. Who looks after it?"

He sat up and looked at the counselor alertly.

"And can I trust those people? I inspect it myself. I would not let anyone touch it. I know whether it is in proper condition."

Mihaly squatted on his heels, Hindu-fashion, in the entrance to the tent. A flap rippled and nudged him in the back, but he did not notice. His eyes were riveted on his hero.

"How I hate them all!" Krishan lay with his head thrown back, beating his fist against the bed frame.

"Whom?"

"Those people waiting in there." He lifted his chin defiantly. "Those people in the gallery. Hundreds of times I've thought: You want a terrifying spectacle—all I need to do is pour out a canister of gasoline and those dried-out boards would go up like paper. The narrow aisles—they would trample each other to death if the fire blocked their way. I know those voices, I know how they would shriek. Look: impregnated wood, heated by the sun. A splendid funeral pyre!"

"Krishan, you must stop doing this for a while."

"No. Not yet. They are just waiting for an accident, so I can dream of evening the score."

The noisy music and the gongs clamored; the reverberation drifted around the treetops. Sometimes the glare of the sun burst through a chink in the greenery and kindled like a fire on the walls of the tent. The reflected light glided quickly over the foot-worn grass.

"The ambassador would be very happy if I died. He would even give ten rupees for wood for my pyre."

Istvan looked around. Mihaly was listening with his mouth open, frightened. It seemed to Istvan that the boy was absorbing knowledge about the dark side of life—that Krishan's words were sinking into his heart.

"Buy us some candies or nuts, only choose well." The counselor threw the child a coin; the little hands caught it in the air. When the boy had run out, he leaned toward Krishan. He sensed that the man was eager to get something off his chest.

"Now, Krishan, tell me what really happened. Only speak quickly, before the little one returns. Surely you needn't be constrained on her account." He nodded toward the young woman.

"No. She will not understand half of it." The chauffeur made a wry face. "And you will keep silence as well, because the honor of your embassy demands it. We drove to Uttar Pradesh at the invitation of the governor of that state. I do not know why the boss was dawdling. I waited for a long time in front of his residence, and then we rushed as if to make up for the delay. First we were held up on the bridge over the Yamuna. Then on the Ganges, narrow bridges, one lane of traffic. I saw army supply columns, carts, and tongas moving along opposite us and a wide line of foot soldiers walking in front. 'Push ahead of them,' the ambassador shouted. 'We have the right. I am traveling with the insignia, on official business.'

"And they were already coming onto the bridge. I knew they would not let us through, for what did they know about who we were? We waited, and they crawled along. Crawled along. Sometimes there were breaks in the lines and it would have been possible to shove in, but a sergeant with a flag was leaning back against the hood. He paid no attention when I blew the horn, and when the ambassador jumped out he told him to sit quietly or he would catch it! I know these Gurkhas. They are not joking. What they will do to a soldier with a chest full of medals . . . Would they block our way out of anger?

"Finally the last tonga rolled by and they let us go. The boss was furious. He pushed me away with his elbow, roared like a buffalo, and sat down behind the wheel. As soon as he started the car I knew that something would happen. He was running it at better than eighty miles an hour. Even in the villages he never slowed down. 'I will show you how to drive,' he wheezed.

"And then the cow scrambled out of the bushes. She walked onto the middle of the highway and looked around in our direction. She felt that something was wrong. She hesitated; should she turn back? 'Pass a woman from in front, pass a cow from behind'— I remember the ambassador saying that to himself, not breaking his speed, aiming for the tight space between her hindquarters and the ditch. I was afraid a wheel would go onto the sand and pull us down. He must have thought of that, too, for he pushed harder on the gas, and then that man jumped out—"

"Man?" the counselor asked hoarsely, and a chill went down his spine.

"He wanted to drive the cow away. He waved a stick and stared at us. It all happened in a fraction of a second. We knocked the cow's hind legs from under her. Glass shattered on the road. I did not even feel the car strike the man. He hit his head lightly and was thrown into the ditch like a cat. We drove a hundred meters more, perhaps farther, before the boss put on the brakes. We leaped out. The cow raised herself on her front legs and dragged her broken back. A little feces dribbled from her. She opened her muzzle but no sound came out."

"And the man?" he asked, hardly able to breathe.

"I ran to him, but I knew at once that he was done for. He lay twisted, with his head down, in the ditch. The boss knew, too, for he stopped a long way from the ditch and stretched out his hands as if he wanted to push away what had happened. 'Don't move!' he cried. 'To the car!' Peasants were running from the field with rods and hoes. They had only seen the cow, but that was enough to put them in a frenzy. They would have beaten us if they had caught us. They threw stones but we got away.

"The ambassador ordered me to drive. He did not even look around; he only swallowed very noisily. Then he said, 'Krishan, you were driving. I will protect you. We will get a good lawyer. I will make it worth your while.' I was afraid of him then and I agreed. He wheezed again and seemed to be planning something. Then he laid a hand on my shoulder. 'There will be no problem,' he said. 'Only be quiet and listen to me. You will not regret it.'"

"I got some anise candies, uncle. Try one!" Mihaly burst in. Gleams of sunlight played on his bare legs, and his eyes were full of happiness. He looked with surprise at the somber men and the woman who was curled up, resting her elbow against the edge of the bed. The tent breathed lightly under a wave of humming noises punctuated by clanging cymbals.

"Well done. Have a munch. Don't bother us just now."

With the candies in a little horn of twisted leaf, the boy went over to the bed on which the stunt rider was resting, but Krishan forestalled him.

"No, Mihaly. I told you about the horoscope. I have to beware of sweets. Give them to her. She will eat for me."

"Why didn't you tell me this before, Krishan?" The counselor steered the conversation back to the confession Mihaly's return had interrupted.

"I wanted to. I tried. But you said that you knew the whole truth, sir, so what was I to do?"

"It's well that I know now." Terey sighed deeply. "But what can be done? They will believe him, not me."

"And that is not all," said the driver, sitting cross-legged on the bed. "We went straight to the governor and the boss filed a complaint that the peasants had been lying in wait for passing automobiles and throwing stones. He named me as a witness. We went outside so the governor could look at the broken headlight and bent fender. He apologized profusely and sent out a truck with police. I sat by the driver. I had to show them where it had happened.

"The peasants were still standing on the road. Some were praying. The cow was lying under a canopy with garlands of flowers. Little lamps were burning all around her. When they saw us, they began running toward us and shouting. They surely wanted to make accusations. But the driver charged at them with the truck and they had to move aside. When we had barely passed them he stopped, and the police jumped out of the truck with bamboo sticks and began beating. I only heard cries and the thwacks of the sticks on their backs. People were running in all directions. I stole a look at the ditch—the man was not there. Probably his family had taken his body."

He breathed uneasily as he relived the incident, and rubbed his forehead and the back of his neck with a towel. "Just as they had chased the peasants away, the officer summoned the head man of the village and filled out a report. The policeman shouted at the man so that he could only bow and apologize. He spoke endlessly about the cow—well, because that to them is the most sacred object—" he thrust his lips out scornfully and rubbed his brush-like mustache with one finger—"and I eat that sacred object."

"Perhaps that man is still alive?" Terey asked without much confidence.

"No. I heard what the women were saying. I wrote down his name and the surname of his father. They were poor people. They did not even know that they could institute a claim for damages. All their lives they have had their noses in the dirt. When we went back, I told him everything." He looked at Mihaly's rapt face and wrinkled forehead. It was clear that the little boy was struggling to understand the meaning of what was being said, so he did not mention the ambassador, but looked significantly at the counselor. "He only said, 'I will not give a penny. It is very bad to begin that way, for then I will never extricate myself.' He reminded me, as you did, that I had signed a statement—that I should not change it, because it was there in black and white—that I was driving the car. And then, as if he had lost his trust in me, he set Ferenc on to throw me out at the first opportunity."

"But why did he do that?"

"Because then if I retracted the statement, it would seem that I was getting revenge for being fired from my job. That is perfectly clear."

The counselor sat hunched over. I know the truth, he thought bitterly. That is what I wanted. And I could have lived on without knowing anything. Ignorance is bliss. After all, I cannot change anything! I have no proof. They will believe the ambassador, not me.

And who would benefit, now that the matter was closed, if an investigation were begun all over? To be silent so no one would speak ill of us, of the embassy . . . to be silent for the good of Hungary? He clasped his hands and clenched them until it hurt. When all was said and done, this was evil! Does the law in this world always serve to entrench the injustices of those who know how to use it to their own advantage? And suddenly he thought of Chandra and was tempted to lay the whole affair before him. There was the man, he felt, who would be able to catch the culprit by the throat, perhaps force him to request to be recalled, to flee. The man who would flay him, fleece him of his last rupee, poison his life.

They gave a start: shrill, imperious bells clanged. The requisite number of viewers had arrived and it was time for Krishan's next appearance. He raised himself reluctantly. His wife handed him his jacket, gently pulled it together in front, and did up the zipper. He stood suddenly stiff as if in a suit of armor, adjusted his helmet, and put on his goggles. The wings, the fluttering strips of leather, rustled dryly.

Before he left the tent Istvan saw that the young woman knelt, seized her husband's hand, pressed it to her cheek and kissed it with her eyes closed.

As he was sitting behind his desk reviewing some newspapers and periodicals, the door opened discreetly and Ferenc walked in.

"I am not disturbing you?"

"Since when do you have to concern yourself about the value of my time? Surely there is no hurry; the reports have been sent out. The boss is waiting for the Indonesian, for his return visit, so relax. We can chat. Sit down. Tell me what brings you here."

Ferenc turned his slender face toward the window, frowned, and thought for a minute as if he had forgotten why he had come. Then instead of taking a chair, he pushed the stack of publications aside and sat on a corner of the desk. Istvan saw himself reflected in the man's sunglasses as in a fun house mirror, with large hands and a little head like an insect's thrown back in expectation.

"Don't you smell a foul odor?" His nostrils twitched and he looked Terey closely in the eye.

"Here, among us? Or are you thinking of our country?"

"No. I smell the stench of war in the world."

"Big news." Istvan waved belittlingly. "It has been smoldering for years. Time to get used to it."

"I am thinking of something worse."

"Of a third?"

"And probably the last."

"You must have slept poorly last night or eaten something spoiled," Terey jibed. "Why are you favoring me with this discovery? Go to the boss, that consummate politician. He will shout at you, he will give you a shot of plum vodka to relieve the pressure, and the evil premonitions will vanish like magic."

"I came to you as one man to another."

"I have risen in your estimation."

"I, too, have moments of weakness." He looked with irritation at Terey lolling in an armchair.

"Well, speak, though of course I never know if you have come of your own volition or if the boss sends you to keep a covert watch on me." He put a hand to his temple.

But Ferenc turned away again and looked through the window at the wall of the storage room over the garage. It was covered with plaited vines and shaded by leaves which, like water, the breeze alternately smoothed and ruffled. "You were not born yesterday," he said. "You know how to read."

"And even how to write. Word of honor. The critics acknowledged it. It is no idle boast."

"Stop clowning. Lay out a couple of news items from the last few days—not from the front pages of the newspapers," he said reflectively, still looking at the flickering lights and shadows on the fleece of greenery.

"What do you see there?" Istvan asked edgily.

"The wall. Look," he pointed to the rippling mass of leaves, "over the surface, the soft tremors, beautiful to the eye, and underneath it, the wall. One man said to me—a man who had stood with his face to such a wall—'You have thick, grainy plaster under your nose, and you see perfectly the whole configuration of things; you see your whole life. Then you know what you could have done with it. And it is too late.' Say—what can you do so that someone, someday, does not suddenly shatter your life? So that it will not become evident that those little tricks, that promotion, that perquisite or that excessive obligingness, obscured the fundamental concerns that make it worthwhile to live? And do you think that you are the only true Hungarian? That you have a monopoly on honest impulses? Istvan, I don't want them to shove a gun barrel into my back and march me away because the time has come to pay for the actions of those who chose the right moments to duck, who hauled down the flag."

Istvan looked at the secretary, uncertain if he were encouraging him to make a confession or share a confidence in order to accuse and stigmatize him publicly at some later time. "Well? Well?" Ferenc urged.

"You who are several years older had a war. You are proven—to yourselves, at least. You know by now what you are capable of. Today we walk along together, but you can use that experience as a point of reference anytime, and we . . . We give way one step at a time. We acquiesce to compromises, we bungle things, we founder. Ah, if we even knew the depth of our mediocrity! Don't pretend not to understand in order to spite me. You know what I'm talking about."

Ferenc took off his glasses and toyed with them like a woman at a costume ball playing with her mask, but his eyes were full of strain and apprehension.

"I repudiated comrades, not for a career. I cannot live without the party." The admission carried the ring of sincerity. "I was young. I believed blindly. Now I am crushed that Beria's gang, that criminal clique, sent our best sons there." He motioned with his chin toward the wall hidden under leaves full of uneasily shifting light.

"What has come over you?" The counselor tilted his head back, resting it on his clasped hands, and watched as Ferenc raked his fingers through his thick, wavy hair.

"What do you think about as you read the newspapers?" He leafed through the pile of publications on the desk. Throwing some of them open, he ran his eyes over the headlines as if he wanted to assure himself of something. Then, evidently dismayed, he crumpled them carelessly.

"A day after the report that Nasser had seized the Suez Canal, a hundred million pounds were lost on the London stock exchange. And the crisis continues. Stocks are plummeting. France and England put on pressure to no avail. What does a strike by the lock operators and a revolt of the pilots prove? We sent our ships, ships that were under contract, and the canal worked. The West has no cause to complain that transport will shut down, that there will be a stoppage. So they are trying an inside tactic.

"Yesterday in Cairo several Englishmen were arrested. Intelligence agents. There was an inquiry. I heard on the radio today how they stopped an Israeli troop transport vessel and before they escorted it to harbor, it sank for no visible cause. What was the cargo? Cement. Do you understand? A wreck loaded with cement to block the canal. Do you want blood? Scuffles on the border between Israel and Egypt. Of course those killed were Arabs; they pounded the fellaheen. Did you notice that there is an English fleet on Cyprus? The Greeks protested; that was suppressed instantly. To cow them, to silence them, the English shot eight. There had not been such verdicts there in the past."

"So you think . . ."

"And why did Queen Elizabeth call up two yearly army-lists? They are shifting the commandos to Cyprus. Look—today's short communiqué: 'Bomb squads on Malta at full complement.'"

"You will say next that it is autumn, the crops have been harvested, so a war could begin." Istvan forced a laugh.

"You absolutely remind me of our peasants, those born politicians, especially when they are sipping their fruit brandy. You, consummate politician, will overlook the Soviet Union and the United States, powers not inclined to jump at each other's throats, for they know what the other side has up its sleeve. Heavy. Very heavy. The wrestlers pat their muscles, they flex their biceps, they garner applause from the audience and listen to those who shout to urge them on, but they themselves are cautious.

"Look"—Ferenc slapped an open newspaper—"and think like a politician, not like a poet! They are waiting for a moment of weakness on our parts; they want to exploit it. If they intend to seize the Suez, to stifle Nasser, it can only be now, when things are at the boiling point in our camp, when we are hard at work imposing order and sweeping out the rubbish . . . They are not well acquainted with the Russians. They think that Khrushchev talked away all that concentrated energy, that he dismantled the engine piecemeal in order to inspect it and change the screws and gaskets. They do not know that there are people who can be called up in a flash, that in the face of a threat the party and the nation would be one. Let Russia shove its fist under their noses and the West will soon come to its senses and be polite."

He is right, Terey thought. We have more knowledge, wit, and resourcefulness than character. That is why he speaks so freely: because he does not have to take me seriously. He feels that he has the upper hand. He knows that I write, but only poetry, not notes on private conversations, not confidential reports.

"What do you say about the nuclear weapons tests announced by TASS?" Ferenc threw out.

"Well, they have made it clear that they are ready to stop if the United States signs a treaty. Many Americans cannot get it through their heads yet that someone else holds the atomic dragon on a leash, and sometimes pulls its tail to force it to growl. They were accustomed to think that all the superlatives—the largest, the best, the deadliest—always belonged to them. Now a rival appears and not only goes neck and neck with them, but in rocket technology surpasses them."

"The experimental explosions are a warning. So they are taken by the Pentagon, at any rate." Ferenz waved a hand. "You are right: they did not believe the seismographs. They sent a plane to take samples from the stratosphere, to see if there was dust. Well—there was. Perhaps they are beginning to think and to include this in their calculations."

"Enough of this discussion of the global picture." The counselor clapped a hand on his thigh. "No guessing games. What brought you here? Are you giving a lecture to the locals? Doing a review of international politics?"

Ferenc looked closely at him. A little smile of approbation flitted over his lips.

"No. No. Now you are not such a poet." He sighed approvingly. "You do have your feet on the ground. But you would rather we took you for a poet, for you are more comfortable that way. You have greater leeway. You see, Istvan, there is an official communiqué about the removal of the minister of internal affairs. They have thrown Farkas in prison. He bullied our people. The Central Committee surrounded him on tiptoe; I know something about it because . . ." he hesitated, looked Terey in the eye again and waved weakly, as if he were brushing away an untimely impulse to make disclosures.

"Because you went from them to the Ministry of Foreign Affairs."

"How did you know that?"

"Are you afraid? Or do you envy him, because in the end—before the procurator, at least—he may talk about what pains him, may spew it up and feel relief?"

Ferenc trembled like a man caught in the act of committing a crime. He leaned over the desk and cried, "No one has a right to accuse me! I believed. I was under orders. Moreover, they explained to me that it was necessary, that it was essential for the good of the party."

"Believe, listen, don't think, and we will meet there." Terey pointed to the wall outside the window.

"And what do you have to do with this?"

"The information came and I did not believe it. I did not want to believe. Those being led to their deaths screamed in the hope that I and others like me would hear. I heard; the secrets leaked out. But I said, it is impossible, at least among us, in Hungary. I thought I knew Hungary."

Ferenc stopped playing with his glasses and hitting them against his pursed lips. He put them back on as if to camouflage himself. In their green lenses Terey saw only a curved likeness of himself, like the abdomen of a carrion-eating fly, and something like a star belching fire: the reflection of the glare-filled window.

"You know, Terey, I'm glad they sent me here. Budapest is seething; I feel it in my bones. If I could do anything there, I would want to prove myself different—better. I would jump like that grasshopper and any hen would peck me up. I tell you, it is better for us to wait out the hottest time here."

The counselor was almost lying in his chair with his hands under his head, watching with profound concentration as a blade on the large fan turned slowly under the white desert of the ceiling.

"I tell you, Ferenc, neither God nor the world likes the lukewarm. I'm afraid we will not attain the grace of absolution. And you will have no opportunity to know what gifts you have. Who you really are."

They sat for a moment in silence. The secretary turned abruptly and moved toward the door. As he gripped the handle, he thrust out his lips and said sarcastically:

"Likewise, you had better beware lest God send a test beyond a man's strength. So why raise a clamor, why be keen to volunteer?"

"You have caught the Indian disease. That's a comfortable philosophy, especially for a Marxist."

The secretary did not reciprocate but quietly closed the door behind him.

He writhes like a fish on a reel, Istvan sighed. Conscience. A fearful premonition of the truth about oneself, which He Who knows us reveals. Ferenc came here hoping that we would exchange secrets as hostages used to be exchanged, to be certain the conditions of peace would be observed. He thought I had heard more about him than he wanted to disclose to me. He does not know, and I will not tell him, that I am weary in my harness, I am struggling. No—it is not even the matter of that peasant they ran down. How to find his family and help them without casting suspicion on the embassy? Krishan will not agree to take that on himself a second time. Margit. The problem of Margit. If Ferenc knew about that, how much calmer he would be.

I am robbing her, he accused himself. I am a miserable little—I am taking advantage of her weakness for me, her defenseless yielding. When it seemed that she had freed herself from me, I went, I abandoned the embassy, I lied—anything to be sure she was still mine. She comes to me, simple and trusting. She makes no stipulations. She has no plans. But I had already had a warning. I whisper: I love you. I love you. But that justifies nothing. She surely knows that. It is better that she knows. Until now she has not asked what would happen with us. She entrusts the matter to me to decide, with the calm reliance of one who deposits money in an armored bank vault. What is she counting on? Only on my love for her? Or on this—that we will be together. Together. Two joined in one; a shared life. And only death can part us.

More than once in the night, after all, I felt for her in my sleep. I wanted her to be there—always, always. And that wretched fear when she told me she was expecting a child! Did I love her less then? No. So what alarmed me? Would I have been afraid to tell the world that I had chosen this woman, that she was the one I loved? Was that a feeling that could not bear the light of day and witnesses? That flees in the face of "complications?" Even those who have not lived with their wives for a long time, who have mistresses, will be eager to play the role of accusers; they will judge and condemn me. Well, what of it? Can't I withstand pressure? A year will pass and the world will forget. Love that does not outlast such a time is not worthy of the name.

If she really had a child, I would get a divorce, he thought, wishing to soothe his conscience. Now that it has happened—a child—if only I truly want it, I can have it. A little red-haired girl with dark eyes, a little Margit.

He did not think of a son, perhaps because he had sons already, only of a daughter. She would love me; in his dreams he felt the tiny hands on his neck, the touch of the cool nose and the warm breath on his cheek. He even seemed to hear words of playful irritation: "Daddy, you're poking me!" He caught himself thinking in English. But she would have to know her father's language. Would he allow her to grow up far from Hungary? In Australia?

Divorce: it was easy to say. From here, from New Delhi, from India I would write, forewarn Ilona, prepare her somehow. "You see, I have fallen in love"—that hardly sounded serious. Better to go to her, to put his hands on her shoulders, step back so their eyes would meet, and lay out the whole truth. "I have found the woman with whom . . ." "And what about what we had together?" Ilona would ask. "And what about me, and the boys?"

"I made a mistake," he would say then. And suddenly he was trembling as if he had heard her say simply, a little sternly, "No, Istvan. I made a mistake, because I married someone else."

There would be no tears, no scenes. Ilona would be silent. She would grow somber. She would look for the fault in herself, not in him. She was like that. She would nod her head as if she pitied herself a little.

In her letters there were hardly any questions about his work, or indeed about him at all. The writing of verse—it was a kind of malady that might occur in the best of families, but it was well not to make too much of it. He writes, his work is printed, why, fancy that! They even pay him for it; good.

Her letters were filled with reports of trivialities: what the boys were doing, how they were studying, how they passed their time, the state of their appetites and what they were eating. He found them touching and a little tedious. Her heart belongs to our sons. I have a place in it only inasmuch as I am their father. He felt that she was not doing him justice.

It was easy to say, I will get a divorce. If the information found its way to the ambassador, he would order him to be recalled immediately, and a notation would go out about Margit: she would never get a Hungarian visa, and they would not let him out of the country. They would be cut off. Passport . . . To go abroad for whole years was only a dream for many. How the few who spoke of Paris or Rome were envied by their less happy rivals, and what slurs were whispered at the expense of those privileged ones! He had a feeling too deep for argument that he must keep Margit out of sight or he would lose her. His throat tightened at the very thought, and he clenched his fist as if to defend himself.

I must have her. All his fiber stiffened. I want to keep her.

To get a divorce and legitimize the new relationship, I ought to return to Budapest and obtain Ilona's consent. And then they have me like a bird in a cage; they can do as they please. I can count on no support. How could I? The wider world smelled sweet to you, in particular the Australian woman, they would say; are our women inferior? You singled her out for yourself, they will say, because she is an only child and her papa has money. You want to cross over, Comrade Terey? We have had our eye on you for a long time. Be reconciled to your country; we will keep you in the bosom of the fatherland. You will have time enough not only to write your informational pieces, but poetry as well.

In his mind's eye he saw the official who would conduct an investigation of his intended flight and, perhaps, of allegations that he had betrayed state secrets. They knew that it was impossible to go over to the other side empty-handed, that one had to have a financial base. They also liked to pump people for information. The face he saw was amazingly like the ambassador's: puffy, yellowish, with a grimace of good-humored shrewdness. It was a good thing that Grace had married the rajah when she did; in Ferenc's eyes that friendship was already a count against him. Information leaks from various sources, but since they would not see him among foreigners, it would be harder to form suspicions and accusations.

The telephone rang. It was Ram Kanval, timidly probing for information about whether the counselor had filed a statement supporting his request for a stipend to travel to Hungary. An exhibit in Budapest, perhaps even a courtesy purchase for a museum of contemporary art, and he would be able to see Paris. His voice rang with barely concealed fervor as if he were saying, I will immerse myself in glory.

Terey reassured him, explaining that the matter was in progress, that he could count on the ambassador's endorsement, so nothing more than a little patience was needed before a decision would come from Hungary. Then they would establish the most convenient schedule, for it would be necessary to transport several dozen canvases; to find an available exhibition hall; to print invitations and a catalog. It all required time and synchronization.

The counselor heard a sigh of relief. In his mind he saw the painter looking down with the receiver at his ear, drawing lines on the dusty coffee-house carpet with the tip of his sandal.

"Have new problems arisen?" he asked cautiously. "Perhaps you will call on me. No, not today. In two days I will have more time."

He was afraid there would be a desperate request like the clang of an alarm bell: Save me, I am in dire need of money. But either the artist was restraining himself from following up his request for sponsorship by pressing for a loan they both knew would be a gift, or someone was standing near him, for his reply was short and wry.

"Problems?" His chuckle was like a hiccup. "No greater than usual. My wife demands that I set about finding some work, that I begin earning money. Would you mind asking your colleagues at other embassies if they could use someone to make drawings and graphics when they publish their bulletins? I do not need much money, only somewhat more than a housecleaner, and certainly less than a cook," he said ironically.

"I will speak to them. I will find out," Istvan promised, full of good will.

He was not very hopeful, however. The diplomats were not especially trustful, and each was concerned about his own group of "foundlings" who had to be fed crumbs of gainful employment simply to give them a livelihood. He hung up, then called Judit to ask if a document concerning Kanval had passed through her hands. To fill stomachs, to have enough money for the daily rice: that was the fundamental problem. The bellies importune, the children scream, the wife weeps because she married an idler. This is real drama, not your romantic perplexities . . .

If such a document had gone out in the last mail, Judit did not remember it, so he called the ambassador.

"What news of you, counselor? You are obviously avoiding me. No cultural developments worth telling me about? No book? No film, play, concert, no other impressive event? Or perhaps some celebrity hanged himself? Not that, either? So what are you calling about? That painter? He is no painter in my book. I did not sign the request. Do you think, Comrade Terey, do you really think that in Budapest they have nothing more serious on their minds than arranging an exhibition for that shirker from Old Delhi?"

"It is a matter of humanity. The man is very well disposed toward us. He is a distinguished painter."

"'Well disposed,' my backside!" the ambassador growled. "'The man'—spare me! There are four hundred million of them! If we began slobbering over every one of them, we wouldn't have time to blow our noses."

"I did what is precisely spelled out in my job description. He is a good painter. I attached press clippings."

"You were an editor. Don't you know how such packs of banalities are fabricated? Coffee and cognac are all it takes. The newspaper lives a day; why not heap on the praise? All right, all right, Terey. I will sign if you say it is worth it. Let him make his trip and you will take the responsibility. Only do not run to tell him right away. Don't make a to-do. This Kanval can wait. Do you know what I am going to tell you? Take a towel, fold it twice, wet it, and put it to your head."

"Thank you, my head is fine. In fact, I understand quite a few things very well."

Bajcsy was silent for a moment; he was unaccustomed to resistance. Finally he said in a completely different tone, "Give me a moment of your time, counselor."

Istvan heard the receiver fall heavily under the ambassador's beefy hand, with its patches of thinning black hair. I must use my better judgment, he thought. I must not exasperate him, for everything may have consequences that affect Margit. He has me in his hands.

"Sɪᴛ ᴅᴏᴡɴ." Kalman Bajcsy seemed immersed in work. Newspapers open to the pages with economic reports and stock market quotations lay before him; he had underlined some items in red pencil. He remained in his chair, in his shirt sleeves, with his collar open and his tie loose and crooked. He was smoking a pipe; involuntarily he pushed the mouthpiece between two of the buttons on his shirt and scratched his chest with an expression of relief. As was his habit, he left the person he had summoned to his own anxieties, as the confessor leaves a penitent to a moment of concentration so he may discern his hidden faults.

"Terey," he began carelessly, "you gave me a timely warning that a law prohibiting the transfer of rupees was coming into effect. I failed to take it seriously, I counted on diplomatic privilege; unfortunately, I was asleep at the switch. We are about to go to Ceylon with the minister of trade. I would like to feel free, you understand."

The counselor nodded sympathetically.

"You spend time among those who may have similar problems: the rajah, that father-in-law of his, the wealthy members of the club. Do you not know someone who could shift a few rupees over to Colombo to be exchanged for pounds?" He looked at Terey from the corner of his eye and sucked on his pipe with smacking noises.

"For a decent fee, of course," he added cautiously. "Can you do me a service and ask, without mentioning for whom or what the sum in question is? But perhaps you already have such a person within reach."

"Yes," Istvan answered in spite of himself. With devilish delight, as if he were pointing the way to a trap, he gave him Chandra's name, adding, "People I am acquainted with have used his services, and no one has complained."

"What does he have to do with Ceylon?"

"I don't know. But he is a man of discretion. Not long ago I heard at a cocktail party that he was asking members of the American embassy staff if one of them were flying to Colombo, because he had a little packet to send. It seemed that he would let others in on profitable transactions."

He noticed that Bajcsy raised his head and blew a wavering veil of smoke upward.

"So it's your belief that this Chandra could—"

"I believe nothing," Terey said firmly. "I am repeating what came to my ear. You know very well, comrade ambassador, that these are business transactions that are carried on face to face. If they were very much talked of, that would mean that the intermediary was not to be taken seriously or that the methods mentioned had been abandoned long before, and were alluded to only for the pleasure of it, like a historic battle a man comes out of without a scratch."

If Chandra gets him in his clutches, he will square accounts with him. He will repay him for everything. I really don't know why I gave him Chandra's name. But perhaps he will not trust him or use his services. He is a free agent.

"Why don't you ask Ferenc, ambassador? Rather he, I think, than—"

"How do you know I have not asked him?" He leaned over the desk, but added after a moment, "No, Terey, I have not asked him and I will not, because he is too smooth, he gives way too easily. And then I say to myself, Be careful, Kalman, that they do not ease you out without your noticing, while thanks to those obliging fellows who say Yes, yes, you make some blunder that will have you packing your bags and shuffling off to retirement, to the scrap heap. I even like you, Terey, for your scrappiness, for your own interest doesn't come into it. If you strain at the leash, it's for our sake"—he tapped his chest with his pipe—"for the sake of our country."

The state and he are the same, Istvan thought fleetingly, but already I feel that he hasn't much longer to go. He is at the peak of his career; he will not be a minister, they will transfer him, they will send him somewhere, but a couple of years and then it is the end. For him, retirement will be worse than death. He is beginning to be anxious about what will be left to him when they edge him out, what he will live on. The pension, even the pension given those who have served meritoriously, in relation to his needs, to the verve with which he is accustomed to live, would not seem enough to save him from privation. That situation creates a genuine moral crisis for some of those who were active in our national affairs.

When they arrive at a certain age, they reach the ceilings of their careers, and then they become vulnerable to the temptation of fast money: to pluck something, to wrest away something for themselves, to drag it home to the den, to have some independence. If he is planning something, Chandra already has him.

"Perhaps I am bothersome now and then, Terey," the ambassador said meditatively, thrusting out his thick lower lip, "but, remember, I have the prerogatives of the captain of the ship here, for the embassy is like a little ship on strange, perilous waters, is it not?"

"Except that when a man disembarks, I assure you, ambassador, he will not drown," the counselor smiled. "It is easy to feel the ground under one's feet."

"What did you say?" the older man bristled, indignantly rejecting the analogy. "Do you suppose it is possible to disembark at any moment?"

This had a strange ring. Istvan realized that a perverse impulse toward repartee had led him to say, unintentionally, something that might have been taken as an audacious affront.

He walked out of the office feeling displeased with himself. Judit, who was bent over her typewriter, lifted her hands from the keyboard. The sudden silence of the machine and her look full of encouragement did not stop Istvan, so when he opened the door to the corridor she asked in a low voice:

"Did anything happen?"

"No. Don't worry."

"What did he want?"

"Oh, some boring business." Seeing that he was putting her off, she began striking the keys quickly and irritably, as if to say, No, then. All right; we will see who will be sorry.

Vengeful satisfaction lay on his heart like a layer of slimy silt. It seemed to him that he had only fulfilled the decrees of eternal law, that he had been the intermediary in that cry for justice: blood for blood. Through his agency the reckoning would come. After all, he had washed his hands of the matter; he had not dared to bring judgment on Bajcsy himself. He had usurped no prerogatives.

The death of that Hindu? Along the way Bajcsy had run over more than one person; he had crushed others, not with a car, exploiting his friendships, his position, his past. Without hesitation he had pushed and shoved, had broken people. Now his time was drawing near. Fate had lavished gifts on him, had indulged his desire for power as if it were allowing him to be elevated, even to thrive in an unexpected career, in anticipation of this heart-wrenching fall and the attendant abasement. It was as if destiny were mocking him: you want this, you have it, take it—and see how far you have come from that zealous activism for the good of those who believed in you, who entrusted the leadership to you.

Yes, he was betraying them even by not taking account of every aspect of this matter. Today, years later, he assesses those maneuvers with the political acumen derived from participation in a hundred collusions, in the gymnastic exercise of raising hands that is called voting when he knew already who wielded the power, knew whom to follow in speaking or how to remain silent at someone's expense—the silence heavier than the stone slab marking a grave after the innocent were condemned. No; Istvan brushed away these thoughts that clung like spider webs. Don't be God's policeman. Look to yourself; see that you don't make worse mistakes. "Let each perish through his own folly"; the old words echoed with bitter wisdom. And that applies to me as well; he felt the thought soothe his conscience. I too have my black card file; I do not even want to look at it.

He closed his desk. He reached for the last swallow of cold coffee, but two half-drowned flies were twitching in the thick sludge at the bottom of the cup.

I WAS SUFFOCATING in that embassy, he thought, exhaling deeply in the radiant azure of the day. The green fringes of the palms swayed, stroking the luminous sky. As he drove the Austin he was still deliberating about whether his conversation with the ambassador had been beneficial or whether there was cause for worry. But he fell under the spell of the sunny afternoon, dazzled by the clusters of flowers that drooped from behind low garden walls: sprays of little roses, the scarlet and purple of feathery bougainvillea. His eyes began to clear after laboring through swarms of black print, through columns of information crowding against each other in newspapers and periodicals—accounts of violence and unrest in a world tormented by anger, covetousness, and hate. He saw the red earth, the hot greenery of burgeoning trees, the bluish-brown ribbon of baked asphalt. The warm air stroked his temples and he recovered his peace and equilibrium.

It was a beautiful time; he savored the moment of oneness with that exotic earth. How good it was to be alive. It was almost like prayer, this deep thankfulness for that gift beyond price. How good it was to love the world, to retain the capacity for delight in the beauty of this sunny hour.

When he arrived at his house and drove the car to the garage, he was surprised at the behavior of the cook, who was sitting on his haunches like a fired clay statue, deep in blue shade.

"Is dinner ready? Why do you look so troubled?"

"Everything is in order, sir," the man muttered without looking him in the eye.

"Everything is in order," affirmed the watchman in his linen hat like a boy scout's, striking the paving stones with his bamboo rod. "I am keeping an eye on it."

Passing through the dining room, Istvan saw the table set for two. He felt a rush of hope; he hurried to his room and nearly collided with Margit. At once he understood why the servants had been acting so strangely.

She threw her warm, bare arms around his neck and reached up to kiss him on the lips. "How I have missed you!" she sighed heavily. "I have dropped in for such a short time . . . and I have waited for you for so long!"

"You should have called."

"I didn't want to. You can't even guess how good it was to sit in your room and wait. I ordered the servants not to say a word to you, because this was going to be a surprise. Did they manage to keep quiet?"

"Yes, but there were two places at the table."

"That silly cook—he had to give me away!" She laughed joyfully, like a mischievous girl.

They stood locked in a close, tender embrace. Her red hair, warmed by the sun, gave off a light fragrance. Through the thin linen she wore he felt the pressure of her breasts, her belly, and her thighs, could almost feel the light pulsing of her blood. He fell on her lips, pushed them apart and kissed her.

"I'll tell the servants to go away."

"Don't leave. Don't leave," she begged in a whisper, pressing him hard with her fingers. He did not even notice when she managed to unzip her skirt; it slid off easily. She jumped out of it with a nimble movement like a child playing hopscotch.

"I've already told them to leave," she murmured as she unbuttoned his shirt and laid her cheek on his sunburned chest.

"I must have a wash. I'm wet all over."

"If you knew how I like you that way, hot, sticky . . . well, pull this off." She tugged at his shirt sleeve.

Their desire was wild, unrestrained, as if they had only one short minute to themselves and would never be together again. When her fevered breath burned on his neck and she stiffened, moaning with delight, he realized that mutual possession is like a struggle—that he was pressing her down with his arms as if she were an opponent, hurting her, leaving her breathless. Slowly, very slowly he became conscious of her again, and she too recovered her awareness, felt the coolness of the stone floor under one dangling hand. At last he rolled over hard, as if he had been hit, and lay supine with the back of his neck on her hand, feeling her pulse as he pressed against the blue veins under the golden skin. They rested; each one's fingers found the other's, entwined with them and remained locked there.

Margit pulled her numb arm from under him and leaned toward him, resting on her hands. Two waves of hair brushed his cheeks. He saw her straight nose, her smooth forehead, the opaline blue of her eyes, her slightly swollen lips. He wanted to have her lolling above him like that for all eternity. A stream of light falling through a chink between the curtains kindled like fire on her hair and lent a glow to the little drops of sweat on her upper lip. He knew her mouth would be fresh, spiced with the aroma of cigarettes, and that her skin would be salty to the taste, and he did not hurry to kiss her, to confirm these things. He remembered and did not remember; it was enough to bend her toward him, and he did not kiss her. He was happy; he felt peace, a deep satisfaction like swarming flecks of light at the bottom of a gushing spring. Exultation filled with gratitude: Margit, Margit, sang his speeding blood, from you, in you is my great, joyous silence. I will never, never have too much of you. And that thought was confirmed by ineffable delight.

He disengaged himself from the lustrous shower of her hair. He reached for a glass and a bottle of vermouth and dropped in some ice. Lightly shaking the glass, which was growing cooler, he looked at Margit, still lying nude on the carpet. Her body was golden brown, but the rosy tan changed to a white with violet shadings on her slim chest and the flat curve of her belly. He thought of the flesh tents of Renoir's nudes—of the magnetism that made the hands long to encircle those lazy, elongated shapes. He saw her face, with the large blue eyes that made his heart beat faster. The eyes, wide open, wandered around the ceiling, following the languidly rotating blades of the fan. The breeze disturbed her hair, which was strewn in a rust-red circle around her head. How intimately the body of the young woman blended with the rug—the forest greens, daubs of blue, and interwoven floral motifs in coppery red! He had dreamed of such a moment. It seemed to him that it was for this very composition of line and color, free from all sensuality, for pure beauty, that he had acquired this carpet of rust and green—as if half-consciously expecting that he would savor her loveliness against that background. She is beautiful, his inner delight told him; she is changed, she is different. It is as if I am seeing her for the first time. She is worthy of self-effacing adoration and desire.

Margit raised her glass and drank with small sips—uncomfortably, for she was unwilling to make the effort to lift her head, now lavishly covered with swirls of chestnut hair shot through with a streak of light.

"Why don't you say something?" She turned toward him with a worried air, leaning on her elbow.

"I am looking at you," he answered in such an altered voice that Margit caught his internal tremor—caught it unerringly, as the varnished wood of a violin intensifies the tone drawn from the strings.

"What is it? Why have you gone so far away from me?" She pushed heavy locks of hair away from her face.

"Stay there, just as you are," he begged. But instead of speaking from his heart—"I want to hold you this way in the core of my mind, to fix in my memory this mosaic with flecks of light and color, this moment beyond naming"—he said too simply in this foreign language, English, "I want to remember you this way."

The girl looked troubled. But seeing that he smiled gently at her, she fell back with relief on the rug with its autumnal colors. Slowly she curled up and seemed to be falling asleep, with her coppery hair still rippling luxuriantly around her face. Then for the first time that day Istvan heard the ringing of the cicadas and felt his heart wrenched by the flight of time, for it could not be stopped, nor the past retrieved. The glass he raised with a trembling hand struck dully against his teeth, and premonition sent a tremor through him.

WHEN MARGIT HAD SMOOTHED her skirt and was looking around with a perplexed air, hobbling on one sandal, Istvan, who was helping her search for the other under a chair, broke into a loud laugh.

"Look!" The sandal was hanging on the door handle, shielding the keyhole from the servants' eyes.

"For the life of me, I can't remember doing that!" she exclaimed, embarrassed.

"All the worse if you do such things reflexively."

"Don't be a nuisance," she said, rubbing his cheek with her forehead.

They went to the kitchen together and brought out the half-cold dishes. He uncorked a bottle of wine. They ate, teasing and joking. They drank wine and peeped into each other's eyes like students in love.

"Why were you looking at me so strangely?"

"When you were on the rug I discovered you again. You were terrifyingly attractive to me."

"Oh, you're laying it on a bit thick. After all, you know me to absolute boredom. What did you see there that was new?"

"You looked like Eve in a Flemish tapestry."

"You like that rug."

"I like you."

"I wonder how much it cost."

"I didn't pay very much."

"I wasn't thinking of money"—her eyes were bright; he was drinking in their light—"but of the children who wove it. Have you, expert on India, seen how carpets are made?"

He shook his head. Incessantly, like the droning of bees, happiness sang in him: I love her neck, her lips, her little ear brightened by a streak of rose-tinted sunlight. He was choking with a tenderness beyond measure.

"But I have seen it. There was a shed of woven trunks and branches with a clay roof so overheated from the sun that even the vultures stepped from one foot to another on it. The warp stretched from the ceiling to the ground. Six children sat on the clay floor, pulling colored wool from spools as fast as they could and tying tight knots. The old master read out something from the great book; I glanced over his shoulder. The pattern of the rug, the floral motifs, were written in secret signs. He knew how to decipher the old book, and he sang out: red, red, yellow, black, black. To keep the work going at a steady tempo he beat a drum with a rod.

"You can't imagine how fast those little fingers tied that yarn! The children's eyes brimmed with tears; they were smarting. Time after time they rubbed their irritated eyelids, but the old man quickened the rhythm. The knots had to be set in closely and evenly; the more knots per centimeter, the more they get for the rug. The little ones are not paid, only their parents, and sometimes the value of their work is simply taken in lieu of an installment on rent for a field or interest on an unpaid debt. The children have a moment's rest when the old man has a coughing fit and spits between his callused feet. They must be glad that his old lungs are diseased; anyway, that is the most common ailment among weavers."

"Where did you see this?"

"I was in a village doing surveys. Cottage weaving workshops are still transmission sites for trachoma. I wonder how many eyes have been ruined to create the beauty of the old pattern, the paradisiacal blossoming tree on that carpet."

"Are you going to issue a decree prohibiting child labor? Will anything help?"

"No. It is certain that they would weave clandestinely, and in Europe and the States there are enthusiasts, connoisseurs of the traditional patterns. Prohibitions would only drive the profits to the middlemen, the dealers."

"What then? Not to buy them? Then we push them to the lowest level of misery," he said bitterly. "Margit, forget for a moment that you are a doctor. Don't think of the suffering of this starving country. At least let me enjoy the beauty of the rug, for they create it mechanically and are unable to delight in it."

"I have hurt you." She held out a hand and he took it in his. "I know, art is born of inspiration and difficulty; suffering heightens the work's greatness. But understand: there is anguish here that is undeserved. Neither the children nor their parents know the price they will have to pay. When the weaving is carried out under these conditions, eyes sting and children cough. It was always so and will be so for a long time yet."

"We are both unsuited to this country." He stroked her hand as it lay on the tablecloth embroidered by diligent fingers. "We were brought up differently. For us, to love means to act, to help, to transform, and here it means only to be together in a somnolent trance, to accept, submissively, the verdicts of fate. Here one can make a fortune—there are enough hands and labor is dirt cheap—or a revolution. Everything else is temporizing, a sleep of one's conscience."

"Connoly says that India will make a communist of him. And I, before I traveled around the villages, didn't think people could be so cruel to each other."

"The conditions force them into it. To live means to stifle others."

"Istvan," she said, "truly, they are good. Gentle. And they work so hard."

"That goodness is their weakness. Undernourished for generations, hobbled by faith that in some other incarnation it will be better for them, beaten down by heat, they wait, they hope."

"I would so like to help them." She clasped her hands. "Do you know why? Because I am happy here, thanks to you. I almost feel guilty when I think of them. I am from a wealthy family; I don't have to be concerned about money. I only have the obligations I set for myself. And I have you . . . I want to pay with good for this undeserved good. I would give a great deal to help even one person here, to save him, to give him joy."

She spoke so ardently that he walked around the table, entwined his fingers in her red hair, leaned over, and kissed her.

"You have given me joy," he whispered tenderly.

"All the more reason why I must work, I must treat them. Do you understand? I am afraid for us."

He looked adoringly at her. "But, Margit, you do that." He lifted her hand and moved the tips of her fingers around his lips.

"Not enough. Nothing is enough." He felt the pain in her words. "Istvan, indeed I'm not a silly girl in the throes of her first attraction. I know what I'm doing. I'm not talking with you out of cowardice. Why should I distress you? You have a wife and sons, after all. You are alone here by chance, a chance that was favorable for me. But I haven't forgotten about them. I am the other woman, a stranger."

"Why are you torturing yourself? For the time being nothing is threatening us."

"For the time being." She sighed bitterly. "Don't tell me not to look farther than two months ahead. I must think about what will happen to us later. The stronger my attachment is to you, the more anxiety I feel about our future."

He was ashamed that until this moment he had not spoken with her about the possible solutions he had thought of, and what they would risk if their relationship were known to the world.

"Margit, until I have a divorce, I have no right to begin this conversation. I can get a divorce when I return to Budapest. I want to make the decision alone with my wife, with no intermediary. She has a right to expect that she will learn about it first from me. They cannot let me out of the country. Are you prepared to come to me there? To remain there, perhaps for whole years—"

"Istvan!" she cried, her voice ringing with gratitude and readiness. After a moment she added, "After all, I will be with you."

"Remember: a foreign language, unfamiliar customs, different conditions. I don't earn much. You will be cut off from your family—sentenced to be with me."

"My father will not disinherit me. I have a profession; I can work. It would not go badly with us." She clasped his hands, eager to embrace what lay ahead. "But—will she agree?"

"I cannot answer for her. She is brave. And she loves me. Yes, for just that reason she should not create difficulties. There is a different issue, much harder." He stopped speaking and looked her in the eye. "I have never mentioned this to you. I have been silent, for it was more comfortable for me. The pronouncement of the court is merely a formal dissolution of the marriage. I am a Catholic, and for us there is no release from vows we have called God to witness."

"Is that so important to you?" She pulled her hand away in astonishment and held it to her head, entangling her fingers in the coppery strands of her hair. "I am a Christian as well, but I don't understand such scruples."

"I vowed, 'Till death do us part.' Only death severs the bond of marriage."

She looked at him uncomprehendingly. At last her face broke into an indulgent smile.

"So it is said. Surely you are not telling me to wait for her death. You would not want me to wish her that. There must be a solution. And perhaps you are looking for an artful way to hedge yourself from me; your love is not strong enough. Can you think of the future, of your life when we are not together? If you really loved me, there would be no obstacle that we could not overcome together. Istvan, Istvan, it would be better not to talk about this, not to make plans—to live as they do here, taking what comes and hoping—" She covered her face with her hands.

It seemed to him that she was weeping. He hurried to her and took her in his arms, kissing her hair and the back of her neck. He whispered entreaties and begged her forgiveness. He knew he had caused her pain.

She lowered her hands and her eyes sparkled. Her lashes were plastered together by tears, but she was smiling. "I won't let you go," she said doggedly. "For how long did they send you here?"

"Two years. Three. This is my second year."

"Well, we have a year ahead of us, at least. What is there to worry about? We Australians don't give up easily. If only you also want—"

"How I want you. I desire you," he whispered straight into her parted lips.

"I promised the professor that I would be back today. If you want to be with me longer, drive me to the airport."

"Stay the night," he pleaded.

"I can't. I had to see you. That's why I dropped in for just a couple of hours."

Incredulously and with a trace of hope he asked, "Do you have a ticket?"

"I have, I have. I had that to begin with. Well, are you coming or must I call the Excelsior for a taxi?"

Her hair was dazzling in the sunlight that was stealing into the room. The sadness had gone from her eyes.

"Let's go." She tugged at his hand. "I don't like to rush."

When they were off to the city, driving on asphalt that glowed with the reflected fire of the sunset, he accelerated the engine. They crested out on the summit of a barren hill overgrown with large thistles that seemed hewn from silver. Far ahead of them, irradiated by the low sunbeams, a half-naked Hindu alternately walked and fell. He raised his hands as if pleading and collapsed on the ground, only to rise immediately, take three steps and extend his arms again as if seeking support. Then he dropped to the ground at the edge of the road.

"What has happened to him?" she asked worriedly. "Slow down. We must take a look."

The lean man, wearing a dhoti and a strap from which hung a jug made from a bottle-gourd, fell down and rose to his feet like a broken toy.

Istvan caught up with him and put on the brakes. They both got out of the car and waited hand in hand until he drew near. He paid no attention to them, but rose and fell as if he were using his body to measure the distance he was traveling. His forehead and chest were gray from the ash that had been smeared on them. His face was serene and full of concentration; his dark eyes flashed with a look of such rapt attention that it was disturbing.

"A sadhu," Terey said softly. "A holy pilgrim."

"Is he demented?" she asked. "His movements are orderly, rhythmical. There is something about this that is unsettling to a normal person. Why is he making his walk so difficult? What sense does it make? He must be mad."

She spoke out loud, certain that the man did not understand English. They trembled when the wayfarer said calmly, even with a tinge of irony in his tone, "No, Mr. Terey. Please explain to your companion that I am no more mad than you or she."

The counselor went up to the man and peered into his eyes, but the Hindu only dropped to the ground again with his hands outstretched. Terey could not recall the hollow, hirsute face. Drops of sweat made furrows on its dusty cheeks; the gray forehead rubbed with ashes made a strange mask of it.

"You know me?"

"Yes. You came to the ministry. You are from the Hungarian embassy. And I . . . The official with whom you still had business not long ago died, and I was born."

"I don't understand."

Still holding hands, they walked beside him, by now somewhat accustomed to the throwing up of the arms and the sudden falls. Their long shadows lay on the asphalt and the red line on the side of the road.

"I was called," he said in a mild voice, as if he were translating into a children's language. "A light entered into me. I understood the senselessness of the work in my office. I realized that I was squandering my life instead of perfecting myself. So I closed my portfolios, shut the books, and walked out. I am going to meet the source of light."

"But why in such a strange way? Isn't a pilgrimage on foot enough?"

"I will show my body that it is subject to me, as a corporal teaches a recruit discipline—as you, sir, give an order to a recalcitrant servant. For a long time I myself was the servant of my body, so it did not try to rebel. It pretends that things are bad—difficult—that sharp gravel pricks it. It begs for food and water, and I force it into a longer march. Now it is quiet. It listens meekly. Once again it has taken its proper role in my life."

He stood up, then fell forward as far as his outstretched hands could reach. He allowed himself to take three small steps and raised his arms again as if to measure off a section of road.

"But this insanity—you are exhausting yourself. You are doing a disservice to yourself and your family, if you have one."

"I have. My wife and sons accepted my decision, for neither tears nor anger altered it. They do not beg me to come back. I am not compelling others to do as I am doing. If I am injuring anyone, it is only myself. This is my body and I have the right to do as I please with it," he said calmly, his even voice at odds with the rhythmic steps and falls that resembled the movements of a mechanical clown. "Leave me at least a little freedom. If I perish, it is only I; and you? In your world there is not even a place for such a journey as mine. And all your technology and science—to what do they lead humanity but to violence, fear, and annihilation? I am harming no one. Respect my will."

Suddenly Istvan remembered an official sitting in the corner of a room, behind a table with a large fan, tidy, even-humored, smiling agreeably. But that man had worn spectacles.

"Did you wear glasses?"

"Yes. By now I do not need them. I do not look for the truth in books. I make my way toward the light, I go to the East—"

"You are Balvant Sudar!" Terey cried. He was about to seize the callused hand, covered with grains of sand, but the man continued his seizure-like movements without even noticing Istvan's friendly impulse.

"Sudar died some time ago, and I was born, thirsting for truth. I know what I desire, and you do not know. You wander, you are tossed about. I walk my own road toward the light, and you must return to your automobile and race on. You will pass me, but I have already passed you. I have outdistanced you. I am the spark which consciously returns to the fire while darkness envelops the others."

"Let's go, Istvan." She pulled at his hand. "The airplane doesn't wait."

They turned and hurried toward the car, which stood on the edge of the highway. The sun was setting; the sky burned a blinding red.

"Do you think what he said about us should be taken as an omen?" she asked with superstitious foreboding.

"No. We may not wallow in the dust, but we, too, pursue our truth, Margit, and I tell you, we will find it."

They sped past the gaunt, half-naked figure stretched on the ground.

"And what is between us—isn't it all the will of the flesh?"

"I wouldn't be so sure," he smiled. "Anyway, that's probably not so bad."

The corrugated aluminum roofs of the hangars flashed between the trees. The blue and white windsock rode the shifting streams of air.

Chapter X

Istvan glanced at his watch again. The hands seemed to be dead, though the second hand twitched as it moved around the face. It was seven minutes past three. The work day ended at four, but their "contacts" were only received until three, so the business day was, for all practical purposes, over. But it was not good form to make one's exit before the ambassador without a definite reason. The boss did not like it.

"As long as I am here, everyone must be at their posts. That is my wish, comrades, and you must abide by it," he had said in a briefing.

He kept them all in this state of readiness a little out of spite. He preferred his office in the embassy to the tedium of his house. The dinner there was not entirely to his liking, for his wife struggled to have Hungarian dishes served, but the cook could not learn to prepare them. Judit had had to listen to the ambassador's complaints more than once, and repeated them to Istvan with concealed enjoyment.

The ambassador's wife, a stout woman, had been accustomed to drudgery from childhood; lately she had put on weight, and, clad in brocade gowns that were too tight, grated on others' nerves at receptions with her puffy face and her everlasting frown of dissatisfaction, especially when she stood beside supple Hindu women, beauties draped in saris. If one of them were equally heavyset, she looked majestic, never merely commonplace. Diplomats' wives from the Anglo-Saxon circle called her "the huckster" because of the shrill voice in which she doggedly complimented the refreshments and extolled her husband's merits. Istvan himself had heard this and was rather ashamed that he had not said a word in her defense.

The servants pretended that they did not understand her broken English and played malicious little tricks on her. They knew she would make no accusations, because her husband and sons would laugh at her. Displaced from her ordinary activities, she wandered around the house with her forehead covered with lemon plasters and her eyes swollen from weeping when no one could see. She suffered from chronic headaches. "With those plasters she looks like a sadhu of some arcane rite," Kalman Bajcsy would quip. "India is bad for her—the heat, the food, even the smell of the phlox that she ordered to have mowed down in front of the house. Her head always hurts so that when we arrived in Budapest, she had to have a maid. She only recovered her spirits during the days when she had thrown one out and not yet engaged another. She is sick without women's work. She grumbles about India; she tries to induce me to go home. I explain that our country pays us very well for her aching head, so she should not complain. She has no faith in doctors. She looks to the local healers for help. Her faith in the wisdom of the occult is equal to her stupidity." He burst out laughing in his hearty bass. "Once again I had to throw out one of those strapping, good-looking masseurs whose specialty is glands. I know those quacks and I know who found him for her."

The ambassador did not hurry to the residence, as they called the small palace leased from a rajah who had been guilty of some malfeasance involving commodities supplied to the government, and banished from the capital. It was difficult to be certain what Bajcsy did in the afternoons. Ferenc alluded vaguely to scholarly work in the area of economics, as indicated by the underlinings in newspapers—stacks of which were cleared away once a week by the caretaker—and English dictionaries piled on his desk. Judit surmised that it was crossword puzzles. Just prior to his departure the ambassador would be exceptionally active, would give orders, call people in for talks, instruct the staff to act on matters that might have taken another week in the files to be ripe for completion. It seemed that he wanted to keep them working all night, until morning, until the very hour that he reappeared.

He thought—not inaccurately, as a matter of fact—that the moment he crossed the threshold of the embassy and made his way home, the entire operation went slack or, properly speaking, ceased to exist. When he had to go away from Delhi, he hedged their authority and decision-making powers around with so many reservations and conditions that, in effect, all matters waited for his return. Listening to reports, he gloated, "You see! Without the boss, work comes to a halt. I know you complain about me behind my back, but you yourselves know that things do not go well without me. It is better if I take the leadership on my shoulders and on my conscience. Give me those papers."

Istvan had not seen Margit for a week; she had been called away. Before that they had seen each other often, even if only for a few hours. By now he had grown used to her flying in at two and flying out again to Agra at seven. A week of silence, of unannounced interruption to their meetings, brought back his old uneasiness. So he was electrified when her voice came on the telephone, and even more when she informed him that if she flew into the city with the professor, she should be free to see him around three-thirty. He wanted to drive out to the airport; she preferred that he not do that, and they agreed to meet at Volga.

He had to wait a quarter of an hour. When she was in New Delhi, even if she could not meet him on time, she would let him know where to pick her up. He glanced out the window at the open gates of the garage, but the ambassador's wide Mercedes stood motionless inside them; its signal lights shone red in the sun.

He sat where he was. What was the man waiting for? he sighed. If he doesn't come out in five minutes, I don't care what happens, I'll be on my way to the city.

Though he could have found ten reasons to go out, it would have been proper to inform the front office and call the ambassador in case he had any urgent assignments. Istvan wanted to avoid that. He knew all too well that he would be summoned and made to listen to a handful of precepts interspersed with reminiscences about the party; he had heard variants of some of those edifying object lessons already. Once they had been about the experiences of loyal comrades with whom the ambassador had been in prison for Horthy. Another time Bajcsy had trotted out anecdotes that demonstrated his own courage or cleverness. He was relieved when he looked through the window and saw the squatty figure of the ambassador. The cryptographer's son, little Mihaly, toddled beside him. He was telling the ambassador something and waving his hands earnestly. Their shadows fell on the white garage wall that gleamed from under festoons of wisteria.

Suddenly the ambassador stood still, as if the boy's words had finally penetrated his mind. He turned toward him and asked something. Istvan looked at the little fellow's uplifted hand as it made circles in the air. He is selling me out—the thought darted through his mind—he will boast about the visits to Krishan. Mihaly was talking; in the end he extended his hands and clapped them together with all his might. He has blurted out everything, the silly little Judas. He has no idea what he is doing. Istvan forgave the child at once. Intuitively he was almost certain that something had happened, and that its sinister effects were unforeseeable. He sat still, stricken with fear and a sense of utter helplessness: nothing could be stopped, salvaged, retracted. It had happened. But what? He heard no words; he could only decipher what was being told from gestures.

Kalman Bajcsy raised his head and looked into the embassy window. Even through the screen he must see me; Terey's lips tightened. I will not hide. Through the thick wire mesh coated with dust he saw the ambassador's forehead shining with sweat, saw his bushy eyebrows and his eyes squinting from the painful glare of the sun. For a moment they looked each other up and down. Then Bajcsy waved a hand to summon him.

He ran down quickly. The ambassador stood with legs slightly spread, leaning forward. He was exhaling heavily, as if he were short of breath.

"You go out for chats with Krishan, Terey?" he asked gloomily. "Who told you to do that?"

"You have also been there, ambassador. It is a circus."

"Be brave enough to tell me to my face."

"What?" Terey looked at him and recovered the sense of having the upper hand. Bajcsy could do nothing, after all, nothing. In the worst case, they might recall him; the thought came to Istvan like an alien voice, the voice of a coldly calculating person. The thought of losing Margit floated up on a wave of anger.

The other man only wheezed. "Don't try to jump on my back, Terey," he said menacingly, raising a finger yellowed from nicotine. "I have halted the careers of better men than you. They have cursed the hour the thought of doing battle with me first lodged in their minds."

"What do you mean, comrade ambassador?" he said a little too loudly, and reproached himself inwardly for it.

"Don't be God's policeman, Terey. You have no proof. None. It is not healthy to know too much. I even liked you, Terey. I spoke to you as to an equal, and I see that it went to your head. Think twice before you do something you would bitterly regret."

"I don't understand." He took a step forward. "What have I done?"

The ambassador moved back a step, rested his hands on the overheated body of his car, then motioned with his head toward Mihaly, who was standing between them. Astonished by the altercation, the boy raised his dark eyes first to one, then to the other.

"If I have stopped you in time, so much the better. You know; keep it to yourself. I am not afraid when I say: Keep quiet. I am not thinking only of your good." He aimed a piercing stare at the counselor's composed, suntanned face.

"Is there anything I can do for you, ambassador?"

"No. Go to the devil!" he roared in his deep voice. "I can't stand a fool."

Istvan turned, walked the few steps to the Austin, and opened it with his key. He was calm, even gratified that he could leave in time to meet Margit. He will do nothing to me. He will not dare meddle with me. Perhaps it is better that he knows. So I had an enemy in him. Suddenly he heard Bajcsy's voice almost pleading:

"Terey, what do you suspect me of? It was an accident, really—an ordinary accident. It could happen to anyone."

He turned around. The ambassador was leaning wearily on his car. His face had lost its bellicose expression; it looked bloated, as if he were unwell. A light breeze ruffled his grizzled hair. The boss—the epithet suited him exactly. Only the dogged, alert eyes seemed to put one on guard. His posture as the toilworn revolutionary grown gray in the fight, prevented only by his character from stepping down from his post of responsibility, won him the indulgence of his Hungarian staff and the young women on whose slender necks he laid a heavy hand, engaging in somewhat insistent caresses which he called "fatherly."

His merits and faithfulness were much talked of; he himself had put many anecdotes exemplifying them into circulation. He counted on the press of business and the impatience of party activists, for when all was said and done, who had the time and desire to inquire about how it really was under the dictatorship of the admiral? Enemies would, no doubt, but he had pacified them by speaking of his heart ailment, deluding them with the hope that he would soon have an attack that would bring all disputes with him to an end. Why waste energy fighting him when they need do nothing but wait a little? The thick, partly open lips, the shallow breathing suggested that it would not be long. He knew how to awaken the sympathy of those more powerful than himself, that still vague benevolence—"We must be helpful to him, we must accommodate him, for he will not hold out for long"—and he pushed down those weaker by using his connections, by issuing brutal refusals and open threats.

Having struggled to gain an ambassadorship in an important country, in the pound zone, he worked diligently to consolidate his political position. He wanted to be one of those who would not move down in rank, who could only be transferred to other foreign postings. They were conscious of their privileges and aware that to represent communism and the homeland and feather one's own nest in a wealthy, stable capitalist country constituted true happiness. His sense of advantage gave rise to a gracious superiority with a trace of contempt for the people crowded into buses and tramways or standing in line, running from shop to shop in search of goods. "We must fatigue ourselves a while yet, comrades," he said indulgently as in his thoughts he escaped with relief to his residence, to his private automobile that was maintained at the nation's expense, to the cook and the band of submissive sweepers, guards, and gardeners. We are poorly remunerated—he retained an absolving feeling of solidarity with those who labor every day that was in harmony with his most sincere convictions. He could return with equal pleasure to Budapest or to Paris, Rome or London, to say nothing of New Delhi.

Bajcsy seemed to be making a claim on Terey's pity. He appealed to his sympathy for people who were worn out and prematurely old, for the stigma of illness on the pale forehead. But his eyes harbored malicious flashes like the eyes of a predatory animal in a cage, ready to leap at the throat of the tamer who drove him there.

"I swear that I am innocent," he panted.

The counselor nodded as a sign that he had heard, that the words of self-justification had reached him. He slammed the car door and started the engine. Before the car moved, the other door opened and Mihaly jumped in.

"I will go with you, uncle," he said. "I will guard the car." There was so much guileless affection in his voice that Istvan locked the door and turned the Austin toward the gate. In the mirror he saw a flabby figure leaning heavily against the Mercedes.

"Why were you blabbering?" He was ashamed of the edge of anger in his voice. "Now I'm not going to take you places with me, because you tell everything."

"You didn't say it was a secret, uncle." He raised his arms in fright and curled up, pressing his hands to his chest. "I was only talking about Krishan's stunts. That's all."

"And what were you showing the ambassador?" He took his hands off the wheel, stretched them in front of him and clapped them hard.

The boy looked at him with round, astonished eyes. He could not remember. Suddenly he brightened and cried, "He flew like an arrow!"

"You didn't talk about the accident with the cow?"

"With what cow?"

Istvan understood. Wishing to show the ambassador that he was not afraid of him, he himself had made it clear that he knew. He had given himself away. If I want to hold him in check, he thought, I must have Krishan's deposition in writing, certified. He must be convinced that he should not tempt fate for too long; enough of this risk. Let him buy himself a rickshaw; he has a motorcycle. He could earn good money. I must induce his wife to hector him about it. But he will not take her opinion seriously. He will listen to me, he thought as he drove down the wide avenue.

"Are we going to the show?" the boy asked happily.

"I have business with Krishan."

The barrel-like building throbbed with the vibrating roar of the speeding motorcycle. The din of voices frenzied with delight rose and echoed under the undulating canvas roof. He is riding, he is flirting with danger—Istvan frowned—the sense that he is risking his life has become a narcotic for him. He must be frightened into accepting my advice. I will say that I have come to warn him. That I have had a dream. It would be easy to disable the motorcycle.

He bought two tickets. He wanted to see once more how the machine thundered as it flew around the thick timbers of the barrel. The boy was already gone; he had run onto the ramp leading to the gallery and squeezed between the people leaning through the balustrade.

The motorcyclist was riding downward in a spiral, sailing into swirling blue streaks of smoke. The viewers went mad, stamped, clapped, howled, whistled through their fingers to express their jubilation.

The rider in his black leather costume halted the motorcycle at the bottom of the wooden pit, pushed his goggles down onto his silver helmet, and raised a hand to greet the audience. Istvan watched and was taken by surprise. The motorcyclist's uplifted face was clearly visible in the sun. It was not Krishan's.

Little hands tugged at him. Mihaly exclaimed, smiling as if he had played a trick, "That wasn't Krishan, uncle. Come on."

They went down. The boy shouted something in Hindi to a group of children who were running out in front of him. They answered in guttural voices, making acrobatic gestures with their hands.

"No. No!" He seized Istvan and clung with a convulsive grip. "Ask at the ticket window, uncle," he begged. His face was contorted, as if he were about to cry. "They must know there. Those Sikhs lie, they lie . . ."

The stout cashier only scratched his chest, tilted his head, and stared at them with wide eyes. "You did not see the notice, sir? We have a new champion. Krishan was killed two days ago."

Terey went cold. Too late, he thought. The lead witness is dead.

"How did it happen?"

"Who knows? He was insured. The underwriting agency took the motorcycle for inspection. They promised to give us a copy of the findings. They do not like to throw money away."

"And a new man is riding already," Terey said caustically.

"We always have a few daredevils who want to make some money," the man said deprecatingly, spreading his pudgy hands. "We pay honest wages. And an accident always draws viewers. We have not been so successful for a long time."

"He . . ."

"He has been burned. There was trouble with his wife. How many? One adult, two children." He sold the tickets without interrupting his stream of talk. "She leaped onto his pyre. She wanted to be burned alive. You know, sir, such passion is a rarity today. People pulled her away; she bit and kicked. Anyone with a camera then could have made a lot of money. You understand, sir. Suttee. It would have been an extra on newsstands all over the world."

Istvan wanted to clench his fist and hit the bloated face framed by a black beard with an oily sheen.

"Where is she? In a hospital?"

"In a hospital? And who would pay? She is over it now. She is calm. She has gone to a woman in Old Delhi. If you like, I will find out where she is. The doorman knows her. You are from the press, sir? Or from an embassy?"

"Krishan was our driver. I liked him."

"We did as well. Just a moment." He lowered the window and scrambled out of the cramped booth. He trotted away toward the entrance, his heavy buttocks rippling. Istvan noticed only then that the boy was standing with his face averted as tears ran down his cheeks, forming large drops on his quivering chin.

"I know this is very sad for you, Mihaly." He put his arms around the boy, stroked the back of his neck and quieted him. "We must find her. She needs help."

"She took him," the boy sniveled. "I saw her, too."

"Who?" Startled, Istvan held his fingers in the child's pale hair.

"His first wife. Once I saw her standing behind him, and he knew as well that she was near, because he looked around. He was afraid of her. So was her sister."

"So it seemed to you. You have been listening to fairy tales."

The boy shook his head.

"Behind the Corso Cinema, third house on the left. Best to go through the Ajmeri Gate, sir," the portly cashier announced. "Everyone must know her there. The accident was widely reported."

Istvan thanked him and he and the boy moved toward the car.

He glanced at his watch; it was late. If Margit were there, if she were waiting, if she called, they could spend a long time looking for each other. They would lose an hour. Her time in Delhi was too short.

"We'll go for ice cream. Would you like that?"

"Aren't we going to find Krishan's wife?"

"We will, we will, but not now. I have to meet Dr. Ward. Miss Margit."

"I know her."

"Of course you do. I want to take her with us."

"Maybe she can help us," the boy agreed.

In the low light and pleasant coolness of the coffee shop, the ceiling fans wafted bluish cigarette smoke around in rings. The lamplight played on silks of wine red and sapphire trimmed with gold. Its gleam wandered over jet black hair gathered into great knots and plaited with little chaplets of fragrant flowers. The hubbub of leisurely conversation, bursts of laughter, soft music, and jingling bracelets on dark wrists and ankles eased his tension, almost lulled him. They wandered among the tables, led on by the glances of beautiful gossiping women. Margit was not there.

"Uncle, here is a table." Mihaly lunged toward it. His voice was still hoarse from crying.

A pair of young Hindus had just risen, leaving behind saucers, glasses, bottles, and an ashtray full of crumpled napkins with traces of red lipstick that made them look like cast-off bandages.

Istvan ordered coffee for himself and ice cream for the boy. The door-curtain was drawn aside; every flash of sunlight in the entry disturbed him. He looked impatiently at the faces of those who came in. A waiter moved between the tables, showing the guests a tablet with the names of those who were wanted on the telephone. No. No, he did not see his name.

Mihaly licked his ice cream from his spoon with growing concentration. His cheerful smile was returning; his eyelashes, still sticky from his tears, were drying quickly. His was a happy age, when one feels with equal pain the loss of a beloved toy and the death of a friend, and with equal ease forgets them. At that age everyone is immortal, and the heart is a spring with inexhaustible resources of feeling. It is easy to rationalize the deaths of other people: age, sickness, accidents, mortality, reach for others and touch them, not us, who since awakening from a calm, deep sleep have been nurtured by the measureless, benevolent waters of time . . . Istvan smiled gently as the little fellow blinked with delight and leaned over the stemmed silver compote that was foggy from the cold.

"Good—you're here!" Margit called, making her way quickly to their table. "I'm late, but I have news for you, Istvan. Perhaps you'll even be pleased—" she made a face like a little girl who by chance has found the place in the garden where the hens lay eggs, or spied the first violets of spring, which still smell fresh and cool, and carries them triumphantly to those she loves. "Give me a little coffee. No, pour it into yours." She pushed the cup toward a glass flagon that hung on a stand, signifying that in Volga the coffee was strong and aromatic, prepared as if in an alchemist's workshop.

"Order another portion of ice cream for Mihaly. Let him share our joy."

"Well, don't wait. Tell us what happened." He looked lovingly at her.

"Nothing certain as yet." She drank a little coffee. "It will all be clear in a few days. The professor has given me an appointment as a lecturer for a university course. My subject will be epidemiology, teaching young doctors how to fight trachoma."

"In Delhi?"

"For a whole month. Perhaps longer," she said jubilantly. "You don't even look happy. Why are you two so glum?"

"I am very happy," he whispered. "But there is serious news." He leaned forward and told her about the driver's death; she listened, absorbed in the story. He did not explain why he was in such a hurry to leave the coffeehouse, and he said nothing about the automobile accident. But she understood without words that they ought to go, and was already rising from her seat.

"Thank you," he said, depositing money on the marble table.

"I have caught you!" They heard a warm, low voice. "You do not see the world around you. I nod, I make gestures, and they are as oblivious as if they were bewitched. Ah, Istvan, Istvan, it is not nice of you to lure my friend away," Grace said, leaning over the table. Her loosely fastened sari concealed her condition, but her movements were ponderous as those of an apple tree with branches bent under the burden of their fruit.

"Why didn't you come over before? You were spying on us, you wily thing, and we met by chance." Margit kissed her.

"A happy chance. I saw how he watched for you," she said sullenly. "Well, sit down. Margit, you have something on your conscience, for you have simply been avoiding me."

They were taken aback and said their goodbyes hurriedly. Margit, peeping at Istvan, explained that she had an appointment with Professor Salminen at the clinic and a flight to Agra immediately afterward, and assured Grace that she would visit her at the earliest opportunity. She kissed the Hindu woman, who had suddenly grown somber, on the cheek. There was so much visible joy in Margit's movements as her figure dissolved in the blaze of sunlight from behind the heavy curtain Terey obligingly opened that Grace's lips tightened. It seemed to her that she had been dispossessed, lost her beauty, been affronted. She went pale. Standing by the vacant table, she looked around at the place settings and suddenly saw a trace of pink lipstick on the cup. They had drunk from one cup: it pained her. She had visible proof that her suspicions were not unfounded. Her heart beat hard. She raised a hand and put it on her abdomen; the mother's angry agitation was communicated to the child.

The Austin rolled slowly amid a dense throng of pedestrians torpidly trailing along in the middle of the road. The blast of the horn did not hurry them. They paused and turned their amazed faces toward the car. At the last minute they leaped away like startled birds, their dhotis fluttering.

Istvan drove impassively. After the blue twilight of the coffee shop, the sun hurt his eyes. He disliked sunglasses and rarely wore them. Once he had gotten dark shades from Judit, but on a visit to the Indian Ministry of Culture he had conveniently forgotten them and they had disappeared.

"Best not tell Grace about us," he said. "The fewer people who know, the better."

"Who would have thought she would be roaming around the coffee shops in her condition? Surely it won't be long."

"No. I was certain that she had gone away from Delhi to the rajah's estate near Benares."

Beyond the fortified Ajmeri Gate they drove into a cluster of rickshaws between the vendors' carts. A warm odor like garlic came from the crowd. Men carried flat wicker baskets piled high with yellowish shocks of camels' hair on their heads. Istvan turned aside near the wall, plowing through the crowd, which parted grudgingly. Curious faces surrounded them; anxious dark eyes scrutinized them. People offered their services, proposed to serve as guides and bodyguards in the labyrinth of congested streets. A leper came rolling up on a squeaky cart and held out a coconut shell on hands without fingers; the appalling disease had eaten away his lips and tongue. His low, painful mooing attracted no one's attention. Europeans had arrived; they were important because they had the habit of paying for services. The sight of them aroused the hope of easy earnings.

"Madam, madam, I will show you where there are silk shawls with gold and silver," mumbled a slender young man with pitch-black eyes and artfully crimped hair. "And perhaps jewels, precious stones, rubies, emeralds from Ceylon."

"No. Not today."

"Or perhaps the temple of the monkey god." Another man pushed his bewhiskered face close to them. He would have looked like a henchman of Ali Baba if it had not been for his meek, filmy eyes and languid voice.

"There." He showed Margit the large, chipped letters filled with red light bulbs: CORSO. Above it, secured with wires to the walls and to the sills of windows that were never closed, were gigantic cardboard figures garishly painted: a dancing girl with full thighs and showy hips gleaming enticingly through muslin pantaloons finished with disks and bells at the ankles; beside her, two men stabbing each other with stilettos as streaks of blood half a yard long dripped from the balconies.

They walked in the road, squeezing between baskets of fruit as the sellers napped amid the clamor, hawking their wares almost involuntarily with their eyes closed.

"The third house. That must be it." He pushed Margit into a passageway sticky with soap suds. Their feet sank into piles of ashes and peelings, bitten cores of vegetables, and ragged bags made of fronds. Behind a tenement, workshops covered with rusty tin huddled, and broken-down bicycle rickshaws stripped of their wheels. They heard whistles, the banging of a hammer, the insistent wailing of a child calling for its mother. Starlings in a cage screeched and emitted astonished chirps as they jumped tirelessly from bar to bar.

The first man to whom they spoke—half-naked and bespattered with oil paint as if he had wiped an artist's brush on his brown, sunken chest—knew no English. But soon they came upon three children, and one—a little girl with large crimson bows in her hair—feeling deeply the importance of her mission, explained in charming pidgin English that the stunt rider's widow lived in a room behind the tailors' workshop. So they followed the cadenced hum of sewing machines and the grating of scissors. The tailors sat cross-legged on the floor, turning the cranks of their hand-operated sewing machines, hardly raising their heads to follow the new arrivals with astonished glances. Their backs were bent with hurry; they were paid by the piece.

"Here." The girl curtsied and drew back a patched curtain. The breeze rolled wads of clipped thread along the floor, and scraps of fabric seemed to dart about like mice.

The room was small, and dark, for the head of a cardboard girl covered the windows. A bed stood in the center—the only piece of furniture, doing service instead of a table or chairs. Next to the wall, on a metal trunk, they saw a photograph of Krishan on a motorcycle, with wings streaming from his arms: the flight in the clouds. Other pictures were set in a half-circle in slits made with a knife in wooden bobbins; they bent slightly, like lesser divinities before a greater one. In a small bowl of water a dahlia floated, glowing like a votive lamp in a narrow shaft of sunlight.

An old woman in a washed-out, faded sari, which had been blue long before but today was the color of smoke from burning stalks, was kneeling and baking little flat cakes on a tall copper spirit stove that crackled with a violet fire and hissed malevolently. A heavy aroma of boiling coconut oil lingered in the air. "Namaste ji," she said, bowing and setting a mug with a thin cake on the floor. "She is not asleep. She is drawing him to her. Durga, Durga—" she called in a shrill voice, lengthening the vowels like herdsmen on the pastures.

The girl lay with her arms bandaged from hands to elbows and folded lifelessly on her breast. The smooth brown skin on her bare belly could be seen from under a short jacket. Several pink scars were covered with gauze soaked with grease; flies hopped nimbly over the bandage. When he leaned over and looked into her black eyes, which were dimmed with pain, he smelled the sickening odor, familiar to him from the war years, of burned hair. He could not see it for the shawl in which her head was swathed.

"Durga, a lady and gentlemen have come to help you. Friends of Krishan." Only at the sound of his name did she seem to recover a measure of consciousness.

"Oh, sir," she turned her head slowly, "he liked you."

"Tell me: what can I do for you?"

"Nothing. I need nothing."

"How will you manage?" He looked at her mouth. On the thick, high upper lip, which gave the young woman the expression of a capricious child, he saw whitish blisters from the fire. She had thrown herself onto the flaming pyre, had tumbled hands first into the blaze. Her face had been in the flames before the attendants dragged her out. He seemed to hear the sizzling of the living body and the flames springing to entwine themselves in her hair. He felt an enormous pity for her.

"I will stay here," she answered in a resigned voice. "I will not return to the village."

"She will stay here," the old woman affirmed sympathetically, pouring dough onto a chattering skillet. "She has no money. Everything went for the motorcycle. There are still payments to be made."

"What about damages?"

"I do not know if the insurance was in order. That was the responsibility of the Sikhs who own the circus. And they are in no hurry to give money away." It was obvious that she was intimately acquainted with Krishan's affairs. "Durga has no money to return to the village. A gentleman promised to get her a place in a dancers' house here. Durga sings like a lark."

"And these burns?" Margit asked.

"They are forming scars, but what is most important is that her face is as pure as a baby's," the old lady said caressingly. "She will be successful. People will remember Krishan for a long time. Suttee. Suttee," she clucked with approval. "Not many women love so much that they jump into the fire after their husbands. True love attracts men."

"Did I understand her correctly?" Margit said, aghast. When Istvan nodded, she whispered, "It's monstrous! How they can speak so calmly about steering her into—it is worse than suicide."

"She is a widow. According to the old custom, she died as well as her husband. Her heart, at least," he said, confirming her ominous inference.

Mihaly moved close to the woman. "Durga, why was Krishan killed?"

"He was angry, as he usually was before his appearances. He shouted at me that my cooking was bad. It was true. I had brought him chapati. He threw it at me. The boys were standing in a group by then. They helped him. He liked the way they led him out with an excited shout. He remembered that there was not much gasoline in the machine. He went to get the canister. The lid of the gas tank was unscrewed. The boys were peeking into it. They were smaller than you. They were licking sweets on sticks. They laughed and I laughed. One of them got another to put his stick in and measure how much gasoline there was. It amused him that the smaller boy listened blindly and would be licking a lollipop with the taste of gasoline. Then Krishan pushed them away, though he liked children and very much wanted some of his own. He poured gasoline in and said to me, 'I must be done with this.' He put his hands here," she raised one bandaged hand and pointed to her arms.

"The boys were already pushing the motorcycle to the ring. Then the curtain closed. I have always listened to the roar of the engine and I understood what it was saying. I knew when he was climbing up the walls and when he began riding down. I waited. I could not breathe. I prayed that everything would be all right. Suddenly the motor died. I could not hear when he crashed. I only heard people shouting—a different kind of shouting, like the roar of a beast that was eating him. I was so weak, so entirely without strength; it was as if all my blood had soaked into the ground." She spoke slowly, in a singsong voice.

She recites the story of Krishan's death as if it were a ballad, Istvan thought, and suddenly felt ashamed that at such a moment he could think of art.

"The first one pulled back the curtain. She was in a white sari. Then a pack of boys stormed out of the building, and the people who were carrying him. And I knew he was dead, for she went before the bearers."

"Durga saw her all the time," the old woman interjected. Removing the pan from the stove, she said something to the girl in their language; they understood that she was trying to persuade her to eat. The sick girl made a motion of refusal with her bandaged hand and the old woman began by herself to chew the heavy, half-done cake, pouring cane syrup over it.

"Durga saw her, too," Mihaly whispered, staring.

"Whom?" Margit asked.

"Her dead sister," answered the old woman. Cocking her face like a cat biting a fish head, she smacked and licked the ends of her fingers and the inside of her hand, onto which a few drops of the sticky syrup had leaked. "She came to take him."

Istvan cursed himself for his cruel curiosity, like that of a surgeon probing a wound. It had been strangely gratifying to listen to this duet, with the musical accompaniment of the shifting hum of sewing machines in the neighboring room, a hammer beating metal in the yard like a broken bell, and the twittering of bicycles below, all mingling with the mournful, pleading, hopeless calls of vendors sitting on the edge of the sidewalk. This suffering was satisfying to him, was the food that nourishes the beginnings of poetry: the threnody of the Indian widow. It seemed to him that he had been led here for a purpose, as if a higher power, aware of every step, had ordered him to abandon all sympathy and only absorb, remember—that he would commemorate the fate of the one who had perished, and the young woman who was receding into the teeming multitude that was India. A few days yet and she would dissolve amid the flickering of silk saris, the jingle of gramophone music, and the throbbing of the drum, though today she was bleeding with the pain of her loss.

"They laid him down. They took off his leather clothing. The manager rolled it under his arm immediately and took it away. And I so wanted him to be burned in that costume. He liked it," she recalled in an undertone. "The police took the motorcycle. I saw the bent metal body. I felt as if my bones were broken. And Krishan lay with his head to one side, looking toward me. I tried to straighten him and then I felt that this"—she pointed to the top of her head with her bandaged fingers—"was completely soft. Suddenly a few drops of blood leaked from one of his nostrils." The memory sent pain sweeping over her. "More and more people came running up. They shoved me in the back with their knees. The ones who were near were silent. The others in the back were shouting to be let through. But as soon as they saw, they were quiet—as quiet as he and I."

The sewing machines whirred. The hammer beat. The blackbirds whistled as if in astonishment. The old woman stopped eating and finally turned toward them. Without bothering to conceal her curiosity she scrutinized Margit, her red hair, her white plastic handbag.

"Didn't Krishan leave any papers?" Terey inquired. "Didn't he tell you the name of the village where they had the accident with the cow?"

"No." Durga raised herself, looking troubled. "There, behind the photograph, is his wallet. Look, sir."

The old woman bestirred herself and brought him the wallet. It was dark from sweat, and bent inward; it preserved the form of the chest that was now a scattering of ashes. In its compartments old identification papers were tucked, and a lottery ticket, a couple of receipts, and some slips of paper covered with serpentine Hindi writing. Discouraged, Istvan let them fall onto the bed. Perhaps it is better this way, he thought; it keeps me from being tempted. If I really wanted to, I could write to the office of the governor; they would give me what I am looking for. And if I have to stay in the background, I can put Chandra on the scent.

He shivered with disgust. What am I looking for? Do I want the information in order to feel more secure myself, or will I insist that justice be done? Leave that to Him Who reaches out alike to the defenseless, the oppressed, the small—the cadence of the gospels leaped to his mind—and the great. He reached into his pocket and drew out a wad of rupees—not many, but it seemed to him that he should show a willingness to offer support. Margit also contributed.

"No. I do not need it," Durga demurred.

"Thank them for their kindness," the older woman admonished her, shoving the banknotes into the wallet and replacing it behind the photograph, on the metal lid of the trunk, which gleamed like cut lead.

"What papers were you searching for?" Margit asked when they had gone out into the yard.

"Not now. When we have taken the boy back." He looked into her large eyes and was charmed by their lustrous clarity: eyes like an angora cat. "It is for your ears only."

"If you don't feel comfortable telling me," she smiled gently, "don't. You will have more peace of mind. And I really don't have to know. Sit by me, Mihaly. Let's leave Mr. Terey alone."

Blowing the horn without letup, they drove into a crowd of cyclists. Slowly they pushed their way toward the glowing red brick gate of the old fortified city. He could see, in spite of what Margit had said, that she was hurt by his silence, for she rested her hands on the arm of the front seat and began to speak.

"I was a little older than Mihaly when a fire broke out in our pasture. Not only did the bunkhouse with the shepherds' belongings burn; so did the stone storehouse that held the wool from the shearing. The tramps who had caused it to happen were soon found—drunks who were sleeping in some bushes. Our people went into a towering rage and dragged them off and threw them into the ashes, deep ashes full of smoldering fire. They were roasted alive. Some of our people are very hard.

"Don't be shocked. They had put in a whole year of backbreaking work and their earnings were wiped out, because everyone shares the profits from the sheared wool. I didn't see it happen, only Stanley did, and he made me swear on his knife to keep the secret. I was terribly afraid; he said he would cut out my tongue. He was a devil, not a man"—there was a ring of approval in her voice. "My father didn't know, and I knew, and kept my word. Today I am telling the first person I have ever told—you."

"How could that have happened?" he stormed. "No one saw the burned bodies? Was there no investigation?"

"The coroner conducted an inquiry, but the workers all testified that the fire started in the shed where two vagrants had slept on the wool. They had caused the fire and they had burned up in it. They were guilty and they had brought the punishment on themselves; what more was there to investigate?"

"Oh, the school of hard realities! That's a nice upbringing they gave you!" His eyes flashed.

He did not drive up near the embassy itself, but let the little boy out on the corner of the avenue. "Mihaly, remember!" He put an admonitory finger to his lips and the boy nodded comprehendingly. "You were with me, having ice cream."

The boy pulled up his leg and scratched his calf. "The tailors' shop was full of fleas," he complained irritably. "Uncle, do you think we will be able to investigate? Will we find the clue?"

"Be a smart boy." Margit stroked his hank of blond hair.

"Uncle, who killed Krishan?"

"We don't know yet what the police will say. They took the motorcycle to inspect it. But it was an accident, I think—bad luck. Go now. Run along home."

The boy scampered away, jumping like a goat, borne along by his own energy. He did not even look around as they drove away.

Evening colored the sky a deep purplish red. Great leaves quivered as buoyantly as feathers in the breeze. As they stopped in front of his house, Istvan heard the calm gurgling of water pouring from the open hydrant; the dry season had come again, and the lawns must be watered.

"Everything is in order, sir," the watchman announced, striking the ground with his bamboo stick. His Mongolian face with its good-natured smile gleamed from under the drooping brim of his canvas hat. "Sir, I am getting married," he declared joyfully. "The cook promised to help me."

"Mind he doesn't help you too much. The cook is clever," Terey warned with a chuckle.

"Yes—clever. I will not give him cash in hand. We will go together to buy things for the wedding feast."

They had hardly gone into the house, into the dimness of the hall, when he took Margit in his arms with a firm grip and began to kiss her.

"Do whatever you must to come to Delhi. I need you so."

"I want to as well." Gently she ruffled his short hair, which was coarse as a brush.

"You don't even know what a joy it would be to see you every day, to hear your voice. You must be near me."

"Don't throw good sense to the winds." A little dove's note of excitement rippled in her voice.

"Margit, I am uneasy. I feel instinctively that—cook!" he shouted, as from the partly opened doorway a black hand protruding from a white shirt cuff discreetly appeared and reached for the light switch. Before he could stop the man, a harsh light flashed on. Lizards flitted around the ceiling, seeking shade under a large blade on the motionless fan. He released Margit and found himself somewhat amused by having been caught off guard.

"I am listening, sir."

"Serve us something to eat, and quickly."

Pereira stood in the half-open doorway. His graying hair fell in wisps on his forehead; his eyes were filled with friendly indulgence.

"Good fish, raisin sauce, salad . . ." he counted the items on his fingers, which were ashy gray on the undersides.

"Don't talk, just bring it. Hurry!"

The cook saw the cheerful glint in Terey's eye and was not alarmed by the raised voice. Bowing and loudly shuffling through the hall in his flopping shoes, he made a great show of haste and obedience.

"What is bothering you?" Margit asked as she walked into the bathroom to wash her hands. "Can't you tell me?"

"I can." He waved impatiently. "I just didn't want to say anything in front of the child." He described the accident involving the cow, and the peasant's death. He told her about the words he and the ambassador had had. She listened alertly, mechanically wiping her hands with a towel though they were already dry.

"It's not good." She looked troubled. "If he thinks you are a threat to him, he will want to have you out of the embassy."

"Oh, no. Krishan is dead, after all. There is no witness who knows which of them was driving then, and there is a report written by the police that says the driver was Indian. The case is closed and I will not touch it. Who would benefit? I will not sit in judgment on him."

"Istvan"—she swung her head with its heavy helmet of hair—"I worry so about you. This concerns not only you, but both of us."

"I know," he answered after a long silence

"We must be careful. The world is not on our side. Who will help us? There are a few people who would feel great satisfaction if things did not go well for us."

"Oh, yes. But we will not allow ourselves to be separated." He spoke with bumptious assurance. "He won't dare touch me. I know too much."

"You are a child. You build an unreal world for yourself. It's more comfortable for you. But the one we live in is different: jealous and cruel. Don't be a poet." She laid a hand on his shoulder.

"I'm sorry. Be a poet, be yourself, but I have a premonition that difficult moments are in store."

With a quick, impatient drumming of fingers on the door the cook tactfully signaled that the table was set.

"Yes. And remember about Grace."

"Why?" She stopped and then, as if penetrating to the depths of his silence, pulled up the truth. "She loves you?"

"No!" He denied it vehemently. "She does not love her husband. She married him out of obedience. She has no one."

"She will have a child." Her voice rang with something like envy.

They sat down to the table. Istvan poured grapefruit juice with ice cubes. The cook stood in the door with his hands crossed on his chest, looking satisfied, like a matchmaker. At a rebuking glance from Terey he disappeared into the kitchen, emphasizing his presence there with a clang of the frying pan, which he threw onto the floor for the sweeper to wash.

"Grace told me that you cried when she told you about it . . ."

"What could she understand?" Margit said with a wry look. "Too much was happening at once. A letter from Melbourne, from my father: my stepmother is expecting a baby. He was so glad, it cut me to the heart. Happy Grace, who put my hand on her belly so I could feel how the little one was kicking, and my situation—well, you know how it was then."

"I understand."

"You don't understand anything. Only women know, women who have counted the days as I did. No man knows what it's like to keep a watch on your own body, to feel as if you are pleading with it."

"But you could have come to me."

"And right away you would have felt trapped, hemmed in. I'm not one of those who beg and whimper for sympathy. Don't deny it. Could you have helped? Would you have held my hand and watched me cry? I could have done, well, anything, even break my contract, abandon the sick and go home. They would have taken care of this for me there; I have doctors as colleagues. Or I could give birth there. I may yet decide to do that. Well, don't look at me like that. I'll tell you; you have the right to know."

He gazed at her intently. She came of hard, stubborn stock; he surveyed the boldly drawn eyebrows, the lines of her chin, her open look. She belonged to a race of women who knew what they wanted, who stood shoulder to shoulder with their men when they compelled respect for their property rights with guns in hand, defending their freedom as settlers. He felt enormous gratitude that she had yielded to him, that she had chosen him. His attachment to her was powerful. He was moved by the outline of her lips, not just because they were his for the taking, but because of their varying expressions; by the gleam that wandered over her hair when she shook it impatiently; by the pure, trusting blue of her eyes, in which he bathed as in a mountain stream.

"Why didn't you trust me then?" he whispered reproachfully.

"Because I don't really know you. I don't know what you are like when you are tested. I don't know where my imagination ends and you begin—the real man, with your own past, which is pushed aside, relegated to forgetfulness, but will return in dreams. There are whole landscapes of your life, and they are important, for they reveal things about you as a poet, and they are impenetrable to me. Your creations. Don't frown, I will put it more modestly: your writings, your verse. I'm jealous of it all; I can't be your companion in it, the first to hear it as you read. Couldn't you write in English? You speak it, after all, so fluently, so properly."

"Yes—properly. Of course I could write in English, but it would always be a translation from Hungarian. I am bound to that language. I named the grass under my feet in it, and the stars over my head. I know it is the language of a small nation, that it hedges me in from the world, but it is my language. I feel every tremor, I express everything in it, and I am certain that I speak it unerringly even to you in our closest moments."

"You're wrong." She blinked at him archly. "As often as I can remember, you have whispered to me in English—and very prettily."

"I was translating involuntarily," he admitted with embarrassment.

"You were translating," she said broodingly, putting a hand to her lip. "If neither you nor I noticed that, I swear that the language barrier can be crossed, can disappear. Only you must really want that. You must not avoid speaking, not keep things from me. Oh, Istvan! I would be so happy if I saw your poetry published, even in the *Illustrated Weekly of India*."

He felt her joy.

"I promise to try to translate it myself, but you must help me. You must look it over with an editor's unsympathetic eye."

"You can't even imagine what a great moment that will be for me." She rose, gratified. "A step closer to you."

They went back to his office and settled comfortably into armchairs. The lamplight fell on the stone head; its polished surface seemed to smile sleepily. Istvan thought of Chandra, their disturbing conversation, the grimace of pride on that sleek, undampened face when he had handed Istvan the gift: ". . . one must summon the courage to say, 'I am a god . . .'" It was interesting to think what fate would overtake him. The only truly evil person I have met here. A man who, as a kind of mockery, tries to do people good. He wants to be bad, while others who know they are in error struggle, suffer, and grieve.

He looked at Margit. Her hair was almost black in the dim light; her hands, fixed in a gesture of weariness, looked as if they were sculpted in dark gold. There is no hesitancy in her; she is happy, though she knows she is taking a risk. She is counting on me.

"Do you know what's missing here?" Her eyes ran over the walls. "A clock. A big clock that would chatter and grumble. In the hall of our house there's an old clock in the shape of a woman, with a clock face instead of a woman's under a wooden hat. Don't laugh. I know it's an extraordinary eyesore even if it is an antique. My great-grandfather plundered it from some Dutch brig. But just listening to that unhurried ticking makes the silence of the evening delightful. Anyway, you will hear it and find out for yourself."

"Are you sure?"

She lowered her eyelids in confirmation.

"How nice." She clasped her hands under the back of her neck; the light glowed on her trim bosom. She listened to the distant jangle of cicadas outside the window. "I don't want to go anywhere else, to see anyone else's face. I will have some leisure. I will forget about the sick, treatments, quarrels with Connoly. What peace!"

"That's just what I was thinking."

"In a few days I will come to Delhi to stay. We must think about where I will live."

"Why not with me?"

"Be sensible. I want to have a room for myself, probably at the Janpath Hotel. It is the most comfortable. Not cramped. So I will be here; why are you irritated? Suppose I want to meet with someone from the Ophthalmological Institute, or the professor arrives and wants to find me? At your house? And Grace? She will be so angry that I didn't stay with her, for it was she who induced me to come to India."

"I would prefer—" he began, carefully lighting a cigarette.

"I also," she interrupted him, "will remember the twenty-third of October. From this date we begin to count our days. We will be together. I will go away for a little. I will collect my things and return."

"Perhaps I could drive you?"

"No. You have been running around Agra with me too much. What do you think—that in Delhi they don't know about us? Three hours by car is no distance at all to the gossips. How I shall enjoy these evenings when we sit across from one another! You can even read the paper. I will be preparing a lecture, and whenever I look up, I will see that you are there. I don't need much to be happy. And there will be a long night before us, and we will not be at all in a hurry to go to sleep." Her bare knees, her slender legs when she stretched them, filled him with an immeasurable tenderness.

Someone's fingers ran over the door with a tapping sound.

"Come in!" he called. But no one entered. They only heard the cook's voice through the door.

"Telephone, sir."

He opened the door; there was no one in the dimness. He looked questioningly at Margit, uncertain if he could trust his senses.

"I don't hear it ringing," she said.

"Sir," the cook spoke up from the corridor, "the telephone rang a long time, so I picked up the receiver. Mr. Nagar insists that it is urgent."

With one jump he seized the telephone. "Hello. Terey here."

At once he heard the rapid, excited sentences: "Come immediately! The dispatches are so hot, my fingers are burning! You should be here now!"

"Tell me in two words!" he shouted, full of anxiety.

"An uprising in Budapest. They are sending all the Western agencies. No joke; this is a regular revolution. You don't believe it? Turn on the radio. There will be a newscast from Delhi any minute. They have to put out something. But I'm getting it firsthand. Well, what, then? Terey, are you locked up somewhere?"

"I'll be there right away."

He stood as if paralyzed and unable to breathe. He was still holding the receiver. It had begun. Hungary. The capital. He felt a coolness on his face, like the fateful breath of events yet unknown. The boys. Ilona. What will happen to them?

Margit was half reclining with her long legs in the golden glare of the lamp. A shadow covered her face. He went over to her and buried his lips in her crisp, lightly fragrant red hair.

"I must go right away."

She curled up, grasped his hand and pressed it to her cheek. The way Krishan's wife had told him goodbye when he went to the arena, he thought.

"I'll wait. I won't go to bed. I'll read," she said tranquilly.

"I may be back very late."

Only then did the tension in his voice strike her. She looked up. "Is something wrong?"

"A disturbance in Budapest. That was the bureau chief of Agence France-Presse."

"I'll go with you. I'll wait in the car." She got up, but he put his hands on her arms and seated her in the chair.

"No. Stay here."

Suddenly she felt that there was a barrier between them, that he had set a limit to what they would share. She huddled in the chair. "I'll wait," she said stubbornly. "Even till morning. Go, then."

He ran out of the room. He did not even close the door behind him. She heard a whir; the reflection of the Austin's lights played over the walls of the neighboring villa. She listened to the drone of the motor until there was only silence. She went to the desk and turned on the radio. A Delhi station was broadcasting a program in Hindi, an unintelligible torrent of words. She realized that she would be equally incapable of understanding the Hungarian bulletins. She wandered around the dial and by chance found a Calcutta station. English: she sighed with relief.

"The unrest that broke out at noon today in the capital of Hungary is growing. It began with academic rallies and workers' demonstrations and has ended with lynchings, disarming of police, and takeovers of government buildings. There were even exchanges of gunfire with the Soviet garrison quartered there under the Warsaw Pact. Today in Budapest flyers have been circulated with the speech Gomulka made at the rally in Warsaw. The attention of the world was focused on Hungary . . ." The speaker went on to report that there had been protests over the kidnapping of five leaders of the Algerian Liberation Front, whom a pilot had handed over to the French after landing at a military airport. The Moroccan and Tunisian ambassadors had been recalled from Paris. There had been a sharp letter from Nasser and the king of Jordan.

None of it interested her. She stood dejected, with her hands in the harsh light of the lamp. Only now did the gravity of the news dawn on her. She began searching feverishly for information. She heard a polyglot din punctuated by frequent repetition of the word "Budapest." Her cheeks tightened at the sound of it as if the name were a frost.

"I will not give you up." She leaned with all her weight on the edge of his desk. "You will not take him from me." She moved the hand over the dial, eliciting hoarse, hurried sentences shouted in Arabic, nasal voices from Asiatic stations, as if one were fingering impatient strings, and Portuguese cadences, darkened with pathos, from Goa. It seemed to her that humanity's entrails were heaving with alarm, that it sensed the rhythm of cause and effect leading to . . .

As a race horse feels tension in its muscles before its run, she knew that a test awaited her, and suddenly she saw her great opportunity, never to be repeated: I will have him. I will. She bit her lip. A new hope presented itself: that all Istvan's past might be obliterated, that he would have nowhere and no one to return to and would settle on this shore alone, a shipwrecked man rescued from the elements, with the terrible freedom of those who possess nothing. All bonds with that unknown city that was her rival would be severed. And then, bringing love as a dowry, he could make his entrance to a new continent, Australia, where he would live, to a new language in which he would create, to money and connections that would free him from feelings of strangeness and from the necessity of living on charity and donations. He would become a citizen of her world. He would be, very soon, a person of importance, would feel himself to be at home.

Blue streaks of smoke curled in the lamplight. The stone head looked on with wide, unseeing eyes, with the shadow of a smile that seemed to speak of the evanescence of all human beings' desire to possess everything over which they exercise power and everything they set as a goal of conquest. A hatred of this broken piece of sculpture came over her because it seemed to mock her—to know what awaited her, and already to pity them both.

Several cars stood in front of Nagar's villa. By the time Istvan got out, one had started up. Istvan recognized the Tanjug correspondent; they liked each other. He was sure that when the man saw him he would come over for a moment's conversation at least, but the Yugoslavian, unsmiling and absorbed in thought, only greeted him in passing. "Damned partisan," Istvan thought with exasperation as the man's automobile moved back onto the road, its tires whining.

He passed the speckled setter, who beat her tail on the floor to greet him. Irritated that he did not pet her, she got up and ambled along behind him.

"You're here at last." Nagar ran up to him with short steps, seized him by the arm and shook him with his left hand, shouting excitedly and holding coils of tape torn from the teletype tightly in his right.

"You've done a good deal of mischief there, haven't you? Your Hungarians have gone mad! They may shoot each other, but why be so quick to burn the museum? I remember what a splendid

Breughel was there—The Crucifixion—and what Dutch paintings! The devil knows what was left . . . They could have shot at people through the windows—there are plenty of them—but not burned the pictures."

"Tell me: what happened?"

"Not 'happened'; it is happening," he cried, nearly beside himself, tottering in place like a child who needs to relieve himself but does not want to leave his play. Terey would have caught him by the nape of his neck and shaken him like a rabbit if it would have gotten the full story out of him.

For Nagar this was only information. He was in his element, basking in his role as a journalist. He was one of the first in Delhi to be informed of important developments; he could impress others, arouse their admiration.

"A big rally today at the Bem monument. Who the devil is Bem? Why a rally there?"

"A general of the revolution. A Pole."

"Of what revolution?"

"In '48."

"In '48 I was in Hungary, and I never heard of any revolution."

"Have a heart. In 1848. A hundred years ago."

"Whom did he fight?"

"The Austrians and the army of the czar," Istvan explained in an agony of suspense, trying to snatch the teletype tapes away from Nagar, who was hiding them behind his back.

"The Russians!" Nagar exulted. "At last I understand. After a hundred years you still remember that."

"Maurice, I have a family in Budapest!"

"All right. Listen." He grew serious, but he wanted the pleasure of recounting everything himself too much to let the tapes go. "They tried to disperse the crowd. The police fired. Gerő had to appear and speak, unfortunately, and then the disturbances began."

"Did he make threats? What did he say?"

"Rational things: that they should sit calmly and make no noise, for he would lock them up. But as he could not do that, why talk that way? Button it, keep mum. Since it was not possible, it should have been he who sat quietly and did not exasperate the people.

When they got weapons, they attacked the radio station. Then their call went out not only to the street, but to the whole country. They took control of the Capital City National Committee; the secret police defended themselves, but they killed them to the last man. A mob is a raging beast. It doesn't pick and choose. The blood goes to its head. It is merciless."

"And the army?"

"The soldiers put down their arms or joined the people on the street. Gerő threatened to bring in the Russians; he called them in to help."

"Was the government in control of the situation?" In an agony of suspense, Istvan seized a fistful of communiqués as if he did not believe Nagar.

"Here—read the slogans they are writing on the walls: Court-martial Farkas stop Free all political prisoners stop Expel Rakosi from the party stop Call a plenary assembly of the Central Committee stop Disclose the contents of the trade agreements stop Examine the investment plan stop. Modest enough demands," he added mockingly.

"Monsieur Nagar"—the Hindu assistant leaned in—"the manager of the *Hindustan Standard* asks that you come to the telephone."

"They all flock to me as if I were a rabbi. Nagar ought to know, and Nagar knows," he exclaimed excitedly. "Here. Read. Read." He raked the rest of the dispatches off the table and pushed them at Istvan. "All the world pricks up its ears at the news from Budapest."

A huge weight fell onto Terey's shoulders; he had a terrible sense of impending danger. He knew what these developments would bring. If the West seized the opportunity, they would have speedy access through Austria. Civil war . . . he felt a tremor as if tanks were rumbling by. Civil war. But perhaps everything would take its course as it had in Poland. Gerő and Rakosi would have to back down. The machine would cleanse itself and punish those who had committed abuses and unlawful acts. Perhaps everything would still turn out for the best. Shooting on the streets of Budapest. At whom? Children, a wife, two streets away from the city committee headquarters.

"Yes." He heard Nagar squealing. "Yes, skirmishes broke out almost simultaneously in Győr and Miskolc. All Hungary is in the grip of revolution. Yes! I have confirmation."

The journalist's exuberance drove Terey to fury. He is enjoying this. There, people are dying. Our blood is being spilled.

He sat with his hands dangling between his knees, holding the ribbons of paper with bulletins in short, dry sentences. By now he had almost memorized them. Trompette sauntered up drowsily, her claws thumping, and put her heavy head on his lap. She raised an expectant yellow eye, waiting for him to scratch her ears.

"Go away!" The sound of his own voice made him tremble; he was speaking to the dog in Hungarian. No. Nothing will happen to them. He clenched his fists. Geza and Sandor are sensible boys. Ilona will not let them out on the street at a time like this. But it will be hard to keep them in. Boys are carried away by the music of gunfire; it is alluring to them. That wild, devouring curiosity to see where the shooting is. The rattle from machine guns. He could hear the whistles, the cat's meow of a projectile deflecting from the pavement, vanishing into a cloud that spread from above the Danube. And the trees in the park are full of red and yellow. The earth, sprinkled with leaves, exudes scents: an acrid fermenting smell mixed with the sour odor of explosions and the stifling smoke of distant fires. How well he knew it from there, from the front on the Dnieper, and later from the winter battles when the ring of the Soviet offensive had closed in around the isolated capital. They would not sit at home.

"Sandor . . . Geza," he whispered, his throat tight with fear. The bitch looked at him with mournful eyes and, disappointed in her hope of being scooped up by a friendly hand, sighed like a human being. She walked away, quite offended, to warm herself by the waning hearthfire.

"Too bad, Terey." He heard a voice behind him; he turned to see Trojanowski standing in the doorway and a stout, balding blond man from Tass.

They shook hands without a word. There was sympathy and comfort in their masculine grip; he was assured that they shared his anxiety and wanted to see him through. Yet he turned his face from them because he was afraid of their searching looks. He knelt, threw a pungent-smelling log on the fire, and raked up the ashes. The wrought iron tongs rang on the stone, startling him. He blew patiently, as if the revival of the earlier fire were of great concern to him.

"Do you have family there?" Misha Kondratiuk was bending over him.

"Very close family."

"Istvan, this had to come. You know yourself, this is the storm that cleanses," Trojanowski said by way of consolation. "A few days ago it seemed that there would be bloodshed in our country as well. There were those who shoved guns into the hands of the workers and baited the Russians, but the instinct of loyalty to the nation triumphed. You will see; everything will happen as it should. Be calm. Those you love will be in no danger. This is not a war against women and children."

"I understand you, Comrade Terey." Kondratiuk spoke soberly. "For injustice, for criminal actions, it would have been sufficient to bring the guilty before the courts. Stalin did not like distinguished party activists; he preferred provosts. It is time to drive those people away, but if you begin to beat the big drum and declare holy war against socialism . . ."

Istvan looked up attentively and tried to guess the other man's thoughts. Did he know more than he was saying?

"At the moment no such thing is happening," Trojanowski snapped. "There is more complaining and searching for omens than foresight. But the West is raising a hullabaloo because it sees an opportunity to drive a wedge. You will see. Tomorrow they will begin to give you instructions—" he turned to Terey. "We have it behind us. We know."

"Those who are willing to incite others always manage to extricate themselves," Misha admitted. "But everything depends on how Hungarians behave—on whether a political row is to your liking."

"Everything depends on how the Russians behave," Istvan said defensively.

"And I tell you, what is most important is what the West will do," called Nagar, hearing the end of the conversation. "It can stir the waters, create a situation in which one side or the other moves too fast. Then something will go wrong. If it were only a struggle for power . . . quiet!" He waved to calm Terey, who was indignant. "I know: justice, freedom, sovereignty—catchwords. The serious question is, who will govern? You would bluster, you would shoot, some would be locked up, others would go on the lam; somehow order would be restored. Even if this were a conflict between the Russians and the Hungarians, some solution would be found, for in the end this is an internal matter to—what do you call it? The peace camp. As a camp, it must have order." He lowered his voice. "But when other forces, external forces, get into the game . . . For the time being they have put Nagy on the committee, that philosopher Lukacs, and Kádár. Nagy was the premier. What is he like? Can he do the job?"

Istvan reflected. "In recent years he has been deprived of influence. Rakosi expelled him from the party."

"That is why the street supported him. Clearly they count on him to be different from the others," Trojanowski said thoughtfully. "They have put their hope in him."

"He is different. A man with a heart," Terey put in.

"That is not good." Nagar twisted his birdlike head. "What is needed is a brain, a coolly calculating one that will not allow itself to be carried away. In politics one must think with the head and the stomach and engage the heart least of all. The heart is not a good counselor."

The Hindu appeared in the doorway again, his neck swathed in a woolen shawl. The night was cool for him; from the open door to the garden drifted a mild autumnal tranquility.

"What now?" Nagar stood up.

"They want you on the telephone again."

"Quite a night!" He rubbed his hands like a monkey hulling a grain of rice. "The whole world is staying awake, listening to hear what is happening in Budapest. Gunfire there!"

"Are you expecting fresh dispatches?" Trojanowski asked the Hindu, who was warming his hands over a lightbulb from which he had removed the shade; it gave the blood in them a rose-tinted glow and vividly etched the dark lines of the knuckles.

"I will stay awake, but I do not expect anything before six in the morning. Radio Delhi broadcasts the first news of the day at five-thirty. There will be no information, but we are interested in the commentary. The international pressures will set in."

"Yes." Misha looked sadly at Terey. "What for you is freedom, justice, an outpouring of patriotism, for others is a playing card that can be seized to begin a new round of bidding."

Disturbed by the movement of those who were rising from their seats, Trompette let her muzzle droop onto her front paws and gave a wide yawn.

"There is nothing to wait for," Trojanowski said. "We are going. Terey, you must sleep for a few hours."

"It is nearly midnight." Misha showed him his watch. In his "Good night" Istvan seemed to hear a trace of involuntary malice.

They went out. The dog accompanied them only as far as the threshold. Lifting her muzzle to sniff the aromas of fall, she was put off by the cool of the dew and returned to her place under the table.

"Everyone is asking if it is true that the Hungarians are fighting the Russians." Nagar poured some vodka. "There is a repugnant curiosity in this. Is it possible? It would be a hopeless struggle, after all. Would anyone take your part, offer you support? Would it not set off a wider conflict? Drink, Istvan. You know I rarely urge you, but vodka will do you good today. It has grown cool somehow, and one doesn't feel like sleeping yet."

The mournful whining of jackals floated in from the garden, as if an abandoned infant were setting up a wail. Trompette moved her head, pretending not to hear. With her muzzle snuggled on one front paw, she wheezed. Istvan held his glass high. The amber liquid gave off a smell like fermenting yeast. "Are they really fighting there?" he asked.

"Not exactly. There were a couple of skirmishes. Tanks were burned with accelerants—bottles of gas—so some divisions withdrew to the suburbs, where they are waiting in readiness. The new premier, Nagy, promised to carry on talks about getting them out of the capital completely. The protesters say that the presence of the Russians does not lessen the tension, but aggravates it. It brings back memories of the war."

"Old times. Eleven years ago, who would have thought of this?" Terey took a pull at the whiskey.

"And where were you then?"

"I was defending Budapest. I was wounded."

"Fighting for the Germans?"

Istvan nodded.

"Well, you see. You see yourself," Nagar said worriedly. "There are thousands like you. They remember. It is fixed in their minds. Good thing you are here. You would have been shooting by now."

"No."

"So one says." He huffed skeptically. "But it seems to me that you would shoot. Believe me, it's easier to shoot than to think."

"No. No."

"No, what?"

"I wouldn't shoot at the Russians anymore."

Nagar turned this statement over in his mind as if he were conducting an investigation. "They overran you, after all."

"Not so long ago we encroached on them. I was on the Ukrainian front for nearly two years myself. Villages burned . . . a hellish winter. Frosts of forty degrees below freezing. Burning a cottage was a death sentence for the women we drove into the snow. When we were retreating I saw curled, shrunken figures in snowdrifts. My soldiers shot partisans—anyway, who knows who they were that were caught? I didn't issue the command to fire only because I had half a liter of plum vodka and I bought my way out of it. A friend went with the platoon to carry out the execution. Do you know why I paid him off with the vodka? Not for conscience' sake. Only because he didn't want to drag himself out of the cottage in such a frost.

"My mother instilled in me with prayers that where there is guilt, there must be punishment, and if there is not, one should tremble, for the future will bring something worse. When there is still no punishment, mete it out yourself: atone.

"To love Hungary. Do you think that means to close our eyes to our past? I am one of the guilty. Because of that, I am afraid."

With both hands Nagar stroked the glass he was resting on his bony knee. "That is magical thinking. It smacks to me of India.

Well, then, let us assume, my champion of justice, that you would not shoot. But people would shoot at you. Unfortunately, history does not seek out the guilty. It favors collective responsibility, and sometimes grandchildren pay for the fantasies and grandiosity of their forefathers. Yes, that is the way it is." He blinked with lashless eyelids.

"Do you think there is hope?" Terey held out a pleading hand.

"Quiet. There is always hope. What we have before us is only hope. Get some sleep, Istvan. This is the advice of an old, wise"—he hesitated for moment, then said, smiling apologetically and with large eyes reddened as if from weeping—"Frenchman. We will not be able to think this out just now. It is night there as well. We must wait."

Istvan emptied his glass at one draught. Around the light of an unshaded bulb set low on a wall, deep shadows played over the sides of the room and the ceiling; the horns of the antelope loomed large and the head of the rhinoceros seemed to burst from the wall like a tree trunk gnawed bare by a river.

"Please—" he began, but Nagar flapped his upraised hands.

"I know what family means, though I have been alone in the world. I will remember. I will call you, good news or bad."

The shrubs, which were dripping with moisture, muffled the echo of Istvan's heavy steps on the tiled walk. The Austin's engine had cooled; for a long time it refused to start. At last the motor began to hum. Drops of water crept over the steamed windshield as if it were weeping. He set the wipers going and drove the car almost involuntarily. He was gripped by an uncomprehending astonishment that was charged with grief and fear. How could this be? Battles on the streets of Budapest? Budapest in flames?

In the glare of the headlights he saw a pair of lean, naked old men with slender staves in their hands lurching forward into the light with their eyes wide open. When he pressed the horn, they stopped and extended the bamboo rods as if they were insects' tentacles. Only then did he realize that they were blind. Large turbans exaggerated the size of their heads; their necks, muffled in long strips of fabric, appeared thick. Their bare legs looked like charred sticks. Where have I seen them? Something took form as if in a dream: the picture of launderers carrying bundles of soiled linen on their heads that Ram Kanval had painted. That ill-fated gift to Grace on her wedding night. Blind. They walk through the night which for them lasts forever. He stopped. Their watchful inertia, a torpor like that of insects, fell away. The shadows of canes riddled the white stream of glare from the headlights as they moved forward. They found the automobile with their groping fingers, and passed by. He almost felt their hands moving over the quivering metal body, which was wet from the dew.

Margit. For so many hours he had not even thought of her. She was not there; she had vanished. But—I love her, he assured himself. Yet the sudden exclusion of her from his thoughts vexed and pained him. How could I forget about her? Blind men, indeed. Still, the thought that she was waiting for him, that he would have to tell her what he had learned, to repeat everything, made him impatient. He would have preferred to be alone.

He left the car in front of the gate. He did not want to raise the shades in the garage. From a distance he saw a yellow light in the window of his living room glowing through the curtain. He felt vaguely guilty that Margit's vigilance rather displeased him.

He walked into the dark grotto that was the veranda and bumped against a body. Shuddering, he searched his pockets and finally found some matches. In the rosy flame figures loomed, lying curled up on mats. He saw a hat clutched tightly in a fist and recognized the watchman, who in his sleep protectively embraced a girl slender as a child. Their intertwined bodies were covered with a thick, Nepalese blanket of beet red. The man's brown hand in its gesture of love seemed to rebuke Istvan.

He saw the dusky gleam of long, tangled hair. Just then the match, with its bent red head like a stamen, went out in his hand. He groped his way to the door, opened it as far as the bodies guarding the threshold allowed, and squeezed inside. He walked along a bright shaft of light that shone from under the door of the living room. Margit was sleeping like a child with both hands nestled under her cheek. He took off his shoes and walked without a sound over the rust-colored carpet. He turned off the radio, which was still pulsing with scattered, tantalizing squeals from the shortwave transmitters. He was moved when he saw the ashtray filled with pieces of extinguished cigarettes with lipstick stains. She had worn herself out with worry. She had waited.

He reached for a soft blanket that lay folded on the edge of the couch and covered her, pushing her, or so it seemed, into deeper darkness. He heard her sigh lightly, but she did not waken, and he was grateful. He wanted to light a cigarette, but he put down the pack; the scraping of the match might rouse her. He sat utterly absorbed in his thoughts, racked by tremors of weariness.

Surely his boys were also sleeping. Perhaps there was no great danger. Could the power be slipping from the government's hands from hour to hour? There are people there, after all, who can think, who will not steer the country toward disaster. What is at stake is not one life or even a hundred, but the welfare of the nation, all we won through the transformations that cost us so much. Liberation—the word had a bitter ring. But it will still take years to forget what we lived through. Once again we are calling down thunderbolts on our own heads. There will have to be discussions, accusations, cries for the gallows. Our guilty will have to be dragged by their necks to the wall. All that—so long as in the hurly-burly of justice meted out in anger, like revenge, corrupted by blind hate, festering with the sense of injuries suffered, the overriding good of the nation is not forfeited, the republic itself is not jeopardized.

Who has the courage to confront a street ringing with cries of righteous indignation and give an order for silence? To issue commands that can win the obedience of those who in madness are ready to kill and destroy—who even believe they are storming the gates for freedom? How can a blind element be converted to an intelligent force that will help the cause of progress for years to come?

He chewed the butt of the unlit cigarette. Dispatches would come tomorrow; at such a moment the ministry would not forget the embassies. Perhaps he could manage to get a telephone connection, to hear the boys' voices, to order them to listen to their mother. To threaten and to promise . . . They must not go out of the house. Or, better, should they go to their grandmother, escape from

Budapest? I do not even know what is happening in our neighborhood. Where has the fighting taken place? What has burned besides the museum? In the bulletins, burned homes have not been mentioned.

Homes—opulent interiors, outmoded Vienna secession furniture, portraits of grizzled drunkards with rakish mustaches. Sideboards filled with dishes used only a few times a year. Old Meissen porcelain crunching under boots, green slivers of broken windowpanes glittering, wads of stuffing protruding from armchairs ripped open by grenade fragments. Photographs mounted on millboard scattered, dry and slick, spilled from a family album covered with faded plush. Faces long dead but more enduring than those that were still alive yesterday but today are one with the earth, their forms no longer like those of human beings but staved in by tons of steel and the caterpillar wheels of a tank pushing into the brick rubble. The remains of children, of women, denuded without shame in the crumpled remains of their clothing—lying in tatters, twisted like empty husks, body fluids pooled like wax, exposed by the surfeit of light pouring in through great holes in walls beaten in by artillery fire. Someone had begun to bandage wounds, but he had thrown away the dressings, for they were expiring, slumping helplessly in the arms that held them. A brick under the ear or a volume of Jókai served as pillows for the last sleep. Reed roofing with clots of plaster hung from the ceiling. A mirror, undamaged and unseeing as a pool of water hardening with winter's first ice, reflected the dead emptiness of the ruined dwelling.

He crawled with his grenade gun to a balcony. Its crumpled balustrade had been pushed aside by an explosion. Below, through streaks of smoke, he could see the pavement slippery with dew and quivering tramway cables now severed and reaching the ground. In the distance he heard commands barked hoarsely in German. He saw burned-out ruins, the reddish wreck of an automobile eaten away by fire, its wheels stuck in black pools of rubber: its melted tires. From far off came bursts of submachine gun fire. The street was filled with the stench of smoldering rags, hair, bodies in the rubble of buildings, invisible to the eye, and the odor, exasperating as spider webs in the face, of war.

No. No, he pleaded, shielding his eyes with his hands. Not Budapest in ruins. Save the city. How I hate war! How I hate those who bring it on.

Under his lowered eyelids he felt the pulsing of a fire. A mane of flame pushed outward from the window of a building. It roared. It devoured the house from inside with insatiable violence. The hellish days of service to foreign occupying armies lived on in him. Images pushed into forgetfulness had seized on his first moment of vulnerability to reappear in an ominous vision, to frighten him in his dreams. That was the past. It was over. But for him and millions of others, years later, the dark residue from the war still trickled into the memory like venom. He pressed his eyelids, pressed toward the radiating pain, as if to obliterate the hateful visions. He rested his forehead on the broad arm of his chair and breathed deeply, inhaling a familiar odor: a heavy infusion of cigarette smoke mingled with the saccharine smell of insecticide.

"Papa—" he heard the despairing voice of his son so close by that he sprang to his feet, listening. His heart beat hard. The barely audible breathing of the sleeping woman seemed to deepen the silence in the room. Slowly he regained his awareness that the child's voice was only a bad dream; from the turbulence in his mind had risen a premonition that something alarming had happened to Sandor. The leaping, throbbing fire subsided into its sources—the glare from beneath the shade of a lamp nearby and a large moth fluttering near it, beating in a soft bass key and throwing spots of shadow onto the wall—and he slowly grew calmer.

He glanced at his watch: twenty after five. Instinctively he roused himself in time to listen to the first news reports. He switched the radio on and lit a cigarette. One thought absorbed him.

Just after the hymn in which the prayerful voices of the Indian choirs built to a jarring crescendo, a young, cheerful voice announced that the weather would be sunny and cool with a wind from the northeast. A summary of Krishna Menon's speech before the United Nations, defending the Algerian people's right to self-determination and warning against putting pressure on Egypt, dragged on interminably. A gathering of French and English warships near Malta . . . Everything is more important to Hindus—he clenched his fist—even the appearance of locusts, than developments in Europe.

Margit awoke and gazed around with wide open eyes. He moved to the sofa and laid his hand on her feet, which were hidden under the blanket. Without exchanging a word, they waited until the world news came on.

Suddenly they heard the word: Hungary.

In spite of a call to lay down arms, the fighting was continuing. The government was not in control of the situation. The people were demanding that Gerő resign. The laborers would not work. At the rallies they were choosing factory councils. Armed citizens' patrols had taken up their posts at government buildings.

A crowd had torn down a bust of Stalin. The five-pointed star had been pulled from the public buildings and had disappeared from flags and soldiers' caps. Premier Nagy had called on all the people to preserve the peace, and received a delegation of youth. The hunt for officials of the state militia and the lynchings were still going on. Throughout the nation the situation was grave, and the tension was growing. In the village of Magyaróvár the secret police had shot into a crowd gathered in the market square; the crowd had attacked a building and tried to disarm them. Many victims had fallen. Further deployment of armored Soviet units circling Budapest had been observed. This meager information, he thought, was encouraging. The less that was happening, the better. He breathed deeply. Nothing had been said of fighting in the streets of the capital, of fires and destruction. So the night had passed peacefully.

"I fell asleep," Margit lamented. "I couldn't hold out until you got back. Why didn't you wake me?"

He looked at her pleadingly and stroked her feet; he could feel their warmth through the blanket. "I had to be alone."

Parrots screamed outside the window. Inside the house, people were beginning to move about.

Whenever Terey tried to get a telephone connection to Budapest during the two hours a day when the British cable was in service on "the other side" of Europe, the answering voices tinkled with polite hopefulness, "There is no connection to Budapest today. Please call tomorrow."

He begged the London operator to find out if the number did not answer—if the customer was not there—or if there had been some serious damage to the line. He even heard a garbled fragment of conversation in Hungarian. "This is the military operator," someone seemed to say, and he called into the telephone that he was a member of the staff at the embassy in New Delhi speaking in an official capacity. But the sound grew faint and gave way to senseless gibberish reinforced by amplifiers. At last the friendly voice from London informed him that Budapest was closed to international calls.

His colleagues as well were trying to establish contact with the ministry. When they met early in the mornings he saw their discouragement, and rage and despair choked him. His premonitions grew worse: he saw his home with burnt walls and blank windows. He saw the charred bodies of his children buried with others in a pit with a metal plaque bearing the inscription "Unknown Victims of the Uprising."

On the third day of the unrest the Indian press began publishing photographs. In the embassy people tore newspapers from each other's hands. The pictures were more horrifying than the bulletins; corpses of members of the secret police hung from streetlights, terribly mutilated, their uniforms ripped away. Who had they been? Perhaps completely innocent people—simple soldiers whom chance had made the targets of revenge.

The faces of a crowd, stony masks of hate and anger—they looked at young boys in civilian clothes, with weapons, standing on a tank and waving a tricolored flag with a hole where the star had been torn out. Istvan looked with numb foreboding at a group of women pressing handkerchiefs to their noses, stifling cries of pain and disgust and perhaps shielding themselves from the odor of putrefaction, for a row of bodies raked by a volley of gunfire lay at their feet. The women had come to identify their kin, fathers, husbands, and sons, who had wanted to take up arms, to capture the barracks. Below that was a picture of a captured AVH commander with his soldier's coat unfastened. He sat with his prematurely bald head on his chest, with a blank but concentrated look, as if he had grown impatient at waiting so long to be shot.

Behind him stood a Hungarian soldier with the cockade of a revolutionary on his cap, placing cartridges in the chamber of an automatic pistol.

"See, see!" Ferenc pushed an illustrated magazine toward him. "This is the way it really looks."

The picture filled a page: a Soviet tank blown up and standing on end. The half-burned body of a soldier under a wall, spattered with glass from shattered windows. He knew that stiffening of the body, when death gives the command. The last Attention! He grieved for the young soldier with light hair tousled by the wind. He grieved terribly for Budapest.

The Nagy government's call for anarchy to be brought under control had the ring of a desperate appeal. But how could one make the argument for reason to an armed, infuriated crowd? Too many injuries had festered, too long a silence had been forced on the people, for them to be quiet now. Those freed from prison reminded everyone of the false charges leveled against them. They showed the scars of their torture. They lifted above the throngs gathered in the squares hands from which the nails had been pulled during interrogations. No one remembered the services rendered by the leaders, the gains made by the people, the rapid modernization of the country. They remembered the special shops, the limousines, the informers. The mob was demanding blood; it was not a question of justice but of revenge. And its revenge was murderous in its cruelty. It was enough to shout, "Secret police!", "Collaborator!", "Toady of Moscow!" for a man to be beaten to the ground and trampled to a bloody pulp (so the Western agencies crowed triumphantly).

They gathered in Ferenc's office, analyzing correspondence and reportage, looking anxiously into each other's eyes and asking wordlessly: What next?

"The Austrian border causes me the most concern." Ferenc showed them a drawing in the *Times*. "They could push in agents and insurgents that way."

"You think in old paradigms." Terey spoke loudly and testily. "Why the devil are they going to send anyone when the whole country listens to Radio Free Europe because we are afraid to tell the truth?"

Ferenc looked at him out of the corner of his eye. Locks of wavy hair dangled on his forehead; he pushed them away with an impatient motion of his head, like a colt shaking its mane. They were quiet, mulling over unspoken accusations. Mistrust was growing between them. Judit gazed anxiously into their angry faces.

"And what does the ambassador say to all this?" Istvan asked. "After all, for the love of God, we have to take a position! Journalists called me in the night, demanding comment. I think I'll go mad; they understand literally nothing of what is happening in our country. We must call a press conference, explain, offer some assessment of the situation."

"And do you understand what is going on in our country?" Ferenc retorted. "I would not take it upon myself . . ."

"Are you waiting to see who wins?"

"I am waiting for an official communiqué from the ministry. We are functionaries; it is not for me to amuse myself with crystal-gazing and prophecies."

"We are Hungarians," Istvan elongated his words for emphasis, "and a struggle for our independence is going on there."

"For socialism," the secretary corrected him, adding his own emphasis.

"To me it's the same. But one has to believe in this socialism, not just fashion slogans for the naive—the uninitiated—and commit oneself beforehand to vassalage, to a lackey's obedience."

"Mind your words," Ferenc snapped. "You will answer for them!"

Judit raised her plump, shapely arms and sighed profoundly. "Is there anything to quarrel about? We cannot influence anything this way. We must wait. Bajcsy wanted to inform himself about the situation today, to meet with the Soviet ambassador—"

They both looked up.

"—but the Soviet ambassador said he had no time."

Ferenc made a wry face and rubbed his forehead impatiently.

"Perhaps it was true that he had no time."

But Judit was not through. With wise eyes like an owl she looked around forbearingly, as if to say: Please let me finish.

"Then the boss called the Chinese"—she drew out her words to underscore the gravity of this information—"and the ambassador will receive him today"—she glanced at her narrow gold watch—"in an hour."

"What do you make of that?" Istvan leaned toward her.

"Perhaps the Chinese will support us?" She looked around as if she were at a loss.

"No more of that 'us'!" the secretary exclaimed. "What 'us'? There is the government—and we must listen to it—and a hostile, rebellious mob. There is no 'us' when Hungarians are shooting each other. People must choose. We must be on one side or the other"—he shoved a hand toward Istvan—"one sees that at once. And that will have consequences. We cannot allow anarchy, even in a small enclave. We must not forget what powers it falls to us to represent. An employee is obligated to be at the disposition of the ministry."

"Especially when there is none." Terey mimicked the man's unctuous tone.

"Until there are new instructions, we are bound by the old ones. Otherwise there would be anarchy here as there is in Budapest."

"I wonder what the boss is looking for from the Chinese." Judit brooded. "What can they tell him?"

"They will offer a declaration of friendship with the full ritual of the heating of jasmine tea," Ferenc said carelessly.

"It's not unimportant. The boss won't feel so isolated then," Terey pointed out.

"Don't quarrel. Please." Judit's voice was weary.

"Well, ask yourselves—won't he still be on our hands for a little while?"

"Why do you come to me for an opinion?" Istvan asked truculently.

"Because it is my duty to ask you, as it is yours to answer my questions. I must know whom I have by me."

Terey clenched his fists. In a sudden spasm of anger he lashed out, "Do you know what they're doing with people like you in Budapest?"

"Fortunately this is not Budapest, and you are not leading a gang of rebels." With perfect posture and measured steps, Ferenc left the room.

"Well, why did you exasperate him unnecessarily?" Judit hunched her shoulders deprecatingly; her swarthy body with its matronly embonpoint exuded a maternal warmth. "He will remember this. He saw the photographs of the people who were shot. He feels threatened. Why make him count you as one of his enemies?"

"I was carried away," he confessed. "It's difficult. I said so."

"You have your share of worry as well. I know. Your wife. Your children. And nothing, nothing can help. I know that. But I was alone, and you will have your family. Remember, in spite of everything, one must live. When I was by the Kama, I was jealous of my family because they were living in Budapest. And in May of '44 the Germans took everyone to Auschwitz, put them in the gas chambers and burned them. And I am alive."

"Yes. But you must not forget that it was the Germans who did that. We sheltered Jews. Only when it came to light that we were ready to capitulate to anyone except the Russians did the Szalasi faction carry out a coup—"

"They were Hungarians as well," she said bitterly. "I don't know myself why I was so bent on being one of you. I have no home or kin in Budapest, not even in a cemetery. But nothing connects me to Israel, either. Although you barely tolerate me, I am a Hungarian, for I want to be one and no one can forbid me. Be careful about these wrangles over who is the greatest patriot."

"I said nothing against you. I'm truly fond of you."

"And what does that count for when you do not understand my feelings? You are certain that you had to do these things—first to go with Hitler, then to hand us over."

"What do you want from me? I was in the army. They mobilized everyone."

"Listen, Istvan. I had a friend. He was also in the army: a professor at the conservatory, a pianist. He was not given a rifle, only a shovel. The Jews were segregated; they formed battalions of 'combat engineers.' The ones with rifles were the ones who kept watch on them. Those better Hungarians! Only there did he feel himself to be a Jew."

"But he survived. He was not at the front. He didn't take a Russian bullet," he cried despairingly.

"He survived, but his hands . . . he will never manage to play a chord. He has the hands of a laborer because of that shovel. And a hundred of his companions are buried there. Shot to bits for nothing; a *csikos* from the plains fired at professors, doctors, lawyers. He killed the Hungarian in those who survived. Istvan, I tell you about this because I am fond of you as well. Don't ask me to cry for you because you have family in Budapest. Your family will pass through this. You will have them. Mine are gone."

As if he had just met her, entire expanses of pain and loneliness in her soul opened before him. He did not know whether to embrace her and beg for forgiveness, or walk out as Ferenc had done, visibly offended. But she sat looking at him hard—a large woman, warm and worthy of the deepest sympathy. He bowed his head. "I'm sorry, Judit," he whispered.

"For what? I only wanted you not to be wearing your troubles on your sleeve. Everyone here has his share of pain, though it may not always show."

He almost ran to his office, humiliated, stinging with guilt. He took shelter behind his desk. Hunching over, he plunged into the daily pile of press, trying to gather information.

The tone of the bulletins was favorable to the uprising. The correspondents emphasized its anti-Soviet character and wrote approvingly of the lynchings of communists. Nagy's calls for the Russian armies to leave Hungary made headlines everywhere. The dispatches also carried a warning from the temporary Air Force Command that if the march of the Russian columns toward the capital was not halted, they would be bombarded.

The *Times* did not predict that there would actually be armed conflict between Hungary and the Soviets. The commentator acknowledged that talks between Nagy, Suslov, and Mikoyan might lead to resolution of the difficult situation in which Hungary found itself. He dwelt on the question of what Nagy was like—whether he would display the necessary moral strength and political acumen.

The West had not shown itself inclined to shift the established spheres of influence and military deployments—the so-called "balance of threat," which in the East was commonly called "peace." He was relieved to immerse himself in these considerations. He made special mention of them in the report he was preparing for the ministry. Bent over his work, he sighed with hope that the conflict would quiet down, that further bloodshed would be avoided. He almost did not hear the knock at his door.

"Come in," he muttered, thinking that his colleagues or the caretaker were opening the door without announcing themselves. He was surprised to see Mihaly, with a face full of distress. Something serious must have happened for the boy to have stolen so far into the building in spite of his father's instructions.

"May I come in, uncle?"

"What do you want?"

"The police took her away. She has been arrested," he said cryptically.

"Who?"

"Krishan's new wife. Someone sprinkled sugar in the gas tank and that caused the accident. They think that she—"

"Impossible!"

The boy looked at him with profound gravity. His eyes flashed with tension. "They really did take her this morning. The driver told me."

"Why would she have done that? The charge is idiotic!" He beat his fist on the desktop, not so much talking to the boy as thinking out loud. "She loved him."

"They said it was revenge because he bullied her sister. He took all her silver and sold it to buy the motorcycle." The boy repeated this information in a reproachful whisper.

"They know nothing."

"But Durga confessed right away," Mihaly insisted. "'It was my fault,' she cried. 'I did not take proper care of him. You can kill me. I deserve it.' So they took her. Uncle, is that what you think?"

"No." Istvan took the boy in his arms. "I'm sure Durga is innocent."

"Will you go there? Will you save her?" The boy's voice was so full of hope and pleading that Istvan promised to intervene.

"We must defend her. Now run along before you get a hiding."

The boy looked around the desk and reached for a two-tone colored pencil, then made a chain of paper clips.

"May I take these? They would come in handy for me." He wrinkled his forehead, which could be seen from under his parted bangs.

"Take them and get going."

The boy reached the door, then turned around. "Uncle—you promised," he said.

"Don't worry. I'll have a talk with the police."

Mihaly scraped the floor with one foot and bowed vigorously, then left the room.

How to defend her? He saw Krishan's catlike, cunning face, the small teeth gleaming white under the mustache. After all, his horoscope had told him that sugar would harm him, Istvan remembered with astonishment. All his life he had not eaten sweets, thinking that he had a weak stomach, that it was hyperacidic. And he had not escaped; sugar had been his doom, only, as if in a bitter joke, sugar burned in the pistons.

Horoscopes are rubbish. They provide yet another opportunity to foist off the responsibility for one's life on fate, to tell oneself that what is going to happen will happen as it is written in the stars. But there is a cruel mockery in what befell Krishan, since he never put sugar to his lips.

Durga is most certainly innocent, though in her despair she is ready to accuse herself, and the police are eager to seize on her statement. Suddenly he recalled what she had said in the narrow room full of the whirring of sewing machines about the boys crowding around their hero. Like a revelation it came to him: a lollipop on a stick. The little boy who at a friend's command put a candy into the liquid—the gasoline must have washed it off. He pulled out the bare stick. Istvan was certain that it must have happened so; he marveled that it had not occurred to him at once. He looked out through the dusty screen to the yard. He wanted to call Mihaly; the child remembered every word. He had open eyes and a mind like a sponge. One had to be careful around him, for he repeated everything with an undesigning ruthless candor.

Below his window the new driver, a Hindu, was polishing the ambassador's Mercedes with a chamois. The boss must have returned. With what had the Chinese regaled him?

The telephone rang. He heard Nagar's excited voice. "Turn on your radio. There is extraordinary news. You surely have a radio there?"

"I have. But tell me—what is happening in Budapest?" he demanded, his tension rising.

"Peace is near. Hungary is on the back burner; there is a new bombshell. Armored forces from Israel have struck on Sinai. The Egyptians are fleeing—as fast as they can flee on camels. Nasser is announcing that he will defend his territory to the last round of ammunition, which is to say, not for long. He is calling in help from Yugoslavia and Moscow. Ben Gurion fired off a speech about how that Arab rabble would not give him a moment's peace. He listed the border incidents, the boycott of goods, the arrest of Jewish bankers in Cairo. Naturally he assured the world that the goal of this expedition was simply to maintain order and that the tanks were on the move for no reason except to secure peace in the canal area."

"Do you think they will be successful?"

"Israel? They have the best army. They have modern equipment. They will rout the Egyptians. They will reach the canal tomorrow. France and England have sent an ultimatum to Egypt and Israel demanding that both sides cease fire immediately and withdraw ten miles from the canal. It is too vital an artery to be interfered with by acts of war. The canal will be protected by English and French troops; do you understand their game?"

"And the Americans?"

"Behind their backs Eden and Mollet are trying to take back the canal."

"You said that Israel . . ."

"It is the third shareholder. It has no stock on deposit; it must put in the blood of its soldiers, thus creating a reason for intervention. A beastly role, but very remunerative. Turn on your radio; you will learn the details. And drop in at my place, because everything is at the boiling point just now, and that uprising of yours will no longer be the private affair of Hungarians."

"Has the deal-making begun?"

"The devil only knows. But you must take into account that from this morning you have become a bargaining chip. The tacit assent of the West. Let each keep order in his own back yard. You know what that means. You were a soldier."

"Call me, Maurice. I'll be there this evening."

"What am I doing just now? Am I not calling you?"

Still holding the receiver as if expecting to hear something more, he remained bent over his desk, gazing at the pile of newspapers and cuttings clipped together. Global developments were jeopardizing the struggle for change in his country.

Someone knocked at the door. This time it was the caretaker, who poked his head in and announced that comrade secretary was summoning the staff to a meeting with comrade ambassador, but had not been able to reach Istvan on the telephone. Terey replaced the receiver angrily.

He found them all in the ambassador's office, but his tardy entrance attracted no one's attention, for they were all riveted to the radio, hearing about the crushing force of the armored divisions that were invading the Sinai Peninsula. The ultimatum of both great powers had been met with condemnation by the Arabs; the commentator expressed the hope that the Soviet Union and the United States would be able to restrain the aggressors and prevent a widening of the conflict.

The speaker had sympathetic remarks for Egypt. Nasser, having resolved to fight, was appealing to the conscience of the whole world. Everyone knew that Israel alone would be able to defeat him, let alone two imperial powers such as England and France. But violence should not be allowed to become the deciding factor in international relations.

Budapest was calm; the workers' demands had come before the Central Committee, which was meeting in continuous session. Flyers were being distributed to the Russian armies: "Soviet soldiers, do not fire on Hungarian workers and farmers! Our revolution ousted Rakosi and Gerő and opened prison gates . . ."

Istvan noticed that Bajcsy bridled with irritation and looked alertly at the faces of his staff. But they were listening with praiseworthy composure.

"Comrades," Bajcsy began, breathing deeply and straightening himself as if his self-confidence had just returned, "the government of Premier Nagy has announced a series of reforms which are necessary for the good of the people. Peace prevails in our country. We must not believe the imperialist propaganda that tries to stir the waters—not only to push us into a fratricidal struggle, but to embroil us in conflict with our allies in order to divert attention from the aggression at the Suez. The dispatches which I have received from Budapest say that the situation is completely under control. The party and the government . . ."

The cryptographer was stealthily manipulating the knob on the radio in an effort to lower the voice of the speaker to a barely audible whisper. Ferenc jostled his arm and he turned around. From the radio came a harsh cry, "The Russian armies, which steadily grow in numbers, invoke the Warsaw Pact. 'If they do not withdraw voluntarily, we are prepared to renounce that pact and declare neutrality,' warns the Hungarian premier."

Everyone turned toward the radio. Kereny shrank back like a man convicted of a crime.

"Turn it off!" Ferenc shouted. When the cryptographer moved too slowly, he jerked the cord from the socket. Bajcsy suddenly bent over and went pale, as if a fist had battered him under his heart. He swallowed loudly and stammered something through lips too sticky to part. The office went quiet. Judit handed him a glass of water. He drank it in great gulps with his swollen eyelids half shut.

"Comrades," he said softly, "the international situation may push us . . . but perhaps this government . . . I ask you to avoid unnecessary disclosures. The more distance we keep from the Americans and the English, the better. And from the French," he added after a moment. "On the other hand, I am directing you to meet with diplomats from our camp, especially from the Soviet Embassy. I myself approached . . ." with a limp hand he rubbed his sagging, carelessly shaven chin—"understand: according to these"—he reached for a newspaper, flipped noisily through its pages, then crumpled it—"they may be keeping an eye on our behavior, watching for treason. Use good judgment. Better to feign stupidity, even to appear a coward, than to make a remark that causes something to blow apart for us. What I am saying is confidential."

They stood waiting for more precise instructions, but the ambassador sat heavily in his chair and signaled with his hand that they should leave.

He had been stricken, though he was trying hard to hold the rudder, to pretend he had foreseen these events. Had it occurred to him after that bulletin that he might suddenly find himself with no place to return to? A new Hungary was being born; would he find the strength to reinvent himself again, to condemn his own earlier behavior, to renounce what until now had been ascribed to him as merit? But perhaps the only road that remained to him was the one taken by those who left under a volley of curses—those whom a wall of bayonets had saved from being brought to court.

"Comrade ambassador"—he leaned across the desk—"this evening I will be at Agence France-Presse. So that nothing can be misconstrued between us, I want to know . . ."

"What I said does not apply to you, Terey," the ambassador wheezed. "I also want to know the whole truth. I am in the dark enough as it is." He seemed deserving of pity, close to breaking.

After noon, though he was tired, Istvan did not give way to the enervating drowsiness. He lay down, then got up, searching for news on the radio. He telephoned Kondratiuk, who assured him that an agreement had been negotiated in Hungary, that the movements of the armies were evidence that the old garrisons were being evacuated, and that only troublemakers could see in them a stratagem to encircle Budapest. He alluded to Nagy's private conversations with Mikoyan, who had the power of a special plenipotentiary and who had expressed to journalists his satisfaction with the outcome of the meetings.

"Do not worry, Comrade Terey. We have reassuring signals. The workers will not hand over the factories and the farmers will not let the land out of their hands. The propaganda of the reactionaries was misleading."

But from Radio Calcutta he heard that the Soviet armies had taken over the airports and barred Hungarian pilots from approaching their planes.

"Sir, Agra is calling," the cook shouted desperately, holding the receiver with his fingertips as if it were burning them.

He heard Margit's voice from far away. "How are you? Have you had news from home?"

"No. I'm calmer, though. The situation is becoming clearer."

"Do you need me?"

"Yes!" he said fervently. "You know I do."

"Do you really want me there?"

"I'm waiting. When will you be here?"

"Tomorrow. I'll fly in on the evening plane. Perhaps you will come for me. I'll be alone."

"And you'll be here for good? Will you stay in Delhi?"

"That depends on you. Till tomorrow, then."

"I'll be at the airport. Here's a kiss."

"I wanted to beg your pardon again." The words came to him from a great distance. What could she have done? That night he had abandoned her, pushed her away. In the face of the uprising, the threat to his family, she had become dispensable; worse yet, it had been as if she had not been there at all, had ceased to exist.

"For what?"

"I thought badly of you."

"I took a breath of air . . . it was nothing. This is foolish. Clearly I deserved it."

"No. It is not foolish. I thought you didn't love me."

"I love you. Doesn't that bore you yet?"

"Don't talk like that."

"Sleep well. Think: only one day."

"That's terribly long. A whole day."

"Think of what I said."

"I remember, but it doesn't make it any easier for me at all. I'd like to be with you."

"You are always with me."

After what seemed to be a moment of reflection he heard a whisper full of bitterness, "You are happy if you believe that."

"Goodbye, my sun."

Pereira stood in the doorway to the kitchen, his bristling gray hair sprinkled with glare from the lightbulb, listening for orders. "Miss Ward will come tomorrow?" he inquired, wiping the salad bowl, breathing on the glass and rubbing hard to polish it.

"Tomorrow evening."

"I will make an anise cake," he said dreamily. "Very good." Suddenly he aimed a cunning glance at Istvan and said, "Is it true, sir, that the English are making war on Muslims? They said so at the bazaar."

"No. They do not have the power they had formerly. They are only frightening them."

"The English were true gentlemen. It was an honor to serve with the officers of the queen. If one of them was angry, he might throw a boot at me, but how he paid. Well, and everything was cheaper then; rice costs three times as much since they left. I cannot imagine how such a power could allow itself to be driven from this country. Surely it was a trick. They must have something clever in mind."

"Don't you remember how rice was carried away to Africa, and peasants here died of hunger in their thousands? Do you still miss the English?"

"I lacked for nothing. And today there is not enough rice for everyone. One has, another has not. So it was and will be, whether the English are here or not."

"And which do you prefer now: the Russians or the Americans?" Istvan treated him to a cigarette. The cook did not dare light it in his presence. He tucked it behind his ear and averred with a wink:

"Hungarians. After the English went away the Hungarians took me, and by now I am accustomed to them. One goes away, transfers me to the new one, and I can live. If you have to, sir, please recommend me—"

"You think that I will go away before long?"

"Who can know? For me such an arrival is like birth, and a departure like death. I live because you allow me to live. All depends on the master's generous hand. I remember. I try with all my might."

"For the time being I am not thinking of leaving," the counselor shrugged.

"There are changes in Hungary. They said so on the radio."

"Only at the very top. In the government."

"It begins at the top and ends at the bottom. The stone from the summit draws the avalanche down. The ambassador's driver whispered to me that he heard"—he laid his hand on his chest and bowed his head with an expression of fatuous humility—"that there are going to be big changes. I thought right away—"

"He didn't understand." The counselor laughed dismissively. He moved away so impatiently that the cook, wishing to placate him, said, "I will serve the dinner now."

"Eat with the watchman. I'm going out."

AT NAGAR'S HE FOUND several correspondents; it was like a stock exchange where news was the commodity, where short, shrill Maurice first called out what he had for sale. On the hearth a fire blazed, fed with crumpled teletype tapes and carbon copies. Streaks of bluish cigarette smoke hovered under a lamp. All the chairs were occupied except one on which the spotted Trompette lay snarling, and the Frenchman allowed no one to drive her off it. Misha Kondratiuk was sitting there, and Trojanowski, and the representative of Xinhua, smaller than Nagar, looking like a polite schoolboy in a blue uniform fastened modestly at the neck. Jimmy Bradley sprawled on the sofa, his legs on a pile of waste paper.

"I give you my word that they are attacking without our consent, behind our backs. They did not ask for advice," he said as categorically as if he were under oath. "This is France's doing. They want to repay themselves for Vietnam and save Algeria for the sake of the metropolitan area. The Israelis rushed things a little. They burst in along the old Mosaic route."

"This is not only about the Suez," said Kondratiuk. "If the English are not succeeding in removing Nasser, they want at least to intimidate him, to reduce him to a role as the head of a temporary government that will be in their pockets. They do not like him in the role of a politician who unifies Arabs."

"I tell you, the French have done this to spite us," Bradley insisted, handing his glass to a servant to be filled. "They know that we will be their successors."

"Sit down, Istvan. Well, find yourself a seat—" the hospitable host looked around helplessly. The Chinese correspondent was ready to give up his place, but as if remembering what a prestigious nation he represented, sat stiffly with his untouched glass resting on his lap.

"Don't disturb the dog. She bites," Nagar warned. "She even bares her teeth at me." But Istvan gave the bitch a friendly pat and scratched her behind the ear until she rose, yawning, and jumped down onto the carpet with a gracious wag of her tail.

"Does she have fleas?" Trojanowski asked.

"So many of you come here that I cannot say for sure . . ." Nagar threw up his hands.

"What news?"

"Not many killed, for the Arabs dispersed, while the Israelis took almost two thousand prisoners. There was an exchange of telegrams between the Kremlin and the White House. Neither side wants the conflict to escalate. The Americans are looking out for the Arab oil, and the Russians have trouble enough with Poland and Hungary. The diplomatic maneuvering, however, is backed by force. And they are ready to mediate, to appease. Such mediations enhance their importance," Nagar added quickly. "In the States they are displeased that the French have been proceeding on their own. It is an opportunity to punch them in the nose, to bring Eden to heel, and to refuse to allow Khrushchev to appear as the only defender of the Arabs. The bargaining is coming: do as you like in Hungary, and we will occupy the canal."

"You know nothing of Polish affairs. Be quiet," Trojanowski silenced him, his blue eyes glittering like a bird's. "On the other hand, there will be real trouble with Hungary."

They nodded in agreement, and Misha sighed heavily. "I was there with Tolbukhin," he said. "The Romanians surrendered. The Bulgarians came over to our side, but not the Hungarians. They fought to the end. Budapest fell and they still held the Austrian border without flinching."

"Does that surprise you?" Istvan thrust out his lip. "At that time Szalasi and his supporters had taken over our government. And the impression you made was hardly encouraging. There was no liberation, only subjugation. No doubt you remember."

"You are right," Kondratiuk said after a pause. "In the end we were coming onto enemy territory. There were many Ukrainians with us; they had passed over scorched earth, they had heard what the women said, what your retreat from the Dniester had been like."

"Friends—don't quarrel. These are bygones." Nagar spoke up placatingly. "What should be of interest to us is whether today the leaders of Hungary can still exercise influence over the impulses of the general population."

The Chinese correspondent followed them silently with a cunning look, inwardly repeating—or so it seemed—every opinion expressed by the others.

"Fortunately there is peace in Hungary," Kondratiuk put in. "One wonders: what is the cause of this anti-Soviet frame of mind? Indeed, we Russians have nothing against you, comrade Terey. The Germans also fought against us; they have much more on their consciences, and we make an effort to find common ground with them, to educate them, to win them over, though for many years it was repeated that the only good German is a dead German. In a week we will celebrate together the thirty-ninth anniversary of the revolution. Everything will be amicable and we will drink lavishly to friendship."

Li-Chuan looked at him attentively.

"I know what galls you," Kondratiuk said, winking. "We beat the pants off you. Such a shabby-looking army: ragged dull gray coats, quilted jackets covered with stains, unable to stay in formation, tottering like ducks, but going forward. Humiliating to be defeated by such slovenly scarecrows, eh?"

"We fought well." Istvan turned toward him.

"Very well, even," Kondratiuk admitted. "Only why boast about it? What did you want from us? The Romanians dreamed of a heritage from the Romans—that I still understand—but you? We did not even have a common border."

Terey's expression softened. He understood that the Russian was not mocking.

"After the closing down of the encirclement near Stalingrad, when we took Marshal Paulus . . ."

"Wait!" Nagar broke in. "Now, something for the soul." He raised his hands with his fingers pressed together, like a conductor focusing the attention of his orchestra. "Eat while they are hot."

"That is for you," Trojanowski corrected him. "Words are for the soul."

"Oh! You were poorly brought up, Marek." Their host shook his head sympathetically. "This is too small and too good to be counted as something for the body. This is, in one bite, delight itself. Do you smell the garlic? And the crust light as fluff? Oh, Trojanowski, Trojanowski, you do not know that whole nations are fed only on a word, and they are content, though they do not grow fat—"

"He has silenced you. Sit down: you've been bested." Istvan waved him away. "Well, go on," he said to Kondratiuk.

"We were going along in a snowstorm. Near Stalingrad. Battered tanks streaked with soot, painted with crosses: steel coffins. The dead lying under a dusting of ice crystals, with faces that seemed to be cast in iron. Ammunition boxes and gasoline barrels with bullet holes that the wind whistled through until chills ran down the spine."

"You're right, we should pour some whiskey. Maurice, shame on you; are you out?" Bradley broke in, peering toward the sideboard under the head of the rhinoceros.

"It was a blizzard. We saw a dark line of soldiers walking in rows of four in front of us. They were surely not our men. Different uniforms. Prisoners—they had no weapons. I caught up to them in a jeep; they were Hungarians. An officer approached me, saluted, and asked, 'Are we going in the right direction?' 'And where do you mean to go?' 'To Siberia. When they captured us, they said we were going to Siberia.' I confess that I was dumbfounded; no, it was not funny at all. They impressed me. They were marching in line, listening to their officers. They looked better than the Germans. I pointed out the way to the crossing, for at the Volga there was a checkpoint where prisoners were sorted out."

"Was no one in charge of them?" Bradley was amazed. "Didn't they try to escape?"

"Where to?" Kondratiuk laughed. "The front had moved a hundred and fifty kilometers west. There was no escaping from where they were. Going in a group, they would have been turned back by the first patrol; going one by one, they would have been killed by villagers. Where could they flee without knowing the language, in cold that froze the eyelids together and nipped like pincers? They had lost; they had to go as captives to where they were sentenced. A fine army. Such a shame that they were with Hitler."

"The Soviet army was better when it beat the Germans," Li Chuan remarked.

"They went in en masse," Istvan said dejectedly, "with no consideration for losses."

"We were in a hurry, not only to win, but to return to our country, where we went the day the war ended, because we knew that you"—he turned to Bradley—"would play your game. You would want to establish yourselves in Europe." Leaning on his elbow, Kondratiuk ran his hand through his hair until it bristled. "But when I think of the war, often it seems to me that the women won it—our mothers, wives, and sisters. They carried on the fight, without praise, through years together. And there is no worthy monument for them."

"A woman's mission is to give birth," Li Chuan said serenely. "It is a great happiness to sacrifice one's life for one's fatherland. If there is victory for the people, communism attaches no significance to the losses."

"If one has little, there is little for him to lose." Bradley frowned. "It's easy to die then. Our people are not so eager for death. They only risk their lives if they are repaid a hundred times over. Like racing drivers or acrobats—those, for example, who walk tightropes over Niagara. If they succeed, there is money and fame. Even if not, the family will get so much that papa will be remembered as Santa Claus."

"But you pushed into Korea and Siam, and you have made South Vietnam your buffer zone." The Frenchman in Nagar was aroused. "You were everywhere."

"We are a true democracy. If you cannot attend to everything yourself, give it to someone who has the desire, and sufficient strength; true, Misha?" Bradley still lay stretched out on the sofa. "It is not people who decide these things, but technology: atoms, rockets . . ."

"People will always be the most valuable," said the Chinese journalist. "It is they who make the bombs and the rockets."

"I didn't like Germans, though they have many fine qualities," Trojanowski recalled.

"And who likes you?" Nagar asked sarcastically. "Arrogant, obstreperous, not inclined to keep promises. Messy . . ."

"Women like Polish men," Misha said. "They know how to get around the ladies—puffed up like turkeys. A Pole gazes into the eyes, he sings his own praises, he bends over the little hands and before the girl can look around she has him under the covers. To learn that from them—to learn—"

"It's an insane world," Terey said gloomily. "You're all good fellows; each of you experienced the war in his own way. Each took his losses. Nagar's family were all cremated at Auschwitz. Jimmy's brother was shot at Dunkirk, where he walked into the sea. Li Chuan fought against the Japanese and was wounded twice, then was sent as a volunteer in a new war between the Americans and Korea. There is no need even to talk about the Russians; Kondratiuk was squeezed into a trench near Lake Balaton when his division was trying to stop the Panzer Armies. The Germans were marching to the relief of Budapest. The Russians kept them back, but at what a price. Today tanks are plowing desert sand again, people are dying, and the stench of it is in the air. And it's made light of, because that's the style of the crafty old guard of journalism, which cannot be astonished or terrified by anything."

When they scattered to their cars after emptying another bottle of Nagar's whiskey, Trojanowski, a little the worse for the evening's drinking, stopped Terey and pressed his hand, whispering, "There are ordinary-looking boxes on the streets of Warsaw, and passersby are throwing in money for medicine and food for Budapest. People cannot be sure exactly what it is about, but they feel intuitively that it is a great issue, a matter of life and death."

"Thank you." Terey patted him hard. "I think all the world understands."

"Not all. Not all." The Pole shook his head. "There are divergent interests."

The other cars moved away. They stood in darkness illuminated by a row of lamps half-screened by leafy trees.

"Do you think we will come out intact?"

"And do you think they will crush you as an example, a warning to others? Not in these times, my dear friend!" Trojanowski's hand cut the air. "Khrushchev's dealings with Poland confirmed that it is possible to reach an agreement on anything."

"We have only ourselves to rely on."

"You have, after all, enlightened people as your leaders. Scholars, writers."

"It is those who never saw the world beyond Stalin who cry loudest for freedom today. Already they are pushing to the head of the parade."

"You do not believe that people change?"

"I believe it, I believe it," he said bitterly, "especially those who want to maintain their positions. You know that when all is said and done, there cannot be a neutral Hungary. To jump from the socialist alliance is to fall at once under the protection of America, which will make Hungary a beachhead. It is important to see that clearly."

"Many think as you do. They will hold the crazy ones in check. You will see; everything will arrange itself. You are not alone," Trojanowski said reassuringly. "In Warsaw the workers are donating blood for your wounded. If anyone would take mine here, I would as well—" he pushed out his left hand and made a fist.

Istvan felt a cool breeze on his face: his jaw set. This Pole was not speaking of brotherhood, but he was offering blood. Blood counted.

The warm Indian night was singing with a whisper of wings, with the rustle of moths lured by the blazing headlights of the Austin. Istvan Terey wandered in that night, an atom of Hungary lost on the Asian continent.

The excited voice on the radio the next morning announced that the English air force had bombarded Cairo, Port Said, and Alexandria. A French warship had sunk an Egyptian frigate, and cannon fire over the water had shattered the boats with the rescued sailors. Smoke hung over the bombed cities; there was extensive damage, and the attacks had claimed many victims, chiefly among the poorest populations. Fleeing crowds had been shot by aircraft strafing the area. The international situation had undergone a sudden change for the worse—the speaker's voice was dark with foreboding—and the peace of the world was hanging in the balance. It was as if Budapest had been forgotten. There are no new developments in Hungary, Istvan thought with relief.

Thank God, he breathed, we may be misguided when we look for connections between the uprising and the raid on the Suez.

THE FIERY RED of the railing cut across the broad, grassy field that was the airport. In the distance the setting sun was yellow as if it were cooling; feathery palms looked like paper cutouts against it. Istvan sat at a small table to which a warm breeze brought the smells of dry meadows, cooling concrete, gasoline, and lubricants. Little moths fluttered up from the grass in a cloud, swirled for a moment in the diffuse yellow light, then dissolved into the sky. Terey crumpled a straw in his fingers and sipped a Coca-Cola. Behind him the big hangar was disconcertingly quiet. Two women in red sat hunched beside their bundles—they were certainly not passengers, for their feet were bare and callused and stained violet by dried clay. Probably they had come to visit relatives who worked at the airport, or perhaps only to stare with dreamy eyes at the departing planes.

The song of the cicadas had died away; it would return after a while with its monotonous insistence, which was amplified by the eaves of the aluminum roof. A great calm filled the wide space around him. With no announcement from the megaphone an airplane wafted unnoticed onto the grassy plain, then roared as it wheeled along the concrete runway. Moths rose from the grass in a sudden swarm like gray smoke and tried to flee, but swarmed back, sucked into the rotating propeller.

Istvan waited. This was not the plane from Agra, though that plane was already a quarter of an hour past due. No one in the office could explain the cause.

A group of passengers approached, led by a stewardess who looked strangely awkward in a European uniform. He took a few steps toward the gate; it did not occur to him that he might meet someone he knew. From the interior of the airplane, as if in anger, someone was throwing out suitcases and linen bags done up with straps.

"Hallo! Mr. Terey!" called a portly, dignified man, waving a parasol. Istvan recognized Dr. Kapur.

"Where is that plane from?"

"From Bombay." The dark face had a bronze sheen in the sunset; the distended cheeks were overgrown with wisps of black hair. "But I am returning from the vicinity of Cairo. There are fires; the airport is not receiving flights. Haifa also refused; they ordered us to turn away because there was shooting. Some boats on the sea even opened fire on us—I saw only flashes below us and white points of light moving upward so slowly that we managed to escape." He gesticulated vigorously. "Only Basra—from there to Karachi and Bombay . . . I saw war. I saw real war."

"From a distance, fortunately."

"No, very close. In Karachi a few Jewish shops had been damaged. The Muslims are enraged. They may well raise the cry for holy war. Because of the attack by France and England, Nasser has suddenly gained supporters. He has taken on new stature. Oh, they are bringing my things. The rascals let the trunks crush them." He ran and tugged at a stack of linen bags, which threatened to collapse. "Enjoy the peace of evening. Who knows whether it will be for the last time?"

The megaphone boomed, announcing the plane from Agra.

He saw Margit from a distance. She walked erect in a flame of rust-colored hair. A little boy in wrinkled white preceded her. The rest of the travelers were stopped to allow a group of people with garlands in their hands to greet him. They bowed, sinking at his feet, and he, obviously bored, allowed them to place the garlands around his neck. Immediately he whisked them onto the arm of a servant, which was bent like a hook.

"Please wait." A guard blocked Terey's way while letting through a big Cadillac that sped across the landing field, bouncing on the grass.

"It seems there is a ban on entry to the airport," the counselor said, surprised. "The gate is closed."

"He has the golden keys that open all gates." The guard seemed to be counting on his fingers. "That is the Nizam of Hyderabad. It was he who caused the delay."

"I know, I just found out, who is accompanying you." He kissed Margit on the lips. "I wanted to give him a piece of my mind. He has cars like that and he can't be on time?"

"He was napping and no one dared wake him. His secretary said, 'Fly when you must, but have another plane ready for my master.' And because there was no other, we waited. Anyway, he is a nice little fellow. He was constantly turning to me and sending fruit by way of the servant."

"And you are enchanted."

"Yes"—her eyes brightened—"because I see you."

He handed over the baggage checks. The attendants took them and a moment later dragged the suitcases to the car. Istvan took Margit's hand and looked at the sky; it was drooping under its burden of purple. The intoxicating lavishness of violent tints drifting above them also moved the Nizam; he stopped the Cadillac and leaned out without alighting. Two doors were opened wide and held in place by servants in uniforms fit for field marshals.

Istvan felt the girl's fingers, which he was holding tenderly, entwine themselves tightly with his. Reflected purple light fell on her face, tingeing with lilac lips parted in delight.

"Look. Lose yourself in the madness of the sky," he whispered. "Those fires mean wind tomorrow, strong, hot wind. Do you know what is happening in Cairo? There are glows in the sky there as well, but it is man's doing. Look there, Margit. The sky seems to sing with flame."

She turned toward him. The sky was nothing to her. He saw an enormous devotion in her eyes.

"Listen: if war breaks out . . . would you have to go back? Or perhaps you all would be interned here," she said as if thinking out loud. "India will be on our side. Then you would stay with me."

Chapter XI

If Margit had not wanted to go to the reception—after all, she had no compelling reason to go—she would have resisted their urgings and stayed with me, Istvan argued to himself as he walked out of his house alone. But since she has come to Delhi to stay, and the dean invited her, it's only fitting that she go and mingle with the professors. In the evening I will have her all to myself. How long can a party like that last? She cannot be the first to rush out or they would say straightaway that she was shunning them. Well—an hour and a half. Two at the most.

Perhaps I could drop in on Nagar. Surely he is with the Russians; he was invited. That's all right. I'll wait. I like the barking of the teletype. I'll look over the latest communiqués. I may just find out something. Nagar will tell me how it was at the Soviet embassy, because the correspondents will also be pressing the Russians for information about what is happening in Hungary.

The sixth of November; the thirty-ninth anniversary of the revolution. A coolish evening, with air like the taste of light wine when it leaves a sour bite of fermentation on the tongue. Wide lawns, leaf-sprinkled basins with sluggish fountains, cloying the eye with the melancholy of autumn. A yellowish-green sky with morbid veins of red. Now and then the falling of a heavy drop of dew. The music of the insects, now growing faint. Sometimes from far away, like a paltry imitation of it, the brief, importunate jingle of bicycle bells and the bleating of rickshaws with rattling motors. He walked along the edge of the road. He had left the car at home; he had nowhere to hurry to.

The day before yesterday the party at the ambassador's residence had fallen flat. Bajcsy had unexpectedly arranged for the showing of a film about the experimental cultivation of rice in the floodplain of the Danube. This was a stratagem to preserve appearances. Such information from their country had a calming overtone, so he wanted to draw in members of the corps and a few guests and pretend that all was well, since they were devoting their attention to agrarian matters. He would take the occasion to listen to opinions, to scent out what the Western diplomatic missions were expecting from Nagy's new government. "The gathering took place in a pleasant atmosphere"; that ought to be the tenor of the report for the Ministry of Foreign Affairs.

Damn that party! Istvan winced. A thin line appeared at each end of his lips: the traces of a malicious smile. The ambassador, bickering with his wife, had shifted from one foot to the other; they had waited on the stairs; and no guests had arrived. On the tables stood bottles of Coca-Cola and mineral water, glasses filled with plum vodka and wine, and trays of hors d'oeuvres. The park was illuminated with strings of colored bulbs. There were long rows of empty garden chairs; a white stream of light beat on the screen, which looked like a partly opened shroud. The six people who had cared to come chatted in whispers as if they were in a funeral home.

A terrible day! The showing seemed a mockery. The guests trailed about like specters. From six in the morning cannon had been rumbling around Budapest. Istvan saw red fragments from distant firings swaying in clouds of November fog. Time and again the artillery boomed. The shattering of windowpanes on the sidewalk made a noise like high-pitched sobbing. Wet rust-colored leaves lay scattered in the park. There was an appeal from writers and a call from the Hungarian Red Cross to save the capital.

"If you would take a glass of fruit brandy, sir," Ferenc urged, tilting his head. "It is a cool evening . . ." and a few timid guests took what he held out to them with his obliging air. Trojanowski was there, and the cultural attaché. The Poles did not disappoint them. The Yugoslavians came. So did the president of the Hungarian-Indian Friendship Society, a tall, wrinkled man with a brown cashmere shawl thrown over his head and arms in the manner of poor village women, and a representative of the ministry—a petty official, a person of no importance.

The French and English did not come. They were preoccupied with the Suez and had no interest in parties. The struggles for the canal continued. The Americans were boycotting the embassy because Kádár had called in the Russians. Beginning this morning, TASS's bulletins had referred to the developments in Budapest as counterrevolution. If the Hungarian ambassador arranged the showing of a trivial film, it amounted to an endorsement of the Soviet intervention. The Russians and the Chinese did not come, for they did not know if the showing were a cover for something—a demonstration, perhaps. In a few days it would be known who the staff at the embassy were and which side they were on; better to wait, Istvan thought, smiling bitterly. How many times during the last week had the ambassador called the caretaker in and asked insistently if invitations to a reception at the Russian embassy had arrived? But the large envelopes with gold engraving were not to be seen. "Perhaps they have forgotten," Ferenc said consolingly, though they both knew that such a lapse of memory would be a pretext.

Counterrevolution. The steep, narrow streets of Buda overrun with thundering tanks. They didn't want to see us, he nodded to himself. They didn't want our mournful faces marring the holiday. As yet they have no instructions as to how to conduct themselves toward us. Without guidelines from the ministry, even friendship is temporarily suspended.

Nagy had gone mad. He had renounced the Warsaw Pact and declared neutrality. The Russians know very well what that neutrality means. All the Western publications are triumphantly flaunting pictures of murdered communists. Cardinal Mindszenty openly called on the nation to fight. Neutrality . . . neutrality in relation to what? To socialism? To capitalism? With force of arms, with this revolution, to win—neutrality? A sword in the hand of a madman. The unstable "military balance" at this moment does not favor either side. The Russians are saying clearly: Whoever is not with us is against us. The power has slipped from Nagy's hands. The wave has carried him away; the street has decided. And on the street the blind force of an armed crowd has exploded with festering hate and time-hardened resentment. That confounded Major Stowne, when I met him, tucked his riding whip under his arm and gripped my hand. "Congratulations!" he said. "At last you have decided to break out of the Red bag that was thrown over your heads."

If that is what he thinks, and he has little to do with politics, what must be the Russians' view? Why should they trust us? Why did Kádár disappear with four ministers on the eve of the attack? The West was saying, "Broken in prison, the man lost his nerve, dropped out of the game." He absconded from Budapest. He is beyond the encircling Soviet armies now, in Szolnok. He is leveling accusations at Nagy. He is devising a new government. No doubt he is just beginning to fight—for the highest stake, for Hungary? Or for himself? To which side is he loyal? Time will tell.

In spite of himself he walked faster. Beyond him was an arch of heavy stone—the Arch of Triumph, a symbol of liberation, of the freedom for which his people, too, were striving. Angular knees rose high in parade step, gleaming from under plaid kilts. The last division of Scots marched away to the screech of bagpipes. His glance rapidly swept the wide vista of the avenue leading to the distant parliament building, its dark mass yellowed by the afterglow from the blue vault of the sky. Sacred cattle, their humps red with cinnabar, grazed on lawns; their brass bells started up their familiar rattle when the animals moved.

A wide peace, a drowsiness like that of a sleeping village, emanated from the most imposing artery of the city. Far away, like low stars, the lights of speeding automobiles were winking. Their glare sparkled on a vitreous piece of coral stuck on a cow's horn by a devout hand. Istvan thought with a shudder: I am walking here, while my boys . . . At once, as if he had been carried home by magic, he saw eight-year-old Geza, saw the child push his head out above the sill of a broken window and watch with delight as innumerable orange and green beads cut through the sky over the park; they were firing machine guns with luminous ammunition.

"Move away," he said in an undertone, as if his son could hear him. Dazed, he looked around the sky as it darkened above the enormous trees, looked at the long rows of glowing street lights. He could have sworn that a moment before he had been in Budapest. His head was still reeling. He paused, breathless, like one who has been pushed from a great height and still hears a ringing in his ears.

Two women with children bundled up passed by. He heard the jingle of bracelets and anklets and the soft singsong voices. They came out of the dusk, their red saris gleaming, and dissolved into the darkness under the trees.

He raised his head toward the sky, which was very remote. Only a few stars blinked unsteadily there. From the depths of his heart he pleaded, "Spare them for me. Hide them. Shield them. I so rarely beg You for anything." The stars trembled lightly and blurred as a tear dimmed his vision.

He wanted, after all, to be free. His conscience seemed to remind him of a half-formed wish: if it were not for Ilona, you could . . . You said, I also have a right to be happy. It came to him with a shock: not at such a price.

Desperately he sought the proofs that he was not the worst of men, worthy only to be condemned and trampled underfoot. Like change in his pocket he carried a handful of merits, of constructive actions, but already he felt the enormity of his guilt. You had no time for me, a voice accused him. You demand that I concern Myself with you . . .

In front of him stood the dark building, like a gigantic tub reeking of tar, in which Krishan had been killed. He had not yet come here to remonstrate with the police about the woman they had arrested. And Mihaly had begged him so earnestly, had looked so trustingly into his eyes. Tomorrow, he vowed. Tomorrow. First thing in the morning.

Though it was not late, the streets were empty. The bracing chill had swept the Hindus off them. Only a seller of peanuts napped, crouching over his hot stove with his head covered by a paper bag with slits. Ashes reddened by a gust of air glimmered on his extended hand.

"Sahib," he whined, "sahib, fresh, very tasty monkey nuts."

Istvan bought as if fulfilling the mandate of the goodness he hoped to attain. The little pouch made from fronds warmed his fingers.

If my statement is not enough, I will ask Chandra for help. Poor Durga. Or perhaps it is better that they locked her up; he remembered the avaricious eyes of her caretaker and her cohorts, whose faces were hidden in the shadows. They promised gowns and trinkets and pushed girls toward ruin. She had lost the man she loved and her body had become useless, a vexing burden. She could dispense with it. She had lost Krishan; she had lost the world. With a leap into the fire that had absorbed the visible form of her beloved, she had made her choice: she had died.

Automobiles hurtled past. In the greenish glow of the streetlights he spied red jackets and gold braid: the officers of the president's guard. Perhaps Khaterpalia himself had sped past him. Behind him came a huge black limousine with a small, hunched white figure; yes, it was Nehru, with his beautiful, gloomy daughter. He glanced at his watch. Ten after eight. The grand reception at the Russian embassy was just beginning.

Like a moth lured by a light he made his way toward the park, which was ablaze with the glow of headlights. The large building with its pillared front resembled an ancient temple. Two policemen in white gloves were urging the drivers of the arriving cars to keep them moving. The glow of hanging bulbs dusted the layered branches of trees whose lower trunks glittered with reflected light. Beds of salvia blazed scarlet. From a distance the tinkle of lively music could be heard, and the swelling din of guests eating and drinking.

Istvan stopped in the dusk. A group of onlookers covered with sheets of linen sat on the sidewalk, quivering in the chilly air, drinking in the unusual spectacle. Cars flowed in through the gate, bearing dignitaries over the crunching gravel toward the carpeted staircase. Other people alighted from taxis and walked with dignified steps, splashed with glare from the headlights of automobiles almost in gridlock. Women in saris threaded through with gold seemed to sail on streams of fragrance, sweet aromas of perfume and flowers. On their shoulders some wore fur stoles drooping low so as to reveal necks framed by gold collars sparkling with jewels.

On the grassy island opposite the gate a small, compact group of men in white were rhythmically shouting a slogan. No one hampered them. Istvan thought they were partisans of a new political order demonstrating in support of a revolution. There were about twenty Hindus. All at once he understood their chant and felt a pain so acute that it frightened him.

"Hands off Hungary! Hands off Hungary!"

An embassy official moved toward the wide-open gate—a tall, powerfully built man with a mane of blond hair. His navy blue suit was rather too large; his trousers fell in wrinkles onto his yellowish shoes. He exchanged a few words with the police, who called an officer over and pointed to the group of demonstrators. The officer threw up his hands in a gesture of powerlessness. The group's shouts grew louder; guests alighting from their cars paused to listen before moving on quickly to the radiantly lit park with its holiday decor. They don't want to spoil the festivities, he thought, and clenched his fist. What do they care about Budapest?

The embassy official returned with three Hindus. They carried, as if it were an unknown weapon, a black bullhorn with coils of cable, which they installed by the gate so that the device faced the dark street. A song spurted at high volume from the megaphone, surging with chords sung by choirs at full voice. The demonstrators opened their mouths, but their voices were lost. They stood for a moment more, conferring with each other, huddling together. At last they began to disperse listlessly, scattering into the dusk along the avenue.

He walked behind them. He wanted to know who they were and where they had come from. When he caught up with them and asked, they gathered around him in a friendly way, pressed his hand with cold fingers and exclaimed one after another:

"We are from the university!"

"Today we shouted catcalls at Nehru himself when he began saying that the attack on Hungary was justified."

"He forgot why the English put him in jail." Someone breathed the odor of spicy food and cheap cigarettes into Istvan's face.

"Equivocator!"

"Defeatist!"

A slender boy hung on Istvan's arm, entwining his fingers around his palm like a woman. Long, matted, frizzy locks of his hair brushed Istvan's cheek as he whispered close to his ear, "Krishna Menon said before the United Nations that he could not approve the actions of the foreign armies, and called on the Russians to leave Hungary."

"Nehru said the same thing only a few days ago," declared another student with an angry, accusing air. "Nehru lost his nerve."

"It is true that we are not a military power, but our strength is real. We must be the conscience of humanity."

"How did Nehru explain this?" Terey asked. "He had to give you an answer, after all."

"He said that the issue was complicated, that it was over our heads. That we are led by the impulses of our hearts and not by political acumen . . . That we should study, and leave politics to those older than ourselves," they said, interrupting each other, full of indignation. Their sandals clattered on the damp asphalt; they walked briskly to keep warm in the chilly twilight.

"We had to attack him because he changed his opinion as if it were a banner. Then he admitted that he had only gotten the full reports today, and he said it was an act of courage for him to alter his assessment of the situation now that he knows a great deal more; that he has learned better than to rush to judgment about matters concerning which he has not thought deeply."

"Then we began to whistle."

"He called us a band of fools."

"He is burned out."

"He is afraid of the Russians and the Chinese."

"He is in the pocket of the Russians," they sniffed with sudden malice. "He has sold out for the steel mills they are building for us."

"We agreed among ourselves that we would go and protest at the embassy. They wanted to give us five rupees each to go away."

"And that fellow who wanted to pay us more to protest?"

"But what a beautiful car he had . . ."

"An American."

"Not one of us took a rupee from him, either. We are independent."

"We are young. We can afford to defend the truth for its own sake."

They accompanied him to Nagar's villa. They made an appointment to visit him at the embassy the next day, and asked for informational brochures. They wanted to sign on with the Hungarian-Indian Friendship Society. The boy who had held him so tenderly by the arm whispered, "And I would like to get a few Hungarian stamps, for I have a collection . . ."

Istvan was touched. Their impulses were so childlike, but they were sincere and full of zeal. "We are for socialism," they assured him, seizing his hand in the darkness. "But violence is contemptible."

He had hardly shut the gate when Trompette, bored with solitude, bounded out with a joyful bark. She tried to climb onto his chest and lick his face.

"Stop wiping your muddy paws on me." He held her affectionately by the back of her neck, though she wriggled with delight in his presence and her pink tongue, like a slice of ham, quivered with readiness to kiss him in canine fashion.

"Mr. Nagar is not here." The young Indian stepped out of the office with movements like a woman's. With a gentle gesture he invited the counselor to come in for a rest if he liked.

"What is happening in Budapest?"

"The situation is under control."

"That's what I heard a week ago."

"There is a new government. In the course of six hours the streets were cleared. Tanks demolished the barricades."

"And what of the previous government?"

"They protested. They appealed to the conscience of Europe. But before it was aroused"—he spoke with a mocking, melancholy air—"the tanks rolled through to the parliament and the premier sought asylum in the Yugoslavian embassy."

"And Mindszenty?" Terey saw that the secretary did not even know the name. "Well, the cardinal. The one who was let out of prison."

"You have strange names, hard to pronounce or remember. He has taken refuge with the Americans. In Budapest there is a curfew. Meetings are prohibited. The military is disarmed." He spread his hands in a sympathetic gesture. "After the Russian forces were called in, the West gave no help. Even diplomatic protests were very measured. The press has already turned its attention away from Hungary, Mr. Terey. It is not important to them," he said emphatically.

"And what is important?"

"Suez. Incoming bulletins say the march of French and English units has been halted. Israel as well is prepared to withdraw its troops. They have gone lax; they have lost the momentum for battle. Khrushchev has won." The Hindu seemed to pause and think, to remind himself of what he had heard. "They calculated that he would be drawn into an altercation in Hungary. In the meantime, he delivered one blow with a fist, then at once supported Egypt. He threatened to send weapons and volunteers, and that would have meant—war, a third world war. So what could the Americans do? Support the Arabs, for otherwise the Russians would have garnered all their sympathy. The French and English themselves were on the battlefield. The cat jumped at the mouse and found itself nose to nose with the watchdog, so it looked around to see which tree to run up in order to feel safe."

His long eyelashes fluttered. He bustled around the hall preparing a drink for the counselor. Istvan thought of a woman who, in her husband's absence, entertains a visitor and, finding herself at a loss, repeats opinions she has heard, stretching her mental horizons and wounding and intimidating without knowing what she has said.

Istvan sank between the cushions of the chair, gazing despondently at two slivers of wood in the fireplace that were bristling with little combs of flame. Suddenly everything became oppressive to him: the black head of the rhinoceros that Nagar had not shot, only bought. The room tricked out with hunting imagery for show. The purebred setter not trained for hunting. The French cuisine to efface the memory of years of hunger. The masks that hid the lonely, hounded man longing for peace and a comfortable life, a man who had been born on the cusp of three empires: the kaiser's in Germany, the emperor's in Austria, and the czar's in Russia. A man who had been cut off from his native country, the religion of his childhood, and the memory of his murdered family, and for those losses had gained so little in exchange.

Perhaps even his homosexuality was a façade, an indulgence that eased him into a circle of refined snobs, of artists full of eccentricity and ennui. What do I hope to find here? he wondered, suddenly disconcerted. No; facts are facts; only commentary can change them to half-truths, quarter-truths, stuff them with sweet lies. I came here for bulletins, nothing more. Nagar gets them sooner than anyone else. And he likes me, so he does not withhold what for several hours is exclusively his property. Tomorrow I will hear the same facts on New Delhi radio; I will read them in the papers. They will grow old terribly quickly. Their significance will last for a little while, and in that hour—the hour when they astonish and dazzle us with the Hungarians' extraordinary devotion to their cause—they will also leave us shocked by the forces that threatened them. The next day, after we have grown used to them, they simply *are*—they only add to the sum of our ineffective knowledge of life, of what is behind us. Of the past.

There is no way to overwhelm the opposing forces. A nation of twelve million, and it is only a chip in a game. Human life, the highest good, ten lives, a hundred thousand, have no significance . . . What can be done? How to help one's own? Whose side to be on?

No. He shook his head as if answering a question put to him suddenly by someone else. I will not shoot at the Russians. They mobilized me then. I was in uniform. The gun barrel showed who the opponent was. I had no choice. It became clear that there was no compass unless you looked into your conscience, unless you acknowledged other people's right to food and freedom. We wanted, after all, to save our country. And we returned from the war mutilated, written into the register of enemies, alongside those humanity judged to be criminals. They made us into . . . no. One must have the courage to say: we became, having paid with enormous sacrifices, with the ruin of our country, their partners.

Now, after this ill-fated uprising, what will become of us? The facts say that we rose up against those who had to subdue us in order to liberate us. And we had our chance in our hands. Do we still have it? Who has the nerve to speak of friendship again over freshly spilled blood? Friendship—Rakosi and Gerő were always declaiming about it, and they built prisons, they sowed hate. Who will stand before the nation after what has passed and say, "Trust me, I am a communist?"

Kádár will form a government? And what sort of person is he? On what grounds did he call in Soviet tanks against Hungarians, he, who is Hungarian himself? What was he trying to save? Today he has everyone against him except for a handful who think as he does—think that they will rescue Hungary, or what remains of it after the madness and slaughter. Can the nation believe him now that cannons have pled his case? The Russians cannot trust him, for he came out of prison. He was tortured. He had his brush with death. He had been falsely accused. He came out of that prison his comrades had built. He came out alive, but was his faith in socialism intact? Has he outlived the memory of the injustice he suffered? Perhaps he called in the Russians so as to have the opportunity to even accounts with his old tormentors at last. Now he will take revenge . . . Does he have within himself the greatness not to aggravate the situation, not to condemn but to unite, to support, to rebuild what has not been destroyed? How can the Russians trust him, since his country let him out of his cell? He is, above all, a Hungarian.

Istvan rested his head on his hands and gazed at the winking, dancing flames. The burnt wood burst and a handful of sparks shot into the dusky funnel of the chimney. The dog exhaled heavily, as if she shared his anguish.

If Kádár brought about the recent coup in order to seize power and square personal accounts, in a hundred years a crowd will drag his bones from the burial ground and throw them into the Danube. If he truly wishes to rescue Hungary, taking on himself the terrible burden of responsibility—of being an object of suspicion and hatred—the nation will not only pardon him but will number him among its heroes, whose names generations to come will utter with gratitude and adoration. The next few years will make it clear. Time wounds; time heals.

There were many crises in the government. He was left alone on the field—he and the Russians, who were watching him closely. Is it possible to know what he really wants?

One thing is certain: the third world war will not start because of us.

The Hindu appeared in the doorway. Tilting his frizzled head, he announced, "I have the latest information. In spite of the occupation of the Austrian border by the Soviet armies, around two hundred thousand have left Hungary, according to provisional estimates. The United States has convened a special commission that will place them in camps and expedite emigration from Europe."

"Well, I have my answer." Terey's knuckles whitened. "The exodus is beginning. Kádár lost. We all lost."

He stared at the winking flames that lent a red glow to the cavern of the fireplace. He seemed to see, from a great distance, Budapest ablaze. He stared until it hurt, until a dull feeling of strain came over him. At last he shook off these painful imaginings and said under his breath, "No. I don't want this."

The dog turned her spotted head toward him, awaiting commands. He had forgotten the Hindu, who stood leaning on the door frame.

"I won't wait any longer. I'll call from home. Goodbye."

"Mr. Nagar will be inconsolable if I let you go." The young man gave him a limp, narrow hand.

Fear tore at Istvan. He lifted the curls of tape from the floor. The information that had been milled through the telegraph concerned—already!—other countries. No sooner had the cannons gone quiet in Budapest than the world, it seemed, had lost interest in Hungary. The uprising had fallen into an abyss of silence. The eruptions of passion, the battles, the blood, the hasty tamping down of dirt on fresh graves, were slowly dissolving into memory.

He was in no mood to meet Nagar, with his irritating sprightliness—his jaunty exhilaration, like that of a surgeon who exclaims, "What a fine tumor, a beautiful growth!" Or a painter who is arrested by the shriveled face of a beggar and his varicolored rags in a stream of tropical light, and finds the lines and the juxtaposition of colors worthy of perpetuation.

He did not even notice when he found himself in front of the brightly lit garden of the Soviet embassy again. The party was ending; the guests had begun to stream away. A megaphone interrupted the music and called up automobiles that docilely, with a crunching of gravel, rolled toward the stairs. This was not the official closing, for the ambassador had not said his goodbyes to those who were departing and the music was still playing in the pavilion in the park. A few onlookers sat here and there, looking sleepily at the greenish fires of jewels, at gold chains like glittering serpents, and at the odd dress of European diplomats.

He stood on the opposite side of the street under a spreading tree, in a chilly deep twilight like frozen ink.

The cars moved out, cutting the darkness with their beams. For a split second they uncovered a little cluster of Hindus in the darkness . . . policemen's white gloves . . . tree trunks. He blinked warily, anticipating the glare before it washed over him. He was standing still, blinded, when he felt cool fingers above his elbow and heard a familiar voice.

"I counted on meeting you here. But no one came from your embassy. A groundless demonstration. Since it already happened . . ."

"How did you spot me?"

Attorney Chandra smelled of Yardley. The Asian stamp of the man was camouflaged by his dinner jacket.

"There was no trick. I wanted to see you and you appeared to me in the glow of a headlight as if you were on stage. Are you waiting for someone? Can we walk around? I drank a little. They have good vodka. But the cold penetrates when one is standing still."

"Let's walk. I don't know myself what brought me here," Terey said candidly.

"I did." The lawyer rubbed his hands together. "I thought of you all the time."

They walked in the darkness, rather hearing than seeing each other. At long intervals they passed through lamplight that sprayed through overgrown branches. Then Terey could see the Hindu's set lips and the gleam of his smooth, glossy hair.

"What is your connection to Khaterpalia's wife, counselor?"

"There is none. Well, I know her," Istvan answered, surprised.

"Is none—and was none? There is a difference."

"I know her husband from the club. We are friends. I have seen them, as you know, from time to time."

"She hates you," Chandra said in a tone of absolute certainty. "Something must have happened. Think. Search your memory."

"No. They are both friendly to me."

"This morning I had an appointment with your ambassador. You were right: he is a sensible man, he knows something about business, and we will surely arrive at an understanding. She was there before me."

"Madam Khaterpalia?"

"They were concluding a conversation. My presence did not hamper her; she considers me a partner of her husband's. He has confided in me on difficult matters, and she knows that I manage to conceal them in the depths of my mind as in a well. Are you not curious as to what they were talking about?"

"Curious? Yes—" he stopped and turned toward Chandra. They were wading through the darkness, through the bitter smell of withering leaves.

"Evidently she was warning the ambassador that you want to be on the other side, that you would not return to Hungary. Is that true? Do not be afraid to tell me. Only I can help you."

"I?" Istvan chuckled harshly, indignantly. "Rubbish! You must have misheard."

"So I thought. Pity. You would have managed it. She said something about your plans to marry, your intimacy with the English."

"Did she mention a name?"

"Well, but this has struck a nerve!" It seemed to Istvan that the attorney's lips were half parted in a soundless, mocking smile. "In my presence, only Major Stowne's . . ."

Istvan breathed easily. His jaws relaxed.

"That means nothing. A retiree. Of course I know him."

"He was an officer of the Intelligence Service. Such service never ends; it is almost a calling," Chandra remarked discreetly.

"I didn't know. Stowne is a man of few words, though he is fond of drinking."

"One must not trust appearances," the lawyer admonished him

gently. "If we walk confidently, it is because we do not know what traps are hidden around us."

"Did she say anything about—" Terey began, then abruptly went silent. No! Chandra could not know about Margit.

"Well, speak up."

Istvan moved easily like someone who wants to stretch his legs after a day's work, to fill his lungs with cool evening air. With his steps he measured the silence that was lengthening, deepening between them. Chandra waited, then ventured as if to encourage him, "I do not know what she had said before my arrival, but you have an enemy in her. A dangerous one. She is not a docile Hindu. English blood . . . She is calculating. Well, will you tell me? No?"

Twelve. Thirteen. Fourteen, he counted. Automobiles filled with party guests still in high spirits flew past them. Bright light washed over lawns wet with dew.

"Madam Khaterpalia ought not to be leaving home. She is expecting a little newcomer," Chandra continued. "But perhaps it is more important to her to do someone harm. How have you offended her?"

Istvan shrugged. He wanted to forget the incident on her wedding night. He had pushed it aside; he had thought little of it for so long that it seemed insignificant to him, but it remained, like a festering splinter.

"I told you about the miraculous rescue of the dead brother of our mutual friend, the rajah. Surely you heard that the matter was successfully concluded. For all parties, the deceased as well. He lived for a few months a life that he had not known, which the gods had not given and will not give him. Pity you did not hear the negotiations. The father-in-law and the man's own brother demanded my assurances that he would never return, for he was even ready to go out to his place of seclusion. Do you understand what their idea of assurance was—what could ease their minds once and for all? Delightful bargaining—" he laughed quietly. "And all for the good of the yet unborn child. How can one not believe in predestination? It will come into the world burdened with guilt, for Grace heard all that passed without a word of protest. She loves that little one. She prefers that it not be forced to share its wealth with anybody."

"And you talk about this with complete freedom?" Istvan bridled. "You did this for them?"

"Impossible cases are my specialty. I did it, and I was remunerated. The rajah and rani, I must say, knew what they wanted; the honorarium they paid left them fully conscious that they were requiring me to violate the laws of God and, what is more difficult, the laws of man. Your holy book speaks of Cain. Nothing is new! Properly speaking, does humanity know any other kind of homicide? People ought to be brothers, but dress them differently, give them a stick with a varicolored rag on it, and they are ready to murder each other.

"What is happening in your country? Before they overran you with tanks, Hungarians were disemboweling Hungarians who had been hung by their feet from streetlights. What do you call it? A just verdict," he sneered, "which makes a man fighting for freedom an executioner. If you were there, I wonder where you would find yourself: among those trampled on the pavement, or among those they hung because somebody didn't fancy their faces or the identity card with the star? And what right do you have to judge and condemn me?"

He spoke with an ominous mildness, but Istvan felt that he was incensed. "Is it because I am frank with you and your friends are not, although they are a close-knit family and make up a most hospitable circle: the rajah, his father-in-law, and the charming rani Grace, full of expectation and absorbed in the fruit of her womb? You had best try to remember how you got off on the wrong foot with her. Then I will try to rectify matters."

Istvan caught his breath. He felt as if he had been beaten about the face. And he could not strike back, for one does not fight with a reptile, one only kills it. Or shuns it, walks around it at a distance.

They walked in the darkness under a sky like a net knotted with glittering stars. They stepped in rhythm. He sensed that Chandra had told him about the matter of the dead brother to encourage him to make confessions of his own, to admit faults—to feel that in this moral twilight they were accomplices. Confess without absolution? The joy of the condemned that there are so many of them, the dense throng with despair biting into it like pincers.

Be careful: he is pumping you for information. He wants to trap you, an inner voice warned. In spite of himself he slowly formulated sentences, evading the disturbing truth.

"Did rani Grace say where I wanted to escape to?"

"Yes." The blow fell. "It was difficult for us to believe; she chose a strange place for you. She seemed to overlook Paris and London. Do you want to escape to Australia?"

Istvan's shoulders hunched as if he had been hit in the chest. He walked like an automaton.

"You wanted to know. Now you do. Well, you have heard the truth. Someone has given you away. Now you must beg for mercy."

"Oh, God!" he barely breathed, but the other man, whose head was tilted toward him, caught it.

"You have remembered after all!" he said triumphantly. "Well, you must not take it all so seriously. You have only to say to me, Help me, and mean it, and I will do everything you wish. Or almost everything," he corrected himself. "At any rate, I will surely help you. Not for nothing do they call me a philanthropist. There is no predicament with no way out; it is only necessary to make up one's mind. To know what one wants. For oneself. You should think of yourself, of yourself exclusively. For no one loves us but ourselves. No one; you may be sure of that."

They were walking amid the caustic smell of swirling smoke. From both sides of the path countless fires appeared, a few with sharp red tongues licking at the night. Others hardly glimmered pink from under cooling ashes. Now they saw bodies wrapped in sheets like grayish cocoons, lying like unborn infants with knees tucked up.

"What have we come upon?" Suddenly Terey was conscious that the lights of the city were far behind them. "Do they bury the dead here as well?"

"No. But it is natural to think so, though those people are still living. It is a cool night. They sleep by the fires. These are the homeless. The poor—beloved of God—'Harijan.' That is what Gandhi named them," Chandra sneered.

They stood for a moment, gazing at the vast encampment. They heard the far-off crying of a baby and the snoring of the sleepers. Little flames seemed to whisper curses and bite hastily at the thorny branches and stalks that were scattered over gray ash. "A cold night." Chandra shivered.

Istvan looked at him. In the low reflection of a fire his white shirt front, his jacket, and the gloves he had doggedly pulled on created the impression that he was disguised as a magician—that in a moment he would appear on the dais, cheap, not worth the price of the ticket, not even worth applauding.

"Let's go back," he agreed. Then, oblivious to his companion, he began to walk faster and faster, as if to escape.

AT THE JANPATH HOTEL the porter pointed to a key hanging on the board where the room numbers were displayed.

"Miss Ward returned only for a moment and went out again at once."

Worried, he caught a taxi and ordered the driver to take him home.

The fusty interior of the cab reeked of sweat and cloying incense. He felt nauseated. The potbellied driver in a ragged sweater was brazenly holding a young boy by his left hand; the boy giggled ingratiatingly. Clattering and grinding, the old Ford moved ahead, permeated by a smell of burning oil. It seemed to Istvan that the two in the front seat were too preoccupied with each other to remember where they were taking him. He got out with relief and noticed a blur of yellow light in his living room. Beside the door the watchman, half awake, was stretching. The girl lay almost hidden in a corner of the veranda, curled up on a blanket.

He could not fit the key into the lock, though he tried to be quick so as not to disturb the lovers. His hands trembled.

Margit came to the door and they fell on each other with desperate eagerness, as if they were about to separate forever. They embraced silently, her forehead resting on his already rough cheek, while under his lips a crisp wave of hair darkened in the deep shadow. He felt the pressure of that dearest flesh now touching his—near, yielding. He felt his own heart. Through the coarse wool of her suit he found her familiar, warm body; he stroked it, clasped it with inexpressible tenderness. All the world lost its meaning. There were only the two of them, predestined for each other.

"Why didn't you go to bed? You'll stay here."

"A telegram came for you," she whispered, touching his cheek with her lips. He did not let her go.

"What's in it?"

"I don't know."

"You should have opened it. I have no secrets from you."

"I opened it, but it was in Hungarian," she breathed, holding him tightly. He quivered. Releasing himself, he went to the desk and shoved a creased slip of paper into the harsh glare of the lamp.

We are well stop do not worry dear stop peace here now stop Ilona.

His lips parted as if in a prayer of gratitude. They were alive. It had passed them by. He looked at the date: it had been sent the day before yesterday. He raised his head and was pained by Margit's despairing look. He had been distant from her again. He had left her on the far side of a threshold she could not cross.

"All is well." His smile was shadowed with anxiety. "They are alive."

It seemed to him that she had expected something else. Her eyes were full of anguish. "Well," she said. "You are calm."

He embraced her, but he felt that she had gone stiff in his arms. The oneness between them, the overflowing adoration and surrender without reserve, were missing.

"You will stay?" It was a question, not an order.

She felt the difference keenly; she caught it, not with the ear, but through the pulse of the blood.

"As you like," she answered sleepily. She went over to a chair, unfastened her tweed jacket, and began to undress. "Turn out the light." She motioned with her head. "I thought I saw someone standing near the window."

"The watchman. He wanted to be sure he could lie down and not go on making a show of guarding the house."

"Take me home later," she whispered, touching him to feel whether he had undressed. He took her in his arms. He trembled as he touched her firm, cool breasts, her slightly swelling belly. The distance between them dissolved.

"No . . . No . . . I want you by me when I wake. Before I open my eyes, I must know that you are here. Margit . . ."

All at once he wanted to confide his anxieties to her, to tell her about his conversation with Chandra and his premonition that a threat hung over them, but her nearness drove other thoughts away. He ran his fingers through her luxuriant hair as if it were spring grass. His hand traveled over her back as if it were a stone on the bank of a stream, warmed by the sun. He heard the soft murmur of her breath. It seemed to him that he was in a forest with treetops swaying in the wind. Again she was his whole world. What happiness, he thought, choking with gratitude—that I can love so intensely.

At the embassy the telegram from his wife made quite a stir. It was taken as confirmation that a general calm had ensued and that the destruction must not be farreaching, since the postal service was operating efficiently.

"If nothing happened at your house, as I was certain was the case, the Western press has outdone itself in magnifying the disturbances." Ferenc gazed at the telegram. "All is well with my family, too. My mother and father live around the corner near Lenin Road and a few houses down."

A trio had gathered: Istvan, Ferenc, and Judit. Istvan tried to penetrate Ferenc's drawn, dogged look. His eyelids were dark with sleeplessness. He is worried, Istvan thought. For the first time he is showing anxiety about his parents. He has never spoken of them. It was as if he had given birth to himself and had himself to thank for everything.

"The boss is breathing more easily. In the night Kádár's declaration came; he read as much of it as he wanted and walks around proud that he did not go off in a rush of adulation for Nagy. He repeated the same sentence to me three times, 'Whoever demands the withdrawal of the Soviet armies knowingly or unknowingly proclaims himself a counterrevolutionary and impels the nation toward the loss of independence.' I foresaw this. From the beginning this uprising stank of counterrevolution to me."

"That means that he understood nothing." Istvan looked Ferenc in the eye. "Either he didn't hear or he didn't want to know why the unrest began. He would have had to beat himself as penance."

"You think that blood was not shed in vain?" Ferenc hesitated. "Certainly there were mistakes, but not such as to necessitate smashing all the machinery of government, disbanding the party. On whom is Kádár leaning now? On those who hid away at the crucial time and were not slaughtered by the crowd? Or on the rebels who shot at the Russians? I know one thing: there are too few of them to make a government."

"You speak harshly." Judit turned her head. "Something in that text must have nettled you."

"Me?" Ferenc frowned. "I have a premonition that there will be an evening of the score, and how that will look you may see in any American newspaper with coverage of Budapest. It only takes a moment to hang someone, and then everyone can commiserate for as long as they like because it was a mistake." He thrust a finger behind his collar and pushed as if the starched linen were pinching him.

"Don't work yourself up. We are in India. In the meantime, things will sort themselves out at home," Judit said.

"Radio Free Europe has thrown out a slogan, 'Destroy the factories, sabotage the machines, so Russia will have no profit from your workshops.' Nice, eh?" the secretary said pointedly. "I heard it myself."

"Well, who is going to pay any attention to them? After all, the workers would be hurting themselves," Istvan shrugged.

"As they did when they began to shoot," Judit said dejectedly, "and they had reasons. There is nothing more tragic than for honest outbursts to be exploited by enemies and turned to our undoing. You can't expect a mob to think; a mob is elemental. It praises, elevates, and destroys with equal ease."

"Give me that declaration to read," Istvan requested. "I am arguing when I haven't seen it in black and white."

"The boss is certainly learning it by heart, but go to the cryptographer. He will give you a copy," said Ferenc. "It shows clearly that we were on the brink of a precipice. The plan of the West was that we would throw our force against the Russians, and that it would incite us, promise help, in the meantime accomplishing its goals with respect to the Suez. This is the logic of these events. I begin to understand Khrushchev's haste. He had to have peace in Budapest. He seized the trump cards from the opponents who were trying to play the game at their own pace. He did not give them Hungary and he did not allow the Suez to be taken away from Nasser."

They were sitting in the corridor on the second floor. The light fell on Judit's luxuriant hair and worried face. Outside the window in the hot Indian autumn, spider webs sailed about. The gardener was raking away crisp leaves. Yellow butterflies flew over the scarlet salvia.

"What did you mean, 'He did not give them Hungary'?" Terey challenged Ferenc. "Hungary is not a spoon to be tucked into the top of a boot! He didn't give us away because we didn't let ourselves be led away by the West, for our people don't want magnates in the Csepel mills or hereditary owners on land that is parceled out. Socialism, whatever we make of it, is our own affair; it is indivisible from independence."

Ferenc tilted his head slightly and looked at him with a barely perceptible smile. "You are quite the chess player," he said, pushing out his lower lip. "So you like a new configuration of things . . ."

"Player? I'm sorry for you if you look at what is happening to us and see only a game, and our politicians as pawns on a chessboard. Damn it! Aren't you Hungarians?"

"Perhaps you are going to start in again talking about how many books were published before the war and how many are published now, about the amateur ensembles and museums open to the public. I tell you: write a revolutionary's notebook, not verse. Write, write and you'll be running a newspaper—you'll be the head of *Szabad Nep*," Ferenc snapped.

"Listen, Istvan"—Judit tried to divert his attention—"that painter, your protégé, called me. He wanted assurances that he has a chance to receive a stipend."

"Hardly the most pressing issue," Ferenc said sarcastically, "when all Hungary is in convulsions."

"It is important to Ram Kanval. Surely the paperwork has gone out? The main thing is that he has hope. They are taught to wait patiently."

Judit looked at Terey with something like pity. She started to explain something but shrugged and sighed, "He will wait until the next incarnation. You are a good fellow, Istvan." It was as if she had said, You are naive, even a fool.

"I wanted to apprise you that your other protégé," Ferenc began maliciously, "well, you know, the runaway from Ceylon, the writer . . ."

"I did not support him at all."

"But he came to the embassy and you gave him gifts. You loaned him money."

"He printed two articles for us. You yourself gave him entrée, comrade secretary."

"He lifted those articles from our brochures. He can do that much. I am not reproaching you, Istvan, but it would be better if you knew whom you were taking under your wing. In a few days he is going to the Bundesrepublik. He will write flattering reportage from there."

"And you said he couldn't write!"

"They will write for him. They will write; it will be enough for him to sign the articles." Ferenc turned the knife. "You are a poet. You look for true art, and you despise the ordinary bullhorn because it is a bullhorn for hire. That is how Jay Motal should be treated. The Germans bought him. They beat us to the punch."

"They won't get much for their money."

"That is our only comfort," Judit said, and, wishing to end their quarreling, added, "Has either of you been to the cinema?" Seeing their surprise, she explained, "The film was not important. It was the newsreel. Yesterday at the Splendid Palace I saw barricades on the streets of Budapest, and dead insurgents. I tell you, for those few minutes of footage, you have to go. It wrings the heart—the scarred center of the city. Burned-out houses standing amid the rubble."

"Shall we go, Istvan?" Ferenc suggested, scribbling on the windowpane with a finger.

"What are you drawing there? The gallows?"

"No. Your initial," Ferenc rejoined. "A capital T, though it may be similar . . ."

"Go at eight," Judit begged them. "Must you be eternally sparring?"

"I don't know if I will have time," Istvan said evasively. He wanted to take Margit.

"What work do you have that is so urgent?" Ferenc's interest was aroused. "You are avoiding us, isn't he, Judit?"

"Yes. He was different before," she said with a baffled air. "You have changed, Istvan."

"That's rubbish!"

"You used to drop in for coffee. We always had something to chat about," she chided him.

"The counselor no longer trusts us." Ferenc tightened the screw. "Evidently he has found other confidants."

"You know yourself that that's not true." Istvan turned away and, wishing to break off the conversation, went to his office.

He wrote a letter regarding Ram Kanval, warmly praising his art. When the clattering of the typewriter keys had stopped, he heard voices from the corridor: they were still talking. He sensed that they were speaking of him. His left ear felt hot. His old aunt had always warned, "Left ear burns you, they speak ill of you; right ear—good news."

An insistent fear reasserted itself: what does Bajcsy know about Margit? Should he believe what Chandra had said? How could he profit by the warning? He could not sit still. He reached for the telephone and when the operator answered, he asked to be connected to the prosecuting magistrate. For some time the Hindu woman searched for the official who was investigating the accident involving the motorcyclist Krishan. At last he had the right man, a man who listened patiently to him and asked for his name letter by letter. When he had finished, the official informed him, to his great surprise, that his intervention was unnecessary, though of course information from a counselor at the embassy would have been highly valued; the woman who had been arrested had been set free the previous day. It had been irrefutably determined that she had nothing to gain by ridding herself of her husband, and she had accused herself as a result of the shock she had experienced.

Feeling relieved and a little disappointed, he hung up. "I acted too slowly," he half-whispered.

Someone knocked at the door. Before he said distractedly, "Come in," the balding caretaker had slipped into the room.

"I am here to clear away the papers." He ran a hand over the desk, on which rose piles of bulletins and newspapers. "Indeed, counselor, you have no room to move. May I straighten up? What is put aside I will take to the archive, what is not needed will go to the stove, and you will have breathing space."

"Very well. Take the stacks from the floor. From the desk as well. What I need I have cut out and put in my briefcases."

"I know that an official needs papers, but you were a military man before that, counselor. Why rustle like a mouse in old newspapers? I will take them away. New ones will come." He waved his hands as if he were about to fly up over the choked shelves. "I also came here on a temporary basis . . ."

He glanced at the nail on which the portrait of Rakosi had hung and winked knowingly at Terey. "I thought I would be in India for only two years and then back in our country, and in the meantime I have outlasted these great ones," he said. "They fell off their high pedestals, and I keep my seat. I mind my own business and I have nothing to be ashamed of."

He smiled shrewdly. He looked at his hands as if to be certain they were not dirty. "I gather up the trash . . ."

"Haven't you been drinking a little?"

"Yes," he admitted. "I can tell you, sir . . . everyone here has a mouth full of high-sounding words. They fight for socialism, but in the soft way, with their comforts, for good money. And I, with this very hand"—with his left hand he struck the open palm of his right—"I killed four fascists. That much I know for sure."

"When?"

"When I went from Sallaumines to the Reds, to Spain. I did it in a mine with Poles, Italians, Algerians—the rag, tag, and bobtail. We had nothing to sell but ourselves."

"And what happened there?"

"By the Ebro? Those I killed? One was a Spaniard, an aristocrat, a very handsome fellow; when I blindfolded him, he spat at me. I understand: an enemy is an enemy. And three Moors . . . they were skilled at fighting with knives."

"What has brought on this deluge of memories?"

"I cannot speak English very well. I do not read the newspapers. Sometimes the cryptographer will tell me how things are, but he looks around three times before he speaks. Maléter has been shot. I knew him."

"Would you have preferred that he shoot himself in the head?"

The caretaker looked nonplussed.

"Do you think there was no way out, sir?"

"My friend, I don't know. I can only speculate. It's wearing me out as well. Do you think it's easy for me?" Terey sprang to his feet. "What if that death saved thousands of other lives? Think of it as a loss sustained in battle."

The man tilted his head and scowled at Terey. His lips twisted in a bitter grimace. "No, counselor, I cannot. That would be putting too good a face on it. You people, as soon as something happens, will always get around a fellow with your talk of how there must be different ways of making sense of it. I know my own."

He looked at his own hands again with a sternly appraising glance, as a father looks at his sons when they return from work in the field.

"Though I have killed, I have clean hands." He straightened his back. "I go around the embassy and I look at the comrades. They feel that there are changes and each one thinks of how to find a place for himself."

"That's human, after all."

"And I don't worry that they will let me go because a better set of people come. I can always manage. Only I would like to be certain to the end that what I do not only puts food on my plate, but serves the nation. I would not measure out my blood drop by drop; what is needed is needed. What more can I give, except for my life?"

Terey went over to him and gripped his hand—a broad hand that even after many years was knobby and hard.

"I think as you do. So do thousands of others."

"Why is it so hard for them to speak up and stamp out these lice who are crawling all over us? All my life I thought that one party—eh! We have seen how it is." He raised his chin abruptly. "You may say that it depends on such people as I. I would rather go to the weapons depot and shoot one of them. For what am I or you or the ambassador? It is Hungary that is important! Hungary must be protected. And they have already shrunk us so that you cannot spit or it will fly over the border and annoy good neighbors."

He moved toward the door and said, bowing half facetiously, "I beg your pardon, counselor, for being so forward. I am not well educated. Perhaps I have offended."

Terey listened attentively as the caretaker's footsteps sounded down the long corridor. If he himself had not had words with Ferenc, this man would have taught the secretary a lesson! He began to pace around his office as if it were a cell, moving diagonally from the door to the window. He looked through the window at the blind wall of the garage, which was covered with a shaggy blanket of dusty leaves.

How many times they had jeered at the caretaker, calling him a drunkard who deserved well of his country. And he was one of those who could be counted on when sacrifices had to be made. It is not with "comrades," but with nails, he thought, that you hammer into place, join, reinforce the walls of the house. They go into the soft wood and hold it, and they do not even ascribe it to themselves as merit. They simply consider it the reason for their existence. And we? And who am I? he reproached himself. What right do I have to teach him?

Suddenly he felt that he had not yet reached the crossroads—that a test was before him, a test he had tried not even to think of. The face of a man aged beyond his years, rigid as a fist, was reflected in his mirror. "You are thinner, Istvan. You are torturing yourself, and I can't help you. I can't give you any relief, though I know what is preying on your mind." Margit's voice, full of deep, caressing kindness, came back to him and he felt her fingers moving over his tightly set cheeks, which were bluish from the razor. At the thought of her his eyes closed like a cat's in a streak of sunlight and his tension eased.

I ought to master myself, or for some trifling reason there will be a quarrel and it will grieve me. I must always remember not to exasperate Margit. I must use my judgment. I must fight for her and for every day I share with her.

In his dreams Budapest collapsed in ruins, full of the smell of burning. He was choked with vague, inchoate images that brought on an unbearable sense of helplessness. He woke as if someone were tugging at his arm. He listened, terrified, to hear the telephone if it should ring. His heart contracted violently. With inexpressible relief he found Margit beside him, felt the pressure of her thigh, smelled the beloved fragrance of her skin and the hair at her temples. He knew that she was not asleep, only pretending to be so he could rest, if only for a little while—so he could forget this anguish. She lay as one who lurks in wait, watchful, her wide-open eyes gleaming in the flood of darkness. He was grateful upon discovering that she was keeping vigil over his nervous dozing, his abrupt disconnection from consciousness, as if a switch had been pulled. He wanted, after all, to satiate himself with her presence forever, to hear her breathing. The rhythm of it gradually calmed him, though sighs still went through it like ripples on windblown water, and spasms of choking, as if she were holding back tears.

Suddenly his head sank deeper into the pillow and he slept. But in his sleep he lost her, though he had vowed to stay awake, to accept that hour of oneness in the dark as an affirmation of their love. Far away beyond a corner of the window loomed the greenish, cratered autumn moon. "Sleep," she begged gently, her hand tracing lines over his wide chest. "You must try to rest. I know this is dreadfully hard for you, but try to sleep."

Full of gratitude and ashamed that he had abandoned her, he kissed her drowsily and, without a word to express the tenderness that overwhelmed him, fell instantly asleep.

He woke, assuring himself that there would be long nights when they would be truly together, like man and wife. The certainty nourished his heart and quieted the hunger of body which was never satisfied, only fleetingly muted by the caresses, the yielding, when Margit opened to him like a book of warm secrets.

He dreamed of long nights unshattered by the crowings of roosters like brass trumpets, of sleeping, then waking only to assure himself that she was there, that she was steadfastly beside him. He had passed, had crossed at one bound the obstacle which had long ago ceased to be important, had diminished, changed into a dry ear of corn broken across the path, not worth noticing when one is quickening one's step, marching in double time. In these dreams Ilona was lost, pushed into the past among bygone experiences, like aged, faded photographs that remind us that we camped under the trees, sang beside the campfire, but all of that is past, remote from the present, of no consequence.

And a great astonishment broke over him that he could have felt himself happy then, since only today did he truly know what love could be. All his life until now had only been a long waiting, a preparation, though he was unaware of it, for meeting Margit. From opposite ends of the globe fate had unerringly led them toward each other, and from that wedding night they had begun to number their happiest days. Grace did not exist. She did not exist; their encounter had been an accident, a mistake. I must have been blind. After all, I met Margit that very evening, and still I did not foresee what she was going to mean to me.

Grace . . . the capacity for intrigue and gossip with which Indian ladies poison life, and the cool calculation of the English. She is not a woman who can be confined to the distaff side of the house, sentenced to a life between the kitchen and the bed. She has her unspoken plans and she herself is capable of carrying them out. Even the expectation of what is called a blessed event has not mellowed her. The repugnant family council on the matter of the claimant to the inheritance exhumed from the funeral pyre . . . she had been there. She knew, she kept silent, so she condoned the rationale that underlay her father's and her husband's actions.

How had she found her way to Bajcsy? She knew him from official receptions, but she had not met with him simply out of revenge. Perhaps her father would do the ambassador a favor and execute the transfer from his foreign account. What would he gain in exchange? If he, Terey, wanted to ask to talk to Bajcsy, Kádár's appeal would create a fine pretext; best to meet danger head on. What had Ferenc read in that declaration that made him lash out blindly? Kádár—the man of the hour. If he makes the old party machine his base, they will all support him for the time being, happy that he demands no squaring of accounts.

I grieve for Hungary. My country. Kádár called on those people for help . . . help for whom? He wanted to save the revolution. Already there is peace in Budapest. Bitterness rose in his throat. Revolution is a two-edged sword; let no one deceive himself. People not only get their just deserts, they learn to think.

Time will tell . . . he noticed that he was talking to himself, gazing at the garage wall with its burden of fleecy greenery. If only it doesn't cost us too much. It seems that our own country has its veins slit and blood flows unchecked. And then what? To refer the case to the just judge, and wait half a century for the verdict?

With a firm step he walked to the cryptographer's office and knocked at the armor-plated door. Inside stood a radio set, a bulky safe, and a narrow table with a draftsman's lamp—in every particular like a telegrapher's cabin on a ship, not omitting a narrow wooden foldaway bunk fastened to the wall.

Kereny turned a pale, puffy face toward him. Hungarian voices came from the radio speaker; the cryptographer almost involuntarily stifled them.

"Are you picking up Budapest?"

"Sometimes late at night there are clear signals. One can catch them randomly," he explained, tracing a line in the air with his finger.

Istvan inquired no further. It was clear that the cryptographer was listening to Radio Free Europe. "What news?" he asked.

"Shepilov has said that the Soviet armies will be leaving Hungary any minute. It would be enough for Kádár to demand it. There is no question of arguing with him."

"And he will not demand it." Terey shook his head.

"Because he would be gone tomorrow." Kereny looked at him sleepily, almost indifferently.

"They have just said"—both knew who, though they did not name the station—"that the uranium mine sustained serious damage. They were satisfied that it could not be reactivated in less than six months."

"So Hungarians have been duped." Istvan beat a fist on the table. "The ruse started a wave of emigration. They urged them on to destroy the factories, for what does Hungary matter to them? All the hired dogs bark as they are told to, and our people blindly believe everything."

"Radio Free Europe gets information so quickly that it is astonishing," the cryptographer said reflectively. "They must have connections in high places."

"That's not difficult at the moment. For two weeks they had open borders. They went in and out. And the people themselves don't know who wants the best for Hungary, or who is right: Nagy, who bolted to the Yugoslavians; Mindszenty, who decamped to the Americans; or Kádár, who yesterday came out of Rakosi's prison and today brings in tanks. Everyone is in a daze. It's lunacy! I came to you for the declaration because I know from talking with our colleagues that each one read it differently. They all looked for what they wanted to find."

"They issued two pages. I have produced a written copy." He pulled a briefcase with carbon copies out of the drawer. "But I am not permitted to let it out of my sight. Read it here, sir."

Istvan walked over to the grated window, turned his back, and quickly perused the communiqué. Kádár explained that his decision had been influenced by acts of unbridled terrorism, lynchings, which did not bring the lawless to justice but took as targets communists who, like himself, had just been freed from Rakosi's and Gerő's prisons. A mob had murdered the secretary of the Budapest Committee, Imre Mező; the director of the military museum in Csepel, Sandor Siklay; and comrade Karamara, who was devoted to the cause of Hungary. Power had slipped through Nagy's fingers; his government was impotent. The incursion of the Russians had been a historical necessity if Hungary were not to become another Korea. But the secret police were disbanded and the old Stalinist measures would not be reinstituted; the guilty would be called to account.

Terey nodded. It must have been this that had disturbed Ferenc, for the services that had opened the door to diplomacy for him might be seen as offenses, depending on who would be evaluating his previous career. Istvan raised his head and met the dogged, watchful glance of the cryptographer.

"Well, and what do you make of it, sir?"

The counselor shrugged.

"The devil only knows what's behind a statement like this." Kereny bent over a drawer and pulled out a pack of cigarettes. He offered Terey Kossuths, lighted one for him, and remarked casually, "And a quarter million have gone into exile, or so they say. Not only rebellious students but our whole team, world champions in soccer. Gone."

He spoke so bitterly that the counselor had to smile. "We will get over that," he said.

"There you had boys worth their weight in gold. Anyone will take them and pay what they ask. They will not be playing in our colors. It is worse than defeat! Do you know what an impression that will make on the world? Millions of fans are watching. The Hungarians—finished!" He blew out a wisp of smoke indignantly. "I don't care if whole embassies cut and run. The workers can be replaced with anyone at all. But goalkeepers or wings! Where will we find such talent?"

Terey did not share the man's disappointment, but he understood his agitation. "Radio Free Europe spoke of people defecting from our missions?"

"Yes. They counted those from New York, Paris, London. They attacked the embassy in Vienna, where our people barricaded themselves and would not allow emigres in. That is a vital point, it is on the route. A long list. I wonder, has anyone left here? But who would want to stay in India?"

"They would not have to stay here. They could go where they liked. For such people, Kádár is not a Hungarian, and they see the country as lost. Fine feelings—for rats. I'm curious: how many of those who fled the country waving the Hungarian flag sat high behind their desks for a long time as censors, in the courts, in the security apparatus? An occasion arose and they sailed away, avoiding the court, having the forethought to smear their faces with the blood of the fallen. They made themselves into great revolutionaries. Tomorrow we will hear them on the radio accusing the party, broadcasting the details of dark doings, and well they know them, for they themselves—"

"If I did not know you, comrade"—the cryptographer turned his cigarette in his fingers deliberately—"I would think this was a smokescreen. Have you been talking with the caretaker?"

Istvan nodded.

"He has been doing a bit of drinking and has begun putting our people under the microscope. There's not a one that doesn't have some reason to say goodbye if the right moment comes. Even the boss, for he can go no higher, and what he put aside he transferred to Switzerland. Kádár will not take that away from him."

"And you?" The counselor did not spare the man. "You have a wife and child here, and a good profession—" he pointed to the metal-clad safe. "You could parlay it into something else. The Counter Intelligence Corps would take you with open arms."

"Certainly . . . but I would have to want that, and I am in no hurry. I have no quarrel with socialism."

"And what do all of you say about me?"

The cryptographer hesitated, but snuffed out his cigarette and spoke his piece.

"You have a wife and child in our country, but that is an uncertain anchor. How many lately have been happy enough to tear themselves away from their families? You will stay, but you may yet be burnt, comrade. I speak frankly, for you go for the jugular sometimes. You do not watch—"

"Don't worry about me."

"I have traveled abroad for a good few years and I tell you, counselor, there has been a change. We would never have chatted this way before. One of us would have been afraid of the other. It's good that a man can open his mouth—though one must still know to whom. And with us there are plenty of people who are schooled to have no scruples about pushing others around so the authorities will prefer them, will exaggerate their merits. But I know what a person is. They may say yes, they will do something; they may say no just as sweetly. But they cannot pull the wool over my eyes anymore. Once they did, and it was enough."

"And what convinced you that I could be trusted?"

"Comrade counselor"—Istvan understood that this form of address had a special meaning for the cryptographer—"you saved my child."

"I?"

"Mihaly told us everything. It was even in the newspapers: 'mad elephant.'"

"I? That's just prattle!" Terey tried to trivialize the incident. "The elephant turned back by himself."

"But he might not have turned back"—the cryptographer looked keenly at him—"and the boy would have been crushed to a pulp. Mihaly does not make things up."

"Very likely ghosts appear to him sometimes," the counselor smiled.

"When Mihaly says he saw something, it means that he did. He learned Hindi as well, more quickly than his father. I don't know when."

Suddenly Terey saw Kereny's animated face grow somber and take on a decorous gravity. He turned around. The door had opened noiselessly and the ambassador was standing there.

"What are you talking about, the two of you by yourselves? Well, you must not stand on ceremony with me," he said indulgently, putting out a pale hand.

"We were just talking of ghosts," Terey began jauntily. "At a time like this, better to talk of ghosts than politics."

"About what?" The ambassador's thick eyebrows bristled.

"I was only talking about Mihaly's apparitions."

"Yes!" the cryptographer added hastily. "He saw Krishan's dead wife. Even before the accident."

"You are talking nonsense." The ambassador was angered at being reminded of the driver he had discharged. "Let the dead rest in peace, comrade Terey. You yourself are doing nothing; do not barge in on others. You hinder their work."

He rested his heavy, hairy hands on the table, next to the radio. "Is there anything new?" he asked. The cryptographer shook his head.

"No? What are they thinking in the ministry? They ought to give us a tip first so we could influence the press, shed a little light on things for the politicians—do something, at any rate, and not find out everything only from our opponents. Not stick out our backside and wait to see who wallops it first."

He pulled a wrinkled piece of paper covered with writing out of his pocket and laid it on the table, as a gambler puts down a trump card. "Send this right away. And you, comrade Terey, don't run away. I want a word with you."

He forced Terey against the door frame and put a hand on his shoulder, puffing the sour odor of his pipe into the counselor's face. For a moment they looked each other in the eye.

"Better to go to your office. We would be more at ease." He pushed the counselor forward with a matey shove that nevertheless asserted his own dominance.

Now comes the business of Margit, Istvan thought. He mustered his defense, waiting uneasily to see from which direction Bajcsy would try to ambush him.

The ambassador settled into the counselor's chair, took out his pipe and a leather tobacco pouch, and tamped the tobacco for a long time, looking askance at Istvan. Finally he asked, "Whom did you call this morning, Terey?"

"I?" He was genuinely surprised. "Ah, yes, I called the prosecutor. You already know, sir? Our information systems are working well."

"The line was busy for so long, the operator had to explain why," the ambassador mumbled, holding the pipe between his fleshy lips and gazing at Terey morosely. "What kind of collusion is going on here?"

"I called about Krishan's second wife. They arrested her wrongfully." He spoke as if the matter were of no importance. "They accused her of putting sugar into the gas tank."

"And you can swear that she did not?" The ambassador shifted his bulky torso until the chair creaked and rested his elbows on the desk. "Why the devil do you care about this?"

"I spoke with her."

"What for?" His voice suddenly rose to a roar. "I've had enough of this! Cut it out, Terey!"

The counselor was silent. He looked at the older man as he wheezed with rage, his puffy jowls quivering.

"Tell me—what is happening with you?" The ambassador spoke in an abruptly altered tone, full of friendliness. "Look at yourself in the mirror."

"I see myself every morning when I shave," Terey murmured

"There are changes, eh? You are simply not the same man. Black rings around the eyes. You're goggling like a lovesick fool. And always looking for a fight."

"Me?"

"Are you worried about your family? You had a telegram from your wife, after all. I'm sure we will get her over here now. You'll sleep better. One must keep a grip on one's nerves, Terey. The tropics wear us down. Do you know what I propose? I truly regret that this has been a painful time for you." He grimaced sympathetically. "When things are a little calmer, take two or three weeks off. A trip will do you good."

In spite of the ambassador's reassuring tone, Terey caught a guarded glance from under the half-closed eyelids with two yellow spots like clots of tallow. He knew instinctively that the ambassador had something more to get off his chest.

"Thank you, ambassador, but won't it be an imposition on my colleagues—"

"Ferenc will be more than capable of taking your place. I am not saying that you should go tomorrow. Comrade Terey, I am making an accommodation for you; you ought not to be testy with me. It is time for a rest."

He rummaged through a file of clippings. "They slander decent comrades. They drag them through the mud. Their only fault was that they wanted socialism and the nation could not keep pace. Whose side are you on, Terey?" He pointed his pipe stem at him; it gave off a little haze of bluish smoke.

"You know, sir. It goes without saying."

"Kádár adopted all the slogans of the insurgents in order to keep himself in power, but between declarations and implementing them, fortunately, a good deal of time elapses. The people finger their bruises, reckon up the damages, and soon it all passes; their fanaticism cools. To me these great changes are like putting on a new cap while the head remains the same, and the head knows what it wants. You may take it for opportunism when you see how I spit on my finger to test which way the wind blows. I tell you, Terey, that is what life has taught me. We must hold to the golden mean."

Seeing that the counselor was disinclined to join in this discussion, he puffed at his pipe and inquired, "What did you think of our film showing? Not a great success? Still another proof that we must bide our time until the commotion quiets down. Then—dribs and drabs: a little article in the press. Send a Hindu to us for reportage. Place a couple of photographs of the grape harvest, pretty girls, for everyone to salivate over. But a little time must pass first. When you come back rested, we will devise a campaign."

I must irritate him so he will show his true colors, Istvan thought. He leaned toward Bajcsy. "Did you manage that transfer? Was Attorney Chandra of any help?"

Bajcsy swung around as if he had unexpectedly been hit, but saw nothing in the counselor's face but the readiness of a functionary dependent on his chief and devoted to him.

"Chandra—" he gave a low whistle of approval. "A magisterial intellect. I had no idea that you were acquainted with such people. He said complimentary things about you. In the end, however, I took care of it without him. You can forget about that conversation." He rose, his heavy hips pushing the chair aside. He tapped his pipe on a corner of the desk, then flung out one foot and crushed the ashes.

"Speak to Ferenc and establish a time for your departure. In December, perhaps, so you will have free holidays."

Then, standing in the doorway, he asked, "And where would you go?"

"South. To the shore. I daydream about the ocean."

"A true Hungarian," the ambassador mumbled half sarcastically. "Bombay? Calcutta?"

"Farther. Cochin. A small port."

"Small, but important. It is a port of call for all the shipping lines from England and Italy on the routes to Malaya and on to Australia."

He turned around and went out, leaving the door wide open.

Terey looked at his broad shoulders and sloping back. Was the mention of Australia the warning signal for which he had waited?

"I'll go," he whispered. "I'd be a fool not to take him up on it."

He started up the fan. The great blades scattered the pipe smoke that still hung like a blue veil under the ceiling. He set to work with such a passion that it startled him when the telephone rang. He heard a name and grew calmer.

"Ah, it is you, Ram Kanval. Only today I was asking about your case."

"I am Kanval but I am Ram's brother. I am a translator. I had the honor of of meeting you, sir." The fluty voice had a pertness like a crowing rooster's. "I did not know that you would still be at work, counselor. I called your house."

Istvan looked at his watch; it was past four. "It really is rather late," he said.

"Would you not like to visit my brother? Today, even?"

"What has happened?"

"I am speaking from the shop. Perhaps you will come to us, sir."

"It is that urgent?"

"Yes—as a matter of fact."

"But may I eat dinner?" he said humorously. "That will not take long. I will be there at five."

"Do you remember the way, counselor? At all events I will come out to the corner of the avenue, in front of the new blocks."

The man's voice was clear but full of concern. "Something has happened to Ram?" Terey asked.

"Yes—but he is already better. He is conscious. You have shown him so much kindness, counselor."

"Very well. I'll be there."

What had happened there? Why had Ram not called? No doubt he was starving himself to spite them. Perhaps he wanted to borrow a few dozen rupees. No, one of his paintings is enough for me; I will buy no more. I have no walls to hang them on. In Budapest? Ilona would say, "Our boys paint better." And Margit? Did she really like his work, or had she bought a painting out of pity, or because it would give me pleasure? No; her taste is very contemporary.

It seemed to him that Kanval's pictures would be beautifully suited to the interior of a little house with fiery nasturtiums in boxes under the wide windows. They would remind them both of summer in India, of the year they met. Already he could see the bluish-gray wall and the flat surface, the color of flame, with painted figures emerging from formlessness. On the hearth there would be a black pitcher and a spray of rust-colored branches, and beside them the stone head he had been given by Chandra. Our house—Margit's and mine. Through a large window there would be cornfields, a sky of powder blue, and one cloud with a well sweep against it. He smiled: the Australian landscape he had sketched in outside the window embodied his recollection of the countryside that had been home to his family, the land of his happy boyhood.

He locked the drawer and hurried, whistling, down the stairs. The caretaker was napping in the hall. Istvan put the key down on a little table with a loud tap to wake him. The man opened an eye, hardly nodded by way of goodbye, tucked the key in his pocket and fell to dozing. His mustache twitched drolly as flies crawled over it. He must have had a good pull at the bottle. The embassy was silent and empty; the staff had left long ago.

He kissed Margit and quickly told her about the telephone call, even holding the door open with one foot as he washed his hands so as not to lose sight of her. He was happy that he could follow her with his eyes—happy that in his presence she did not simply walk but seemed to dance.

"Can you take me?" she asked cautiously, against all contingencies placing medicines in her bag and ordering syringes to be prepared. They finished dinner quickly, much to the satisfaction of the servants.

As he drove the Austin he managed to read a large poster: *House of Wax*. It was a horror film. "I forgot to tell you"—he touched her thigh—"you're going to the movies with me today. I must see a newsreel. There will be pictures of the uprising with views of Budapest."

"What time do we go?"

"At six, when we are back from Kanval's. We won't meet anyone we know at that hour. Only local people will be there because that's the low-price showing."

They cut through streets lined with villas. The air smelled of the country, of stables and hay loaded on the creaking tongas. Already in the distance he saw the familiar figure, the navy blue blazer with metal buttons like those worn in English boarding schools, the full, starched white trousers.

"What happened?" He looked at the small face in which only the eyes flashed, full of reproach, and the mustache, long untrained, drooped, with shaggy hairs falling to the mouth. Kanval's head swayed with happiness that they had met—that he had them in tow and could lead them to his brother.

"He drank some poison. He is better now. I could not speak freely by telephone, for everyone's ears were open and the people in the shop know our family. I do not want to say what he poisoned himself with. His wife is with him."

"Suicide?"

"We did not even want to think of that." Shame darkened his voice as he tried to dismiss the idea. "But so it seems. His brother-in-law had been speaking very hurtfully to him lately, and his father-in-law had set his wife against him. They think that he does not want to work. According to them, painting is not work, and he gets no other work, though I myself have seen how he runs from place to place in search of it. He dreamed of escaping from here, of putting India out of his mind for a few months. You, sir, promised a stipend. He was counting very much on a journey to Hungary." Suddenly he squealed, "To the left now, through the ditch! They finished the water main and they are excavating to lay cable."

The car's wheels ground through clods of baked clay that sent red dust flying upward. In front of the house a cluster of children were playing marbles, noisily cheering the well-aimed strikes. A slender girl in flowered slacks squatted in the middle of the road, triumphantly shaking a bag that held her winnings.

Rapidly they climbed the steep stairway with red blotches of betel juice to Ram Kanval's family's apartment. A huddle of relatives with saddened faces awaited the counselor, whose hand they quickly pressed. They looked respectfully at Margit, for the little translator managed to communicate to them that she was a doctor.

In a shadowy room the sick man lay wrapped in blankets. The outline of his emaciated body could hardly be seen under the folds of fabric. A clay bowl holding a white liquid stood by the bed. Istvan pushed back the window curtain and the westering sun struck Ram Kanval's face. It was yellowish-green and glittering with sweat. His open mouth sucked greedily at the air. He lay inert; only his eyes darted about as if with an uncontrollable life of their own.

"His wife gave him curdled milk," the brother explained. "But everything came back up."

"Very good," Margit said encouragingly. "Milk is an antidote to some poisons." She listened to his heart with her stethoscope and counted his pulse. She peeled the cover from a syringe and drew an oily yellow liquid from an ampule. "I will give him something to build his strength. What did he take?"

"An infusion of some herbs." His father, a stout gray-haired man, threw up his hands in desperation. "If we had known that it would come to this, none of us would have said a word to him."

"He must be left in peace—above all, in peace," Margit ordered. "Do not come in. Do not lament over him. He will sleep. His convulsions are stopping. Has a doctor been here? Where is his wife?"

A small woman in a peasant-style cotton sari leaned against the door frame. Her head hung so low that Istvan saw quite clearly the scarlet-tinted parting and the wings of unplaited hair that were a sign of mourning. The tight sleeves of her white blouse cut into her arms.

Ram Kanval recognized Istvan. His face, with a smile on his rigidly set lips, resembled the face of one dying of lockjaw. The counselor leaned over the plank bed and took the man's cold, limp, sweaty hand.

"Nothing is lost, Ram. You will go yet. I promise."

"No." The word came through his labored breathing. "They are lying to you. They said today that they do not want me or my pictures." He spoke in a broken whisper, coherently, but suddenly he looked walleyed at the ceiling.

"Did he poison himself with alkaloids?" Margit said worriedly. "It is too late for gastric lavage. What was in the stomach would have come up with the milk. The dose was not lethal, but even now I can see the effects of paralysis. Not much can be done to help. I believe he will survive."

"He will live?" his brother demanded, picking wisps of his mustache from between his lips with a bent finger.

"If he has the desire—if he will fight," she replied, coiling up the rubber pipe of her stethoscope. "Whether he will have a reason to live depends on all of you."

"Listen, Ram"—Terey jogged his hand—"I swear that if you don't go to Hungary, you will go to Czechoslovakia, to Romania. All the attachés are friends of mine."

"They said my pictures are decadent, opposed to socialism," Kanval said in a gurgling whisper. "They said that the uprising was not quelled so people's minds could be poisoned with such an exhibit."

"Ferenc," the counselor snarled.

"No. The ambassador himself. It is the end of everything."

"It is the end of nothing!" Istvan cried, nearly beside himself. "You will go to Paris! I will move heaven and earth."

Ram Kanval twisted his lips into a misshapen smile. His eyeballs rolled and the pupils darted into the corners of his eyes; he could not control their movements. He must have been growing tired. A sweat heavy as foam broke out on his forehead.

"You must live, do you hear? Live! You will go!"

"Do not shout. I hear you . . . in red," he whispered.

All at once he began to choke. Spasms bent his body until whitish clots showed on his lips. His wife knelt by the bed and rubbed his face with a wet towel. "He is dead," she whimpered. "He has left me."

Margit pushed her hands off him roughly. "No. He has gone to sleep. Leave him alone. Don't tire him with questions. Cover the window; the light bothers him. Noise makes him see colors. I would prefer that he be sent to a hospital—" she turned to an older man in a camelskin vest whose bare knee could be seen from below his wrinkled dhoti, shaking nervously.

"What for? Here everyone keeps watch over him. He is well cared for. It is better not to fatigue him. A hospital is costly. And the whole building would raise a cry and say that we killed him." He tugged at the arm of his daughter-in-law, who was hunched over beside the bed, and commanded, "Put hot water bottles on his legs. Have you been tending him or not? He is your husband!"

"You all wore him out. You know nothing!" She leaped at her father-in-law, waving her open hands like talons in his face. "A while ago a merchant was at the barsati and wanted me to sell his pictures. He put down ten rupees for each of them."

"And did you sell them?" the brother asked worriedly. "That is quite an opportunity."

"I am not stupid. He gave ten rupees; he will give twenty."

Istvan saw that the painter's eyelids had parted a little. His eyeballs moved uneasily. His lips were forming, not a grimace, but a hint of a smile. "The paints themselves cost more. Do not sell them," he whispered.

A gaggle of children peeked into the hall, where a gray-haired woman was talking about the case. When they had jostled their way onto the stairs, a little boy jerked at the bag that belonged to the girl with bows in her hair and the marbles fell in a cascade, striking each step hard. The children jumped around, shrieking, to catch them.

"Thank you, sir." The translator bowed. The ends of his mustache were sticky with saliva. "You have given him hope."

"Not I. That merchant. He doesn't believe me."

They went out to the road and he turned to Margit.

"Yet another casualty of the trouble in Budapest. I'm not joking. If it hadn't been for the uprising, we would have given him a stipend." He glanced at his watch and was silent. He hunched over the steering wheel. It was past six.

"I'll park the car. You run to the box office for the tickets. Cut in front of the line; no one will object. These colonial customs—sometimes I think they like to feel abased."

They made their way in without difficulty and reached the balcony at the moment when the lights were dimmed. They sat in the first vacant seats they found. After an advertisement in color showing a sleek young man suffering from a headache and a kind soul offering him the wonder drug Aspirin, the newsreel began. They sat nestled against each other; Margit's hand found Istvan's, stroked it, then rested on it with a gentle pressure as if to say: Don't torture yourself, I'm with you. What you will see has already happened. It is the past.

The building of the dam in Bhakra Nangal; the modern city of Chandigarh; in windows, glare breakers that looked like empty honeycombs or thinly sliced Swiss cheese; a palace of justice with gigantic columns like an Assyrian temple; oxen wading in thin mud at a snail's pace, dragging a wooden harrow with several children standing on it so that the wheels ground more deeply into the churned mire.

Suddenly Istvan trembled. Three hunters flashed on the screen and moved precipitously toward the ground. A city that seemed to be made of white blocks appeared, smothered in a fleece of smoke. A crowd that from that elevation looked like a liquid overflowing fled into gardens and palm groves. He sighed heavily: this was not Budapest or any Hungarian city.

"An attack by the Israeli Air Force on Port Said"; the speaker's voice penetrated his consciousness. They were shooting from airplanes and the crowd dispersed, dissolved into individual particles, darting figures running in zigzags before they fell, as if they were simulating the deaths of insects. But Istvan knew it was real. On the screen it even had its own aesthetic; people toppled over like ninepins, and a low murmur of something like approval ran through a hall inured to such scenes by American battle films.

A view of Budapest from a monument by the Danube burst onto the screen. He saw General Bem in a hat with a curling cock feather and the crowd with uplifted heads listening to a speaker who had climbed onto the stone plinth. There was nothing unusual in this frame, but Margit, with her hand on Istvan's, felt Istvan's fingers lock onto the arms of his seat. His breathing quickened. He raised his head. All his emotion seemed to be drawn to what he was seeing. The commonplace faces, the bared heads of the singing crowd were profoundly moving to him, for they were his countrymen—Hungarians.

He felt a bond with them that was incomprehensible to her, a connection she would never share. She looked furtively at him; his reactions gave her clues as to the significance of the images that changed like clouds driven by a windstorm.

A closeup of a half-torn away plaque with the inscription Stalin Road and under it the old name, Andrássy Avenue: the camera gave a view of the streets over which the crowd was surging. Long tricolor flags with holes ripped out of their centers where the stars had been torn away hung from buildings. Batteries of cannon in the park fired among houses. Soldiers in uniforms like those of the Russians, with cockades on their caps, held long missiles in their hands; at a command the missiles' mouths emitted clouds of steam. The film had no sound, only a music track. The picture trembled. Evidently it had been made by hand by an accidental witness.

A crowd stood on a small square, heads upturned. Suddenly a man flew out of a fifth-floor window and struck the gleaming wet pavement heavily as a sack of flour. Others in uniforms were led out and driven to a wall with kicks. A young man in a hat with an aigrette and a double-barreled shotgun in his hand hit an officer who was leaning on the wall—with a whirling motion hit him in the back so hard that the butt of the gun broke. The enraged man went on hitting with the barrel while the butt, broken off but dangling on its long strap, skipped on the pavement. Those in uniform standing by the wall stretched out their hands, explained, pleaded.

A sudden convulsion distorted the faces; they looked like children curled up in terror, calling in the darkness, "Mama . . ." But they had already taken the bullets. Some fell dully, their faces unshielded by their arms as they hit the paving stones. Others lurched against the wall, their backs leaning on it, marking the place with a pooling of liquid black, for blood appeared black on the screen and a cry for mercy is the black stain of an open mouth—a harbinger of the night that would envelop them.

"No. No." A voice tense with repugnance came from somewhere in the audience. Istvan turned his head as if to see who had shouted.

Houses in flames. Tanks. A long column photographed by stealth from behind blinds. The segmented crawling wheel of a tank turning little by little to vanish beyond a house on a corner.

"I live not far from there," he whispered in her ear, and again lost himself in what was being shown on the screen: the interior of a room; a stern, fanatical face. The cardinal was allowing himself to be interviewed in the American embassy. The sound came on, and the first words in Hungarian were followed by a voiceover in English. Margit was pleased; at last she could understand, and she nodded as if in agreement. But then she caught Istvan's whisper:

"He summoned them to fight and escaped himself. Their blood is also on him."

People passing over the border, a throng dragging suitcases and bundles. In the cold, in the pouring rain, their breath steamed. There were accusations, tears. Soldiers laid down their arms before an officer of the border guard. The Austrian nimbly felt the thighs of the defector, shook the inside pockets of his coat, and demanded in a terse German dialect, "No grenades? All weapons surrendered?"

Women in white caps with crosses on their bands were carrying meals to children from a field kitchen. The screen was filled by a close-up of a small, smiling face with tears on its cheeks seen across a steaming mess kit. Margit felt her eyes brim with tears; she sniffled. He could have been there—she squeezed Istvan's hand—they could have killed him and buried him among the trees that hovered grimly, stripped of their leaves. And if he had managed to flee over the border, he would have been among those the West was hurrying to help. Joy kindled in her that he was, after all, here in Delhi, in another part of the world, far from Hungary. And he would not return there for she was stopping him, blocking his way.

"Did you see how it was?"

"Terrible." She felt him quiver, so she corrected herself, "Awe-inspiring."

"You cannot understand us—" he began, then went silent. From the screen a girl waved her hand toward them; she was speeding along on water skis, leaving two trails of foam. "Come on." He caught Margit in a grip that was a little too strong. "We're leaving."

She rose obediently. The lights went on, illuminating the empty chairs and the tardy viewers packed around the edge of the theater, who now moved in a wave in search of seats. Steering them toward the exit, Istvan spied the pale, altered face of Ferenc, who saw him as well and followed him with his eyes. Istvan let go of Margit's arm and whispered, "Walk faster."

When they were in the car, he sat for a long time without starting the engine.

"What is it?" She leaned over him apprehensively. "Let me drive."

"All right," he agreed easily. They changed places and Margit gave him a lighted cigarette.

"Istvan—which side are you on?"

He inhaled and answered quietly, "When I talk with Ferenc, I know the insurgents are right. The same when I talk with the ambassador or with Judit. Talking with others, I think: What should be done to save Hungary from being torn apart? The survival of the nation itself is at stake. We can cease to exist. They will divide us; we will disappear from the map. It has happened even to larger countries."

"Can it be as bad as that?" she asked incredulously, frowning. "You haven't answered. Whom are you for?"

"I don't know. I don't know. I say that in all sincerity. And it wearies me, it drives me mad. I simply know too little about what has happened."

The watchman with his bamboo rod lying tight against his arm welcomed them in military fashion.

Istvan sat in a chair with his head tilted and took a long time to light a cigarette. "I'm sorry you had to look at that," Margit said.

"No. I must know. Only now do I grasp the scale of the disaster."

"Even if you were in Budapest, you could see only a part of what was happening. Don't despair. Think of what can be salvaged, how to get clear of this trap. Those who crossed the border have not stopped being Hungarians. They can do more for your cause than those who are gagged."

He looked at her, blinking.

"Yes. So it would seem. For the time being, the world is moved by the tragedy of Budapest, but tomorrow they will have had enough of the refugees; they will only be burdensome foreigners. To remain in Canada or Brazil, which are offering hospitality to defectors, they must work, become like others, stop flaunting these bleeding wounds—in a word, year after year they must downplay their origins, put them in the drawer with their hidden memorabilia. It will come to this, that they renounce the very cause for which they took up the struggle."

"So you believe they really shouldn't have left?" She grew somber. "And you? What would you have done? Would you have taken a chance and returned to that Kádár?"

"What do I care about him? I would have been returning to my homeland. Understand: your country has never really been threatened. Your Australia is not just a nation but a continent. Only a man who is suffocating knows what an open window is. Kádár had to adopt the slogans of the uprising because the nation was calling for reforms. If he is honest enough to follow through with them, we must make every effort to support him. If he lied, nothing will save him. But that is in the future. Only time will tell."

"You prefer to wait here—" her lips were parted. She held her breath.

"That doesn't depend on me. I care most about something else. Margit, I love you. Remember that."

She smiled, but there was anguish in her face. She lowered her bluish eyelids. He saw how fatigued she was, how overwrought. He felt a deep tenderness and gratitude. In her own way—a different way than his—she, too, was disturbed by what was happening in Hungary.

He got up and sat on the arm of her chair. She rested her head on his chest for a long time and they sat in a comfortable silence.

"Tell me," he whispered, stroking her springy red hair, "how are things going at the university? Handsome fellows, those students? Are you nervous before your lectures?"

After seven he began to pace about uneasily. Suddenly he announced that he had something urgent to attend to, something he had forgotten about. Though the cook had set the table, he reached for the key to the car.

"I'll be back in half an hour. I'm very sorry."

Margit nodded to say that she understood, she would wait.

"Will madam eat? Everything is ready." Pereira was perturbed. "Shall we wait for the master?"

"I'm not hungry," she said calmly, but her hands trembled when she poured some whiskey and the siphon, under pressure, wheezed.

When he returned as he had promised, she did not have the courage to ask him anything. Only as they were lying close together and he was sleepily stroking her smooth knee as it rested on his thigh did he confess in an undertone, "I didn't tell you the truth, Margit. I was ashamed. I went to the cinema again to see that newsreel. I went in without a ticket; I gave the doorkeeper a rupee. I stood in the dark and watched it. It seemed that the first time I overlooked some details that are important to me. I looked at the faces to see if I recognized anyone."

She listened, curled up as if she were cold. This will always be closer to him than I am, she thought despairingly. He pats me mechanically, as one pats a dog.

Her calm, her sudden torpor, he read a different way. "You are wise, Margit," he said. "Very wise. It's better not to speak of what happened there."

"No." Her head shook on the pillow. "We ought to talk to each other. When you don't speak, I'm not sure if you've learned anything. Did you understand that this was a useless sacrifice? I'm terrified at the thought that tomorrow you might be tempted to do something self-destructive. The experience of others seems to mean nothing to you. Must everyone give his back to the lash?"

"That's not the way it is," he said indignantly, kissing her hair. "You see that I'm not doing anything foolish."

"I want you—I beg you—not to go back there," she said passionately. "I want to save you. I believe in your talent. Do you think they will allow you to write without constraints? To write as you wish?"

"At the moment—certainly not."

"Well, be brave enough to say, I am not going back to that cage."

It was the first time she had spoken so brutally. The sight of that river of refugees gave her added courage. If so many had made their way across the border, why did this one, her chosen one, hesitate?

"I'm not going back," he whispered, touching her temple with his lips. "I'm not going back, and as yet nothing is pressing me to."

"I wanted to remind you that I didn't renew my contract for next year. As of January I'm free."

"What will you do?" He leaned on his elbow.

"Wait. For you. I will patiently cut the threads that still bind you to this lost cause. The strongest tie was burned away by the uprising. You saw yourself that those who were keen for the struggle, the real patriots, have left Hungary. They won't let the complacent ones be at ease; they won't let the free world sleep. They won't let it forget. Australia waits for you—a whole continent that you can move, wakening sympathy for your country."

Istvan listened, choked with emotion.

"Certainly I am not ordering you to decide in an hour, or tomorrow. I know this will be terribly difficult for you, but I will be with you then. I won't let them destroy you. You have to write, to create. In your literature, were there no poets who went into exile and returned to find themselves famous, to see their books being passed from hand to hand like torches?"

"Of course there were."

"Well—you see. You see yourself," she said triumphantly.

They lay in the dark. Passing automobiles threw dancing splotches of light on the walls, as if someone were shining a flashlight and trying to peer into the house. A feeling of loathing came over him, spawned not by thoughts of India but by memories of whispers, the furtive looks with which he had measured the distance from hostile ears. Some colleagues warned against others, dropping words like stones: agent, spy, informer. The quip ran through his mind: if you want to be a member of the writers' union, you must put out two books and put away three friends. Awards, favorable notices in the press, the thrusting of names and titles into the limelight, even undignified celebrity, and the disappearance of other writers—the silencing of their voices, to the astonishment of readers—all took place at the push of a button, at the express direction of people who had nothing to do with culture.

He remembered all that, yet his resistance was aroused by Margit's demand that he share her aversion to Hungary. It was his country. It was not decent to speak ill of it, as it was not decent to speak ill of one's mother.

"You think I'm too stupid to know what happened in your country," she whispered. He felt her warm breath on his neck. "I wanted to understand you better. I've read everything that has come out in English about the countries behind the Iron Curtain."

This admission moved him, even amused him a little. She must have felt this, for she added hotly, "That's not funny at all. You will say it is all propaganda and slander, and I remember what Krushchev said. Nothing need be added—"

He took her in his arms, rocked her on his chest and tried to soothe her. Silence deepened throughout the house. Even the great blades of the ceiling fan were motionless. Only in the flashes from the headlights of the few passing cars did the shadows swing around and silently elongate.

"Great Britain is covering up some murky business as well, but there is this difference: no premier has yet dared to speak of it so openly," he said tersely, bitterly, as if he were bringing charges. "Let these Hindus tell about the weavers whose fingers were cut off, about the murder of the family of the last mogul, about how here in the Red Fort a major of the Queen's Lancers shot even little children and for that was made a peer of England. And the way they fed dissensions among the Arabs, because oil is more precious than blood. And General Templer, who led the Dayaks to battle against the Malayan partisans and applauded them for beheading prisoners . . . well, and Suez. You saw, after all, that a brazen crime has been committed, but the poor don't count. You can shoot at the villages as if you were on a firing range and get away with it."

She grew tense in his embrace; he felt her alienness. It hurt him, but he had to defend the world in which his life was lived—to which he was connected by the twin forces of struggle and creation.

"If I didn't understand you, my dear one—so dear!—if I didn't know when you spoke that you were filled with anxiety and suspense, that you want the best for me and that you believe that you are rescuing me, it would be hard, after what I've heard, for us to talk to one another." He weighed his words carefully, holding her in his arms; it was not easy for him to put all his bitterness into words.

"You are good to me, very good, not because you are submissive, but because you really do think of me, of Istvan Terey, who has only one life. You don't even know if what I write has any value, but you believe in my ability, you believe in my behavior as you see it. In my words and gestures of tenderness you find certainty, the confidence that you aren't making a mistake. Love makes you perceptive. Often it seems to me that you know more about me than I know about myself.

"You have premonitions about a poet, Istvan Terey, who could be born only if he were with you. You know the power of love. You know its force, that ardent readiness to surrender. Sometimes I wake up at night because I dreamed about you, and I look for you. My throat is tight and the taste of blood is on my lips. I'm ready to scream because you aren't beside me, because the thought has come to me that I've lost you somehow or that you have left me. Margit, I'm sure that no one has ever loved me as you do, or ever will, and that I have in my hand a gift that is priceless, unique. If they were to tell you, 'If Terey lives, you must die,' you would show no shadow of hesitation. You would say, 'Take me.' Can there be a greater sacrifice than life?"

She relaxed a little and nestled her face against his arm. When he stopped speaking, she seemed to beg him, with a light touch of her lips, to say more in this language which was not his own. She remembered that and agonized at the thought that in Hungarian the words would have a different, perhaps more beautiful ring; they might lead her closer to what she wanted to understand, to sound to the very deepest level.

"If it were only that you had given yourself to me, I would be grateful to you. I would desire you, for you're the most beautiful woman on earth to me, but that isn't everything. It's a precious gift, but not unique. Margit, there's not much true love in the world, though so much is said about it and still more is written. Those who haven't known it swear it doesn't exist. You're a mature, intelligent woman. You have a profession; you have some experience of life. Tell me: how many times have you loved as you do now? You yourself have said, only two times that count. Years ago there was—Stanley. You were full of passion and girlish naivete. That passion was unconsummated and untested. It was a presentiment of the element, like the hum in the shell you put to your ear that lets you imagine the ocean.

"There were men in your life. You crossed out their names because, as you say, they didn't count. At last I was here, blown into your life from the far side of the world, from a country that's strange to you, putting thoughts into your language with difficulty. There are thousands of matters that absorb me that you know nothing about, and yet you say without hesitation, 'You are the man. I was waiting for you. I only want to belong to you. I want more: to help you become what you ought to be.'"

Her thigh moved over his knee; she rested her head on her hands. He hardly saw the moist gleam of her wide-open eyes. "Speak," she begged. "Speak."

"The last evening in Agra you said—sitting by me, for I had just awakened—you said, with a world of goodness and devotion in your face, 'I wish you were a leper.' I was taken aback. I was seeing the stumps of those people on the carts with their hands and feet eaten away—those poor stammering wretches to whom one gives alms. 'Are you mad?' I shouted. I was angry at you. Then you stroked me tenderly and said, 'For then all the world would disown you except me. Then at last you would know that I love you.' It seemed an eccentric metaphor to me, but now I see the truth in it. You are capable of that sort of love—of deep, even painful joy at devoting yourself beyond human endurance, recklessly, without calculation."

"Speak," she whispered when he was silent.

"Very well, Margit." He put his hand on her warm, receptive one. "This will hurt. I warn you."

"Go on," she breathed, moving her lips over his chest.

"You thought of my boys. You know that I have two sons. You bought them, Geza and Sandor, carved animals, elephants, buffalo, tigers. You chose very carefully. I remember it all: your defiant smile, for it had to be a surprise for me, and it was. You put me to shame; you had thought of them and I, their father, hadn't. I remember every move, the funny way you wrinkled your nose when you looked closely to see if they were really sandalwood. A box of toys from you, but you kept yourself in the background, so they came from me, and you were happy to do better than I had, to fulfill my responsibility for me. And now you demand that I go away with you and take away their father at a stroke. Margit, I love you, but I don't want to lose them for—"

She writhed like a fish when it feels the hook.

"No, Istvan!" she cried in desperation, pounding the pillows with her fists. "You know me, after all. Don't think badly of me. I had one desire—to save you from the fate of those people in the film. I was trembling all the time we were in the theater, thinking that you could have been one of those who were shot or mangled. Or one of the exiled and homeless who fled as refugees, feeling bitter because they had lost, or because they had not understood what they were doing and had brought destruction on the capital they love. You want to be free. A creative person must be free. I only wanted to help you in that. I'm stupid, stupid. Forgive me, Istvan. I'd never have dared demand that you give up your children."

She beat her forehead against his hand and her hot tears flowed over his skin. He stroked the back of her neck and felt sorry for them both. He clenched his jaws until it hurt.

"I don't want you to suffer like this."

"You did right! You should beat me if you see me being senseless and wicked. I had the best intentions, and only now I see that I didn't love you enough. Don't remember it against me, please."

"I'm like a leper, Margit, at least for one-third of humanity, because I come from there, from the Red camp. You would like for me to repudiate my country, and it is there. To abandon my family, and it is there. To forget the language they speak there. You want me to advance by betraying my homeland. Think: you yourself would lose your respect for me. You would never be able to trust me. You would wonder: since he renounced all that, how can I be sure he will not be untrue to me as well?"

"Don't distress yourself," she moaned. "I know the way I spoke was horrid, but I was truly not thinking that way."

He was close to her. She felt his presence with her body, which was touching his; his open palm was under her forehead. But she felt that he was far away, looking at her contemptuously. The bitter taste of her mistake was in her mouth.

"It's my fault, Margit," he said, suffering as much as she was. "I shouldn't have loved you, shouldn't have met you on it with every gesture and every kiss vowing faithfulness. I couldn't renounce you. I didn't know how. And I can't do it today. I'm so happy that I found you. That I have you. Don't ask me to hasten the hour that must come. I ought to beg for your forbearance, for when I say, Stay with me, I'm not speaking of the last day, the hour of death. That is how it should be . . . I'm only pushing the day away, like a coward. It's not far off: a year, two years—the threshold we can't cross together.

"I believe I know you, and I know how much you're worth. Sometimes I pray: God, let her be happy. To do that, after all, is to pray against you and me. For since I can't bury the past, I can't say: Istvan died, a father died, Hungary died, and someone was born who—apart from pain and self-loathing—has nothing to offer. After all, the one you would take with you would not be me. Do you understand? I would despise myself. Could you be happy with me?"

"Istvan! I shouldn't have said that," she sobbed.

"You should have. We've avoided this conversation for too long. You thought: it's his decision. I don't want it to seem that I am trapping him. I won't urge him; it will happen of itself. And I steered around the questions that needed to be asked, for honesty demands that they be asked. We must both answer them in good faith, supporting each other. You must help me in this, and I must help you."

"That is just how I have always thought about this moment," she gasped out, wiping her tears. "Nothing is final yet. Everything can still change." There was a ring of resilient hope in her voice. "After all, you still haven't given me anything to be despondent about. I see how happy I can be. I want the deep peace I find in you. Will that be taken from me? To mock me? He could not play with us so cruelly."

She breathed fitfully. Her words were tremulous and broken from her crying a moment before. He knew that she was not making her argument to him, but bargaining for him with the One they both, though they knew He existed, wanted to leave out of their considerations. He stroked her head, which shifted heavily on his chest as if it had become severed from her body. There was nothing sensual in these caresses, only tenderness and the hope of quieting the sobbing that was going away like a storm driven by the wind—the sobbing that tore at his heart.

They lay side by side, breathing on each other. Her fragrant hair was spread lightly against his temple. The shadows deepened above them and pressed down so heavily that breathing was difficult. He thought he heard the rustle of flying flakes of invisible soot, but perhaps it was only her eyelids brushing his chest. It seemed to him that they were like a pair of freshly hatched chicks whom the brooding hen has not taken under her wing, who are put into a pot full of gray down and feathers and, terrified by their unknown fate, cuddle together, searching for courage in their own warmth.

He heard the brisk ticking of his watch on the table; the metal face emitted a low tinkle as if the squeaks of a greedy insect were tirelessly cutting into the congealing dark. Margit's breathing grew even; she must have closed her eyes, for one last tear, pressed from under an eyelid, flowed onto his chest, tickling him. His arms were growing numb, but he avoided the slightest movement so as not to rouse her. He thought she was sleeping when she said softly, taking him by surprise with her cool, wakeful tone, "Let's not talk now, Istvan. We've wounded each other enough."

"Yes."

"I want you to sleep. You're showing the strain of the last two weeks. You must rest. You must sleep."

"I can't."

She moved her hand over his forehead as if to wipe away the disturbing thoughts that repeated themselves in his mind. "Think of the boys. They love you, though they may not even know it. They have you, even if they don't appreciate it. Think of them. They are alive. They need you."

"I'm thinking of you."

"You'll have plenty of time for that. Until the end of your life, when I won't be with you."

They were silent, listening to the rapid beating of their hearts, terrified by the words she had spoken. The sleepless nights of the lonely, separated from each other, when pictures bleed from the memory to torture the heart, and insistent questions return. Why? Could it have turned out differently?

He kissed her warmly as if she were a child, covered her carefully with the blankets, and, lying on his back, listened to her breathing in the darkness that teemed around them, rose and then subsided into black atoms. It seemed to him that the gnawing insect in his watch was working faster, boring into time, cutting indefatigably. Its tiny rasping bit Istvan to the heart.

"You must go away." Margit was handing him a cup of morning coffee.

"That's what the ambassador recommended. But I can't just now. I don't know if things have really quieted down there."

"What did you say to him? When he lets you, go."

"I told him I would go to Cochin."

"Where is that?"

"In the south. The very tip of India."

"But why there?"

"Out of cheek, to take him by surprise. Soon after I arrived in India I saw a color film: the ocean, palm trees, white beaches. Little houses, the water, and sails like kites on the horizon. I said to myself, I must go there. The winter is a good season, not too hot."

"Well—go."

"I don't know yet."

"I'll be free the fifteenth of December," she said thoughtfully. "I didn't extend my contract."

"Would you go?"

"Yes. Though I know it would be senseless, trailing after you to the end."

"Don't talk like that."

"Cochin. Cochin," she whispered. "Surely that's far enough from the embassy. Do they pester you very much about me?"

"They don't know much about us, fortunately. I've stopped spending time at the club."

"That must seem strange in itself. It will be harder and harder for you to hide me. You must be seen among people. You can't avoid them like this. They really should see you. That's only common sense. Promise?"

"When I'd rather wait for you. I think . . . I'm at no loss for company."

"You're dreaming," she said sorrowfully.

"Do you forbid me to dream?"

"When you dream, you are preoccupied with what you are creating. I, a living person, am less important to you. Istvan, you are much happier than I am. When you are suffering, you can tell the whole world in your writing. And I . . . I only have you, and still I hesitate before I say a word." She took his hand and put it on her heart. "We will go to Cochin together. If you like."

"We'll steal away and be out of sight. We'll have no one but each other."

"You don't even know what you're saying." She was defending herself against the vision of that joyous solitude on the sparsely peopled beaches of the south. "That's terrible."

"We'll be happy."

"So that afterward we can push each other away into despair?"

He kissed her hair and whispered pleadingly, "Don't talk that way. Please."

She was quiet. She only held him desperately, as if the future were going to tear her away and carry her to a place from which there was no return.

"Listen," she said in a peremptory tone. "Salminen is arriving Saturday. He's giving a lecture on Sunday. He asked me to assemble some material for him and develop some statistical summaries. I'll be busy."

"Two whole days?" he burst out, annoyed that the old doctor with whom he felt little connection was taking away what was his.

"He's coming by car. I must wait for him at the hotel. I certainly won't tell him I'm staying with you. It's only decent for me to be with him on Sunday. Imagine how affronted he would feel if I weren't in the hall! On Saturday you can entertain your colleagues. On Sunday, go to the club. Surely you don't want their attention to be drawn to us."

"I don't want to see anyone. I'm not up to talking to people."

"I'm not asking you if you want to do this. You must," she said with emphasis, "for our sakes. I really want to go to Cochin with you. All the holidays; just the two of us."

"Good!"

"And Sunday?"

"For a few days now Nagar has been after me to go out for duck with him. But not a real hunt. A club picnic."

"So much the better. Everyone will see you."

He only sighed.

"You don't have to murder ducks. Let them live," she whispered. "And in the evening I'll come to you and you will tell me everything. Remember—it must be a cheerful story. Do you hear?"

"Yes."

"And now kiss me," she murmured, pretending that she was brave, that she had already forgotten about the night's conversation—that she was thinking only about the next few days. That she was carefully forming plans, believing that there would be many such days, so many that both of them would begin to speak not of days to come, but of years.

THE YAMUNA FLOWED LANGUIDLY through a wide valley. Its moving surface sparkled with scales of light. Its shoals were overgrown with willow and clumps of reeds three meters high, with tassels of violet seeds curved like cocks' feathers. The marshes dozed, their slimy pools like windows surrounded by a wall of bulrushes—a wall partitioned by miry streams that could hardly be seen under clumps of matted grass. The sharp edges of the rushes attached themselves to clothing; the hand careless enough to catch one was cut as if with a razor. Even on the tops of the high hunting boots there were white scratches.

These thickets were the ducks' breeding grounds. Their only enemy was the jackal who, lured by sleepy squeals, could steal the young from the nest. But when the mother led them to the water, they were safe in the shadowy corridors of streams hidden by the mane of riotously overgrown grasses, and the fecund slime assured them of plentiful food.

The birds that were not shot burst into flight reluctantly. They liked to forage among the rushes and bide their time while the hunters wandered along the streams, plunging into the labyrinths of grasses, into the tall reeds, which emitted the fusty odor of rotting weeds—the sickeningly warm, heavy stench of decay.

Under a high sky dimmed by a melancholy autumn fog, the shotguns popped without echoes. They sounded almost harmless, as if someone were shooting into a paper bag for a joke.

"Hold the dog. Don't let her go!" Nagar squealed, and two servants dragged along the spotted Trompette, who tugged at her leash after every shot, barking frantically. Her eyes were bloodshot and her teeth chattered as saliva leaked from her muzzle. "She is like a wife who does not see the ducks that have been shot, but only scolds at every miss," he said chattily to the Partridge twins.

Fanny, freckled, plain but energetic and full of the journalist's temperament, wrote for women's magazines and traveled a great deal. Her specialty was exotic customs—in short, erotic practices of Papuans and Polynesians, wooden codpieces elaborately carved by tribes in Borneo, matters bordering on witchcraft, primitive medicine and poisoning, which very moral, wizened Englishwomen read about with blushes.

Her sister was always in her shadow, a homely, obliging girl whose blue eyes were perpetually wide with astonishment, whose frizzy hair was the color of straw and whose name was Anna, though everyone called her Moufi—even her sister—and she placidly assented. She helped her famous twin; she was something of a photographer. She adored Fanny, whom she regarded as a woman with no equal. Neither shot; they only helped start up the birds. Fanny stepped watchfully, beating about the high grass, while Anna waited for her sister's orders with her camera at the ready.

Nagar, in a light linen hat and carrying his bag, wearing field glasses on his chest and a belt gleaming with the brass cartridges he had tucked into it, seemed most impressive to them, particularly with his endless narrative of tiger hunting. They exchanged significant looks. Moufi signaled to her sister: there's a story for you, and Fanny responded: I already noticed that, but you remember, too, because it might come in handy.

The twins had never parted since their parents had died in the bombardment of London. Rumors circulated about the pair: they were called "the Partridges" like a married couple, and one was never invited anywhere without the other. Jokes at their expense they took in good part, and often told racy anecdotes about themselves that made them almost universally popular.

In the listless air, sluggish lines of smoke spread like gray cobwebs. Cooks, surrounded by a cluster of people from the villages, squatted by the fires, stoking them with thorny branches and sheaves of stalks. Vultures kept watch from the bare tops of old trees, clapping their sides with their hard wings after the shots as if registering their approval of the slaughter of the birds.

Istvan had not brought his cook, since he assumed that Nagar would insist that he join him for dinner. He had come with Dorothy Shankar, who was turned out in hunting garb. Instead of a sari, she wore a plaid flannel shirt with pockets over her small breasts. Her outfit, completed by a belt and riding boots, aroused general delight. In her hand she carried a light single-barreled fowling piece. She was excited; she talked so unstintingly of her home and family that Istvan did not need to exert himself to entertain her. The driver, a gloomy Sikh, kept looking in the mirror to see what Terey was doing, since he was silent while the girl burst into seductive laughter. Her huge eyes were a velvety black; her cherry-colored lips and the dimple on her swarthy cheek lured with a virginal freshness.

Yet it was with relief that he left her to the Partridges, who, delighted with her beauty, unceremoniously forced her to let them take her picture with the gun raised.

"I'm ordering photos!" From behind a strip of tall grass the American reporter raised two fingers. "I'd rather have them than ducks."

"I'm not giving you any, Bradley!" Fanny declared. "You'll use them to impress your friends and tell them that she is your fiancee."

Miss Shankar listened blushing, with the barrel of the gun aimed at the sky, paralyzed from waiting for the click of the shutter. "Is it over?" she asked, like a child playing hide and seek. "May I move now? I would like to shoot one round at least. Mr. Nagar is cracking away like a machine gun, frightening the ducks for miles."

Terey slipped quietly in among clumps of plants with wilting leaves; the fermenting vegetation smelled like tobacco. He waded through grasses, yellowed from the summer drought, which crunched under his steps. He made his way toward an old stream bed where rapids glistened like a freshly sharpened sickle through the dun-colored weeds.

The spongy quagmire, streaming with water that made sucking noises, gave under his rubber soles, but on the layered webbing of enormous grasses it was possible to step securely. Through denim pants that fit closely around his ankles he felt the rough, sticky edges of the grass scratching like innumerable claws. Sometimes something rustled in the reeds; his ear caught the fluttering and then it subsided again. Only the crickets twittered in two tones as if commanding him to be watchful.

I've lost the knack for socializing, he reproached himself. I've grown unused to being with people. It's just as well they haven't noticed yet how much the last months have altered me. I really am avoiding everyone! I'm not looking for ducks, only the chance to be alone.

Behind him walked a young Hindu in a turban formed from a soiled rag, carelessly wound. The end fell to the back of his neck, shielding it from the maddening flies. He followed at a distance of a dozen paces or more, now dropping back, now moving forward, always keeping Istvan in sight but never intruding. Even his footsteps created no distraction.

"Sahib"—he put his hands to his mouth, but alerted Istvan in a whisper—"there. Two fat ducks."

In the shadow of overhanging branches, hardly rippling the olive-colored water, a pair of teals swam close together. Istvan shook his head and waved, then took down the gun he had hung from his neck and leveled it as if to shoot into the air. The other man nodded and bolted into the bushes. He raised a hand, then threw a piece of rotting root into the undergrowth so that it splashed. The ducks flailed in the water, which seemed to cling to their wings, before sputtering into the air over the thicket. Istvan let them fly up so the ricochet from his shot would not graze the Hindu; they struggled to rise high above the clumps of reeds. The shot swished through the air. One duck fell like a stone, rattling dully on the ground. The other flew on, quacking in mortal terror. Whitish down stripped away by the lead pellets lingered behind her in the air.

Suddenly, as if her beak had struck a windowpane, she whirled and, hammering with her wings, burrowed into the dense mesh of grasses.

"Beautiful shot." He heard a husky voice behind him and saw Major Stowne in washed-out denim standing motionless in the reeds. With the dark barrel of his shotgun protruding, he reminded Istvan of a heron.

"I'm sorry," Terey faltered, embarrassed. "I didn't see you, sir. I wouldn't have barged in."

"That was just the point: for me not to be seen. You will pass on; I will stay. You all scare the birds and they move over here, where it's calm—just under my barrel. Have a look." He pushed aside a shock of overhanging grasses with his boot and showed Istvan several birds that he had killed. "I have no complaints. See, there on the wing. Shoot."

From the direction of the camp, where the chatter of gunfire never stopped, flew a little flock of ducks—five, seven, Terey counted, moving his barrel into position. He had no qualms now as he drew a bead on the first three. He fired and one began its fall, finally striking a shrub amid a shower of yellowed leaves.

Stowne did not even bend over to collect his birds. He only whispered to summon the villager. The Hindu was caked with mud to his thighs; the sash on his hips was soaking. He held the upturned lower edge of his shirt in his teeth and shook the spoils of the shooting. He stood in the sun, trembling from the chill and perhaps with excitement, for he grinned broadly.

The shooting by the river never let up. It was as if someone were throwing stones at the bottom of a barrel.

"Monsieur Nagar is crazy." Stowne's florid face creased in a frown. "You were a soldier, so you instinctively avoid him. Sometimes I've gone out with him for quail, and I had to crawl because he was shooting like a tank in all directions. I was never under such fire on any front in the war."

"He wants to be king of the hunt," Terey said mockingly.

"And you'll see: he will be. I know him. A real fox. He told the lads who retrieve the ducks for us that for each one they brought him they would get half a rupee. Well, didn't I tell you? And where is yours?"

Istvan looked around the bushes. The Hindu disappeared; the tufts of reeds swayed almost imperceptibly. He lifted the bird he had just brought down. It had lain with wings outspread, its blue patch dazzling, its neck iridescent. He fastened it to a strap on his belt.

"Eh, what? Did I get it right?" the gray-haired major said triumphantly. "You can stay here as long as you don't disturb the ducks or, above all, me. It's a good place. It will do for us both."

But Istvan only tipped his hat, pushed the tangled reeds apart and moved wordlessly away.

He dodged and wove for a long time, wrestling with the undergrowth that clutched at his feet like a snare. Time after time he heard the flapping of ducks' wings in the air and their quacking, but reeds and shrubs twice his height covered his field of vision. He came upon a swampy depression—a tiny stream was trickling somewhere under the layers of colorless grasses—and he had to get around it; he had no wish to emerge drenched and plastered with mud. He had gone so far away that he could hear no shots. He was tired and the sun, though invisible, was broiling. He decided to go back—to make his way to the high bank, circle through the fields, and approach the camp from the road by which they had come.

I am at the hunt, as Margit requested. But she would not be satisfied, because I am alone. After all, she wanted me to enjoy myself, to break out of my solitude.

As he came onto the dry meadows he shot one more bird, which had flown recklessly near his barrel. It was not a clean shot; the cluster of pellets had been too large and had ripped apart the belly.

When he picked up the duck, warm blood ran over his hand. He wiped it on the grass but it stuck to the butt of his gun. Swarms of flies swirled around his face and settled around the open beaks of the birds strapped to his belt.

"Hello, Mr. Terey!" He heard an elated voice behind him. From the direction of the bare, rocky fields and patches of corn stripped of its ripe ears, from among the stalks whitened by the sun, Bradley heaved into view. He looked like an overgrown peasant with chubby cheeks and bristling, tousled blond hair. "Look what I bagged! Not just any silly duck."

Above the American's fist a small head was sticking up amid a comb of pertly waving royal blue feathers. A long sheaf of shifting, fiery colors—the tail—swept the dust.

It was a peacock.

"Hide that this minute!" Istvan commanded.

"Why? This is a tasty bird."

"But sacred."

"I never dreamed—"

"There will be trouble. We all could be stoned. These people are not so docile."

Bradley let go of the peacock and stood over it, hesitating.

"Tear off the tail. Cut away the wings and legs. Wrap the rest in anything you have and put it in your car right away."

"Damn! It was the tail I wanted most." He nudged the bird with his shoe. "Curse this country! They won't eat these things themselves and they won't give them to anybody else."

Terey did not wait but walked rapidly on. Bradley caught up with him.

"Are you afraid or what?"

"No. I'm just hungry."

"And my throat's burning. God! I'd drink three cans of beer as long as there was ice. Surely they have it."

"Of course they do. Nagar does—I'll vouch for it."

"For beer on ice I'd give him the Suez. But the French got hit where it hurts there, though they took no losses. A defeat with worse repercussions than Dien Bien Phu: they have all the Arabs against them. They've taken a kick."

"Don't bother me about politics," Terey snapped.

They walked along the path side by side. Shadows lay on the decaying grass from which whitish stones, worn smooth by the river, protruded like bones. Lizards warmed themselves on them—darting little skeletons sheathed in greenish skins.

"You know, Fanny's not so bad," Bradley began. "But that other one—some fellow made a move on Fanny and she invited him home. They did some drinking and went to bed, and when the guy had finished, Fanny called, 'Come 'ere, Moufi. Come, sis, and I'll show you a real man. That's a rarity today.' Well, and what was a fellow to do? He saved his honor. He took the poor little dear in her quilted housecoat with forget-me-nots, and Fanny perched on the couch and watched to see that everything happened as it ought—" he burst into a loud laugh.

"He told you that himself?"

"No," he admitted, frowning. "Fanny was bragging. She's a lot of fun."

"That's just publicity."

"Probably. Everybody likes her, but as a friend, not as a woman. Sure, she told it to make an impression. But Miss Shankar could be in a Coca-Cola ad. Oh, the delightful smell of roast duck!" He rubbed his big palms together. "Istvan"—he clapped him on the back with a heavy hand—"we'll knock back a few."

"We'll hit Nagar up. I'm ready to give him my ducks if he'll just break out the whiskey. The king of the hunt must stand everyone a drink."

"I like you, Terey. One must make sacrifices for the future. Especially when it smells so good."

A joyful hubbub greeted their appearance. Girlish voices asked how many birds they had shot. Istvan shook the few undistinguished ducks that hung from his belt, and Bradley roared, "I shot a great big bird, but it flew beyond the river—"

"The Air India plane, no doubt," Nagar said. "And you certainly didn't hit it . . . I have fourteen ducks."

"Long live the king!" Bradley called in a thunderous voice. "Hey, fill the bumpers! Only—can Comrade Terey drink a toast like that?" he asked in a stage whisper. "Maybe I'll drink for him."

The guests lay on blankets under shady trees, relaxing. Nagar dismantled his gun and tried to impress them by tooting on the barrel as if it were a trumpet, but the sound was not at all similar, which sent Bradley into spasms of laughter. Fanny Partridge added to the merriment by proposing to the American, announcing that it would be a marriage with something extra, and pointed to her blushing sister. Even the Hindus smiled, though with restraint.

"I have to eat first," Bradley stipulated. He sat crosslegged, balancing a tin mess plate on his knees and eating rice soaked in spicy sauce with a spoon. "When I have eaten, you will draw straws"—he licked the spoon with a knowing wink—"to see which one of you will have the honor of chasing flies off me when I'm lying down."

Major Stowne leaned toward Terey and said an undertone, "A gentleman does not behave this way." He shook his head ruefully. "Many things may be said, but not in front of the servants."

The villagers who had retrieved the ducks stood in a group under the trees. Each had a ladleful of rice in a bowl made from a leaf. They ate with their fingers, looking over the faces of the picnickers with eyes full of astonishment and bovine mildness.

"Soon, soon, sahib," a cook assured Terey. "I am heating the meat." He squatted, blinking, and blew on the ashes of the dwindling fire. White flakes of burnt stalks flew up, swirling. "The rice is surely warm. I wrapped the pots in thick coverings of newspaper."

Rattling their wings, the vultures jumped to the ground and walked about, moving their long necks up and down. They were looking for bones, for scraps scraped from mess plates. They plucked shreds of greasy paper from each other's beaks.

"Why don't we just shoot at them?" Bradley made a face. "They stink when I'm trying to eat."

"That isn't done," Stowne scolded him. His face was red from alcohol. "They are repugnant but useful, in contrast to journalists. Wherever there is shooting, straight away there are plenty of you. But the vultures—they truly clean the world."

The sun shone benignly. Veils of haze hovered over the broad river bed with its sandy shoals. Ducks flew overhead, settled amid the rushes, slid softly into the water, shook their rumps and quacked as if for joy that the hunt had stopped.

"Trompette!" Nagar said anxiously. "Where is Trompette?"

She was running with great bounds, carrying a teal in her mouth. She trotted up to her master and looked him in the eye for a long time, not even wagging her tail.

"One more that I shot but we could not find. Fifteen," he exulted. "Put her here—here, at your master's feet." His finger pecked the air, pointing down.

The dog hesitated, then moved a step forward.

"That is the only one he managed to shoot!" Stowne whispered.

Istvan, lying on his side, reached for a little pot of rice packed in newspaper and took off its wrappings. Steam rose from under the cover. He took a helping and waited for it to cool.

Suddenly his eye fell on the grease-smeared headline of a short item of news: "Death of a Hungarian Journalist." He reached for the paper.

"UPI. The well-known Hungarian journalist Bela Sabo was shot yesterday as he attempted to cross the Austrian border. Though he received assistance, he died. Bela Sabo, born Bela Fekete, was a distinguished reporter; his book on liberation movements in Africa, *Where the Devil Is White*, was translated into many languages. Sabo's tragic death has evoked an outpouring of grief in the world of journalism . . ."

He stared at the rumpled, soot-stained newspaper with the circular indentation made by the bottom of the pot. Without knowing what he was doing he smoothed it, trying to find the front page.

Bela is dead. Killed.

Stupefied, he gazed at the great blue smoky space above him and the flashing current at the bends of the crawling river. The glare from it made his eyes smart.

"Here, Trompette, little doggie, dear," Nagar coaxed, reaching for a collar to restrain the resisting bitch.

Bela killed. The dog lays the duck at Nagar's feet. Bela is not there. Not there. And never will be. The duck opens its wings, springs onto Nagar's chest, flutters in his face, and from his shoulder flies into the air. Bela killed. What is that roar of laughter? Everyone is going off in gales of giggles, howling and clapping. With his hand Nagar wipes his muddy cheeks. The dog watches with reproachful bloodshot eyes; her muzzle is full of feathers. Where did the feathers come from? Why are they laughing? Bela is dead.

"She wanted to save the honor of our king of the hunt!" Bradley bellowed. "She grabbed him a live duck!"

Bela. Bela. Why did I have no premonition? He buried his face in his hands.

"You'd hardly call this a hunt," he heard Major Stowne beside him murmuring and smelled the aromas of curry and whiskey, "but I must confess, it's been a first-rate frolic. Even that sad Hungarian is about to choke from laughing."

Istvan walked away, staggering. The Indian attendants stepped aside at the sight of his blanched face. He walked blindly; he stumbled into a tree trunk. He wanted to hurt himself, to feel physical pain, since anguish was tearing his heart so that he was standing with his mouth open, hardly able to breathe.

Over the smooth bark of the tree, white as if it had been bleached, ran a little line of red ants. They crept to his hand, which was grasping the trunk. They gathered, seemed to hold a council, and then circled around, peeping and examining the spaces between his spread fingers with their antennae. Bela is not there. Whom could he talk to? Whom could he talk to, who would understand? They had sworn to be together always.

He went back to where he had been sitting. He did not believe this. He must check. Perhaps he had made a mistake. Perhaps there was another surname, another first name. Only a pack of vultures, crunching torn paper in their beaks, were walking over the pot and rolling it, shaking out the remains of the rice.

He wanted to kick the birds, to take them by their nude, squirming necks and strangle them. Around the rattle of wings rose the stench of carrion. He stood over the tatters of the newspaper, the overturned pot. He heard Bradley's easygoing laugh:

"They ate it all up. There's nothing left."

Chapter XII

In neither of Ilona's letters was it possible to find an evocative image, or even a sense of the climate created by developments in Budapest. He had the impression that she had written cautiously, conscious that her letters would be read by many eyes before they reached the hands of the addressee. The most important thing was that all the family were still alive. Only Sandor was ill, with flu. He had gotten a chill because it was hard to get a glazier. Windowpanes everywhere were broken. There was no lack of food; bread was supplied in timely fashion, meat could also be found, and they were not suffering severe shortages because her parents had sent a large parcel from the country with real salami, salt bacon seasoned with paprika, mutton, and a tin box of eggs which arrived without breaking, having been half buried in sawdust.

He smiled as he read this scrupulous recounting of trifles. He liked Ilona's exactitude; he seemed to smell the pungent rawness of the beechwood shavings around the eggs as if they were clinging to his hands. He saw the table under the window that looked out onto the narrow yard with landings off kitchen stairs; he heard the stairs rumbling under the feet of packs of gleeful children.

The letter in which he had asked for details relating to his friend's death must have crossed hers in the mail, for she had not written a word about Bela. Perhaps she did not know what had happened to him. She could have telephoned the editorial department. But were any of the old staff there—any of those with whom they both had been friends?

He remembered years when such a question would have brought ambiguous, evasive answers, words carefully screened as if to avoid upsetting someone seriously ill, and the conversation would have concluded with a phrase that was almost ritualistic: I will tell you when we meet; it's best not to speak on the telephone. In that case, what the devil were telephones for? Just to assure the caller that there was life at the other end of the wire? Or were they only for the ears of eavesdropping authorities?

The letters brought him a feeling of relief. So the worst was over; at last there was calm and a measure of order. He stared at a short sentence: "It has been very difficult lately." Then immediately the subject changed, as if Ilona were trying to cover her tracks, feeling that she had already said too much, particularly about glaziers and windowpanes, which were in short supply throughout the city.

To all appearances the functions of the embassy were being carried on normally. But close observation revealed that other embassies were avoiding contact with theirs. At receptions, conversations broke off and groups dispersed into the crowd when the ambassador or Ferenc came over. It seemed that the world around them was waiting impatiently for pronouncements, demonstrations—that official connection to any government in Budapest had deprived them of their standing as representatives of Hungary's true interests. That was not only galling but humiliating.

It was rather different in his own case. At the club, in the press corps, they simply liked him. But the friendliness and tolerance he met with, the advantage he seemed to enjoy, was baffling to his colleagues and aroused their suspicions.

There was genuine excitement when his poem appeared in Bombay's *Illustrated Weekly*. He had translated it himself. For a long time he had wanted Margit to become acquainted with his style. She had suggested several improvements; she had been able to select the appropriate English expressions. The poem was about Budapest, about his nostalgia for the beauty of the city.

He was summoned to meet with the ambassador. He passed quickly through Judit's office, since he found Bajcsy's door open and saw the boss's curmudgeonly face beyond the threshold. He was sucking a pipe that had gone out. Judit could only glance at Istvan with fear and sympathy, as neighbors look at an acquaintance with whom they have exchanged words every day and who has suddenly been found to have murdered his wife, set a fire, or at the least indulged a perversion.

The door had not even closed when Kalman Bajcsy pounded the pages of the thick weekly with the back of his hand and growled, “What is the meaning of this, Terey?”

“A poem. They invited submissions. I sent one.”

“Who cleared you to do that?”

“You yourself, comrade ambassador, recommended that we begin to draw the attention of the press to Hungary again.”

“A poem about Budapest? Do you know how this will be read just now?”

“Does the name of the capital have to be left out because there has been an uprising? I wrote this a long time ago.”

Bajcsy fixed him with a stony glare. “And what does this mean, ‘bloodstained leaves,’ ‘banks in shackles’?” He read the words with damning emphasis, turning the stem of his pipe. “Don’t make a fool of me.”

“Metaphors. In the fall, leaves turn red. The suspension bridge on its chains binds both banks of the Danube together,” he explained with impertinent precision. “You remember the Chain Bridge, comrade ambassador?”

“But who knows about it?” the older man thundered. “You will regret this, Terey. Who called my attention to this antic of yours? An ambassador who happens to be a friend of mine.” He jabbed the pipe at Terey’s chest as if it had been a knife. “He congratulated me on having people on my staff who could write poetry. I know very well what he meant. I will not have you making a laughingstock of me.”

“Perhaps he knows something about poetry?” the counselor ventured to remark with a show of disarming naivete.

“He? How? We must be watchful here. There is no time for us to amuse ourselves. And I will tell you something else, Terey: don’t publish anything without my consent. You may be a great poet in our country, but it is different here, where every word has to be held up to the light three times before it is printed. You are with the service; you are an official of my embassy. You will not play politics on your own hook. They put me here for that.”

If he could have, he would have given an order to have me flogged, Terey thought fleetingly. He looked at the burly hands with their curling black hair as they clenched into fists and opened again in powerless rage.

"Well, why are you looking at me like that? Did you understand my order?"

"Yes. I only wanted to put you on notice that another poem of mine will appear in the Bengal literary monthly with my biography and list of credits."

Bajcsy caught his breath. "And there will be more about bloody leaves and shackles? You will withdraw that poem this minute."

"I'm afraid that would make a very bad impression. I will have to furnish some explanation, and I will write them that I declined publication at the ambassador's wish."

"You will attribute nothing to anyone except yourself."

"That's impossible. I want the poem to be published. These are the first pieces of Hungarian poetry to appear in India."

Bajcsy's eyes bored into Terey. He breathed as if he had been running. "And what is this other poem about?" he asked more calmly.

"About love."

A vein throbbed in the ambassador's neck. He nodded skeptically. "About love? It depends on what you put into it. About love for a woman?" he asked suspiciously.

"Yes."

"And will that one have metaphors as well?"

"Politicians also use metaphors, not just poets. It will be translated into Bengali."

"That's better." Bajcsy exhaled. "Let them print it, but you will be responsible for the consequences. In the future, however, everything you publish goes through this desk. I want to see every scrap of paper you send to the Indian editors."

He sat pressing his hand into his beefy cheeks. At last he asked wearily, "Terey, why do you take such delight in upsetting me? I will prick you once and that fame of yours will burst like a balloon."

"You can shout at me, but that's all. And send me back to Hungary. But there have been changes in the ministry there. You think that they love you, ambassador—that you can speak a word and they will all be on their knees. Not in these times. You know well that I fill my own balloon, if I may use your figure of speech. I glide under my own power. Your boys may learn about me in school. Well, yes—they will take the qualifying examinations. You know that just as well as I do. No one need inflate my balloon. I have value outside this embassy."

Bajcsy's creased face glistened with sweat. Suddenly he croaked, "Get out."

"Have I satisfied you on the points in question, comrade ambassador?" Terey rose.

"Take yourself off!" the ambassador roared. "Get out of my sight or it will be too bad . . . I can't stomach you, Terey." He sprang up and stood by the window with his back turned. He did not even look around when the counselor closed the door to his office.

"In a hellish humor, eh?" Judit leaned across her desk. "Did he try to bite your head off?"

"Yes, but he realized in time that he couldn't stomach me." Istvan winked. "Do you know what sent him into such a fit? A homeopathic dose of poetry—just one poem of mine in *Illustrated Indian Weekly*."

"You're not behaving sensibly."

"If I had been sensible, I would never have been a poet," he admitted ruefully. "The boss doesn't know what he wants. First he calls me in, then he says he doesn't want to look at me. It's not as though I'm forcing myself on him."

"You're in a good humor," she said, surprised. "Have you had news from home?"

"They are alive. They have enough to eat, a roof in one piece over their heads, and glass in the windows. What more do you want?"

For a moment she did not speak, but brooded with her fingers against her lips. Finally she whispered, "Ferenc has a letter for you. It's best that you get it from him, but don't mention that I told you."

His mind filling with fresh agitation, he went straight to the secretary's office. He tugged at the door handle, but the room was locked. Ferenc had gone out.

At his own desk, beside the newspapers rolled up and secured with bands of thick paper—the daily allotment of press brought by the caretaker—he saw a narrow envelope with words stamped in Hungarian: air mail. He looked carefully to see if it had been opened. The back bore no sender's address, but the handwriting looked familiar. He tapped the envelope on the desktop and carefully cut the edge with scissors. He drew out sheets of paper covered with unsteady writing. He looked at the signature on the last of the folded pages and suddenly had to stifle a scream of grief. The letter was from Bela.

Not a day goes by that I don't think of you. I miss you terribly. I caught myself, as I walked through Heroes' Square, in a dialogue with you, as if you were here. A huge statue lay pulled down on the pavement, the larger-than-human face turned toward the sky, the crown of the head white with bird droppings, like a graying of the hair invisible to us until now. As long as it stood, it was not subject to the ravages of time. It did not age; it grew in fame. Some fellow was battering its head with a hammer on a long handle until the bronze shell groaned, but the head did not give way. The chap grew warm from his exertions, threw off his jacket so that his suspenders could be seen crisscrossing his white shirt, brandished the hammer, and banged away like a madman. No one was near, but little groups of passersby watched furtively in front of the half-opened gates of houses. Amid the metallic ringing of his blows came the high whistling of stray missiles fired from beyond the zoo toward the suburbs.

I walked through the square, where there was hardly any light, only the soft luminescence of the wet paving and tramway rails. I felt as if I were in a dream. A small, disappointed man was taking his revenge, pounding with a hammer like a child beating his fist on the corner of a table that had given him a bump on the head. I wanted to watch him at close range. I admit there was some journalistic curiosity in this: a monument on the pavement, a body in a bronze uniform groaning under the hammer head. What was this fellow trying to avenge by shattering it? Had he lost someone close to him? Or was he only disappointed because of what he had imagined about greatness, infallibility, divinity? Perhaps he was punishing it for his own blind trust, for his love and attachment.

Perhaps he was one of those who had marched chanting the name on the monument, at the calls to action forgetting their grievances, for only the man in bronze would think on their behalf and establish laws.

I felt no joy in the frenzied toil of the man with the hammer. It was easier to shatter this monument without leaving a trace, except for the clinking of bronze, than to change the convictions of people, to straighten bent necks, to get it through their heads that the violence the fallen leader employed, just by virtue of its being raised to a legal norm, was a crime three times over. Death took him, and his colleagues stripped him of his merits; they exposed him for what he really was. But they did not root out the poisonous old antipathies, and contempt for the ordinary man, who was supposed to listen and admire. They hate the demigods from an older time before whom they groveled, but today in the depths of their souls they would take a lenient attitude toward "wet work," for indeed there are situations in which it is simplest to have recourse to those unpleasant but effective methods and—at a stroke—do what must be done.

So I said to you, and today I will recount everything. I was walking to the stone pedestal when a tank came from the avenue, shooting into the square with automatic rifles. I tell you, it was like a bad dream. I was not even afraid. It was as if I were incapable of being touched by what was happening. I looked out from behind the granite plinth; above me stood gigantic jackboots from which wisps of straw protruded as if in mockery. Only the statue lay on the empty square, the dead face with its mustache turned toward the lowering sky. In the wavering glare of rockets from over the Danube, it seemed to sneer. The tank rolled onto the square and peppered an abandoned tramway car until shards of glass sprayed from the broken windows. They had been afraid of an ambush. Tons of rocking steel crawled toward the park; wheel belts left a wale of indentations in the asphalt. Flashes came from beyond the railroad bridge, and round after round of machine gun fire ripped the air. I was alone by the fallen statue on the darkening square. Suddenly I saw the attacker, the avenger, crawling out of its hollow interior, dragging his jacket. He had taken cover there. He spat on his hands and hit the head with his hammer. The head moaned like a bell that has burst. The noise of the blows lured the curious to the gates. Traffic started up again; people slipped by quickly along the walls.

I am writing this for you. I have not succeeded in finishing the letter. I am writing now after a two-day interruption. Today by the cemetery wall I saw the bodies of people who had been shot. They lay one by another, as if looking to each other for warmth. I was told they were informers, agents. Someone seemed to know who they were. He summoned people from the street who brought them in and handed them over to the workers' guard. They had been beaten with no investigation. I am going with the people of the capital. That strong current carries me along, but there are moments when—condoning impulses of hate, hurriedly explaining to myself that it must be so, that this is the price that must be paid—I feel a chill as I think which way this turbulence will drag us.

Istvan, the mob is terrible. It is good that you are not forced to watch what is happening. Stalin said, rather ten innocent be punished than that one enemy elude us. That was a crime, but today, just as hastily, people are unjustly punished. They have already told me of people hung without justification. There is an appalling momentum on the street; they are squaring accounts as if they did not believe that law would re-establish itself and tribunals mete out justice openly. The crowd wants retribution now, this minute, blood for blood. In return for the humiliation they have suffered they beat the interrogation officers, the former masters of life and death. They spit in their faces and their victims do not even dare wipe the saliva that trickles from their foreheads. They look back with lifeless eyes as if they know what awaits them.

What should be done, Istvan? Should they be pardoned? Tomorrow they will recover from their fear and take our magnanimity for weakness, or, worse yet, stupidity. They will muster their forces. Their concern is not the nation or socialism. They want power. They wallow in their sense of immunity. They despise those in whose name they wield authority but whom they consider human dung. Say: what would you do with these judges who con-

demned the innocent, who began the hearings with the verdicts in their briefcases in accord with instructions received by telephone, with the findings of specialists in interrogation who tore out fingernails, maltreated prisoners physically and psychically—who tortured them into signing depositions in which they confessed to crimes not committed? What would you do with doctors who sentenced political prisoners to confinement in bunkers smaller than coffins, in cellars with water to their knees, cynically attesting, "This is a man, not a horse; he will endure it. And if he should kick the bucket, we will write that the cause of death was influenza, heart failure. The coffin will be sealed and all is done."

Would you let them go free? Wouldn't it be better to strangle them while we have them in our hands? While the workers' fingers are lodged in their beardless, greasy chins so that they shriek with terror?

Today we would revel in the investigation, the trial, the lawful verdict. And tomorrow they would grant them amnesty! They destroyed not only people, but socialism. They ruined the moral fiber of human beings. They frightened and bought off the younger generation. Everything seethes around me. I flail; I do not know whom to believe. There is so much conflicting information, and all from eyewitnesses, shouted angrily, affirmed on oath. People see what they want to see. Istvan, you can be happy that you are far away from this. You will come back, you will return when conditions are right. Desperation forces people to strike blindly. I hear tank patrols thundering around the boulevard; the motors are droning. If only they would let us cleanse ourselves! We ought to do it with our own hands, with no one's help. The Poles are trying. How much they are spoken of and held up as an example, but they have no conception of how it was with us through all those years. They never went with the Germans. They were not poisoned.

Istvan, the committee deliberates without recess. Day and night lights burn and angry voices spar. Delegates come in armed. Rifles hang in the cloakroom instead of coats. One feels that the earth is trembling under Hungary. Momentous hours. Under the windows a parade passes. Young people cry, "Don't believe Nagy. He only babbles." "Power to the committee of the Revolution!" I walk along the street. I go into the crowd. It is a raging river. I entrust myself to its current. I want what is good for this nation. I want what is good for Hungary.

Warmest regards,

Your Bela

P.S. Two more days have passed. It is calm, and that is gratifying. I do not trust the mail; it is still not working properly. I am giving this letter to the correspondent from Vienna, who leaves today, for nothing unusual is happening here. Thank God; I dream only of such bulletins.

November 3rd, 1956. Budapest.

P.S. One word more: believe me, we will emerge whole from this chaos. It is impossible that in our camp two socialist countries, two countries bound to each other by a defense pact, would turn their gun barrels on each other.

Your red Bela

Dazed, he looked blankly at the map of India, at the outline of a triangular land like a dried cheese. Outside the window the sky glowed and a car horn blared. The Austin was open. No doubt Mihaly was sitting behind the wheel.

The next day at dawn, the dreadful memory confronted him again. How could you trust them, Bela? The nation is not the mob that stamps on portraits and roars in the squares, brandishing weapons torn away from soldiers. Yes—it is easy to say that now. And with every day, as the date memory clung to grew more remote, it would be easier to recognize the signs of hate, madness, provocation, and obvious counterrevolution. But they did not want to see, as the comrades who were carried away earlier by airplane from their positions of power did not want to hear the voices of protest, the complaints and calls for justice. Bela is dead. It cannot even be said that he died for the cause. UPI only reported that he had been wounded as he tried to cross the Austrian border. And so you let yourself be swept away by the mob, the outflowing human river, by mindless forces. The suffocation was too much for you. You abandoned Hungary.

Was the letter that dangled from his fingers a call to arms, a testament? Or, now that it had reached him, was it only a warning? Was it a sign that he should not go back? If there were no homeland, to what would he be returning? Or was it wrong to think that way, even at the worst of times?

If the Western newspapers were putting out the news of Bela's death, they must have buried him in Austria—not even on Hungarian ground. Anyway, was that important? Magical thinking: the ground is the same everywhere. No. No. The ground on which we took our first tottering steps . . . In that grass I hid my face, I wiped away the tears of my first humiliations. I beat it angrily with my powerless fists. I tugged at it so it would not slip away from me, for it whirled so after the mad chase that my ears rang. The ground I named in the most beautiful of languages, for it was my own: Hungarian. It is waiting for me, I know—not a large place by my standards.

Bela is dead and I am foundering, crumbling. Now there is no one who remembers the enjoyments of childhood: bathing the horses, camping on the island in the Danube that was overgrown with willow when the river rose without warning and nearly drowned us as we slept in the cabin. Bela was the only one I told that I loved Ilona when we were still schoolboys, before we had taken the final examinations. I wanted to beat him to death when he grabbed her photograph from me and laughed as he hopped from bench to bench and held it over his head. Then when I caught him, he threw it to the other boys, and they gave it back with a mustache and beard drawn on her face. I wished he would die. And now he has.

Indeed, I loved him because he knew me. He shared my anxiety; so many times we talked the night away, chatting until dawn. We had bitter mottos for those nights: Fun shall make us free. Revelry revives the nation. A devoted friend. A splendid colleague, full of the joy of life. Always ready for adventures, full of madcap inspirations. Impossible that the air has closed over him like water, without a trace.

Words about a lost friend from childhood . . . about my own death in the passing of my loved ones. Istvan was ashamed. Was he ready to exchange every motion of the heart for words, calculating unconsciously that he would print them the next day and throw them to the world as one throws seed to birds?

Fervently he set about conjuring up faraway images. The meadows by the Danube loomed before him—the doleful cry of the startled lapwings. Willows: big cats with the downy golden coats of spring. Branches swayed in the wind, jostling tiger-striped bumblebees who protested in bass rumblings. The water was a strident blue; it whirled away into little streams and slowly filled each of the horses' hoofprints with quicksilver. Suddenly he heard a heavy step in the corridor and noticed that the handle of his door was trembling.

"Come in!" he called, sitting erect and alert.

"I do not want to disturb you. That is why I listened for the sound of the typewriter," mumbled the caretaker.

"What do you want?"

"Nothing. I would only like to ask if you received your letter, counselor."

Istvan grasped the thin sheets, which were folded accordion-style, and showed the man the envelope.

"Thank you. I have it."

"No, not that one. Among the old newspapers I cleared from here I found a letter you had written by hand. Tom brought it here, but the secretary met me and said that he himself would give it to you, and sent me to the warehouse."

"Why do you think he couldn't give it to me?" The counselor tilted his head.

"I saw him read it, and then he took it off somewhere. Where, I don't know. But I could see that you had written it and laid a newspaper on it, and then something happened and you forgot about it. But a letter like that had better not get into the file."

"Did you read it?"

The caretaker squirmed uncomfortably and shifted from one foot to the other.

"My English is weak. It was not in the envelope. I read—counselor, sir—I read the letter, so nicely written . . ." He put a hand on his chest. "Comrade Ferenc is in. Perhaps just now you could—"

Istvan moved toward the door.

"Wait here."

He went to the secretary's office. Ferenc brightened at the sight of him.

"Give me the letter," he snarled.

"In good time. Sit down. What is your hurry? I have been wanting to have a personal conversation with you."

He groped in a drawer and drew out an unsealed envelope. Istvan saw the address: Miss Margaret Ward. Agra. He did not dare glance inside and see which of his letters it was and what declarations of feeling it contained. Heat flowed along his spine. He could have choked with rage at himself. All those evasions and concealments, only for this—that all should be lost for such a stupid reason, everything given away. He tucked the envelope into the pocket of his jacket. He would have given anything to be able to see its contents.

"Take a seat," Ferenc said invitingly. "Whither away so fast? Surely not to the post office; that is dated two months ago. It can wait. When are you taking your furlough?"

"Before the holidays."

"For long?"

"As long as I can!" he said vehemently.

"Have you found us so trying?" Ferenc said regretfully. "Well, what next?" He took out his wallet and carefully counted out ten banknotes. "Here is a thousand. Take it; don't be tiresome. It is honestly earned. Your commission from the firm for cases of whiskey delivered at your order. Don't be coy. Take it as I give it."

Istvan did not look at the money, only at the ingratiating smile on the secretary's face. What stratagem was hidden behind it?

"You have no reason to be offended by the money. By me, you may. Surely you cannot think that I am a Judas so upright that I share the silver with my victim. I have not shown the letter to anyone. It is your private affair. In your case I have other reservations." He looked at the pocket into which Istvan had put the letter as if he wanted to touch it so as to divine the content of the message. "But remember this: I will not dig a pit under you."

"Thank you," Istvan muttered after a pause. "There is no point in my not taking it. Since you charged the order to my account, I suppose I am entitled to it. The first business I've done—through no wish of my own—thanks to you."

"If you would not be so hotheaded," Ferenc sighed, "we could look around for more. Profits are there to be made, but it is difficult to count on you."

"Best not to count on me." He gathered up the notes. "I'm not a businessman."

As he was walking out the door, a whisper reached him: "And I am not your adversary. I would gladly help you if you had decided to—"

"To what?" He whirled around.

But the secretary only waved.

"Nothing. You are so distrustful of me, there is nothing to say."

"Did he give it back?" the caretaker asked worriedly.

"All is well." He pulled out the wrinkled letter, and when the door closed he held his breath as he glanced through a dozen lines. He read it with a critical eye, suspiciously, looking for hidden connections between simple words and his actions, plans, the decisions which, in their judgment, he might make. *You know, Margit, I have no secrets from you. I tell you everything as it really is.* These words might be read as referring to the professional secrets of the embassy, real and imaginary. *It will be as you wish. Only call me and I come . . . You are my whole world.*

Yes, these turns of phrase might attract Ferenc's attention, might arouse suspicion that by chance a confession had fallen into his hands—the confession of a man who was about to betray and desert his country, who had caught a glimpse of freedom and chosen it. My flight would be convenient for them. A deserter—anyway, we suspected it a long time ago. Our collective (that word takes on luster in this case!) showed true devotion to the cause of socialism, and to you, Comrade—here for the time being a space must be left for the correct name, since no one knows if Kádár will remain in power a month.

Never! He bit his lip in impotent rage. Already he felt a despondency suffused with bitterness. Why not listen to them? They are afraid of independence; they depend on their positions. Yet two hundred thousand have left the country. Bela, on whose integrity I would have staked my life, died trying to pass into Austria. By what right do I judge myself wiser than they? How can I doubt Bela's patriotism? Because they killed him?

His letter described events that had occurred hardly a month ago. Terribly long ago; the distant past. The letter, like a twig pressed into coal, says little about the murmur of the primordial forest. A lost epoch; perhaps in years to come posterity will search out and retrieve those buried memories. We must go forward. Looking behind me will not bolster my courage. Bela's grave in an Austrian cemetery offers no hope; it puts me on guard. No bullet will reach me here. I put the country's borders behind me long ago.

But as he pressed his fingertips against his eyelids, he felt that that border was in his heart, and had not been crossed.

To go away, to break this tether . . . enough of the embassy, of the same faces, conversations and rancors, which wore on him like the stench of burning feathers. He rested his head heavily on his hands and shut the world out. Fate, after all, hides events in its sleeve, and death is not the worst of its surprises. I am prepared. I am ready for that final meeting.

But even as he passed judgment on himself, other solutions occurred to him. If Ilona . . . We all would be saved, we all would benefit, even You. I would not have to shatter Your stone tablets. One may shake the Ten Commandments in helpless anger, but no one is exempt from them. They are always with us, etched on our consciences; they weigh every action, affixing their sign of approval or condemnation so as to crush us in the last hour and accuse us for eternity.

Why should I not shake myself free of the past and begin a new life, cut off from all that had been—from myself as well? Let the new poet, Istvan Terey, be born on the shores of Australia, writing in English. Indeed, I can write in that language. I have proof that I can reinvent myself. My work is being printed.

Perhaps in years to come someone will ferret out the fact that I came from Hungary and feel that he has made a discovery. And that is all. People are quick to forgive the abandonment of one's past. They forget that their speech was supposed to be the yes that means yes and the no that means no, like border stones between good and evil. And they long for leniency for themselves; they want us to be tolerant of each other and not take notice of faults, because we are, at bottom, accomplices.

Since no bullet shot in Budapest brought me freedom, I have a wife, obligations. What is unfolding in my mind is hideous. How many times my eyes have slid over brief news items under small headlines: he killed his wife, he stabbed his wife with a knife, and I shrugged them off, thinking, can two sensible, cultured people not find a simpler solution, not separate without losing respect for each other, not remain friends and part without insults and curses? Is death really the easiest way? Or perhaps the convicted murderer was more honest: he killed because he wanted to be free. She was blocking his way, so he thrust in the knife. And I am convinced that one of those bullets, blindly shot, could bring me freedom. I am a murderer, though my hands are clean. I find pleasure in these hypothetical solutions. I assent too eagerly to these possibilities. Moreover, I attribute them to Him Whose will is discreetly called fate, coincidence, or chance.

I am angry at Ilona because her existence reminds me of myself years ago, when I was mawkishly and absurdly in love. If only it were possible to forget that! To say: I did not know yet. I embraced her in a breath of jasmine, as yet understanding nothing of life. A blind puppy.

Chandra would absolve me with a simple explanation, with light mockery: that one who long ago took his vows and meant to keep them is not you. Cells die in the body and others replace them. Every so many years we change completely. Your wife is accustomed to you; she did not notice that a stranger lived beside her—not at all the same man she had exchanged promises with, but another. How can you, a living man, take responsibility for someone who a long time ago ceased to exist, only because you have not changed your name and you still look around when they call: Istvan Terey? But you can be someone else entirely. You can create yourself. It is only necessary to have the courage to say, I can, therefore I will.

Only the first step is difficult. After that you will see that you yourself created the constraints. There are no impassable barriers. None. If He exists, let Him try to stop you. After all, you created Him for yourself from ten commandments, and you carry Him like a crushing burden. Instead of wishing for your wife's death, kill Him; that's no great trick. It's enough to say that He does not exist, and I myself will be the master. At once everything becomes simple.

To escape, to go where we will be happy. To take Margit by the hand and lead her. To return to my country. Let them say what they like. The whole world is of no concern to me. It does not exist apart from us. Only our looks waken it to life, and words can consolidate a more perfect, unblighted world.

One must have the courage to say: I decide. My happiness is the law. I. Margit and I. Because I want her. For her adoration, the surrender in which she herself takes such delight, has become indispensable to me.

Yet a plea arose from deep within him: Help me, I don't want . . . But he did want; he wanted painfully, desired, craved. In this torment there was a disingenuous calculation: he was trying to force God's hand, to blackmail Him. If You cannot find me a way of possessing this woman that is compatible with Your law, do not be surprised if I must break it, and it will not be my fault. I went to great lengths to find a solution.

He banished these troubling thoughts, these whinings of deceitful logic, like arguments from the chambers of hole-in-corner lawyers where dark goings-on are forever being whitewashed. Chandra greets me. Chandra offers me his services, he thought irritably. The telephone rang and he lifted the receiver, out of temper at being disturbed.

"Istvan? You invited me for today. Nothing has changed, has it?" He heard a tinge of sourness in Trojanowski's voice.

"No. I'm glad we can chat a little."

"Your wife is well? Your children doing well in school? Windowpanes being replaced in Budapest and scarred façades on buildings beginning to be repaired? Are you in a better frame of mind?"

"Everything is all right at home."

"And with you?"

"Nothing wrong. I'm tired. They've promised me a holiday."

"Will you dash over to Hungary?"

"No. I'm going to the seashore. A furlough in the country of posting—" he repeated the conventional form of words.

"You were born under a lucky star. I envy you. Till tonight. I am ordering the 'wooden plate' and red wine."

"What time will you be here?"

"When I have sent some telegrams. One thing more—or perhaps you know already. Madam Khaterpalia's child was stillborn."

"What?" he cried, as if Trojanowski had accused him of something.

"Nagar said so, and he knows everything. After a visit from her doctor she felt some discomfort, and an unexpected premature birth ensued. The child was dead."

"What happened? Such a fine-looking woman!"

"The devil only knows. Perhaps old indiscretions on the part of the rajah? How do you know that he is healthy? Money does not cure everything. Have I caught you unaware with the news?"

"It's terrible. She had been so happy—" he whispered.

"Like every mother. Very difficult. Predestination."

"You don't know where she is? In a hospital?"

"Call Nagar or the rajah. I don't know. Until tonight."

"Goodbye."

He put down the receiver. Poor Grace. Misfortune aimed its blows at her with appalling accuracy. So many cunningly considered measures to ensure that the one whose birth the family awaited would receive the entire inheritance: plans and calculations now set at naught. All for nothing. He remembered how, on the veranda at the club, Grace had pressed his hand to her belly so he could feel the baby's movements. Was it mine? He trembled with alarm. No. No.

He strode nervously around the room, then called the rajah. A servant answered and promised to notify his master. His voice was serene and obedient, as if nothing had happened in the house.

"You already know?" He heard Khaterpalia's voice. "Thank you. Grace does not wish to see anyone. Even me. Do not come."

"You have my deepest sympathy."

"I know. You like her." The man sighed, and after a long silence stammered hoarsely, "She is most upset and angry that this happened within two hours after a visit from Kapur, who said that everything was okay, that the baby would be born in two weeks. There might be light pains, for the placenta was dropping, but all was well. Because of that I made light of her discomfort. Grace was suddenly frightened because it was not moving. I calmed her; I assured her that it must be sleeping. She insisted that that could not be so, that it had never been quiet for so long. The doctor did not hurry, either. And then he groped around her with his stethoscope, growing more and more apprehensive. 'I cannot get a heartbeat,' he said. 'I cannot hear anything.' And very soon the birth occurred. It was choked by the cord, which was twisted two times around its little neck. As if someone had deliberately choked it."

Istvan could tell that the rajah was suffering, was seeing what had happened to him as a horrible injustice, as if fate were sneering at him. The hand with which he was holding the receiver was slippery with sweat. If I feel this so acutely, what state must he be in?

"Is there anything I can do to help?"

"No. He had a tuft of damp black hair and a small face contorted as if he were crying. They said he resembled me and not Grace. I have lost a son."

"How does the doctor explain it?"

"Does it matter? He cannot bring the child back to life. Kapur says that the fetus was small, as is usual with the first child. The mother experienced some emotional upset and the stimulus was communicated to the infant, who rotated and became entangled. But Grace was in no distress. She was so happy!"

"This is terrible. Please convey my—"

"Very well," the rajah interrupted. "When she is calmer I will let you know. I must create a cheerful situation for her, gather friends, leave no room for thoughts of . . . She did not even see that child. Let the whole incident be like a bad dream. I have ordered that everything be removed that could remind her of him: the little carriage brought from London, the layette, the crib. She had already been walking around the hall with that carriage to see what it would be like. It is gone. It was not there. We did not have a child at all. These were only dreams.

"Thank you, Istvan. I knew that you . . . You will be the first of those I wish to see at her side. Only I warn you: speak of anything, even that you were a little in love with her, as long as you do not allude to this. Do you understand?"

"Yes."

"Now a few days' quiet. Until she is herself. I will let you know. Remember, a child is in her future. It will come in a year, a year and a half. That one did not exist."

Istvan was speechless. Magical thinking: he believes he can expunge pain from memory, make it disappear like that tiny curled body that the water of the Yamuna swallowed up.

Outside the window the garish sun beat down. The wind carried clouds of red dust and caressed the heavy coat of leaves on the tangled vines that covered the garage wall. Out of sheer force of habit he completed the last bit of writing for that day. He left the embassy with relief. Mihaly in a jockey cap with upturned visor was swinging on the unlatched gate, which scraped mournfully.

"Uncle, take me. I will go for a ride with you, uncle."

"I'm not going home," he answered through the lowered window of the Austin.

"You don't like me like you used to! We don't have any secrets anymore."

"Get in, you little blackmailer." He opened the door. "But I can't bring you home for quite a while."

Behind the small moss-covered temple, besieged by brambles and with its roof chipped like a bitten apple, the city's gardens began. They saw long swatches of red snapdragon and green mignonette. Fields of salvia blazed such a jubilant red that they seemed to shimmer. Autumn did not hamper the luxuriant plant growth as long as hoses sprinkled the ground. He bought an armful of huge violet gladioli; their sleek chalice-like blossoms were open. Blinking in the sun, Mihaly cradled them carefully

"They smell like wet dirt!" His face puckered with disenchantment.

Istvan attached an envelope containing a note: "I share your pain, Grace." It was not true.

He felt a fear, a vague presentiment that the hand of judgment he had invoked might also reach into his life. If You want me to settle the question, very well, so it shall be: the thought returned like an ominous musical phrase sung by distant choirs. Grace lost the child she longed for. The most agonizing blow. He knew what to take—and what will He take from me? He shuddered. Distant song, and the dull beat of drums slapped by a scrawny hand, streamed on the air like black ribbon. Do I not have the right to reach for what is most precious to you, since you call Me your Lord?

He stopped the car in front of the park gate and sent Mihaly to deliver the bouquet and the note. The watchman who always guarded the entrance, circling about like a dog on a chain, was not there. The doorway to the palace was open, and dark; the small windows on the second story were tightly closed.

The boy was already running back, his knees catching the light.

"No one was in the hall, so I put the flowers on the table," he panted, full of elation. "They will be surprised!"

When the automobile had started again, he turned to Istvan with a flushed face and begged timidly, "Since we are here, couldn't we have ice cream? It is so awfully hot."

"It's not nice to trick me, Mihaly," he said sternly, but he did not have the heart to refuse. "Have you had dinner yet? I don't want to get in trouble with your mother."

"Ice cream isn't food. Anyway, I won't brag about it. If you like, that will be our secret today."

In the colonnade at Connaught Place, vendors of illustrated American and English publications had spread their wares on a brightly colored carpet on the walk. Terey stopped; he was always drawn to books. A gaunt Hindu with a sunken chest and a graying mustache detached himself from a pillar and said in an exhalation of garlic, "I have banned items: *Secrets of the Black Pagoda* and *Indian Nights*. I have photos. Thirty classic positions."

Istvan shrugged. The man looked tearfully into his eyes. "Sahib—perhaps the address of beautiful girls?"

From habit, so as not to kill the hope in eyes glittering from hunger, Istvan put him off. “No, not today. Another time.”

The peddler bent in a respectful bow. It seemed that his slender, veined neck would break under the burden of his enormous turban.

In the sweet shop the curtain was drawn back. Sunlight from the windows shone through the layered cloud of bluish cigarette smoke. The fans were not humming, so the din of voices divided itself clearly into Hindi and English. The quiet laughter of women, the jingle of spoons and the clapping of hands to summon the waiter drew their attention to the neighboring tables. The exquisitely pleated turbans of Sikhs clustered thickly in the snug booths. Their tightly rolled beards gleamed oily black. It was difficult to find seats. Terey looked around uncertainly.

“I will take it on a waffle, in my hand,” Mihaly said helpfully. They moved toward the buffet, which was shrouded in a haze of steam from the balefully hissing coffee warmer.

It seemed to Istvan that as he moved through the narrow space between the tables, he caught himself on something. Then he felt a hand detaining him.

“Come and sit with us.” He heard the voice of attorney Chandra. “You know Kapur. Doctor, please make a little room. What for the boy? For you, strong coffee, I know.”

“Ice cream,” he answered mechanically, taking a seat with relief. He pressed the lawyer’s cold, bony hand and the doctor’s warm, strong one.

“The child must eat slowly,” Kapur advised, puffing out his full cheeks. “He could easily take a chill, you know? And I predicted: too much good fortune all at once.” He rolled his eyes. “A fortune. Youth. Health.”

“And love. Love,” Chandra prompted sarcastically.

“It is written on her palm: she will give birth to two more.”

“And if they are daughters?” the lawyer asked.

“They must try until the end is achieved.” The doctor threw up his hands as if to say that there was nothing more to discuss. “They are both young, after all. Nothing is lost. She can still bear children.”

The waiter brought a tall, slender silver bowl of ice cream with coconut cookies stuck into it. He poured coffee from a glass globe that he set above a spirit lamp. Its blue flame pierced the dimness with a sepulchral glow.

"Doctor"—Chandra leaned on his elbow—"pay the check, and in exchange I will furnish you an opportunity for substantial earnings. A great opportunity: decide quickly."

Kapur smiled distrustfully and shook his head as if to say: I will pass it up.

"I think, however, that it cannot be done without my help," the attorney began in an undertone.

"I might have known!" the doctor retorted. "I see what awaits me. The risk, mine. The profit, yours. I will not be taken in. I do not agree to it." Then he said appeasingly, "In any case, I will pay the bill."

"I have not finished yet. The rajah has lost his son. The important thing was, after all, a son. A great deal of money was waiting for him; a fortune! Undivided."

"Well, and they need not hurry. It is still waiting. We will not receive the legacy: not you, not I." Kapur thrust out his thick lip.

"Be calm. I tell you, it is already too late. And we both can profit handsomely if we act in concert."

Kapur grew sober. He leaned across the table and looked deeply into the lawyer's placid face and his eyes, which concealed a catlike somnolence. His fleshy nose scented business. Suddenly he turned his head as if he had remembered that there was an unwanted witness.

"Later, perhaps?" He opened his sticky lips with a smacking noise.

"Mr. Terey is not hampering us. The more who know of this, the better," Chandra drawled emphatically. "The widow of Khaterpalia's older brother is expecting a child."

"Impossible!" The doctor bridled. "He was repulsive. The terrible burns, the scars. I saw him!"

"When one loves, one wants to have a child. And she conceived one. She needed to. She will not be a barren widow but the mother of a young rajah. Of the elder heir."

"But that man died!"

"And was burned. But he managed to beget a successor. That he was the rajah's brother I have proof in writing: the statement of the court and the protocol signed by all the members of the family who have an interest, including the father-in-law Vijayaveda. The decision cannot be reversed, though they could try. I will see to it."

"In what month is she?" The doctor leaned forward, devouring every word.

"She says she has not bled for two months."

Istvan nodded toward the boy, who lowered his eyelids and busied himself by chipping at his mountain of ice cream.

"Nothing is certain yet," Kapur said with a worried air. "It is still possible to bribe the servants, to give her an herb. She could lose it."

"That is why we will draw up an agreement with her, and you, doctor, will take her under your most scrupulous care." Chandra tapped the table with his bony fist.

"The rajah will not forgive us. You helped him . . ." Kapur hesitated. But his eyes were opened to the possibility of unbounded influence and of gaining the widow's trust.

"In any case, you must be by her side," Chandra said in a low voice. "That is your function, doctor. Mine is to ensure that it is paid well. Royally. A fortune is at stake in this game. Khaterpalia and his father-in-law are seasoned merchants. They will not haggle."

Istvan looked at their faces, which were brightening with the smiles of partners refining a strategy. They had come to terms; they understood each other. "You are a formidable man, Mr. Chandra," the counselor said quietly. "After what you told me that night—"

"I? Ah, yes." The lawyer waved a lean hand, ruffling a stream of smoke. "Do you mean to say that business ventures with me are hard to bring to termination? Well, yes. But, indeed, you know my specialty: I am a philanthropist. Should I not occupy myself with the affairs of a poor woman who is expecting a child and who has twice lost her husband—especially when I see danger threatening her?"

"An unusual case." Kapur turned his head, puffed out his hairy cheeks, and sniffed.

"Only unusual cases interest me."

"Does the rajah know of this yet?" Istvan asked.

"The later he finds out about it, the better for everyone. One worry is enough for him. I am not asking you to keep it a secret, though I think good judgment dictates that we keep it confidential for a time. Why put pressure on him? Am I right?"

It seemed to Istvan that he knew what the lawyer was thinking.

"It will be safer that way," the doctor affirmed. "I will go to the widow today. I will examine her. I want to be certain."

"Conditions vary with women. But since she wants a child"—Chandra seemed to be talking to himself—"she can always have one."

"Time has passed since the death of her husband," Kapur reminded him. "A child cannot be born too late, for they will question it. And they will win."

"And in the seventh month?"

"It is easy to recognize a premature one," the doctor warned.

"These considerations are theoretical at this point," Chandra cut in. "In case . . . For the time being, she expects a child. A normal pregnancy. The third month. I want to have that from you in writing."

Istvan listened with aversion. After all, they did not have to hide what they were saying from anyone. They spoke of assistance and care—matters which were not in conflict with the law.

"Attorney, you enjoy appearing in the role of fate." He looked into Chandra's dark, murky eyes.

"Fate? And what is that, properly speaking, if not my intention?" Arrogantly he tilted his face upward. "Faith . . . gods . . . I am not the tool of predestination. I direct it, my dear sir. I can enlist the gods in my service."

"You are fond of money, however, and in the end it is the goal," the counselor insisted.

"You wound me! For me it is only a means. I despise it, so it is pushed into my hand. I punish some by taking it from them and reward others by giving it to them. I love to prepare surprises. I thought you appreciated my disinterestedness. If you found yourself in a predicament . . ."

Suddenly there was a clink as the boy put down his spoon.

"Let's go, uncle."

"Perhaps you would like one more helping?" Chandra tried to pat him but Mihaly moved back, avoiding the touch of the bony hand that, like a reptile, executed a half-circle in air blue with smoke.

"No, no. I want to go back now."

"I often think of you, Mr. Chandra—" Istvan said under his breath.

"Good. I also have a sense that you are trying to summon me," the lawyer cut in.

"I think you are very unhappy."

"I? That is foolish! I have everything I want."

"You would like to be loved, adored. All you possess is paid for. You buy friendship, women, even the blessing of a beggar."

"Not true!" His voice rose. "They must be grateful to me. I fulfill their desires."

"Uncle, I will wait in the car." Mihaly pulled away as if in terror.

"We're going now. Goodbye, doctor. Goodbye."

Chandra squeezed his hand with unexpected force.

"Before long you will be the unhappier one. That is my prediction. You will always find a confidant in me." He looked Terey in the eye almost beseechingly. "I myself will attend to your affairs."

Istvan turned and moved impatiently toward the door. Mihaly ran ahead, dragging him by the hand. "Uncle, that is a bad man," he whispered. "He will do something awful to you."

"He can't do much. The worst injuries are those we inflict on ourselves."

"Uncle, you heard about the girl who was given an apple by the witch. She bit it and slept as if she were dead. Or she gave her a comb that she fastened in her hair and forgot who she was. Or she pricked the girl's little finger and squeezed out a small drop of blood, and then she put that finger to her mouth and drank all her blood . . . and there was no trace of a wound. Or she took hold of her blouse and twirled so long that it strangled her—the girl's own blouse—and she was sitting between her parents, but they could do nothing to help her. Or the witch led the girl to a great mirror, and when she looked at herself, the witch gave her a push and the mirror closed behind her. It was mute and never told anyone where she was. I know he would be able to do that, and even worse things," Mihaly insisted. "That's why I wouldn't let him give me anything."

Terey listened uneasily. Mihaly seemed to be babbling like a child with a high fever, muttering to himself. He touched the boy's head: it was cool.

"After all, you know, those are fairy tales," he said. "You weren't afraid of an elephant, but you run away from an old gentleman who wants to treat you to some cake? Mihaly, what happened?" he asked, trying to calm the boy. He looked at the street full of bicyclists and motorcycle rickshaws and scattered them with the blare of the horn.

"I was eating my ice cream," the boy stammered, curling up on the seat of the Austin, "and suddenly I was afraid. His eyes seemed to suck the life from everything, even your smile and the taste of my ice cream. Because of him my heart seemed to stop and even the spot of sunshine on the table went dark. Something cold comes from him. He's like a dead man."

"No. He's just an unhappy man. He has a great deal of money. He helps people."

"His money is a part of the plot," the boy whispered with fear in his eyes. "It takes more money from other people's pockets and it returns to him before midnight strikes. And if you tried to stop it, it would turn into dry leaves or cockle shells."

All at once Istvan realized that Mihaly had a gift he would look for in vain in his own sons: fantasy, the ability to create. He was moved by the receptiveness of the boy's imagination. Perhaps India had embedded itself in him so that in years to come, when he was a grown man, he would remember today's encounter and a feeling of dread would creep over him, with Chandra in the character of a servant of dark forces. Were his instincts already telling him that? After all, Istvan himself also had moments of unmitigated loathing for the attorney who was so ready to be helpful.

The sky took on a green tint and began to cool. A gust of wind shook the huge papaya leaves. Young Sikhs with topknots like girls' released a red kite in the form of a vulture. A pair of spotted puppies nipped at each other's tails. A benign chill rose from the earth; the brief twilight came on and the first stars, as if just washed, appeared above the horizon as the heat dissipated.

I would like to live on in this boy's heart . . . Suddenly it seemed to him that it was not in his sons but in this child that his legacy would remain—that it was not through blood or genes, but through words spoken in confidence, intimate revelations, that the boy could inherit his traits, his desires and hopes. I am like a cuckoo, pouring into the absorbent mind of the child my own restlessness, goading him to spread his wings. Indeed, Mihaly had once said with a rending sigh, "I want to be like you, uncle." Anyway, he doesn't know me, he thought, smiling to himself. He creates his own version of me. He imagines someone much better, much purer: his ideal.

Or was he always missing his sons? He stole a glance at Mihaly, who was now in a sunny humor as his gaze followed the kites. Two—three—they glided like fish, falling through the glowing sky toward the darkening ground.

"Uncle, can we stand here and watch for a while? Oh, that big one is flying over to eat the others! It will bite holes in them."

They got out of the car. He put his arm around the boy, and with upturned faces they watched the dance of the orange and yellow kites dragging tails like garlands. The strings were invisible, so the motions of the kites, diving in the afterglow from the west, were like the motions of toys in free play—toys of childhood off on a spree, full of a life of their own.

Through the thin fabric of his clothing he felt the warmth of the confiding little body. He heard his cries of delight when the paper vulture lost altitude and fell among the trees. The two smaller kites seemed to climb higher and higher on the mild breeze, over the first beaming star with its greenish twinkle, its light wavering as if it were uncertain of its place in the evening sky.

When he had taken the boy home and returned to his house, he saw two figures nestled together on the steps of the veranda: the watchman and his girl. The man sprang up officiously and turned on the light; it glowed from among the leaves. His fiancee darted into the shadows like a lizard. Passing the soldier, who stood at attention but moved his turned-up mustache as if he wanted to say something, he saw a small body curled up in a thick cluster of climbing plants. Only the deer-like eyes flashed in the shadows of the branches.

"When is the wedding?"

"In a week, sir. The best day. The horoscopes have been checked. The stars favor us."

Terey shrugged and grasped the door handle. The cook had already come running up and turned on the light in the hall. By mistake he had started up the fans, which were whirling under the ceiling.

The stars? And what did they have to do with this? How nice for them that they can foist off the responsibility for their own lives, can pray to the stars or shake their fists at them, and they hang above us, they revolve in the freezing heights, stony, indifferent.

"Madam is not here," Pereira announced, scratching the graying stubble on his face. "Madam will not be staying here tonight."

Istvan nodded as a sign that he knew this, though for a moment he had deluded himself that he would find Margit watching for him in her chair, a little drowsy—that she would take him in her arms, that he would feel her fingertips pressing him before he managed to push the light switch, and he would kiss her for a long time, a long time, resting his forehead against her temple.

The cook seemed to float in the darkness, barefoot, noiseless. He lit the lamp on the desk. The masks with bared teeth grinned from the wall. "There is a letter, sir." He motioned toward the air mail envelope with its striped edge.

Istvan recognized the round letters: Ilona's writing. The envelope opened easily—he hardly had to pry it with the little opener—as if it had been trained to give up its contents. Inside were a sheet of paper and photographs. Ilona: the high forehead, a little childish, framed between wings of black hair. Strong eyebrows; frank, straightforward eyes, eyes that have nothing to hide. Full lips prone to smile. Pretty; very pretty; lovely, he told himself; probably even prettier than Margit. He gazed at her face as if he wanted to remind himself why he had singled her out among so many others, why he had loved her. She is like a Hindu woman, he thought with astonishment. In his imagination he drew a point between the eyebrows, darkened the eyelids, hung a thick silver necklace around the throat.

He set the picture down outside the circle of light and began to read the letter. It was concerned with commonplace matters, like her other letters: stories about their sons' doings, about Sandor's throat, about Geza's dream that his father would bring home a monkey, even a very small one. Then he came upon this sentence: *Do you ever have time to think of us when you think of home? I wish you were here with us.* It was not a cry of longing or a confession of love—only a reminder that he belonged to them. She did not like overt gestures, or light when she lay resting in the nude, or even a mirror when he kissed her in the foyer before he left for the office; he had noticed her sidewise glance at that mute unwanted witness.

He had gone away. He had become a stranger. He surveyed his own past dispassionately, as if it were a book about someone else's life.

Once more he took the photograph in his hand. As he admired the young woman's beauty, a feeling of satisfaction came over him. She can still begin a new life, he thought complacently. She will not be broken. She will easily find a man to console her.

What does she think of me? That really makes no difference. And suddenly, pitying himself and his own anguish, he found himself believing that when friends learned of his departure and began to condemn and stigmatize his betrayal, Ilona would defend him. He could hear her calm voice: Perhaps it is better for him this way. Perhaps he believed that he would be able to write in a different way. Who knows what drove him to this? It is not easy for him, either.

Ilona's large, dark eyes, shadowed by her lashes, looked out without blinking. That angered him: her insistent, inquiring gaze. That's what the fool of a photographer told her to do, he thought irritably, dropping the little piece of cardboard on his desk, for he heard steps on the veranda and the voice of the watchman assuring someone that the counselor had been home for an hour. It must be Trojanowski.

"Hello! Why are you sitting there with a dry snout?" the Pole called from the threshold. "Open sesame—" he pulled at the handles of a carved box with both hands and greeted approvingly the necks of bulging bottles that emerged from under the lid.

"You walk in with no greeting?" Istvan asked.

"Would you like a Chinese ritual? 'Hello' is not enough? Well, allow me—" he folded his hands as if in prayer and bowed low. "*Namaste ji.* Be praised, oh noble one!"

He settled into a chair, stretched his legs and crossed them. He lit a cigarette. "Does the watchman lighten your loneliness by bringing in girls?" He peeked alertly from under his lowered eyelids to see whether he had hit his mark. "He just hid one from me."

"No. That is his fiancee. They will be married in a week."

"Well, well. Now I understand. Mountain people from Nepal have different customs. An Indian groom would not even be allowed to see the girl before the wedding, so he would not defile her with a glance. Parents and matchmakers look over the goods. A photograph is enough. And with us they would want to go off right away to bivouac together with a tent and a kayak. To test things out, to examine them in detail. And they break up almost without regret. There! Just another experience."

The cook poked his head in and, having assured himself that the wine was poured, carried in a tray of hot, peppery meatballs bristling with toothpicks.

"It's looking grim for you." Trojanowski bit into the appetizer. "Today a crowd of workers gathered at the parliament demanding an end to repression. They insisted that Nagy be returned. They took their time about it. Kádár spoke to them. He promised that those who had been driven out would return. The people believe that he will attend to that, but it has been difficult for him in the beginning." He drank a little of the golden plum vodka. "And what do they write you from home?"

"Nothing of interest, really." Istvan threw up his hands. "Everything is all right. They are alive. My wife is working. The children are studying."

"That means that things are hard."

"Why the devil did he call in those people? Couldn't it be the way it was in Poland?"

"Don't be a child. First, they already had their hands on you. Second, Kádár was summoned. I must confess that his courage impresses me. He took on himself the responsibility for Hungary's fate. He feels, after all, the aversion that surrounds him," he said reflectively, "but he has a goal, a great cause, that enables him to withstand pressure. He knows what he has rescued. The struggle for a nation, for the future, is that much more difficult because it is lonely. Well, he has people. But many attached themselves to him for tactical reasons, all the while suspecting that he seeks power, that he wants to pay himself back for being in prison. However, the motives of their actions are not important; only the effects are. The thing is for him to have time—a year or two. Then they will begin to respect him."

His eyes wandered around the room as if the silence had just begun to make him uneasy. "Let's put on a little music. It's dismal here."

He turned on the radio. A melody from some American film about white immigration gathered volume: *Anastasia*. His foot swayed in time to the music; he liked the plaintive song crooned in a soft, husky female voice.

"So you think Khrushchev rushed Nagy's ouster?" Istvan asked, turning down the radio.

"He wanted to make things easier for Kádár"—Trojanowski curled his lips—"to clear the decks for him. He did not take the effects into account. Now he has strikes in Hungary. But that will pass. To eat, they must work."

"I don't like that way of getting things done."

"Who does?" Trojanowski smiled sarcastically. "Agreements. Guarantees. We are grown people. Agreements stand if the conditions under which they were signed do not change—well, and if the stronger party wants to abide by them. In adult terms, if that party still has something to gain. Everyone operates this way except us, except Poles. We defeated the Turks at Vienna, rescuing the nation that invaded us later. We were with Napoleon until the end, though everyone else left him, and at least half of Poland could have been bargained away from the czar. Faithfulness to the end! To the last shot. The world marvels at us for that, and takes us for fools. Crazy Poles, eh!" He waved an angry hand. "Our communists are romantics as well—but they have their feet on the ground," he added as if to himself. He sucked meditatively at the plum vodka.

"If it were not for them, our People's Republic of today would not be," he added, setting aside his glass.

"And you are like that," Istvan mocked gently. "A chip off the old block."

"What can I do? At birth I was burdened with this inheritance," Trojanowski sighed with affected regret. "At times I am even proud of it."

"Certainly Mindszenty would be to your liking. A cardinal, a voluntary prisoner in the American embassy. He did not abandon Hungary."

Trojanowski leaned on his elbow and ran his hand through his dwindling shock of blond hair. His blue eyes glowed belligerently.

"I don't trust such pathetic gestures. Is that a test of my intelligence? We must get this straight: he left Hungary—he left because he is on American territory though he is still with you. He understood nothing about the situation in which he found himself after he left prison. He thought it would be as it had been. Suddenly he felt himself to be not a spiritual leader, but a political one. He urged people on to the struggle. And then he boasted—" Trojanowski looked around for cigarettes, which Istvan pushed toward him in an Indian copper case. "No Kossuths? I prefer strong ones. But the Church has experience. It is a wise institution. It does not approve of desertion."

"You can't demand that anyone push themselves into martyrdom," Istvan protested. "They would have shot him. He's an old man."

"Well, yes. It would have been a worthy ending for his life. The Church acknowledges two solutions for its dignitaries in such cases: endure with the faithful to the end and go to the wall when the end comes. The Church values the sowing of blood. It does not go to waste. As a matter of fact, the communists think the same way: an idea that is not worth dying for is not worth living for."

"And the other solution?"

"It is more difficult, for it requires not only zeal and heart, but good sense. It is a wise, circumspect pact with the victors, for in the end it must come to that, and the Church values that, perhaps even more. But for that it is necessary to love one's flock more than oneself."

"Are you a Catholic?"

"You might say so," he said as if the question troubled him. "In all sincerity, I was. One can renounce it, but it trails after us: tradition, habit, almost magical gestures. I have kept up the hope that the problem exists." He blew smoke at the ceiling. "It would be better if it did. One pushes away these thoughts; there is no time for them. We do anything to deaden that insistent voice."

"And so—only after death?" Istvan whispered, listening intently.

"We are inured to death. We know that life is a fatal illness. But who wants to remember that every day? I tell you, I cannot imagine not lying in the cemetery under a cross . . . Don't tire me. Surely you didn't invite me here for this."

"I wanted to ask for your help," Istvan ventured. Trojanowski turned toward him, surprised. "I have a painter here."

"A Hindu?"

"You know him, so it will be that much easier for you to talk to him. Ram Kanval. He was going to go to Hungary. But you know what those imbeciles call it: decadent art."

"Uh-oh. Something unpleasant comes back to me when I hear that scientific term," the journalist drawled. "Well, go on."

"Bajcsy refused to approve his stipend. You have the greater freedom: take him. He's going to waste here. He tried to poison himself in a fit of despair; I mention that only for your information. Well, think of something. Will you help?"

Trojanowski sat silent with his eyes closed.

"Listen. I'm going away. I put this to your conscience," Istvan insisted. "Try for once not to do this like a Pole, for you wax sentimental, you promise, and the next day your zeal passes and you forget altogether."

"All right. I will speak to our cultural attaché," he agreed at last. "You may count on me, though I can't vouch for the result."

"That's all I ask. Thank you. I know he will be to your people's liking. Enough now. Let's go into dinner. What's your pleasure? Wine? Plum vodka?"

"Let's stay with the same." Trojanowski took the bottle and, still holding his glass, moved toward the dining room. "Ah—the smell! All the time I was missing something: it's just that I'm hungry." He clapped Istvan warmly on the shoulder.

ISTVAN SPOTTED A NOTICE in the press that two well-known journalists who had escaped from Hungary had appeared in Calcutta and Bombay. None of the embassy staff, however, could remember any newspaper or other publication at which people by those names had worked. He would gladly have talked with them and listened to their accounts of the uprising, even if it had inculpated him in the ambassador's eyes. But the route taken by the self-exiled representatives of Hungary bypassed New Delhi.

In bold type on their front pages, the *Hindustan Times* and the *Hindustan Standard* sounded alarms about scuffles between patrols on the border of Kashmir and riots in Tibet. They accused the Chinese of invading territory that had been Indian from time immemorial, though only lightly manned forts on two main caravan routes marked out the zone in question, with its barren highlands and arid valleys in which bands of herdsmen wandered freely, grazing yaks and sheep, or pilgrims on their way to Lhasa or the Buddhist monasteries of Kullu passed to the beat of gongs and the birdlike whistle of fifes. An exchange of fire that was actually insignificant reverberated in the press, conveniently for the government, which welcomed the interrogatories of members of parliament demanding new appropriations for arms.

Hungary had vanished from the front pages, displaced by developments in nearby Tibet. In reports of the deliberations of the United Nations Istvan spied a note to the effect that the representatives of Kádár's regime had been subjected to procedural hostilities instigated by Argentina or by the regime of Chiang Kai-shek, but that it was clear already that the communists had won—had forced the West to acknowledge the new government.

Istvan wandered around the embassy, began conversations, scrutinized his colleagues, only to tear himself away suddenly, escape to his office and shut himself in. It seemed to him that they knew more than he did, that they had access to inside information—that they belonged to the circle of the initiated and he was left out.

"Don't lose your wits. Stop looking for a fight." Ferenc put his hands on Istvan's shoulders. "I swear to you that nothing is going on. I would have told you right away. You are the source of your own anxiety. Take yourself in hand or your nerves will do you in. Go away. Rest up. The boss approved your leave."

"Don't chase me away. I'm going of my own accord." Full of suspicion, he broke away from Ferenc's grip.

"When?"

"In a few days. Understand—I'm always waiting. It seems to me that as soon as I leave Delhi, something will happen to spoil my plans."

"That is the best evidence of nervous exhaustion," Ferenc said triumphantly. "Nothing will happen, I assure you. You are simply overwrought. Otherwise you would not be a poet, only a bookkeeper."

"You're probably right."

When he returned to his house, he was overtaken by fresh misgivings and a feeling that something was threatening him. But the days passed monotonously, one like another, with no surprises. He must be hysterical, he thought. He wrote letters to Ilona, explaining with consummate cruelty that he loved someone else and wanted to begin a new life, and asking her to understand even if she could not forgive. Then he tore them up in disgust, knowing that he was lying in spite of his best intentions, and that the pain he would cause would provide no closure, would not end anything. He sat across from Margit with a glass in his hands and tried to find assurance in her eyes. He drank a great deal, though alcohol did not furnish him the anodyne he wished for.

He nestled close to her. As he dropped off to sleep he felt her knee on his thigh and clasped it sleepily with his hand, only to wake after a short doze. He was instantly conscious; he listened in alarm to her even breathing and the wails of jackals scavenging in the yards of the villas.

Margit did not urge him to leave the city, but she believed that the farther they were from New Delhi and the embassy, the easier it would be to divert him, to tear him away from the centripetal force of his country's anguish.

"I've finished the lectures," she said calmly on the day before the feast of Diwali.

"Well, what of it?" he bristled, as though she had accused him of something.

"Nothing. I'm free." Her eyes were so clear and trusting that he was ashamed of his angry retort.

"Do you want to go?"

"I want to be with you," she said gently. "I have more time for you now. I thought you would be glad."

"All right." He turned his head away as if she had pressed him for a decision. "We will clear the account at the hotel. Pack. Leave a suitcase here. It's time to go."

"Wouldn't it be better to take everything with us?" she said, weighing her words.

"Do you think we won't be coming back to Delhi?" He looked her aggressively in the eye.

"Perhaps that would be best," she whispered, "but I will do as you like."

Under his hostile look she inclined her head as if it were drooping beneath an excessively heavy burden. Her red hair fell in a wave, shielding her face. She did not gather it back with the usual gesture but let it fall in a languid cascade. Finally she said, "Everything you would come back for can be bought. Leave part of the baggage. I understand that you want it to appear that we are only going for the holiday. Do you find it calming that there is still time for a final decision?"

"And you think . . ."

"I don't think anything. I know. I would only like to help you. But you must decide for yourself. Otherwise you would hate me."

In the deep silence they heard the shouting of the cook and the clank of the mortar in which he was beating the spice. Vines worried by the evening wind were scraping the dusty screen in the window beside him.

"All right. Let's go tomorrow," he said suddenly.

A new vitality surged through her. She pushed a lock of hair behind her ear and her eyes began to sparkle.

"Tomorrow. At dawn," he declared, now decisive. "We will be off to the white beaches I've dreamed of. The water will cleanse me of these worries. We'll bury them in the sand. Margit, help me." He bent over her. She put her arms around him and pressed him tightly to her.

"This is all I want, after all."

He buried his face in her disheveled hair with its familiar fragrance, which he drank in until his blood hummed. "You are good for me," he said, kissing her neck.

By the time the bellboys carried her luggage to the car twilight had fallen. On balconies and the stone parapets of terraces leading to gardens, hundreds of small lights twinkled. Little gold tongues licked the darkness. Houses were already lit for the ceremonial opening of Diwali. On roofs, in windows, even on the steps of houses, lights flickered. Wicks in oil blazed in metal boxes before beggars' shanties. Everyone hoped to lure the goddess of happiness to their homes; they marked out the path and lighted the way in. Istvan found it painful. He was supposed to buy flat candles and clay sentries with oil lamps, but in the press of business before the journey he had neglected to prepare for the Indian holiday.

All the city smelled of candles. The dance of lights, the warm, living flame, transformed buildings, lending charm to the scene. Over the treetops the fires of enormous, vitreous stars trembled. The sky seemed to droop among the houses, shaking flashing particles of light onto doorsills, walls, and paths. The goddess Lakshmi, with a lamp in each hand, was leading good fortune toward those who were waiting, begging, in the twilight.

"I wonder if our house will have lights. I didn't give the cook any money. I completely forgot," Istvan said.

But when they drove up onto the grassy square, he saw with relief an unsteady little cockscomb of flame on the low wall. The dusky grotto that was the veranda, covered with its fleece of climbing plants, glittered with golden flames in little lamps. The watchman stood with his legs planted wide apart, leaning on his thick bamboo stick. Three rows of small lights blinked on the grass at his feet, bowing in the barely perceptible breeze. The fiery display lit up his legs, which seemed hewn from bronze. His huge shadow fell on the wall, making him the vigilant envoy of the supreme beings.

"He lit the place." Istvan sighed with relief. "They deserved a reward. And happiness has a shining path to our house."

Margit waited in front of the gate until he had parked the Austin in the garage. The cook greeted them with a triumphant air; he was squatting, straightening the tilted wicks with a stick.

"As good as everyone else's, true, sir?"

"Even handsomer." Terey clapped him on the shoulder. "You didn't stint on the candles."

"We must be generous to Lakshmi so she will come to us," the man answered ingratiatingly, and discreetly handed him the bill for the little votive lamps.

"Very good. Here you are."

"This is too much, sir." The cook cocked his head on his slender neck like a magpie that cannot lift a bone in its beak.

"Take it all. Because you used your head."

"Ah! Sir, your happiness is our happiness, you know. The watchman is getting married because he has a good job. All my family, sir, blesses you. And the sweeper's family, and the gardener's. You are like a strong tree and we are like birds who weave nests in your branches. You have an open hand and do not ration rice as they do in other houses. Sir"—his speech took on the rhythm of an incantation and he raised his hands toward the leafy fringes of the climbing plants—"may the goddess Lakshmi visit this house with gifts for you and madam."

Long shadows fell on the walls. The air smelled of hot oil and candles, like the interior of a temple. The assembled servants bowed to them.

"And we wish you great success," he answered. "I leave the house to your care. Manage our home wisely. Tomorrow I go to the south."

"For how long, sir?"

"For a few weeks."

When he found himself in the living room, he went up to Margit, amazed and anxious. She sat hunched over, hiding her face in her hands.

"What's happened?" He opened her hands and saw that her face was damp with tears.

"Nothing." Under wet lashes that clung together, her eyes were shining brightly. "For the first time you said 'our home.'"

He bent over her, taken aback. Gradually he began to understand, and to feel compassion. She needed so little—an impulsive word—to build the whole edifice of the future. She loves me—the thought recurred like an accusation—loves me.

"I want to hear that always, until my last day," she whispered, nestling against him with damp, flushed cheeks.

Swarms of lights on the neighboring villas shone in blurs through the window screens. An acute sadness seemed to have settled over the city, like crepe over the plots in a village cemetery on the day people light candles in memory of the dead.

"We will go tomorrow." He pushed away painful thoughts. She leaned toward him, rubbing her cheek and blinking with happiness, like a little girl who has no words to express her joy and thankfulness for an unexpected gift.

❧

THEY LAY ON FINE WHITE SAND, close enough to touch each other. A few yards from their feet, turbid waves died on a shore that had been battered and swept smooth as an enormous bowl wreathed with heaps of pungent-smelling seaweed. The ocean swelled gently and tilted, driving water toward the coast. Yellow and reddish sails, appearing almost motionless on the horizon, stood like triangles with their points resting on the gray water.

It was not easy to find a name for the few loosely connected beams, forming something like a beak, that opened like a fan with slits to create a channel for foaming seawater. There were no boats to be seen, only the slowly revolving triangular sails, patched and dimming in the sun, that wandered on the edge of the sky like kites ripped from their strings.

He turned his head and fixed his gaze on Margit's austere, chiseled profile, veiled by her windblown hair. Her bluish-green eyes, squinting a little, glittered with happiness. Her lips parted slightly with her deep breathing. Her small breasts under her wet bathing suit, barely covered, challenged him.

The choked alleys of Old Delhi dissolved and vanished: the crowd pressing blindly, the mass of bodies one had to rub against to walk along the street, the stifling odor of drains, urine, pastilles, fermenting fruit peelings, incense, the smells of flaming butter in votive lamps and palm oil that permeated hair and lingered on clothing.

Here on this great sweep of beach they were alone, deprived of all resources but each other—joyful castaways. Free of obligation to the world, they rested, not even hearing the groaning of the surf that doggedly spilled onto the shore, raking with it the coarser sand and the pink shells. A damp breeze blew over them, allaying the sweltering heat of noon. The air over this expanse of sand untrodden by anyone's feet was veined with flashing green. The leaves of battered palms rose, swelling as if in flight, shaking their leathery fringes.

"Don't sleep." Her fingertips brushed his side, which was plastered with smooth, fine-grained sand.

"I'm not sleeping. I'm thinking," he answered, stretching. "Do you know that in two days it will be Christmas Eve?"

"Are you counting the days? Do you know exactly how many have passed?"

"What for? Our time here will be too short that way. I know about Christmas Eve because I got a letter from the hotel management asking what we would like for the holiday dinner."

"Don't they believe that Daniel will repeat our order accurately? He's a clever chap." Daniel was a young man whose services came with their rented cottage.

"The entire menu was written out. I only had to underline our choices."

"Why did you do it without me? You should have consulted me."

"It will be a surprise for you."

"I'm sure you ordered something awful, as you did in the Chinese restaurant that time. When the chef explained what it was made of, I felt something inside me protesting!"

"But you liked it. As long as you didn't know, you enjoyed it. I've ordered seafood for us."

"And where is the turkey with dates and chestnuts?"

"It's still alive, but there is enough of it to order six servings. They have it figured very closely: chicken, two servings; duck, four; turkey, twelve. Apart from us, there are only two old English ladies. Amazing how empty it is. I expected a crowd."

"Do you wish for other women? Am I not enough?" She scooped up a handful of white sand and watched as it trickled through her fingers.

"Don't talk nonsense."

"I'm glad you rested a little. The solitude will do us good."

"For the time being there aren't many people here because the Suez Canal is blocked. But they will be here for New Year's. The beach will be filled with them."

"I don't need them at all. It's fine with me as it is." She sifted sand through her fingers; it made a little mound on his chest. "I love the sea. There is such peace about it."

"Even though I was half dead from driving, the first night here I couldn't sleep. I heard it," he whispered. "It has so many voices. It chats and it lures. It rumbles as if it were impatient. It seemed to me that it was taking advantage of the darkness to creep onto the shore, scour the dunes, submerge the beaches, and circle around us, all very cleverly. The roar of the water intensifies in the dark."

"You got up. I heard you go out onto the veranda. But I didn't want to open my eyes."

"I saw how it shone. The land was black and the waves glowed like phosphorus, as if they were full of drowned stars. I was as frightened as a little boy for fear the tide would wash us away, cottage and all."

"I'm not afraid of the ocean." She thrust out a cocky lip. "I like the way it carries me along."

"You swim out too far. I call you and you pretend not to hear."

"You swim alongside me"—she peeped into his dark eyes—"and I think you would swim as far as you could go. It's hard to decide when to turn back. It's easy to swim out. It's much harder to go back to shore."

"I saw a map in the harbormaster's office. The bay has shore currents. It's best to remember that. They could carry us a long way out."

"You wouldn't leave me, though." She laid her hand on his sun-tanned chest. "I wouldn't be afraid to swim away from the shore with you."

"I don't like this train of thought!" he shuddered. "It's silly."

The sea soliloquized more loudly, surging and washing the smooth sand on the shore with its thick tongues.

"But there are some disturbances at night," she said, engrossed in playing with the sand, which was as clean as sugar. "The night before last I heard shouts and something like a chase. Last night there were shots."

"I asked Daniel. He said the police had set a trap for smugglers. Think of these empty cottages. I wouldn't be at all surprised if gold or opium was stashed in them. The water near the beach is deep; they could sail close to the very shoreline with a cutter. Anyway, those boat-rafts of theirs can scud about for days."

"You have imagination," she said approvingly. "You are always ready to reconstruct the whole story. It is enough that someone was running along the coast. One rocket fired; perhaps it was for practice?"

"They also smuggle people—refugees from Pakistan. Daniel told me while you were asleep."

"They are fleeing. They will not escape themselves. Freedom is in us. We must muster all our courage and determination and break out of the iron band that was forcibly imposed on us." She turned toward him; he felt her sandy hand resting on his thigh.

"Not forcibly imposed, unless what you mean by 'forcibly' is that you have a birthplace, a language and a fate shared with others whom you should not abandon. The rest of our obligations we undertake voluntarily, and you know very well that they are part of ourselves."

"Primitive blood ties." She lowered her head with aversion.

"No. I'm speaking of the deepest community of interests with the world we find at birth, which we ought to change, to transform."

A wavering trill from a flute could be heard in the distance. At the foot of a layer of rocks, between the leaning coconut palms, they saw the dark torso of a conjurer playing his song. He seemed to have no head, for his white turban was indistinguishable from the bright sand milled from under patches of turf parched by the sun.

"It's easier to change the world than to change yourself," she whispered bitterly. "The world, the world! And what is that but a game in the sand? You've already seen how much of that remains. It's a lesson you should learn."

"And you? What role are you marking out for me?" He raised himself on his elbow and looked into her eyes. The ends of her curled eyelashes glittered in the sun.

"Be yourself at last. Free. Write as you like. Don't be hampered by anyone."

"Even you?"

"Even me," she insisted. "Write about your Hungary, but free yourself from that dog collar that's choking you—from the time you've lived through, from its improvised systems. You don't have to be a bureaucrat whose masters' words are law. Think of what is yours, your own, unique. What do you have to say? To people, not just Hungarians."

"My masters' words are not law to me," he smiled. "They change too often. And what I would like to say to Hungarians ought to be important to everyone who thinks and feels responsibility for the collective fate."

"Time—yours, ours, we must submit to it. Don't let yourself be weighed down. Don't become involved in collusions for a year or two. Your mind is full of words that are not your own. You put out your hands and they are poised to applaud. It's not even like a circus, for force doesn't require dexterity."

"Stop," he said. "Don't torture me."

"I?" She pretended to be surprised. "This hits home because you think the same."

Again they heard at a distance the birdlike squeal of the beggar's flute, until it was swallowed up by the roar of the surging water.

"What is he expecting?" Istvan gazed at the naked body growing still darker among the gnarled, half-exposed roots of the palms. The motionless fronds hung down like roosters' tails in the sky full of trembling light.

"He is like me," she said broodingly. "He wants to attract someone's attention."

"Why has he been sitting so far away?"

"He doesn't want to be obtrusive."

"Do you think he's waiting for us?"

"He is a beggar, not as shameless as I am, but undoubtedly a beggar. We recognize each other at once." She drew curves in the sand with a finger and watched vacantly as a breeze sweeping the beach pushed the sand before it grain by grain.

He turned around quickly and pulled her to him.

"Don't talk like that. Better to hit me. It would hurt less." He kissed her, breathing hard. "Everything I have is yours."

"Except you yourself." She shook her head. "I'm poorer than that beggar, for he doesn't know what he could have, and I know what you have deprived me of, what you withhold from me."

"I?"

"You. You don't want me."

He kissed her bluish eyelids and smoothed her eyebrows with his lips. He found coarse traces of sea salt on her shoulders. He tried to smother her despondency, to dispel it with tenderness, but he made his argument only to the body warmed in the sun that lazily coaxed caresses from him like a tame animal.

"Don't," she begged as he was uncovering her white chest and pressing it with greedy lips. "That man—"

"He is far away." He laid her gently in a warm hollow in the sand, a white cradle. She threw out her arms and he rested his hands on the palms of hers, entwining their fingers until it hurt. They heard the distant notes of the flute, the cries of birds, and the deep restless groaning of the ocean, which crescendoed until the perpetually washed sand received its baptism by water and the foam soaking into it sizzled.

They rested side by side, languid, sleepy, as the glare of the invisible sun bore down. At the touch of each other's hands—the affirmation that they were together, bonded in the amicable communion of bodies—a deep, peaceful joy pulsed in their blood.

"Are you going in the water?" she drawled lazily.

"I must!" He sprang up, seized her hands in a tight grip, and raised her from the sand.

Holding each other, they ran over the level strand of beach, which was licked clean by wind and water. The ocean glittered blue and silver so that it hurt the eyes. It drew back, luring them on, only to raise them on a tall wave that churned up sand from the bottom. The swelling water bathed their heated bodies with its coolness and passed them easily to the next wave. The shore withdrew imperceptibly as if at their wish. It all grew more and more distant: the cottages squatting on pilings as if on little legs, poised for flight; the palms shifting their places. They felt as if they had been cast adrift among these hills of water while the shore was slowly wandering, freed of their presence and their watchful looks. Istvan felt the light pressure of the current.

Around him he heard something like provocative applause—the clapping of wet hands—and the greedy smacking of the waves. He grew alert. Margit's green cap jumped high, then dipped into the deep troughs. She swam calmly, boldly, a few yards ahead of him. She turned her head, frowning as the salt water made her eyes smart. He saw that she meant for him to follow her. She was testing him, courting danger.

They heard the guttural groaning of the buoy, pounded by a wave, engulfed and then floating again with a dull moan of relief.

"Margit!" he shouted. "That's enough! We're going back."

His voice was snagged in the morass of sound that came from the heaving, rustling water. He was not sure that she had heard him. He swam to the buoy and grabbed the ring, which was rough with blisters of rust. A wave dragged him; it tried to wrench him around, to pull him away. He had to be careful to keep it from forcing him against the metal covered with sharp shells.

"Margit!" he cried angrily. She heard; her body shifted, hovering in the deep water. She raised a hand that glistened like a flake of tinfoil as a sign that she understood. He saw with relief that she was turning around.

Blowing water from her nose and mouth, wrinkling her nose in comic revulsion, she clung to the tilting buoy. The current tugged at them. Their bodies jostled each other.

"Have you had enough?"

"At least one of us has to have some sense," he snapped, holding onto the bare cone of the metal float.

"You've lost your nerve." She gloated like a child. "I could swim like that, and swim and swim. The water carries you. It holds you." She patted the smooth, tilted surface of a rushing swell.

"I remember how far away the shore is." He scuffled with the buoy, which, in an unusual burst of animation, tried to shake him like a skittish horse.

THE BRISK SEA WIND flicked grains of sand about and lashed their shoulders. The palms began to bend toward each other and their heavy wings feigned flight.

He heard the crunching of packed sand under Margit's quick step and bit his lip. The lunatic; I wouldn't have been able to save her. Resentment penetrated him like a chill: we both could have . . . I, too. I would have stayed with her. And somehow it was easier to think of that, with the water licking their feet like a warm tongue, than to think: I will sail with her to Australia.

"It's quite a way to the hotel." Margit sounded surprised as she came up behind him. "But it carried us away. You might have waited. You're not very concerned about me."

"It was you who wanted to do it. I'm hungry." He walked faster as he saw her shadow overtake him.

"And I'm happy." She marched along beside him, leaving deep footprints that the sea behind them leveled and erased as if reminding them that only the moment existed, so they ought to enjoy it.

He felt an almost agonizing joy that they were together—together, only the two of them, walking the narrow road the sea and the sun smeared with a shifting coat of silver, mirror-glass, and glare. The two of them, as if it were the first day of creation. They could have wandered that way for eternity. A wave rustled like a chatty friend and their steps seemed to sing.

He looked at glittering crabs no bigger than peas. When he reached out for them, they pulled in their legs and let the retreating water carry them with it, hiding them in its turbid depths. He leaned over, determined to seize them. But even as his hand covered them they burrowed quickly into the sand, and the water, as if in collusion with them, hid their traces. So he collected flat shells like rosy petals of stone flowers.

"For Mihaly?" She handed him her rubber cap.

He filled it until it creaked like a moneybag with bits of calcified sponge, broken branches of coral, and polished pebbles with marble veins. Their colors faded as soon as they dried, until he moistened them in a wave, uncertain if it was an illusion, and the sea gushed suddenly over his open hands and plucked away his booty.

For whom am I collecting them? The thought of the reckoning that would follow this happy hour welled up, tinged with bitterness. No, not for Mihaly. He had gathered the shells impulsively for his boys, or rather on their behalf, looking for treasures with their eyes since they were not with him, they were not wading in the quicksilvered water full of changing fire. A senseless impulse. In any case I will not send them this rubbish.

A wave rushed up, hissing, and scraped the shallow bottom. He turned around and shook the shells out into the retreating water, which was full of ragged wisps of rushes. He waited for an obliging swell and rinsed the cap to a glistening turquoise.

"Why did you do that?" she asked with genuine regret. "You're so contrary."

He looked at the oval of her face framed by the clinging coppery strands of her hair. In her eyes the sea seemed to be brimming in lustrous green. He felt a profound sadness, as if he had behaved deceitfully and she, utterly trusting, had acquiesced to it. He kissed her to comfort her as one kisses a child and whispers, Sleep peacefully.

A wide path between the water and the white beach gleamed

ahead of them, smoothed by the subsiding waves. Far away they saw a twisted black shape like a tree trunk with roots that the ocean had dragged ashore, as if it were throwing off everything that could foul it internally. A dark gray mass of shriveled wild plants, seaweed, and rotted boards with tar stains gave off a rank odor. Two crows pecked at a jellyfish the size of a washbowl, picking out clots of darkening tissue.

"Look." She stopped, pointing with an outstretched hand.

Half embedded in the packed sand lay the blackened body of a drowned man. His skin was cracked. His hair, eyebrows, and eyelashes were overgrown with rust-colored clots of salt. His eyes were sunken as if the sun had blinded him. The incoming tide had washed up the corpse and thrown a garland of little grasses on it. A few flies hovered close to it; their tiny wings glittered like mica, vibrating with a monotonous hum, but they did not light. Foam spattered high.

"Don't touch him!" Margit exclaimed. "The water isn't taking him away. The hotel must be notified."

"He looks like a piece of rotted wood. He's not disgusting at all." He saw that she was startled and repelled. "He has no legs. Exactly like a fashionable sculpture."

"Stop."

"How many days was he carried by the waves? He is not loathsome; he connects us to the earth we walk on. How astonishingly quickly he became a thing, no longer a human being."

The moaning of a gong drifted on gusts of wind like a knell: the hotel was summoning guests for lunch. Margit walked rapidly as if she wanted to run away but the half-obliterated form were pulling her back. She imagined that the corpse had changed position, that the drowned man was trying to rise and follow them. But the hard-packed wet sand had sucked him halfway in, imprisoned him, and would not let him go.

"We will never know what happened to him. I cannot think of him only as a decaying material object. There is the imperative to attend to him, to bury the dead," she reminded him in an undertone.

"To burn them," he corrected her. "There has been no storm for the last week. He must have drowned, or died of natural causes and been thrown overboard."

"But then they would have wrapped him in a winding sheet and attached a stone."

"They would have had to have a sheet." He shrugged. "He was naked. There wasn't even a loincloth."

Another large jellyfish, pecked to shreds, gleamed on the sand. Farther on lay several, then a dozen or more—a burial ground for masses of fibers like short-lived fossils under domes, all dissolving in the sun to a sticky, stinking soup.

They turned and took a shortcut across the beach, which was glowing with heat, wading to their ankles in white sand like the ash from a fire that had just gone out. Turning away from the shifting views of the ocean and of the bay, which seemed to be covered with fragments of mirrors, they pushed wearily along toward the pavilion. The hotel staff were setting tables on the shady veranda; through a sunny chink white napkins flashed, artistically folded. The melody played by the Hindu sitting among palm roots led them along. Women in faded saris with flat baskets on their heads passed them, bowing and moving with small steps toward the sea, their silver bracelets tinkling.

When they reached their cottage, the slender, boyish servant hurried out to meet them, smiling broadly and handing them bathrobes. Margit went into the shower first; the water, warmed by the sun, dissolved the salt that had pasted her eyelashes together.

"Come quickly! We seem to have run short of water again," she called. "Use it while you can."

When he walked out to the veranda, dressed in linen trousers and a light shirt, Margit was chatting with Daniel. In a simple green dress with white edging she looked girlish; her red hair, tied with a white ribbon, flowed onto her right shoulder, and her skin was rosy with sunburn.

"Smugglers of people won't turn back for one dead man, especially a foreigner," the young man told her with incomprehensible exhilaration. "They dissect him so he is unrecognizable and throw him into the sea."

“Who attends to human remains?” Istvan pointed to the flashing silver crescent that was the bay.

“They will call from the hotel. A policeman will come and order the elders of the village to burn the body. He himself will not touch it, for it is not known what the man died of—perhaps plague—and he is educated and knows what bacteria are.” The young man’s white teeth showed in a winsome smile.

The blistering heat from the sand burned through their sandals and seemed to scorch Margit’s calves. As they reached the central pavilion, Istvan saw that Daniel was hanging the rinsed bathing suits on the railing. The air quivered as it rose; the melody of flutes mingled with the hiss of grasshoppers, the buzz of swirling flies, and the rippling fronds in the palm grove in a mellow symphony of holiday leisure. When they walked into the delightful shade of the hotel veranda, it seemed to Istvan that the opulence of summer was dripping like a honeycomb when a breeze fluttered the pages of the big calendar and revealed a date: December twenty-third.

“Pardon my boldness, but sir and madam are very careless.” The maitre d’hotel, dressed in starched white linen, was leaning over them. “I was observing through field glasses. You swim out too far.”

“Are you thinking of sharks?” Terey said, making light of the man’s warning. “We have become accustomed to your sign: Beware of sharks. Well—what of it? After all, we came for the swimming.”

“It is difficult to return to the shore.” The maitre d’ was still bending over them worriedly. “The current pulls hard. I was not even thinking of sharks. They have never yet attacked a white person.”

“If not to the shore, surely we could swim to a fishing boat. Its men would pull us out.”

“Unfortunately, they would not.” The man’s concern was not to be turned aside as he summoned the waiters to serve the meal. “If the sea takes a victim it desires, it also reaches for a member of the family of anyone who rescues him. After someone is drowned the catch is always better. The sea shows its gratitude. The fishermen would not rescue you, for they want to be in the good graces of the element from which they draw their livelihood. They believe this. They want to propitiate the sea.”

"Nothing is as you imagine," Margit sighed, but just then her attention was drawn to the dish placed on the table and the beer, poured from cans, that left a cool fog on their tall glasses. "And perhaps that sadhu who was playing the gourd fife is not a beggar."

"I don't mind saying that it would have been just my kind of gaucherie to give him alms," Istvan fretted. "I wanted to, but not in my bathing suit."

"That is fortunate. He is a very rich gentleman. This hotel belongs to him, and so do a large number of fishing boats. He has warehouses for coconut meat and houses in the port."

"And he sits by the sea and plays like a pauper waiting for pennies."

"That prayer of his is a hymn of worship to the sea. He sees divinity in it." He explained this as he would to children who comprehend none of the wisdom of adults.

When the waiters had left the table, Margit exchanged greetings with two elderly Englishwomen in the other corner of the veranda and asked them if they liked the place. Looking indifferently around the vast blue sky, they answered that its attractiveness, like that of the other places in the brochures, had been exaggerated. It was true that the weather was good, but it was empty and cheerless. Immediately after the holidays they were going to Colombo.

"Why did you get involved with them?" he said, quelling her friendly impulse. "We won't be able to get rid of them. Eat."

"I don't think they're happy."

"They have bank accounts. They travel. They do as they like."

"Too late. Everything came too late: wealth, acquaintance with the world, even the pleasures of the table. They don't digest their food well; I heard them ask for rice gruel. But they hope to find a chink through which to escape their age. It distresses them. They don't want to resign themselves to it. Sad."

"And they are funny in those girlish dresses, with garish lipstick. Pearls on turkeys' necks. They follow every Indian man with their eyes. Don't they see how they look?"

They walked toward the blue cottage.

"They're terribly unhappy," she said with conviction. "They

don't believe in love even if they once experienced it. By now they only trust money."

"And that is dreadful." Contemptuously he kicked a coconut shell that rolled like a monkey's skull. "They buy men's attentions."

She was silent, stepping lightly along the firmly tamped path covered with streaks of sparkling sand. She shook her head reproachfully and whispered almost to herself, "Everyone buys love somehow. I do, too."

He whirled around, took her by her arms and looked deep into her eyes, where he saw the lustrous reflection of the clear sky.

"Is it so bad for you, being with me?"

"No. You know that very well," she answered soberly. "I want only one thing: that we go to Australia and this seesawing finally ends."

They stood in the full glare of the sun. The warm wind ruffled Margit's skirt. Curving, feather-like palm fronds swayed above her red hair. He felt the pulsing of her blood, the fragrance of her skin, and the slow, infuriatingly calm hum and rumble of the ocean.

"Margit, you're wise, after all."

She gazed with anguish into his dark eyes. He looked forthrightly, defenselessly back at her. She saw the heavy line of his eyebrows, his tanned forehead, his windblown hair.

"Wise?" she repeated reflectively. "Do you mean that I feel nothing? When someone drowns, he calls for help, he thrashes about. Even when he goes under, you can see his hand grasping at the air. I know, Istvan, that you would rush to rescue him. To rescue anyone. But you don't notice me. I eat, I drink, I sunbathe on the beach, and I sleep with you, but I'm drowning. Understand, Istvan! I'm drowning."

He was silent. He hung his head. Their shadows joined and formed a single silhouette on the white sand at their feet.

"I understand."

"No. At least spare me that. If you understood, you would not leave me in uncertainty. After all, I dragged you to the very tip of India. My strength is exhausted. Let's go to Colombo. Decide on that one step."

He looked at her with profound tenderness.

"That's why you attached yourself to the English ladies. They are flying there." He patted her and whispered, "Don't distress yourself. I'll go with you."

Though it was a beautiful day, her eyes were clouded with sadness.

"You must not talk that way. You know it isn't true. I am buying you. You have my body; you forget about me. You say, You are good, you are wise, you love me. And then it goes against me. You want me to end it because you don't have the courage. I know what lies behind all those reasons you invent: Ilona, the boys. I only veil her at the moment because I am here."

"Please understand."

"I understand more than you." She pushed his hands away. "That's why this is hard for me."

"But I'm with you," he cried, clenching his fists in a gesture of powerlessness.

"Do you think that a condemned person is much happier if the sentencing is delayed?" she said in an undertone, turning her head toward the ocean, which advanced tirelessly toward the white beaches.

He took her, resistant and upset as she was, and kissed her temple. Gradually she relaxed and, leaning forward a little, let him lead her toward the cottage. He felt a tremor run through her; her lips were hot and dry. The sun, he thought. We lay in the sun too much. It seemed to him that she had a slight fever.

They drew near the little blue house in silence, reconciled, leaning on each other. Through the open door came the slow tapping of typewriter keys. They stood still, smiling indulgently. Turning his head back and forth, utterly absorbed, the attendant was striking the keyboard with two fingers. The breeze lightly ruffled the bundled mosquito netting. Daniel was alert; he looked around and, startled, jumped away from the typewriter.

"I am very sorry." He cringed like a dog that has gotten into mischief and now waits for a hiding.

"What are you writing?" Istvan looked over his shoulder, but the boy quickly pulled the paper out of the machine.

"Nothing. Really, nothing."

"Show us."

It looked like a song written in English, not polished but fresh and full of feeling. Its subject was the star of Bethlehem that shone in the eye of an ox and on the silver neck of an ass. Their breath warmed the bare, helpless feet of the baby. The animals sympathized with him, for they knew the world: the stony roads, the long journeys in the dust and heat, the blows falling on the back, the lashes with the whip and the burdens too heavy to bear, the premonitions of death when even a damp sponge does not moisten the cracked lips. The few beasts pity the newborn who desires to conquer the world with love.

"Well, what next?" Istvan asked, surprised.

"Only wishes. Joyous holidays—" he was embarrassed. "I wanted to lay the letter on the table with the present for memsahib. It was going to be a surprise."

He pulled out of his shirt a long strand of tiny opalescent shells, well matched and strenuously polished. He laid them on Margit's outstretched hand. The necklace retained the warmth of his skin.

"Who taught you the song?"

"No one, sahib. I composed it myself. I am sorry for disturbing the machine. I thought it would be more elegant this way." His gentle eyes were soft with humility, his long, dark fingers entwined pleadingly. "I wanted to prepare a gift, for I will be receiving something from you, after all," he explained with childlike candor.

Terey was ashamed; he had not thought of a gift for Daniel.

"And what would you prefer? A gift, or money to buy yourself something you want?"

Daniel raised his shapely head. He looked troubled. Margit shook the string of shells softly; they chattered and tinkled. Outside the window the ocean was keening. White streaks of foam rushed toward the shore and dissolved on invisible beaches. Dunes swept by the sea wind glinted uneasily. Now and then the dry rattle of palm fronds, as if someone were ripping oilcloth, drifted into the room.

"Of course Daniel wants both." She dispelled the young man's worry. "You will give him a tie—the mango-colored one. And a few rupees, as you said."

"You will go to church? At midnight there is a Christmas mass. Many fishermen will come. And there will be a crèche in which everything moves. The people have been working on it all year."

"Let's go, shall we?" Margit suggested. "There is nothing to do here. And you're probably tired of this solitude—just the pair of us."

"We'll see." He felt trapped and defensive. He had forgotten, completely forgotten. Was this a subtle invitation from the One he had pushed from his thoughts, driven away from the sunny beach and shut into the chapel, as a troublesome suitcase is left in a baggage room? "And where is it?" he asked rather coldly.

"Not far from here. Beyond the village, in the palm grove. And the priest is from Europe. A real monk with a beard."

"Of what nationality?"

Daniel's long eyelashes fluttered helplessly and he threw up his hands.

"I don't know. White."

Margit said encouragingly, "We'll go and we'll see."

Outside the window figures appeared with flat baskets on their heads. They spoke in husky voices. Daniel answered them, and announced with a smile of satisfaction that displayed his charming dimples, "They have brought the star. I ordered a star of the sea for you from the fishermen. I told them to catch a big one. I can dry it so it will not lose its color. You can fasten it to the hood of your car as the English do when they drive away."

Leaning on the railing of the veranda, they could see into the baskets. Crabs half a meter across, tied together and strewn with seaweed, fumbled with their legs. Yellow cuttlefish swelled like living money bags, rippling arms that seemed both animal and vegetable. Like the leaves of the century plant, Istvan thought. Sometimes from under the seaweed a goggling lashless eye flashed disquietingly.

"They ask you to buy lobsters, sir. They can prepare them in the hotel kitchen. Freshly caught; live." He took them carefully in his hands and raised them to show how the tails fluttered in their hard shells. "Not costly, sir. A very good dish."

The women stood still, not even raising their faces toward Istvan. They seemed to be intermediaries. The glare of the sun fell on the shallow baskets and kindled rainbow-tinted points of light on the wet scales of the fish and the crabs' shells. It flashed on bare breasts, empty, sucked-out bags hanging from under saris carelessly thrown on.

"Surely you will not force me to eat these appalling things." Margit stepped back. "Especially after what we saw on the shore."

They raised their heads and looked at the long expanse of beach. A smudge of smoke rose from among the dunes: a body was being burned. A tall man swathed in white stood there, guarding the unseen fire. The funereal chirping of flutes floated back to them. "The sadhu apologizes to the sea," Daniel said drowsily and began, without aversion, to rake through the seaweed with his hand. He selected lobsters and held a whole cluster by their long antennae.

In the silence they heard the crunch of the shells, the rattle of the angry tails. The intonation of the sea was fainter, as if it were farther from the land. Squeezing Margit's hand tenderly, Istvan whispered, "To your next holidays—in Australia."

"I want to be there sooner," she replied impatiently. "And with you. Well, please—say it again. It's terribly important."

In a low-necked white dress accented by a necklace of irregularly shaped hunks of turquoise that complemented the color of her eyes, she was captivating. Her hair glowed with coppery highlights like tiny living, shifting flames from a candle; it cast a shadow on her forehead. A light shawl with gold threads was slipping from her arms.

"You know that's what I want, too," he whispered, gazing into her cool eyes, which were now sparkling with joy.

"But say it again," she insisted, leaning toward him as if drawn by an irresistible force.

"With you. With you."

On a silver tray sat a dish with leftover shells and the crisp red husk of a lobster. Its antennae threw a darting shadow on the white of the tablecloth, while the painstakingly arranged claws the color of coral wallowed among leaves of curly kale. They ate filet of turkey breast with fragrant nutmeg stuffing, sweet and biting, and pineapple salad, washing it down with chilled wine. Far away over a sea burnished with shifting light a row of golden points glided along: a passenger ship making its way south. It was sailing to where Margit wanted to go. In the quiet they followed it with their eyes until it was lost in the darkness.

"I would give anything for you to be happy."

"I will be. You know very well that it depends on you."

Under palm fronds the cheery English ladies raised their glasses, forgot for a moment the coolly expectant young Indians in white dinner jackets who were leaning solicitously over them, and called to Margit, "Merry Christmas!"

Istvan and Margit lifted their glasses. In the dark, outside the windows that opened toward the bay, the Angelus bell rang with an insistent, rapid rhythm. As if it had summoned him, Daniel appeared on the steps of the terrace. Margit noticed with satisfaction that he had put on the new tie, the gift from Istvan.

"Do you really want to go?" Istvan said, still resisting. "Wouldn't it be better to go to the beach in front of us, to the ocean?"

"No. No." She shuddered with aversion. "Let's see the chapel and how they pray."

When they were walking away from the radiantly lit hotel veranda, the night seemed milder. The sand glowed and a soft breath of warm wind drifted from the dunes. Fireflies flew over tufts of dry grasses. The bell urged them on, clanging beyond the palm grove.

"I told the priest you would be coming," Daniel said with a self-satisfied air. "He was very glad. This way, please. Be careful of the roots. The path takes a turn."

Between the gently sloping trunks of the coconut palms the sky teemed with stars—large stars that glittered nervously and hardly pierced the dusk. Now they could see the faithful, women and children, their figures moving noiselessly among the trees. Only a little lamp suspended from a black wrist made a splash of color on a sari donned for the holiday. Little lights arrived, converged, and gave off a soft glow through the open gates.

"I did not believe that you would come." A friendly voice spoke up and a tall figure detached itself from the wall. Istvan felt the hearty, coarse pressure of a workman's hand, a hand accustomed to wield the ax and shovel. "It is rare that any of the tourists drop in. They prefer the sea."

They stood before the chapel gate. By the warm twinkle of the candles they could see a gray uncombed beard, a sharp glance from under bushy brows. The priest wore an orange linen habit—the color worn by Buddhist monks—and sandals on his bare feet.

"You are from England?"

"No. Madam is from Australia and I am from Hungary."

The monk held Terey's hand as if he were afraid he would wrest it away and escape. "Good heavens! What a surprise!" he said in a choked voice, and suddenly began to speak rapidly in Hungarian. "I also am a Hungarian, from Kolozsvár. A Salesian. I have been here since 1912."

"Hungarians were still not free then."

"Hungarians were always free. Only the kingdom . . . Are you an emigrant?"

"No. I am here temporarily."

The priest looked him hard in the face. "And can you return there?"

"Can't you?"

"That depends on the will of my superiors. They are accustomed to having me here, and I am reconciled to it. I had not thought that God would give me such joy on the holiday. I can speak in my native language! I even taught a pair of boys here. They picked up the words like a recording tape, but they are not Hungarians. It was as if I had taught parrots."

"Are we detaining you, father?"

"No. Father Thomas Maria de Ribeira, an Indian from Goa, is saying mass. I will hold one later for the fishermen when they return."

"What are you speaking?" Margit moved closer to them; they had almost forgotten her. "Is the priest Hungarian?"

"Yes."

"Well—you are glad!"

"Yes. Don't be jealous. Have you been in contact with our embassy, father?"

"No. They sent me the registration document, but I put it aside and there it lies."

"And your passport?"

"Everyone knows me here. No one asks about documents. I have no intention of going anywhere. And for the last road no passport is needed. Heavens—what happiness, to speak Hungarian! Are you man and wife?"

"No."

"But you are a Catholic—you came here—" the priest was troubled. He raked his beard with his hand.

"Yes."

"Perhaps you both would like to join—"

"We have just finished dinner. It is impossible. Perhaps another time."

They stood in silence for a moment. The monk seemed ashamed of his insistence. "I am sorry," he said. "I would so have liked to hear a confession in our language. How I would enjoy being an instrument of grace to a countryman! Here—in India. It is no accident that has brought you to me."

Margit stood leaning against the door frame, peering into the church. Warm light fell on her cheeks, which were tinted rose over her tan, and kindled on her hair. From inside came singsong voices repeating the litany, and the spicy smell of the warm throng.

Women entered, apologizing for their tardiness. They bent gently and touched the worn threshold with their foreheads, kissing their fingertips as they placed them on the floor. They threw lace mantillas over their hair, glancing at Margit as if she were not well brought up, then slipped inside.

"Then you will be able to see our Budapest?"

For a moment he did not answer.

"You know nothing about the events of November, father? About Kádár?"

"Who is he?"

"Or about the revolution, the fighting in Budapest?"

"No. I have no radio. I do not read the newspapers. But tell me: what happened there?"

Where to begin? How to tell him in a few sentences? Suddenly Istvan lost the will to speak. One would have to begin with the entire history of the last forty years. "Well, there is peace at the moment," he said bitterly.

"And I was so upset. Praise God! Better not to read the papers; the reporters write such screaming headlines now, you begin to think there will be war tomorrow. And in the meantime nothing so terrible is happening. Nothing. And that's good."

Deep in the chapel a bell tinkled. The old man turned around and dropped heavily to his knees. He waved an admonitory hand, cutting off the conversation, urging them to fix their attention on the altar. Over the kneeling crowd Istvan saw, between the dark fingers of the priest, the golden flame of the chalice and the fragile white disk.

Women crept forward on their knees, suddenly stood erect, then sank down with their foreheads to the floor, hunched, breathless. A crowd of figures draped in white surged to the altar. The men shuffled on bare feet; the bundled fabric that secured their dhotis swung to the rhythm of their walk, falling like loose skirts below their knees.

Are they truly aware of what is taking place here? Do they understand the mystery? I believe. I know—but I have cut myself off, I am not being nourished from the source. In that moment he was stricken at the thought that he was excluded from this community, that he was under indictment. He himself was the prosecutor and judge. As long as I am with Margit, there is no forgiveness.

The Lord will not afflict his servant, will not retract the word that saves for eternity.

He raised his hand and covered his face, which was contorted with stinging remorse and anger at himself. Indeed, I knew all this, or should have known, if I feel so superior to fellow Catholics from this village in Kerala, fishermen, gatherers of coconut meat and fiber, peasant women wading in rice fields, girls bending under the burden of little brothers and sisters. Each of them could come here in a trustful spirit for the blessed bread; I alone cannot, as long as . . . Of his own will he condemned himself to estrangement, he abandoned them: yet another betrayal under the pretext of gaining freedom.

Margit slid closer to him and leaned gently against his arm. He felt her touch through his light clothing and his pain intensified. "That was beautiful," she whispered. Her hair tickled his neck.

Does she comprehend nothing? She looks at the altar and the praying crowd as if it were a pageant full of light and color. And I will not try to explain it to her; I would have to say something detrimental to myself. He exists—we are even prepared to reconcile ourselves to that—so He can serve as a cane to lean on and then put in a corner so we have both hands free to seize the world. To visit in church as in a museum. We admire the statuary, the stained glass, conceived in a transport of humble adoration. His memory was bursting with images from tours of churches; he saw the upturned heads of people gazing at the frescoed vaults, hardly hearing the smooth recitation of the guide, who was extolling the choreographed gestures of the baroque saints or the agonizing tension of the dark figure at the moment of death.

He pulled Margit close, as if he were afraid he would push her away. She turned toward him trustfully, tenderly. She is good, he thought.

"Are you here for long?" the missionary queried in English. The light that fell on the open gates made a yellow blur on the edge of his frayed cassock and his bare feet in worn sandals.

"Two weeks. We would be happy to visit you." She extended a hand. "It is so peaceful here. And it would be so nice for Istvan to speak his own language."

"Will you come?" The monk spoke directly to Istvan, for he was troubled by his silence.

"No," he said in an undertone. Ignoring Margit, he turned around and plunged into the deep twilight among the palms, where the elongated figures of Keralan fishermen disappeared amid whispers and the light jingle of bracelets. The warm light of swaying lanterns slowly floated away.

"What is it?" There was a note of anxiety in the girl's voice.

"Why did you drag me here?" he burst out, knowing his anger was unjustified. "I had a feeling it would go badly."

"I thought it would give you pleasure. What did he say? What did he want from you?"

"Oh, nothing. It's my problem." He took her hand and raised it to his lips. "I'm sorry."

"What is it all about?"

He turned so unexpectedly that she almost bumped into him. "Do you really want to know?"

The tone of his voice gave her pause. "If it's something painful," she said hesitantly, "perhaps not tonight. But I'm with you. I can share the burden. It won't overwhelm me."

"We have to talk about this sometime." His voice was subdued. The attendant walked a little way behind them; he knew the paths, so he put out the lantern, but his finger played with the button. Bright patches of light exposed rough palm trunks running toward the sky, clumps of dry grass, and dusty, almost black branches of shrubbery.

"After all, there is always—a solution." He could hear weariness and a drowsy sadness in her voice. "But don't demand that of me. Let's leave it to fate, like the Hindus."

"What are you talking about?"

"If I weren't alive . . ."

He clamped his fingers on her arm and shook it desperately. "Don't even think of such a thing!"

He kissed her forehead and her eyes, pressing her eyelids hard with his lips and ruffling her eyebrows. Her cheeks were flushed and salty, her mouth dry under her lipstick.

"My life," he breathed, rocking her as she clung to him.

"And Ilona?" she whispered. "Please, Istvan, at least don't lie to yourself. So many times we've talked about the future without taking her into account, as if she were already dead. Well—be brave enough to think that I might leave and release you."

"I don't want to. I can't."

She trembled as if a chill had run through her. A salty breeze from the sea carried the smell of rotting heaps of plants and wet sand. They heard the reluctant drumming of the waves. She pressed his hand to her lips and cheek. He felt her tears.

"Here is the path, sahib." White light spurted between the bristling dry grasses.

"Go first, Daniel," he ordered, letting go of Margit.

"You did not see the crèche, the three kings, the elephants. They shake their trunks," he said proudly, speaking very low. "After mass the villagers turn the winch and all the figures walk around the manger. The star shines. Saint Joseph smokes a hookah just like a Hindu."

"Madam doesn't feel well."

"I have a little fever," she admitted, licking her dry lips.

"Memsahib lay in the sun too much," the servant murmured admonishingly. "Too much time in the sea. The sun and water sap your strength. Sahib should not allow it."

They stepped in among the dunes and floundered in the deep sand, which squeaked under their feet. The white eye of a lighthouse winked far away in the dark. Long ridges of talus glimmered like rotted wood in the breeze. Daniel put out the light. The darkness was not impenetrable; in the sand, washed to a sheen, they could see their half-effaced footprints.

They made their way, unhurried, toward the orange-tinted windows of the hotel restaurant. The guttural voices of the bay drowned out the barely audible tinkle of music from the pavilion. They caught the blare of a saxophone, the syncopated beat of percussion, like lost radio signals. Daniel walked confidently and, it seemed, faster. He took off his sandals and held them in his hand. Margit followed suit. Under its surface the sand had not cooled; it gave under the pressure of their feet, and warmed them.

It seemed to Istvan that this had happened before—that he knew this landscape, obscured by darkness and sprinkled with glassy stardust, knew the figure of the guide outlined by the warm glow of the distant lamps. Perhaps he had waited in a dream for a friendly hand to lead him away from his fears, to point out a refuge. He took Margit's hand. She trembled.

"Are you cold?"

"I'm sad," she answered thoughtfully. "I'm sorry. I'm not good company."

They were near the cottages, whose rear walls rested on the steep bank; their fronts were raised on poles that faced motionless waves of gray sand. In the windows, as if in black mirrors, whirled a rain of stars. The shrill voices of cicadas pursued them like alarm bells. They bored into the ears; they were a torment.

"What is it, sir?" Daniel said suddenly, startled. He lit the lantern, but it was only a hindrance; his eyes were accustomed to the dark. A large animal leaped from among the dunes and ran in a zigzag until it was lost in the shadows. The cicadas shrieked madly.

"It was a man." The beam of the servant's lantern fell on a partly dissolved footprint with a small circular hollow around it. Wet grains of sand clung together. Istvan felt the moisture with his fingers as he checked for blood.

"He came out of the water."

"Leave it be." Margit gripped his sleeve. "He ran away and we have peace. What concern is he of yours? Please—let's go back to the house."

But the footprint lured them. Daniel caught it in a white stream of light. "He ran on all fours like a dog," he said. "He must be here somewhere."

"Don't be afraid, Margit. We'll be back."

They walked quietly, alert for the slightest sound. The wheezing of the sea quieted; there was the blast of a trumpet. The cicadas marked the men's passing with a long cadenza of rasping. The declivities in the sand disappeared and they found themselves on parched, gritty ground with sparse dry grass that prickled like fish bones.

"Wait," Margit called, putting on her sandals.

Istvan stopped. He saw the lantern's beam brush against their cottage, lick at the window, fall on the veranda steps, and creep among the piles that held up the floor. He heard Daniel's triumphant call.

"Sahib, we have him! He was hiding here."

He left the girl and came running. He squatted by the servant, resting both hands on the sand. In the circle of harsh light, squeezed between the piles and the sloping hill, a Hindu in wet rags caked with sand was cowering. His teeth showed from under his short mustache like a snarling dog's. He did not cover his eyes. Holding a pebble tightly in his hand, he uttered a throaty cry.

"Did you understand what he said?"

"Yes. He asks us not to kill him," Daniel answered in amazement.

"Tell him who we are. Ask where he came from."

Daniel repeated this in an earnest voice and began serving as interpreter. Margit sat beside them and gazed at the Hindu, who turned his head away when the cone of light was fixed on him.

"Turn that off," Istvan said.

"No need." She restrained Daniel. "He's blind."

"He ordered me to swear by Durga that we will do him no harm, that we will not give him away." The servant's voice shook with excitement. "He escaped from a boat and swam toward the noise on the shore. He thought we were chasing him. Madam doctor is right: he is blind. He begs us not to kill him, for he saw nothing. He says that he has a rich brother who will repay us if we hide him."

The appeals to take the man into their cottage went on and on. Margit sent Daniel to the hotel kitchen for a bowl of rice. The blind man's eyes, covered with a film, gave his gaunt, tanned face a look of dull stupefaction. Finally he crawled out, admitting that he was hungry. He did not lunge for the food, but asked for water, washed his hands, rinsed his mouth and spat on the threshold, which he found by feeling for it with his toes like a monkey. He sat cross-legged, placed the bowl of rice between his thighs and ate slowly, listening to the far-off sonorous beating of the sea and the band from the hotel. Daniel crouched in front of him like a dog before a hedgehog, uncertain whether to attack him or acknowledge him as a member of the household.

"Ask why his brother doesn't take more of an interest in him if he is so wealthy."

"He is a singer, sahib. He composes verse and recites ancient poetry from memory. Among us such people are respected. He wanted to reach Ceylon, to go to the temple of Buddha. Everywhere people feed him and give him lodging for the night. He is a true sadhu," he explained proudly. "He was in Benares. His brother does not restrain him; he goes his own way. He asks us to send a telegram to Bombay tomorrow and his brother will surely come."

"Can he recover his sight?" Istvan leaned toward Margit. "You wanted to truly help at least one person in India. You have an opportunity if his brother turns up here. You can advise him as to how this man might be cured."

"There would have to be an operation. He would see a little. I'm not a fortuneteller, only a doctor. I would have to do a thorough examination."

"He asks for a few bottles, a pot of water, and two forks," Daniel announced. "He will sing for us."

"Where will I get bottles at night?" Istvan shrugged.

"I will look for them, sahib. I will bring some from the hotel kitchen. I will find them." Daniel slipped away into the night.

Seven empty wine bottles were placed before the blind singer. With startling dexterity he filled them with water to various levels, struck them with a fork held flatwise, and, listening attentively to each tone, established a scale of crystalline notes. When he passed the fork over the glass, barely touching it, the bottles sang like a xylophone. He checked the positions of the bottles with his hands and tapped them as if to assure himself that he could strike them accurately. At last, now in command of himself, he gave Daniel an instruction.

"He will sing, and I will translate. He begs that you will ask no questions, for he himself does not know if he can do it. It will be the voice of the dead."

"Do you want to listen to this?" Istvan asked Margit, but she only put on a shawl and nodded. She sat still, leaning hard against him. Suddenly she quivered.

"What is it?"

"Nothing." She put a finger to her lips.

"Among us it is said: someone is walking on my grave," he said, whispering, for piercing trills were rising with the fork's firm strokes and the singer, inclining his head, began his monotonous recitative. Daniel translated it in a colorless voice, hesitating now and then and searching for an English word, trying not to fall behind the blind man's cadences. Deep shadows appeared on the walls; between the pure chiming tones of the glass came the moaning of the sea and the boisterous sound of the band. But little by little the whole world began to recede while nothing remained but words like the wailing of mourners.

"The Kingdom of Lanka, the music of streams that never dry, trees with the smell of wet mangoes. Reviving rain lashes the great banana leaves; bunches of fruit smooth as a maiden's skin await the hands of the hungry. On the palms, coconuts bump like young goats butting each other. In the fertile mud, ears of rice tickle the hand like cats' whiskers. Birds fill the air and the sea rings with the scales of fish. Gods walk on the earth of Lanka, the island predestined for the just, given in possession to the meek and industrious . . . Land of plenty.

"They who escaped the knife of the Muslim, they who moved among burned houses, looked for work; they whose eyes cried out all their tears and were empty as the palm of a beggar. Fathers, feigning hope, went away every morning so as not to hear the weeping of hungry children timidly asking if they would eat today. They went away, they fled as far away as they could. They sat in the shade, grew feeble and dozed. Then the palm trees murmured in their ears; a hand combed tufts of rice ears, the mango touched the dry, cracked lip, and they dreamed of the Kingdom of Lanka, the land of plenty beyond the sea.

"A stranger came by night, and they whispered long, taking counsel while the children slept. The news went round that there was a ship that would hurry over the sea to the Kingdom of Lanka.

"They would only find rescue if they could pay. They counted long and carefully. Ornaments stripped from women passed from hand to hand: hoops of silver wire, gold coins on chains ripped like leaves from bosoms, lighter than butterflies' wings. Little, too little gold to pay for the journey to Paradise.

"They touched the heads of their sleeping children. They chose victims. They sold their daughters as slaves to houses with no doors, only curtains of clattering bamboo rods, houses in which a woman does not sleep. Their sons they sold to peasants who felt their arms and inspected their teeth with their fingers, as they do with oxen. Their money, their treasure—and you could have held it in your fist—they gave the nocturnal visitor. He laid out a receipt which they could not read, but they trusted him, they believed. It was not the first load or the last of pilgrims longing for paradise, for the island of Lanka.

"I wanted to sail with them. To walk in the footsteps of Siddhartha, the prince who did not fear death. They did not want to take money from me. They knew me; I paid with a song. I listened to their quick breathing. I touched their hearts. We were led by night; the grass clutched at our feet, the branches snagged our hands as if to call: Do not go! But I was with them. In front of me, women carried their little children; men marched behind me with bundles of rice and clothing. We walked into water that slowly rose. I held the hand of a friendly wanderer bound, like me, for the land of plenty, the Kingdom of Lanka.

"'Do not fear.' They took me by the arms. 'It is not deep here and the boat can be seen.' I was not afraid. I had already heard the wave boom against the ship. I was pulled into its wooden bottom and tucked tightly into the passengers' quarters. I felt the warmth of their bodies; they were overcome by sleep. The sail, swollen with the sea wind, creaked on the mast. The helmsman took me under his care. He ordered me to sing about the battle Hanuman waged with a pair of giants. The yardarm whimpered. I smelled the odors of tar and of the beneficent sea. When I was silent, they gave me milk from young coconuts. They fed me rice in a leaf twisted like a buffalo's horn. They were good to me; they asked only that I sing again of the land of Lanka.

"We sailed two days, for I felt the sun's breath, and the third night, when the gulls squealed like wakened children to greet the dawn, the helmsman ordered us to disembark. They tested with a pole; the water around the ship was shallow, the land not far. They left the ship quietly. They lowered themselves into the waves without the clink of a bracelet, blessing in whispers those who had smuggled them to paradise, to the Kingdom of Lanka."

The glassy clink of the bottles struck with metal made Margit shudder. The hoarse voice with its cry for the country all the hungry so longed for was unnerving. The singer seemed to forget his hearers; his unerring strokes fell harder on the bottles, and with the uplifted face and white eyes of a statue he lamented to heaven and the distant sea.

Daniel crouched beside him and translated in a whisper. He did not hinder the blind man, but conveyed the sense of the cry which reverberated in them both—as if they were remembering it—in a secret language. Margit's hot, dry fingers pressed Istvan's hand hard, like the fingers of a child who hides behind its mother so as not to see something frightening. The music in the restaurant stopped; they did not notice at all. Only the voices of the ocean seemed nearer, as if they had been called as witnesses.

"I wanted to go down into the water, but they held me back. They ordered me to be silent. They had been good to me, after all; I believed that they would take me to the shore. The ship sailed lightly without people. And then the first moan floated from over the waves. The betrayal was discovered: there was deep water farther on, and the shore was distant—the shore, or perhaps smoke. I heard weeping, shrieking, pleading. Already the sharks were cutting the wave that surged toward them. They beat as if with oars. They snorted like oxen. They smacked like pigs at the trough. So the partners blotted out the traces, drowning the cry that died away beneath the sky of Lanka."

Suddenly the light blinked and the glare began to leak from the bulb. It was only a red wire; at last it went out. Istvan wanted to go for a candle but Margit held him lightly with her arms around his neck. Then he remembered that to the singer, darkness was no hindrance.

The bottles jangled like gravel on a windowpane as he hit them. He struck without hesitation; the chords sang in the dusk. All at once they were overtaken by a dreadful suspicion that the tale they were hearing was true. The night encircled the walls of the cottage, murmuring and humming. Among the distant stars the lighthouse blindly waved its yellow sword like a giant at bay.

"Before a wave extinguished the last voice, the helmsman paced up and down, looking out. They must have watched the spectacle; I thanked the gods that I was blind. I heard the sharks thrashing. I felt death near. I did not fear dying, only the rending of the body that is alive, pulsing with blood, terrified, naked and defenseless. Those who had been devoured had paid for their faults. Whimpering from ignorance, free of the past, they would be born anew in the beautiful land of Lanka. I waited for death—and the helmsman demanded that I sing to them. The vessel quivered in the fair wind and the lines creaked. They gave me fish to eat; no one refused the water that smelled of mildew.

"That night I heard the bargaining for my head. The helmsman swore he would not betray a blind man. They landed here and threw a stone instead of an anchor. When I heard the sounds of the shore amid the clatter of the surf, I waited for night. The water carried me onto the hardpacked sand, but the sea, not satiated with victims, suddenly changed its mind and dragged me back. Nevertheless I emerged and ran through the dunes in fear that it was pursuing me. And you are the first I have told of that flight to the earthly paradise—of the people who will never accuse the living, for they, reborn, are unaware of the fate that met them at the very gates of Lanka."

He struck one clear note. As its tremolo hung in the air, he clapped his hand on the floor boards twice with a dull boom like the sound of a drum. Then the deep silence was only measured by the sighs of the drifting sea. The singer hung his head in inexpressible weariness. Daniel trembled with emotion, as if he had only grasped the meaning of the ominous narrative as he translated its final words.

"Ask him if he will tell the police all this tomorrow. I'll take him in the car. No one will find out."

"No, sahib. He says he will not speak. The police will not believe him."

"But is this possible?" Margit squeezed Istvan's hand so hard her fingers seemed to be biting it. "Is what he is saying true? It's not just a poem?"

"That is the truth concerning earthly flights to paradise," Daniel answered, still thrilled and appalled by the blind man's recital.

"Where is this isle of happiness?" she demanded.

"It is Ceylon," Istvan said, adding hastily, "We cannot leave him like this. We must . . ."

The blind man spoke insistently to Daniel, demanding something.

"He asks that we hide him until his brother arrives. Two days. Three. He is certain that his brother will put aside everything and come. He swears that the gods revealed this secret to him so he would sing of those who were swallowed up by the ocean, devoured by the sharks."

"Damn it! Nothing will save those people. The pirates must be caught and hanged!" Istvan stormed.

"He says: We leave justice to the gods. The pirates only enforce the will of the one who gave them ships and enabled them to engage in smuggling. Sahib," he added after a moment, "we do not have a death penalty. Even Gandhi forbade us to execute his murderers."

"I've had enough of this 'he says,' 'he wants,' 'he doesn't want.' I make the decisions here. Is that clear?"

Daniel and his countryman spoke rapidly to each other. At last the young man rose and said earnestly, "I have heard nothing, sahib. The blind man gives good advice. Before there would be a proper investigation they would poison him, and me as well. Best to be silent."

"Who would poison you?"

"The pirates. The smugglers of people."

"Do you understand any of this?" Istvan turned to Margit in helpless exasperation. "How can we help them when they don't want help?"

"Night is not a good counselor. He should not stay here. They will surely be looking for him."

"Where can we hide him?"

"I would take him to the mission now that it is dark," Daniel advised. "Let the fathers attend to him. Perhaps you will go with me, sahib. I am afraid."

"I'll go, too." Margit rose, then quickly gave up the plan. "Go. I'll wait. I'm terribly tired. Go yourself." She sat slumped and weak in the darkness under the looming white bundle of mosquito netting.

"Lie down."

"All right," she agreed easily. Alarmed, he touched her forehead. It was hot. Her hair was damp with sweat; it clung to her temples. He was seized with a fear that she was ill—very ill.

"There's nothing wrong with me. A little fever," she insisted. "It's giving me a pain in my joints. I'll take an aspirin and it will go down."

"And the blasted light had to go out. Can you find the aspirin?"

Daniel took a flashlight from under his dhoti. A stream of white glare hurt their eyes.

"Turn it out," she begged in a whisper. "The aspirin's in the drawer. Well, go on. I need to be alone now. The sooner you go, the sooner you'll be back."

The blind man stood up, jostling the bottles so that they chimed briefly. They listened: it seemed that in the echoes of the sea they could distinguish muffled noises, the stamping of many feet. It was so quiet that they could hear grains of sand dropping from the man's wet rags and scattering on the floor. Their own pulses beat painfully in their ears. The blind man whispered something. Daniel translated, "He says that we can go. That is only the sea grumbling."

"Take this. I'll be calmer," she breathed into Istvan's ear. He felt her push a long, cold object into his hand; it flashed in the dark with a moist, vitreous sheen. "Be careful. It's a lancet."

He shrugged. What was she imagining? We are on the hotel's beach; the staff are sleeping alongside us. A patrol is even walking the shoreline. The mumblings of the sightless visionary have frightened Margit; the night and the fever have conjured up phantoms. We are in no danger.

Irritably he took the bare arm, which was still caked with sand, and helped the blind man down the steps. The cool skin, rough with sand, reminded him of the lifeless form the waves had left on the beach.

He turned around and saw with relief that Margit had disappeared under the tent of mosquito netting.

Gripping the lancet, he waded across the beach as if the sand were cold ashes. He smelled the greasy, briny odor of the blind man's windblown hair. What have I become involved in? Certainly I'm not going to fight anyone. A diplomat with a knife, at night, on the dunes . . . A smuggler runs from a pirate ship: a madman's story. He would gladly have thrown away the lancet, but he was afraid he would not be able to find it later. The roar of the sea crashing against the beach soothed his anxiety with its measured rhythm.

As they passed the last cottage, which was empty and bolted shut, Istvan laid the lancet on the step. Under the sky with its burden of stars, the whole tale seemed no more than the raving of a fevered mind. Another day, he thought, and I'll be laughing at my gullibility.

He waited, hidden among the palms in darkness black as thick smoke, until Daniel had given the blind man over to the care of the mission. He heard the dry clashing of the great ragged leaves, the sleepy grunting of the tall trunks. He was worried about Margit. He was already eager to go back when the servant slipped silently out of the shadows.

"I told the fathers that it was at your direction, so they took him at once," he began in a whisper. "His brother will pay."

"If he has a brother," Istvan muttered skeptically.

"I believe him. He does not lie." After a moment's hesitation Daniel added, "Fugitives from Pakistan came, then left, and no one worried about their disappearance. They had a layover in the port. They begged; now they are gone. They are nowhere to be found. So much the better. Now there is no more trouble. Ceylon protects itself against people from India, but there are chinks, so they leak through."

"And no one knew of this?"

"Perhaps something was said about it, but who would believe? To believe is to kill hope, sahib. And that is to acquiesce to death—a slow death from hunger."

They walked in darkness filled with stars. The sand crunched under their feet. The sea groaned like a mute, trying clumsily to utter something with plaintive rumblings and splashes. All the coast was dark. Only one lighthouse nodded toward them, beckoning with a stream of brilliance.

"I think they all perished, sahib," Daniel whispered. "That is why no one brought an accusation against the pirates."

"But there was no confirmation that anyone had sailed safely to port. What about their sons and daughters?"

"They did not want to write, for it would have betrayed them. Or perhaps they did not know how. And where to write? They waited for word, and then they forgot. When the parents sold their children into slavery, they foreordained them to ruin."

"And you can think so calmly of all this?"

"That is human life, sahib. We all delude ourselves that where we are not, it must be better."

Istvan was furious. He could have taken the man by the arm and shaken him. You fool. You damned fool. Why don't you rebel? All the servant's logic seemed senseless to him, yet he acknowledged that his explanation of the crime they had stumbled upon might be correct.

"Think, Daniel! Is it worth it to kill for a handful of silver—a pair of rings and necklaces?"

"They do not do it for the booty. They must collect the fee or no one would believe that they would take them," the servant whispered, holding on to Istvan. "They offered those people to the sea."

Istvan strode on with clenched jaws. The insane lie: one devised it and the other stupidly believed it!

"The sea gives fish, the sea feeds us. We must assure ourselves of its good will. Otherwise it will be angry and reach for victims itself. Fishermen for generations, their fate depends on the sea, so is it any wonder, sahib, that they want to propitiate it?"

"And you are a Catholic?" Istvan tugged angrily at the young man's arm. "Don't you understand that this is a crime and those thugs are ready to lure new victims?"

"The runaways would have starved to death. And so—I did not push them into the water. They themselves wanted to go away. Best not to meddle. I am a Catholic. I also want eternal life. Let each save himself as he is able. Everything that happens happens because God permits it. If He had not willed it, He would not have allowed them to die."

Daniel understands nothing, and certainly thinks that I understand nothing. Caste and fate. He does not think of such people as his neighbors. He manages to anesthetize his love for God in Indian style. To anesthetize himself from cooperating with God, from co-creating himself and the world that exists, which after our death can be better, more beautiful because of what we leave behind.

From the long beaches washed by waves drifted a wet odor like the smell of a dog being chased in the rain.

"I would not involve myself in this. I would leave vengeance to God. It will find them when the time is ripe," Daniel said softly.

They had reached the line of cottages on piles; they were dark and quiet as hives of hibernating bees.

"First thing in the morning you will send a telegram. Perhaps his brother will show better judgment and convince him to file a deposition."

"Very well, sahib."

"Until tomorrow, Daniel. Give me your flashlight."

He ran up the steps, covering the stream of light with his fingers. He pushed aside the mosquito netting and leaned over the sleeping woman. Margit lay with her fists against her half-open mouth, from which trickles of sweat and threads of saliva gleamed. Her breathing was choked as if she had been sobbing not long before.

Something crumbled under his foot—something like a grain of sand. He uncovered the flashlight and saw white pills scattered on the floorboards. He was terrified that she might have poisoned herself accidentally, dizzy with fever and reaching for another bag in the dark. He raised one of the pills and was relieved to see that it was stamped Bayer. Like an echo her words returned: If I died, everything would be simpler. Since you cannot make the decision yourself, cannot make the final choice, you will leave it to fate. You will call in the arbiter.

No. No. Trust me; give me a little more time. I will resolve my issues myself. With his hands resting helplessly on his lap, he saw the swarm of stars framed in the rectangle of the open door.

As if she sensed in her sleep that he was near her, she rolled onto her side and groped for him with her hand. The blind, trusting motion of her body moved him. He put out his hand and she took it in her fingers; they were weak, hot and sticky. Let her be angry; I'm going to get the doctor in the morning. This may be something serious. Margit is not versed in tropical diseases.

He remembered that there was ice water in the thermos; it only remained to squeeze in a couple of lemons. Above the monotonous noises from the bay he seemed to hear the dull, labored beating of her heart. He looked at the dark swirl of her hair and the faint outline of her body under the sheet. His ankles were smarting with mosquito bites; they stung like sparks from a fire. He scratched them with the sole of his sandal. The last tugboat heaved a long groan, reminding him of twilight over the Danube.

He bent over her and then fell into a short doze. He did not lose the sense that she was by him, that he must help her. When he was younger he had not experienced such oneness in love—a love not impelled by the cry of the body, but deeper, quieter. And then he spied the lancet he had forgotten lying on the threshold like a silver fish thrown up on the shore, but it was the threshold of another cottage, not this one. He must bring it back in the morning or children would find it and take it away.

He woke with a feeling that something terrible had happened. The light of the lamp was barely visible under the ceiling, irrelevant in the brightness of the rising day. Margit lay beside him with her eyes open, watching him as if she were ready to burst into tears. A white sky without a single cloud hung over a quiet sea. Only a flock of gulls rocking on a wave screamed with voices full of amazement.

"Have you been awake long?" he asked.

She shook her head and whispered, "Merry Christmas. I've spoiled your holiday."

"Don't talk that way." He touched her forehead. Her temperature had not gone down. "Do you want something to drink?"

"Give me another nightgown. This one is all wet. And move away. I'm disgusting."

"We have to call a doctor." He kissed her dry, coarse lips.

"Don't kiss me. I don't know what I have, and you might get sick, too."

"We would lie here together," he said, trying to joke as he pulled garments smooth and transparent as water from a cabinet. He helped her change her nightgown; for an instant he saw her small breasts, naked and defenseless.

"What could a doctor tell me? I'm not in pain. There is no rash. We have to wait. The disease will have to manifest itself."

They spoke very low. She looked through the open door toward the sea.

"Such a beautiful day! Go for a swim before breakfast."

Her eyelids closed. She looked like a tired child; the glare of the sunny day dazzled her. She took the thermometer from the corner of her mouth and tried to shake it quickly, but he managed to read: 39.2. She tried to smile but only distorted her mouth. "Go on," she urged tenderly. "You'll be back in a few minutes."

"You're weak. I'll help you."

"I can get to the bathroom myself." She lowered her narrow feet and stood up, leaning on the bed. He saw the outline of her tanned body through filmy fabric; the deep cut of her nightshirt exposed arms bronze from the sun. I must remember her this way, he thought—dependent on me, yielding, undefended. I supported her and she accepted that with relief. She let herself be led.

"Let me be," she whispered. He kissed her temple. He wanted to encourage her, to assure her that he was there.

He undressed quickly, throwing his pants on the chair. He turned off the useless lamp. As he stepped down onto the cool sand, a tremor ran through him. Dampness, chill, and diffuse light—the luminous blur of dawn—mingled in the air. He ran, breathing deeply the smell of the sea, delighting in the dexterity of his muscles, the responsiveness of his body. He stopped before the last cottage and was astonished to see that the lancet was not lying on the step where he had left it. He saw no footprints; the morning wind had erased them. He knelt to see if it had fallen into the sand. A brown rat lurked among the pilings, polished by the flagellating wind, that supported the floor. It looked out fearlessly with yellow-ringed eyes. He ran on and splashed into water that tilted gently with an invisible wave. It parted reluctantly, sleepily. The gulls swam as if they had grown tired of the unpeopled shore and abandoned it.

Just before his eyes, on a smooth expanse of water, he saw a fine dust carried from the land—light particles of soot from the tugboats. Beside it loomed, like a globe of violet glass, the circular form of a great jellyfish that was making its fateful way to the beach. On that dark belt of sand, the sun would kill it.

His brown arms cut the water. He did not swim so much as loll in the surf, roll, fall into the trough, then beat the water and rear up to the waist like a bird rising into flight. He was filled with the joy of a new day, of the love of a woman, fulfilling desire and transcending it, drawing the soul aloft as if on wings; he felt an immeasurable tenderness and gratitude that she wanted to be with him, to share the day. In the distance, like children's laughter, the cries of gulls were borne on a slow wave. A ship in the port bellowed in a bass key.

THE DOCTOR, wearing a painstakingly pleated turban, left his stethoscopes hanging from his neck and moved a hirsute ear over Margit's back. He pressed it with his cheek and she bent under the weight of his head. Because her temperature had not fallen—and this was the third day—he suspected that it was a paratyphoid fever, which was usual enough on the coast. Memsahib's system would soon get the better of it. Wishing to show that he was conversant with modern medicines, he suggested penicillin, for he had just received a fresh supply. But Margit only shrugged. She was weak; her hair had lost its coppery sheen. She tried to comb it, but there was no strength in her hands. She sat as if eaten up with fever, perspiring, her eyes flashing with an unhealthy brightness.

"I've grown awfully ugly." She put down her mirror. "You are truly in love if you can look at me without loathing."

He sat in a wicker chair and read aloud an entertaining short story from a thick edition of the *Illustrated Weekly of India*. Within himself he felt an unfamiliar serenity and order; it seemed to him that they were an old married couple and that what connected them was embodied in their surroundings, confirmed and reinforced by experience. He stole a glance at her: she had grown ugly. But when all is said and done, he thought, I love her not only for her grace and beauty. Through her I have this gift of peace. We understand and trust each other.

"Sahib." Daniel was standing in the door to the veranda in a white linen costume that made his face and hands seem even darker. "Sahib, the wealthy brother is here."

"Just don't do anything foolish," she begged.

"I'll talk with him on the veranda with the door open. You'll hear everything. You can put in a word at any minute."

In front of the house, in the sun, stood a man in European dress: a white shirt and tie. His face was olive; his eyes looked out watchfully from under thick brows. He held a light straw hat in his hand.

"I am not intruding, I hope. I will only take a moment. I have already seen my brother. He told me everything. I had to come and thank you."

"Please sit down, sir."

He bowed and pressed Istvan's hand tightly. He walked lightly up the steps and seated himself with catlike grace. Daniel brought a tray with Coca-Cola, ice in a wide thermos, lemons sliced in half, and a metal squeezer rather like a nutcracker.

"Will you drink whiskey?"

"With pleasure. I beg your pardon, but who is in there?" He pointed to the bedroom door.

"My"—Istvan hesitated as if he were being deposed by investigators—"my wife. Unfortunately, she is ill."

"Ah, I know. The lady doctor. I asked because we are speaking of intimate matters. I do not like it when there are too many ears. Fortunately we can see all around us."

"Someone may be under us."

"No one is there. I checked." He smiled with satisfaction because he had already thought of that. "I wanted to ask you to leave this matter to me."

"Have you informed the police?"

"No. Mr. Terey, one should not forget that you are from the Red embassy, while I am from the Congress Party. Here in Kerala the communists are in power for the time being—a coalition supported by the votes of 'wild delegates,' or, if you prefer, 'independents.' The communists enjoy a certain popularity because they want sensible reforms. But that would mean that someone must give up something, must lose so others can gain. And those who have are not at all eager for redistribution.

"This government will not sustain itself. Delhi will remove it. If the matter of smuggling people to Ceylon should come to light now, it will only be a card in the game; at least that is the way the opposition will treat it. They will say the communists are concerned about whipping up the passions of the voters, not about justice. Those drowned refugees from Pakistan—from another country—are people from nowhere."

"Do I understand that you are against the communists, and yet you have not given up on seeing justice done?" Terey brandished his glass. The sunlight rested on his bare, sandaled feet caressingly, like a fawning cat.

"You have put it well. If you file a deposition and my brother does not confirm it . . . after all, you do not know Malayalam."

"But Daniel . . ."

"Your attendant translated a classic poem. Right, my boy?" He turned to Daniel, who was sitting crosslegged in the shadow of the house, gazing with longing at the undulating vastness of the sea.

"Yes, sahib."

"When one has money, one can do much. I am here a day and I know almost everything. Even if they were arrested, they would escape the ultimate penalty. Trust me a little."

"When it is not right for me to be silent—" he said in a hard voice.

"You have already been silent for three days. I know; you were waiting for me. There are other justifications. It is not necessary to trumpet everything one knows right away. Silence is not a lie; it only leaves room for deliberation. If you file a statement, they will treat it as a pawn in a political game: you are from the communist side. Please trust me. I will attend to this."

"What guarantee do I have that they will not load a new cargo of runaways tonight and leave them to be eaten by sharks?"

"None, except for my word."

"I don't even know your name."

"And what is the point of your knowing it?" The dark eyes looked sternly at him and the lips under the close-clipped mustache narrowed in a malevolent smile. "They meant to kill my brother. He was saved because he is a sadhu, a singer of the gods. The gods allowed the blind man to see the truth. You are only one link in the chain. You received him, fed him, conducted him to a safe place, and summoned me. The rest is my business. My brother's life is worth more than that ship full of beggars. Just now I have hurried here; I am not like him. He has greater riches, riches inaccessible to me, but I have rupees enough to find hands that will assist the cause of justice. Do you believe me?"

He leaned toward Terey and gazed into his face. On the fingers of both his hands were thick gold rings with rubies.

"Yes. I believe you. I have no choice."

"How much should I pay you for your help? Answer without restraint. I have plenty, and what you did for my mad, saintly brother is beyond price."

Terey saw that Daniel had raised his head and was looking tensely at him, moving his sticky lips as if he wanted to shout something.

"Nothing. I really did nothing for him."

"I apologize," the man whispered, "for speaking in front of them." He motioned toward Daniel and the open door to the bedroom. "Here is a notebook; write something here. You are with the diplomatic corps; you are afraid that there will be trouble. I swear, no one will know."

"No. I would have taken in anyone in need of help."

In the silence gulls uttered nagging cries. A flock of gray crows shrieked hoarsely as they snatched with their beaks at the jellyfish that gleamed like clouding glass in the sun.

"If not with money, how may I repay you?"

He heard a quiet call, as if Margit had suddenly thought of a way: "Istvan, come here for a moment."

He jumped up, almost stepping on the hat the wind had blown off the windowsill without anyone's noticing.

"What do you want, darling?"

She sat with her head tilted a little like a listening bird, her matted hair pulled back and held tightly behind her ears with small combs. Her blue eyes beamed exultantly. She motioned for him to lean over.

"Tell him to take his brother to a good oculist. I'll give him the address. Surgery can remove the cataracts and his sight will be restored."

He kissed her forehead, which was a little cooler now. He repeated her suggestion to the Hindu, who was smoking a cigarette. The shadows of gulls tame as doves, gliding toward the rubbish bins behind the hotel, flitted over his knees and his face, which was bathed in glare.

"We have spoken of this more than once. After all, I am not a peasant from the countryside with the hindquarters of a buffalo obscuring my view of the world. No, dear sir, neither I nor my brother would agree to that. Are you sure that what I can offer him is better than what he creates? I know the beauty and greatness of it. More than once I have been brought to tears listening to his songs. He is a poet. All India is his. All that charms us would be lost without him. His song is like a blossoming branch."

"Have it written down and publish it."

"I have tried, but the resonance and the gestures are not there. The parts that cannot be reproduced fall away like petals from boughs in bloom."

"There is still the tape recorder. The tape will preserve it forever."

"And where will you find the light of that hour, the glow of clay walls, the dust soft as a carpet, and the cry of the thirsty hawk? The faces of the peasants listening with rapt attention, who abandoned their unsatisfied bodies—he carried them away, he involved them in the fates of the warring gods. No, that is not my brother," he said loyally. "None of this concerns you: your kindness is devoid of understanding. To you he is just one blind man. But you are cripples. You hear his songs and do not understand them, for you do not know Malayalam," he burst out, clawing the air. "I went to the mission school. I know who Homer was. I want you to understand! Would you dare suggest to Homer that he try to recover his sight? Do you understand what a pathetically ludicrous idea that is? What can you give him that is more than what he has, what he brings from inside himself?"

His brother must be the object of his love and pride. It seemed to Istvan that the man could tear an opponent to bits like a tigress defending her young if something threatened the singer. The two of them are mad. It is impossible to arrive at an understanding with them. They have the advantage over us; they are in no hurry. They believe that they will live on innumerable times, drawn ineluctably into vortexes of change.

"So you want nothing from me." There was a note of irritation in the man's voice. "I do not like being a debtor."

"Support the mission. They gave him shelter there."

"They are not our friends. They teach that we live only once. They implant an alien sense of hurry. I cannot give a paisa to that mission."

He bent to retrieve his hat, but Daniel, standing on the sand below the steps, was already handing it to him.

"Thank you again." He seized Terey's hand like a beast of prey and pressed it until it hurt. He must be a practitioner of yoga, he thought. Strong—and he seems so unimposing.

The Hindu nodded to the attendant, who ran behind him eagerly and listened deferentially to his orders. His head with its curly black hair bobbed in zealous agreement, like the head of a bird pecking grain.

A sea of tilting mirrors gave off silver fire. The two Englishwomen were returning from the beach under parasols as light as those in paintings by Renoir. They were accompanied by a young man with a bronze tan who waved colorful bathing suits and wrung rainbow-tinted sparks out of them.

"Unhappy thought," Margit said apologetically, extending her hand with a meek smile, "we will never come to understand this India."

He sat down beside her. He picked up a weekly newspaper that was warmed by the sun and smelled of printer's ink, but he did not read it. He was unconscious of everything but the girl, hot from fever and with dark rings around her eyes—rumpled, wan, and so desired.

"Come," she whispered and put his head on her shoulder, holding him to her like a child. "Stay this way a moment. No, don't kiss me. I'm sticky. Lie against me. I want to enjoy knowing that you're here. You will never understand that hunger."

"I understand," he murmured, and it seemed to him that he really did. His eyelids touched her bare neck, with swelling greenish veins under her golden skin. He saw tiny wrinkles, or rather their distant harbingers—the signs of the way she would look when time lay on her. Now only sweat and the dust of the moment outlined them, dust sifted from the shifting white dunes through the warm, gusty air that rocked the coconut palms and rattled their fronds like a fire close by.

"I'm better. Tomorrow I'll try to get up. Istvan, forget about that blind singer. Leave that to the people here. Let them see to it that justice is done."

"Did you want me to say that?"

"No." She was silent for a moment; they heard the whishing of the tide, the squawks of startled gulls and the cautious scratching of a water rat who was climbing on a pole under the floor. "I was thinking of our old house, of all our family. If you knew them, you would know at once why I am as I am. My grandfather held tight to his money to the last. My father trained under him as a bank executive. Grandpa never spared him humiliation; he would give him tongue-lashings in front of the staff. On Christmas Eve, instead of presents, he would give us checks in envelopes—a gift that didn't require him to think about us. He didn't have to find out what we wanted, go to the shops and buy things; it was simpler just to fill out the checks.

"I remember Christmas on the yacht, spending the night on the bay. A huge turtle baked in its shell, stuffed with bananas. As long as mama was alive, we observed tradition: a festive dinner, the men in jackets, I in a long white dress with lace—the kind of dress I thought I would be married in. But that's in the past for me; don't worry." She stroked him jokingly as if to reassure him.

"It's terrible—the way time obliterates the past. Whenever I was rummaging in the cabinet and came across a handkerchief of mama's, the smell of perfume would bring her back so vividly that I would cry like a little chit of a girl. Our cousin Donald . . ."

He saw tears on the ends of her lashes, but she was smiling. His look encouraged her to speak.

"I told you about the old clock in the hall."

"The one in the shape of a woman with arms akimbo and the clock dial for a face," he whispered, knowing that she would be glad.

"Yes. Donald took an air gun and shot at the pendulum. Grandpa caught him and was furious, not because the clock was a precious family piece, only because the target was so large—as big as a saucer—and he had missed it. Grandpa took the gun, put in the bolt, and missed as well. 'You can't shoot with that. It will ruin your eye,' he yelled, and threw the gun out onto the street. Before Donald could run down the stairs, some little scamps had taken it away. It's foolishness I'm telling you about, but that was my home—my real home. The others were just places to sleep.

"One returns home. That is where I want to give birth to our son or daughter. Best of all, one of each. You'll like it. You'll see. It will be ours. My father prefers a more modern house; I prefer the old one. Anyway, my father only thinks of his new child now. I've been pushed into the corner, and I annoy him; he stumbles over me as something that belongs to the past. I can't manage to be happy about this little brother, probably because I haven't seen him. Besides, I'm used to being an only child—and perhaps you make it hard for me to see anything else."

He was touched to the quick by the memory of a rambling whitewashed house with streaks of bluing bleeding through. The high, chipped doorsill: how hard it had been for him to crawl over it! For whole years they had split the kindling on it. Sharp splinters had stuck in his bottom. He saw the hall, with its smell of dry clay, inlaid with flat stones. His ears rang with the squeal of a swarm of chicks, yellow with brown stripes on their backs, which fled at the rattle of the wrought iron door handle in the form of a ram's horn. Dim light: windows filled with myrtle and pots of impatiens. Piles of pillows on the beds and a light scent of fresh air and moisture, for the linen had been taken to the orchard to be aired in the breeze and warmed by the sun. He had been born in a bed like that, and he could have slept for ever, listening to the placid chat of the neighbors and the whinnying of horses, the far-off barking of dogs and the creaking of the well-sweeps.

But he could not live in that house anymore. In Budapest, where the boys were, and Ilona . . . that was only the place where he hung his hat. He could change it with no regrets, move into another street. Even to Buda, near the castle. If a house had lost its significance—changed into a temporary stopover—could a country as well? Is it not enough to be a human being—free, without roots?

"Listen." Margit was worried. "Did you send holiday greetings to your people?"

"To the boys? Quite a while ago. Two weeks ago."

"I was thinking of your colleagues in Delhi. Of the ambassador."

He shrugged. "They're not thinking about me, either."

"But you should be thinking of them. Send New Year's cards. You'll shame them."

"You're a good girl." He rose, for he heard footsteps on the stairs to the veranda.

"Sahib!" Daniel called softly. "He took me with him on a special errand. I am to give you a present. He has already gone."

"I told him I didn't want any presents."

"He was certain that you would accept this trifle." Daniel grimaced in the glare of the low sun and held up the round green center of a young coconut. "Perhaps you will drink the fresh milk. It is very healthy. Shall I cut into it?" he asked, reaching for a knife.

Istvan looked undecidedly at the smoothly gleaming green heart of the coconut, which was the size of a soccer ball. Several scratches could be seen in it—evidence of the coconut's having been cut with a chopper. He raised it to his ear and shook it. There was a soft splashing inside.

"The blade has to be driven in three times at the base, where the shell is still soft. You remove the piece you cut out like a three-cornered cork." The servant demonstrated; the fibrous tissue crunched under the point of the knife. He brought a tall glass and Terey poured in the cool, cloudy liquid. Suddenly something emerged from inside the coconut: a gold chain with a pendant in the shape of a leaf like a hand.

"Margit!" he called, then asked in astonishment, "How was that so cunningly placed in the center?"

"A surprise, sir." Daniel doubled over and slapped his thighs with excitement. "He is wise. He knew that you would accept the coconut. We stuck in two knives and pushed apart the pulp. The chain slid in as if it were an alms box and the nut closed with hardly a trace. Sir, a medal with the hand of Buddha brings luck."

"Go and give it back to him right now." He fished out the necklace with a knife. Drops of coconut milk trickled from the metal.

"I told you, they are gone. Perhaps memsahib likes the necklace?" he suggested with a friendly, knowing wink.

"Do you want it for a souvenir?" Istvan held the chain on his fingertips. The gold hand with the lineaments of a lotus flower flashed red in a stream of sunlight.

"Beautiful work." She was holding up her hair with one hand and trying to do up the zipper at the back of her neck.

"They touch it up, they polish it, because they have time. The form has been consecrated for ages. Do you like it?"

She nodded, drew Istvan to her, and kissed him on the cheek. He sat on the edge of the bed and held her as she rested against his chest. They listened to the dry scraping of the palm leaf broom as Daniel swept the veranda, the angry buzzing of flies drunk on sticky drops of Coca-Cola and the protest of one trapped in an empty bottle—the shrieking vibrato of a terrified insect. The sea, as if exhausted, emitted sleepy wheezes. He held the girl tightly; his lips were on her tangled rust-colored hair, which shone in the glow of the setting sun. The fly played its quivering treble note. Margit must have heard it as well, for she whispered, "Go. Let it out. Or kill it."

He did not hurry. He sighed tranquilly.

"And bring the coconut milk."

Reluctantly he stood up and turned the bottle on the tray so its neck faced the westering sun. The fly found its way out of the bottle. The desperate buzzing stopped. As he carried the glass, he stealthily sampled the refreshing, slightly salty liquid. Margit drank it in large gulps. He saw the trembling of her tense neck.

"The taste reminds me of tears," she whispered. He saw the clear blue of her eyes and almost moaned.

For three more days he did not let her lie on the beach. Though the breeze from the sea tempered the heat, the invisible sun would have sapped her strength. He himself only plunged into the water briefly and swam out for short distances, knowing that she watched him constantly, apprehensively, half-hidden in the shade, resting her head on the warm wall of the veranda.

He hurried toward the cottage through the dry exhalations of fire that came from the white sand. He brought her a rose-colored shell as big as two hands, a crab shell, a green fragment of bottle glass, its roughness rubbed smooth by the waves—frosted, as if every trace of civilization and mechanical production had been rubbed away, leaving a glassy pebble through which the world appeared completely different than before. The crab shell, bristling with spines around the edges, served as an ashtray for them. The rose-tinted shell lay on the windowsill; the glass, like a bookmark, was buried in a volume laboriously read.

These acquired treasures Daniel cleaned away without their noticing, removing them from view, and they forgot about them like children who abandon their pails and shovels when they are called away to other enjoyments.

On New Year's Eve automobiles arrived and powerfully built men in clowns' caps, with balloons fastened to the backs of their trousers, ran between the cottages in the twilight, trumpeting squeaky notes on paper horns. Elderly ladies with dyed hair sprinkled with gilt offered bare arms to young men, hoisted the edges of their long gowns as if they were fording a stream, and pulled their escorts along, tittering and hopping about like little girls. The dining room was ablaze with yellow lights and alive with quickened rhythm and jarringly loud conversation. From the cicadas in the bushes came a frenzied jangling, as if they were trying to be heard above the music.

In the night he sat on the veranda with Margit. They felt no wish to be part of the crowd that was shouting in defiance of the music. When in the pearly glow from the sea they spied roaming couples, silhouettes locked together as in mortal combat, they smiled indulgently. Istvan found Margit's hand and stroked it lightly, nourished by the peace in his heart. They sat late, gazing at the little lights of passing liners, so far away that they seemed to mingle with the enormous stars. They talked without hurry; the undulation of the water measured off long spells of silence. Only the mosquitoes, lured by the fires at the restaurant, finally drove them into the cottage and under the netting.

But the next morning was, as before the holiday, quiet and empty. The guests got into their cars almost unseen and stole away toward the town, as if they were ashamed of their escapades the previous evening. The cottages stood open on the shore; he could hear the thumping of wicker furniture in rooms from which mattresses had been dragged out, and the singsong lament of the staff as they restored order.

Adroit as a circus performer, Daniel carried in their breakfast on a tray on his head. Margit settled into a chaise longue, propping her bare feet on the railing of the veranda. Her cretonne dress, in a geometrical print with green and violet fish, was unfastened from top to bottom, revealing her close-fitting turquoise swimsuit and her body, which in the scorching sunlight seemed to be made of reddish gold.

They talked of the future—the future he wanted to believe in.

"You will write about your Hungary and no one will stop you. You forget that you won't have to support me," she explained as if he were an obstinate child. "At last you can be yourself, not looking over your shoulder at the jury box, the self-appointed authority on what you ought to write and how."

"You said that I am taking Hungary with me." He spoke quietly, reflectively. "That's true. A movie cut short. I can look back at it all, write my commentary on images recalled, be moved that I was there—a participant in those events. Up to the time of my leaving. And then I'll begin to collect, to fish short bulletins and notices out of newspapers—traces of events, so I can imagine what's going on in my country. The rest will be guesses. And if predictions are misleading and my people show themselves different than my cherished image of them, I will not be able to understand their behavior and may begin to feel hatred or contempt for them."

As the sun on her knees became unbearably warm, she flicked her straps down and partly uncovered her small breasts. Droplets of perspiration sparkled between them. She pushed up her hair, which was sticking to the back of her neck, and tossed it over the back of her chair. She remained for a moment in that pose, hands above her head, sighing deeply with half-closed eyes.

"Not many of those who are fleeing stop to think that they are no longer sharing the fate of their country. They have wrenched themselves from that common bond. Even if I could see the forces that threaten Hungary better from a distance and make my arguments without interference, I sense an unspoken stricture: 'But you will not share the future with us. You will not risk your neck. You have already walked away. You have said your No. Well, that is enough; we can understand your decision, but at least spare us your preachments.' In spite of sentiments, attachments affirmed once in a while, with every year I would become more estranged. And that's the truth. Everything I would write there about Hungary would be about the past."

She took his hand and laid it on her heart, stroking it. "And must you drag the past with you? You will find a hundred themes, another country, new people. You will rediscover Australia even for us, for Australians, because you will see it for the first time, with new eyes. You are poisoned with politics. Do you have to be the dog at the heels of the sheep to block their way, to bark and turn them back?"

He took his hand away.

"You know whose dog I can be without losing my dignity."

"Mine?" she whispered, stroking his hair.

"No. Not yours."

"It's terribly difficult to communicate with you. You're becoming tiresome. You can always write about yourself; you say, after all, that a person is a universe. Artists are never tired of telling about themselves. Go. Swim. Cool your head, my great writer on the five-year plan. You're bent on suicide. Well, why are you looking at me like that? You'd be ashamed to admit even to yourself that you're destroying your own talent. You believe that an angel will fly down and take you by the hand like Abraham when he was about to kill his own son. But you Catholics don't like to glance into the Bible," she jeered maliciously.

"And perhaps you're shifting some of the responsibility to me? I will take you on my conscience, free you from your shackles and carry you so far away that you can absolve yourself. I, you hear, I." She beat her fist against the frame of her chair. "What you want is for me to become the voice of destiny. I will be. And I swear to you, I will save the poet in you." Her lips tightened in a grimace of pain and angry impatience. "Only don't make me beg too long. It's humiliating. Now go."

She curled up and put her bent hand under her forehead. She seemed to be crying. He stood over her for a moment, ready to kneel and embrace her and whisper words of comfort, but a sense that he had been insulted grew within him and he stiffened with resentment.

He went down to the water. He slipped off his beach coat; the sun touched his arms like a trainer examining an athlete's muscles. He broke into a run, threw himself into the water, and did a hundred meters of crawl. He did not look around. He felt the need for intense exertion, even risk. As his breathing grew steady and he changed to the breaststroke, the surface of the tilting waves flashed as if with mica, pricking his eyes. Water the color of laundry bluing, bitter-tasting, stuck on his lips. He swam doggedly, putting distance between himself and the shore, though he was sure Margit had come out of the shade and was leaning on the railing, watching his head as it disappeared time after time in the troughs between blue ridges.

She would be beckoning to him to come back; that was just why he did not look around. It occurred to him that he would have to wage a determined struggle to get back to the beach. The current was stealthily, imperceptibly pushing him before it. It was as if Istvan, carried out from wave to wave, was not catching foam in his hands, but the mane of a thrashing horse.

Suddenly something told him: enough. He put his legs down into the water: they trembled like a cork on a fishing line. He looked around. The bank was far away. The veranda was empty. He counted the houses; he had not erred. Margit had gone in. She was not looking out at him at all. He let himself drift calmly; he swam in a long diagonal toward the beach. An hour later he stumbled onto the shore, collapsed onto the hot sand and breathed with his mouth open. He had no saliva.

I have not set a date for our leaving, so she thinks I don't love her enough. She lashes me like a horse to make me take the hurdle. Poor thing; why is she so tormented? Hasn't she had enough proof?

The sky was like a sheet of zinc, with no gleam of white from a cloud or a gull's wing. He walked slowly back to the water's edge. Gushing wavelets ran up to his feet, streaking them with foam when he stepped in them. He strained his eyes looking for shells or branches of broken coral to take her as a peace offering.

The first taxis were coming into the palm grove. Out of them scattered whole Hindu families, mothers and children—groups of six or eight, so many that he marveled that they could have packed themselves into the cabs. Women in long saris, covered by parasols and guarded by their men, waded in the water, jumping back with squeals as warm spurts darted from the mischievous waves. Brahmins from wealthy families shunned the sun, shielding their light skins to avoid the tanning that would make them resemble the despised Dravidians.

Three girls wrapped in pink tulle went waist-deep into the water. Crouching and slapping their hands on the surface, churning up sparkling droplets, they bathed like old Hungarian farm women who had worn long shirts fastened between the legs with safety pins. He stood there for a moment, ready to jump in if help should be needed; he knew they could not swim. But they came out of the water, which tugged at them, sucking at their transparent dresses; the soaked tulle clung to slender thighs. A man in a blue shirt thrown over narrow trousers smoked a cigarette, not watching over the bathing women but only looking into Terey's face with a hostile expression, as if he wanted to push him away.

He shrugged and ran along the wet strip of beach. A heap of seaweed smelled of fish and iodine; loose scales glittered like sequins on the dried plants. At last he found a forked branch of coral, white as if from salt. His heart warmed with a childish happiness that he could give it to Margit.

Under the leaning trunk of a palm the elderly Hindu was sitting with a flute, playing an evening greeting to the sea and the setting sun. Istvan passed him at a distance; even his long shadow did not graze the feet of the hunched old man. He remembered that the shadow of an infidel could contaminate, offend, render one unworthy to mingle with the divine.

The room seemed empty. Margit lay without speaking behind the lowered mosquito netting. He pushed aside the nets and at once met importunate, anxiously questioning eyes.

"I'm sorry." She extended a hand. "I was unbearable."

He took her hand, turned her palm upward and put the branch of coral in it. It flushed pink in the low light; outside the open door the sky was bursting with brilliant wine red.

"Do you feel unwell?"

"No. But I didn't have the strength to watch while you were swimming in the ocean. If you loved me . . . I knew you were swimming a long way out to spite me. I came in from the veranda, but I saw you all the time, here, from behind the netting."

"I didn't think you had such an imagination."

"Imagination!" she sighed. "I simply have a heart. I don't want to lose you. I don't want to, Istvan."

"What are you afraid of? You're so impatient."

"Perhaps you could call it that," she whispered, running her fingers over the lumpy excrescences of the coral. "But I'll be calm now. I won't cause you any more trouble. I swear it."

Suddenly he was jealous of that piece of coral that she was caressing with her fingertips. The tender pursing of her lips, the hungry concavities of her cheeks, were so familiar. The red liquid evening had spread over the sky; he heard the soughing of the sea of molten copper, the challenging cries of gulls who were settling down to sleep.

"Anyway, I'm with you." He kissed her, opening lips that clung greedily to his, and found the taste, bitter from nicotine, of her tongue. She huddled close to him, not letting the spiky branch of coral out of her hand. It jabbed his arm.

He bore down on her with his bare chest as if he were smothering her. They were oblivious to the open door that framed the violet sand, the red water of the bay, half motionless as if clotting, and the lazily wavering sun, small as an orange. He took her with angry impatience, forcing his way. She tried to resist, then against her own intentions gave caress for caress. When she threw back her head and moaned melodiously, he rose on a wave of immeasurable delight. He had drawn from her a voice as of a string tightening to the utmost—to the breaking point, the brink of a great silence.

They rested; they were tired out. He stroked her breasts, tasting her arm with the tip of his tongue. It was as salty as if she had come out of the sea.

"You think it's enough to pat me, to kiss me, to caress me and forget about everything worrisome," she whispered with drowsy rancor. "And you're right. I forget, though only for a little while, when I'm filled with you, when I can take you into me. And afterward the anxiety returns, all the keener because I know what I might lose. Istvan, Istvan, I want to sleep by you even if it were the last sleep, the sleep with no waking."

He stroked her in silence, feeling a vast emptiness. He could not find a word of comfort that did not ring false. Despair closed in on him.

The sun had fallen until it seemed half submerged. Its molten light blazed on the horizon. Nestling together, they pushed aside the netting that gleamed rose in the sunset and watched the last beam as it plunged behind the water. At once the early evening came on, and their eyes, still dazzled, were full of rainbow-colored sequins; in the sudden dusk, they oriented themselves by touching each other lightly, like the blind.

"It's good for me, with you." She put her arm under the back of his neck and rocked it lightly. "Very good."

To be part of the pulse of his blood, to anchor myself in his memory. I must be very tender to him. If ever I must lose him, I will still be part of him. He will know that I loved him. One may have a wife, may have women and not be touched by love, not know that great sense of devotion, of oneness. After all, I've awakened beside other men—she thought with a jarring clarity—and it was good with them, but none of them gave me what he has. If he reached out for another woman, he would have to judge her by me, compare her with me, remember, remember.

But she did not say a word, for she was afraid that it would annoy him, that he would misunderstand. She felt powerless; she only snuggled up to him and pressed her cheek on his chest. And he, roused from brooding, at this beckoning kissed her eyes as if she had only that moment returned from a long journey—as though after yearning for her through a long absence he had found her again.

"Sahib. Sahib." Daniel, standing on the veranda steps, clapped. "The *chaprasi* came with the mail."

How did he know that he shouldn't come in? Terey thought approvingly. Intuition, or tact? Perhaps just good English training. He freed himself from her arms, which fell away slowly and lay like torn vines that have lost not only their support but their sense of existence. He felt for coins in the pants that hung in the wardrobe. He threw on a robe and went out barefoot to the veranda.

"Give it to me."

The boy came up the steps and with a deep bow laid a telegram on the railing. He was from the lowest caste. He believed that he might defile even a European by his touch, Istvan thought.

He opened the rough paper with its inelegant lettering and, turning his back to the sky with its failing light, read with difficulty:

Istvan Terey. Cochin. Hotel Florida. Imperative that you return to Delhi Stop Serious personal matter Stop Ferenc.

He went back to the bedroom, turned on a little lamp, and handed her the message. He read it over her shoulder, wondering what could have happened.

"Will you go?" she asked as if expecting him to say no.

"I must. I'm still an official with the embassy."

"You're with me, at the very tip of India. You could say now, 'I'm staying. I'll be there in two weeks to settle my affairs.' Tell them goodbye—if they deserve that courtesy."

"You forget that this is just a furlough. It's only decent of me to go back."

"Shall I wait here?"

He was silent. He lowered his head.

"How long will you make me torment myself?" she whispered. "Perhaps you would prefer that I go with you?"

"Yes." He brightened. "Definitely. We'll go together."

"I'll be following you around to the end." He was struck by an alien, unwilling note in her voice.

"What do you mean?"

"And if they want to send you back to Hungary?"

Anxiety froze his face like ice.

"No. They would have made that announcement with joy." He set his lips. "They wouldn't begrudge me a friendly kick."

"Call, at all events. Demand an explanation."

He dressed hurriedly. Before he drove the car around she was already standing by it, self-possessed, ready to offer help and advice.

When they reached the asphalt highway, he put the brake on hard. A long black car was hurtling out of a palm grove. Its driver saw the danger and slowed down a little too late. In the raw glare of their headlights, which flooded the interior of the other car, they spied the old Hindu, the sadhu who had been serenading the sea with his flute. The look on his shaggy face with blinking eyes brought to mind the grimace of an enraged cat. The automobile sped away; its red taillights brightened and then faded.

"Did you recognize him? The peasant dhoti looked like a disguise. And I didn't believe Daniel."

"Keep going." She clasped her hands. "They told us to wait at the post office."

Great moths glowed in the stream of light, crunching against the hood like chestnuts from slingshots, leaving spatters on the windshield.

The town greeted them with distant plumes of smoke and the odors of burned oil and stagnant drains. Lights glowed in little shops here and there, then more frequently, before they drove in among brick houses. The low post office stood dark and empty; only one frosted window was illuminated. Istvan knocked once and again. Someone uttered a hoarse question but did not step forward.

Suddenly the blind screen was raised with a hard shove and the mustachioed face of a clerk peered out. "Oh, I am very sorry." He assumed a ceremonious smile. "I did not know."

He handed Istvan a form to be filled in: from whom, to which state, which city, how many minutes. "Delhi," he read, shaking his head. "That is far away. You will have to wait."

They sat in the stuffy room on a grease-stained bench, speaking in whispers. The man lowered the window and seemed to have gone back to dozing when the phone rang unexpectedly.

"Sahib will go to the booth, or speak from my telephone, for it is better. There where the riffraff speak, they have to do something with their hands, and they pluck at the cord as if it were a dhoti, they pick at the receiver as they pick at their ears. In the booth the connection breaks off."

Eager for his conversation with the capital, Istvan glared at the telephone. In spite of the clerk's assurances that it was a good one, he barely succeeded in forcing a distorted voice out of it.

"Hello! Hello!" he shouted. "Istvan here. Istvan Terey. Do you hear me? What's happened? What do I have to come back to Delhi for? Something serious?"

At last through the hum and crackle they understood each other and Ferenc realized who was speaking.

Margit sat motionless on the bench, pressing her hands together and resting her chin on them. She listened in suspense, trying to guess from Istvan's shouted words what the voice at the far end of the wire was saying, since its responses might affect their future.

"I don't understand. I'll start tomorrow. I'll be with you on Thursday. But what does the boss want with me?"

The clerk's face looked as if he were sucking juice from a lemon, he was so worried for fear the words would be lost, would not reach the receiver at the end of the wire.

"Tell me, though: is it good news or bad? Tell Judit hello for me. I'll be there on Thursday without fail."

He held on to the receiver as if deluding himself that now he would hear what was most important. That Ferenc would change his mind and blurt out the whole truth—would perhaps dispel misgivings and burst out laughing. Then his eyes met the girl's anguished look and he forgot about the Hindu, who waited as if in ambush. He hung up hastily and thrust the telephone through the window as into the maw of a ravenous animal that could not close its jaw.

"What did you find out?"

"Nothing. When you come down to it, nothing. He said that it would be a surprise. That I should come without delay. The ambassador had instructed him to say that. You heard what I asked him. He said that there was important information for me. That I would not be alone. What do you make of that?"

He paid impatiently, though the clerk was still checking the bill, which seemed staggering to him. The telephone call had cost a quarter of his monthly salary from the post office, so he was alert for information that confirmed what he imagined to be the earnings of foreigners from the capital, and the revenues of large businesses.

When they were sitting in the car, Margit, filled with grim premonitions, put her hand on his arm.

"Perhaps your family has arrived? Your wife is waiting in Delhi?"

"He'd have let that cat out of the bag. He wouldn't have kept it a secret."

"He gave you a hint. He said that you would not be lonely."

"You know, that's possible." He seized on her explanation. "They may be that idiotic with their idea of a surprise."

In the darkness the car sped along the highway by the sea, which reminded him of a plowed field. White moths floated about obliquely like the first flakes of snow.

"Tell me—what is she like?"

"Who?"

"Your wife."

He caught a glimpse of her chiseled profile, the stubborn line of her chin and the shadowed waves of her hair, which seemed to be submerged in water rather than in darkness.

"She's different," he began cautiously.

"I know: above all, she's the mother of your boys," she said enviously. "But if you want it this way, so do I. Will you have the courage to tell her that she will return to Budapest alone?"

"Don't worry. I can tell her."

"Are you still hesitating? Surely you won't make me talk to her."

"Leave it to me."

"Remember—I'm with you." She spoke as a friend speaks to bolster the courage of one who is about to meet a powerful opponent. "It's the end of our holiday. When do we start?"

"In the morning. As early as possible."

They drove onto the white sand on which the hotel stood. It glittered a little ominously, like camphor sprinkled under the lid of a trunk. Daniel appeared in the glare of their headlights and showed them where to park the car so it would have the most time in the shade. He had no idea that that was no longer necessary.

"Turn out the light and pull down the netting."

"I won't sleep tonight. Let's listen to the sea," she urged him. "Our last night . . ."

"That's a thought." He brought out a blanket, spread it on the steps of the cottage and covered her legs. "Do you have cigarettes?"

The zipper on her bag made a grating sound and she handed him a packet wrapped in crinkling cellophane. For an instant he saw her downturned face in the little yellow flame of the lighter.

Far in front of them the sea was a luminous white. It moved with a wet scraping and rustling as if it were diligently shifting the gravel and the sticky sand, from which water was streaming. It sighed and stuttered like a man engaged in heavy work. He put his arm around the girl. In spite of the cigarette smoke he caught the fragrance of her hair—the exciting fragrance that was so distinctively her own.

His eyes roamed over the shoals of stars and their shifting brilliance as they rose, sank, and reappeared in shimmering powdery sprays. Water rats scurried among the piles that supported the cottage, scattering the sand. The paper they had dragged in to line their dens in the furrowed edge of the mound rustled.

I have her. He stood stiffly, holding his breath. I truly have her. I have her because she wants to be mine. I find the confirmation of that in her: I have her. If Ilona has come, I must tell her honestly; I have already made my choice. It's simple: all that's necessary is to stand by Margit openly, in front of everyone. Let them see.

When they sat nestled together on the wooden steps in the friendly dark, it all seemed easy to him, though he knew that he would suffer, and that he would inflict pain.

She was smoking, saying nothing. Suddenly she flicked away her cigarette; it sizzled in the sand amid a spray of sparks. Fanned by an imperceptible breeze, its red tip glowed as if someone had picked it up and was finishing it greedily.

"What are you thinking?" He touched the back of her neck.

"That I'm still with you. That these days have passed so quickly that I feel cheated. Tomorrow we're going back, and I still—what did I want to find here? What eluded me?" There was resignation in her whisper.

"You wanted to break the ties that bind me to my country."

"And it didn't work."

"It did work. You got in the way of them. But it only took one conversation for them to tighten around me again."

"One conversation, with that Hungarian of yours," she said slowly, brooding. "And I didn't even think . . ."

From behind the mane of black palm fronds the rim of the moon emerged, filling half the sky with a white glow. It floated straight toward the lighthouse, as if the flashing were drawing it irresistibly. They were silent.

"Have I lost?"

"No!" he said hotly. "You have me."

"If only that were true. You love me, but I have no real place in your life. You even put yourself before me: you have honor and integrity, a deep sense of the obligations you've taken on. You respect the law. Perhaps that's why I love you. Though I don't want to admit it, the verdict has been pronounced."

"Are you thinking of Delhi?"

"Yes. After all, you've procrastinated. You didn't want to pronounce it yourself. You preferred that the decision come from beyond us both. You invoked it, and now you have it."

"If a hundred ambassadors were breathing down my neck, I would decide for myself in the end," he said with a catch in his breath. "This only hastens our departure."

"Do you know what you're going to do, then?" She looked straight ahead at the white windmill-like tower of the lighthouse.

"I knew from the beginning."

He expected her to ask the next question, to probe for the truth.

But she only leaned on his arm and reminded him, "All day tomorrow behind the wheel. You must rest before the drive."

His hand was on her erect back. He led her into the bedroom; neither turned on the light. His ear caught the familiar rustling, the steps of bare feet, before she appeared out of the darkness naked, vulnerable. She stood with hands lowered as if transfixed by a sudden chill. He knelt half a step in front of her. She stood motionless so as to be near him, so his cheek could rest on her flat belly and his arms encircle her hips. "Margit," he whispered. "My love."

When he touched her she trembled, nestled to him, and pressed her lips to his. "I'm taking you to me as if these were the last moments of my life. As if it were all I could take into eternity."

"Don't say that!" he pleaded. He stroked her hips, then encircled them tightly with his arms.

She put her hands on his arms and dropped to her knees. Her firm nipples moved against him. Her cool skin slid softly against his, and in a cloud of hair her temple rested against his shoulder. Her forehead pressed against his pulsating neck and she heard the hammering of his heart; she felt his trembling. They knelt for a moment, listening to each other like horses that stand in a pasture head by head gazing at the setting sun, and only a shudder runs through the glistening reddish coats.

Morning broke, washed by a short, hard rain. The palm fronds gleamed as if they were freshly polished. The ocean danced in silver and green. "It's as changeable as your eyes," he said when they had emerged from the water and a light breeze was drying them.

"Our last swim." She stood still, luxuriating for one more moment in the tranquillity of the bay.

"Stop," he begged. "Be glad a beautiful day has begun. It's like a good omen."

"It will be sweltering. We'll drive in shifts, shall we?" She bent to brush sand from her feet. "I liked that bay. I felt happy here."

"Perhaps we'll come back."

She looked at him with enormous eyes that seemed to say: Do you believe that? The Angelus bell warbled plaintively; someone tugged at it as if in anger. Suddenly the ringer stopped dead, and the bell clanged off key.

Among the slender trunks of the palms, at the feet of the furrowed mound, stood a jeep. Police in shorts and red turbans were standing motionless; the high bank was swarming with half-naked fishermen swathed in white. Without going far out of their way, they saw what had drawn the crowd. The peasants' eyes were riveted on the actions of the police as they examined faint tracks awash with loose sand.

Between them, his body curved as if he were bowing, lay the old sadhu. His forehead rested on the ground. Both hands were pressed to his chest as if he had wanted to hold to himself something very precious which was slipping away from him. A few steps farther on were a gourd with black holes, decorated with glass and bits of crushed tinfoil stuck on with a resin, and a common flute of the type used by snake charmers, beggars, and sellers of peanuts.

"Please do not come near." A policeman stopped them. "We are waiting for the photographer."

"What happened to him?"

"He is dead. He was a rich man. He was an important person in these parts. There will be trouble."

"Especially for the family," another officer grinned, his white teeth gleaming under his mustache with its twirled-up ends, "when they try to establish the amount of the inheritance."

"Accident? Suicide?" Istvan demanded. The wind stirred the gray wisps of hair on the dead man's sunburned neck.

"He is holding both hands on the haft of a knife, but that might simply be a reflex: someone may have thrust it in and he wanted to pull it out, and fell as you see. We would all have preferred that it be suicide. He had extensive business interests, not always above board. But a believing Hindu does not commit suicide. Even those in misery endure hunger and difficulty beyond human strength. They wait for the end; they want to be purified by suffering and attain a happier life. To be born into a wealthy family," he explained sourly.

Fishermen stood on the talus, which exposed tangled masses of brown palm roots. They surged and pushed to get a better view. Suddenly the bank gave way with a dull ripping sound and the ground opened. Dark, slender figures sprang onto the sand.

The officer put his whistle to his bluish lip, but already the police were brandishing clubs. The fishermen were shouting and running in all directions to escape the bamboo cudgels. Those who crawled along the bank, hiding behind the palm trunks, snorted with laughter like boys being chased.

"Wait." Margit held on to Istvan. "Here is the photographer."

He fixed his tripod in place, took various views of the remains, then knelt, lay on the sand, and seemed to be prostrating himself before the dead man. Finally the corpse was turned over. The legs straightened as if with relief, the hands dropped and the black handle of the knife with its copper decoration showed from under the ribs.

"We can go," Margit breathed. "Did you see how they looked at me? As if they had never seen a woman. I was sorry all the time that I didn't have a beach coat."

"What were you waiting for?" They waded through the loose sand. "Perhaps he sent those runaways to paradise."

"A worshiper of the sea. I thought of that at once. Would you like to know why I stayed? I had to see the knife. You went out during the night; in my sleep I felt the coolness of your skin when you came back. And you didn't give me back the lancet."

"Do you think . . . I could have . . ."

"You believe it is your calling to hasten the verdicts of justice," she said with emphasis. "If you had been certain that the old man was responsible for the deaths of those defenseless people and might evade judgment because he was a sadhu, because he was rich and the police preferred not to fall afoul of him, you wouldn't have spared either yourself or those you love. I know you."

He looked at her set lips. She was walking so fast that a red hank of hair that had escaped from under her aqua bathing cap swept her back. The sand parted under her narrow feet.

Before they went under the shower to rinse away the saltiness of the sea, he took her in his arms and turned her toward him. They stood that way, breathing rapidly. Her eyes were full of a cold fire.

"What do you want?" she asked. "You've killed, after all. You said so yourself."

"It was war then."

She tilted her head and suddenly he understood that she was like him: hard. She had been able to hate. She had come to India. She wanted to help people in misery. She had come to have her chance at life, to challenge fate. Well—she had had him. She had plunged into love, into the measureless element, but he knew by now that he was the stronger of the two.

"You don't need a knife to kill," she said pointedly. "Now let me go."

She went into the shower and pulled down the straps of her bathing suit. A hail of bright drops beat on her breasts, which were paler than her arms. She immersed her face in the silver stream and closed her eyes: beautiful and distant.

"Sahib!" Daniel called from the veranda. "Murder on the beach! He was not a good man. Sahib, I have filled the petrol cans. He left a fortune. There are sandwiches in the basket and a mountain of oranges. They will probably arrest his nephews, since they would inherit it."

They saw a dried red starfish on the hood of the Austin.

THE RAINS, THE MONSOON downpours, had not destroyed the roads. The beds of the mountain rivers were not flooded. The wheels of the car churned shallow, sparkling water; they could imagine that the tires were relieved to settle into the swift current that made streaks in the yellow sand on the bottom. They plowed their way between mountains with dark brownish-red walls like clotted blood. The slopes were overgrown with matted, thorny bushes. Patches of earth parched from drought, lashed by winds, scratched and swept bare, gleamed over cracked subsoil. The sky had retreated upward and was empty, marked at long intervals by a black cross—a hawk that circled slowly and escorted them without bothering to move its wings.

A dry wind blew in the hollows. Invisible dust floated on the air; its vapid taste was in their mouths and it soaked into Istvan's sweat-stained shirt, turning it red. Air streaming through the lowered car windows, heated as if by a stove, rippled through Margit's light dress. She responded by removing one by one, with a little struggle, her underthings. Sighing, she lounged against the hot back of the seat and pulled her dress open at the top. Her hair, stiff with dust, swathed her forehead in a lusterless sheath.

They stopped beside a little brook and threw off their sandals. The water flashed cheerfully. A school of small fish scattered like shadows. Istvan raised the hood of the Austin and put water into the radiator. The steep wall of the gorge gave no shade; lizards scurried over it, shriveled as if the red clay had parched them. They panted with open mouths, looking stupefied.

Margit took a stick and picked out incrusted wasps and grasshoppers that the wind had blown into the cells of the radiator. Lost in thought, she turned the shimmering wings of a butterfly over in her fingers. Istvan poured gasoline into the tank; its vapors formed a trembling mist in the heat.

They hardly spoke to each other. They sat dazed by the noon heat, holding their bare feet in the briskly flowing stream. They smoked cigarettes that tasted bitter and gave no pleasure. They gazed blankly at the swarm of little fish that came swimming up until the water seemed to boil with them. The fish beat against their feet, fluttering as if there were an electric current in the water.

"We have to push on"—he threw a cigarette butt into the water—"and get to Hyderabad if we're going to stay the night in a decent hotel."

"Good. Only let me have a dip."

She threw off her dress, knelt, and shattered the glare that lay on the water, splashing her skin with sparkling droplets. Her slender body took on the golden gleam of the late afternoon. She sank down softly with a deep sigh, half reclining on the sandy bottom of the shallow river. Around her the water was stained rose from the dust that washed off her skin.

"Margit!" he shouted. She opened her eyes reluctantly; the sun hurt them. "Sit up!" He gave her his hand and lifted her. She clung to him; he felt her weight and the coolness of her skin.

"Look! There, around the white stone. It looks like a root with the current breaking over it like glass, but it moves on its own and is ready to spring."

Startled, she pulled in her legs. The moisture on her breasts, her bare, paler belly and her brown thighs dissolved in the hot breath of the red rocks as if she had rubbed her skin with oil. Istvan reached for a stone.

As if sensing his intention, the snake vanished under the water. The surface, veined with the current, pained the eye with its bright silver sheen and the crimson reflections of the mountainsides.

"It disappeared," he said without anger, skipping a pebble that threw up glittering droplets.

"Do you think it was poisonous?" Margit hastily pulled on her dress; the hot fabric clung obstinately to her wet back.

"Shall I find it and check?"

"Let's go. You've spoiled it for me."

Istvan soaked his shirt in the water, wrung it out, and slipped it on. In the opposite lane garishly painted, overloaded trucks were rolling up and stopping in the center of the riverbed like oxen at a watering place. Disheveled drivers climbed down into the water and drank from cupped hands; snorting, they rinsed their noses and mouths. All the gorge rang with their shouts. They watched curiously when the Austin moved out onto the broken rocks, but the engine, after its rest, carried them out effortlessly. The truck drivers began to splatter water on each other like romping children. They had already forgotten about the foreigners.

The smell of mildew and dry grass rose from the superheated marl. On the trees by the road, which were red with dust, the throbbing chime of cicadas drilled the air. The road twisted, sinking between the hills, rising, falling again into large valleys, forcing him to be alert. He concentrated; he kept a hand on the horn. It was hard to tell if, beyond the next clump of trees, they might not meet a truck charging along, piled high with cargo.

He slowed down. Women with round vessels on their heads were coming down a steep path toward the road. They wore only skirts; their suckled-out breasts dangled like drying socks on their sun-charred torsos. Three-layered necklaces of silver flashed in the sun. They pointed to Margit's coppery hair and spoke to each other rapidly, shielding their eyes with their hands and immersing their faces in the deep shade. The curve of the road carried them behind a sparse clump of bushes.

"You'd have liked to photograph them." He turned toward Margit. "They had beautiful adornments that you don't get at the goldsmiths', but you still see them in the villages, in places far from the cities."

"No." She peeped drowsily into his eyes. "I won't buy anything. I don't need cheering up."

"They had ugly breasts," he added a moment later, as if it had just occurred to him.

"You managed to notice?"

"I was thinking of you." He drove on casually, holding the wheel with one hand. With the other he touched her thigh and the hand that lay limp on it. His dry shirt puffed out and fluttered in the hot wind. He withdrew his fingers, fearing that their sticky weight would be hot and tiresome.

In Bangalore they found themselves stuck in a crowd of automobiles invaded by swarms of bicycles. Gardens seemed to doze; dust tarnished the lacquered surfaces of leaves. Only the white walls of villas glared in the sun. They wanted nothing to eat. They drank strong, sweetened coffee boiled with milk. The seller cooled it by pouring it in a long, narrow stream, as if he were juggling the copper vessels and spinning out viscous threads.

It was still too early to settle in for the night. They checked their route on the map. The racket in the city was wearing; the air carried the odors of fermenting rubbish heaps, the smell of grease from frying, the sweetish reek of excrement. They decided to travel on toward Hyderabad. Istvan knew night would overtake them in the mountains; he thought they would stay in some village inn. When he went to fill the gasoline tank and the spare canister, Margit, wanting to stretch her legs, walked across the street, which was crowded with dark-skinned figures in blue and white shirts hanging over carelessly fastened dhotis. Young men accosted her gently but persistently, offering to help her, to accompany her, to advise her. They gazed at her, remarking on her gestures, her clothes, the color of her hair. The narrow shops exuded a strong, spicy fragrance. Dust and streaks of smoke from little stoves hung in the air, and the sour stench of heated cow dung.

In a kiosk she found local newspapers in English and old illustrated weeklies from abroad. She bought cigarettes and matches; undecided, she spread yellowed pages of print and her eyes fell on the headline "Demonstrations continue in Budapest." She checked the date; the information was ten days old. The correspondent reported that a crowd of workers had gathered before Parliament demanding that those arrested be freed. She was happy to read the commentator's opinion that protest rallies were still going on, and that Kádár would face many difficulties before he gained the confidence of a society outraged and embittered by recent events.

She began rifling through the files of newspapers, perusing page after page, searching for news from Hungary. She bought several papers, rolled them tightly and pushed them into her travel bag.

They drove for a long time through a thirsty valley. The sun reddened; when once they let it out of their sight, it retreated among the shaggy ridges of a jungle faded from drought. Among the huts—clay nests clinging to rocks—they looked for water. A half-naked old man with a face of ebony led them to a well, or rather a deep stone cistern. The water was drawn with a leather bag. The rope scraped as it wound; water spattered heavily into the stone throat, jangling and singing, and the sounds of its generous pouring whetted their thirst. They pushed the spokes of the winch impatiently with the full weight of their arms.

"Don't drink it!" Margit blocked him. "See? That's not water, just a soup of drowned beetles."

"It won't hurt me," he insisted, feeling a delightful coolness trickling through his outstretched hands.

But the old man raised a warning finger. He pulled the bag onto the wide brim of the cistern and drew out round, almost black watermelons. A knife plunged deep with a crunching sound, cutting out a juicy pink half-moon. The refreshing juice trickled over Istvan's chin and chest. He bit in eagerly, slurping and smacking. Swarms of red midges swirled over him, pushing blindly into his eyes and mouth.

"The best I've eaten in India!" he said with profound conviction, rinsing his hands in a stream of water that leaked from a hole in the leather bag.

The old man would take no payment. He gave them two more watermelons for the road. But an hour later, weary with the ride, they tried another and had no taste for it. The unpleasantly tepid flesh, souring in the heat, was repulsive. Even the juice had spoiled; it gave off an odor of fermentation, like the offscourings of fruit.

The sky hovered close to the earth; its glow faded. Languidly, as if with a sword, the distant blaze of the sunset pierced the violet. The ground still panted from the heat of the day. He drove without turning on the headlights. On the horizon the sun was burning out, and though its light spurted in long radiant streams like a despairing call for help, a low moon ambled out and steeped the valley in a bluish afterglow.

"Drive carefully now. Shall I take over?"

"No. My sleepiness has passed."

A stooped elderly man hobbled along the edge of the road, leaning on a long stick. He raised a hand in the glare of the headlights, but lowered it when he saw that this was not a truck. Istvan gradually slowed down. They passed him standing behind a clump of trees with trunks that gleamed as if they had been whitewashed.

"Shall we take the old man?"

"I've heard so much about the *dacoits*," she began. She saw through the rear window that the man had one leg swathed in fabric and was dragging it like a piece of baggage.

"The *dacoits* don't touch Europeans. I think they consider us beneath them. We are outside the sacred order, the castes, worse than the worst. Or they see us as a kind of natural disaster which must simply be waited out."

The lame man stopped, unable to believe his eyes. He did not understand what they were saying to him; he knew only his own dialect, and the few words that Terey managed in Hindi did not reassure him. At last he understood. He got in, but let go his stick and crouched close to the car door as if ready to jump out any minute. He breathed with the shallow panting of old age. In the lazy air of the sultry evening an odor of pus rose from his leg.

"What's wrong with him?" Margit wondered. "Leprosy, perhaps?"

"No." He smiled cruelly. "Haven't you recognized it yet? It's a mortal sickness called life. It runs various courses, but it always finishes in death. He's coming to the end."

They drove in a haze of moonlight. The mountains sparkled as if they had been sprinkled with snow; perhaps even on the high slopes the starry sky had shaken down a dew. The glow of their headlights on the road cut a red wedge of clay packed down by wheels and baked from the heat.

Suddenly a flock of sheep loomed in front of the car; the animals, in a jostling mass, kicked up a reddish cloud of dust. Men drove undersized cattle into the ditch, forcing them to jump like goats. The smells of cow sheds—of milk and dung—burst onto the air. Women stopped along the road, tall women with shawls thrown over their heads. Dogs ran about in the light from the car, their black lips and white teeth flashing.

A gray streak of wood smoke hung in the air over the startled sheep. The women carried copper vessels suspended from fire hooks. The charred brands slept in their ashes: eternal fire. Istvan caught the familiar fragrance of home. Then the lame old man began to shout. Men with long spears ran up to the car. One had a rifle on his shoulder.

"He wants to go to his people. He wants to get out," Margit guessed. As soon as she pressed the door handle, the crippled man pushed himself onto the road and snatched his stick out of the car. He caught up to the herdsmen and spoke to them, waving his hands.

The left side of the road was already empty. Istvan drove the car in among the gray woolly backs, pushing the flock apart. As they vanished in the cool blue of the night, he asked, "Did anything strike you about the movement of those nomads?"

She said nothing.

"They were walking quietly, as if they were driving stolen animals. The sheep wore no bells. The cows had no clappers. The dogs didn't even bark. They seemed to dissolve in the dark."

"Only the smell of smoldering wood was left, and the odor of wounds running with pus—as if he were still sitting behind us." She hunched over in anger. "I'm not even sure he didn't think we meant to kidnap him! The herdsmen didn't seem happy that he returned."

"They had thrown him out. He's a burden to them. They're looking for new pastures, for water. They can't lose animals for the sake of one old cripple. The animals are their living, so they must care about them above all. Meadows not burnt up with drought—they make it possible to have milk from the cows and sheep, for they don't butcher them for meat. They would die of hunger first. Milk is life. They had to leave the old man. They wanted to live."

"And we took him to them again," she whispered.

"No doubt they've already left him." He spoke without turning his head; he was gazing at the reddish fragment of road the headlights were tearing from the darkness. "They live according to the ruthless laws of nature."

Before eleven they stopped in a large village. Peasants smoking pipes lay on beds in front of the cottages, wrapped like mummies in white sheets. Their fires glowed red in the breeze. The smoke, like a veil, sheltered them from the mosquitoes that were breeding in the half-dried-up cisterns. They surrounded the car; a couple of the younger ones spoke English. A tall man volunteered to show them the way to an inn and guided the car along a footpath. Istvan had to turn around because the Austin could not squeeze between the clay walls on which cow dung had dried.

"Too narrow," said the young peasant with as much pride as if he had made a great discovery.

Above silver water the horned heads of buffalo protruded, their eyes blazing like jewels in the headlights. Temple steps, notched and interspersed with clumps of coarse grass, led to the silent reflecting surface. An enormous low moon lurked behind the mangrove. The spreading branches grew in the earth like ropes of aerial roots, creating caves filled with diffuse light.

They turned around cautiously. The pungent smell of rotting herbs, muck, and slime drifted from the water. The shore was a band of black and silver, pocked with innumerable hoofprints.

They drove around the village. They passed a forge that gave off a glare sprinkled with sparks and rang with the cheerful beat of a hammer; the blacksmiths were finishing their work in the cool of the night. They drove along a thick stand of sugarcane near an octagonal building of masonry with windows narrow as loopholes. Behind a closed screen door the light of an oil lamp brooded.

"Here, sahib, is lodging for the night," the man said comfortingly. "In the old Methodist chapel."

The dying murmur of the engine summoned an old man wrapped in a patched blanket. Behind the building sat a shed containing the inn's kitchen and a hencoop. An open hearth threw a shifting glow onto the ceiling; fringes of spider web shaggy with soot hung from the beams. A half-grown boy was sitting cross-legged by the fire and cutting an old piece of gutter into V-shapes with shears, bending the pointed ends up. At his feet lay a scrawny bitch with sagging teats. The boy tried to fit segments of the armor he was making, with its comb of bristling spines, onto her back. He beat a nail into the metal to make holes and secured each section with a wire. At every summons the dog rose meekly and heaved a sigh.

"The water will boil shortly." The caretaker threw sticks onto the fire. "You surely have your own tea. I invite you: we have only local tea, smoke-dried. I will dress the chickens quickly."

He went over to the poles where the birds were sleeping with their heads tucked under their wings and felt them, gauging their weight with his hands. As he wakened them, they cackled. He chose two, carried them away as they flapped their wings and squealed in desperation, and took the shears from the boy's hands. He stopped in the doorway, which was splotched with moonlight as if with chalk.

The chickens had squawked themselves hoarse and were paralyzed by their sense that death was near. They dangled lifelessly. With one grating snarl of the shears he cut off their heads and let the bodies fall onto the heavily trodden grass. The headless birds lunged about as if to escape, spraying black blood against the moon. They jumped, dragging their wings, staggering drunkenly in circles. Before they went rigid they burrowed into clumps of weeds.

The dog walked out in her strange armor with its protruding points like a beast in a fairy tale. She licked up the blood from the dried grass as if from necessity—as if overcoming an aversion.

"Why have you got her up that way?" Terey asked.

"A panther has already taken two dogs from my son," the old man blurted out. "This dog has pups too small to live without her. My son wants to protect her. He understands that it will be good for her."

He did not pluck the chickens. He only tore off the feathers together with the skin. They stuck to his fingers, which were dark with blood. The bitch snatched the entrails as they were ripped out and gulped them down with one snap of her lean muzzle.

"I won't eat," Margit whispered. "I want to wash up, have some tea, and sleep."

"I'll watch to be sure he doesn't skimp on the spices."

"The water is in a barrel under the ceiling, but it is cool. You need only pull the cord and it will pour. The other barrel, the one by the wall with the dipper beside it, is for washing after. The water closet is here—but who except in a case of great urgency would come out to the yard—only please flush. One guest from the ministry is already sleeping: a Hindu, not important. If I had known that you were coming, I would have purchased more vegetables and some tinned foods and set aside the best part of the hotel," he said proudly.

The moon shone brightly; it seemed to stare unnervingly into their faces. Weariness came over them, and they shivered from the chill of the mountain night. The flickering light gave the walls of the shed a greenish tinge and glimmered on the disemboweled chickens. The dog sniffed the severed heads and munched them, choking on the beaks.

The boy came out of the kitchen to help Istvan spread out the bundles of bedding that were strapped to the roof of the car. But, enthralled by the green globe that was the full moon, he stood for a long time with his head turned up as if he were bewitched.

Margit slipped into the shed and sat on a block of wood behind the caretaker, who was tending the fireplace. He ran his hands over the hot embers as if his skin were fireproof. The feathers that still stuck to his fingers sizzled; the stench of them drifted through the room.

Why did I feel the slaughter of those roosters as an injury to myself? Nothing really happened; the rest of the chickens fell asleep again. They will not realize tomorrow that there are fewer of them. Does some ruthless hand also snatch us away for some reason that to it is self-evident? An evil vision—as if I press blindly on toward something that I don't yet comprehend, but that will overtake and seize me. Is it possible to hear in the cries of slaughtered birds the voice of one's own fear of death?

She pressed her fingers between her teeth and bit until it hurt. It was a relief. That herdsman, lame, thrown aside by his people—we took him back to be thrown aside again, to live through the despair of isolation a second time. They will leave him on the road. They will betray him. He will try feverishly to catch up with them, dragging his ailing leg. The long shadow will gain on him, a whine will urge him on: the craven sob of the hyena, walking along as if with a broken back, sneaking from one windfallen tree to another, under bushes, in the twilight, lured by the decay of the body. It also wishes no man to be wronged; it wants only the carrion, the rotting meat. Its jaws snap; they can crush the thickest bone. And that cripple knew it was waiting for him to die, if not tonight, then tomorrow. The next day. Shouldn't I have stayed by him, torn away the rags even if he resisted, made an incision, put on a dressing? Did I do all I could have?

She reproached herself for the relief they had felt at letting him go, at giving him back to his own people, perhaps his own family. The sick should be treated by force here. Women swinging vessels with embers in front of their eyelids, men guarding flocks with spears in their hands. It may even be that they are happy; it is enough to accept the premise that this is the only life possible for them, inevitable as fate. Does it matter how one dies? We pass through that black gate alone, slipping from the arms that want to hold us. Is it worth it to form bonds in this life, to cling with all one's might, to struggle?

Perhaps that man who sat on the edge of the road threw away his stick because he knew by then that one does not defend oneself—that he was doomed because he was already dead in the eyes of his people, who had walked away. Perhaps he was reconciled to it. She smelled the scent of a hyena whining with the lust to tear and devour the still-warm body.

She prayed, she hid her face in her hands and prayed, for rescue for the lame man. After all, some truck might come along; he might shout, might stop it. A will to struggle might awaken in him. But she felt a bitter certainty that the sick man would not cry out, and that the hyena, frightened away by the truck's headlights and the roar of its engine, would return.

In a drowsy burst of weeping she accused herself and begged for mercy for the man whose kin had abandoned him. And they will feel no guilt; their hands will be clean. Because they won't know. Blessed ignorance.

In the leaping firelight the old man turned his brown, furrowed face toward her. "The chickens will be ready soon."

The door opened. Istvan said that the bed was ready. He was baffled when Margit rose and clung to him desperately.

"A sleepy little girl?" He stroked her back and held her close. "I'll tuck you in in a little while. I'll feed you."

"Do you think"—her tense whisper demanded an answer—"that they took that man with them?"

"Who?"

"The old man with the infected leg." She was angry that he had not understood at once. "I saw a hyena slinking along behind him."

"Of course they took him. You were dozing. That nightmare tired you. But surely you wanted to exchange me for him and devote your life to him," he said with an indulgent smile. "You know the devout principle: nonviolence. Change nothing by force. Let evil destroy itself, and let us perfect ourselves. Let the world not hinder us in this. Nor any hyena."

She was appalled. "You can't be serious."

"Of course not. I wanted to remind you of the law of this country in which we are only guests. They must deal with this themselves—not as individuals but as ethnic groups, as a state."

"Mother India!" she sighed.

"Exactly. Remember how those mothers by the walls of the dung cottages raise locks of their daughters' hair in the sun and delouse them. They comb out the lice and let them fall into the grass. To kill them is not allowed, for life is sacred. Calm down. Don't castigate yourself. What is one cripple in the scheme of things? Life goes on."

The old caretaker, busy with the reddening chickens that were roasting on a wire net over hot charcoal, seemed not to notice that the visitors were waiting. The dog scratched with its paw, pushed aside a creaking partition, and stepped into a dark corner. They heard the thin, mournful whine of a puppy.

Margit hurried to help. The bitch lay by her pups, impaling one on a sharp point of the armor. She would not allow the whimpering little dog to be freed. Istvan lit the corner with a flashlight. The dog growled at Margit, ready to bite. Her lips were curled and trembling; her fangs were bared. The oppressive armor, unnecessary inside the house, pressed against her back. The puppy was damp and soft as dough; she licked its lacerated belly and turned the others over with her paws. They pushed their way unerringly toward her teats. Her downy coat swarmed with translucent yellow fleas.

"Stop worrying about the whole world." He drew her firmly to him. "Come and eat."

She rose obediently. A savory smell was coming from the roasted chickens. The juicy meat with its crisp surface held the pungent aroma of spices. She hardly bothered to taste it before biting eagerly into a leg.

The bitch left the mewling puppy and drew near them, waiting, tense with anticipation, to be thrown a bone. The gleam of the open fireplace played on her tin spikes. The flames glimmered; red sparks flew up, tracing zigzags in the air. The remaining chickens squeaked in their sleep, sometimes stretching their necks and cocking their heads to look out with eyes like rubies, full of wonderment, only to tuck them under their wings again. Perhaps they had seen an apparition; perhaps they had heard those cries again.

They went into the servants' quarters; the screen door stuck on one of the tiles in the floor, scraping harshly. Behind the partition of boards plastered with wallpaper the light was dim. Smoke floated over the makeshift wall as an unknown man puffed at a cigarette. The portable mattresses, pillows, and linen spread on plank beds were covered by old army mosquito netting painted with green and yellow spots.

"Which do you want?" she asked, yawning.

"Does it matter? I'm sleeping with you."

"No." She shook her head, motioning with her thumb toward the wall, which was rickety as a screen. Tiny rays of light burst through holes in the wallpaper.

He showed her a hook affixed to a beam at the end of the corridor. A cord was attached to the hook: he explained the mechanism. Water ran boisterously from a gasoline barrel. In the drain, covered with a slimy grating, something was scratching. She pulled down her dress, asked him to run the water again, and bathed, suppressing her aversion. The medallion in the shape of Buddha's hand gleamed, throwing a golden blotch like a birthmark on her breast. When the water began to flow into the drain as if from a watering can, there was a scraping in the hole under the floor and a rat fled, squealing.

In the dark, invisible mosquitoes flew over them, spinning out their tremulous hungry whine. Their bites burned like sparks from a fire. They communicated in whispers, since under the barrel ceiling of the old chapel voices were amplified. When they returned, their neighbor's curtain was pushed aside and they saw a slender, balding man in striped pajamas.

"Do not let my presence constrain you"—he inclined his head—"since we must share accommodations. Please behave as if I were not here. I have shown myself so you can see that I am not asleep."

"Are you still working?"

"Who can sleep when the moon is full? It draws me outside. Do you hear, madam, how the jackals howl? They, too, are restless."

It was clear that he was waiting for them to prolong the conversation, but they bowed politely and made their way to their quarter of the room.

They undressed in the dimness. There was nowhere to hang things, so Margit laid her dress over the foot of the bed under the mosquito netting. Istvan sat lost in thought, feeling to the bone the fatigue of the long ride that had demanded alertness and concentration. When he closed his eyes, he saw orange cliffs in the harsh sun; blue shadows and thorny ashen-colored brush on the slopes; watermelons almost black, with water streaming from them as if the rinds were coated with wax; Margit's pale breasts ever so slightly brushed with tan in the flashing shallow stream.

"Are you thinking of what will happen in Delhi?" she whispered. She was as invisible under the spotted net as if she were hidden in a treetop.

"No. I feel calm."

"Budapest?"

"I'd give a lot to know what's really going on there. It's quiet as a cemetery. Everyone wants to forget what happened."

"There are demonstrations at the Central Committee again. The workers went with torches of burning newspaper."

"How do you know?" He raised his head, suddenly alert.

"I bought some papers. There's been unrest there for quite a while."

"Why didn't you tell me at once?"

"I didn't want to upset you."

"Where are the papers?"

"In the car. You're not going to read them by flashlight, after all."

She heard only the screen door frame scraping the floor. A moment later the other man was shuffling about as well. She lay with her hands under her head, half asleep. With a crackling sound the rat tore splinters from the wooden grating over the drain. It squeezed through with a squeal of relief and scampered along the wall. Margit, hidden behind the mosquito netting, did not see it. In the deep shadow its claws scratched on the stone; furiously it set about tearing at some paper. She thought solicitously of Istvan. No doubt he was sitting in the car reading the news briefs by flashlight for the hundredth time. Without knowing it she fell asleep.

Istvan could read by the light of the full moon; he sighed tranquilly. If the workers could hold rallies and march in the streets burning the party newspaper, and no cannon fire dispersed the crowd, that meant the new government was confident. Things were not so bad. He breathed more freely. Around him the world was white with luminous, shifting moonlight. Dung houses slept below him like cast-off building blocks. Monkeys sat on the peak of a small pagoda, and it seemed that they might easily jump onto the enormous face of the moon, which was all too near. The pond bristled with two-headed monsters: the heads of ruminating buffalo were reflected in water heavy as mercury.

In the distance, mountain ranges shimmered in the starlight. The quivering air was filled with lustrous, disquieting blue dust. Roosters hoarsely announced the midnight hour; a vast silence lay on the heart, unmarred by the sobbing of the jackals close by who slipped past in pairs, disturbed by the unusual brightness of the moon. In the yard, in a puddle of rippling silver, the dog in its weird armor, trailing a long, misshapen shadow, circled quietly this way and that like an antediluvian beast. Leaning against the wall of the inn, the Hindu was sitting crossed-legged, peasant-fashion, wrapped in a blanket. His bald head glistened in the stream of moonlight.

"Are you in a hurry to seek oblivion, to lose yourself in sleep?" he asked, wishing to detain Terey. "Sit on this stone. Let us talk for a while. What a splendid night! Surely madam is asleep already."

All at once the captivating loveliness of the night was laid bare to Istvan. He was moved; he felt a warning twinge of sadness. Feast on this, he thought; drink in the beauty of the full moon over India. This may be the last time you will see such a night in the Ghat Mountains. His feelings choked him as if he were saying goodbye. He wanted so much to call Margit to him, to have her share the silence in the shifting radiance of the moon.

"I came here to fight against the greatest plague in the country." The Hindu's glasses gleamed like ice. "People do not even know about this, and after all, they are being devoured."

"You hunt tigers?" Terey said in amazement.

"No. I am thinking of cows."

"Sacred cows?"

"They are all sacred, the ones that go about the cities wearing garlands and the wild herds that roam by night and graze on cultivated land, destroying fields. A fifth of the crop is lost. Think: a cow for every two residents of a teeming nation of four hundred million. A cow, which gives a modicum of milk, eats as it tramples fields and is not permitted to be killed, so its meat will be eaten by dogs and jackals. Its hide can be pulled off only by untouchables, and not until it collapses from old age, at which time the leather is not worth much. These millions of cows are our downfall. They lay waste the fields and starve the people, depriving them of life. These wandering herds in effect devour people."

His thin hands, like greenish bronze in the moonlight, stretched toward the sleeping village in the valley. His voice had a fanatical ring. Long shadows lay on the white wall of the old chapel.

"Do the peasants understand this? Aren't you afraid they might stone you?"

"If I told them that extermination—selection of the stunted beasts—is necessary for their good, they would surely beat me to death." His tone was bitter and sarcastic. "But I say that it is for the good of the cows. I speak of their hunger, of their agonizing deaths when the vultures rend them while they are still alive. And the peasants cry, more than they cry over their own starving children! Indeed, they have seen the cows when they are sick—ill with consumption, poisoned with bhang hanging down on half-decayed plants. They know very well what I am talking about, and they admit that I am right. They want to help the cows more than they want to help themselves."

"And has your campaign brought results?"

"Yes. They must allot pastures, pave the watering places, set the healthy animals apart—I do not dare say the farm-bred animals—and remove the sick for the time being, for treatment. The veterinarians' assistants must be Muslims, for their religion counts it no sin for them to kill without hesitation. And everything takes place with all protocols observed, painlessly. The animals must be coddled so that a fanatical crowd armed with sticks, stones, and sickles does not beat us to a pulp. I know that I am acting against the will of the people; any of them would joyfully sacrifice his own life to save a half-dead cow. If they saw my true intent, I would be a demon to them, a destroyer of the source of their sanctification. The cow, mother of goodness, the nourisher. The cow, which cleanses from guilt. It is enough to receive, to swallow—*Panchagavya!*—five ingredients of magic medicine that come from her: sweet milk, sour milk, butter, dung, and urine."

"You are an unbeliever?" Istvan leaned toward him, surprised.

The man opened his shirt and showed him a sacred thread that made a loop on his chest. He was a Brahmin—perhaps a rebellious one, but still a member of the highest caste.

"I want to help people, to save their lives," he said reflectively.

Istvan noticed that he was smoking a cigarette, puffing with his fingers wrapped around the end of it so as not to touch it with his lips, and he smiled almost imperceptibly. Even this iconoclast was afraid the cigarette might have been made by a machine operated by one of the unclean, or packed by one, and he preferred to avoid contamination.

In front of them the moon went its way, foundering in the tops of trees hewn from old silver. Its round face shone, then seemed to dim; it pulsed with radiance like a living thing. Jackals wailed, choking with spasmodic sobs. Yes—this man with his English education, bold, resolved, valued people's lives above the lives of cows, but those he wanted to save from hunger he preferred to keep within the old divisions of caste—in the place birth, fate, and the gods had appointed for them.

He saw on the Hindu's slender fingers the red reflection from the burning tip of the concealed cigarette when he pressed it to his lips. The dog in its armor sat in the middle of the yard; raising her head, she echoed the jackals' whining note. Then, as if frightened by the dead face of the rising moon and worried about her pups, she scratched at the door. It opened slightly under the pressure of her paw: with a jarring clank the metal spines caught on it.

An overwhelming vision of this world in its captivating wholeness came over him and he loved the man, the enemy of cows, who sat crosslegged beside him; loved the dog, who was forcing her way into the sleepy dimness of the shed; loved the old man, though he was a slaughterer of chickens; loved the living chickens who squeaked in their sleep, awaiting their turn. He even loved the voices of the jackals, as if their lament, wrested from their famished entrails, was part of that world's entreaty. The actions of all living things seemed incalculably precious, though he knew they were like words written with a stick on a path trodden by feet and hooves and sprinkled with dust by the wind.

For he was convinced that one must undertake the troublesome task of transforming the world, and carry on until the last heartbeat, the last breath. He felt that he was close to a great, enchantingly simple secret that would be revealed to him that night so that he would tremble with amazement that he had not guessed it long before. A few minutes more . . . The silver mask with its obliterated features seemed to rustle in the treetops in the gap between the mountains, to shatter the boughs. He had never been so close to the truth; he longed for it, and he feared that it would change him.

And then the roosters in the village began to crow raucously, as if with alarm. The younger ones in the shed chimed in in immature, broken voices. From inside the building came Margit's voice, filled with sleepy alarm.

He went inside. When he pushed aside the mosquito netting, she seized his hand and pressed it to her hot chest. Her heart was pounding.

"Were you afraid? After all, I'm here," he whispered. She relaxed and fell back on the bed with relief.

"Something was crawling near the bed. Probably a rat. I called and you were nowhere to be found. I was frightened. Outside the screen in the door I saw that dreadful moon and someone sitting hunched over, lurking there as if to tell me something awful," she mumbled, not letting go of his hand.

"That's our neighbor." He laughed lightly. "It's the full moon. An exceptionally beautiful night. We chatted for a while, sitting on the threshold."

He noticed that her breathing was regular, that already she had ceased to hear him. Though she held his hand involuntarily, she was in a deep sleep. He went to his bed and undressed slowly under the netting. Mosquitoes flew over him and bumped into the screen. Their neighbor shuffled in, cleared his throat for a long time, and spat. Istvan fell asleep, still hearing a light splashing; he remembered with relief that water was spattering from the barrel a few drops at a time. He closed his heavy eyelids, then half-opened them. The light still glowed through the holes in the wallpaper.

It frightened him that this moon, bathed in its own glow, was merging with the whole world and overlooking, displacing, the woman he truly loved. He listened to her calm breathing. The scratching of the rat's feet, the scraping and rustling, disturbed him. The truth. What is the truth in my case? Did I love less when I pledged to be faithful to Ilona? Perhaps in a different way, and I was different, he thought, hoping to justify himself.

He saw the white river, full of its own sheen, and someone warned him that that was just the truth. Simply to spite himself, he made his way to the water with an angry fearlessness, plunged a foot into it, and was appalled to realize that that white-hot metal, moving as from a blazing invisible furnace, would cool in unknown forms. He had seen such a pouroff of steel in Csepel, in Budapest. He felt no pain except that the leg with which he had stepped so confidently, which he had trusted not to fail him—a part of his very self—gave way and he lost his balance. He flew toward death in blinding light.

He woke, involuntarily feeling with his hand to be certain he still had a leg. His foot stung; he must have thrust it out from under the netting when he pushed himself onto the mattress. He scratched himself for a long time, happy that he had a leg. He dozed and dug at the bites with his nails again. The mosquitoes must have squeezed in under the mesh, for it seemed to him that they were trumpeting straight in his ear, grazing him, tickling him with their wings. But he did not fight them; he only covered his head with his hand and slept.

In the morning they drank strong tea and in delightful weather drove to Hyderabad. Their Hindu acquaintance had already risen at dawn so as to perform his ablutions on the steps of the temple above the smooth surface of the cistern, over the edge of which the sky seemed to have been poured. Though they had not slept through the night, they were not tired. The sun, not yet in full glare, sparkled through the trees beside the road and seemed to breathe in their faces.

At noon Margit took the wheel and something like a daze, a somnolence, came over him. His head drooped. He knew they were riding through plains tufted with sparse clumps of trees. Real images blended with dreamlike visions and he slept, breathing in the fragrance of dry leaves, fires dead in their ashes and the girl's light, elusive perfume.

He awoke feeling embarrassed and scrutinized her for a moment from under his eyelids. He caught her solicitous look as she checked to see if sudden jolts disturbed him. A smile, momentary but full of warmth, appeared on her face like a burst of light. He felt deeply anchored in this state of peaceful happiness, and in her unobtrusive presence; she was simply beside him, taking over the driving, ready to share an hour's tiring journey with him, or a day's, or even fate itself.

They talked about simple things: about rest, food, lodging, the condition of the car and the supply of gasoline. At night they fell briefly into each other's arms, exchanged wordless caresses, and fell asleep at once. The Asian moon, orange-tinted in the early evening, was frightening, like a face rubbed with chalk. White light splashed on the mosquito netting and the whining of jackals woke them for a while. They listened and then, profoundly relaxed, nestled together and settled gently back to sleep in the fecund darkness.

Two days later just at noon the Austin, red with dust, drove into the suburbs of Delhi. A railroad track crossed the highway; as if for spite a guard with lanky legs protruding from under his long shirt beckoned a group of children over, blocked the iron gates, and secured them with a large padlock. Though the train was not due for twenty minutes, there was no power that could force him to let the car through. The instructions were written for slow-moving tongas harnessed to oxen. Several were standing there, with the animals' heads dully drooping. Istvan and Margit could hear the sticky switching of tails soiled with excrement.

The drivers squatted over a ditch and relieved themselves, chatting drowsily. A stork with a head that looked very old and a pouch under its beak stood on one leg above the whitened bones of a dead cow. No one looked for smoke on the gleaming rails. No one hurried. A light wind sprang up, driving clouds of dust, and scampered over the stony fields. Far in front of them rose the chunky shapes of houses with flat roofs. Flocks of circling pigeons flashed like handbills shaken from the faded sky.

"First, take me to the hotel," was Margit's plan. "Then find out what surprise they have waiting for you at the embassy and let me know. I'll wait."

"Wouldn't it be better for you to come to my place first thing?"

"No."

"Hope for the best."

She said nothing. Her hands clasped her upraised knees. Her eyes were sad.

He got out and wiped the windshield with a chamois. The glass was covered with starry bloodstains where horseflies had smashed against it. The bass-toned whistle of the locomotive, like an organ chord, flew over them. The train streamed past—only a few cars, nearly empty; two with cooled air for Europeans and the rich.

The train had long since passed by—it was hardly even a speck on the horizon, blowing smoke like the horsehair brooms the tonga drivers used to beat away the flies—before the guard saw fit to unfasten the padlock and open the iron gates. Istvan leaned on the horn and passed the tongas. Amid yells and the creaking of enormous wheels, the Austin sprang across the tracks in front of the line of wagons and sped toward the city.

He dropped her off in front of the sunlit façade of the hotel on the shady street where Tibetan women had spread their rubbish heap of fabricated antiquities on mats under the trees—fragments of busts, imitation bronzes, and wooden masks. He heard the young men at the reception desk call joyfully, "Kumari Ward. Doctor Ward."

The suitcases bumped into the revolving door as their knees pushed against the flashing plates of polished brass. Istvan felt that he was returning home. Suddenly he began to hurry. He breathed in the urban smells of asphalt, scorching paving stones and dust, the odors of exhaust and pastilles.

The car sprinted on. Before him stretched the avenue leading to the Arch of Triumph—a compelling perspective boldly conceived. The India Gate was a soft rose against the wan sky. In the distance stood a clump of tall trees and circus tents respiring in the wind. He had looked for Krishan there. Farther on lay the road to the embassy, to Judit, to the place that in this country he called home.

He was surprised that the watchman was not standing in front of the gate; the entrance to the yard was open. A goat with udders protruding at her sides and knocking against her shaggy legs looked at him with a malevolent yellow eye and went on nibbling colorless flowers that had long gone unwatered.

After all, they must have heard the murmur of the engine. But no one came out to greet him. On the veranda he bumped into a pallet and a blanket. A clay hearth stood there, full of gray ash, and a small pot in which flies swarmed. Leaves shriveled with drought crackled under his feet.

All the joy of returning to his old haunts left him. The house had fallen into disorder. Ilona and the boys were not waiting there for him, that was certain. The door to the hall was unlocked. He walked into the stuffy interior, following the din of voices, angrier by the moment at the slovenliness he saw. From a distance he recognized the half-senile grumblings of the cook and the languid voice of the sweeper, the peculiar effeminate sniveling.

He took them by surprise as he stood in the doorway to the kitchen. Apart from those of his own household he saw the neighbors' servants, all of them sitting in a circle, conferring with each other as their hands reached into a large pan of rice and vegetables. The kitchen was filled with a stifling odor of something burning, of sweat and cigarette smoke.

"Sahib!" exclaimed the frightened sweeper. "*Namaste ji!*" Old Pereira wiped his soiled fingers on his patched, unbuttoned shirt and folded his hands, bowing so low that his bristling tuft of gray hair bobbed.

"What is this desertion? What's going on here? Why is the house neglected, dirty? Open the windows, sweeper!" he barked. "You have an hour to get things in order."

The other servants slipped away stealthily on all fours. Only in the heat of the yard did they straighten to their full height. Their bare feet fluttered dully on the stones.

"We were told that you were not coming back." The cook looked furtively at him through eyes welling with tears. "We have not been paid for the new month."

"Who told you that?" He nearly choked with anger; it throbbed in his temples.

"Mr. Ferenc. He was here and took all the mail." The cook sounded terrified.

"The devil! What mail?"

"Letters that came for you. The ambassador told him to."

"Who told you to let things go like this? What have you been up to without me? I'll chase down the lot of you!"

He strode to the hall, where the sweeper had flung open the windows and dust gleamed gold in trails of sunlight. He saw the watchman in front of the house. He saw the small figure of the girl, whose falling hair covered her face as she leaned over, hastily rolling up the bedding, like a dog digging a hole in the ground to bury a bone. The light streaming in through the windows exposed layers of dust on the top of the table.

All at once it seemed to Istvan that he was an intruder—that he was causing confusion, like a dead man who had been carried out and buried and had suddenly claimed his place among the living. Pereira was standing before him, wringing his hands, exuding worry.

"What will become of us, sir? Will the new man keep us?"

"What new man?"

"He is not here yet. He is just flying in."

Istvan was stunned. Now he understood.

"How do you know?" he asked quietly.

"From the ambassador's staff. I took the liberty of asking the secretary when he was here. After all, it is a matter that concerns us—whether we will have a living—and he confirmed it." The man with his aging face looked at Istvan to see if there was any remedy, any hope.

Istvan felt himself filling with bitterness; rage and grief stabbed his heart like a glass splinter. They have disposed of me. Smeared me. The dispatches have gone out urging that I be recalled. I have been pushed out of Delhi by some clandestine maneuver. Like a stupid, naive puppy I believed they were well disposed toward me. I went away with the girl; I put the evidence in their hands myself. Only one of their calculations failed: I came back. Now I've caused trouble for them.

He looked at the sweeper. The thin dark arms wielded the broom and wiped the dusty window screens with a damp cloth. Istvan thought of wind-up toys with broken springs; a few movements, a few shudders, and they stop as if astonished that the end is already here, that they are suddenly lifeless. The sweeper wrung out the cloth and reddish dust colored the water so that blood seemed to be dripping from the rag onto the windowsill.

He was grieved for the servants. He was the only source of subsistence for them and for their families, whom he had never met—the whole contingent of wives, mothers- and fathers-in-law and more distant kin. They were assured three times a day of a fistful of rice carried quietly out of his kitchen; he was, as Pereira said obsequiously, their father and mother. Even apart from the matter of food, he was a gift from fate.

What would happen to them now? For the time being they had a little savings; they could parcel it out, ration it, use up what remained from the past—and then? In clean, starched shirts they would make the rounds of the embassy staff, press bribes into the hands of people as much in want as they were themselves, speak ingratiatingly, plead in servile accents, for cooks are powerful; their patronage leads to the kitchen, with its delightful aromas of dishes cooking, where rice is not weighed before being poured into the pot or the heaping spoonfuls of flour for the *chapati* counted. To live is to attach oneself to a foreigner again. Files of effusive testimonials are not enough; one must promise a steady stream of payback from one's wages to those who can help one to a job. They will pay for the very promise of work, for the hope that will keep them alive.

"Before I leave, I will try to find you a place," he told Pereira, who repeated and translated the words. A glow seemed to fall on their faces; they bowed, raising prayerfully folded hands to their foreheads. They thanked him and blessed him.

The telephone rang. Margit wanted to know if everything was in order in the house.

"I've been recalled," he said helplessly.

"Very good!" Her voice was clear, even challenging. "I expected that. Surely you're not worried about it. Yes, Istvan, it's time to bring the issue to a conclusion." After a moment's reflection she added, "What do you intend to do? Don't decide anything until I come to you."

"I must see the ambassador. And they are just beginning to clean the house. Margit, I'll let you know when I get back." He was almost pleading.

"Be calm. Keep your anger under control, do you hear? Remember, I'm with you. I'm waiting. Think: already they're unimportant to you. You don't need them. You're free, do you understand? At last you have the upper hand. You can be yourself! They are afraid to speak, afraid of their own shadows. What are you worried about? If you're really upset, I forbid you to go there just now. Do you want to give them any satisfaction? To show that they have struck a nerve, that it hurts? Istvan, it's not even worth it to despise them. You can only pity them."

He said nothing. He rested a hand on the light blue wall. He was calm again; a cold doggedness was growing in him, a desire for a reckoning.

"Do you hear me?" She sounded distressed. "Istvan, after all, they have done you a service. You should even be grateful to them. They have decided for you. You have this behind you. Do you hear?"

"Yes."

"They can't separate us."

"No."

"So nothing has happened. Do you understand?"

"Yes. I am calm. I'm going to the embassy to give them a surprise. They thought I wasn't coming back."

"Well, you see, they were thinking sensibly. Call first before you go. Stiff upper lip, darling."

"All right. I really am calm."

"I believe you. Go!"

Without replacing the receiver he pressed its holder and disconnected the call. His self-possession really had returned; he dialed the number for the embassy. Judit picked up.

"Is that you, Istvan?" She was amazed. Obviously troubled, she asked, "You know already?"

"I found out from my servants. I'd like to talk to the boss."

"Half an hour ago he went to his residence for lunch. He has the new Japanese ambassador with him. Ferenc is sitting in. It's empty; there's no one here."

"And what's going on," he asked sardonically, "except for my recall?"

"I must talk with you. You have no right to accuse me. You know nothing. Istvan, are you coming back? I'm sorry to ask you that, but everything depends on how you act. Don't burn your bridges. Come—your salary is here. It would be a shame to let it go; it will come in handy. You can exchange rupees for pounds. Don't cheat yourself to make a stupid gesture. Take what belongs to you."

"I can pick it up anytime. I'm going to the boss."

"Be careful. He can't stand you," she whispered. Then she added hastily, "He's afraid of you."

He did not care what else she might say. He hung up. Now she was ready to help him out with good advice, but had she said anything when they were destroying his career? I am calm, he repeated. I am utterly calm. His sweaty hand cast a shadow on the wall.

The telephone rang again, but he did not pick it up. He was sure that it was Judit, wanting to make him see things her way. She is not bad. And Ferenc? And the cryptographer? None was bad in his own right, but taken together . . . One goads the other, making sure no one hesitates. They are not bad, but they are not good, not only to me but for each other or for themselves.

He came into the hall, followed by the servants' watchful looks. "It's one," he said, looking at his watch. "Don't bother with lunch. Put on an early dinner, at five. A good one; make an effort. For two people. Here's some money." He laid out a bill, forestalling the cook's wheedling. "I'll pay you tomorrow."

"For the whole month?"

"Even if I leave."

There was no need to explain that. He walked out to the car, which was still unwashed and bore traces of the long drive. The watchman obligingly opened the door, stamped one foot, and stood at attention. On the grassy square his wife was waving a branch, chasing away a goat that had climbed onto the garden wall and was savoring a little flower. His tension was gone; release had come suddenly. Had the issue taken on its proper proportion and stopped tormenting him?

Margit is right. Nothing has happened. He smiled at himself unexpectedly in the dusty mirror. Nothing—yet.

He made his way, unhurried, through the streets of Delhi toward the ambassador's residence. He passed motorcycle rickshaws with little canopied roofs. Hirsute Sikhs with puffy cheeks, leaning on their steering wheels, squeezed their pear-shaped horns with languorous smiles.

He left the car at a distance from the gate. The white columns of the residence were garlanded with passion flowers; the Bajcsys' younger son was careening around a flower bed on a bicycle. Crinkled leaves rustled under its wheels and flew among the melodiously humming spokes. The boy nearly collided with the counselor.

"Look out!" Istvan exclaimed, jumping out of the way.

"You look out!" the little daredevil answered. "This is my yard." He sped on along the paths, lowering one foot to steady the bicycle at the sharp turns.

Hidden in the shade behind the palace stood a car carrying a small white flag with a red circle in its center. The luncheon with the Japanese ambassador was not over yet. The guard, a short man with sinewy bowed legs, blocked Istvan's way. The sun flashed on the handle of a knife thrust into his belt.

"Whom do you wish to see, sir?" he asked. Seeing that Istvan was moving confidently toward the stairs, he became disconcerted. "The ambassador is not free," he said.

Istvan felt as if he were trespassing. He did not know this new, recently hired watchman. A thought stabbed him: had he really found himself excluded from the group, set apart, stigmatized? The boy on the bicycle flew straight at them, forcing them apart.

"Let him in!" the child shouted. "He is one of ours."

He went up the stairs to the spacious hall and sat in a comfortable armchair. He decided to wait until the guest had left; he wanted to talk with the ambassador alone. From the open door to the dining room came a laugh in a bass voice and fragments of sentences basted with unctuous politeness. No doubt I'm here for the last time, he thought with relief.

So many times he had stood on the stairs greeting guests as they arrived, shaking hands as the park flashed with colored lights, the orchestra played old waltzes, the gravel crunched under the wheels of automobiles, and the smell of fuel blended with the perfumes of women sewn into glossy silks. Now that was behind him, like the lamentable film showing during the struggle in Budapest—the rows of empty chairs. The memory of the embarrassment they had endured grazed him like a bullet.

But other parties had been successful. Plum vodka and Tokay had livened up even the phlegmatic Hindus: they danced. They sang. They did not want to leave. When at last they were left alone, the ambassador with one jerk had pulled off his snap-on bow tie—for he had never learned how to tie one like a man in the higher sphere of society—unfastened his dress shirt, which was softened with sweat, and poured himself some wine. "Well, drink up!" he had invited graciously. "Well, Ferenc! Terey, go ahead! We've flushed out the crowd; it's gone. We can breathe easily. There's no one here except us."

On the walls hung pictures of steel mill workers in the red glare of a blast furnace, masons on scaffolding, a woman mixing feed for piglets swarming to a trough; pictures like color photographs, approved and purchased, and no way was found to display them, so they were packed off to the foreign post. Lent—but no one would demand their return. They were relieved to write them off as a loss. The chairs and the red carpet had come from India. The great vase full of freshly cut branches with nondescript violet blossoms seemed to have been put in place randomly, with little relation to what was around it, for this house was not a home but a transient accommodation.

He lolled in the chair, smoking a cigarette, and was just walking out, saying goodbye to his life as an officer of the diplomatic corps. Margit was right: nothing has happened. Really, nothing.

"So you've arrived." The ambassador's wife came up. He had not heard the steps on the thick carpet. Evidently she had been bored with the conversation in a language she understood only poorly. She gave him her lumpish hand without a welcoming embrace, as if she needed support.

"Please sit down. They will be through directly." She nodded toward the dining room. "You do not harbor resentment toward my husband? I want you to understand him. He had to." She tried to penetrate his impassive expression. Her large eyes—hazel, even pretty—looked tearfully at him. "Instructions came to purge the mission, on the quiet, of a 'doubtful element.' He did not single you out; it was a collective decision. My husband said he would do nothing to injure you. After all, he has to be careful. Do you understand?"

"Yes. I understand too much."

"No one believed you would come back. If you had not gone away it all would have gone differently. But that feeling persists. Talk to my husband, only please spare him. He has so many worries just now." She confided in him, misled by the calmness of his manner; she almost took him for an ally. "He sleeps badly. His heart suffocates him."

She leaned toward the counselor and laid both hands on her lap palms up, like a gossiping peasant woman. Her features were plain, honest.

"There are great changes in the government. Other comrades, not all of them friendly, went to the authorities. As long as he had the party behind him, he knew whom to go to and how to make his case; he always prevailed. More than once I was afraid—because he is so self-asserting, he demands so much—that he thought I was silly. And he was probably right, for he bore up against everything so that I was frightened sometimes. If that is reversed, he will not hold up well. Do not be hard on him," she begged.

Voices drifted in from a distance; they were saying goodbye. Luncheon had ended, and she knew she ought to put in an appearance before the guest left.

"You can return to our country. To Budapest. Do you believe that I envy you?"

"I believe it."

"There are no people here. We see diplomats exclusively." She sighed heavily. "And one can be ever so careful, can handle them with kid gloves, and still they backbite, they make fun. But we must receive them. When you leave, think of your wife. I know where one can get beautiful silks in Old Delhi and lizard skin for sandals and bags. I would gladly go with you when the ambassador is not here."

Bajcsy appeared with his guest. The ambassador, large and heavyset, seemed to be hustling the little Japanese man along with every breath. He spied the counselor and threw his head up, nodding to signal that he would be right back. Istvan was relieved to see his fleeting troubled look. His wife sailed up to the visitor, who stood with his head inclined. His smoothly combed hair gleamed as if the crown of his head had been brushed with lacquer.

The car engine rumbled; the hum died away on the gravel. Istvan welcomed the sound as a boxer welcomes the sound of the gong that summons him into the ring.

"Well, here you are at last, Terey." The ambassador did not offer his hand; he only walked around with a ponderous step as if he were sniffing something. "This is a surprise. You're being recalled."

"As you wished, ambassador."

Bajcsy was morose. His eyebrows were knit. "Yes, as I wanted." He admitted it; he was courageous enough not to evade responsibility for the decision. "Well, now. Will you go back?"

"And when you are recalled, ambassador—will you go back?"

"Don't bait me, Terey," he said slowly. "I warned you in time. I asked you for your own good—" he looked around and, seeing that his wife was standing by, waved a hand. "Go. Leave us alone. I have something to say to the counselor."

He waited until she disappeared into the dining room, then turned to Terey. He looked at him dourly for a moment, licking his drooping lips. "You wanted to investigate on your own hook, and there are no witnesses." He spread his hands.

"There are none," Terey admitted calmly, taking out a cigarette with a rustle of its cellophane covering.

Bajcsy cut to the chase. "You wanted to do me in."

"No. Why would I?"

"So you say now"—the ambassador loosened his tie and unbuttoned his collar as if he were short of breath—"only now. And I have you in the palm of my hand." He shoved a clenched fist at Terey. "There is proof, black and white." He waited a moment, then said abruptly, "I know who you were with at the shore."

"Well, and what of it?" Terey said without batting an eye. "What concern is it of yours? For two years you've promised to bring my wife here and she's not been here yet."

He hated himself for saying it, but the argument had its merits. The ambassador reminded him of a country blacksmith, an old gypsy who was disguised in a light blue suit of raw silk but had forgotten to bathe. His fingers were soiled; there were traces of soot on his white collar. The comparison amused him, though he knew the stains came from the pipe Bajcsy was involuntarily tamping down.

"I'll cut you down to size, Terey. I'll cut you till you bleed. I've not yet written an opinion. It's enough that I will attach a report of our meeting—of what the comrades said, and they had their eyes on you more closely than you think. You'll be sacked from the ministry before you know what hit you."

"I haven't the least desire to stay. That's a misconception," Terey broke in, lounging carelessly in his chair.

"I'll crush you, Terey," the ambassador said gleefully, winking. "You'll be squealing. I've taken bigger people than you down a peg."

"If I were in your place I would be more careful about making categorical statements, ambassador. Try . . ." He was embarrassed at having said too much, for the other man had the upper hand and could injure him, accuse him—and explaining himself would bring down more blame. "There are comrades who remember your merits."

"I was in prison. You can't take that away from me." He thumped his chest until it seemed to rattle.

"I wouldn't think of it." Istvan sat cheerfully erect. "It's just that those merits are somewhat more common now. You liked the uncompromising way of doing things. Budapest is what it is because of people like you."

Bajcsy was too good a player to be shaken; he took these blows.

Could it be that this measly poet, this little puling cad, this detestable piddling intellectual, had his own channels of information? Was he reaching high? Did he know something the ambassador did not know yet? Had he received some signal?

"Do you want to know what the comrades attested against you?" He counted, seizing his heavy, soft fingers one by one with his other hand. "First: you hardly work. You're lazy. And this is a country for conquest"—he quickly corrected himself—"a country that could be won over. You had nothing in your head but women, outings, amusements. No one but you belonged to a club; you're a social climber. That circle of friends: you spent time with them, they invited you places, you became intimate with capitalists, for what is Rajah Khaterpalia? And his father-in-law? And that pettifogger Chandra? And Major Stowne, who works for the intelligence service, and everybody knows it but you? And what is she doing here, that Australian who's attached herself to you? You picked a fine set of friends!" he intoned. "These are not just suspicions. I have evidence in hand. It was the last minute; you would either be recalled, or"—he weighed his words—"we would push you out. Cut ourselves off from you."

"Groundless accusations," he said with feigned indifference.

"Groundless? You foisted your trashy connections on me. On me personally." He jabbed his chest with a finger. "And your suspicious inquisitiveness? I caught you in the cryptographer's room, where entry is not allowed."

"I wanted to read the proclamation of the new government."

"You should have come to me. I would have given you access. And the strange pretexts, the sounding people out, feeling for their weak places. Who got my personnel to drinking? Did you give the caretaker whiskey? Six bottles. What did you want out of him in exchange?"

Istvan put out his cigarette. Stay in control. Next he will certainly be brandishing the invoices I gave Ferenc. I set myself up.

"Is that all?" To his own surprise, he sounded calm.

"Isn't it enough? What would you do in my place? I only asked that you be recalled." He leaned toward Terey, his face drooping as if in good-natured solicitude. "I didn't want to destroy you. I wrote that it was at your request—that you have had enough of being separated from your family."

Istvan was not certain whether Bajcsy was mocking him or overwhelming him with blame, humiliating him so he could raise him from his knees like a prodigal son with a gesture to all appearances forgiving, compassionate—raise him and press him to his bosom so tightly as to smother him.

"That's right," he admitted politely. "I think, ambassador, that they will not count that as a weakness on your part."

"My dear fellow"—his fatherly tone was almost caressing—"why did you go behind my back? What were you prying and digging for?"

"I like to know things." Istvan's face tightened into something like a grimace.

"But for what purpose?"

"I was looking for the truth." The admission had the ring of a concocted lie; it embarrassed him.

"At whose direction?" Seeing that Terey was silent and found the question distasteful, the older man explained as if to a stubborn child, "I will remain here. It's impossible to move me; it isn't even proper. If they cut Bajcsy, soon they would be asking, Why not the others? I've attained too high an elevation. To censure me is to discredit the party. Only those who do nothing are unblemished. Do you understand? I don't want to yield my place to some fool! When they wanted dirty work done, they turned it over to me. And I was good then. Now they look at me as if I were a criminal. Though after people like me, something remained. It stands. It—is. Doesn't that count? Have I ever said I am an innocent lamb?" He breathed with parted lips. Mechanically, angrily he shoved tobacco into his pipe but did not light it, for he knew the smoke would stifle him.

"I want to be a vice-minister. I will be. I want to rest, to go to a small, comfortable country—to a country like Holland—and I'll bide my time. They won't push me lower. Perhaps I won't be read by schoolchildren as you will, but such people as I made the history of the republic." The sagging fold of skin under his chin quivered with his shallow breath. "They won't put me out to pasture. I won't be buried alive. I'll be where the party puts me." Yet he spoke as though he would give orders to the party.

Istvan remembered the ambassador's wife's anxiety, the instinctive fear that the taut string would break. It was the tale of the golden fish: the boss knew the magic words and he knew in which ear to whisper them. And they had been fulfilled, but the party of today was not the golden fish. On his doughy hands, damp with unhealthy sweat, it would be difficult today to feel the corns, the traces of hard labor, for they belonged to the distant past. He had grown stout; his broad hindquarters filled more and more capacious chairs. He had lost his immunity, though he thought he still had it. The first failure would break him; he would sink into despondency. He would be like a rag. Istvan did not feel hatred for him. He was almost grateful that he could feel sympathy.

"You wanted the truth? And for what? Will things be easier for you when you know it? You insist on your right to it, and you don't know what it is. Truth corrodes like acid. That is the price of power. Some of those who rule know the truth. And they must keep it hidden inside themselves, for if they shouted it to the nation, the people would stop their ears and run away. And they must open their mouths in order to issue commands every day, to lead, to govern. How I envy you that boyish ignorance, Terey!"

His hands shook. He noticed it and rested them heavily on his parted knees. "I don't want to scuttle you," he whispered furiously. "Just get out of my sight. Go to Hungary. Go to Australia. Go to the devil. Anywhere I can't see you and those good, stupid, inquisitive eyes of yours."

Istvan knew that Bajcsy was too distraught to play the game. He had crushed him; he knew he held the advantage. He heard his wheezing. He saw the fold under the unevenly scraped chin, the gray and black stubble; the cracks in the baggy skin showed through. The conversation must have taken a toll on him. No, I'll not attack him. I'll not inflict a blow. I don't want to. I don't want to.

Suddenly he seemed to see the ambassador in Budapest, walking with the shuffling steps of an old man. He stopped and leaned on a tree, oblivious to people who looked at him as they passed by, gasping through parted purple lips. Light air washed by a spring shower, wet, gleaming pavement and sparkling leaves, wrought iron garden fences, a boundless sky—and a man unable to get his breath. His feet slid along the ground, which had long since ceased to be a battlefield and become, in spite of the paving stones, soft and slushy. He shuffled, and if he still felt the earth under the soles of his shoes, it seemed unfriendly; it had become insistent. It reminded him that it was there, that it was waiting.

A servant brought a tray with coffee in two small, brittle cups. "Drink." The boss's tone was peremptory. Roused from his thoughts, Istvan looked at Bajcsy's crumpled face. The older man reached for a cup and lifted it to his open lips. His hand trembled and drops of brown liquid fell onto the rug.

"So I shouldn't go back to work?"

"That would be best."

He looked back from the doorway. He saw the bulky, stooped figure, in a jacket hitched up too high, crammed between the arms of the chair.

"And my letters?"

"I ordered that." He took the responsibility for everything on himself, certain that he was equal to it. "They are in the safe. Tell the cryptographer to give them to you. I don't need them. I think we understand each other."

Istvan passed through the shadowy house and walked out between the pillars on the porch. He sighed deeply and inhaled the clean, fragrant air as if he wanted to escape the dust, the weightless suspended particles, the ashes blown from the pipe that was stifling the ambassador. The watchman pulled aside the heavy gate; the garden seemed to be sleeping in the winter sun.

Fragments of sentences came back to him and he brooded over gestures and tones of voice, thought of more pertinent, incisive answers, marveling that they came to mind only now. He shrugged with a dissatisfied frown, like a man who should have provided crucial information but procrastinated, and an evaluation was written. But Ferenc didn't pin the business he had going with the whiskey bought with the diplomatic certificates on me, and he could have; I wouldn't have been able to explain. They would have believed him. In the end he preferred that nothing be said about it; he was saving his own skin. Unconsciously Istvan wanted to see his colleagues in a better light. He was hungry for goodness and congeniality.

His feet scraped on the paving stones; the sound echoed from the embassy walls. The working day was over. The caretaker stood among the palms in green-painted pots, keeping an eye on the Indian sweepers to make sure they took up the matting that served as a walkway and beat it, rather than simply brushing its surface as the usual cleaners did.

"Is it you, counselor?" The caretaker lunged toward him with such unfeigned joy that Istvan could not push away his extended hands. "I said I would bet my head that you would come back."

"But you accused me in the matter of the bottles."

"How could I be quiet when they all pounced on you? I spoke because no one else gave me a wretched bottle. I told them what kind of man you are, and right away they turned it into something to blame you for. I meant to defend you. A person has to bite his tongue before saying a word. I, after all . . . Surely you believe me," he said pleadingly, pressing his hand.

"I believe you now—but it was painful for me."

"I would have been on your side, comrade counselor. But when the ambassador said that he knew from a certain source that you had bolted, I kept quiet. I had my tail between my legs."

"And you signed," Istvan said bitterly.

"I signed. And not only I. It happened in such a way that there was no holding one's own ground."

"Very well, old friend. There is no more to say. The most important thing is that you didn't go back on me."

"The way it came out it was as if we had been slapped in the face."

"Is the cryptographer still here?"

"Yes. In his office. The secretary is in, too."

He hopped over the roll of matting that lay in the middle of the steps as if it were a threshold that was too high. He had hardly opened the door when Judit rose from her desk and threw herself on his neck as if he had been saved from impending death. She kissed him. He did not hug her; he stood with his hands lowered. He felt her warm, ample, friendly body against him. He saw, close to his face, her blue-painted eyelids and mild hazel eyes.

"Are you angry? Won't you forgive us? Understand, Istvan, Bajcsy had information from some woman, absolutely certain information that you had sailed from Cochin with that Australian. Listen! I called you at the shore. They told me at the hotel that no such person was there. They always mix things up, mispronounce our names. They said—though I persisted—that a married couple had been there and gone away. No doubt they said that to get rid of me. A call from Delhi startled them. Then there was the meeting. The ambassador was so sure when he said that he knew the facts, that he was notifying us . . . that woman . . ."

Grace. It flashed through his mind. Grace, surely.

"I was with her." He put a hand on Judit's arm.

"Istvan, do you love her?" she asked in alarm. "What will happen to you both?"

He stood without a word, as if he had been struck by a hammer. Only now did the question cut him to the very heart. He turned around reluctantly, brimming with bitterness. He caught her look; it was full of pity and kindness, as if she understood—as if she had the same kind of test behind her and, feeling her own scars, wanted to buoy him up, to whisper: You see, I eat, I dress, I work, I live, do I not?

When he drummed with his fist on the armored door, he felt a hard spasm in his belly, as he had in wartime before an offensive. I'm wounded. The mournful refrain repeated itself. I'm wounded.

Little by little the door opened. Smoke billowed from behind it as if the room were burning. When he saw the metal box full of crumpled cigarettes on the table, the fumes suspended in the air—the tilted blue layers the other man stirred as he moved about—he realized that something serious had happened.

"I've come for my letters."

The cryptographer looked around alertly. He asked no questions. Taciturn as usual, a little sleepy and absent-minded, he opened the safe and took out a thick envelope with a number.

"Was it a disciplinary recall?"

"No. At your own request. The date of your departure is at the discretion of the management of the mission. Have you spoken with the ambassador?"

Istvan opened the envelope and shook a handful of letters out onto the table. He recognized Ilona's handwriting at once. He was enraged to see that they had all been opened. On some he saw something written with a red marker on one corner: the letter P.

"What I got I'll give back." His anger leaped ahead of events. "What does that mean?" He pointed to the marking.

"To photograph it. You probably want the films and the pictures. I have them in a separate place. Please just sign for them. I must do things by the rules."

It isn't his fault, Istvan thought. He only got an order and carried it out. Controlling his feelings with difficulty, he wrote his name in the open book. He saw the other man's tremulous blink and suddenly it dawned on him that the cryptographer had deliberately not asked on whose authority he was collecting the papers and photographs. He had simply obliged him by returning them. Perhaps he had even taken a risk.

"Did you read the letters as well?"

"I sit here. I wait for hours. I get bored. I read them. Have a look at the ones that are marked. The parcel was waiting for the couriers. You withdrew it just in time."

Istvan unfolded one letter. At the top he saw the inscription AFP. Nagar had written.

My dear fellow,

The news has reached me that you have taken leave of the embassy. Reportedly you are marrying, in spite of previous experience. Will you be going to Melbourne? I will miss you; you know how fond of you I am. If I can help you in any way, remember, you may count on me. You are not going back to Hungary: good judgment won out. I endorse the decision. Follow my example: I lost my homeland and gained the whole world.

Yours affectionately,

Maurice

The next letter was from Chandra. He proposed on behalf of a partnership including Rajah Khaterpalia, his father-in-law, and Chandra himself that Istvan assume the role of overseer of investment in Australia—of the construction of a modern cotton weaving mill and spinning factory which they had entrusted to their old partner, Mr. Arthur Ward.

"Knowing your interest in his daughter, I think that my, or rather our, offer—for it is the result of serious deliberation, and evidence of trust—may be suitable for you. Conditions remain to be negotiated."

Why do I hesitate, then? I would make so many people happy. How comfortable it would be to say: We predicted this. This flight has been in the planning for a long time. He is guilty. At last we have the culprit! The mission was purged of a questionable element. The ambassador was not duplicitous when he said: I have evidence. There was proof enough. One does not write such letters if some shared secret does not lie behind them, some plan for the near future. Bajcsy knew what he was doing; he generously returned the letters but kept the photocopies.

Chandra's letter was balm to his bruised self-esteem; it held out the promise of restoring his financial independence. He would not feel like a prince consort. It would be a beginning. He felt an urge to spit into the open safe, then rush to Margit, press her to himself, cradle her in his embrace and whisper, "Let's run away from here. Let's go. Let's go now!"

The cryptographer looked at him out of the corner of his eye, puffing out blue smoke that swirled in the light of the draftsman's lamp that was burning though it was daytime. The hand in which he held Chandra's letter fell as if the paper were lead.

"Attractive offer, eh? Will you accept it?"

He said nothing.

"When will you leave?"

"I don't know."

The cryptographer smiled as if he had heard a choice piece of wit.

"Perhaps you two will fly out with the ambassador." He leaned forward and exulted. "An hour ago a message came. He was recalled."

"Does he know?"

"No. For the time being only you and I know. Amusing, no?"

His face looked a little like the face of a cat who holds a mouse in its claws: it betrayed a vein of startling cruelty. He is sure that I, too, have reason enough to hate the man and he wants, for a little while, the company of someone of like mind.

"When will you tell him?"

"Tonight. He will be more susceptible. Believe me, he will not check to see what time the wire came. He will have something to think about until morning. So many times he kept me here like a dog on a leash because he thought something would come in. He made me watch here whole nights. He treated the machine better! Now I will take this night from him. I will pull the pillow from under his head and sprinkle hot coals on it. He will not sleep tonight."

In this submissive man, not given to conversation, condemned to loneliness because of the nature of his work, lurked undiluted rage.

Istvan brooded. If Kádár is replacing people, the change of course will not simply be a maneuver, a subterfuge, but a sign that there is life in our country, that there is hope for Hungary.

"If they shove him off the teat, you will see him spit on Hungary, and soon he will be sick of socialism. Fly out with him and bring him in by the scruff of the neck so they will make his tongue wag about what he did. But I am afraid that while they are making sense of the situation, he will become ill and put in for treatment in Switzerland, where he stored his money. And when he is close to the money, he will recover his health. He will disappear and they will forget about him right away, but the evaluations he wrote up will still affect the fates of people like me. That is why I gave you the photocopies and plates, though you did not even know about them. He will not give you a hiding. He will have to save his own skin." The man spoke in a voice thick with anger long suppressed.

Suddenly he went quiet; they heard a knock at the door. The

cryptographer put a finger to his lips. He listened: he recognized Judit's voice and pushed aside the bolt.

"Come. Take your pay for January," she said. "You'll need it."

Istvan pressed the cryptographer's hand and went with Judit to the cashier's desk. He signed the only blank space on the list, which was filled out with no room to spare by the embassy staff.

"Can I help you with anything?" she asked timidly.

"Yes," he said vehemently. Seeing her face riveted on him and her eyes filled with suspense, he smiled slightly. "It's nothing difficult. I wanted to ask you to retain my servants for the person who will take my place."

"Good. That's a trifle. I'll see to it."

"I know. That's why I'm turning to you." He rolled up the slick bills that still carried the smell of newly printed money, nodded deeply to Judit, and hurried down the stone stairs that were bare without the red cocoa matting.

Mihaly stood by the car. He rubbed the fender with the handkerchief he used to wipe his nose, stepped away, and looked with approval at his work. The light on the polished metal was so bright that the eye recoiled.

"How good that you are back, uncle." The boy smiled so broadly that all his being seemed alight. "It was dull without you. No one has time. Everyone chases me away. I get in everyone's way. I get under their feet." He gave a comic imitation of the voices of Ferenc and the caretaker.

"And Miss Judit?"

"She gives me candy as if I were a little tot."

"You're not little at all." He put his hand on the boy's shoulder.

"No, for if there is something to buy at the market, mama sends me, and then I am big. And when I want to go to the cinema alone, they yell at me. They tell me not to go so far by myself. Little, little—" he mocked. "Hindus my age already have wives. Really! A Sikh who plays badminton with me told me that they have already found him a wife, and he is just eight."

Istvan took the boy in his arms. He was filled with affectionate sympathy for the child who, without friends his own age, felt isolated.

"We are very busy."

"But why is it that you can talk to me sometimes? Why don't you think I'm stupid? Stupid—" he frowned as if at those who pushed him forcibly back into the infancy he had outgrown.

"I like to talk to you."

"No." The boy contradicted him hotly. "You like me. Is it true that you're running away?"

"You've got it wrong."

"Uncle, take me with you." He raised his keen eyes trustingly, looking for consent.

"You know that's impossible. Your father wouldn't let you go."

"Yes, he would, and so would mama. Is that lady going with you?" he asked with unconscious shrewdness, groping in the pocket of his pants. "Uncle, I want to give you a present."

Istvan had forgotten the boy, forgotten about the whole world. The question returned like an echo in empty rooms: it reverberated. It rang with reproach. It accused him.

"Uncle"—the boy tugged at his hand—"wake up. Put this to your ear, only don't open it or it will escape." He took a cardboard box from his pocket and thrust it toward Istvan. The lid had been pierced by a pin.

Istvan looked at the boy—at his outstretched hand holding the gift—as if he did not understand. Finally he forced himself to smile. "You have another bird," he said, remembering the fun the boy had had with the grasshopper.

"No. I have a cicada. I caught it on the mirror. I set it between some leaves and it flashed like a piece of the sun and the cicada flew over. It walked around a leaf and jangled and then saw why the other one didn't answer. Will you take it, uncle? It likes orange juice and the center of the lettuce best. It takes a leaf in its little hand and looks funny when it drinks. And it will wink at you if I don't take it back."

He tied the box with a thread and put it on the seat of the Austin. "Uncle," he said thoughtfully, "why aren't I your son?"

"Because you have your father." He took the boy's hand and squeezed it. "Thank you."

"He is not mine. He belongs to the embassy. Do you hear how it jingles? It is saying goodbye to me." Happy again, he waved to Istvan as he drove away.

For a moment longer he saw the little boy in his mirror. His hair bristled over his forehead as he stood alone in the sun on the red road.

When he reached the avenue he had to slow down. The whole width of the lane was filled by a crowd of shouting ragamuffins; dust rose from under their bare feet. Above the swirling streams of boisterous humanity a red banner with white curvilinear words in Hindi hung on two poles. Demonstrators peered into the car and rubbed its body with their fingers, leaving smudges. One threw him a flyer of thin paper that read, "Private sweepers of New Delhi: Demand payment of your whole wage, not just installments." So something was stirring; for their work they were demanding the agreed-upon payment from their employers, not just a subsistence.

Pereira, rustling in his starched clothing with flat expanses where the iron had pressed hard, stepped around the table, waiting for the signal to serve the meal. In the center of the tablecloth stood a brass vessel holding a clump of cloyingly fragrant mignonette.

"Here you are at last!" Margit exclaimed. "What did the ambassador have to say? Do they want to send you back?"

"Yes," he said in a voice that was not his own. He was like a man cut in two. He heard a command: Look. Well, look. You have her. You can do with her as you wish. And another: It is over. You chose, after all, long ago. Don't be a coward.

"They want me to go back. As soon as possible. I'll fly."

Though his expression boded nothing good, she was still smiling gently, as if she were hiding a pleasant surprise.

"Fine. You should have a frank conversation with your wife. I'll go with you."

"No." It was a stone being wrung from him, not a word. "You can't."

"I've been thinking of this for a long time. I can." She waved a hand impatiently. "When all is said and done, they won't eat me there."

As if for the first time, she saw his gray face, dogged and full of pain.

"Surely you don't want—" she whispered.

"I don't."

"So where am I to wait?" she cried fearfully.

"Don't wait." They were not words. They were boulders that took all his strength to push.

She still did not comprehend, but gazed at him in immeasurable astonishment, as if he were only now revealing himself to her and appearing shabby, detestable. She looked at him as if she could not recognize the familiar face, as if someone were impersonating him. But it was indeed her Istvan, who loved her, whom she trusted and to whom she was giving not only herself but all the future—life. Her life.

"Please understand, Margit. I—"

She shook her head and stepped back, standing erect.

"Enough. Don't touch me. You liar. You miserable little liar." Her tone was cold, superior. "Call me a car," she commanded in a whisper that was worse than a shout. "Did you hear? I should have known it would be like this."

He was silent. He did not try to defend himself. He only looked at her in despair as her breathing grew uneven and her eyes closed. She leaned against the open door.

"I don't lie to you."

"No. You don't lie." She measured out the blows with cruel calm. "You believe what you say—when you say what's convenient."

There was a knock on the window frame.

"A taxi is here," Pereira called obligingly. "I have hailed it. What shall I say?"

They stood opposite each other, neither daring to take a step forward. He was racked by the pain he had inflicted.

"Didn't you ever love me?" She bent over as if she were going to fall; she seized the door frame and steadied herself. Her head reeled as if she could not fathom her own blindness or the enormity of his actions. "Why didn't you kill me? I could have drowned there, where I was so happy," she moaned. Suddenly, with quick steps, she went out to the veranda.

He started to run after her, but the cook had already slammed the door of the old taxi shut and was standing with his gray head down, up to his knees in blue exhaust. Popping and roaring, the automobile started up and disappeared around the corner.

The sun, spilling through ragged leaves, hurt the eyes. Passing his hand along the wall, he went back into the living room, slumped into a chair, and hunched over. He poured some whiskey and immediately set it aside untouched. He swallowed as if something were stuck in his throat. From far away he heard the voice of the cook as he bustled about.

"Has something happened, sahib? Did I do wrong to call the taxi?"

He shook his head no, for that did not matter now. As if he had just awakened, he waved away the tiresome chatter.

"No. Don't serve the meal. Eat it yourselves. Nothing for me later, either. Not tonight. Go. I want to be alone."

He noticed with amazement that his face was calm; he saw it in the mirror. He managed to pay them their wages, to listen to their thanks, to assure them that they would still have employment, that nothing they feared would happen to them.

How could she say that I didn't love her? What is this sea of pain I'm drowning in if not love? She is my life, and it is torn away from me. Most terrible of all, I myself—and she so trusting, so yielding—did it with my own hands . . .

Desperately he tried to remember the first step: when had he seen, been led aside by the certainty, that he was exempt—because he was different from others, because perhaps it would not count? I create the law, so I can break it. And I broke us both. One may, in a rebellious rage, break the stone tablets, tread them down in fury with a feeling of joyful liberation. One may free oneself from them. But they will block the way, threaten, speak in signs of fire.

"Till death do us part . . ." He heard his voice, for the organ pipes were silenced; Geza and Sandor chanted. For from the Danube country I took my strength and I will be her son—and then the words whispered by foolish lips thousands of times: I believe. I believe. I believe. Millions repeated words of commitment and did not even know why they kept those vows. Two hundred thousand went abroad; perhaps half would still return. Others believe as they breathe, without knowledge, happy as the ox and the ass over the manger. Their prayers are heard; they are not led into temptation. They would become lawmakers, they would judge, and they would forget that they will be judged.

I would have been happy with her. I would have been. I know. At the price of triple betrayal. I understood the last ring of Dante's *Inferno* in the night; I knelt on the sand before the gates of the chapel built of pugged clay and cow dung, like Hindu ashrams. I heard the singsong rhythm of an unknown language, and I knew very well what they were saying—I, a future excommunicant. I don't want it at that price.

She said that I had never loved her. After all, I did that for love, a love that embraced and assimilated her. She takes me for a madman. If only it were true! I wish I could believe it. How can I explain to her—or is it possible to explain to a person who has been stabbed why it was necessary? Why a loving hand thrust in the knife? I was not lying to her when I said that she is my life. Only mine, mine and hers. We could have turned our backs on all the world and been satisfied with each other.

He bent over, pressing his fingers into his eyelids until he felt a radiating pain and saw red spots. He muttered, "I had to. I had to."

He stiffened with alarm for her. He counted the stages of their advancing intimacy; he remembered the other man who had hung with bound hands in a raked-up fire as his hair sizzled in the flames. But enemies had done that. Today he himself, whom she so loved . . . A hundred times worse. And if in that hour, pushed to the very edge of despair, she saw no relief except in oblivion?

He raised his head defiantly and stood up. Bumping against his chair and pushing it away, he ran to the telephone. He dialed her number at the hotel. She was in her room; he breathed more easily as he heard, after the rattle, the click of the receiver as it was raised.

"Margit," he whispered into the forbidding silence. "Margit." He had to beg. "Can I see you?"

"What for?" He heard a voice in which there was no longer any hope.

"I want to tell you . . ."

"I've heard everything."

And a sound like the click of scissors. She had hung up.

He went back to his chair. Her words, gestures, decisions repeated themselves and though he explained and clarified them to himself time after time, he was afraid. Her pain was greater than his; it was holding her at bay like an animal, engulfing her in a thickening wave of darkness. Hopelessness. He understood. She had stopped waiting. He realized with terror that she had not been exaggerating when she whispered, "Why didn't you kill me?"

It was impossible, impossible to explain. What did it matter that he had also reached the depths of despair? Suffering does not unite. It pushes people apart, awakens aversion even to loved ones. Something about it embarrasses, makes one wish to hide it, like sickness.

He hated himself because he could think and act so coolly, even adjust his tie with a deft motion and remember to lock the door. The startled watchman rose abruptly from the veranda steps and stood at attention as a concealed cigarette glimmered in his left hand. The girl nestled by the balustrade like a young animal, half-disappearing into the cascade of climbing plants so he would not notice her. He pretended not to, but he knew very well that they had been sitting together, embracing. He did not envy them. He enjoyed indulging their happiness, which again, thanks to his intervention, had a future.

He drove the car out as if he were in a trance, involuntarily—as if he were dozing behind the wheel. He went into the hall. At the reception desk they knew him. Yes, Miss Ward had asked for her bill; she was leaving. They had gotten her a ticket from Air India. She had given an order to be wakened at five; before six there was a plane to Bombay. She was upstairs now. A moment ago she had asked not to receive calls from the city. They knew everything; they knew more than he did. He hesitated, reassured by all these directives of hers and what they indicated. And he could still come unexpectedly, and suddenly all these measures, these preparations to decamp, would be unnecessary.

He did not dare go upstairs. The inquisitive looks of the staff who had seen them so many times . . . He could not bear the garishly lit hall. The big reel with slides: the red fortified walls of Fatehpur Sikri, the white marble domes of the Taj Mahal, the blue ocean and the placid tilting palms, like the long necks of birds, that reminded him of the places where he had been with Margit. He turned his eyes away and saw them even under his closed eyelids. He escaped to the car and huddled in a corner of it. It seemed to him that she was beside him, keeping watch just a step away.

He peered at the hotel windows: some blazed gold and rose, others were dim and colorless. He gazed at them until he realized that he was looking for the window of her old room. Now she would have another one, and he did not know which. She ought to know I'm here, he thought. Or perhaps she was calling him now, again and again, and he was nearby but unable to hear, in the metal body of the automobile as in a crustacean's shell, shrouded in the shadows of the trees.

In the wavering glow of the streetlights he saw a small band of men passing by—a pair of Englishmen trailed by a Hindu in an enormous turban who was chattering incantations, muttering that today was an exceptionally propitious day for omens, that the stars were revealing the fates of people. But the Englishmen knew what awaited them; what they were already certain of was enough. He gave up hope and turned to the drive leading to the hotel. He peered at Istvan and called softly, "Sahib."

But seeing that Terey was sitting with his eyes closed, he did not dare rouse him. He walked slowly away, disappointed.

Events take their inevitable course, exposing the logic of connections. Even Grace had only accelerated their course.

Was it precisely for Margit that fate had brought him to India? He was immovable in the conviction that he had been born for this test, had matured for it through the years. They had come to each other from two extremes of the globe, led unerringly so that . . . It had to happen as it did. Any other choice would have been a denial of the truth. Had he known from the beginning how he must proceed, though he had not wanted to admit it to himself and had delayed, had put off the fatal hour?

It was not at the moment when he had stammered out "I don't want—" but earlier, much earlier, that he had doomed her and himself. He had reached the decision in anguish, always resisting, dragged step by step.

Then by the sea at midnight, when he felt that there was no appeal from the verdict, and she slept with her face pressed into her bent arm and he heard in her breathing a quiet choking like the smothered echo of recent crying, he had needed to be alone. Alone. He had waited until her breathing grew soft and regular. He had extricated himself from the mosquito netting. The stairs of the veranda creaked. Under his toes there was the cool, grainy sand. The wide beach slept in the dark; the sky with knots of stars hung like netting flung unevenly above it. The ocean rushed onto the sloping shore and streams of water flowed down, scouring millions of shells. A ridge of dredged-up seaweed, parched by the sun and black during the day, teemed with a shining powder of alien life.

He moved as if without volition, slipping over the tilting dunes, walking in the beam of the lighthouse—the lowest of the stars, set aglow by human hands.

He was only a step from the sea. All his senses were attuned to the vast surging and subsiding of the water, the exhalations of salt and decaying plants. The breeze ruffled the hair on his chest and blew around his legs. He felt a light warning chill. At the water's edge, where the hard-packed ground was licked clean by the tides, he stopped. Foam died away at his feet with a hiss like a stifled sigh.

The world. A vision of the world: a writhing mass of suffering. Terrified creatures murdered by bestial toil and hardship. What was his despair compared to that abyss of pain and misery?

It seemed to him that he was hearing a remote swelling wail, but it was only the calls of distant tugboats signaling to each other. So many die at this hour. They don't live to see the dawn. A heartfelt tear of crystallized grief. They can do nothing more. To the last breath they are disturbed by the certainty that they could have accomplished more; they are pained by the enormity of good left undone.

I stand in the darkness, naked before the sea, the sterile earth and the stars—alone, as in the moment of death. Let me count the days that are left to me and stifle the thought of myself, of the body's joy, of approbation fleeting as foam.

As if he were feeling around him those who were departing the world that night, as if he were one of them, he dared to raise his head. Great stars hung like the points of raised spears.

Help me, so I may accomplish even a part of that which You began, from which You stepped aside—so I may advance a few steps farther on the road You abandoned. Take my eyes if they see only superficial things.

A sacrificial flame kindled in his heart.

Change my tongue into a coal if it speaks idle words. Let me have one thought, one desire: to give myself without calculation, without receiving a word of gratitude, even without hope, to the last spasm and the bottom of my heart, to the renunciation of myself in Your name, Who are love. To serve You by giving myself over to the most miserable, to those who never know satisfaction, to the jealous, to those with a cruel thirst for love and those who don't believe in it. They wait for me, though they know nothing about me. They: those nearest me, those from my country and those from distant continents. I see them as if with one face, breathing hoarsely through its open mouth, pouring with sweat—a work-worn, sorrowful human face. Yours.

He was accustomed to the darkness now. On the smooth, gleaming sand he saw thousands, hundreds of thousands of crabs no bigger than peas, rolling yet smaller globules from the mud. Another wave came. If it were not to engulf them and wash them away, this was the last moment to burrow in and hide—to wait until the stream of water retreated. They emerged from the packed sand and began again. He thought of time and generations, arduous human building, creation in the face of destruction. All the shore teemed, glimmering with phosphorescence from the unabating, hurried activity.

Though the cry he had flung into the dark went without an answer, in the slow billowing of water white with crests of foam and the swarming of the crabs, which did not pause from their labor, he found new strength.

He went in to Margit, who shivered in her sleep when she felt the coolness of his body. He lay with his eyes open, his muscles contracted with pain.

"What have you come for?"

Margit's whisper. It seemed to him that he was still seeing her at the shore.

"I had to be with you."

The bitter curl of the lips. The shadow, the memory of her smile.

"You were afraid that . . ."

"Yes."

"Did you come out of concern for me or for yourself?"

In the twilight of the avenue her hair gleamed like copper under the streetlights; he could not see her face. He opened the doors of the Austin. She hesitated, then bent over and got in without looking at him. Her eyes evaded his by gazing into the street, toward the long line of trees interspersed with the greenish glow of the lamps.

"That would have been simpler," she said after a while. "For where do I start? You took everything from me."

She said no more. She was overcome by weariness. Suddenly she raised her head and their eyes met in the mirror.

"How little you know me. Don't be afraid," she said in a hard tone. "I won't do that. You can't free yourself from me now. I'll be a weight on your heart through all the nights we won't be together. It's terrible, Istvan, but even after what you've done, I can't hate you. I can't."

"I had to do it," he ventured in a whisper as pain pierced his heart.

"You had to. You had to." She bent her head. "How I hate Him. The cursed idol, faceless, infallible, for He is not material, like us." She was blaspheming, spasmodically clenching her hands. "You've sacrificed us both for Him."

He listened. Every word burned, then turned to ashes. She had cut him to the quick; she could not have wounded him more deeply.

"I will not kill myself, do you hear? Don't torture yourself, go, rest . . . Go to sleep," she whispered, laying her hand forgivingly on the back of his bowed neck. He bit his lips and trembled under her touch. Suddenly a sob wrenched itself from him. The tears of a man broken by pain; it is most charitable not to look at them.

"Will you ever forgive me?" he moaned. "Me . . . You should accuse me, not Him."

She contradicted him with a slow movement of her head.

An approaching car cast a sharp glare over her. Her eyes were wide, as if she were blind. She was numb; she saw days like voids before her, a desert impossible to wade through, time when she would be alone as a stone among stones.

"Go now," she whispered. "End your vigil over the dead."

"Let me stay. Let me take you to the plane. I want to be with you to the last."

"When the porter rang and said the gentleman was waiting, I cried, 'Who?' 'The one who always comes . . .'" She repeated the phrase through clenched teeth. "I sent him to check. I didn't think you'd have the courage. But it was you. And everything came back. You're here."

Timidly he made out the outline of her face in the dark, the straight nose, the pale, narrowed lips—lips he remembered as full, parted, expectant.

"When you go back," she breathed in the voice of one who is dying of an illness and in exhaustion whispers, "When you bury me, I want you to . . ."

He waited, quivering and ready, vowing to himself to do anything she might demand.

"Don't let them crush you. Stand up for yourself. Be hard, cruelly hard, as you are to me."

To the last she was thinking only of him: he and his writing were important. She believed that he was a creator. That with a word he could call things to life, revive them, stop time.

The old peanut vendor shook his smoky stove on its bamboo slat. An imperceptible breath of air bent its five red flames. As if she could not bear for anyone to go away disappointed that night, she let him hand her nuts in a little cone of twisted newspaper that smelled of kerosene. She did not open it; it lay between them. The old man caught the money and walked away a few steps. Then, as if his honesty had gotten the better of him, he turned back and held out another bag.

"I had a premonition that it would end this way." She opened her hands spasmodically as if she were trying to grasp an elusive thread. "And I didn't want to accept it. I couldn't believe it."

"Do you regret everything? Would you rather we had never . . ."

"No." For the first time, she looked at him. "Without you I would never have known how it was possible to be the happiest woman in the world. Should I thank you? Do you want to wring that from me? You gave me a gift and then took away all the joy. You shattered it."

The words lashed him. He cringed and took the blows.

Beggars, some of them women and children, came out of the darkness squealing like hungry birds. They peered into the car. They stood patiently for a long time with fingers outspread. She dug the last of her change out of her pocket. They crowded in, shouting and pushing. In the light from passing cars he saw their thin legs, their tattered, threadbare clothing. They could not shake off the whining crowd; the mendicants shoved their faces through the window and tapped on the car with their fingers. Great flashing eyes gazed from under matted hair, waiting for the hand that sprinkled coins.

"Give them something."

"They'll never leave us alone," he said. When she threw a whole handful of coins onto the walk, he turned on the headlights, blew the horn, and drove on—escaped.

"I'm poorer than they are," she whispered. "I have nothing."

They rode along the Yamuna. Below them the funeral pyres were burning out. He drove her through Old Delhi. On the sidewalks the homeless lay like headless cocoons, wrapped in soiled sheets. Garlands of colored light bulbs blazed as if in derision; gigantic figures of film heroes swung on cables. We were here, he thought bitterly as each place they passed evoked a memory. We visited Krishan's wife in the little room behind the tailors' workshop. We bought sandals. We took our first walk, when I pushed her into the smoke of dried cow dung as if it were deep water—the stench of burned bodies, the smell of unleavened bread baked on tin plates. She was immersed in the real India.

"Where are you taking me?" she asked drowsily.

"Nowhere." Frightened, he hastily corrected himself, "Nearer to dawn . . . Perhaps you will want to come back?"

"I have nothing to come back to."

It was growing cool. The bent grass, trodden down by foot traffic, gleamed with the early morning dew. The sky was going white; behind clusters of huge trees a fiery fissure split the night.

They drove up to the hotel. He waited for her to let him follow her, but she motioned to him to stay where he was. Two sleepy bellhops, yawning and scratching under their arms, went to get her suitcases. He got out of the car and opened the trunk.

"You ought to eat something," he reminded her, but her look silenced him.

He had not had a bite all the previous day, but he felt no hunger, only bitterness—the slimy dregs of bile. As they were passing the gardens outside the city, he stopped the car. In spite of her protests he called an old man from a shed with watering cans all around it and asked him to cut some roses.

"How many?" he asked, rubbing the scratchy stubble on his face and yawning until the yellow incisors flashed in his otherwise toothless mouth.

"A lot," Istvan shouted impatiently. "All of them."

The man brought a sheaf of buds. They were almost black, with stiff leaves; they smelled of the freshness of the night and of wet mown herbs.

"What are they for?" She fixed her eyes on the fleshy petals sprinkled with dewdrops. She held them apathetically on her knees.

The road crawled along, curving gently through arid hills. They came upon a sadhu who had abandoned everything to follow the truth he sought.

And then the airport appeared. The corrugated aluminum roofs of the hangars gave off a white glare. Travelers surrounded them: women with children, carrying bundles with pots tied to them. A megaphone chattered in a foreign language, the voice compelling attention and then wearying the listeners, for they could understand nothing. A beautiful girl with enormous earrings served them coffee from a machine. They drank it and looked mutely at each other.

A mustachioed clerk asked Miss Ward the weight of her luggage and noted it on her ticket. Istvan seemed to feel the girl in his arms—his arms, which had carried her, cherished her. The rising roar of engines could be heard like the voices of winged beasts surging into the air. A bass voice called, "Flight to Nagpur. Change there for Bombay and Madras."

A stewardess with slim thighs, wearing an iridescent blue sari, raised a bare arm and beckoned to them with long fingers. They left the hall, which rumbled like the inside of a barrel, and walked down to the wide, flat, grassy airfield. He noticed that it was a beautiful, sunny day.

The airplane was white in the light. The stairs had been rolled up to it.

Margit pressed the prickly armful of roses, which only now were taking on a red tint. She did not give him her hand and he did not dare reach for it. He saw her face, wan and looking older than her age, her blue-veined eyelids and her eyes, which mirrored despair itself.

"It's wrong, Istvan," she whispered through colorless lips. "Even a dog doesn't deserve this."

She turned around and almost ran toward the plane so he would not see her burst, trembling, into tears. The stewardess took her by the arm and led her inside as if she were ill.

Before the steep stairs were rolled away, the Indian woman appeared once more and put Margit's roses on the little platform. He remembered the prohibition against traveling with plants and fruit: fear of contagion.

The left engine roared first, then the right. The airplane turned where it stood. A hard breeze jerked at the white skirts of the barefoot attendants who bent over and pushed away the stairs.

He gazed at the round windows; the sun blazed on them as on a row of mirrors. The plane moved slowly, hopping lightly. The odor of exhaust hit him in the chest. The breeze ruffled his shirt and nipped at his pants legs like a dog. Clouds of dust drifted about and grit beat his forehead. He shielded his eyes and when he lowered his hands, the plane was a speck sailing into the glistening blue. Then it was lost as if in the depths of the ocean.

When he was sitting in the Austin, unable to put a hand on the wheel, Mihaly's cicada began to sing in its box as if it were insane. He undid the thread, raised the lid and shook it out onto the grass.

He saw that its wings glinted like glass as it flew toward the tops of the trees, from which came a rasping as of metal gears: the overture of the advancing heat.

Her bag with a yellowed newspaper, the tightly twisted little paper horn in which peanuts rattled—she had held them in her hand. He sat unable to breathe. A cry rose in his throat; he wanted to turn his head away, to beat it against the car. He missed that golden hand, the eyes beaming like the sky after the first snow, looking trustfully at him from under waves of coppery hair. Margit is gone. Gone. And I am alone.

I am alone.

A dull pain grew and settled at the bottom of his sickened heart. It wandered through his pulse, then tightened around him. He parted his lips and gasped for air. He closed his eyes; he saw the dry grass bending in the warm breeze, the red stony hills, the sun filling the vastness of space, lashing it with brooms of flame.

Chronology

April 14, 1916 Wojciech Żukrowski is born in Krakow. At the time, Poland is partitioned between Russia, Prussia, and Austria.

1918 World War I ends, and Poland gains independence for the first time since it was first partitioned in 1795.

September 1939 World War II begins with Germany's attack on Poland. Żukrowski serves in the Polish horse artillery and is wounded in his right leg.

1940 With political and economic ties to Germany, Hungary joins the Axis and fights as an ally of Germany. Hungarian troops participate in the invasion of Russia; some fight in Ukraine, like the fictional Istvan Terey in *Stone Tablets*. Hungarian leader Miklós Horthy seeks to negotiate a peace with the Allies, but Germany coerces Hungary to remain in the war by kidnapping Horthy's son and imprisoning Horthy himself.

February 1945 As World War II draws to a close, Roosevelt, Churchill, and Stalin meet at Yalta in Crimea to plan for postwar Europe. Again Poland loses its independence as the Yalta Agreement places it, together with Hungary and other East European countries, in the Soviet Union's "sphere of influence." On May 8, Germany surrenders, ending the war in Europe. On August 14, Japan surrenders, ending World War II.

August 1947 India, under the leadership of Gandhi and Nehru, gains independence from British rule. Nehru becomes India's first prime minister. Independence leads to the creation of Pakistan as an independent state and to revisions to business and currency regulations which will affect characters in *Stone Tablets.*

March 1953 Stalin dies. Throughout the Eastern bloc, political prisoners are released, and citizens in Russia's client states hope for new political freedoms.

May 1955 Moscow formally establishes the Warsaw Pact, a mutual defense agreement between Russia's client states, including Poland and Hungary.

1956 As a result of the end of Stalinist rule, Hungarians are emboldened to demand internal reforms and more autonomy from Moscow. On October 22, university students announce demands for free elections, freedom of expression, and the withdrawal of all Soviet troops from Hungary. A statue of Lenin is toppled in Budapest as clashes occur between Russian troops and Hungarian dissidents. The Hungarian government tries to negotiate a withdrawal of the Soviets from the country. On November 1, Hungarian leader Imre Nagy announces that Hungary has withdrawn from the Warsaw Pact and calls on the West for support, but on November 4, Russian launches full-scale attacks that inflict severe damage on Budapest.

In late October a crisis develops in the Mideast as Israel, Great Britain, and France move to seize the Suez Canal, which President Gamal Abdel Nasser had earlier nationalized. Stalin's successor, Nikita Krushchev, supports Nasser, taking the role of defender of Arabs. The Suez Crisis threatens to bring about a military confrontation between Russia and the West, muting the response of the United States and other Western powers to the situation in Hungary, where Russia succeeds in crushing the uprising.

Żukrowski begins a three-year assignment with the Polish diplomatic corps in India. By this time Communists, including those in nearby China, are eyeing India, with its impoverished masses, as a potential field for the extension of their influence.

1965 Żukrowski, already a well-known author and screenwriter, completes *Stone Tablets.* The Polish censors refuse to allow the book to be published until a confidant of First Party Secretary

Władysław Gomułka, Poland's head of state, persuades Gomułka to override their decision.

1966 *Stone Tablets* is published. The book is extremely popular in Poland, but its criticisms of Stalinist abuses and its sympathy with the Hungarian Revolution cause such a furor in the Warsaw Pact that a new print run is held up. Andrzej Wajda, even then well known in Poland, is refused permission to make a film of the book. Polish authorities try to placate angry Hungarian officials by promising not to allow it to be translated into foreign languages.

1970 *Stone Tablets* is translated into Czech by Helena Teigova, but its distribution is forbidden by the government. Printed copies are stored in a warehouse, but workers smuggle so many out to readers that when the ban is lifted, few or no copies remain.

1984 A film of *Stone Tablets*, with the characters changed from Hungarians to Poles, premieres in Poland.

April 1989 Under pressure from the Solidarity movement, which includes some 10 million of 38 million Poles, the communist government of Poland agrees to allow multiparty elections. Two months later, Solidarity wins 99 percent of the available seats, and its leader, Lech Walesa, is elected president, effectively ending communist rule in Poland. In October, Hungary introduces a multiparty system. Hungary opens its border with Austria, which leads to the opening of the Berlin Wall on November 9. The demolition of that wall by ecstatic East and West Germans signals the end of communist domination in East Europe.

1996 Żukrowski wins the Władysław Reymont prize for lifetime literary achievement.

1997 *Stone Tablets* is published in a Russian translation.

August 26, 2000 Żukrowski dies in Warsaw.

2005 Żukrowski's daughter Katarzyna, an economist and professor at Warsaw School of Economics, authorizes an English translation of *Stone Tablets*.

Wojciech Żukrowski was born in Krakow, Poland in 1916, in the middle of World War I. He was studying Polish language and literature at Jagiellonian University at the outbreak of World War II. Żukrowski then served in the horse artillery and within a short time he was wounded. After Hitler's forces occupied Poland, he joined the Polish resistance as a specialist in sabotage.

From late 1939 until 1945, Żukrowski worked in the Solvay limestone quarry with his friend Karol Wojtyla, who would become Pope John Paul II. The quarry was a haven for Polish intellectuals because it was not closely watched by the Germans. Acting on a shared passion for "cultural resistance" to the detested Nazi occupation, Żukrowski and Wojtyla helped form an underground acting group, the Rhapsodic Theater—an enterprise that could have brought severe punishment if they had been discovered. The two corresponded until Żukrowski's death in 2000.

Żukrowski married Maria Woltersdorf in 1945 and had a daughter, Katarzyna. He first gained recognition for *From the Land of Silence*, a book about life in an occupied country, and *Kidnapping in Tiutiurlistan*, an animal fable critical of war, which became an enduringly popular children's book. In 1953 he became a war correspondent in Vietnam and China and traveled in Laos and Cambodia. The death of Stalin that year eventually led to the "thaw," a relaxation of political discipline that revived hopes for increased autonomy within member nations of the Warsaw Pact. In 1956, as Poles watched the deepening rebellion against the communist regime in Hungary, Zukrowski embarked on a three-year tour as cultural attaché with the Polish diplomatic mission in India.

In 1966 Żukrowski published *Stone Tablets*, one of the first Polish language literary works to offer trenchant criticisms of Stalinism. The book was finished a year and a half earlier, but the censors held up publication until Władysław Gomułka, then head of the Polish state, personally ordered its release. Shortly thereafter, a new print run was delayed due to political pressure from Hungary, whose leaders resented the novel's sympathetic depiction of the revolt of 1956. Renowned film director Andrzej Wajda was refused permission to make a motion picture of the book. A Czech translation was printed but banned from distribution by the government; when the ban was lifted, nothing remained to sell because workers in the warehouse where the copies were stored had smuggled all of them out to readers.

Stone Tablets remained a favorite with the Polish reading public and eventually, like several other Żukrowski novels, became a film. Its popularity continued after 1989, when the seventy-three-year-old author once again found himself in a free Poland. In 1996, Żukrowski won the Reymont Prize for lifetime literary achievement.

Żukrowski died in 2000. He had written forty-four books and won twenty literary awards, including the prestigious Pietrzak Prize for *Stone Tablets*. He was buried with military honors in Powazki Cemetery, the resting place of many notable Poles. The Pope organized a special mass for him in Rome.

—Stephanie Kraft